THE WALKING DEAD

BOOK TWO

a continuing story of survival horror.

created by Robert Kirkman

image comics presents

The Walking Dead
book two

ROBERT KIRKMAN
creator, writer, letterer

CHARLIE ADLARD
penciler, inker, cover

CLIFF RATHBURN
gray tones

RUS WOOTON
letterer (chapter 4)

Original series covers by
TONY MOORE

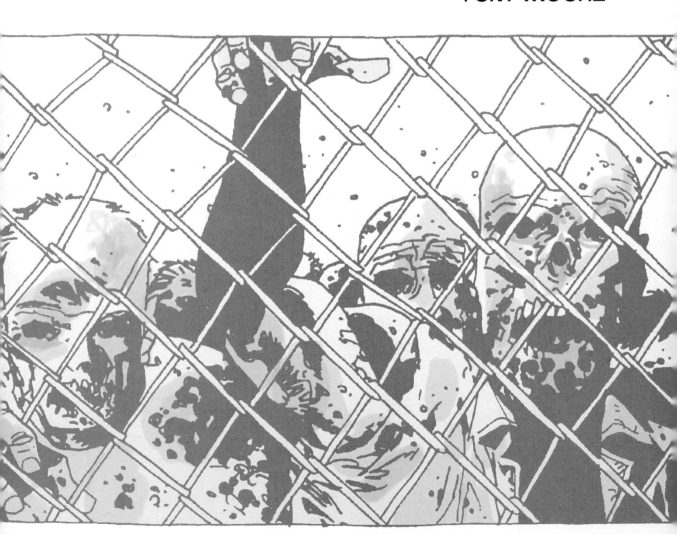

Robert Kirkman
chief executive officer

J.J. Didde
president

www.skybound.com

Robert Kirkman
chief operating officer

Erik Larsen
chief financial officer

Todd McFarlane
president

Marc Silvestri
chief executive officer

Jim Valentino
vice-president

www.imagecomics.com

Sean Mackiewicz
editorial director

Shawn Kirkham
director of business development

Eric Stephenson
publisher

Todd Martinez
sales & licensing coordinator

Jennifer de Guzman
pr & marketing director

Branwyn Bigglestone
accounts manager

Emily Miller
accounting assistant

Jamie Parreno
marketing assistant

Jenna Savage
administrative assistant

Helen Leigh
office manager

Robert Pouder
Inventory Control

Feldman Public Relations LA
public relations

Sarah deLaine
events coordinator

Kevin Yuen
digital rights coordinator

Jonathan Chan
production manager

Drew Gill
art director

Monica Garcia
production artist

Vincent Kukua
production artist

Jana Cook
production artist

Chapter Three:
Safety Behind Bars

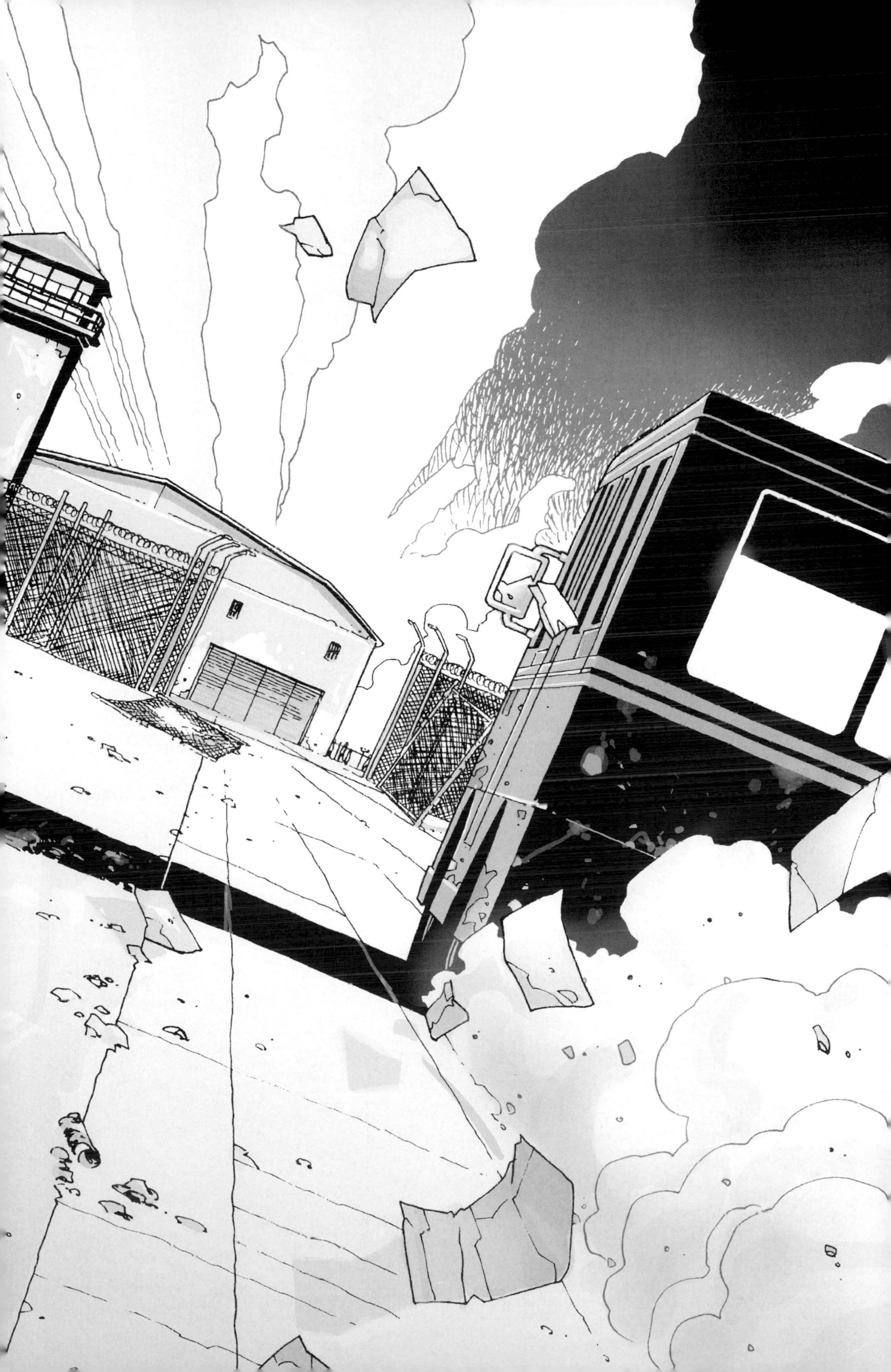

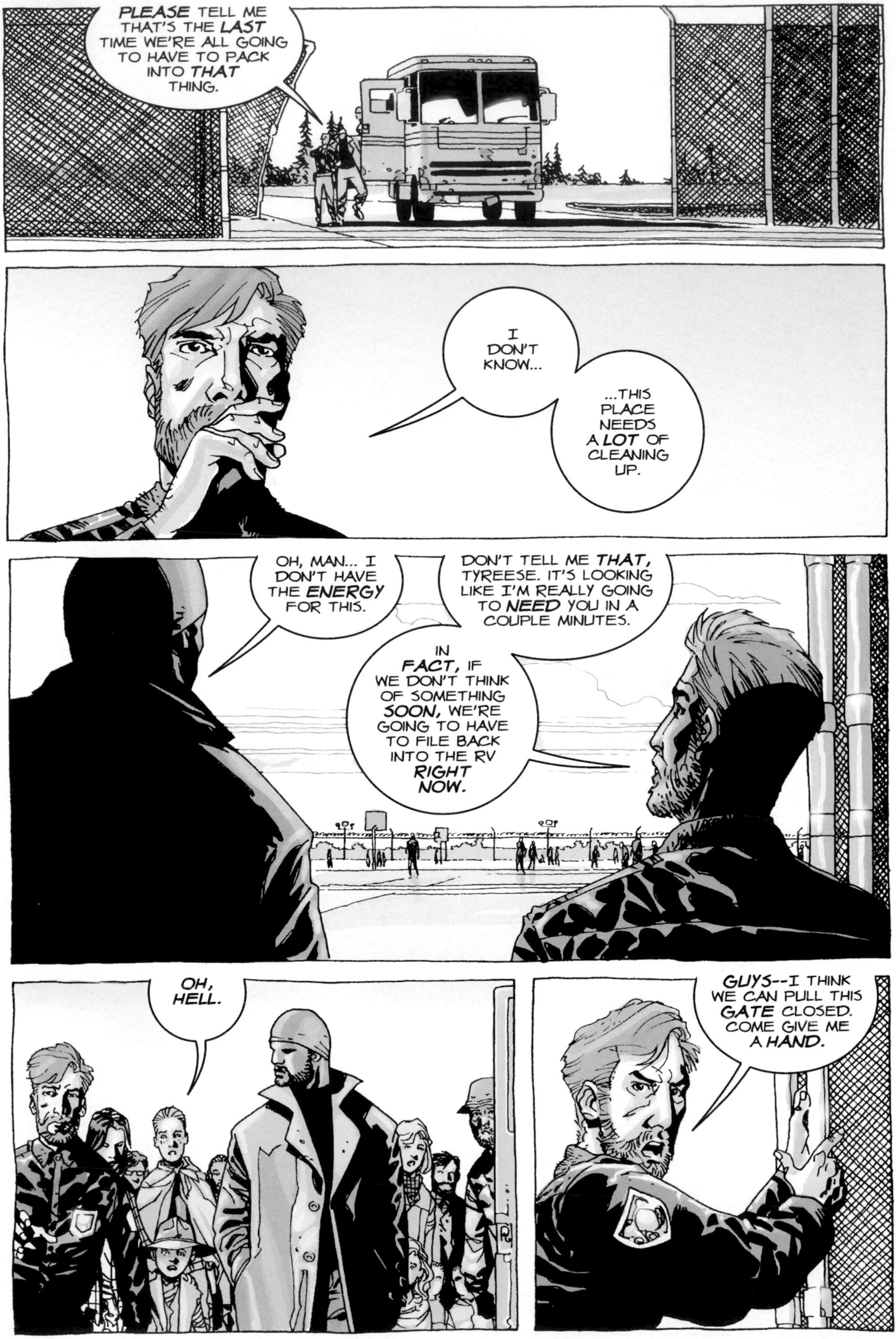
PLEASE TELL ME THAT'S THE LAST TIME WE'RE ALL GOING TO HAVE TO PACK INTO THAT THING.
I DON'T KNOW...
...THIS PLACE NEEDS A LOT OF CLEANING UP.
OH, MAN... I DON'T HAVE THE ENERGY FOR THIS.
DON'T TELL ME THAT, TYREESE. IT'S LOOKING LIKE I'M REALLY GOING TO NEED YOU IN A COUPLE MINUTES.
IN FACT, IF WE DON'T THINK OF SOMETHING SOON, WE'RE GOING TO HAVE TO FILE BACK INTO THE RV RIGHT NOW.
OH, HELL.
GUYS--I THINK WE CAN PULL THIS GATE CLOSED. COME GIVE ME A HAND.

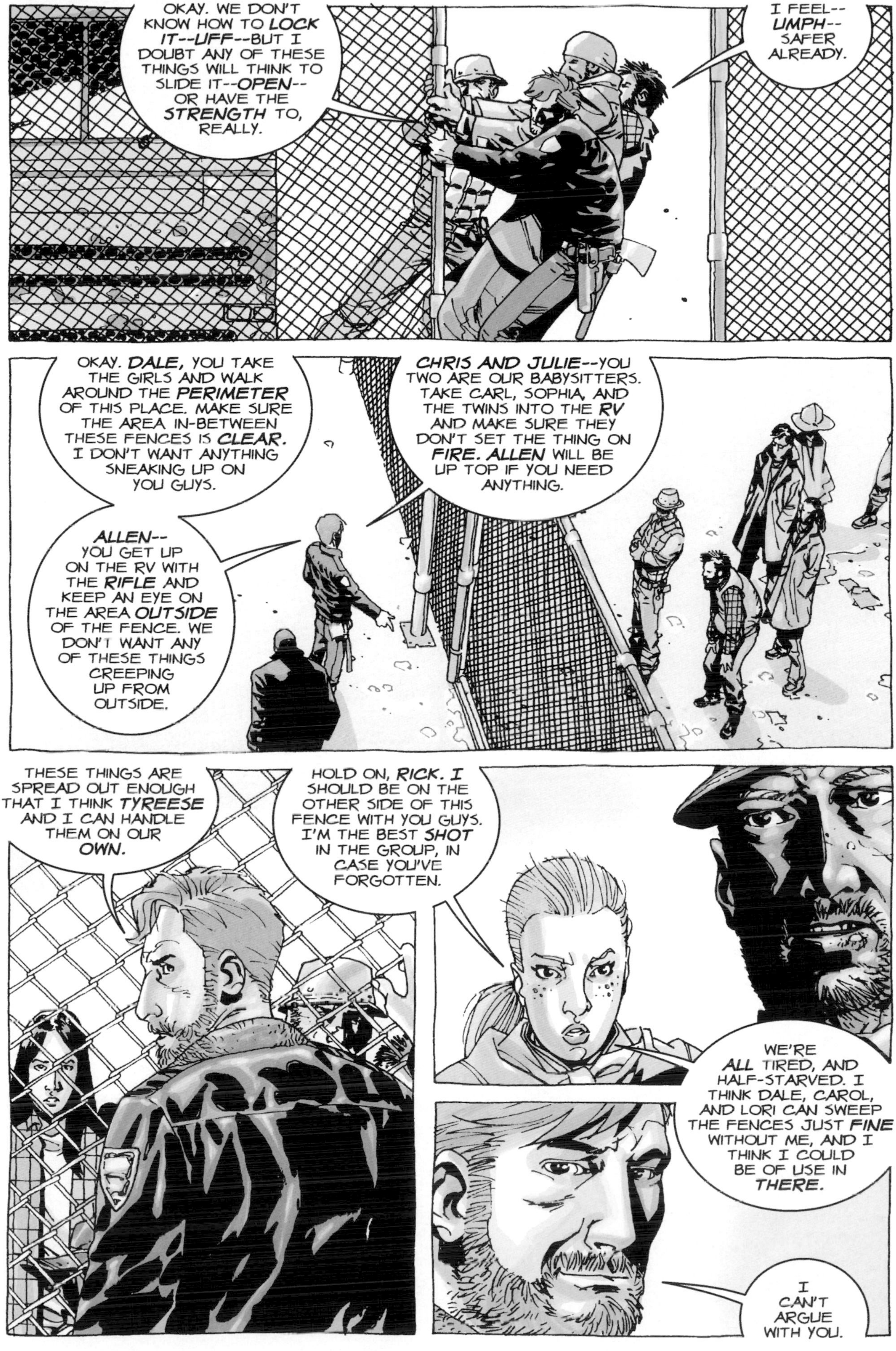
OKAY. WE DON'T KNOW HOW TO LOCK IT--UFF--BUT I DOUBT ANY OF THESE THINGS WILL THINK TO SLIDE IT--OPEN-- OR HAVE THE STRENGTH TO, REALLY.
I FEEL-- UMPH-- SAFER ALREADY.
OKAY. DALE, YOU TAKE THE GIRLS AND WALK AROUND THE PERIMETER OF THIS PLACE. MAKE SURE THE AREA IN-BETWEEN THESE FENCES IS CLEAR. I DON'T WANT ANYTHING SNEAKING UP ON YOU GUYS.
ALLEN-- YOU GET UP ON THE RV WITH THE RIFLE AND KEEP AN EYE ON THE AREA OUTSIDE OF THE FENCE. WE DON'T WANT ANY OF THESE THINGS CREEPING UP FROM OUTSIDE.
CHRIS AND JULIE--YOU TWO ARE OUR BABYSITTERS. TAKE CARL, SOPHIA, AND THE TWINS INTO THE RV AND MAKE SURE THEY DON'T SET THE THING ON FIRE. ALLEN WILL BE UP TOP IF YOU NEED ANYTHING.
THESE THINGS ARE SPREAD OUT ENOUGH THAT I THINK TYREESE AND I CAN HANDLE THEM ON OUR OWN.
HOLD ON, RICK. I SHOULD BE ON THE OTHER SIDE OF THIS FENCE WITH YOU GUYS. I'M THE BEST SHOT IN THE GROUP, IN CASE YOU'VE FORGOTTEN.
WE'RE ALL TIRED, AND HALF-STARVED. I THINK DALE, CAROL, AND LORI CAN SWEEP THE FENCES JUST FINE WITHOUT ME, AND I THINK I COULD BE OF USE IN THERE.
I CAN'T ARGUE WITH YOU.

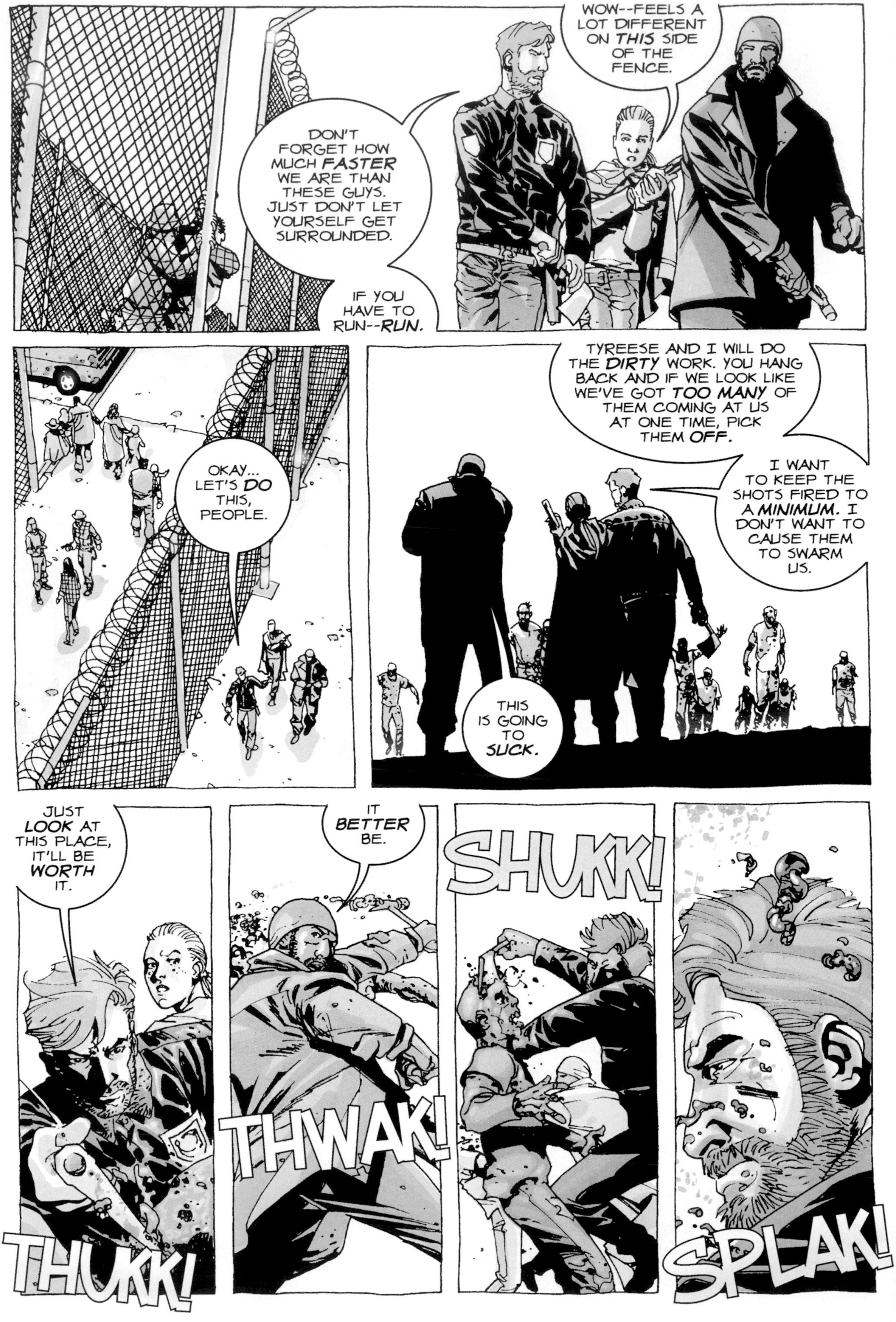
WOW--FEELS A LOT DIFFERENT ON THIS SIDE OF THE FENCE.
DON'T FORGET HOW MUCH FASTER WE ARE THAN THESE GUYS. JUST DON'T LET YOURSELF GET SURROUNDED.
IF YOU HAVE TO RUN--RUN.
OKAY... LET'S DO THIS, PEOPLE.
TYREESE AND I WILL DO THE DIRTY WORK. YOU HANG BACK AND IF WE LOOK LIKE WE'VE GOT TOO MANY OF THEM COMING AT US AT ONE TIME, PICK THEM OFF.
I WANT TO KEEP THE SHOTS FIRED TO A MINIMUM. I DON'T WANT TO CAUSE THEM TO SWARM US.
THIS IS GOING TO SUCK.
JUST LOOK AT THIS PLACE, IT'LL BE WORTH IT.
THUKK!
IT BETTER BE.
THWAK!
SHUKK!
SPLAK!

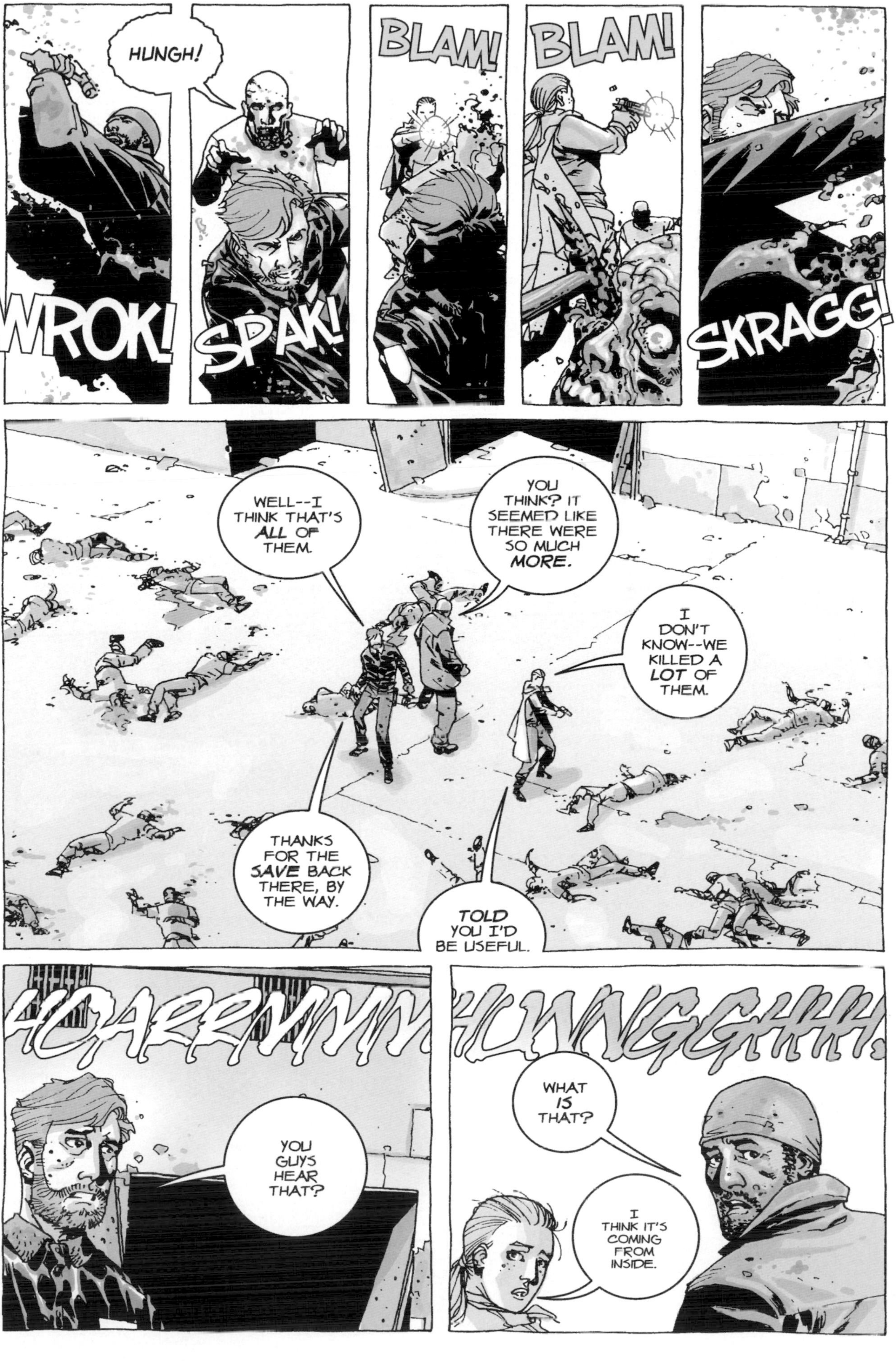

WROK!
HUNGH!
SPAK!
BLAM!
BLAM!
SKRAGG!
WELL--I THINK THAT'S ALL OF THEM.
YOU THINK? IT SEEMED LIKE THERE WERE SO MUCH MORE.
I DON'T KNOW--WE KILLED A LOT OF THEM.
THANKS FOR THE SAVE BACK THERE, BY THE WAY.
TOLD YOU I'D BE USEFUL.
HGARRMMMHGWNGGHHH!
YOU GUYS HEAR THAT?
WHAT IS THAT?
I THINK IT'S COMING FROM INSIDE.

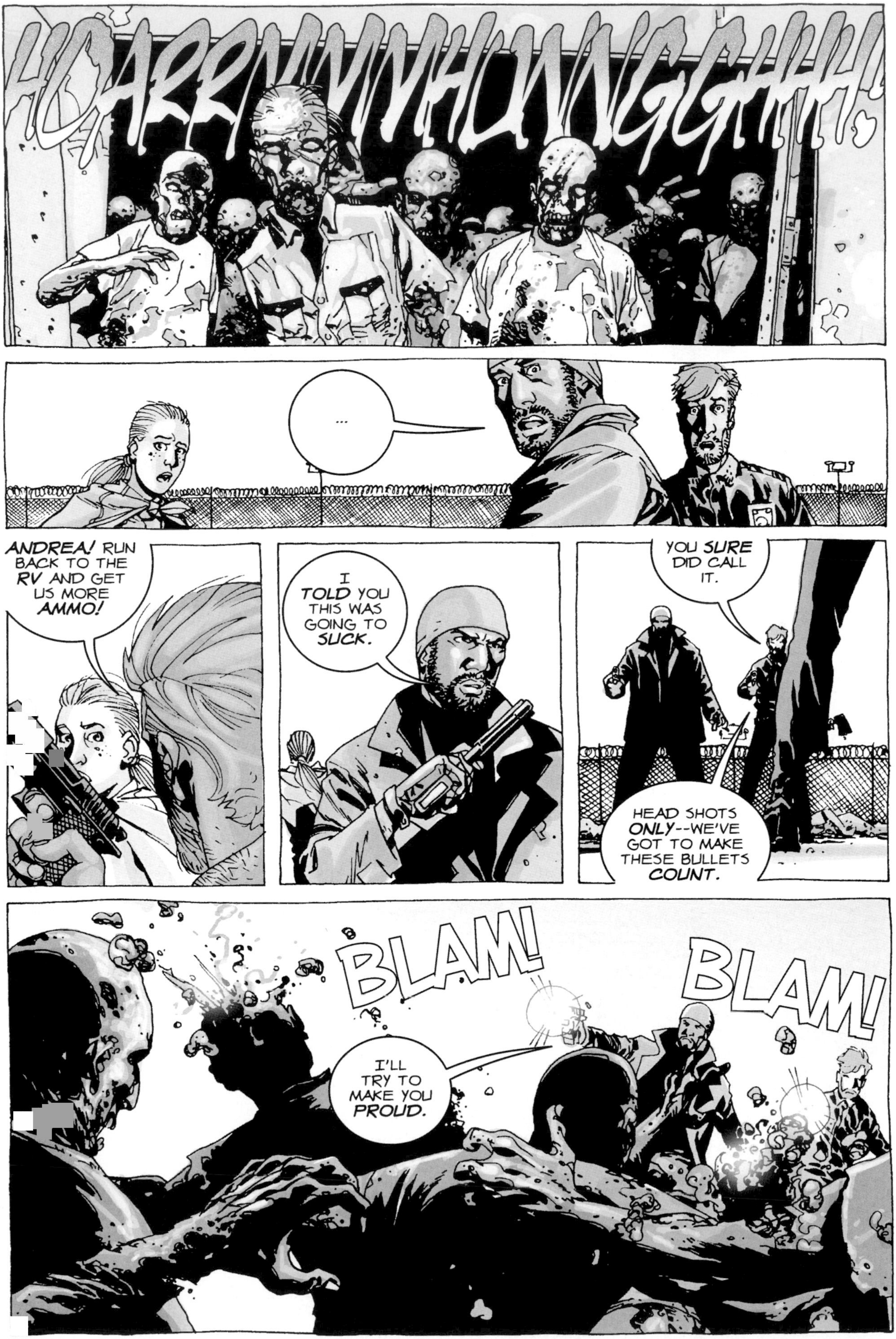

HOARRMMMHUNNGGHHH!
...
ANDREA! RUN BACK TO THE RV AND GET US MORE AMMO!
I TOLD YOU THIS WAS GOING TO SUCK.
YOU SURE DID CALL IT.
HEAD SHOTS ONLY--WE'VE GOT TO MAKE THESE BULLETS COUNT.
BLAM!
BLAM!
I'LL TRY TO MAKE YOU PROUD.

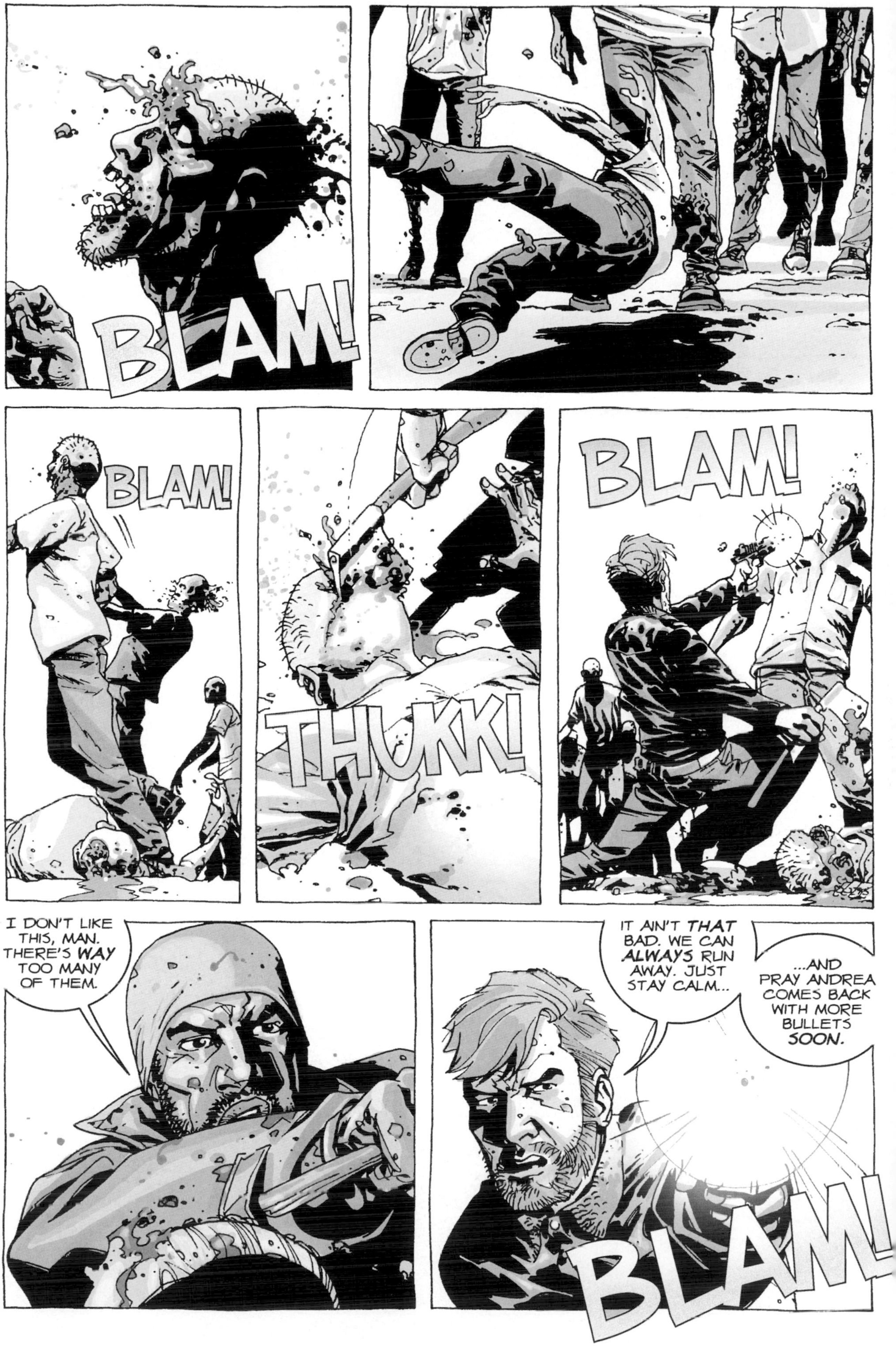
BLAM!
BLAM!
THUKK!
BLAM!
I DON'T LIKE THIS, MAN. THERE'S WAY TOO MANY OF THEM.
IT AIN'T THAT BAD. WE CAN ALWAYS RUN AWAY. JUST STAY CALM...
...AND PRAY ANDREA COMES BACK WITH MORE BULLETS SOON.
BLAM!

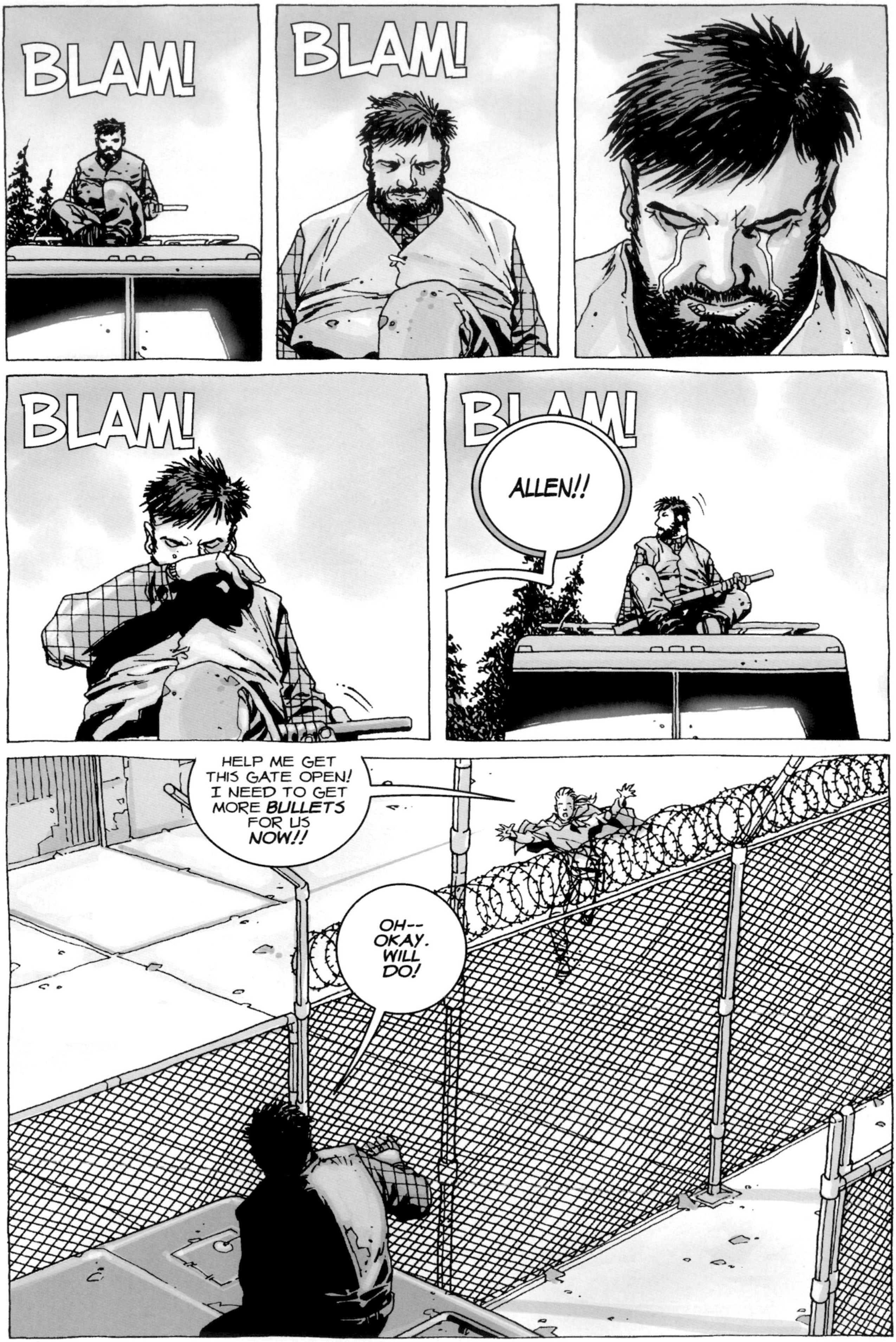
BLAM!
BLAM!
BLAM!
BLAM!
ALLEN!!
HELP ME GET THIS GATE OPEN! I NEED TO GET MORE BULLETS FOR US NOW!!
OH-- OKAY. WILL DO!

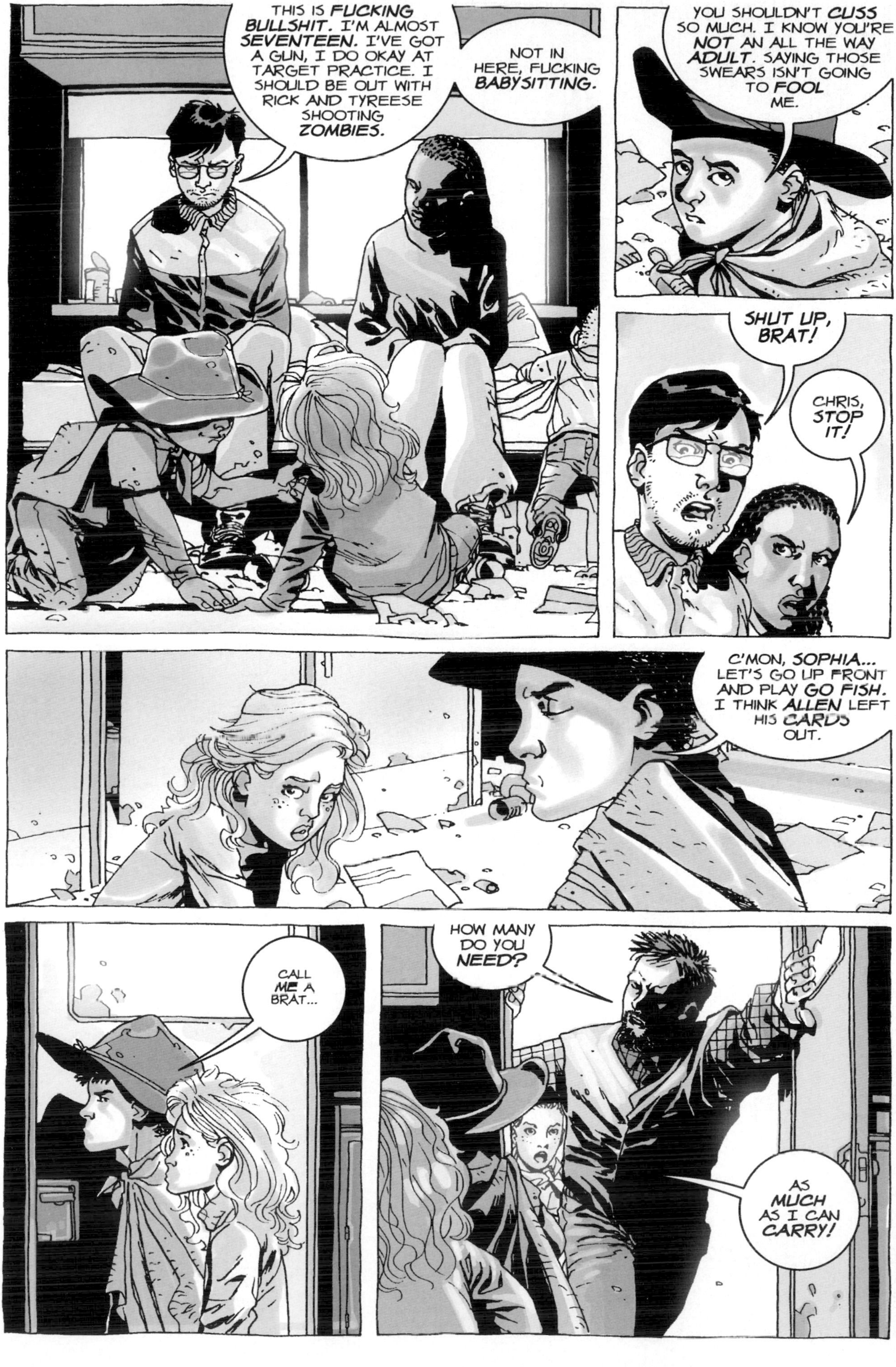
THIS IS FUCKING BULLSHIT. I'M ALMOST SEVENTEEN. I'VE GOT A GUN, I DO OKAY AT TARGET PRACTICE. I SHOULD BE OUT WITH RICK AND TYREESE SHOOTING ZOMBIES.
NOT IN HERE, FUCKING BABYSITTING.
YOU SHOULDN'T CUSS SO MUCH. I KNOW YOU'RE NOT AN ALL THE WAY ADULT. SAYING THOSE SWEARS ISN'T GOING TO FOOL ME.
SHUT UP, BRAT!
CHRIS, STOP IT!
C'MON, SOPHIA... LET'S GO UP FRONT AND PLAY GO FISH. I THINK ALLEN LEFT HIS CARDS OUT.
CALL ME A BRAT...
HOW MANY DO YOU NEED?
AS MUCH AS I CAN CARRY!

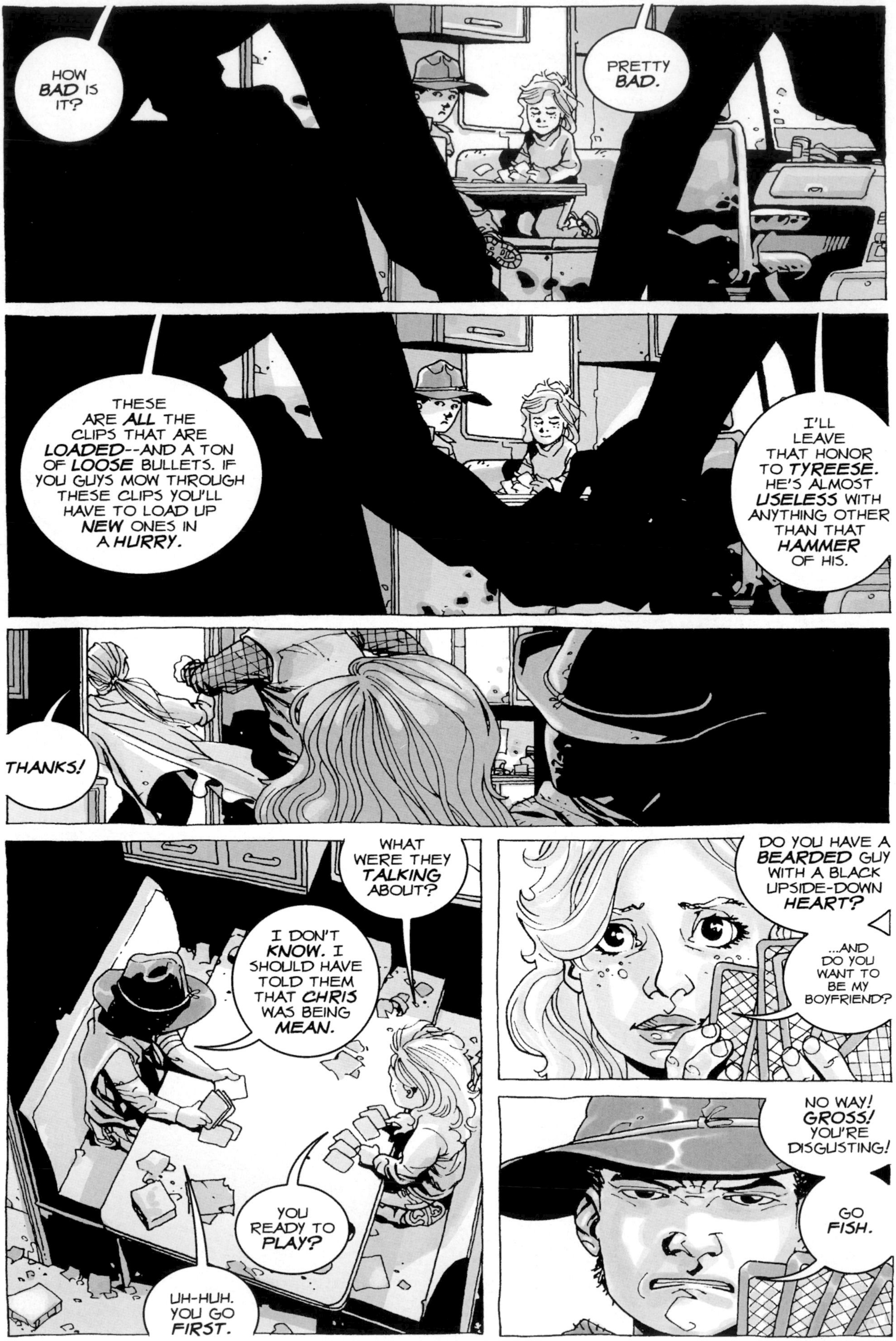
HOW BAD IS IT?
PRETTY BAD.
THESE ARE ALL THE CLIPS THAT ARE LOADED--AND A TON OF LOOSE BULLETS. IF YOU GUYS MOW THROUGH THESE CLIPS YOU'LL HAVE TO LOAD UP NEW ONES IN A HURRY.
I'LL LEAVE THAT HONOR TO TYREESE. HE'S ALMOST USELESS WITH ANYTHING OTHER THAN THAT HAMMER OF HIS.
THANKS!
WHAT WERE THEY TALKING ABOUT?
I DON'T KNOW. I SHOULD HAVE TOLD THEM THAT CHRIS WAS BEING MEAN.
YOU READY TO PLAY?
UH-HUH. YOU GO FIRST.
DO YOU HAVE A BEARDED GUY WITH A BLACK UPSIDE-DOWN HEART?
...AND DO YOU WANT TO BE MY BOYFRIEND?
NO WAY! GROSS! YOU'RE DISGUSTING!
GO FISH.

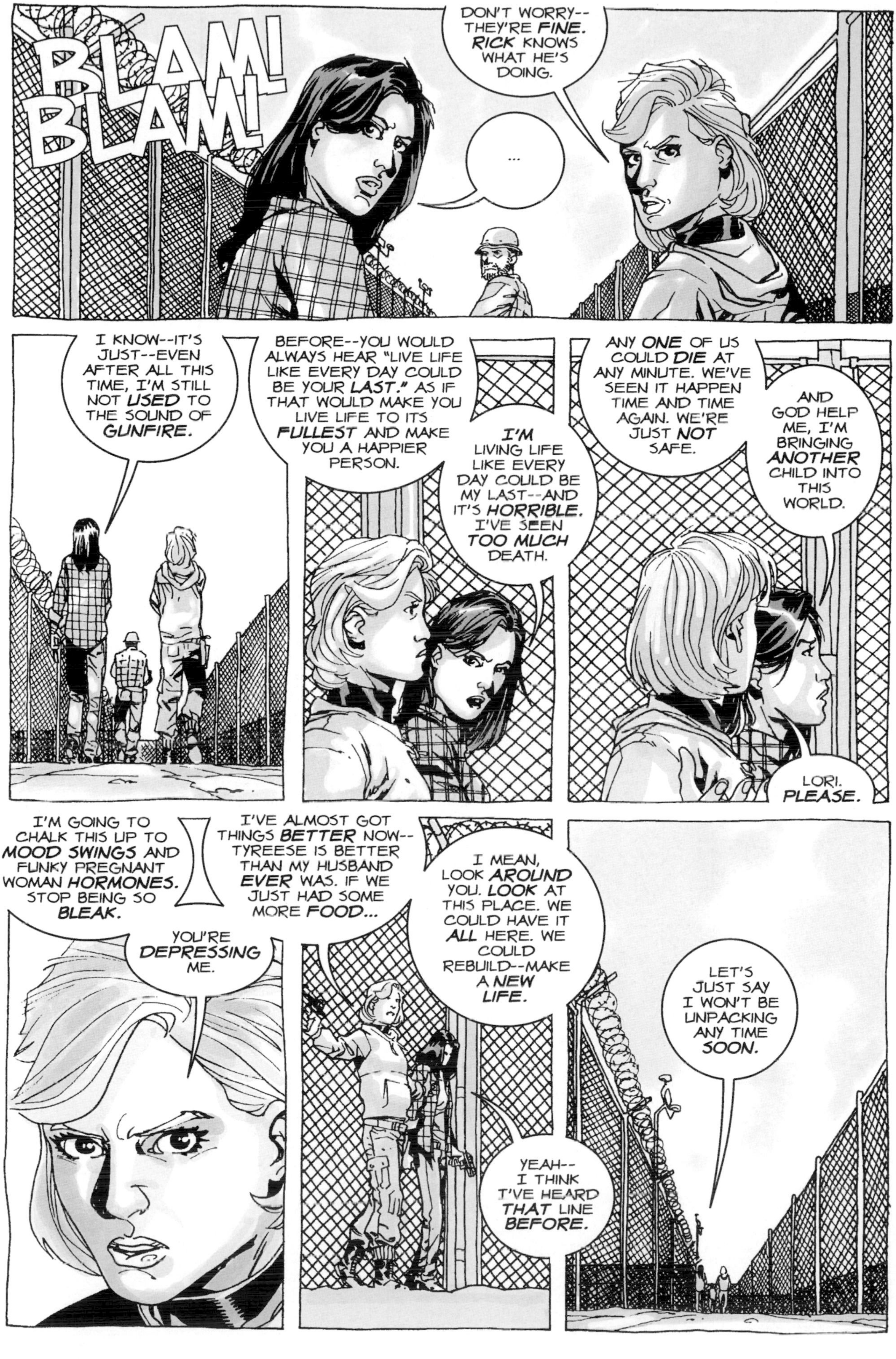
BLAM! BLAM!
DON'T WORRY--THEY'RE FINE. RICK KNOWS WHAT HE'S DOING.
...
I KNOW--IT'S JUST--EVEN AFTER ALL THIS TIME, I'M STILL NOT USED TO THE SOUND OF GUNFIRE.
BEFORE--YOU WOULD ALWAYS HEAR "LIVE LIFE LIKE EVERY DAY COULD BE YOUR LAST." AS IF THAT WOULD MAKE YOU LIVE LIFE TO ITS FULLEST AND MAKE YOU A HAPPIER PERSON.
I'M LIVING LIFE LIKE EVERY DAY COULD BE MY LAST--AND IT'S HORRIBLE. I'VE SEEN TOO MUCH DEATH.
ANY ONE OF US COULD DIE AT ANY MINUTE. WE'VE SEEN IT HAPPEN TIME AND TIME AGAIN. WE'RE JUST NOT SAFE.
AND GOD HELP ME, I'M BRINGING ANOTHER CHILD INTO THIS WORLD.
LORI. PLEASE.
I'M GOING TO CHALK THIS UP TO MOOD SWINGS AND FUNKY PREGNANT WOMAN HORMONES. STOP BEING SO BLEAK.
YOU'RE DEPRESSING ME.
I'VE ALMOST GOT THINGS BETTER NOW--TYREESE IS BETTER THAN MY HUSBAND EVER WAS. IF WE JUST HAD SOME MORE FOOD...
I MEAN, LOOK AROUND YOU. LOOK AT THIS PLACE. WE COULD HAVE IT ALL HERE. WE COULD REBUILD--MAKE A NEW LIFE.
YEAH--I THINK I'VE HEARD THAT LINE BEFORE.
LET'S JUST SAY I WON'T BE UNPACKING ANY TIME SOON.

BLAM!

BLAM!

I GOT ANOTHER CLIP LOADED! WHO WANTS IT?!

I'LL TAKE IT!

BLAM! BLAM! BLAM!

THIS KEEPS UP LIKE THIS-- WE'RE GOING TO RUN OUT!

BLAM! LAM!

I THINK WE'VE LUCKED OUT-- LOOK.

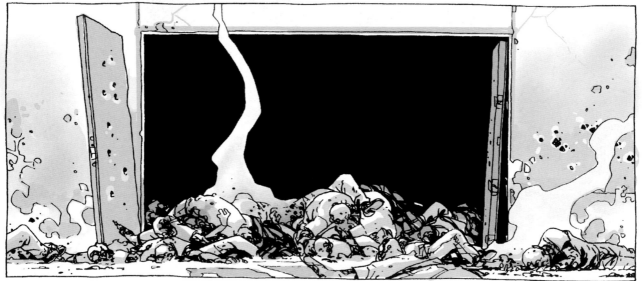

YOU THINK THAT'S ALL OF THEM?

IT'D BE NICE.

ONE WAY TO FIND OUT--

BLAM!

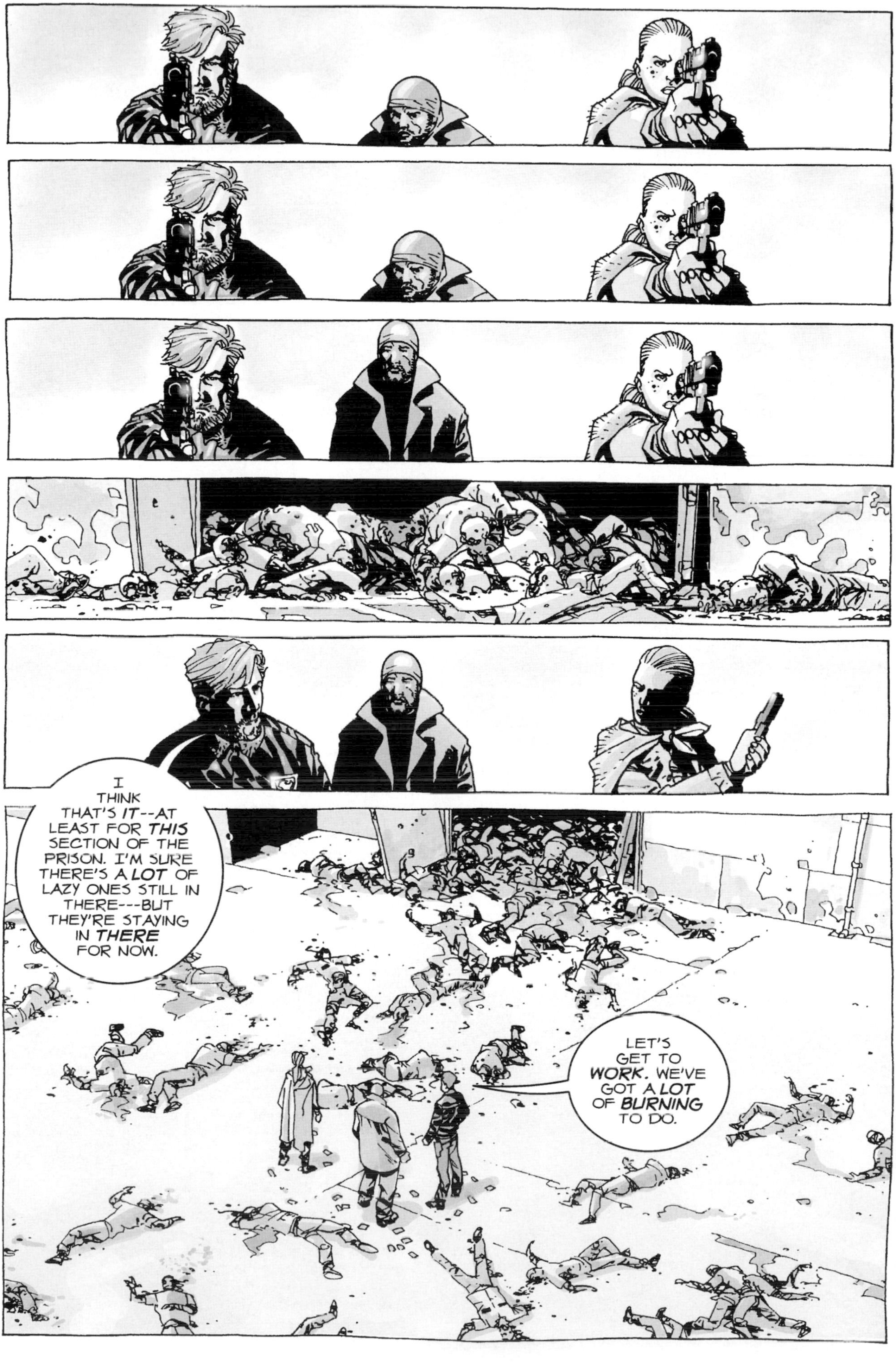
I THINK THAT'S IT--AT LEAST FOR THIS SECTION OF THE PRISON. I'M SURE THERE'S A LOT OF LAZY ONES STILL IN THERE---BUT THEY'RE STAYING IN THERE FOR NOW.
LET'S GET TO WORK. WE'VE GOT A LOT OF BURNING TO DO.

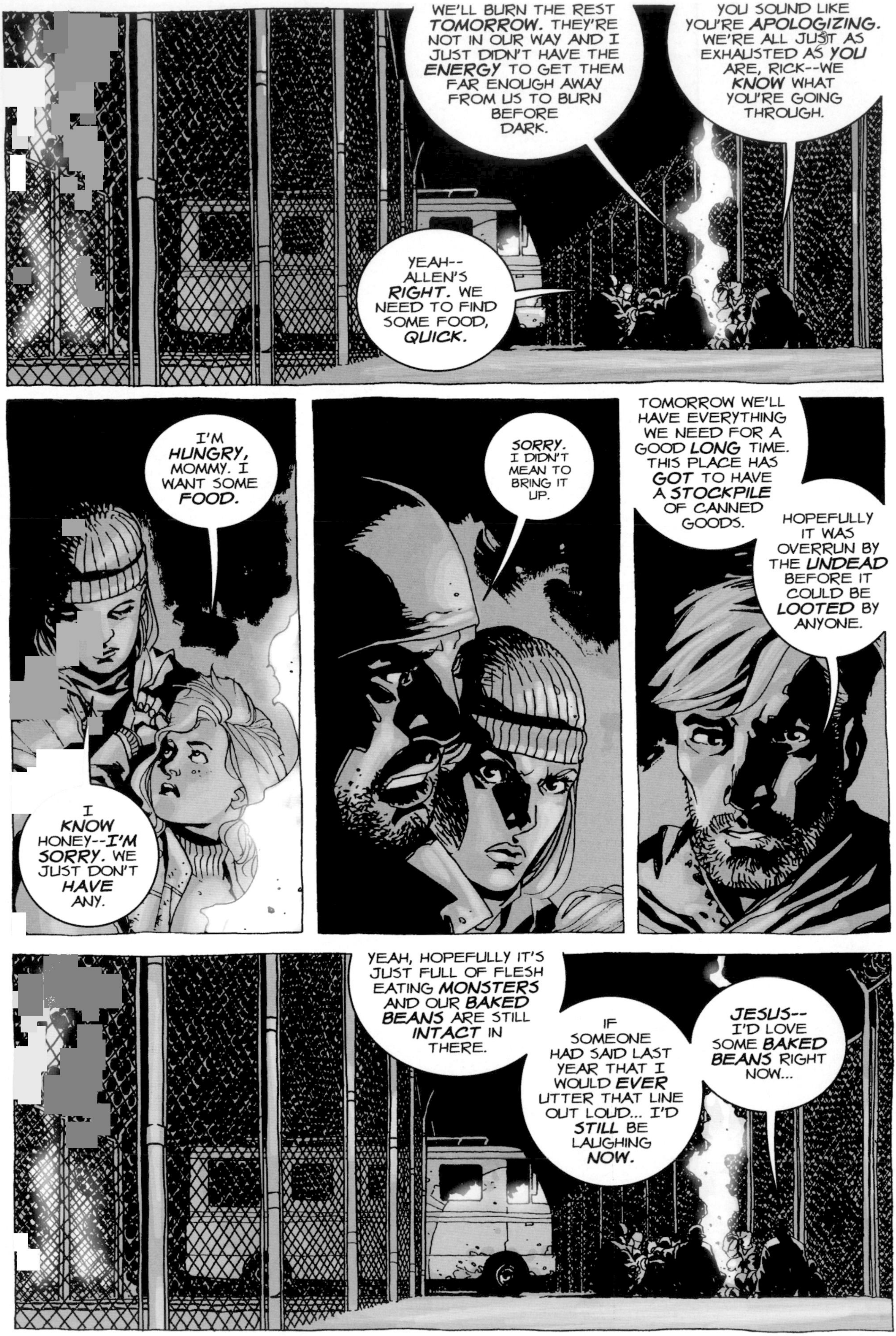

WE'LL BURN THE REST TOMORROW. THEY'RE NOT IN OUR WAY AND I JUST DIDN'T HAVE THE ENERGY TO GET THEM FAR ENOUGH AWAY FROM US TO BURN BEFORE DARK.
YOU SOUND LIKE YOU'RE APOLOGIZING. WE'RE ALL JUST AS EXHAUSTED AS YOU ARE, RICK--WE KNOW WHAT YOU'RE GOING THROUGH.
YEAH--ALLEN'S RIGHT. WE NEED TO FIND SOME FOOD, QUICK.
I'M HUNGRY, MOMMY. I WANT SOME FOOD.
I KNOW HONEY--I'M SORRY. WE JUST DON'T HAVE ANY.
SORRY. I DIDN'T MEAN TO BRING IT UP.
TOMORROW WE'LL HAVE EVERYTHING WE NEED FOR A GOOD LONG TIME. THIS PLACE HAS GOT TO HAVE A STOCKPILE OF CANNED GOODS.
HOPEFULLY IT WAS OVERRUN BY THE UNDEAD BEFORE IT COULD BE LOOTED BY ANYONE.
YEAH, HOPEFULLY IT'S JUST FULL OF FLESH EATING MONSTERS AND OUR BAKED BEANS ARE STILL INTACT IN THERE.
IF SOMEONE HAD SAID LAST YEAR THAT I WOULD EVER UTTER THAT LINE OUT LOUD... I'D STILL BE LAUGHING NOW.
JESUS--I'D LOVE SOME BAKED BEANS RIGHT NOW...

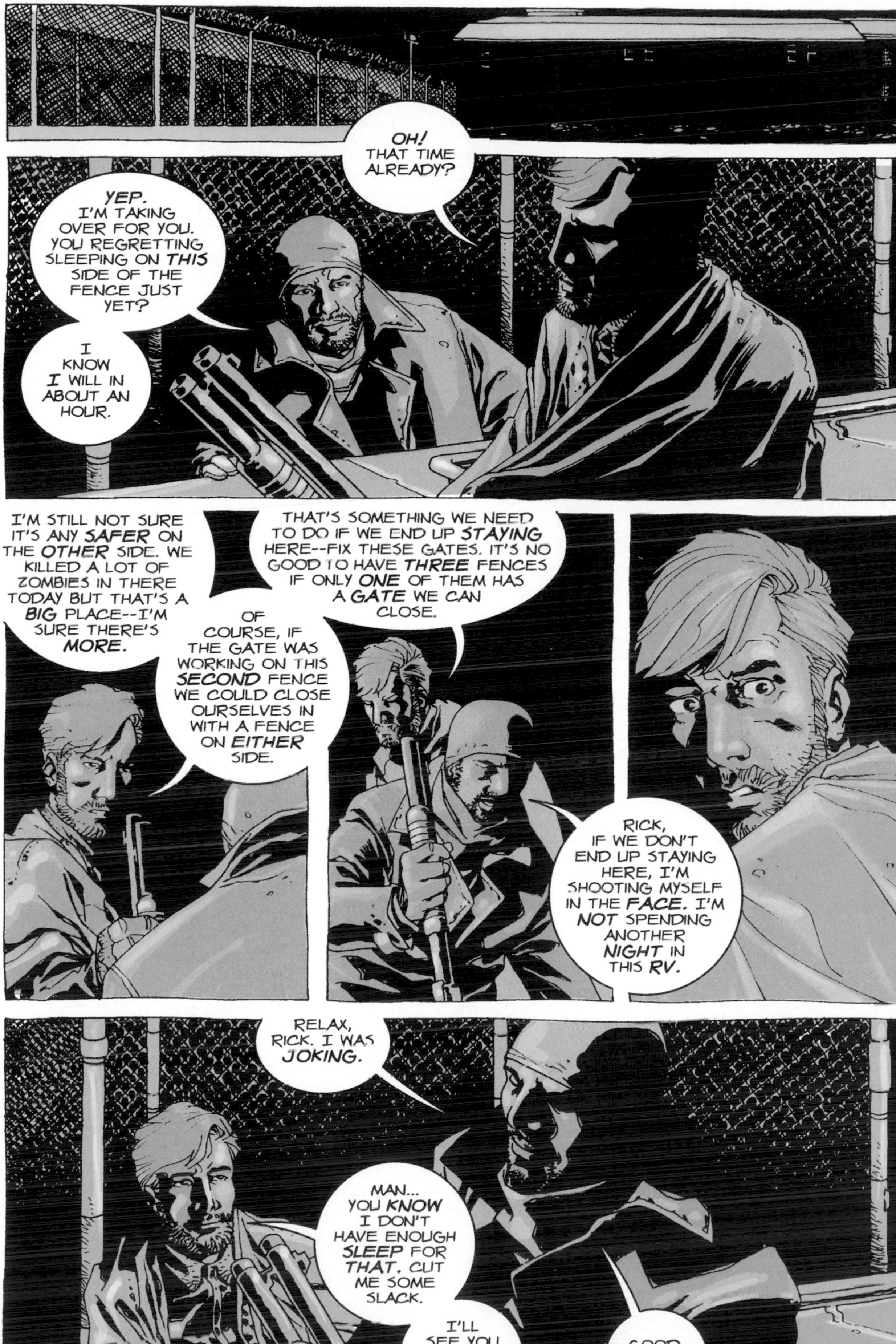
OH! THAT TIME ALREADY?
YEP. I'M TAKING OVER FOR YOU. YOU REGRETTING SLEEPING ON THIS SIDE OF THE FENCE JUST YET?
I KNOW I WILL IN ABOUT AN HOUR.
I'M STILL NOT SURE IT'S ANY SAFER ON THE OTHER SIDE. WE KILLED A LOT OF ZOMBIES IN THERE TODAY BUT THAT'S A BIG PLACE--I'M SURE THERE'S MORE.
OF COURSE, IF THE GATE WAS WORKING ON THIS SECOND FENCE WE COULD CLOSE OURSELVES IN WITH A FENCE ON EITHER SIDE.
THAT'S SOMETHING WE NEED TO DO IF WE END UP STAYING HERE--FIX THESE GATES. IT'S NO GOOD TO HAVE THREE FENCES IF ONLY ONE OF THEM HAS A GATE WE CAN CLOSE.
RICK, IF WE DON'T END UP STAYING HERE, I'M SHOOTING MYSELF IN THE FACE. I'M NOT SPENDING ANOTHER NIGHT IN THIS RV.
RELAX, RICK. I WAS JOKING.
MAN... YOU KNOW I DON'T HAVE ENOUGH SLEEP FOR THAT. CUT ME SOME SLACK.
I'LL SEE YOU IN THE MORNING.
GOOD-NIGHT, RICK.

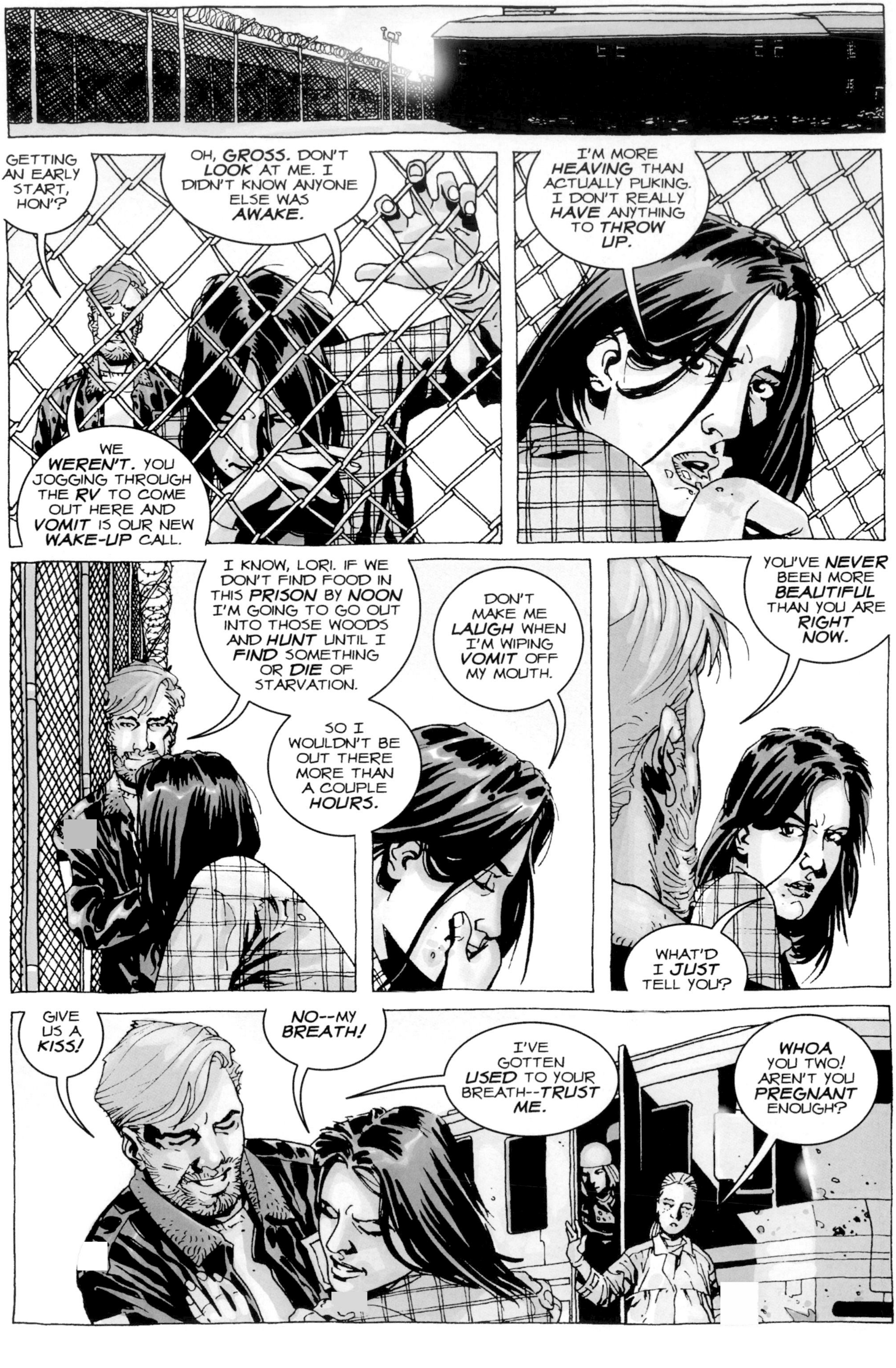
GETTING AN EARLY START, HON'?
OH, GROSS. DON'T LOOK AT ME. I DIDN'T KNOW ANYONE ELSE WAS AWAKE.
WE WEREN'T. YOU JOGGING THROUGH THE RV TO COME OUT HERE AND VOMIT IS OUR NEW WAKE-UP CALL.
I'M MORE HEAVING THAN ACTUALLY PUKING. I DON'T REALLY HAVE ANYTHING TO THROW UP.
I KNOW, LORI. IF WE DON'T FIND FOOD IN THIS PRISON BY NOON I'M GOING TO GO OUT INTO THOSE WOODS AND HUNT UNTIL I FIND SOMETHING OR DIE OF STARVATION.
SO I WOULDN'T BE OUT THERE MORE THAN A COUPLE HOURS.
DON'T MAKE ME LAUGH WHEN I'M WIPING VOMIT OFF MY MOUTH.
YOU'VE NEVER BEEN MORE BEAUTIFUL THAN YOU ARE RIGHT NOW.
WHAT'D I JUST TELL YOU?
GIVE US A KISS!
NO--MY BREATH!
I'VE GOTTEN USED TO YOUR BREATH--TRUST ME.
WHOA YOU TWO! AREN'T YOU PREGNANT ENOUGH?

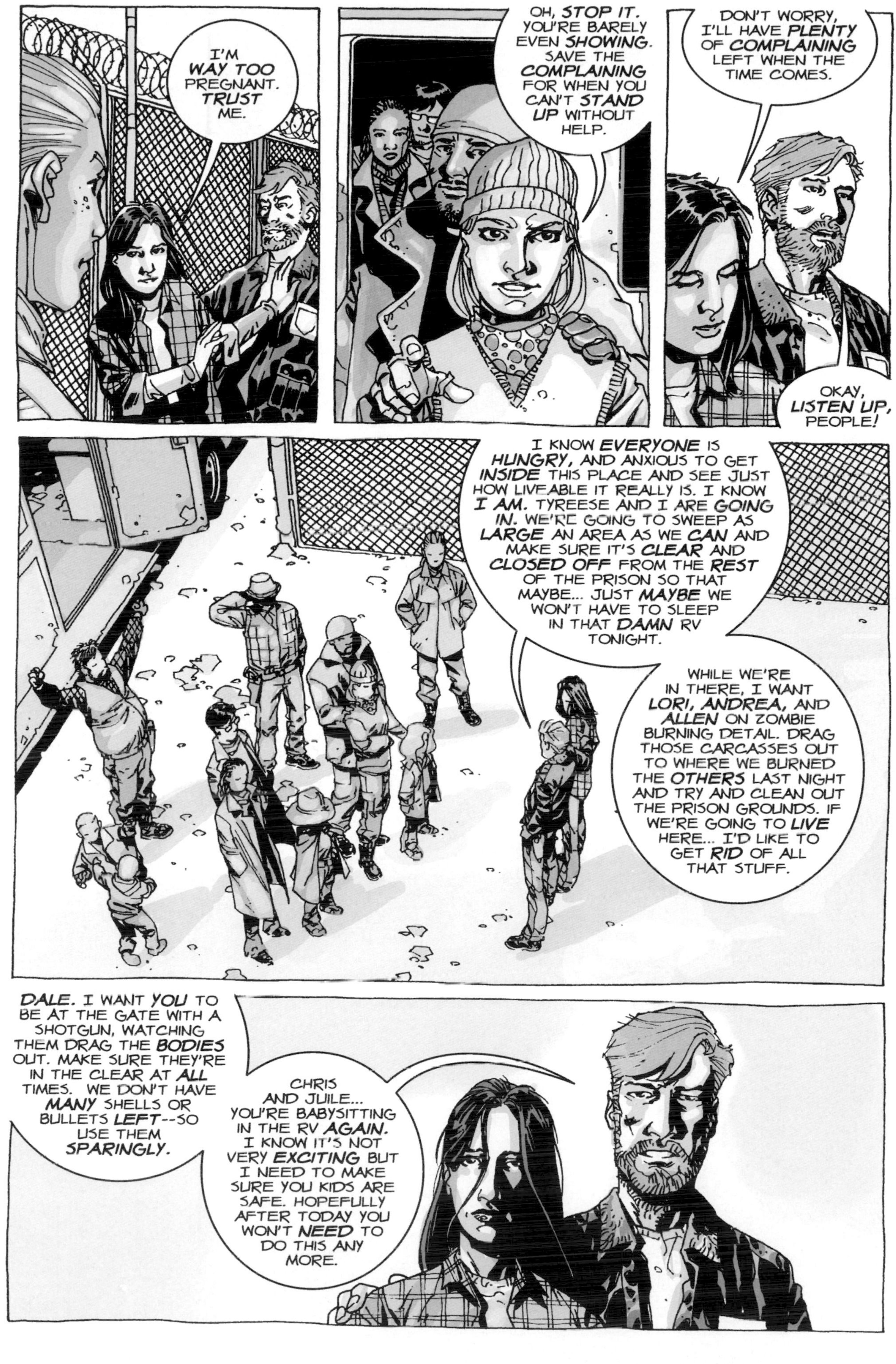
I'M WAY TOO PREGNANT. TRUST ME.
OH, STOP IT. YOU'RE BARELY EVEN SHOWING. SAVE THE COMPLAINING FOR WHEN YOU CAN'T STAND UP WITHOUT HELP.
DON'T WORRY, I'LL HAVE PLENTY OF COMPLAINING LEFT WHEN THE TIME COMES.
OKAY, LISTEN UP, PEOPLE!
I KNOW EVERYONE IS HUNGRY, AND ANXIOUS TO GET INSIDE THIS PLACE AND SEE JUST HOW LIVEABLE IT REALLY IS. I KNOW I AM. TYREESE AND I ARE GOING IN. WE'RE GOING TO SWEEP AS LARGE AN AREA AS WE CAN AND MAKE SURE IT'S CLEAR AND CLOSED OFF FROM THE REST OF THE PRISON SO THAT MAYBE... JUST MAYBE WE WON'T HAVE TO SLEEP IN THAT DAMN RV TONIGHT.
WHILE WE'RE IN THERE, I WANT LORI, ANDREA, AND ALLEN ON ZOMBIE BURNING DETAIL. DRAG THOSE CARCASSES OUT TO WHERE WE BURNED THE OTHERS LAST NIGHT AND TRY AND CLEAN OUT THE PRISON GROUNDS. IF WE'RE GOING TO LIVE HERE... I'D LIKE TO GET RID OF ALL THAT STUFF.
DALE. I WANT YOU TO BE AT THE GATE WITH A SHOTGUN, WATCHING THEM DRAG THE BODIES OUT. MAKE SURE THEY'RE IN THE CLEAR AT ALL TIMES. WE DON'T HAVE MANY SHELLS OR BULLETS LEFT--SO USE THEM SPARINGLY.
CHRIS AND JUILE... YOU'RE BABYSITTING IN THE RV AGAIN. I KNOW IT'S NOT VERY EXCITING BUT I NEED TO MAKE SURE YOU KIDS ARE SAFE. HOPEFULLY AFTER TODAY YOU WON'T NEED TO DO THIS ANY MORE.

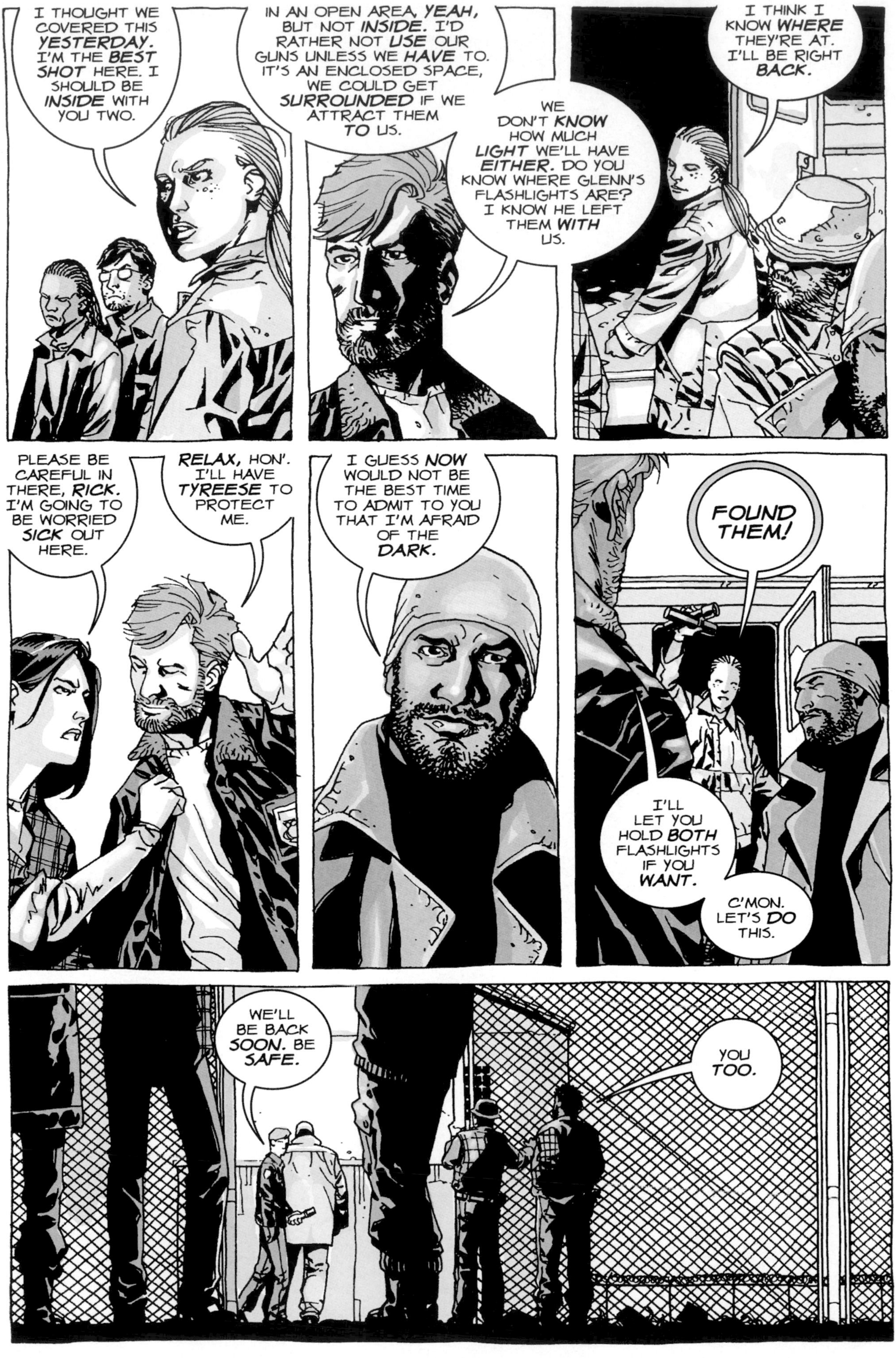
I THOUGHT WE COVERED THIS YESTERDAY. I'M THE BEST SHOT HERE. I SHOULD BE INSIDE WITH YOU TWO.
IN AN OPEN AREA, YEAH, BUT NOT INSIDE. I'D RATHER NOT USE OUR GUNS UNLESS WE HAVE TO. IT'S AN ENCLOSED SPACE, WE COULD GET SURROUNDED IF WE ATTRACT THEM TO US.
WE DON'T KNOW HOW MUCH LIGHT WE'LL HAVE EITHER. DO YOU KNOW WHERE GLENN'S FLASHLIGHTS ARE? I KNOW HE LEFT THEM WITH US.
I THINK I KNOW WHERE THEY'RE AT. I'LL BE RIGHT BACK.
PLEASE BE CAREFUL IN THERE, RICK. I'M GOING TO BE WORRIED SICK OUT HERE.
RELAX, HON'. I'LL HAVE TYREESE TO PROTECT ME.
I GUESS NOW WOULD NOT BE THE BEST TIME TO ADMIT TO YOU THAT I'M AFRAID OF THE DARK.
FOUND THEM!
I'LL LET YOU HOLD BOTH FLASHLIGHTS IF YOU WANT.
C'MON. LET'S DO THIS.
WE'LL BE BACK SOON. BE SAFE.
YOU TOO.

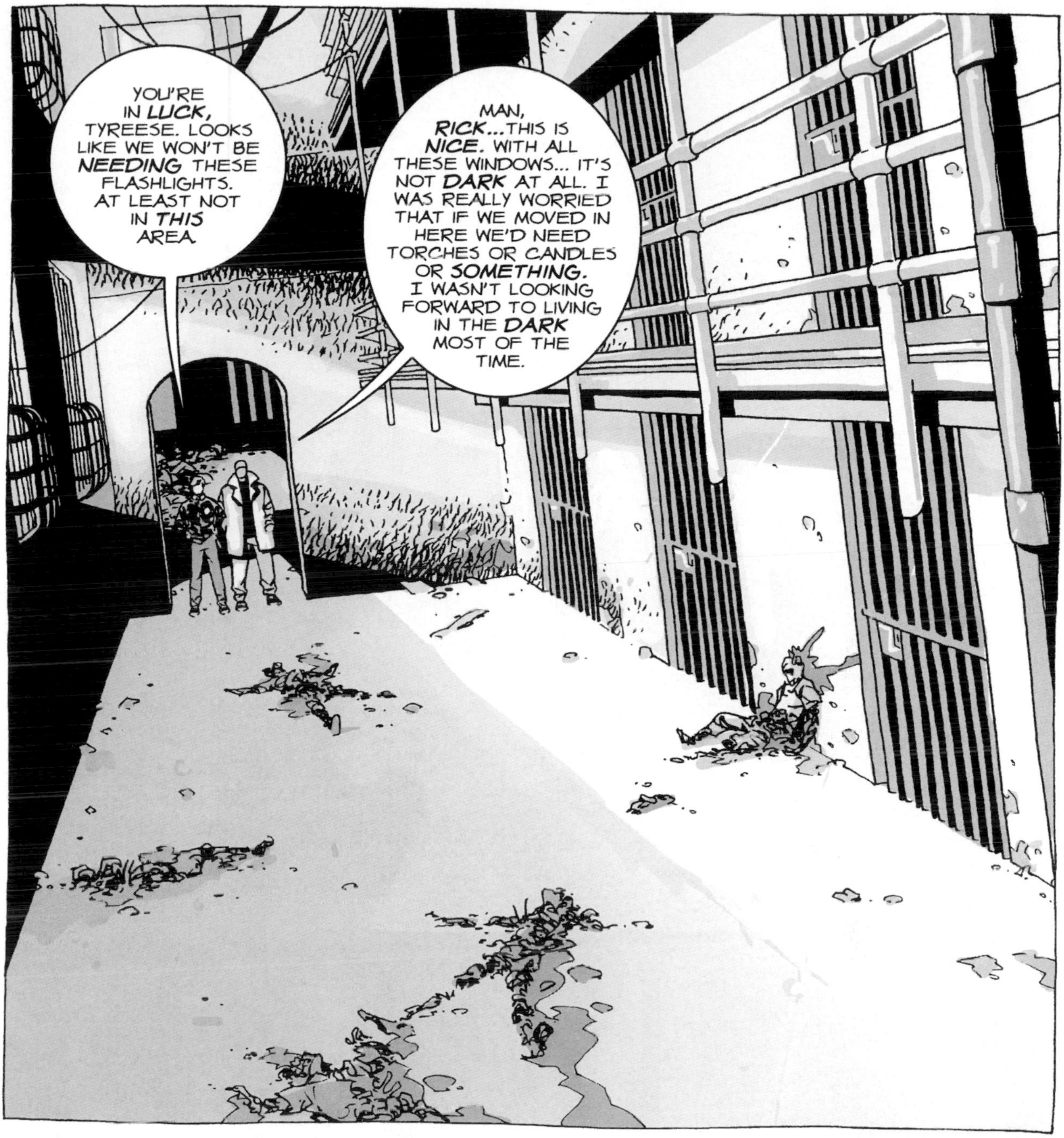
YOU'RE IN LUCK, TYREESE. LOOKS LIKE WE WON'T BE NEEDING THESE FLASHLIGHTS. AT LEAST NOT IN THIS AREA.
MAN, RICK...THIS IS NICE. WITH ALL THESE WINDOWS... IT'S NOT DARK AT ALL. I WAS REALLY WORRIED THAT IF WE MOVED IN HERE WE'D NEED TORCHES OR CANDLES OR SOMETHING. I WASN'T LOOKING FORWARD TO LIVING IN THE DARK MOST OF THE TIME.

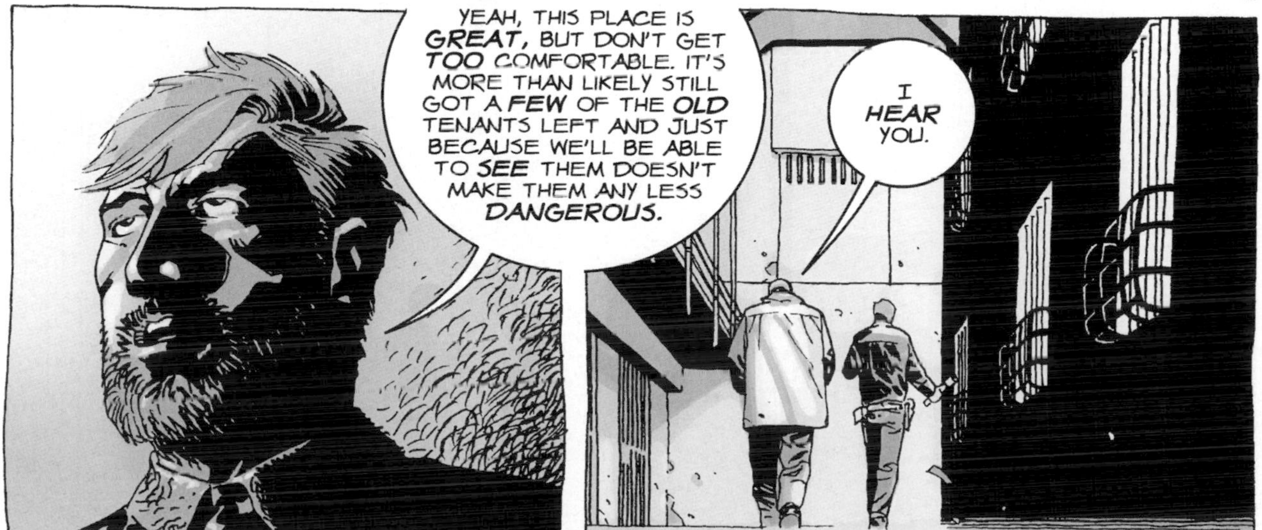
YEAH, THIS PLACE IS GREAT, BUT DON'T GET TOO COMFORTABLE. IT'S MORE THAN LIKELY STILL GOT A FEW OF THE OLD TENANTS LEFT AND JUST BECAUSE WE'LL BE ABLE TO SEE THEM DOESN'T MAKE THEM ANY LESS DANGEROUS.
I HEAR YOU.

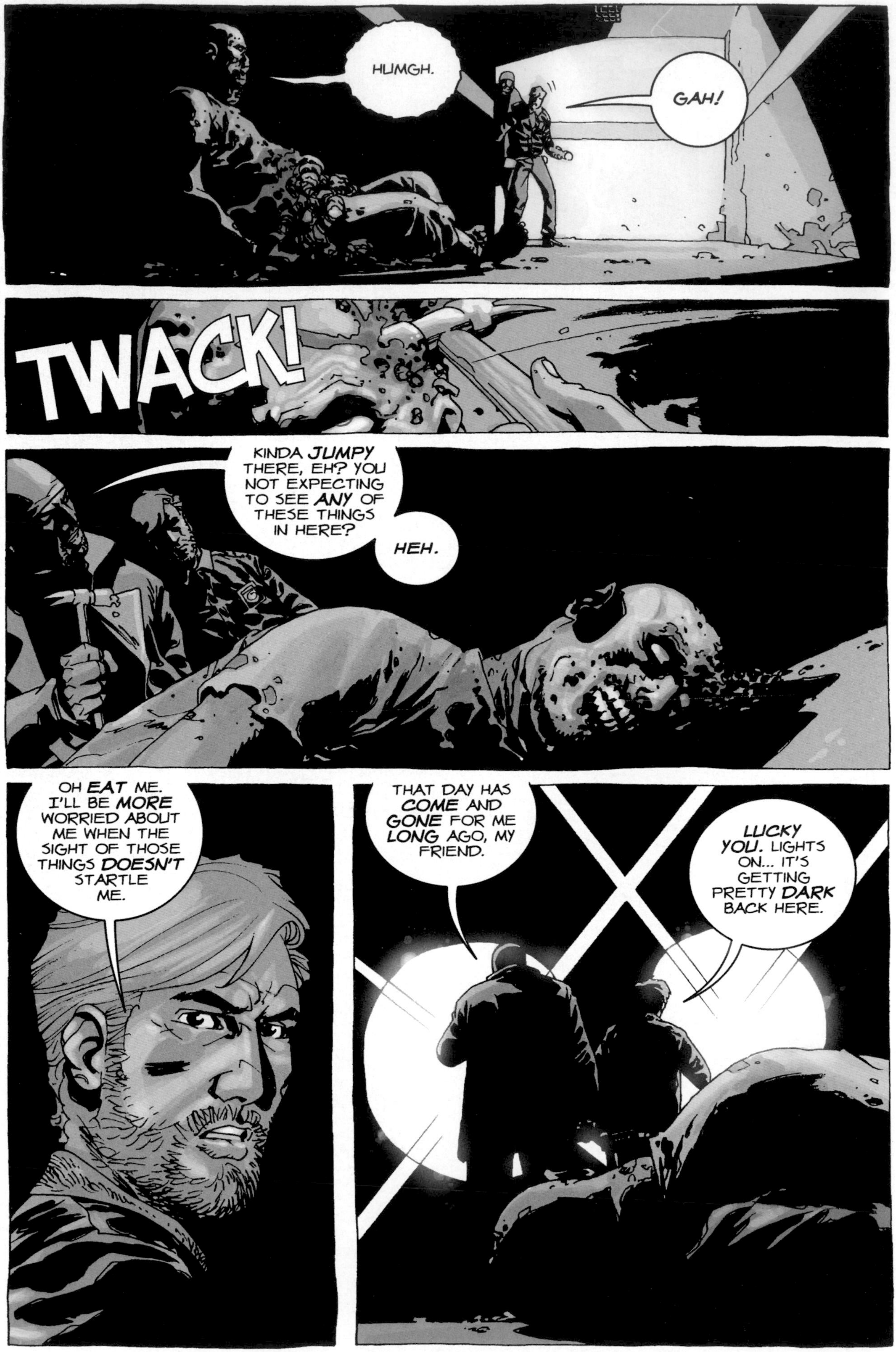
HUMGH.
GAH!
TWACK!
KINDA JUMPY THERE, EH? YOU NOT EXPECTING TO SEE ANY OF THESE THINGS IN HERE?
HEH.
OH EAT ME. I'LL BE MORE WORRIED ABOUT ME WHEN THE SIGHT OF THOSE THINGS DOESN'T STARTLE ME.
THAT DAY HAS COME AND GONE FOR ME LONG AGO, MY FRIEND.
LUCKY YOU. LIGHTS ON... IT'S GETTING PRETTY DARK BACK HERE.

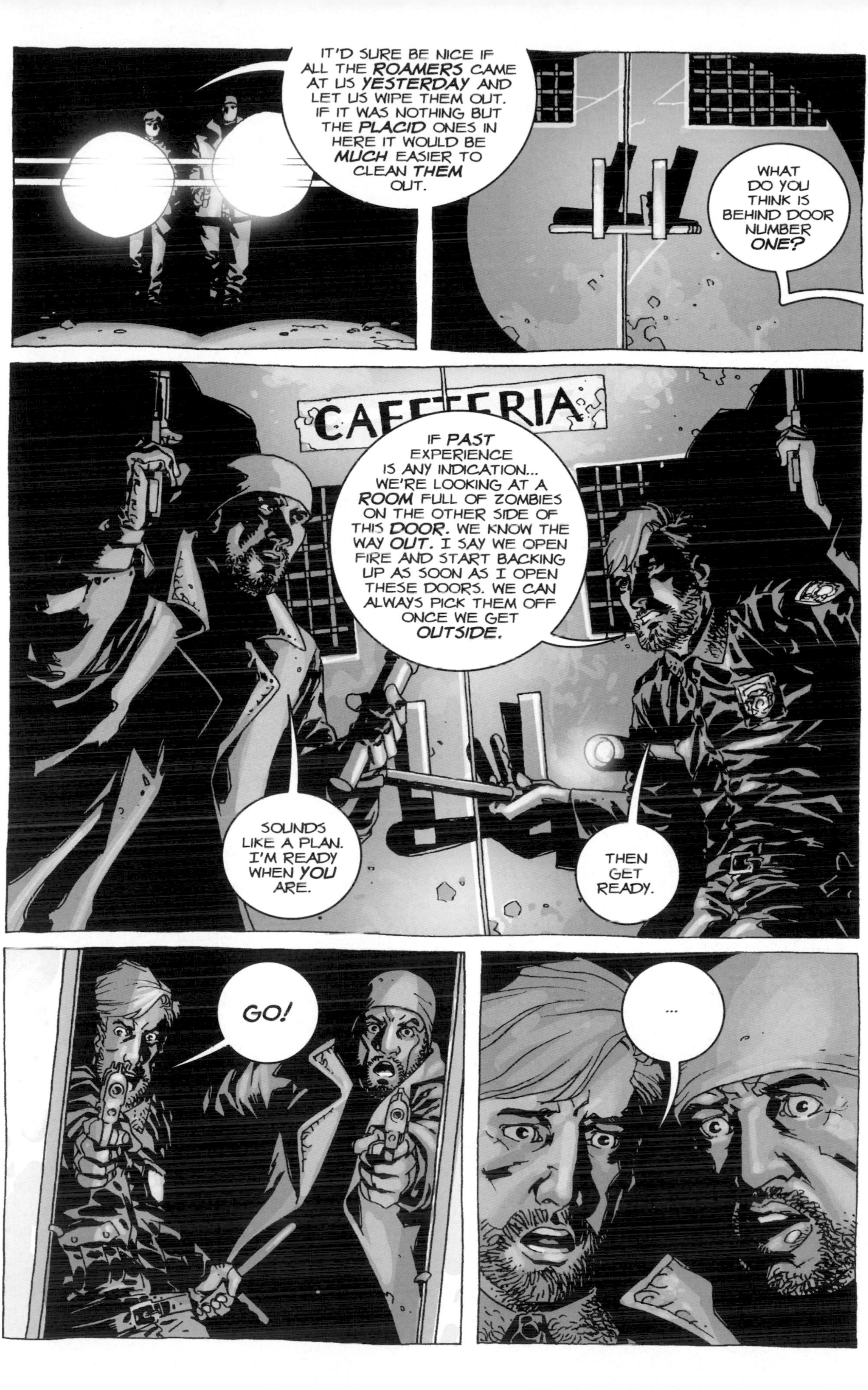
IT'D SURE BE NICE IF ALL THE ROAMERS CAME AT US YESTERDAY AND LET US WIPE THEM OUT. IF IT WAS NOTHING BUT THE PLACID ONES IN HERE IT WOULD BE MUCH EASIER TO CLEAN THEM OUT.
WHAT DO YOU THINK IS BEHIND DOOR NUMBER ONE?
CAFETERIA
IF PAST EXPERIENCE IS ANY INDICATION... WE'RE LOOKING AT A ROOM FULL OF ZOMBIES ON THE OTHER SIDE OF THIS DOOR. WE KNOW THE WAY OUT. I SAY WE OPEN FIRE AND START BACKING UP AS SOON AS I OPEN THESE DOORS. WE CAN ALWAYS PICK THEM OFF ONCE WE GET OUTSIDE.
SOUNDS LIKE A PLAN. I'M READY WHEN YOU ARE.
THEN GET READY.
GO!
...

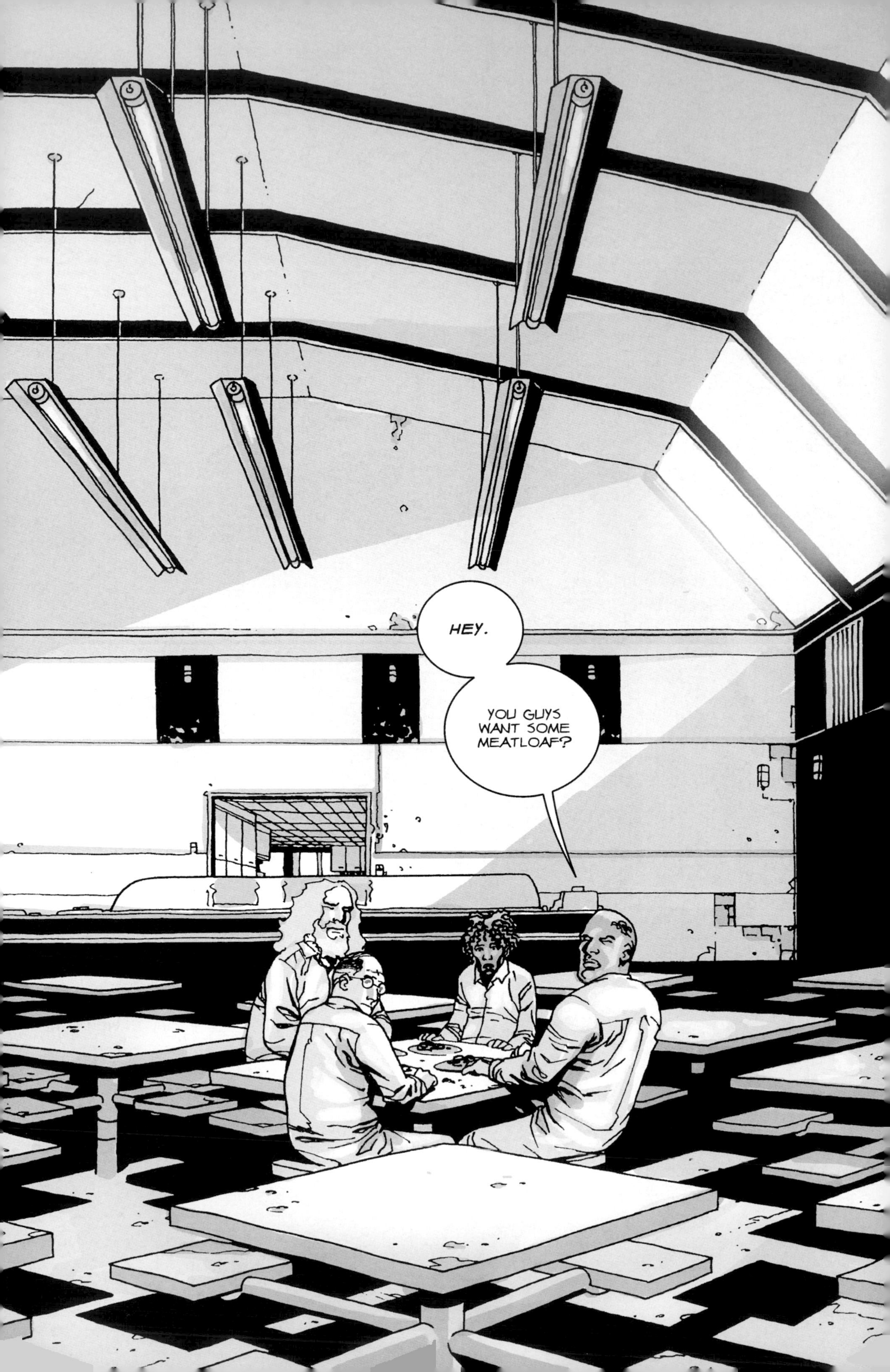
HEY.
YOU GUYS WANT SOME MEATLOAF?

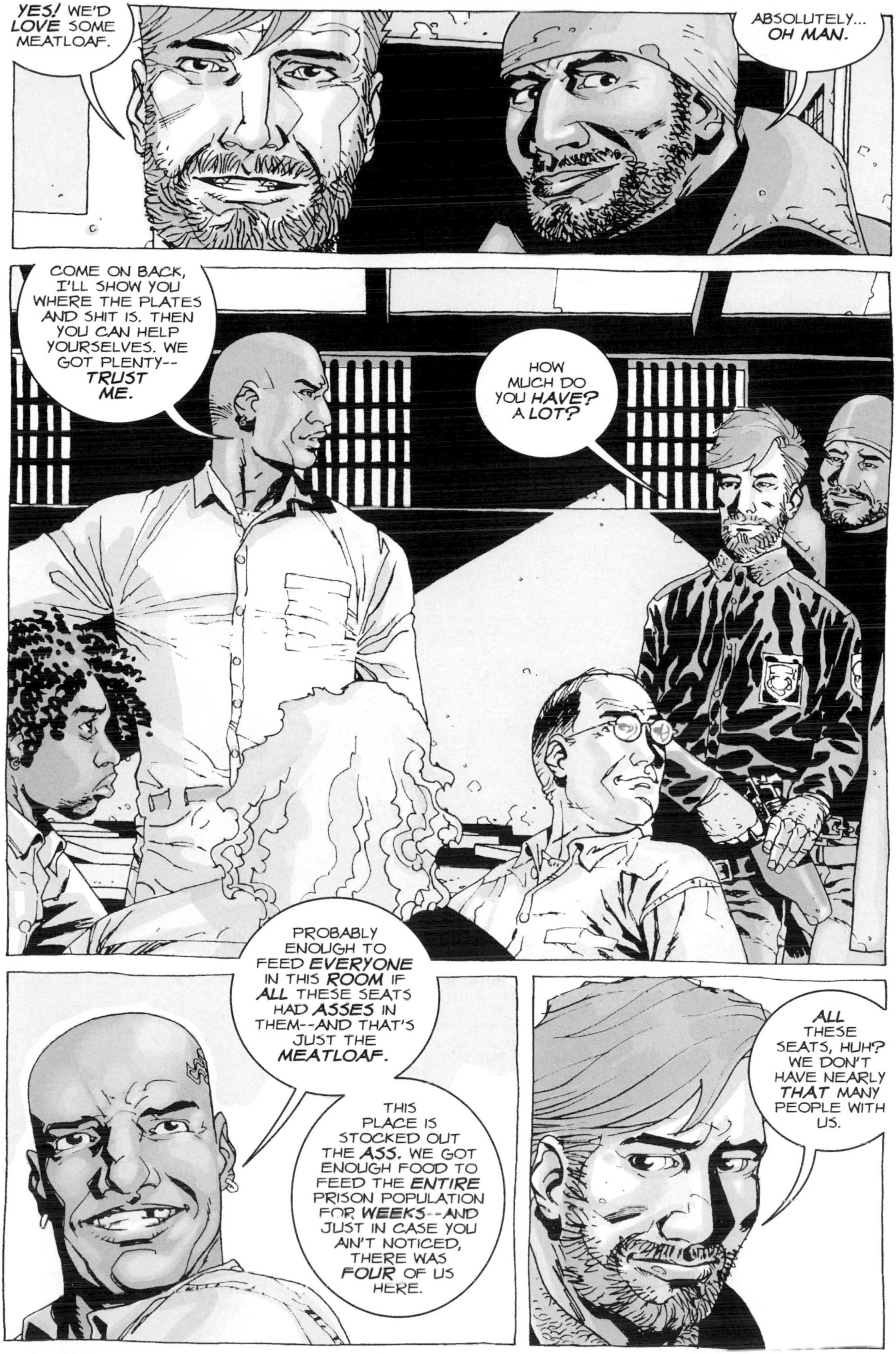
YES! WE'D LOVE SOME MEATLOAF.
ABSOLUTELY... OH MAN.
COME ON BACK, I'LL SHOW YOU WHERE THE PLATES AND SHIT IS. THEN YOU CAN HELP YOURSELVES. WE GOT PLENTY-- TRUST ME.
HOW MUCH DO YOU HAVE? A LOT?
PROBABLY ENOUGH TO FEED EVERYONE IN THIS ROOM IF ALL THESE SEATS HAD ASSES IN THEM--AND THAT'S JUST THE MEATLOAF.
THIS PLACE IS STOCKED OUT THE ASS. WE GOT ENOUGH FOOD TO FEED THE ENTIRE PRISON POPULATION FOR WEEKS--AND JUST IN CASE YOU AIN'T NOTICED, THERE WAS FOUR OF US HERE.
ALL THESE SEATS, HUH? WE DON'T HAVE NEARLY THAT MANY PEOPLE WITH US.

WOW! THIS IS **AMAZING**.

NOT SURE-- BUT I CAN STILL BE IMPRESSED.

CHANGING YOUR MIND ABOUT THIS PLACE YET? YOU THINK WE CAN **STAY** HERE?

C'MON, EVERYBODY-- THEY'VE GOT THE **FOOD** BACK THIS WAY. I KNOW YOU'RE **ALL** STARVED.

NOT **TOO** MUCH, SON. WE'VE GOT TO SAVE ENOUGH FOR **EVERYONE** TO HAVE SOME.

RICK, **LOOK** AT THIS TRAY. I DON'T THINK WE CAN EAT ALL THIS IF WE **TRIED**.

I DON'T MEAN TO **INTERRUPT**--BUT YOU GUYS DON'T LOOK LIKE NO **RESCUE TEAM** TO **ME**. I MEAN YOU ACT LIKE YOU AIN'T EATEN IN **WEEKS**.

YOU FOLLOW ME?

RESCUE TEAM? NO--WE'RE JUST...I DON'T KNOW **WHAT** WE ARE... WE'RE JUST **PEOPLE**. YOU GUYS ARE DOING **MUCH** BETTER IN **HERE** THAN **WE** WERE OUT **THERE**.

WE'RE **NOT** HERE TO **RESCUE** YOU.

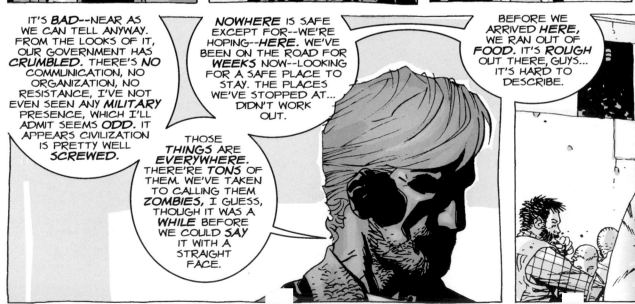

IT'S **BAD**--NEAR AS WE CAN TELL ANYWAY. FROM THE LOOKS OF IT, OUR GOVERNMENT HAS **CRUMBLED**. THERE'S **NO** COMMUNICATION, NO ORGANIZATION, NO RESISTANCE, I'VE NOT EVEN SEEN ANY **MILITARY** PRESENCE, WHICH I'LL ADMIT SEEMS **ODD**. IT APPEARS CIVILIZATION IS PRETTY WELL **SCREWED**.

THOSE **THINGS** ARE **EVERYWHERE**. THERE'RE **TONS** OF THEM. WE'VE TAKEN TO CALLING THEM **ZOMBIES**, I GUESS, THOUGH IT WAS A **WHILE** BEFORE WE COULD **SAY** IT WITH A STRAIGHT FACE.

NOWHERE IS SAFE EXCEPT FOR--WE'RE HOPING--**HERE**. WE'VE BEEN ON THE ROAD FOR **WEEKS** NOW--LOOKING FOR A SAFE PLACE TO STAY. THE PLACES WE'VE STOPPED AT... DIDN'T WORK OUT.

BEFORE WE ARRIVED **HERE**, WE RAN OUT OF **FOOD**. IT'S **ROUGH** OUT THERE, GUYS... IT'S HARD TO DESCRIBE.

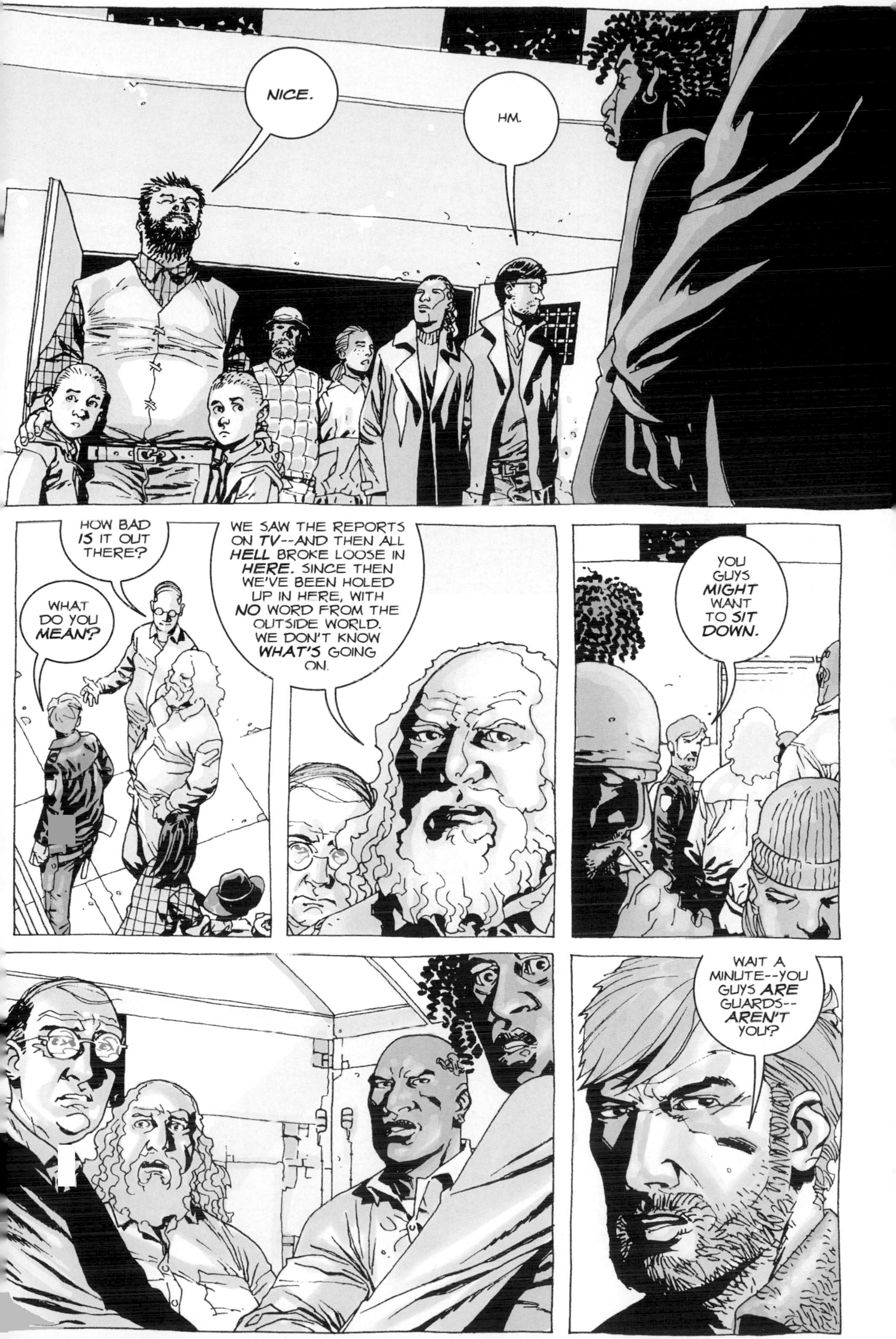
NICE.
HM.
HOW BAD IS IT OUT THERE?
WHAT DO YOU MEAN?
WE SAW THE REPORTS ON TV--AND THEN ALL HELL BROKE LOOSE IN HERE. SINCE THEN WE'VE BEEN HOLED UP IN HERE, WITH NO WORD FROM THE OUTSIDE WORLD. WE DON'T KNOW WHAT'S GOING ON.
YOU GUYS MIGHT WANT TO SIT DOWN.
WAIT A MINUTE--YOU GUYS ARE GUARDS--AREN'T YOU?

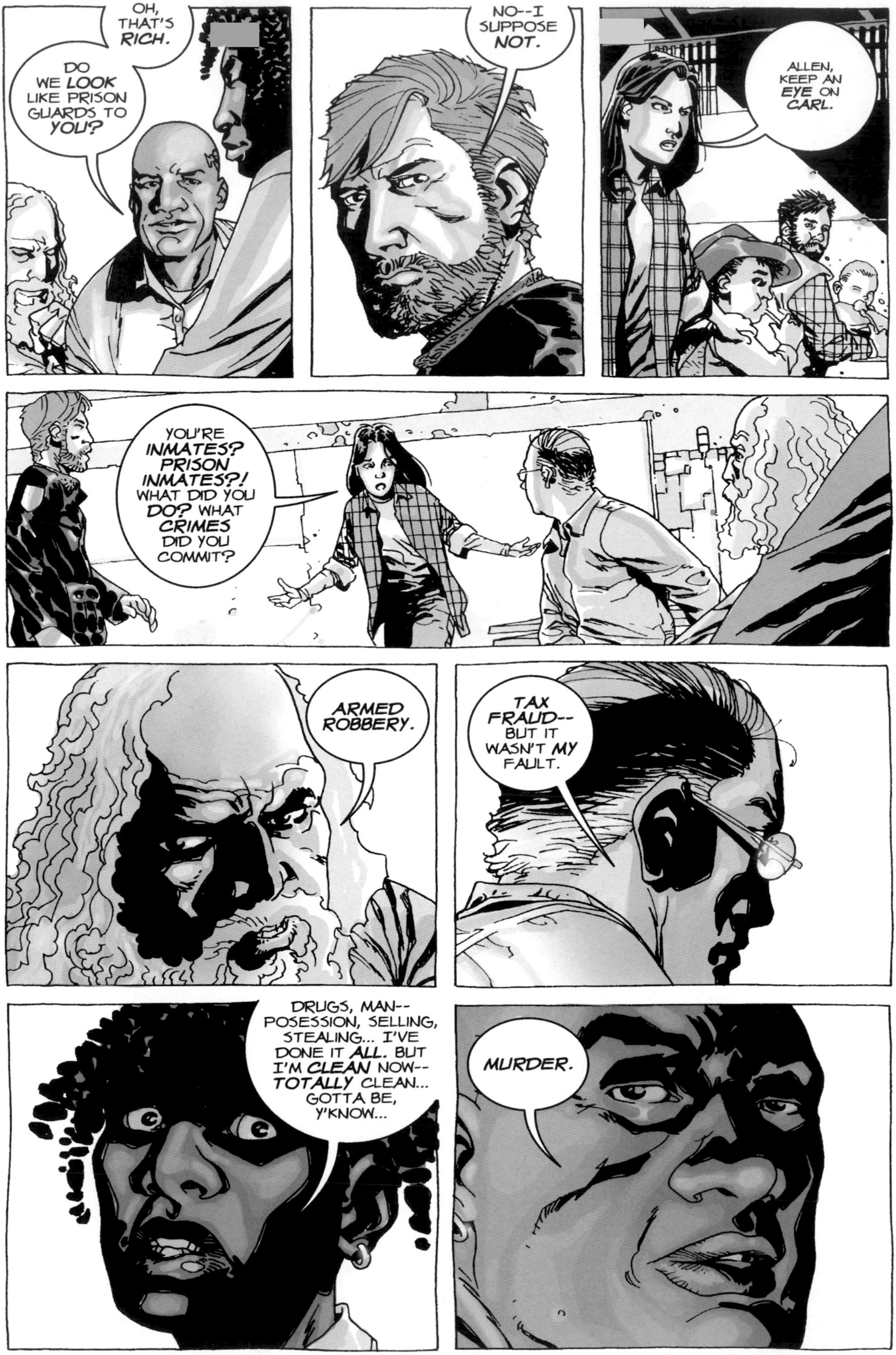

OH, THAT'S RICH.
DO WE LOOK LIKE PRISON GUARDS TO YOU?
NO--I SUPPOSE NOT.
ALLEN, KEEP AN EYE ON CARL.
YOU'RE INMATES? PRISON INMATES?! WHAT DID YOU DO? WHAT CRIMES DID YOU COMMIT?
ARMED ROBBERY.
TAX FRAUD-- BUT IT WASN'T MY FAULT.
DRUGS, MAN-- POSESSION, SELLING, STEALING... I'VE DONE IT ALL. BUT I'M CLEAN NOW-- TOTALLY CLEAN... GOTTA BE, Y'KNOW...
MURDER.

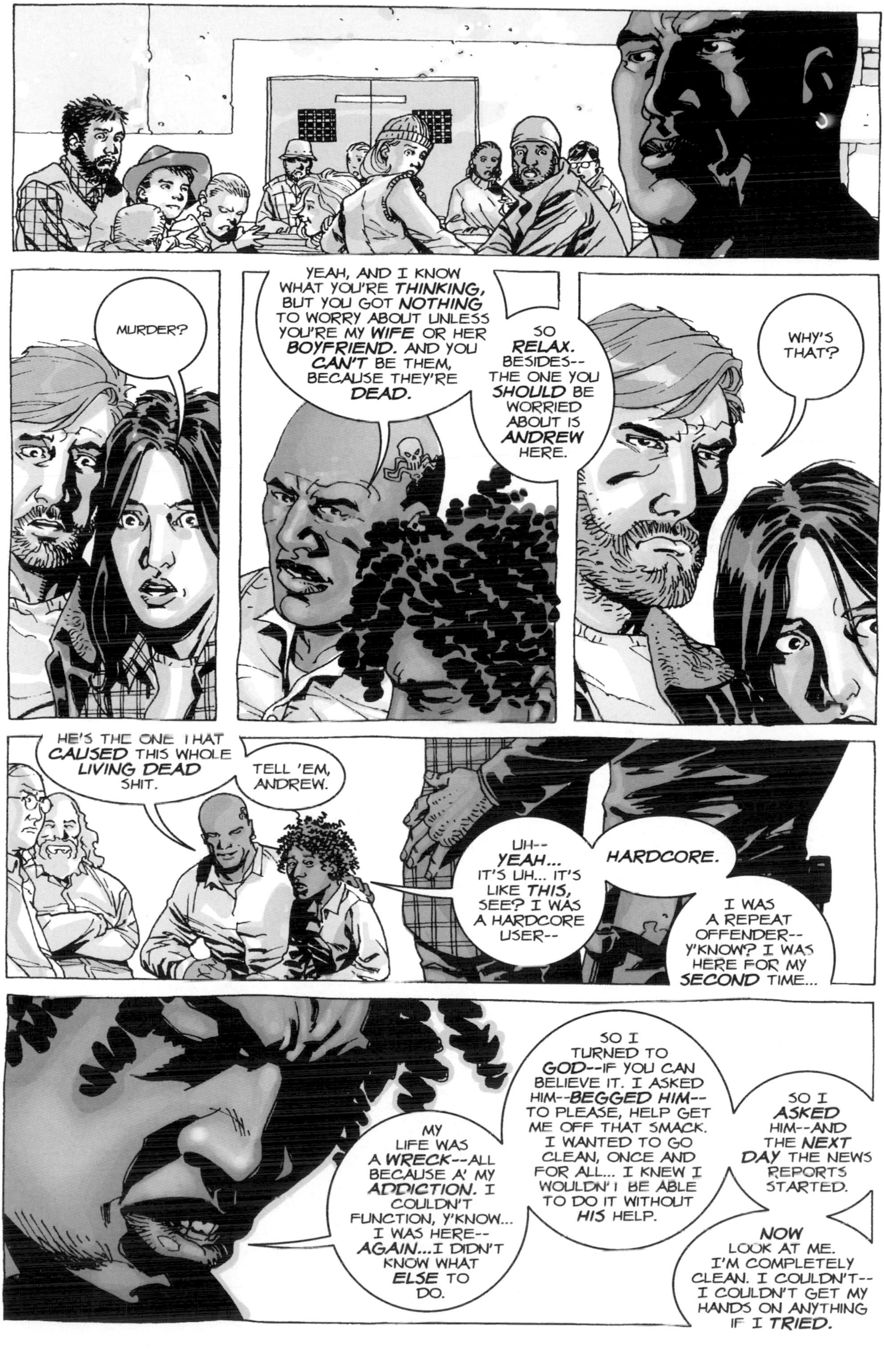
MURDER?
YEAH, AND I KNOW WHAT YOU'RE THINKING, BUT YOU GOT NOTHING TO WORRY ABOUT UNLESS YOU'RE MY WIFE OR HER BOYFRIEND. AND YOU CAN'T BE THEM, BECAUSE THEY'RE DEAD.
SO RELAX. BESIDES-- THE ONE YOU SHOULD BE WORRIED ABOUT IS ANDREW HERE.
WHY'S THAT?
HE'S THE ONE THAT CAUSED THIS WHOLE LIVING DEAD SHIT.
TELL 'EM, ANDREW.
UH-- YEAH... IT'S UH... IT'S LIKE THIS, SEE? I WAS A HARDCORE USER--
HARDCORE.
I WAS A REPEAT OFFENDER-- Y'KNOW? I WAS HERE FOR MY SECOND TIME...
MY LIFE WAS A WRECK--ALL BECAUSE A' MY ADDICTION. I COULDN'T FUNCTION, Y'KNOW... I WAS HERE-- AGAIN...I DIDN'T KNOW WHAT ELSE TO DO.
SO I TURNED TO GOD--IF YOU CAN BELIEVE IT. I ASKED HIM--BEGGED HIM-- TO PLEASE, HELP GET ME OFF THAT SMACK. I WANTED TO GO CLEAN, ONCE AND FOR ALL... I KNEW I WOULDN'T BE ABLE TO DO IT WITHOUT HIS HELP.
SO I ASKED HIM--AND THE NEXT DAY THE NEWS REPORTS STARTED.
NOW LOOK AT ME. I'M COMPLETELY CLEAN. I COULDN'T-- I COULDN'T GET MY HANDS ON ANYTHING IF I TRIED.

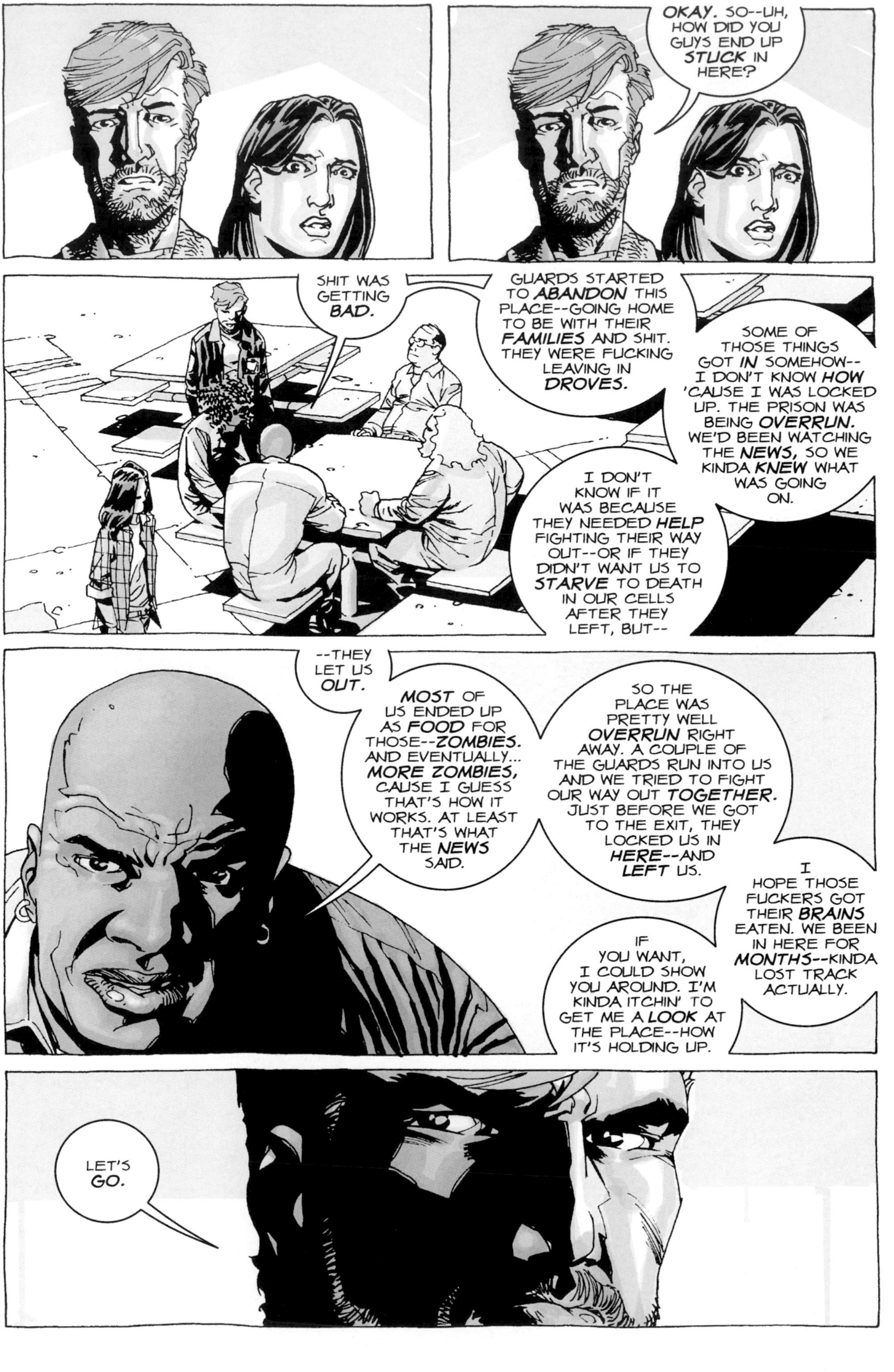
OKAY. SO--UH, HOW DID YOU GUYS END UP STUCK IN HERE?
SHIT WAS GETTING BAD.
GUARDS STARTED TO ABANDON THIS PLACE--GOING HOME TO BE WITH THEIR FAMILIES AND SHIT. THEY WERE FUCKING LEAVING IN DROVES.
SOME OF THOSE THINGS GOT IN SOMEHOW-- I DON'T KNOW HOW 'CAUSE I WAS LOCKED UP. THE PRISON WAS BEING OVERRUN. WE'D BEEN WATCHING THE NEWS, SO WE KINDA KNEW WHAT WAS GOING ON.
I DON'T KNOW IF IT WAS BECAUSE THEY NEEDED HELP FIGHTING THEIR WAY OUT--OR IF THEY DIDN'T WANT US TO STARVE TO DEATH IN OUR CELLS AFTER THEY LEFT, BUT--
--THEY LET US OUT.
MOST OF US ENDED UP AS FOOD FOR THOSE--ZOMBIES. AND EVENTUALLY... MORE ZOMBIES, CAUSE I GUESS THAT'S HOW IT WORKS. AT LEAST THAT'S WHAT THE NEWS SAID.
SO THE PLACE WAS PRETTY WELL OVERRUN RIGHT AWAY. A COUPLE OF THE GUARDS RUN INTO US AND WE TRIED TO FIGHT OUR WAY OUT TOGETHER. JUST BEFORE WE GOT TO THE EXIT, THEY LOCKED US IN HERE--AND LEFT US.
I HOPE THOSE FUCKERS GOT THEIR BRAINS EATEN. WE BEEN IN HERE FOR MONTHS--KINDA LOST TRACK ACTUALLY.
IF YOU WANT, I COULD SHOW YOU AROUND. I'M KINDA ITCHIN' TO GET ME A LOOK AT THE PLACE--HOW IT'S HOLDING UP.
LET'S GO.

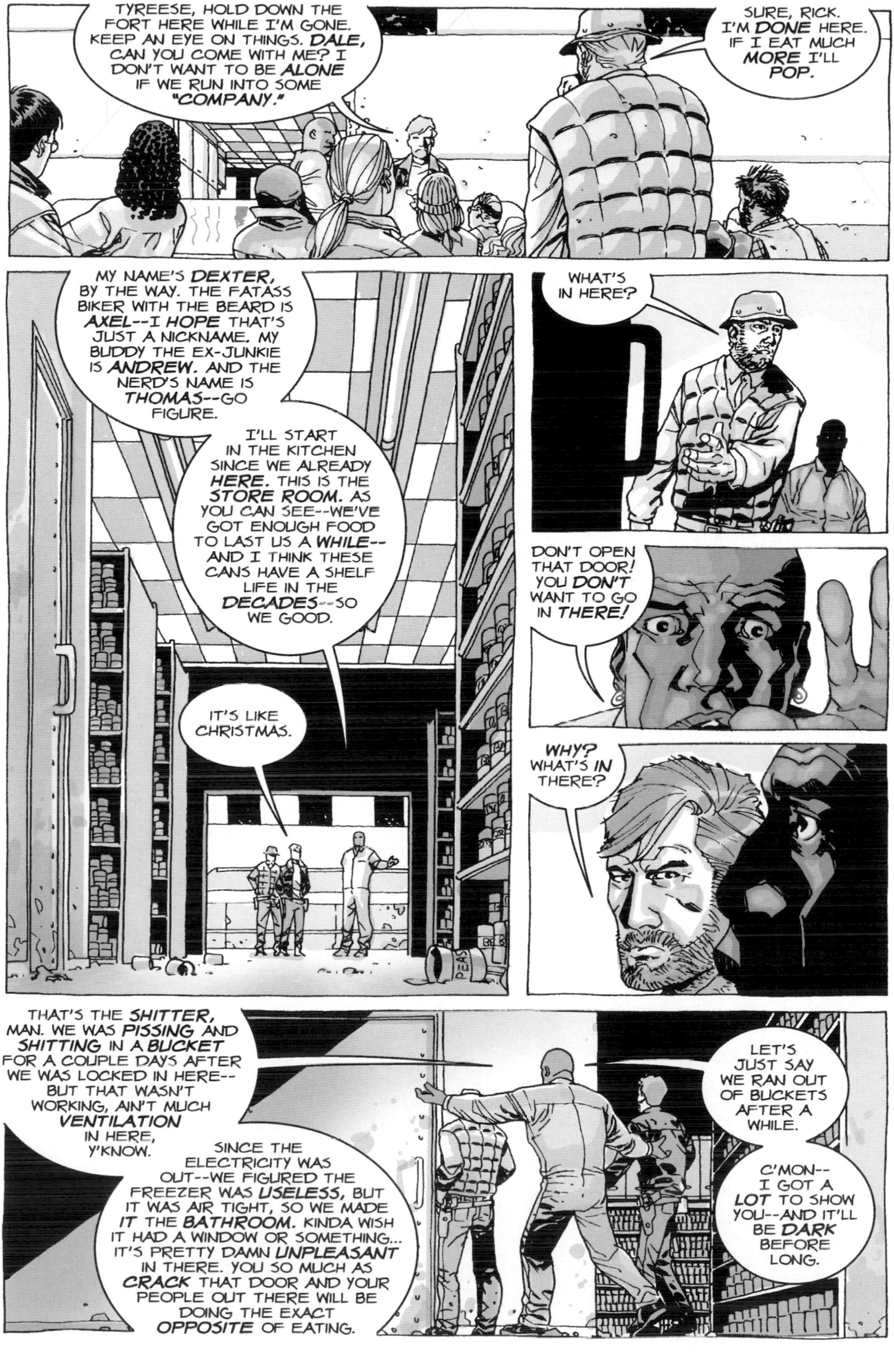
TYREESE, HOLD DOWN THE FORT HERE WHILE I'M GONE. KEEP AN EYE ON THINGS. DALE, CAN YOU COME WITH ME? I DON'T WANT TO BE ALONE IF WE RUN INTO SOME "COMPANY."
SURE, RICK. I'M DONE HERE. IF I EAT MUCH MORE I'LL POP.
MY NAME'S DEXTER, BY THE WAY. THE FATASS BIKER WITH THE BEARD IS AXEL--I HOPE THAT'S JUST A NICKNAME. MY BUDDY THE EX-JUNKIE IS ANDREW. AND THE NERD'S NAME IS THOMAS--GO FIGURE.
I'LL START IN THE KITCHEN SINCE WE ALREADY HERE. THIS IS THE STORE ROOM. AS YOU CAN SEE--WE'VE GOT ENOUGH FOOD TO LAST US A WHILE--AND I THINK THESE CANS HAVE A SHELF LIFE IN THE DECADES--SO WE GOOD.
IT'S LIKE CHRISTMAS.
PEAS
WHAT'S IN HERE?
DON'T OPEN THAT DOOR! YOU DON'T WANT TO GO IN THERE!
WHY? WHAT'S IN THERE?
THAT'S THE SHITTER, MAN. WE WAS PISSING AND SHITTING IN A BUCKET FOR A COUPLE DAYS AFTER WE WAS LOCKED IN HERE--BUT THAT WASN'T WORKING, AIN'T MUCH VENTILATION IN HERE, Y'KNOW.
SINCE THE ELECTRICITY WAS OUT--WE FIGURED THE FREEZER WAS USELESS, BUT IT WAS AIR TIGHT, SO WE MADE IT THE BATHROOM. KINDA WISH IT HAD A WINDOW OR SOMETHING... IT'S PRETTY DAMN UNPLEASANT IN THERE. YOU SO MUCH AS CRACK THAT DOOR AND YOUR PEOPLE OUT THERE WILL BE DOING THE EXACT OPPOSITE OF EATING.
LET'S JUST SAY WE RAN OUT OF BUCKETS AFTER A WHILE.
C'MON--I GOT A LOT TO SHOW YOU--AND IT'LL BE DARK BEFORE LONG.

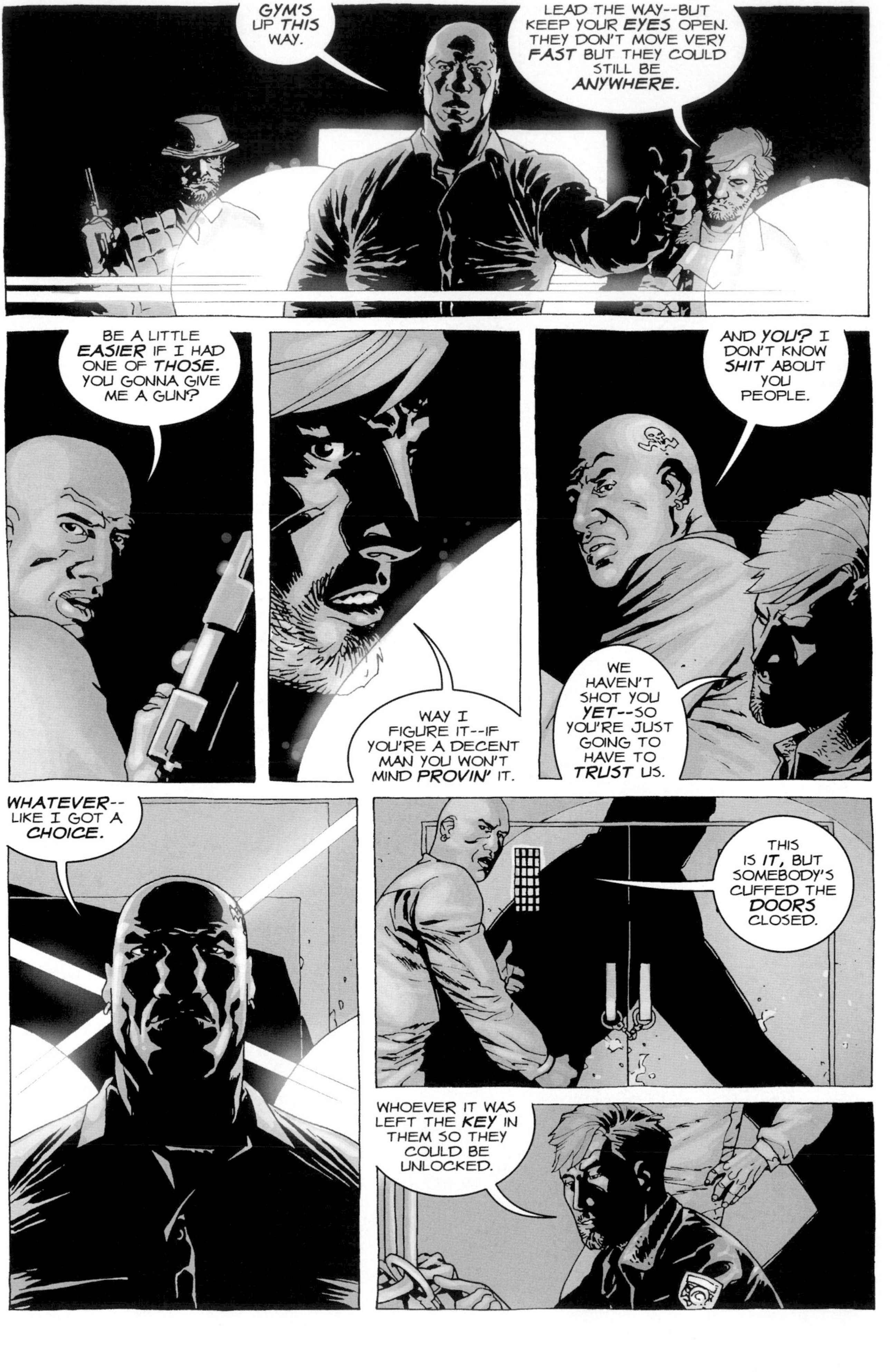
GYM'S UP THIS WAY.
LEAD THE WAY--BUT KEEP YOUR EYES OPEN. THEY DON'T MOVE VERY FAST BUT THEY COULD STILL BE ANYWHERE.
BE A LITTLE EASIER IF I HAD ONE OF THOSE. YOU GONNA GIVE ME A GUN?
WAY I FIGURE IT--IF YOU'RE A DECENT MAN YOU WON'T MIND PROVIN' IT.
AND YOU? I DON'T KNOW SHIT ABOUT YOU PEOPLE.
WE HAVEN'T SHOT YOU YET--SO YOU'RE JUST GOING TO HAVE TO TRUST US.
WHATEVER-- LIKE I GOT A CHOICE.
THIS IS IT, BUT SOMEBODY'S CUFFED THE DOORS CLOSED.
WHOEVER IT WAS LEFT THE KEY IN THEM SO THEY COULD BE UNLOCKED.

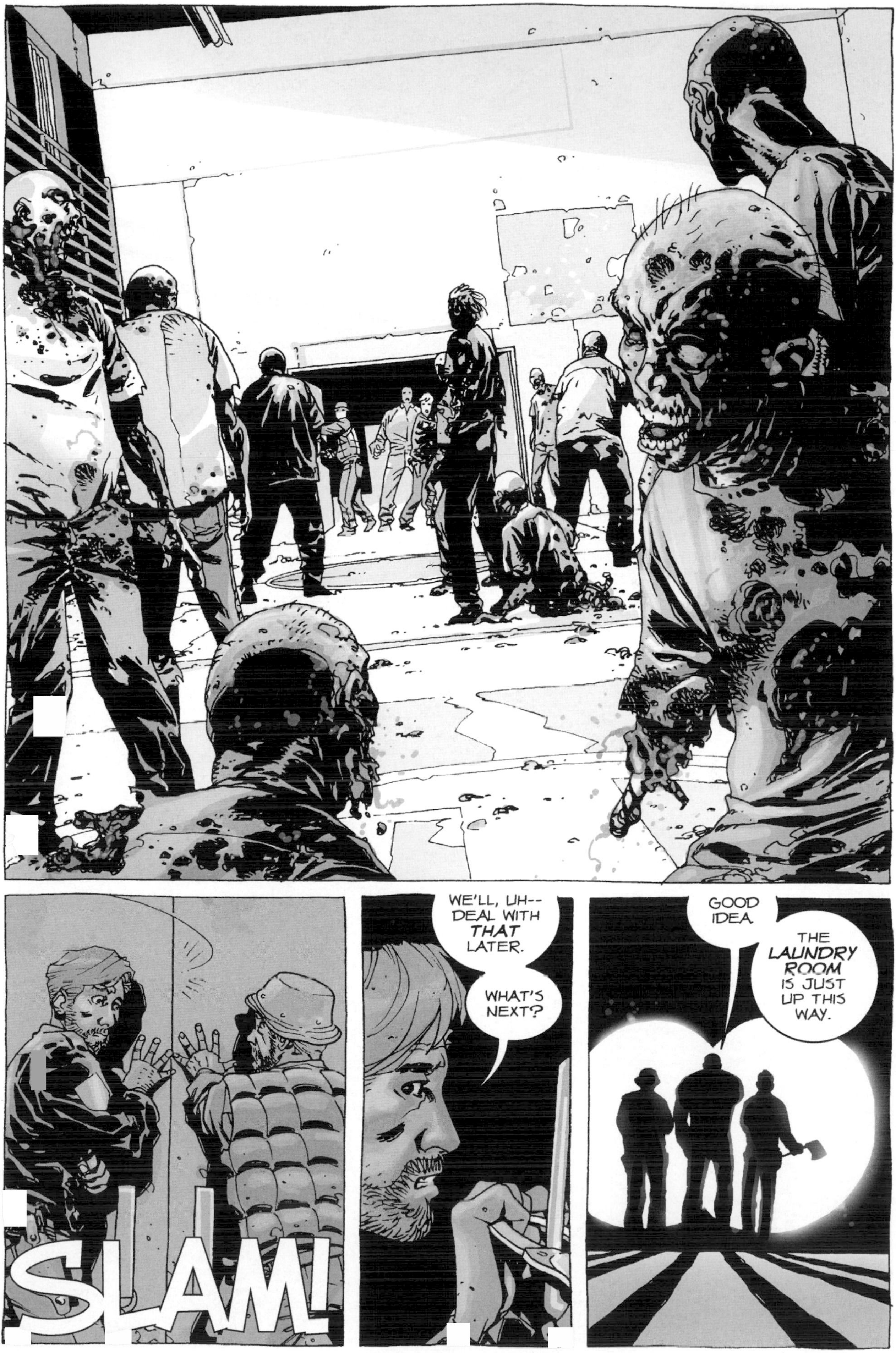
SLAM!
WE'LL, UH-- DEAL WITH *THAT* LATER.
WHAT'S NEXT?
GOOD IDEA.
THE *LAUNDRY ROOM* IS JUST UP THIS WAY.

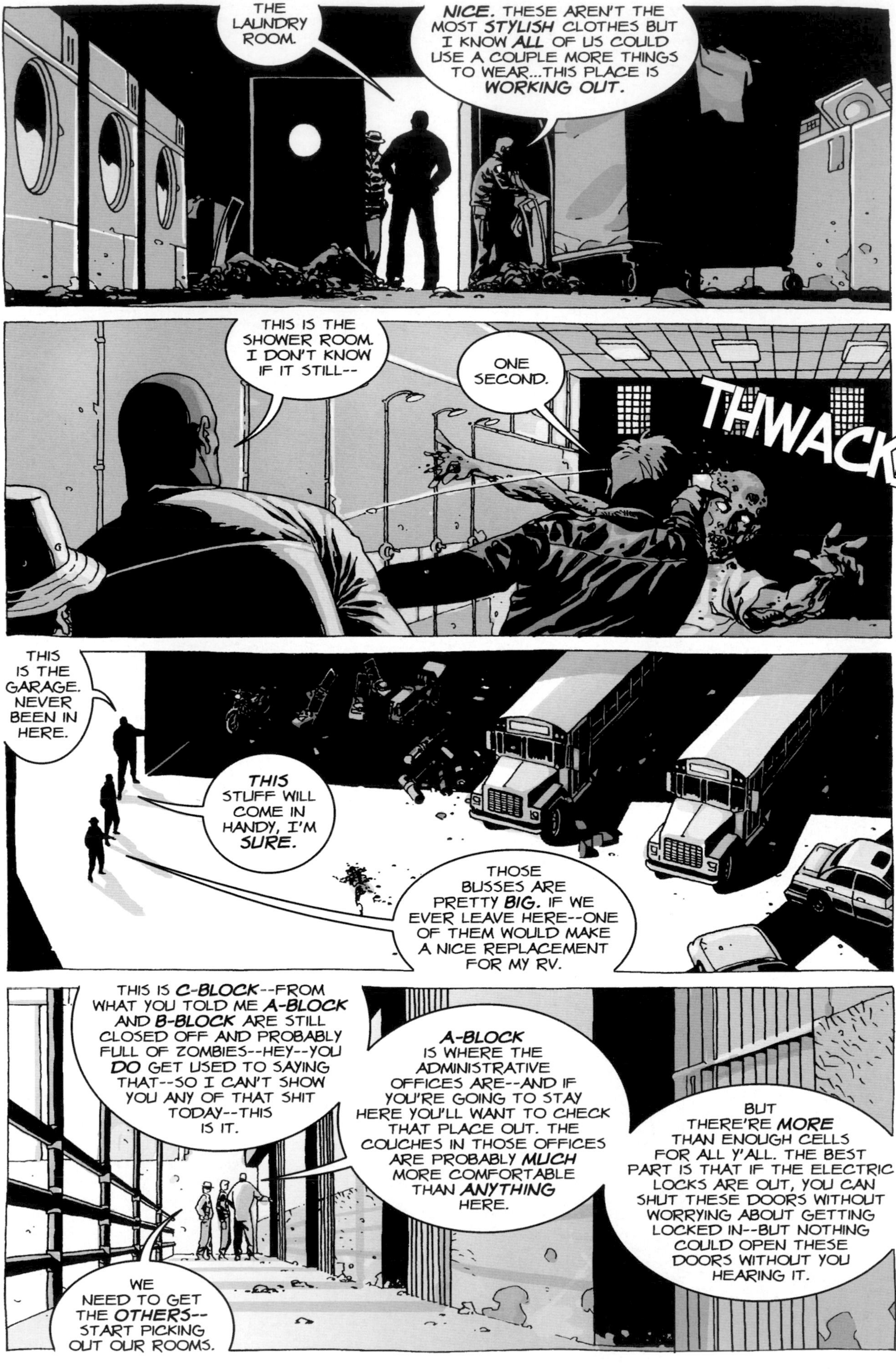
THE LAUNDRY ROOM.
NICE. THESE AREN'T THE MOST STYLISH CLOTHES BUT I KNOW ALL OF US COULD USE A COUPLE MORE THINGS TO WEAR...THIS PLACE IS WORKING OUT.
THIS IS THE SHOWER ROOM. I DON'T KNOW IF IT STILL--
ONE SECOND.
THWACK!
THIS IS THE GARAGE. NEVER BEEN IN HERE.
THIS STUFF WILL COME IN HANDY, I'M SURE.
THOSE BUSSES ARE PRETTY BIG. IF WE EVER LEAVE HERE--ONE OF THEM WOULD MAKE A NICE REPLACEMENT FOR MY RV.
THIS IS C-BLOCK--FROM WHAT YOU TOLD ME A-BLOCK AND B-BLOCK ARE STILL CLOSED OFF AND PROBABLY FULL OF ZOMBIES--HEY--YOU DO GET USED TO SAYING THAT--SO I CAN'T SHOW YOU ANY OF THAT SHIT TODAY--THIS IS IT.
A-BLOCK IS WHERE THE ADMINISTRATIVE OFFICES ARE--AND IF YOU'RE GOING TO STAY HERE YOU'LL WANT TO CHECK THAT PLACE OUT. THE COUCHES IN THOSE OFFICES ARE PROBABLY MUCH MORE COMFORTABLE THAN ANYTHING HERE.
BUT THERE'RE MORE THAN ENOUGH CELLS FOR ALL Y'ALL. THE BEST PART IS THAT IF THE ELECTRIC LOCKS ARE OUT, YOU CAN SHUT THESE DOORS WITHOUT WORRYING ABOUT GETTING LOCKED IN--BUT NOTHING COULD OPEN THESE DOORS WITHOUT YOU HEARING IT.
WE NEED TO GET THE OTHERS--START PICKING OUT OUR ROOMS.

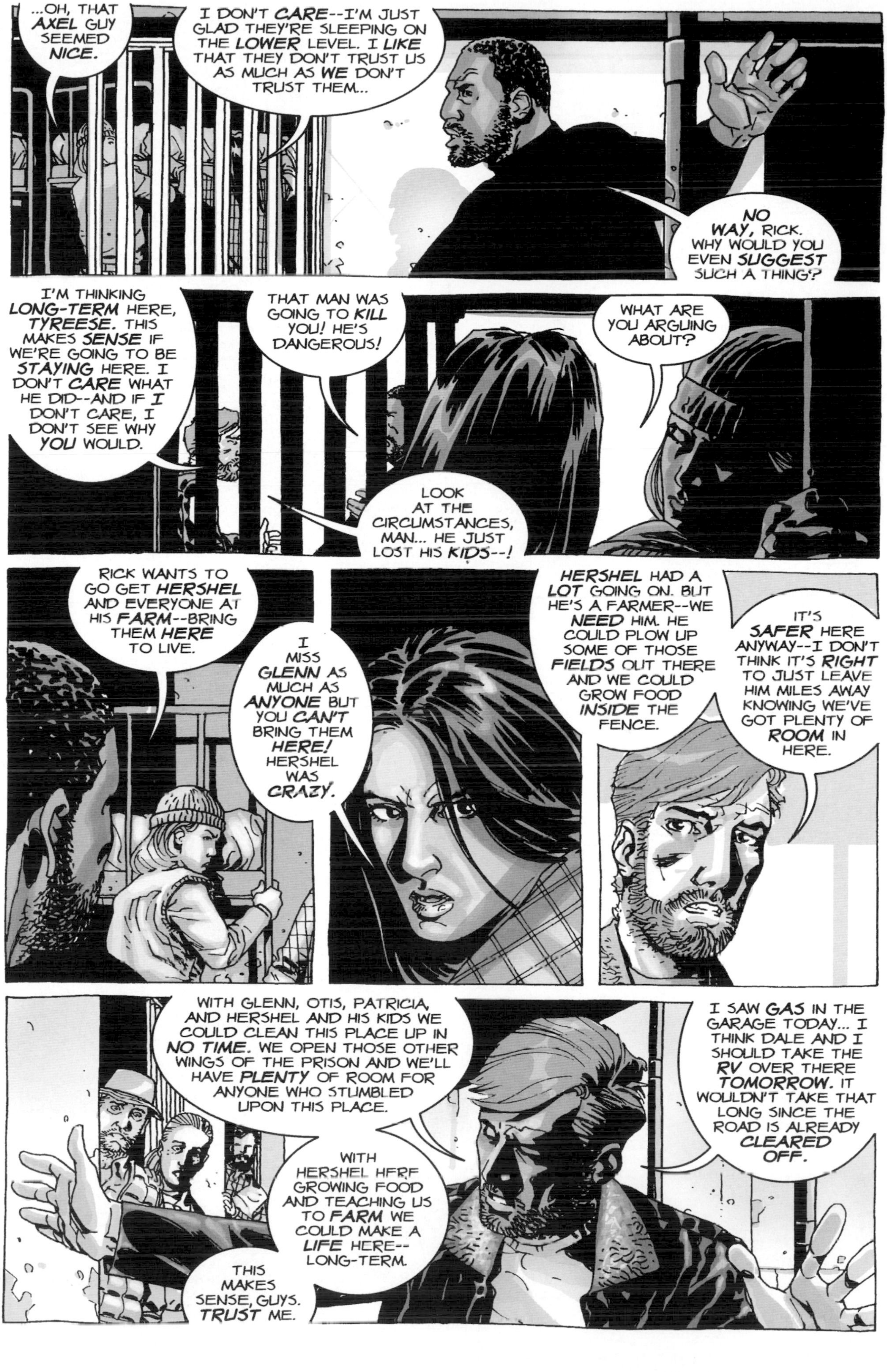
...OH, THAT AXEL GUY SEEMED NICE.
I DON'T CARE--I'M JUST GLAD THEY'RE SLEEPING ON THE LOWER LEVEL. I LIKE THAT THEY DON'T TRUST US AS MUCH AS WE DON'T TRUST THEM...
NO WAY, RICK. WHY WOULD YOU EVEN SUGGEST SUCH A THING?
I'M THINKING LONG-TERM HERE, TYREESE. THIS MAKES SENSE IF WE'RE GOING TO BE STAYING HERE. I DON'T CARE WHAT HE DID--AND IF I DON'T CARE, I DON'T SEE WHY YOU WOULD.
THAT MAN WAS GOING TO KILL YOU! HE'S DANGEROUS!
LOOK AT THE CIRCUMSTANCES, MAN... HE JUST LOST HIS KIDS--!
WHAT ARE YOU ARGUING ABOUT?
RICK WANTS TO GO GET HERSHEL AND EVERYONE AT HIS FARM--BRING THEM HERE TO LIVE.
I MISS GLENN AS MUCH AS ANYONE BUT YOU CAN'T BRING THEM HERE! HERSHEL WAS CRAZY.
HERSHEL HAD A LOT GOING ON. BUT HE'S A FARMER--WE NEED HIM. HE COULD PLOW UP SOME OF THOSE FIELDS OUT THERE AND WE COULD GROW FOOD INSIDE THE FENCE.
IT'S SAFER HERE ANYWAY--I DON'T THINK IT'S RIGHT TO JUST LEAVE HIM MILES AWAY KNOWING WE'VE GOT PLENTY OF ROOM IN HERE.
WITH GLENN, OTIS, PATRICIA, AND HERSHEL AND HIS KIDS WE COULD CLEAN THIS PLACE UP IN NO TIME. WE OPEN THOSE OTHER WINGS OF THE PRISON AND WE'LL HAVE PLENTY OF ROOM FOR ANYONE WHO STUMBLED UPON THIS PLACE.
WITH HERSHEL HERE GROWING FOOD AND TEACHING US TO FARM WE COULD MAKE A LIFE HERE-- LONG-TERM.
THIS MAKES SENSE, GUYS. TRUST ME.
I SAW GAS IN THE GARAGE TODAY... I THINK DALE AND I SHOULD TAKE THE RV OVER THERE TOMORROW. IT WOULDN'T TAKE THAT LONG SINCE THE ROAD IS ALREADY CLEARED OFF.

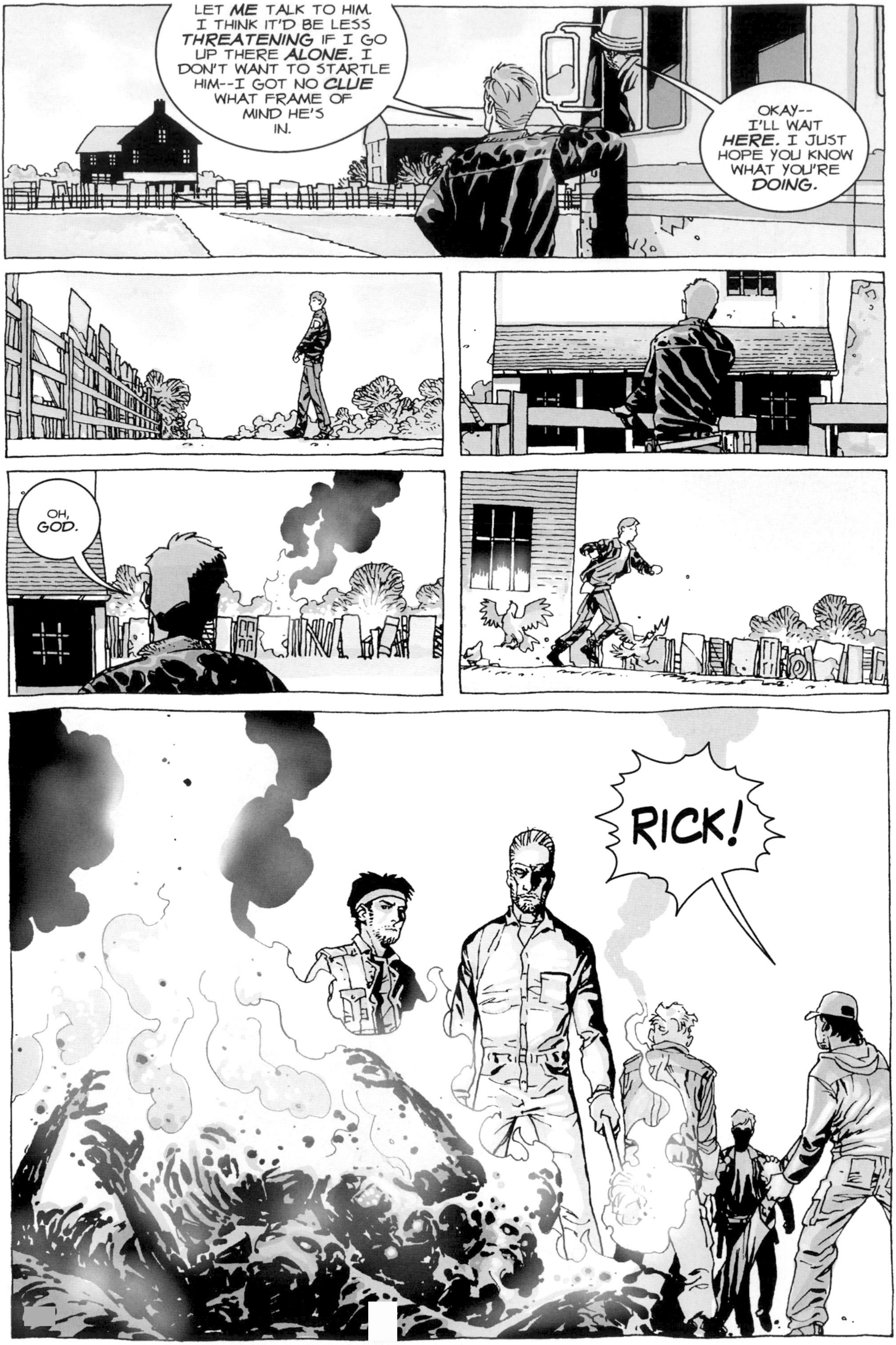
LET ME TALK TO HIM. I THINK IT'D BE LESS THREATENING IF I GO UP THERE ALONE. I DON'T WANT TO STARTLE HIM--I GOT NO CLUE WHAT FRAME OF MIND HE'S IN.
OKAY-- I'LL WAIT HERE. I JUST HOPE YOU KNOW WHAT YOU'RE DOING.
OH, GOD.
RICK!

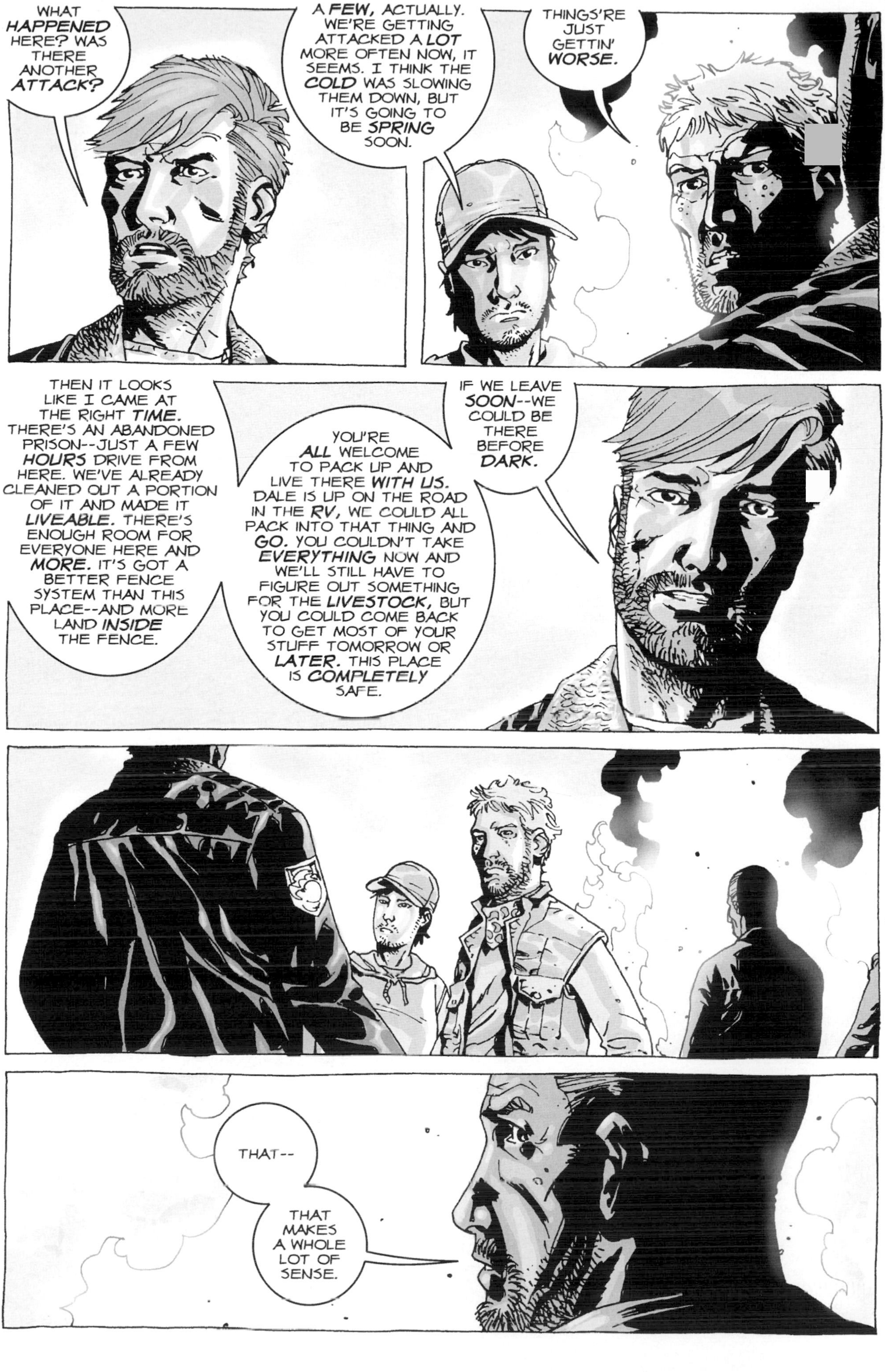
WHAT HAPPENED HERE? WAS THERE ANOTHER ATTACK?
A FEW, ACTUALLY. WE'RE GETTING ATTACKED A LOT MORE OFTEN NOW, IT SEEMS. I THINK THE COLD WAS SLOWING THEM DOWN, BUT IT'S GOING TO BE SPRING SOON.
THINGS'RE JUST GETTIN' WORSE.
THEN IT LOOKS LIKE I CAME AT THE RIGHT TIME. THERE'S AN ABANDONED PRISON--JUST A FEW HOURS DRIVE FROM HERE. WE'VE ALREADY CLEANED OUT A PORTION OF IT AND MADE IT LIVEABLE. THERE'S ENOUGH ROOM FOR EVERYONE HERE AND MORE. IT'S GOT A BETTER FENCE SYSTEM THAN THIS PLACE--AND MORE LAND INSIDE THE FENCE.
YOU'RE ALL WELCOME TO PACK UP AND LIVE THERE WITH US. DALE IS UP ON THE ROAD IN THE RV, WE COULD ALL PACK INTO THAT THING AND GO. YOU COULDN'T TAKE EVERYTHING NOW AND WE'LL STILL HAVE TO FIGURE OUT SOMETHING FOR THE LIVESTOCK, BUT YOU COULD COME BACK TO GET MOST OF YOUR STUFF TOMORROW OR LATER. THIS PLACE IS COMPLETELY SAFE.
IF WE LEAVE SOON--WE COULD BE THERE BEFORE DARK.
THAT--
THAT MAKES A WHOLE LOT OF SENSE.

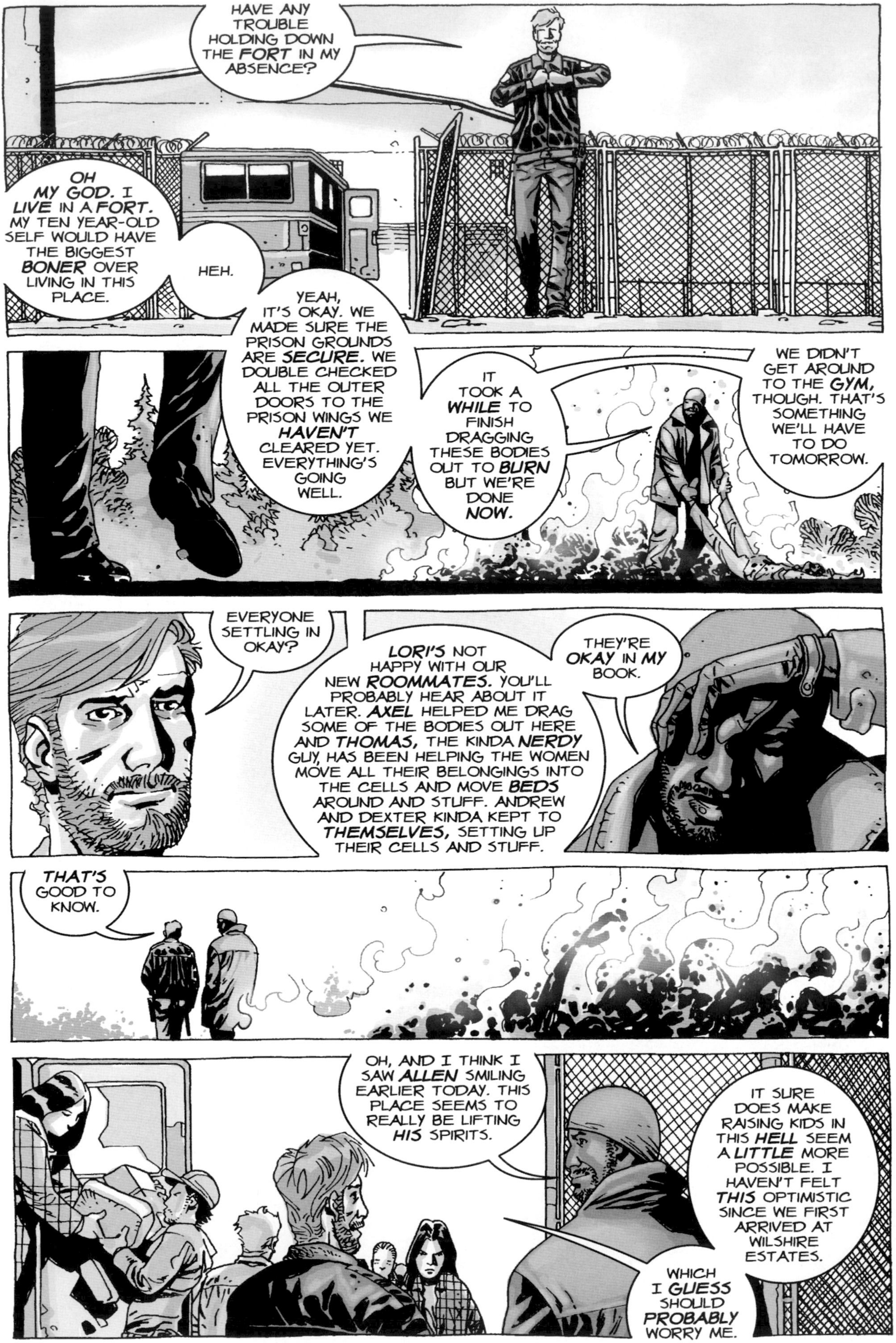
HAVE ANY TROUBLE HOLDING DOWN THE FORT IN MY ABSENCE?
OH MY GOD. I LIVE IN A FORT. MY TEN YEAR-OLD SELF WOULD HAVE THE BIGGEST BONER OVER LIVING IN THIS PLACE.
HEH.
YEAH, IT'S OKAY. WE MADE SURE THE PRISON GROUNDS ARE SECURE. WE DOUBLE CHECKED ALL THE OUTER DOORS TO THE PRISON WINGS WE HAVEN'T CLEARED YET. EVERYTHING'S GOING WELL.
IT TOOK A WHILE TO FINISH DRAGGING THESE BODIES OUT TO BURN BUT WE'RE DONE NOW.
WE DIDN'T GET AROUND TO THE GYM, THOUGH. THAT'S SOMETHING WE'LL HAVE TO DO TOMORROW.
EVERYONE SETTLING IN OKAY?
LORI'S NOT HAPPY WITH OUR NEW ROOMMATES. YOU'LL PROBABLY HEAR ABOUT IT LATER. AXEL HELPED ME DRAG SOME OF THE BODIES OUT HERE AND THOMAS, THE KINDA NERDY GUY, HAS BEEN HELPING THE WOMEN MOVE ALL THEIR BELONGINGS INTO THE CELLS AND MOVE BEDS AROUND AND STUFF. ANDREW AND DEXTER KINDA KEPT TO THEMSELVES, SETTING UP THEIR CELLS AND STUFF.
THEY'RE OKAY IN MY BOOK.
THAT'S GOOD TO KNOW.
OH, AND I THINK I SAW ALLEN SMILING EARLIER TODAY. THIS PLACE SEEMS TO REALLY BE LIFTING HIS SPIRITS.
IT SURE DOES MAKE RAISING KIDS IN THIS HELL SEEM A LITTLE MORE POSSIBLE. I HAVEN'T FELT THIS OPTIMISTIC SINCE WE FIRST ARRIVED AT WILSHIRE ESTATES.
WHICH I GUESS SHOULD PROBABLY WORRY ME.

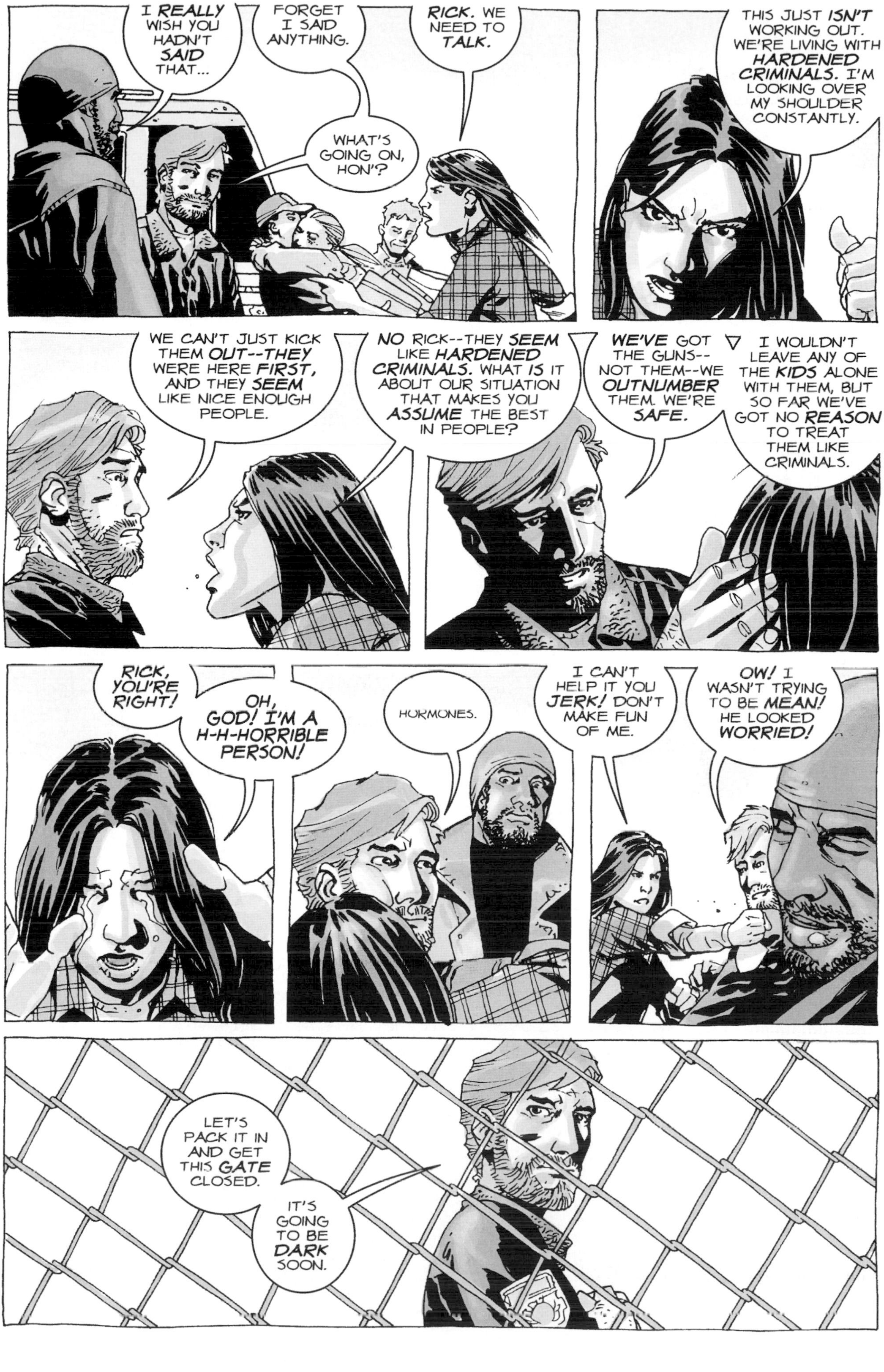
I REALLY WISH YOU HADN'T SAID THAT...
FORGET I SAID ANYTHING.
WHAT'S GOING ON, HON'?
RICK. WE NEED TO TALK.
THIS JUST ISN'T WORKING OUT. WE'RE LIVING WITH HARDENED CRIMINALS. I'M LOOKING OVER MY SHOULDER CONSTANTLY.
WE CAN'T JUST KICK THEM OUT--THEY WERE HERE FIRST, AND THEY SEEM LIKE NICE ENOUGH PEOPLE.
NO RICK--THEY SEEM LIKE HARDENED CRIMINALS. WHAT IS IT ABOUT OUR SITUATION THAT MAKES YOU ASSUME THE BEST IN PEOPLE?
WE'VE GOT THE GUNS--NOT THEM--WE OUTNUMBER THEM. WE'RE SAFE.
I WOULDN'T LEAVE ANY OF THE KIDS ALONE WITH THEM, BUT SO FAR WE'VE GOT NO REASON TO TREAT THEM LIKE CRIMINALS.
RICK, YOU'RE RIGHT!
OH, GOD! I'M A H-H-HORRIBLE PERSON!
HORMONES.
I CAN'T HELP IT YOU JERK! DON'T MAKE FUN OF ME.
OW! I WASN'T TRYING TO BE MEAN! HE LOOKED WORRIED!
LET'S PACK IT IN AND GET THIS GATE CLOSED.
IT'S GOING TO BE DARK SOON.

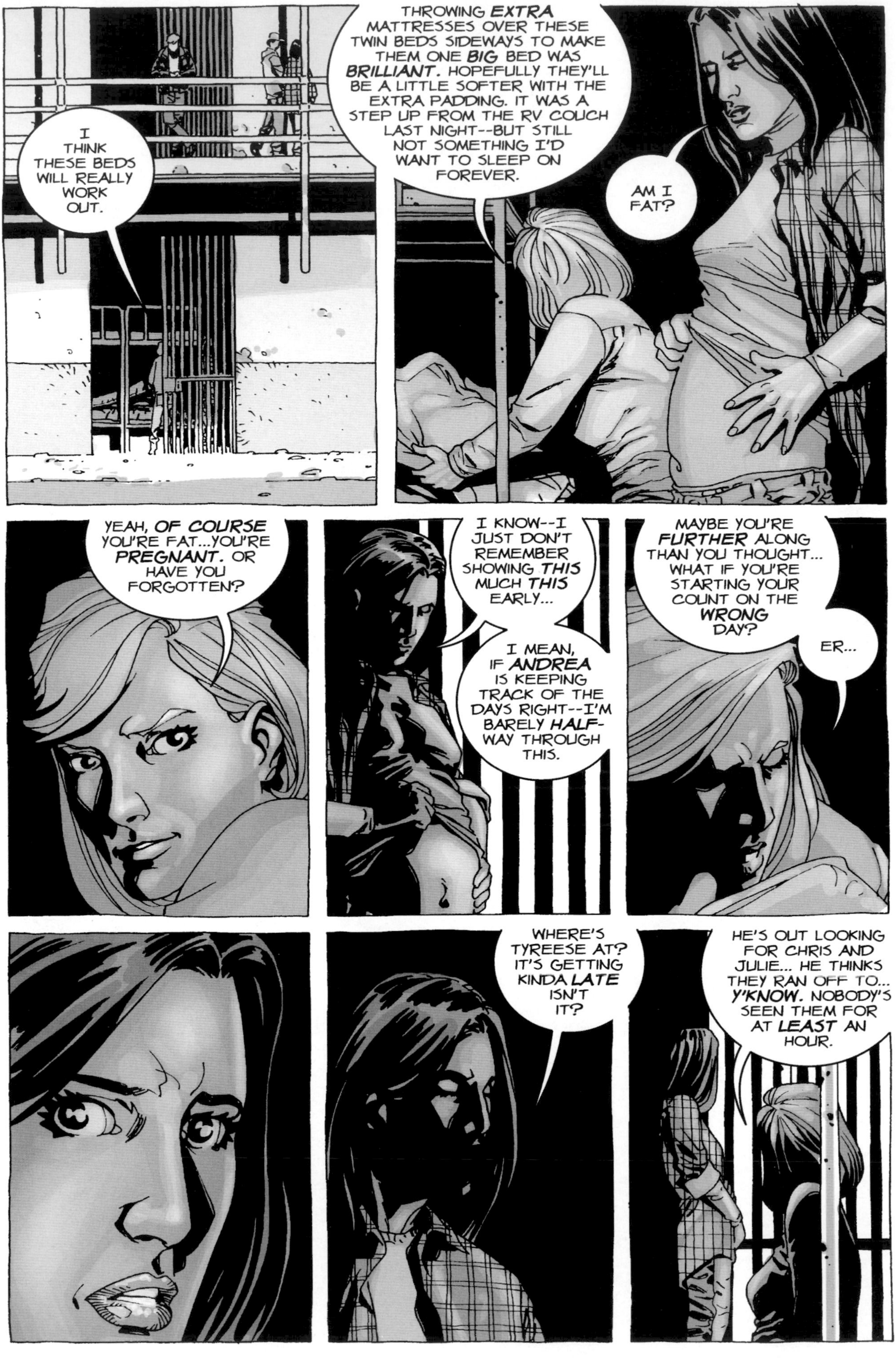
I THINK THESE BEDS WILL REALLY WORK OUT.
THROWING EXTRA MATTRESSES OVER THESE TWIN BEDS SIDEWAYS TO MAKE THEM ONE BIG BED WAS BRILLIANT. HOPEFULLY THEY'LL BE A LITTLE SOFTER WITH THE EXTRA PADDING. IT WAS A STEP UP FROM THE RV COUCH LAST NIGHT--BUT STILL NOT SOMETHING I'D WANT TO SLEEP ON FOREVER.
AM I FAT?
YEAH, OF COURSE YOU'RE FAT...YOU'RE PREGNANT. OR HAVE YOU FORGOTTEN?
I KNOW--I JUST DON'T REMEMBER SHOWING THIS MUCH THIS EARLY...
I MEAN, IF ANDREA IS KEEPING TRACK OF THE DAYS RIGHT--I'M BARELY HALF-WAY THROUGH THIS.
MAYBE YOU'RE FURTHER ALONG THAN YOU THOUGHT... WHAT IF YOU'RE STARTING YOUR COUNT ON THE WRONG DAY?
ER...
WHERE'S TYREESE AT? IT'S GETTING KINDA LATE ISN'T IT?
HE'S OUT LOOKING FOR CHRIS AND JULIE... HE THINKS THEY RAN OFF TO... Y'KNOW. NOBODY'S SEEN THEM FOR AT LEAST AN HOUR.

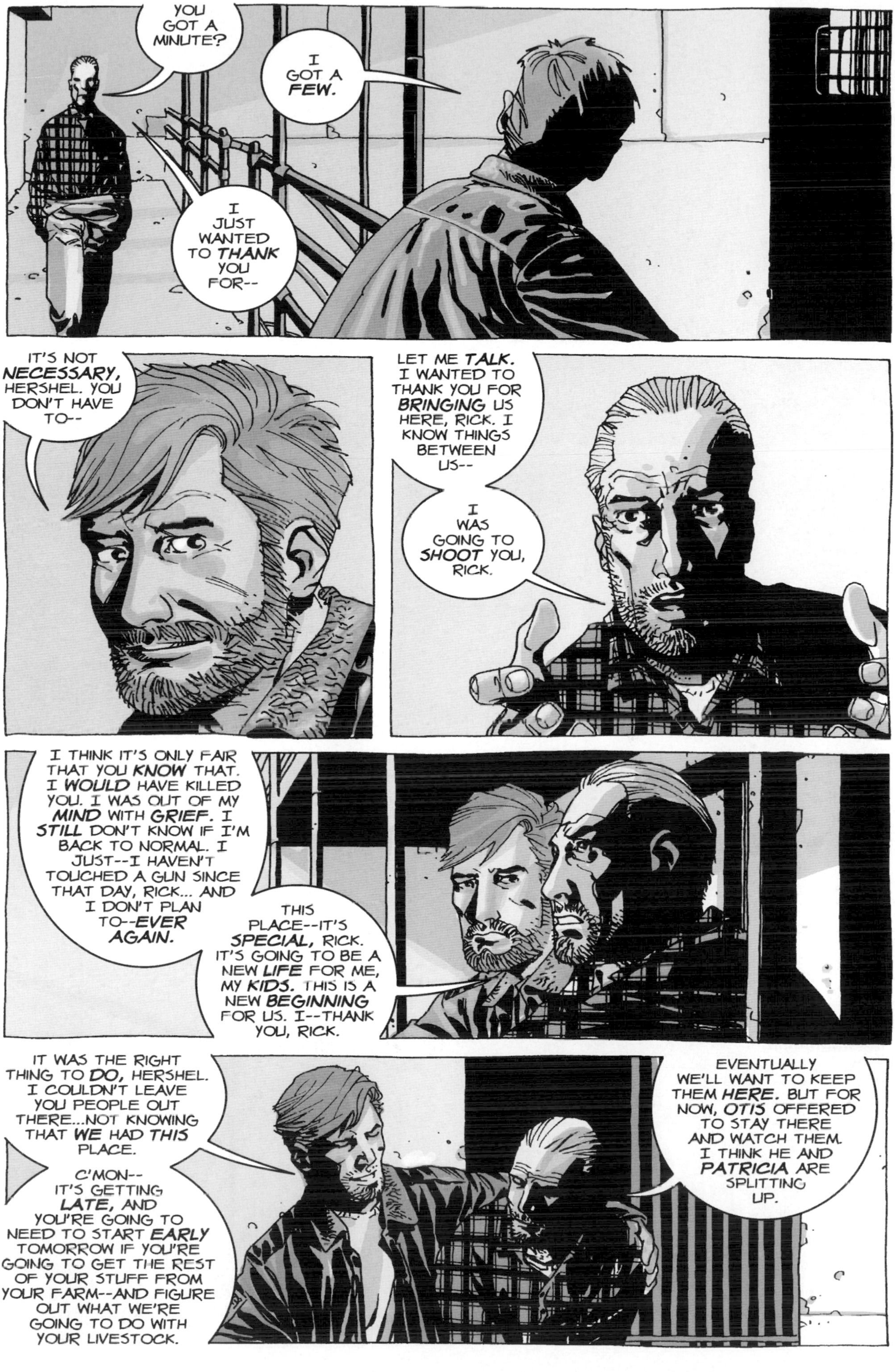
YOU GOT A MINUTE?
I GOT A FEW.
I JUST WANTED TO THANK YOU FOR--
IT'S NOT NECESSARY, HERSHEL. YOU DON'T HAVE TO--
LET ME TALK. I WANTED TO THANK YOU FOR BRINGING US HERE, RICK. I KNOW THINGS BETWEEN US--
I WAS GOING TO SHOOT YOU, RICK.
I THINK IT'S ONLY FAIR THAT YOU KNOW THAT. I WOULD HAVE KILLED YOU. I WAS OUT OF MY MIND WITH GRIEF. I STILL DON'T KNOW IF I'M BACK TO NORMAL. I JUST--I HAVEN'T TOUCHED A GUN SINCE THAT DAY, RICK... AND I DON'T PLAN TO--EVER AGAIN.
THIS PLACE--IT'S SPECIAL, RICK. IT'S GOING TO BE A NEW LIFE FOR ME, MY KIDS. THIS IS A NEW BEGINNING FOR US. I--THANK YOU, RICK.
IT WAS THE RIGHT THING TO DO, HERSHEL. I COULDN'T LEAVE YOU PEOPLE OUT THERE...NOT KNOWING THAT WE HAD THIS PLACE.
C'MON-- IT'S GETTING LATE, AND YOU'RE GOING TO NEED TO START EARLY TOMORROW IF YOU'RE GOING TO GET THE REST OF YOUR STUFF FROM YOUR FARM--AND FIGURE OUT WHAT WE'RE GOING TO DO WITH YOUR LIVESTOCK.
EVENTUALLY WE'LL WANT TO KEEP THEM HERE. BUT FOR NOW, OTIS OFFERED TO STAY THERE AND WATCH THEM. I THINK HE AND PATRICIA ARE SPLITTING UP.

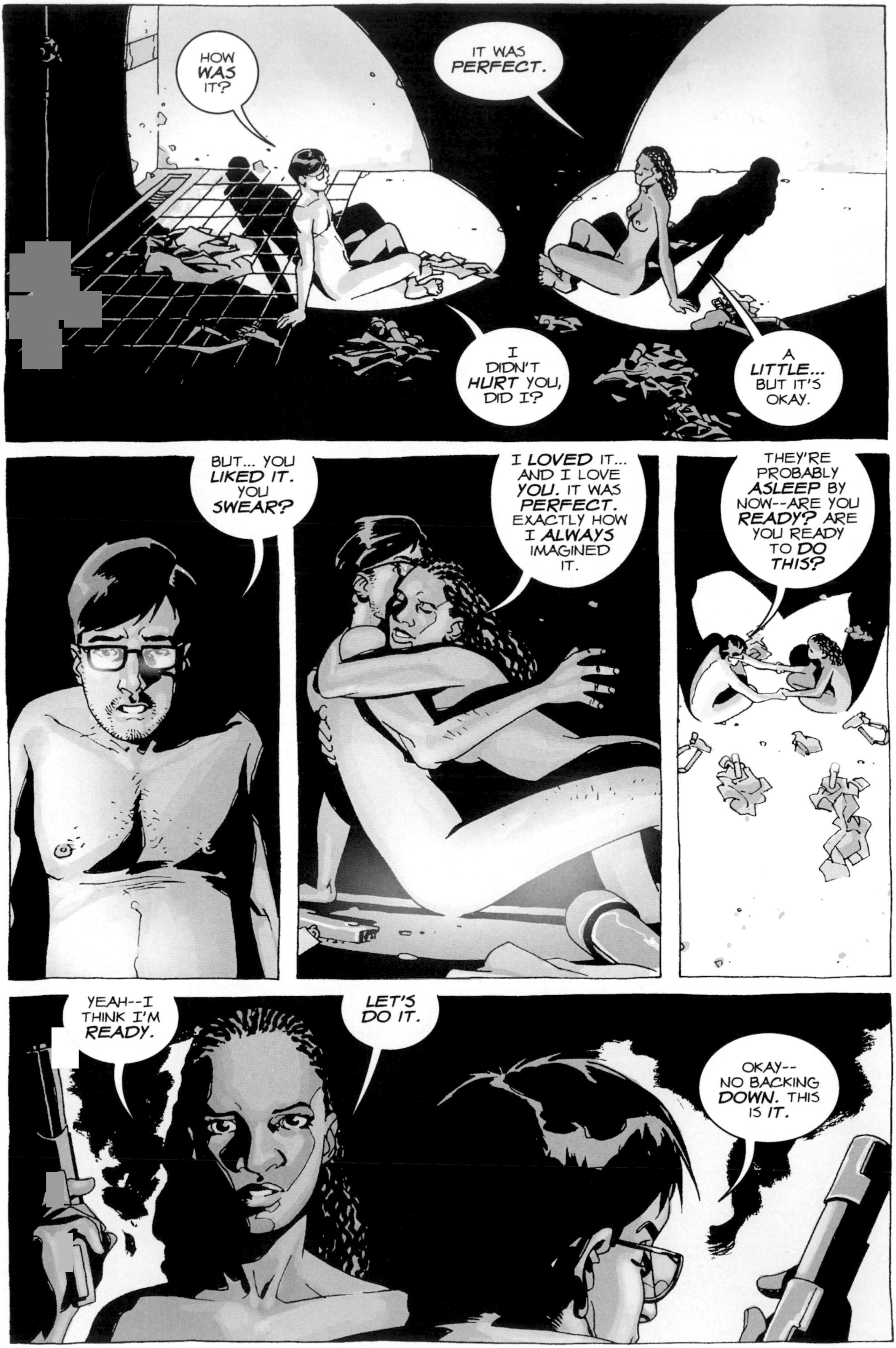
HOW WAS IT?
IT WAS PERFECT.
I DIDN'T HURT YOU, DID I?
A LITTLE... BUT IT'S OKAY.
BUT... YOU LIKED IT. YOU SWEAR?
I LOVED IT... AND I LOVE YOU. IT WAS PERFECT. EXACTLY HOW I ALWAYS IMAGINED IT.
THEY'RE PROBABLY ASLEEP BY NOW--ARE YOU READY? ARE YOU READY TO DO THIS?
YEAH--I THINK I'M READY.
LET'S DO IT.
OKAY-- NO BACKING DOWN. THIS IS IT.

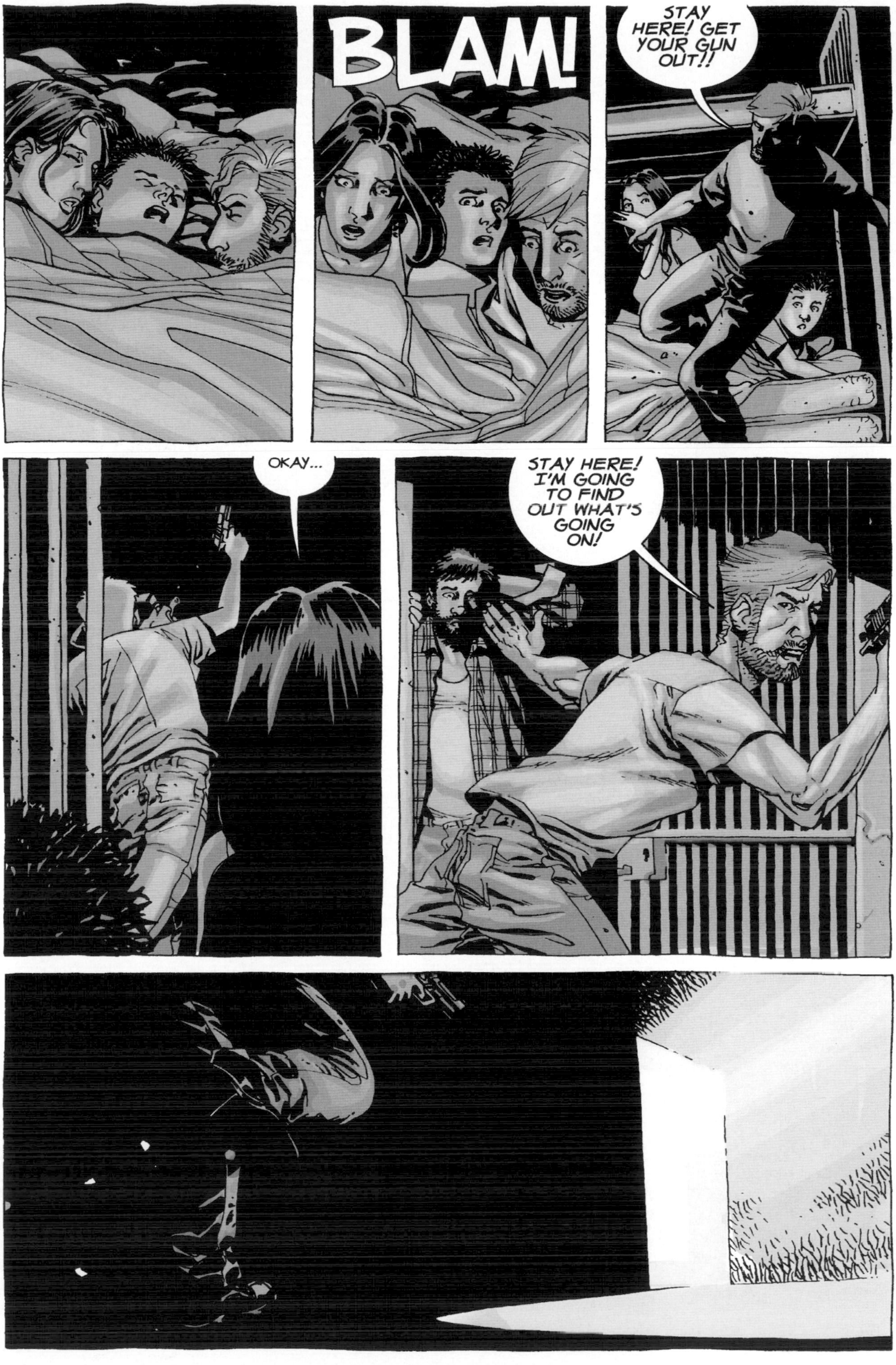

BLAM!
STAY HERE! GET YOUR GUN OUT!!
OKAY...
STAY HERE! I'M GOING TO FIND OUT WHAT'S GOING ON!

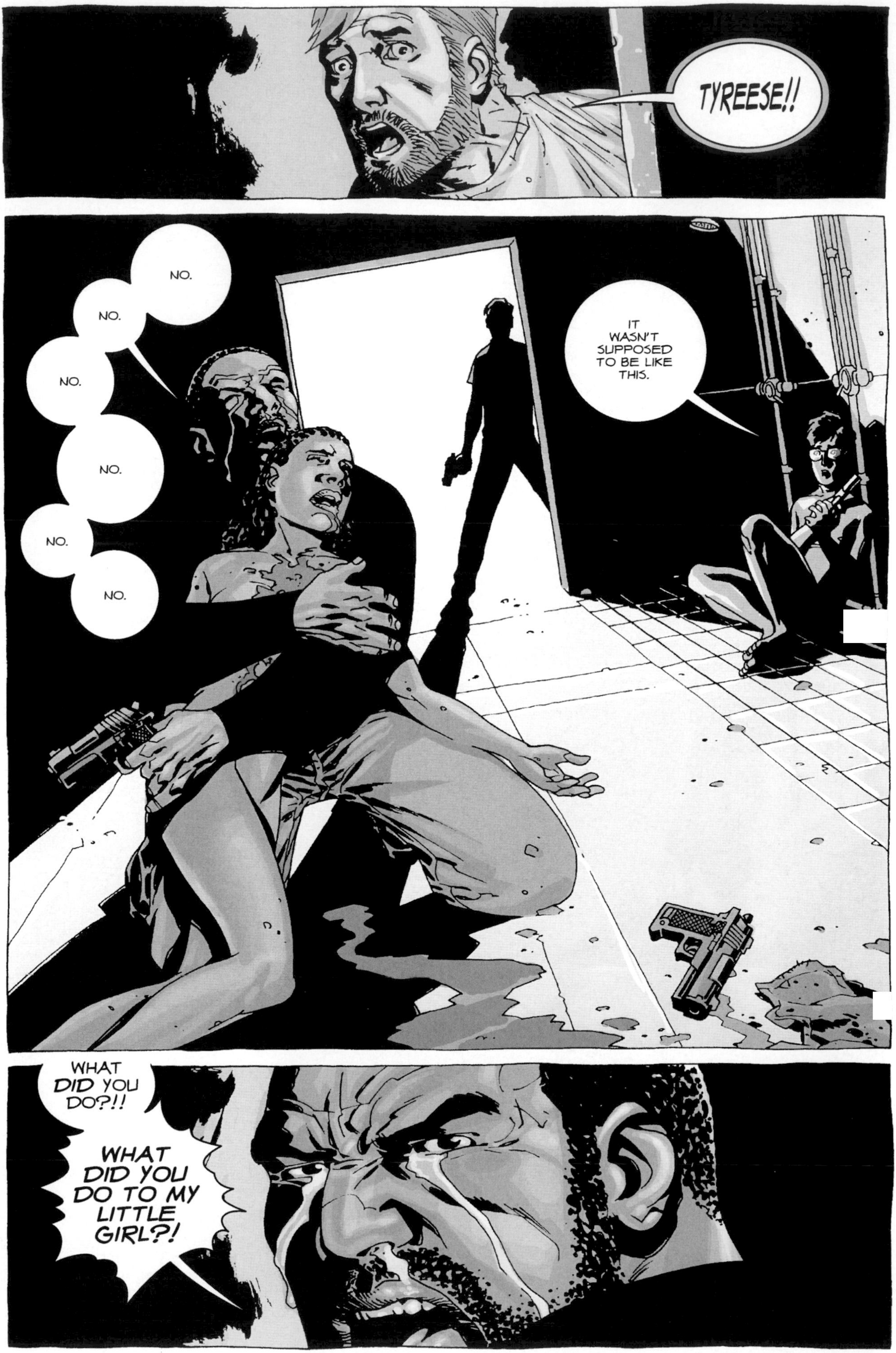
TYREESE!!
NO.
NO.
NO.
NO.
NO.
NO.
IT WASN'T SUPPOSED TO BE LIKE THIS.
WHAT DID YOU DO?!!
WHAT DID YOU DO TO MY LITTLE GIRL?!

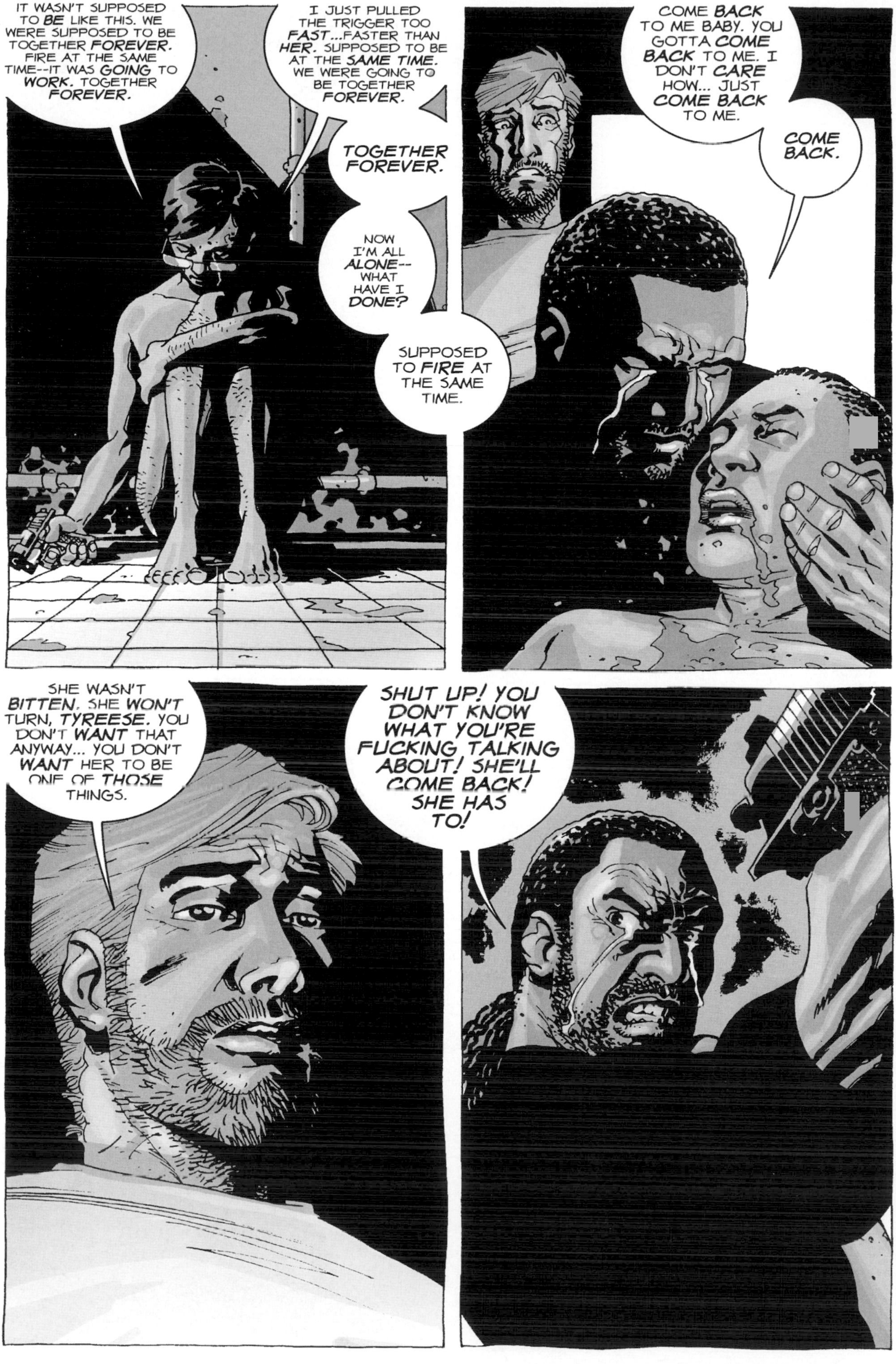
IT WASN'T SUPPOSED TO BE LIKE THIS. WE WERE SUPPOSED TO BE TOGETHER FOREVER. FIRE AT THE SAME TIME--IT WAS GOING TO WORK. TOGETHER FOREVER.
I JUST PULLED THE TRIGGER TOO FAST...FASTER THAN HER. SUPPOSED TO BE AT THE SAME TIME. WE WERE GOING TO BE TOGETHER FOREVER.
TOGETHER FOREVER.
NOW I'M ALL ALONE--WHAT HAVE I DONE?
SUPPOSED TO FIRE AT THE SAME TIME.
COME BACK TO ME BABY. YOU GOTTA COME BACK TO ME. I DON'T CARE HOW... JUST COME BACK TO ME.
COME BACK.
SHE WASN'T BITTEN. SHE WON'T TURN, TYREESE. YOU DON'T WANT THAT ANYWAY... YOU DON'T WANT HER TO BE ONE OF THOSE THINGS.
SHUT UP! YOU DON'T KNOW WHAT YOU'RE FUCKING TALKING ABOUT! SHE'LL COME BACK! SHE HAS TO!

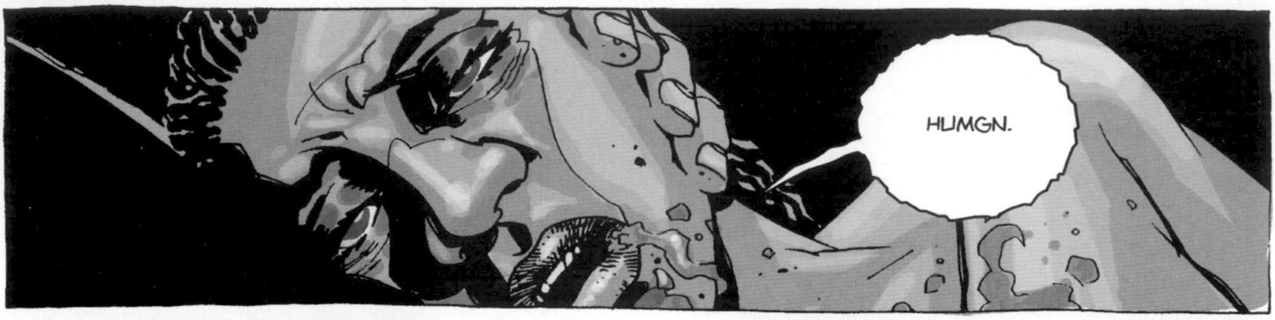
HUMGN.

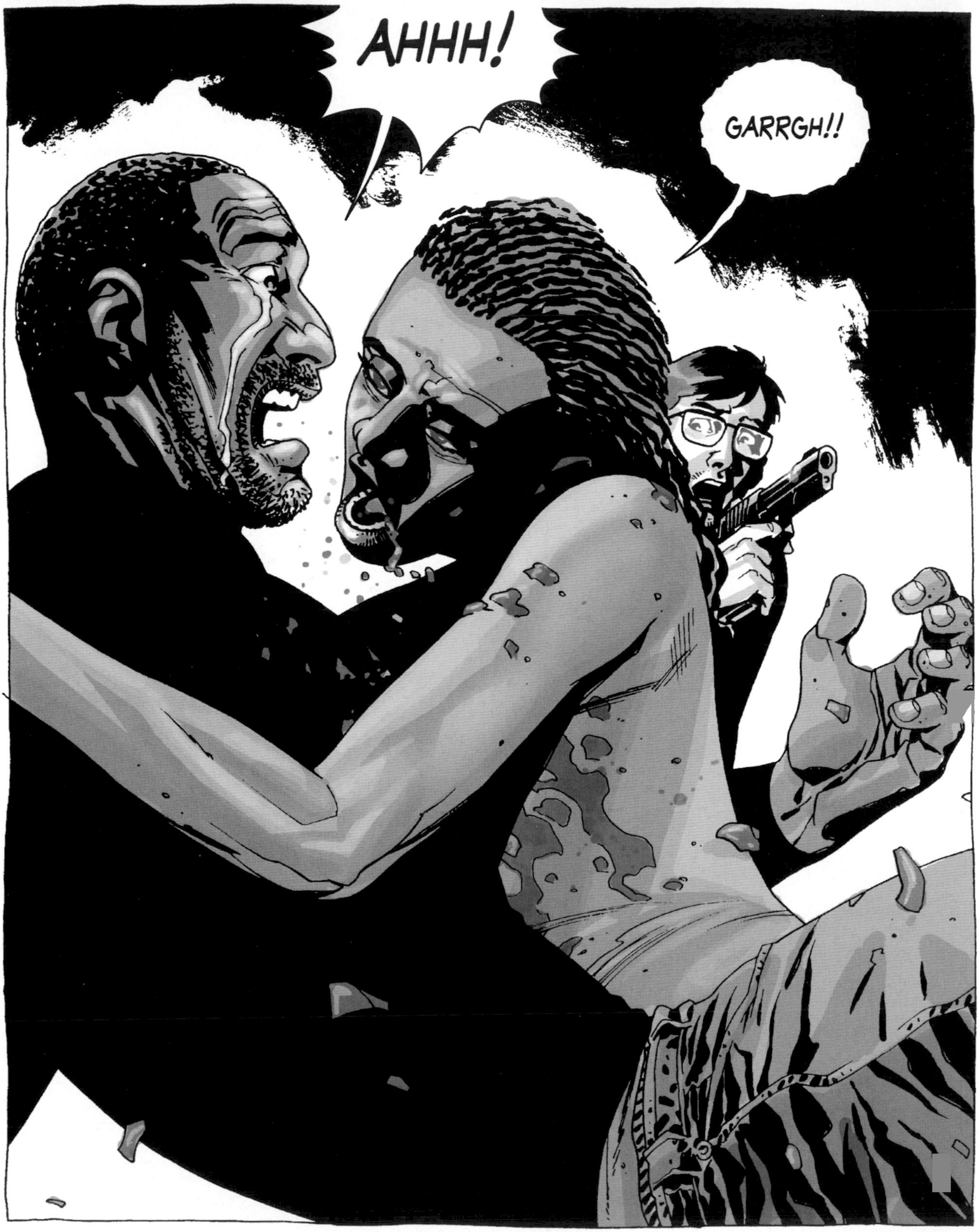
AHHH!
GARRGH!!

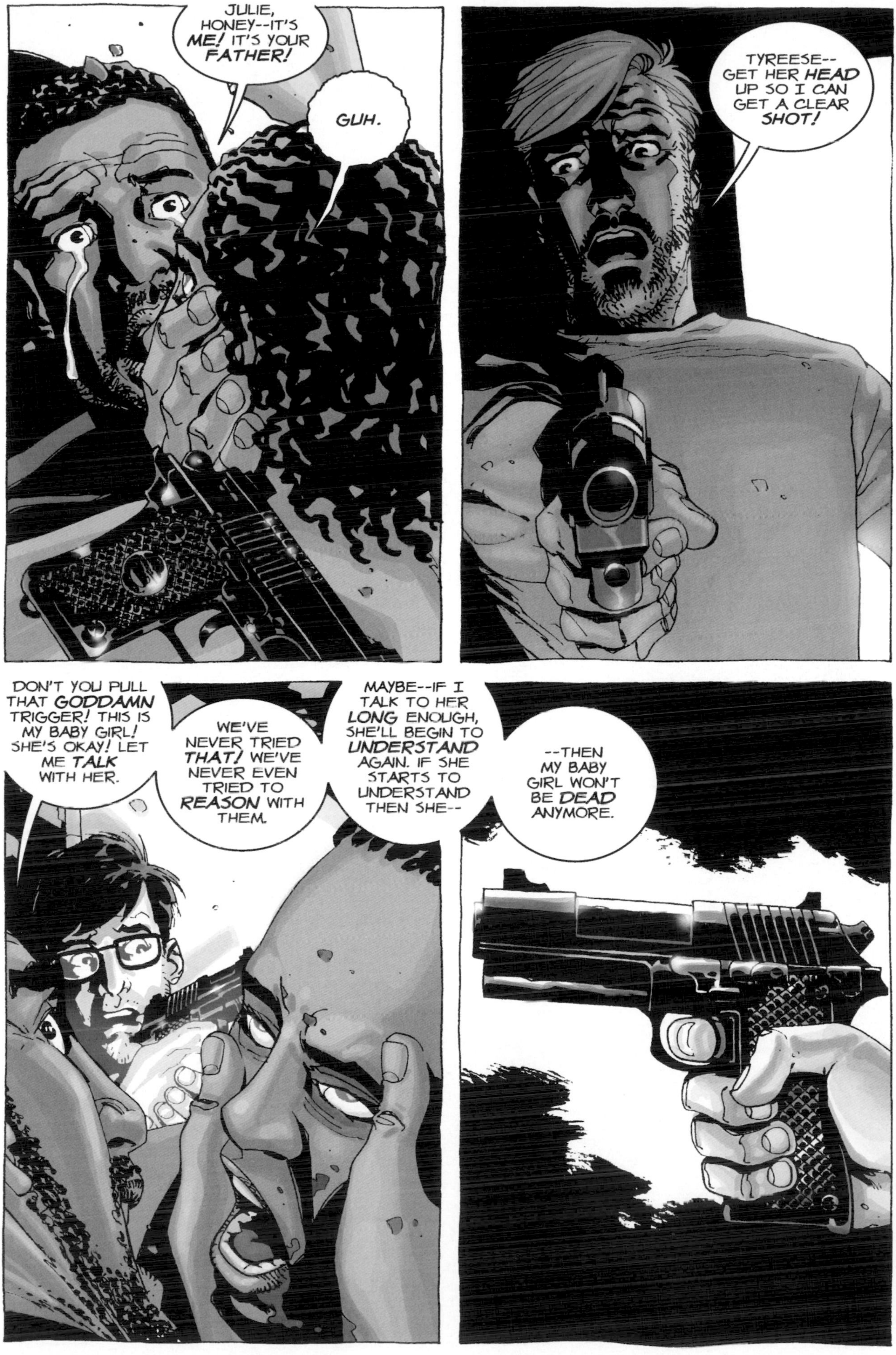
JULIE, HONEY--IT'S ME! IT'S YOUR FATHER!
GUH.
TYREESE-- GET HER HEAD UP SO I CAN GET A CLEAR SHOT!
DON'T YOU PULL THAT GODDAMN TRIGGER! THIS IS MY BABY GIRL! SHE'S OKAY! LET ME TALK WITH HER.
WE'VE NEVER TRIED THAT! WE'VE NEVER EVEN TRIED TO REASON WITH THEM.
MAYBE--IF I TALK TO HER LONG ENOUGH, SHE'LL BEGIN TO UNDERSTAND AGAIN. IF SHE STARTS TO UNDERSTAND THEN SHE--
--THEN MY BABY GIRL WON'T BE DEAD ANYMORE.

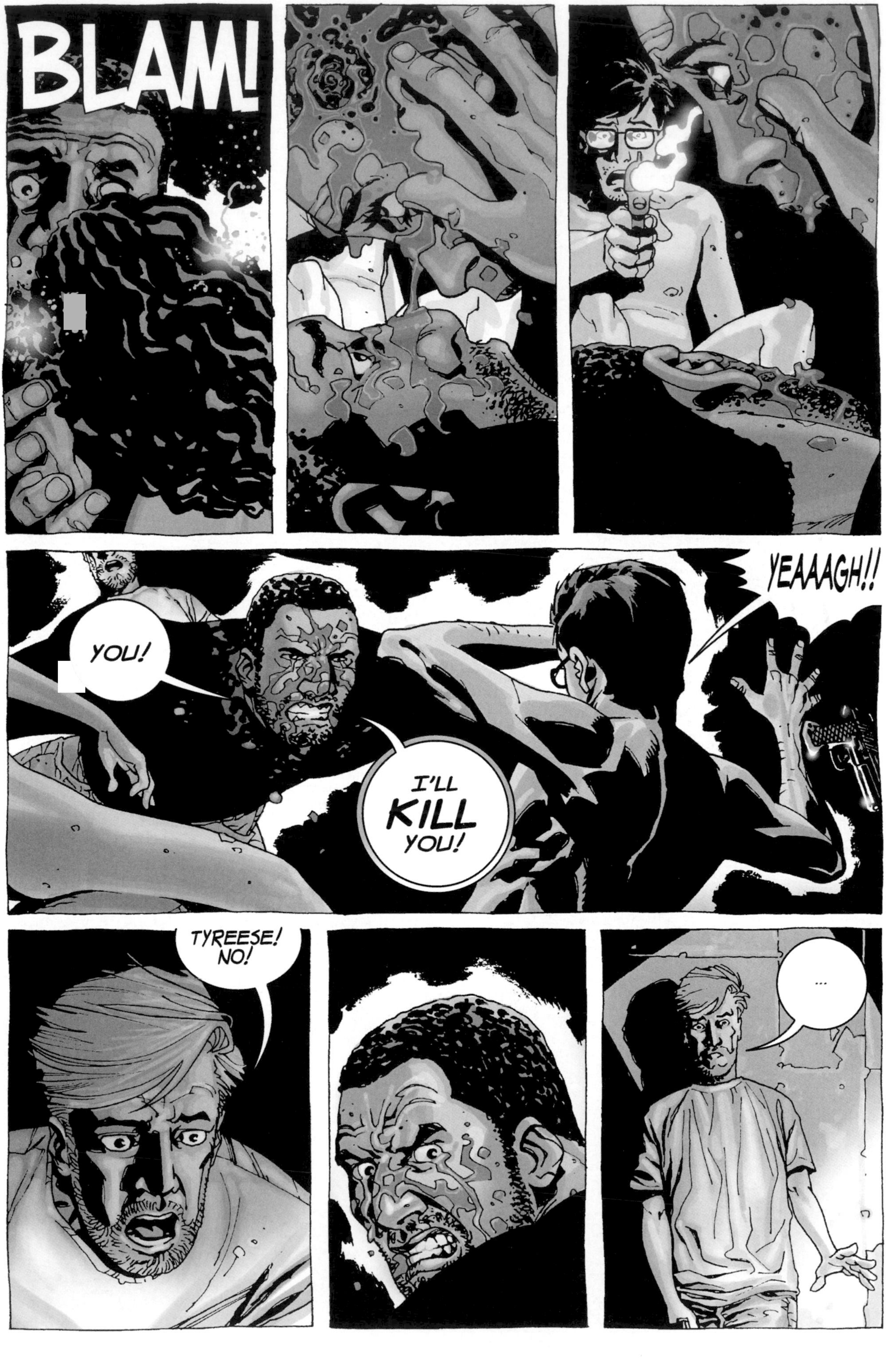
BLAM!
YOU!
I'LL KILL YOU!
YEAAAGH!!
TYREESE! NO!
...

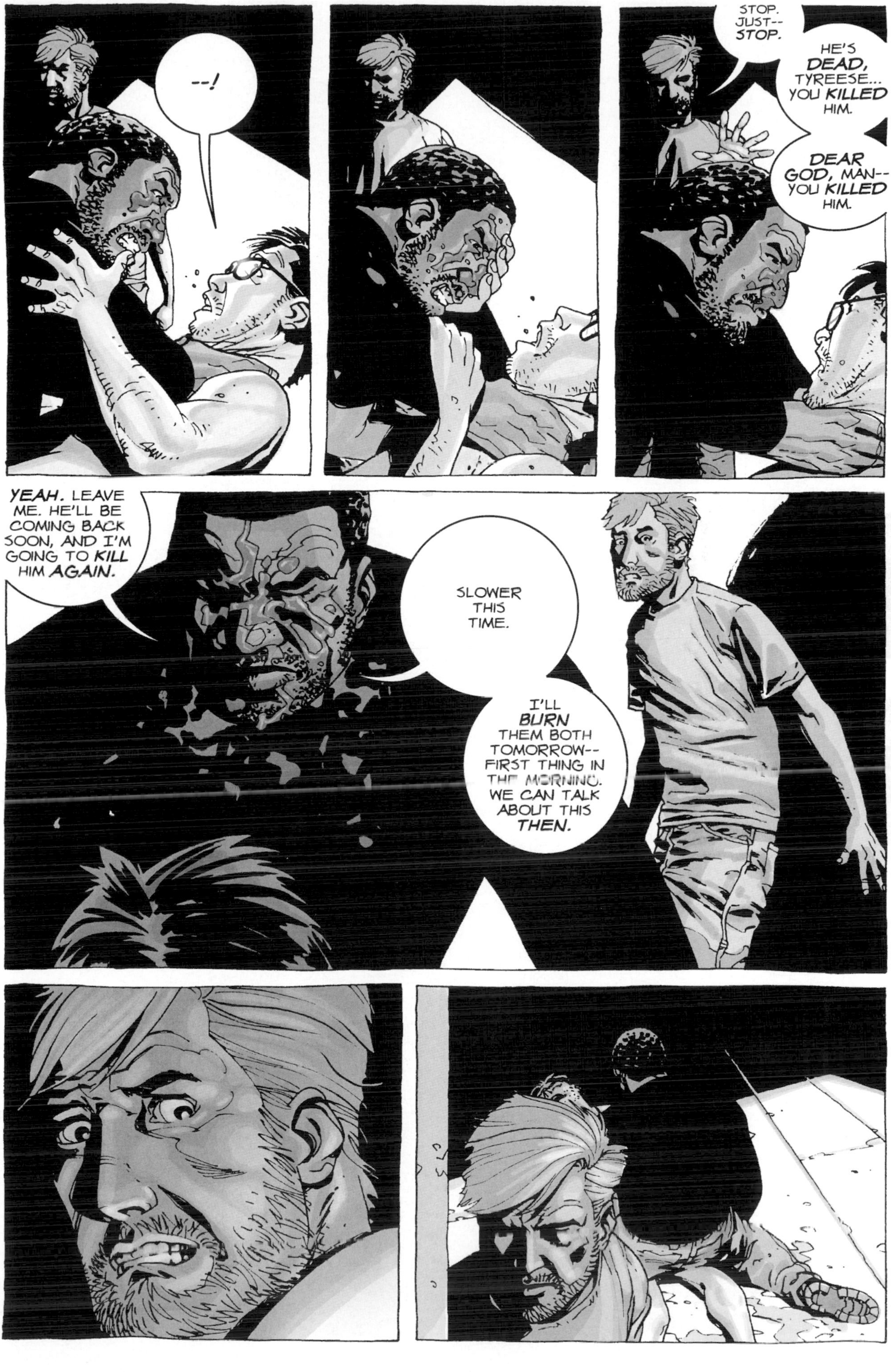
--!
STOP. JUST-- STOP.
HE'S DEAD, TYREESE... YOU KILLED HIM.
DEAR GOD, MAN-- YOU KILLED HIM.
YEAH. LEAVE ME. HE'LL BE COMING BACK SOON, AND I'M GOING TO KILL HIM AGAIN.
SLOWER THIS TIME.
I'LL BURN THEM BOTH TOMORROW-- FIRST THING IN THE MORNING. WE CAN TALK ABOUT THIS THEN.

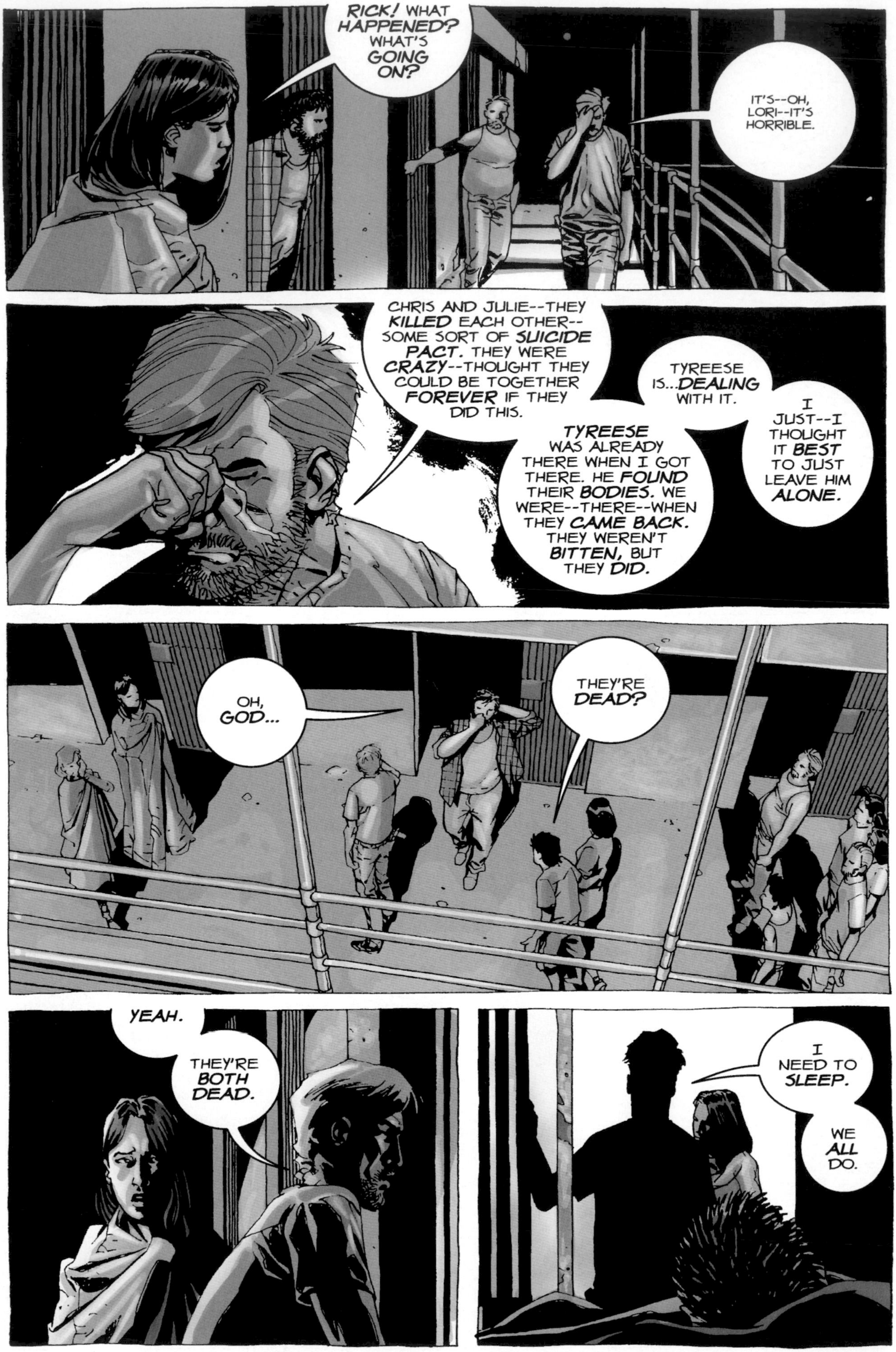
RICK! WHAT HAPPENED? WHAT'S GOING ON?
IT'S--OH, LORI--IT'S HORRIBLE.
CHRIS AND JULIE--THEY KILLED EACH OTHER--SOME SORT OF SUICIDE PACT. THEY WERE CRAZY--THOUGHT THEY COULD BE TOGETHER FOREVER IF THEY DID THIS.
TYREESE WAS ALREADY THERE WHEN I GOT THERE. HE FOUND THEIR BODIES. WE WERE--THERE--WHEN THEY CAME BACK. THEY WEREN'T BITTEN, BUT THEY DID.
TYREESE IS...DEALING WITH IT.
I JUST--I THOUGHT IT BEST TO JUST LEAVE HIM ALONE.
OH, GOD...
THEY'RE DEAD?
YEAH.
THEY'RE BOTH DEAD.
I NEED TO SLEEP.
WE ALL DO.

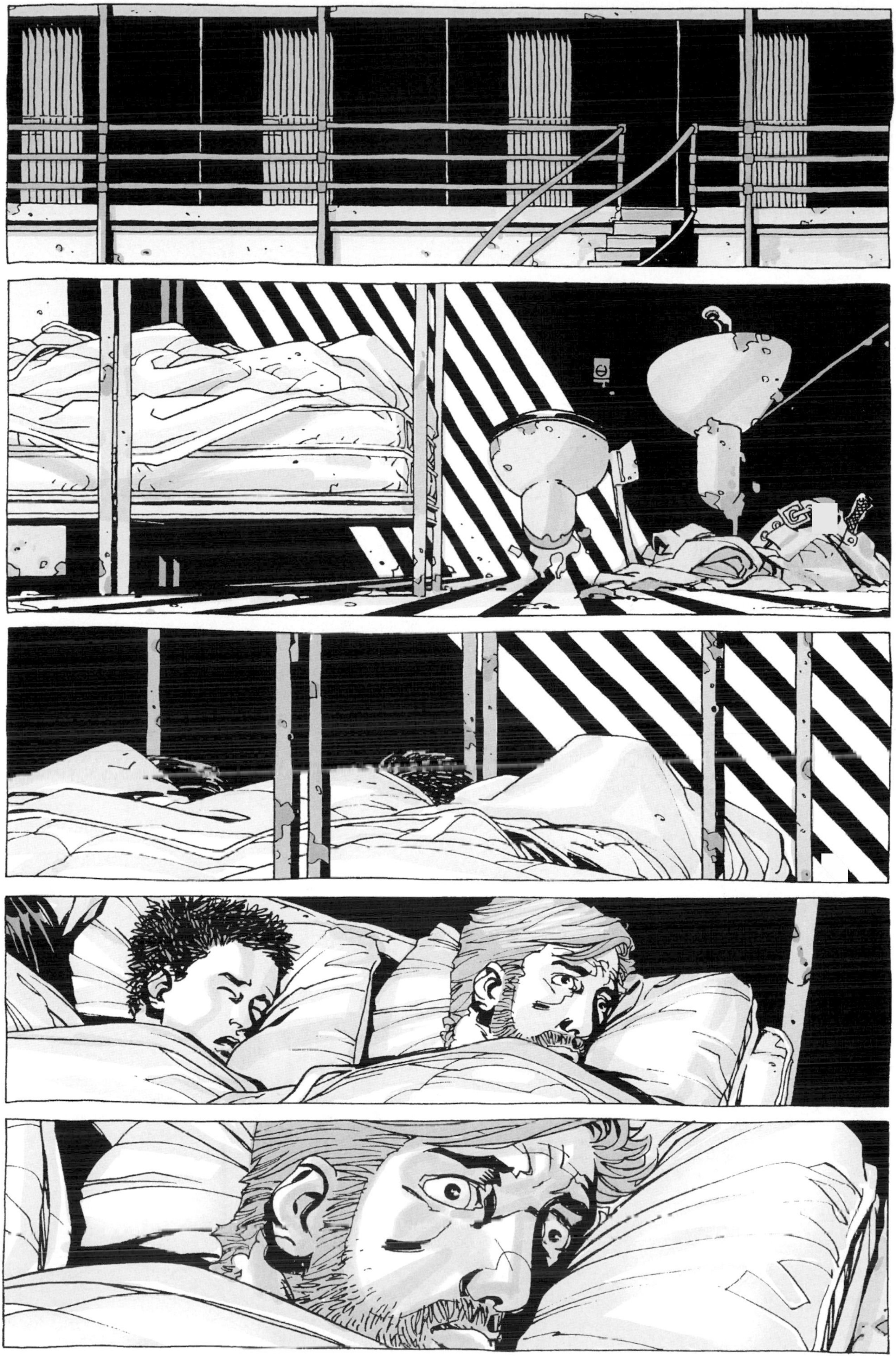

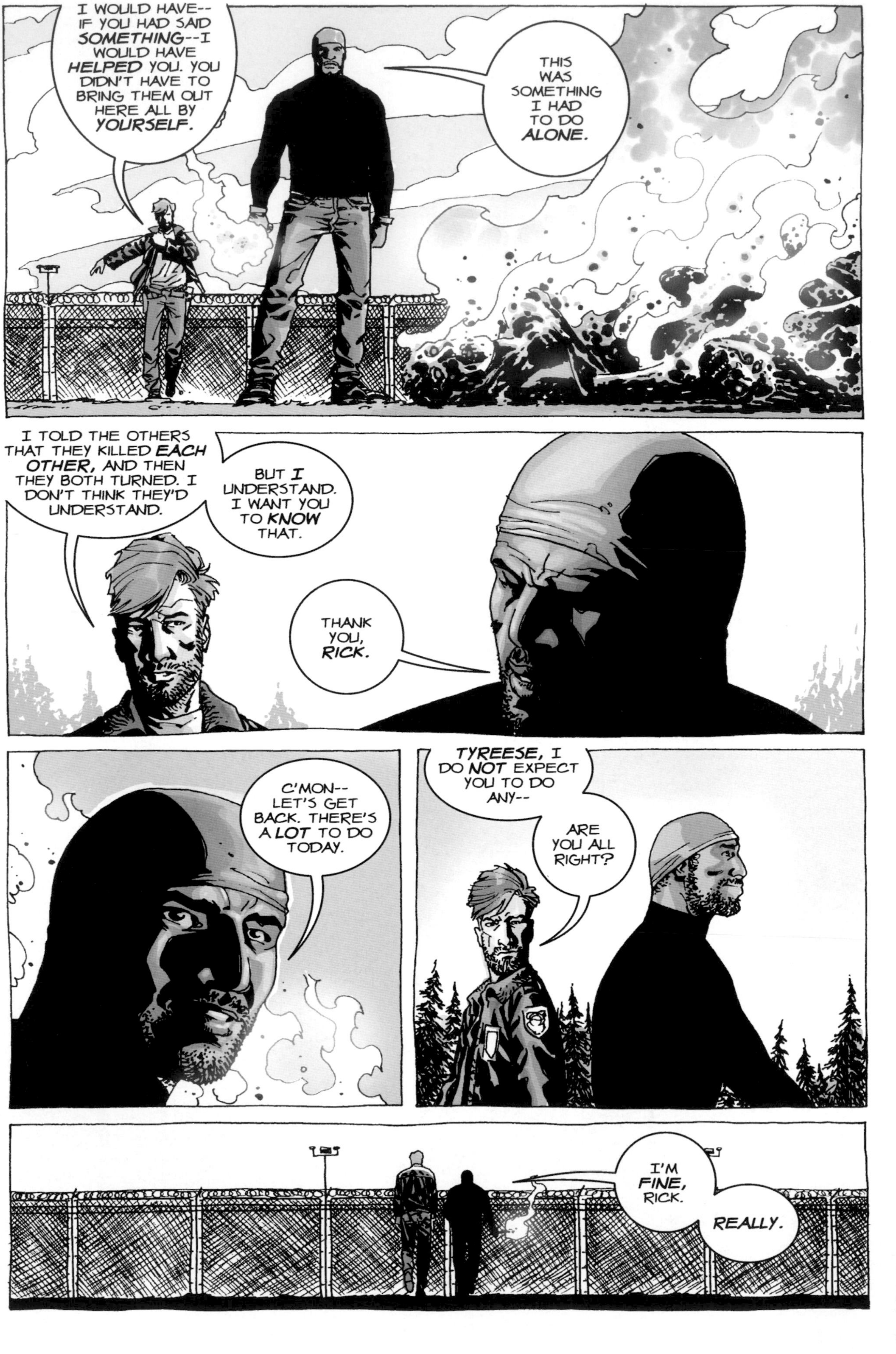
I WOULD HAVE-- IF YOU HAD SAID SOMETHING--I WOULD HAVE HELPED YOU. YOU DIDN'T HAVE TO BRING THEM OUT HERE ALL BY YOURSELF.
THIS WAS SOMETHING I HAD TO DO ALONE.
I TOLD THE OTHERS THAT THEY KILLED EACH OTHER, AND THEN THEY BOTH TURNED. I DON'T THINK THEY'D UNDERSTAND.
BUT I UNDERSTAND. I WANT YOU TO KNOW THAT.
THANK YOU, RICK.
C'MON-- LET'S GET BACK. THERE'S A LOT TO DO TODAY.
TYREESE, I DO NOT EXPECT YOU TO DO ANY--
ARE YOU ALL RIGHT?
I'M FINE, RICK.
REALLY.

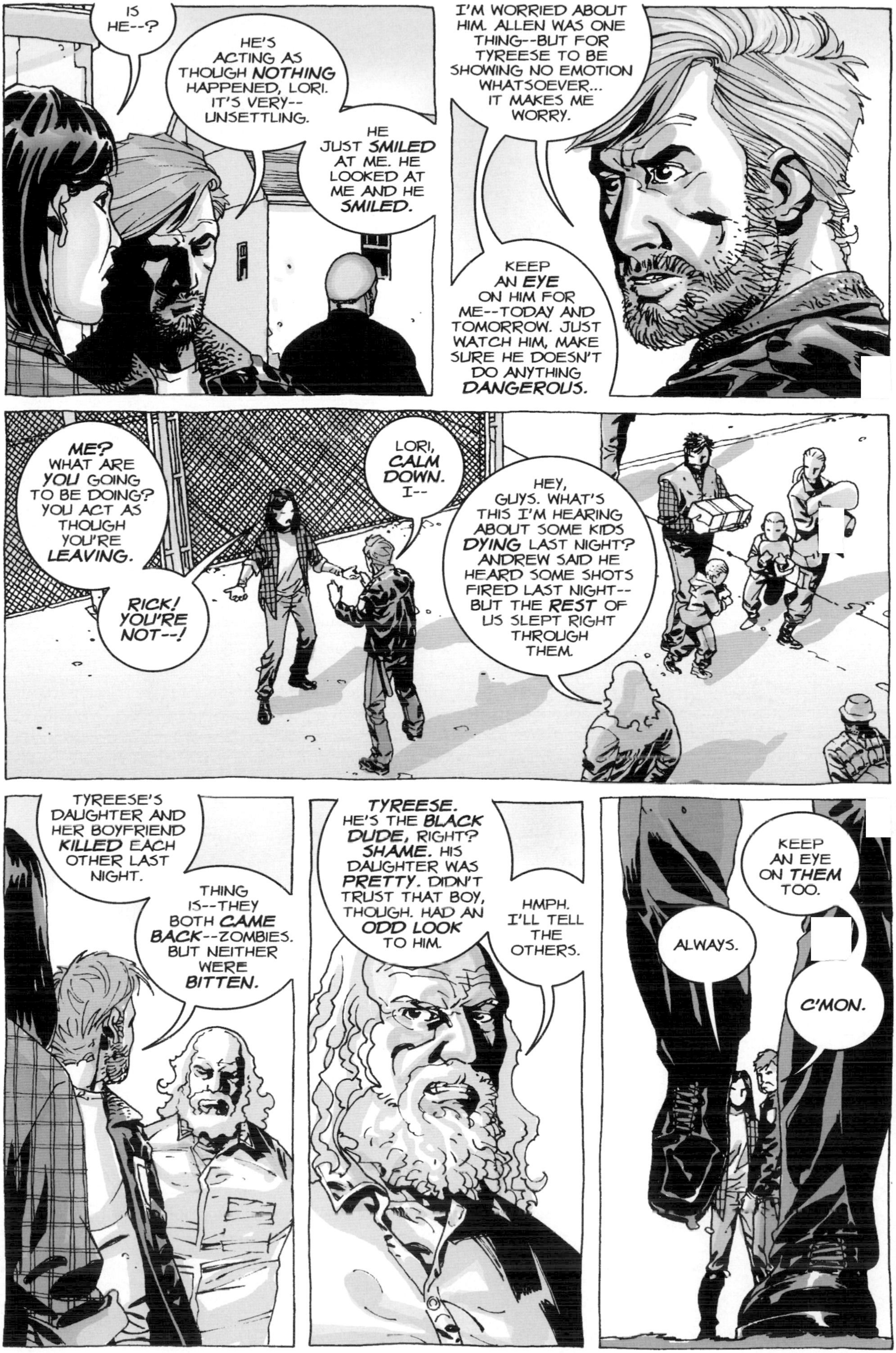
IS HE--?
HE'S ACTING AS THOUGH NOTHING HAPPENED, LORI. IT'S VERY-- UNSETTLING.
HE JUST SMILED AT ME. HE LOOKED AT ME AND HE SMILED.
I'M WORRIED ABOUT HIM. ALLEN WAS ONE THING--BUT FOR TYREESE TO BE SHOWING NO EMOTION WHATSOEVER... IT MAKES ME WORRY.
KEEP AN EYE ON HIM FOR ME--TODAY AND TOMORROW. JUST WATCH HIM, MAKE SURE HE DOESN'T DO ANYTHING DANGEROUS.
ME? WHAT ARE YOU GOING TO BE DOING? YOU ACT AS THOUGH YOU'RE LEAVING.
RICK! YOU'RE NOT--!
LORI, CALM DOWN. I--
HEY, GUYS. WHAT'S THIS I'M HEARING ABOUT SOME KIDS DYING LAST NIGHT? ANDREW SAID HE HEARD SOME SHOTS FIRED LAST NIGHT-- BUT THE REST OF US SLEPT RIGHT THROUGH THEM.
TYREESE'S DAUGHTER AND HER BOYFRIEND KILLED EACH OTHER LAST NIGHT.
THING IS--THEY BOTH CAME BACK--ZOMBIES. BUT NEITHER WERE BITTEN.
TYREESE. HE'S THE BLACK DUDE, RIGHT? SHAME. HIS DAUGHTER WAS PRETTY. DIDN'T TRUST THAT BOY, THOUGH. HAD AN ODD LOOK TO HIM.
HMPH. I'LL TELL THE OTHERS.
KEEP AN EYE ON THEM TOO.
ALWAYS.
C'MON.

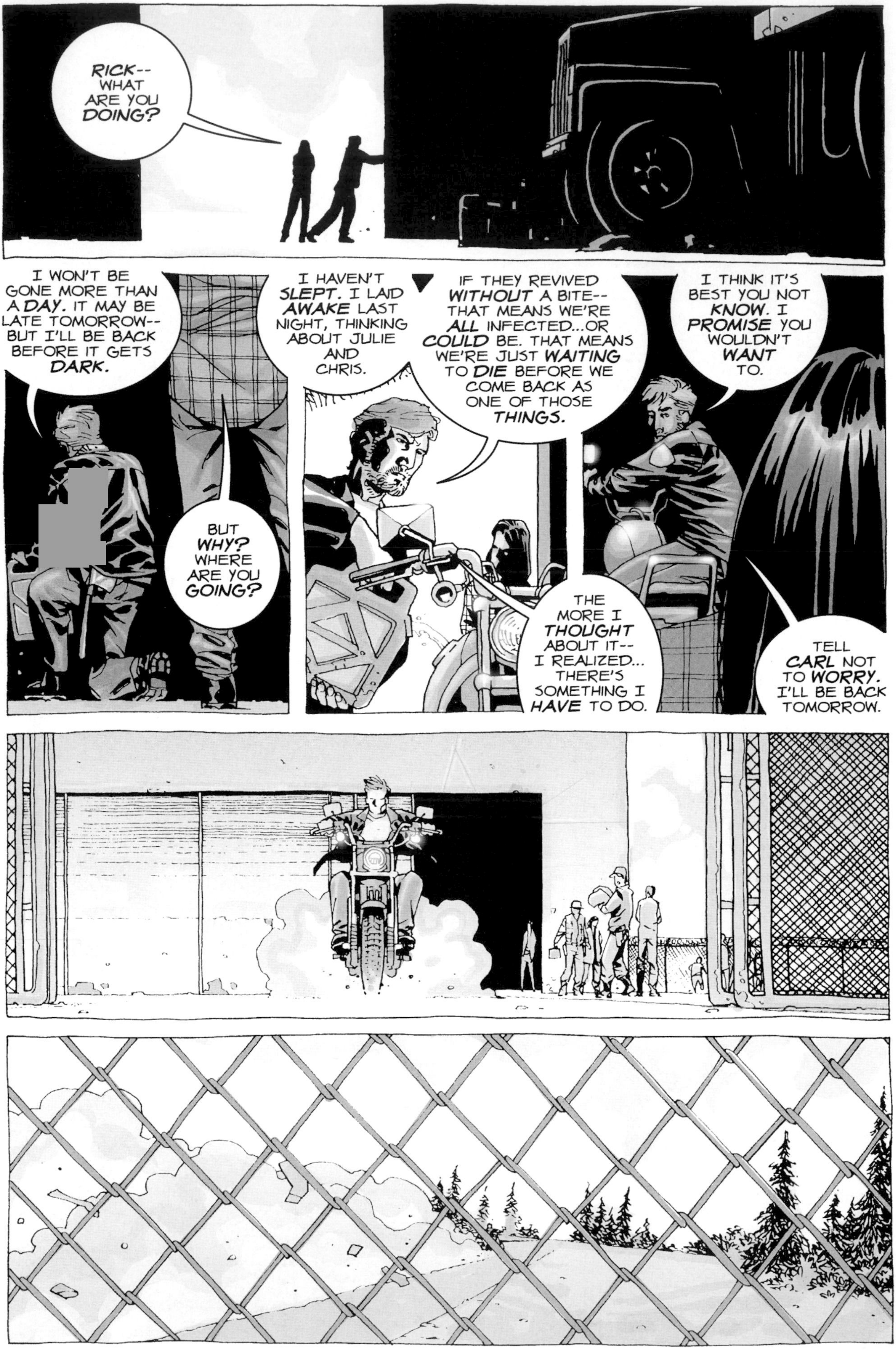
RICK-- WHAT ARE YOU DOING?
I WON'T BE GONE MORE THAN A DAY. IT MAY BE LATE TOMORROW-- BUT I'LL BE BACK BEFORE IT GETS DARK.
BUT WHY? WHERE ARE YOU GOING?
I HAVEN'T SLEPT. I LAID AWAKE LAST NIGHT, THINKING ABOUT JULIE AND CHRIS.
IF THEY REVIVED WITHOUT A BITE-- THAT MEANS WE'RE ALL INFECTED...OR COULD BE. THAT MEANS WE'RE JUST WAITING TO DIE BEFORE WE COME BACK AS ONE OF THOSE THINGS.
THE MORE I THOUGHT ABOUT IT-- I REALIZED... THERE'S SOMETHING I HAVE TO DO.
I THINK IT'S BEST YOU NOT KNOW. I PROMISE YOU WOULDN'T WANT TO.
TELL CARL NOT TO WORRY. I'LL BE BACK TOMORROW.

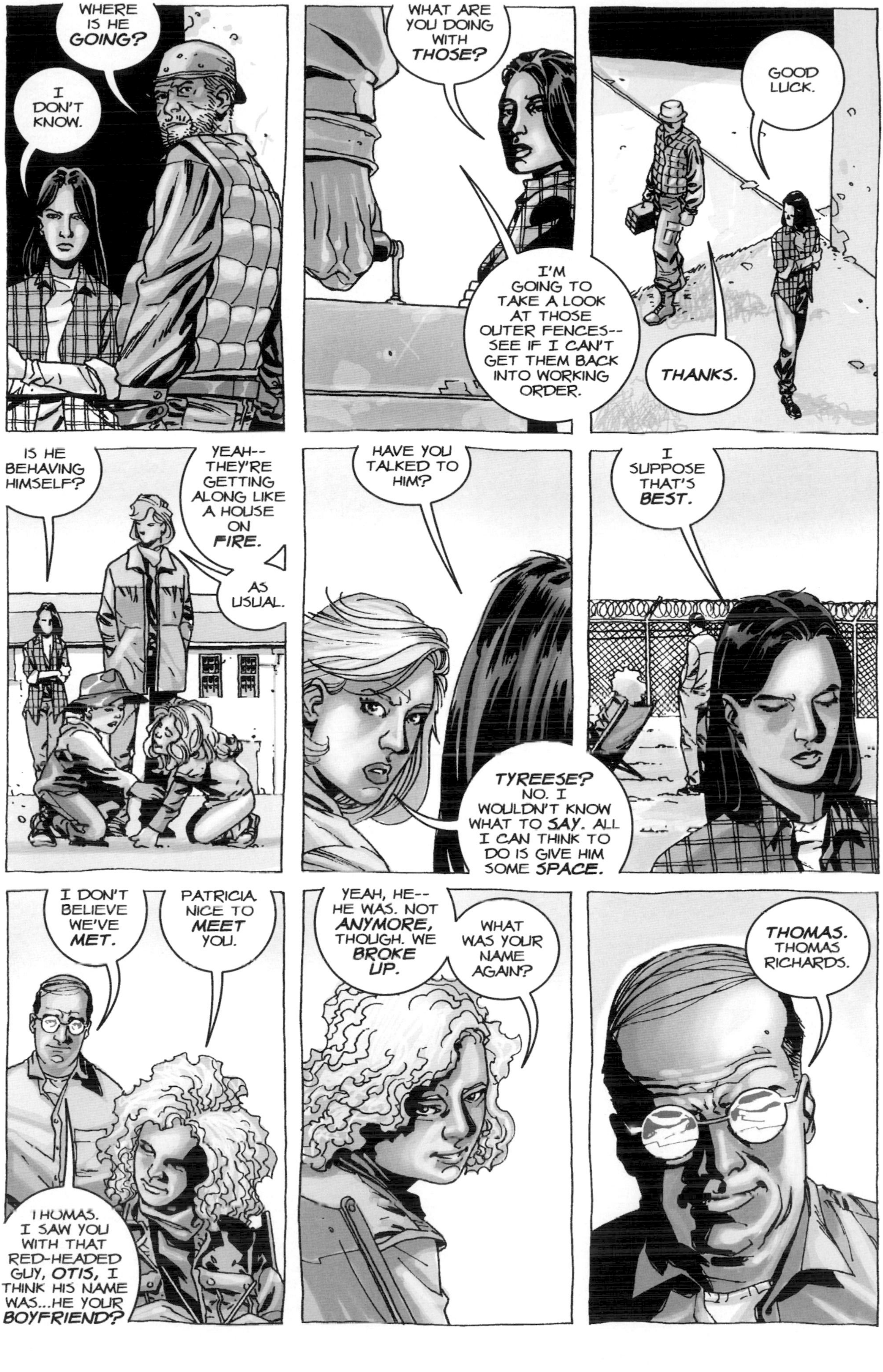
WHERE IS HE *GOING?*
I DON'T KNOW.
WHAT ARE YOU DOING WITH *THOSE?*
I'M GOING TO TAKE A LOOK AT THOSE OUTER FENCES-- SEE IF I CAN'T GET THEM BACK INTO WORKING ORDER.
GOOD LUCK.
THANKS.
IS HE BEHAVING HIMSELF?
YEAH-- THEY'RE GETTING ALONG LIKE A HOUSE ON *FIRE.*
AS USUAL.
HAVE YOU TALKED TO HIM?
TYREESE? NO. I WOULDN'T KNOW WHAT TO *SAY.* ALL I CAN THINK TO DO IS GIVE HIM SOME *SPACE.*
I SUPPOSE THAT'S *BEST.*
I DON'T BELIEVE WE'VE *MET.*
PATRICIA. NICE TO *MEET* YOU.
THOMAS. I SAW YOU WITH THAT RED-HEADED GUY, *OTIS,* I THINK HIS NAME WAS...HE YOUR *BOYFRIEND?*
YEAH, HE-- HE WAS. NOT *ANYMORE,* THOUGH. WE *BROKE UP.*
WHAT WAS YOUR NAME AGAIN?
THOMAS. THOMAS RICHARDS.

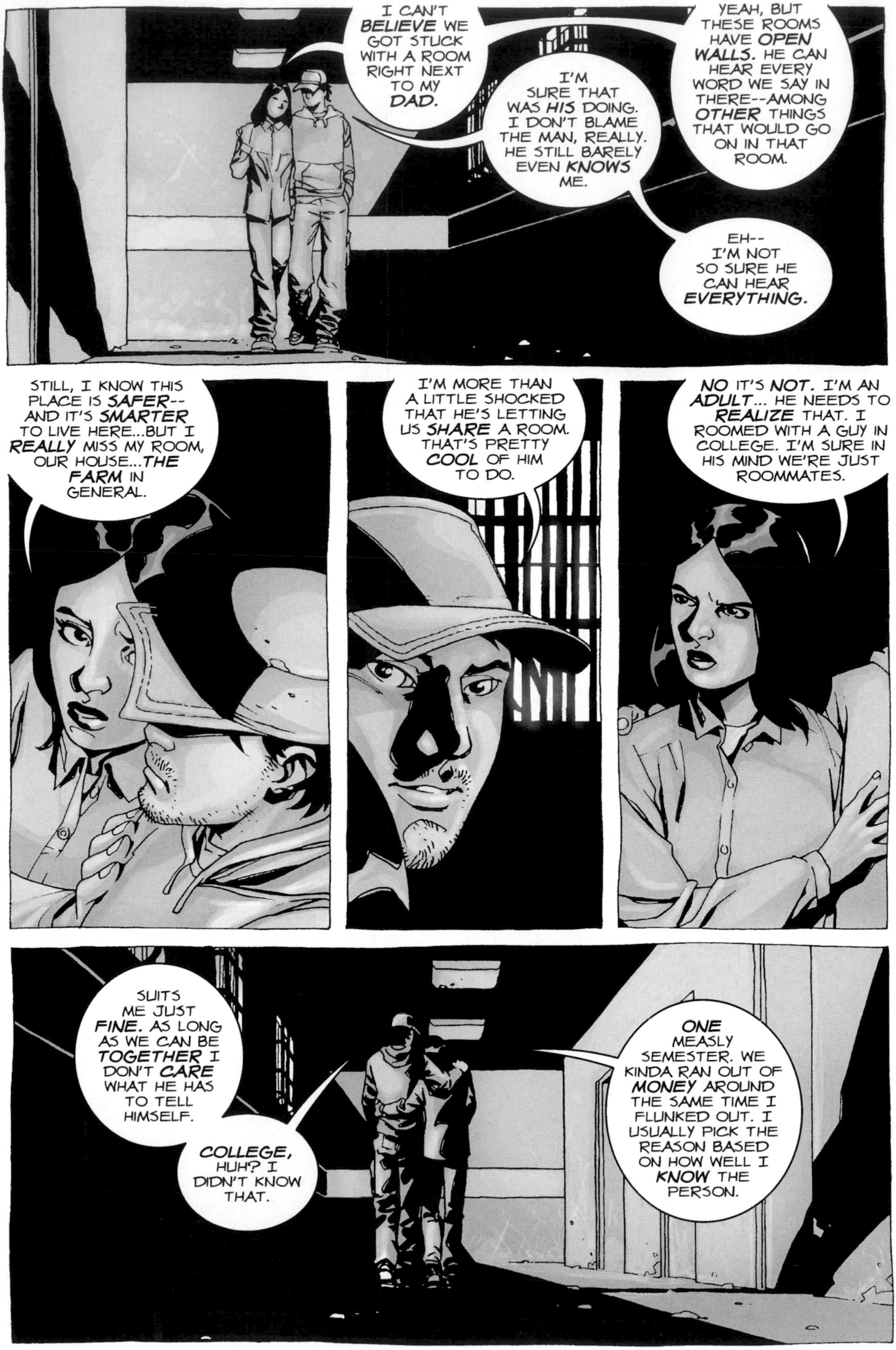
I CAN'T BELIEVE WE GOT STUCK WITH A ROOM RIGHT NEXT TO MY DAD.
YEAH, BUT THESE ROOMS HAVE OPEN WALLS. HE CAN HEAR EVERY WORD WE SAY IN THERE--AMONG OTHER THINGS THAT WOULD GO ON IN THAT ROOM.
I'M SURE THAT WAS HIS DOING. I DON'T BLAME THE MAN, REALLY. HE STILL BARELY EVEN KNOWS ME.
EH-- I'M NOT SO SURE HE CAN HEAR EVERYTHING.
STILL, I KNOW THIS PLACE IS SAFER-- AND IT'S SMARTER TO LIVE HERE...BUT I REALLY MISS MY ROOM, OUR HOUSE...THE FARM IN GENERAL.
I'M MORE THAN A LITTLE SHOCKED THAT HE'S LETTING US SHARE A ROOM. THAT'S PRETTY COOL OF HIM TO DO.
NO IT'S NOT. I'M AN ADULT... HE NEEDS TO REALIZE THAT. I ROOMED WITH A GUY IN COLLEGE. I'M SURE IN HIS MIND WE'RE JUST ROOMMATES.
SUITS ME JUST FINE. AS LONG AS WE CAN BE TOGETHER I DON'T CARE WHAT HE HAS TO TELL HIMSELF.
COLLEGE, HUH? I DIDN'T KNOW THAT.
ONE MEASLY SEMESTER. WE KINDA RAN OUT OF MONEY AROUND THE SAME TIME I FLUNKED OUT. I USUALLY PICK THE REASON BASED ON HOW WELL I KNOW THE PERSON.

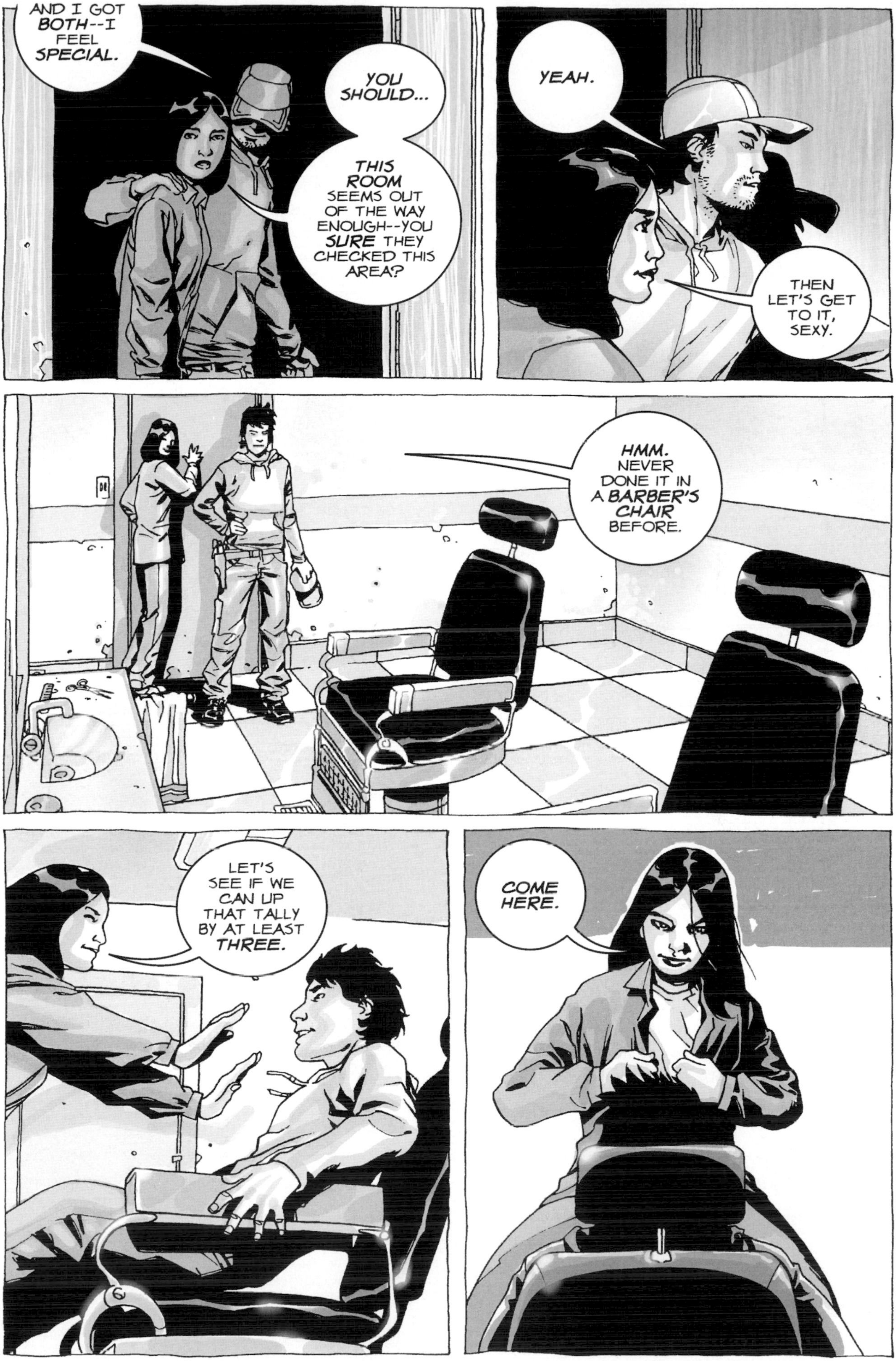
AND I GOT BOTH--I FEEL SPECIAL.
YOU SHOULD...
THIS ROOM SEEMS OUT OF THE WAY ENOUGH--YOU SURE THEY CHECKED THIS AREA?
YEAH.
THEN LET'S GET TO IT, SEXY.
HMM. NEVER DONE IT IN A BARBER'S CHAIR BEFORE.
LET'S SEE IF WE CAN UP THAT TALLY BY AT LEAST THREE.
COME HERE.

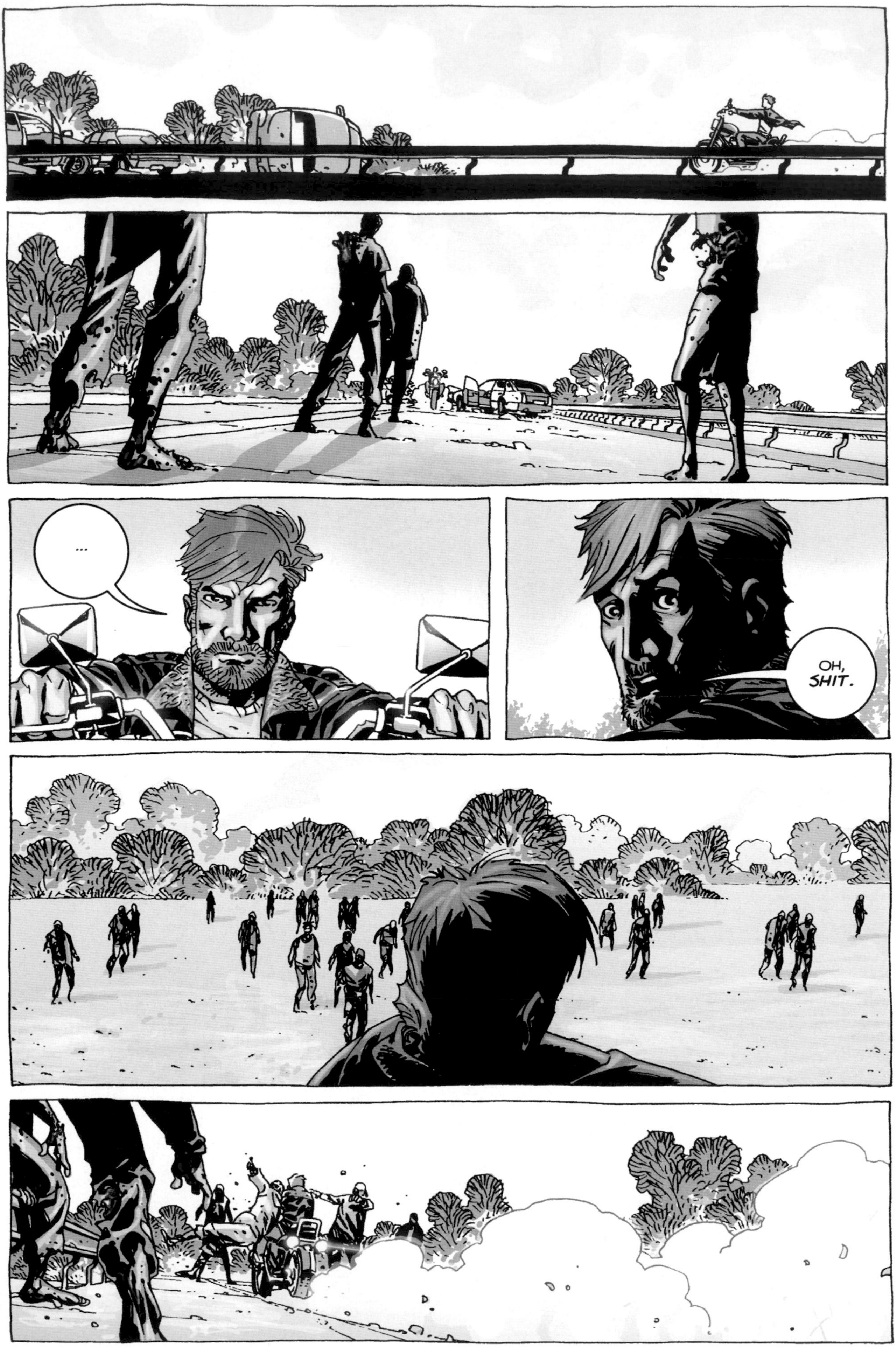
...
OH, SHIT.

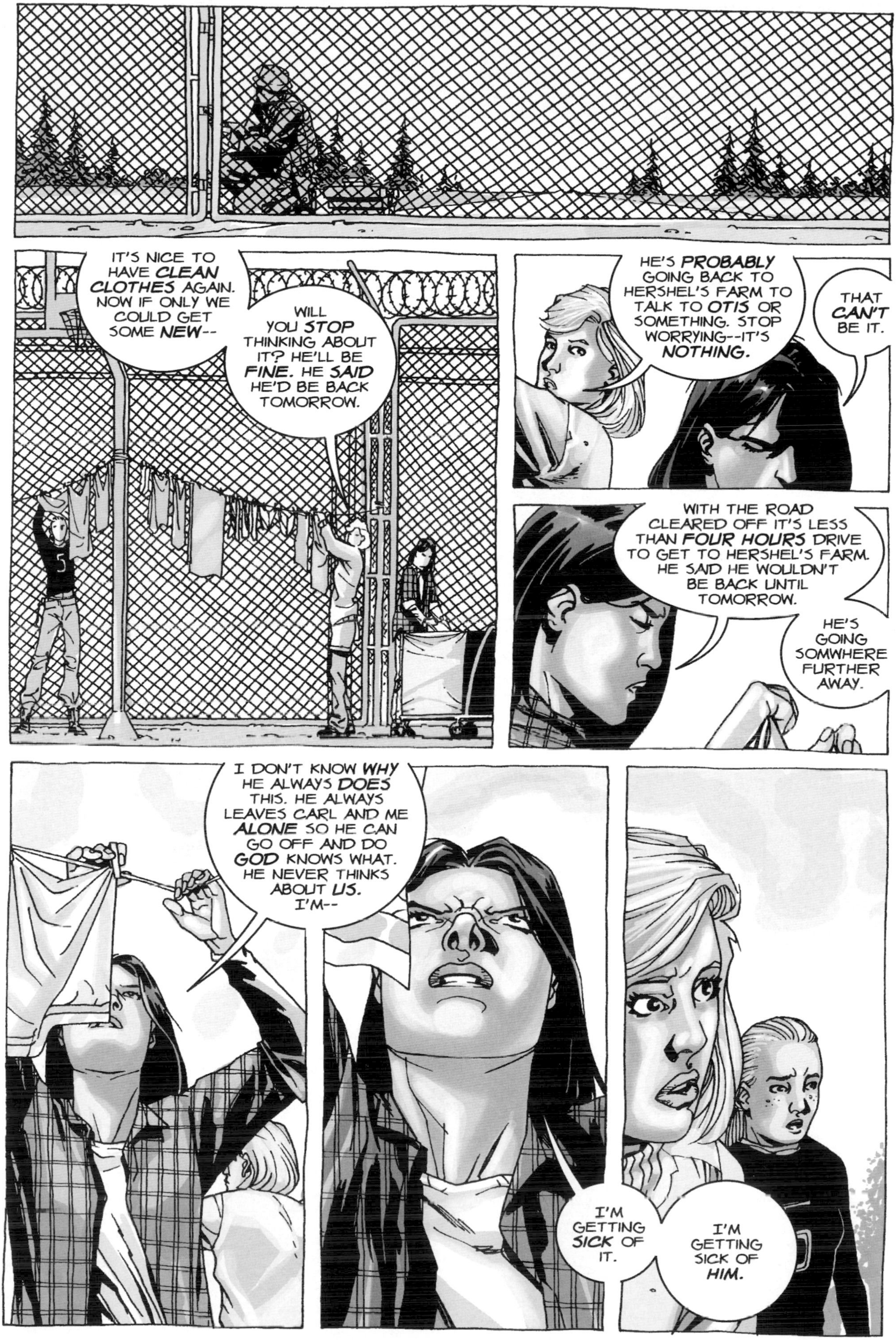
IT'S NICE TO HAVE CLEAN CLOTHES AGAIN. NOW IF ONLY WE COULD GET SOME NEW--
WILL YOU STOP THINKING ABOUT IT? HE'LL BE FINE. HE SAID HE'D BE BACK TOMORROW.
HE'S PROBABLY GOING BACK TO HERSHEL'S FARM TO TALK TO OTIS OR SOMETHING. STOP WORRYING--IT'S NOTHING.
THAT CAN'T BE IT.
WITH THE ROAD CLEARED OFF IT'S LESS THAN FOUR HOURS DRIVE TO GET TO HERSHEL'S FARM. HE SAID HE WOULDN'T BE BACK UNTIL TOMORROW.
HE'S GOING SOMWHERE FURTHER AWAY.
I DON'T KNOW WHY HE ALWAYS DOES THIS. HE ALWAYS LEAVES CARL AND ME ALONE SO HE CAN GO OFF AND DO GOD KNOWS WHAT. HE NEVER THINKS ABOUT US. I'M--
I'M GETTING SICK OF IT.
I'M GETTING SICK OF HIM.

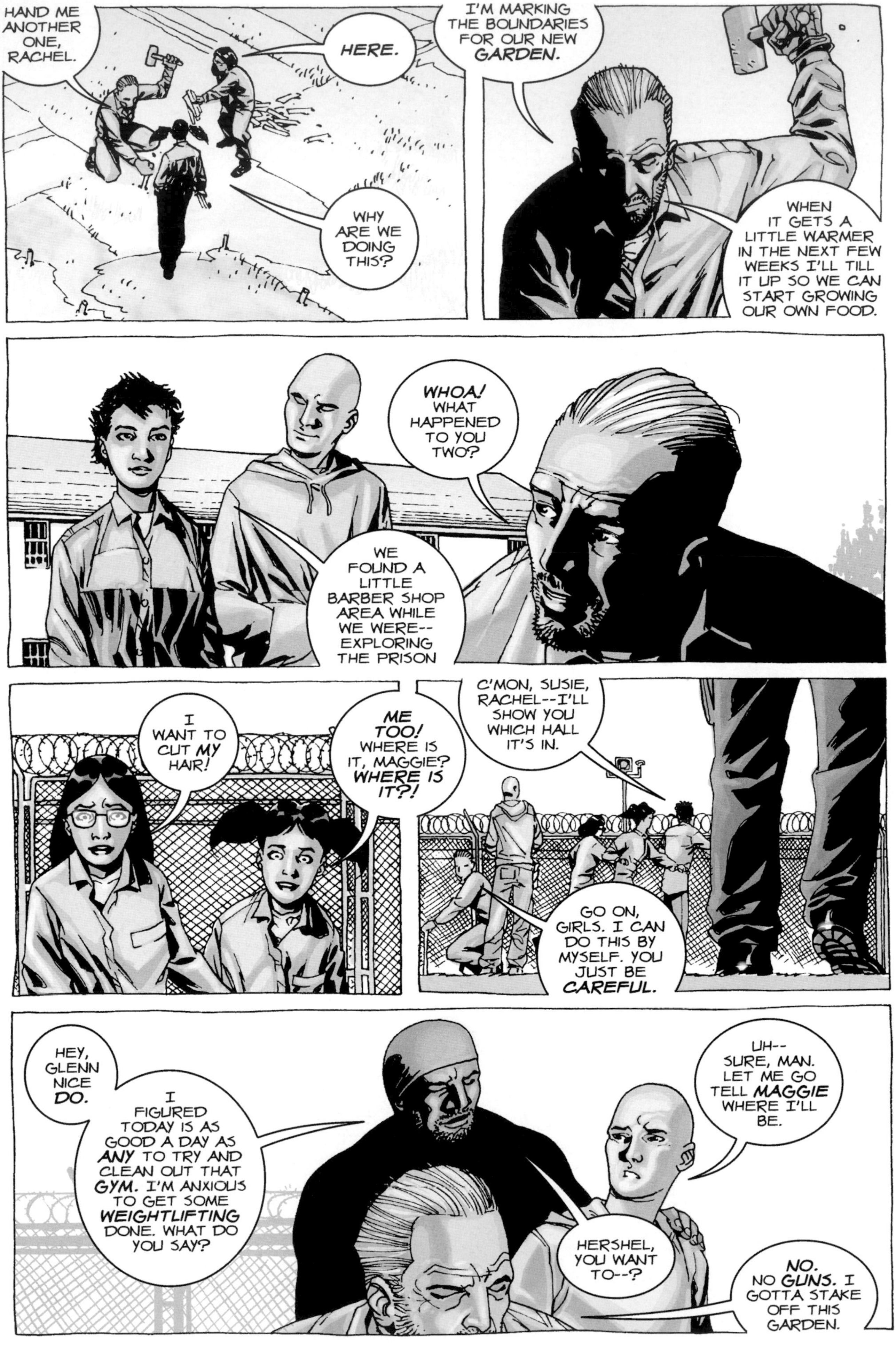
HAND ME ANOTHER ONE, RACHEL.
HERE.
WHY ARE WE DOING THIS?
I'M MARKING THE BOUNDARIES FOR OUR NEW GARDEN.
WHEN IT GETS A LITTLE WARMER IN THE NEXT FEW WEEKS I'LL TILL IT UP SO WE CAN START GROWING OUR OWN FOOD.
WHOA! WHAT HAPPENED TO YOU TWO?
WE FOUND A LITTLE BARBER SHOP AREA WHILE WE WERE-- EXPLORING THE PRISON
I WANT TO CUT MY HAIR!
ME TOO! WHERE IS IT, MAGGIE? WHERE IS IT?!
C'MON, SUSIE, RACHEL--I'LL SHOW YOU WHICH HALL IT'S IN.
GO ON, GIRLS. I CAN DO THIS BY MYSELF. YOU JUST BE CAREFUL.
HEY, GLENN NICE DO.
I FIGURED TODAY IS AS GOOD A DAY AS ANY TO TRY AND CLEAN OUT THAT GYM. I'M ANXIOUS TO GET SOME WEIGHTLIFTING DONE. WHAT DO YOU SAY?
UH-- SURE, MAN. LET ME GO TELL MAGGIE WHERE I'LL BE.
HERSHEL, YOU WANT TO--?
NO. NO GUNS. I GOTTA STAKE OFF THIS GARDEN.

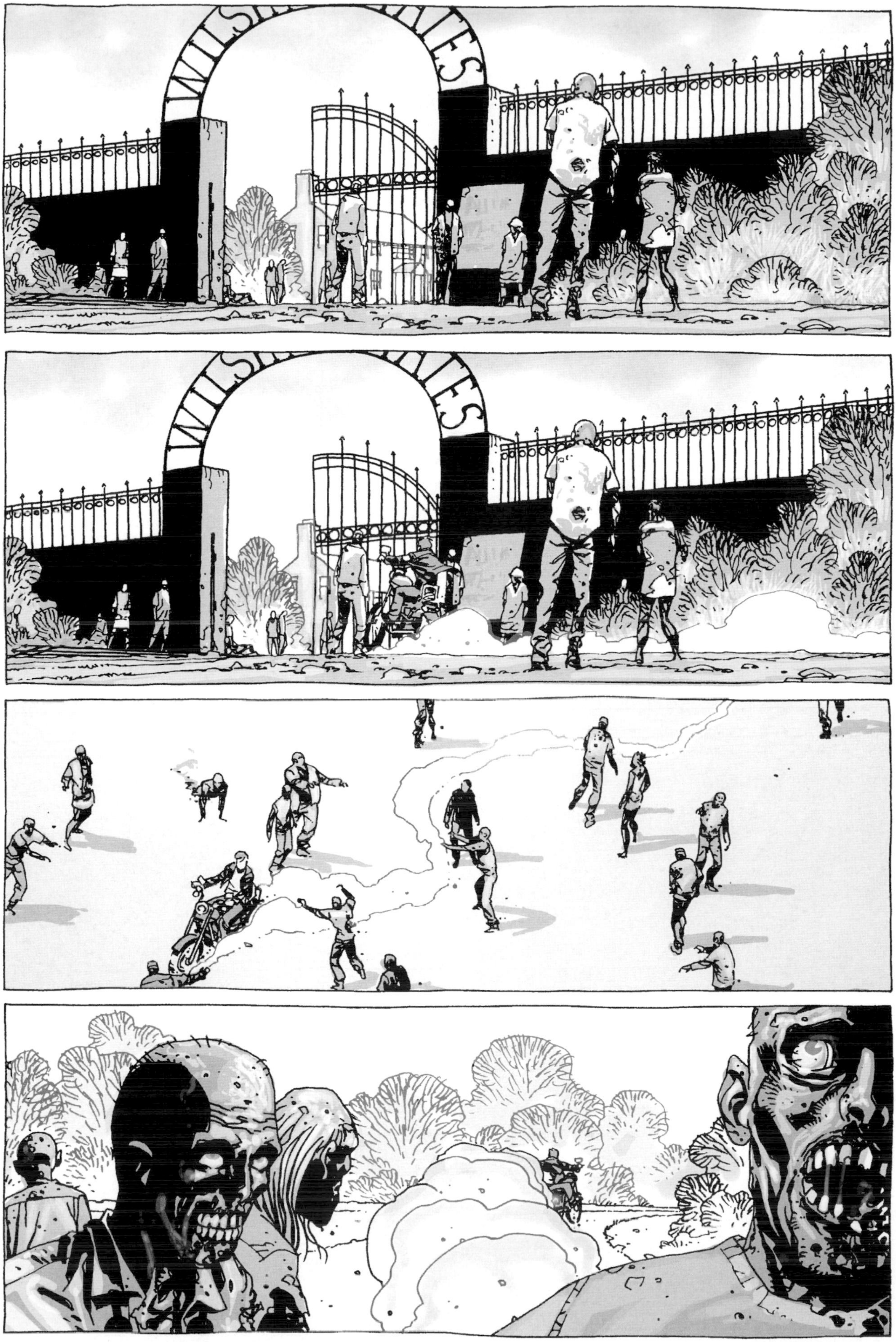

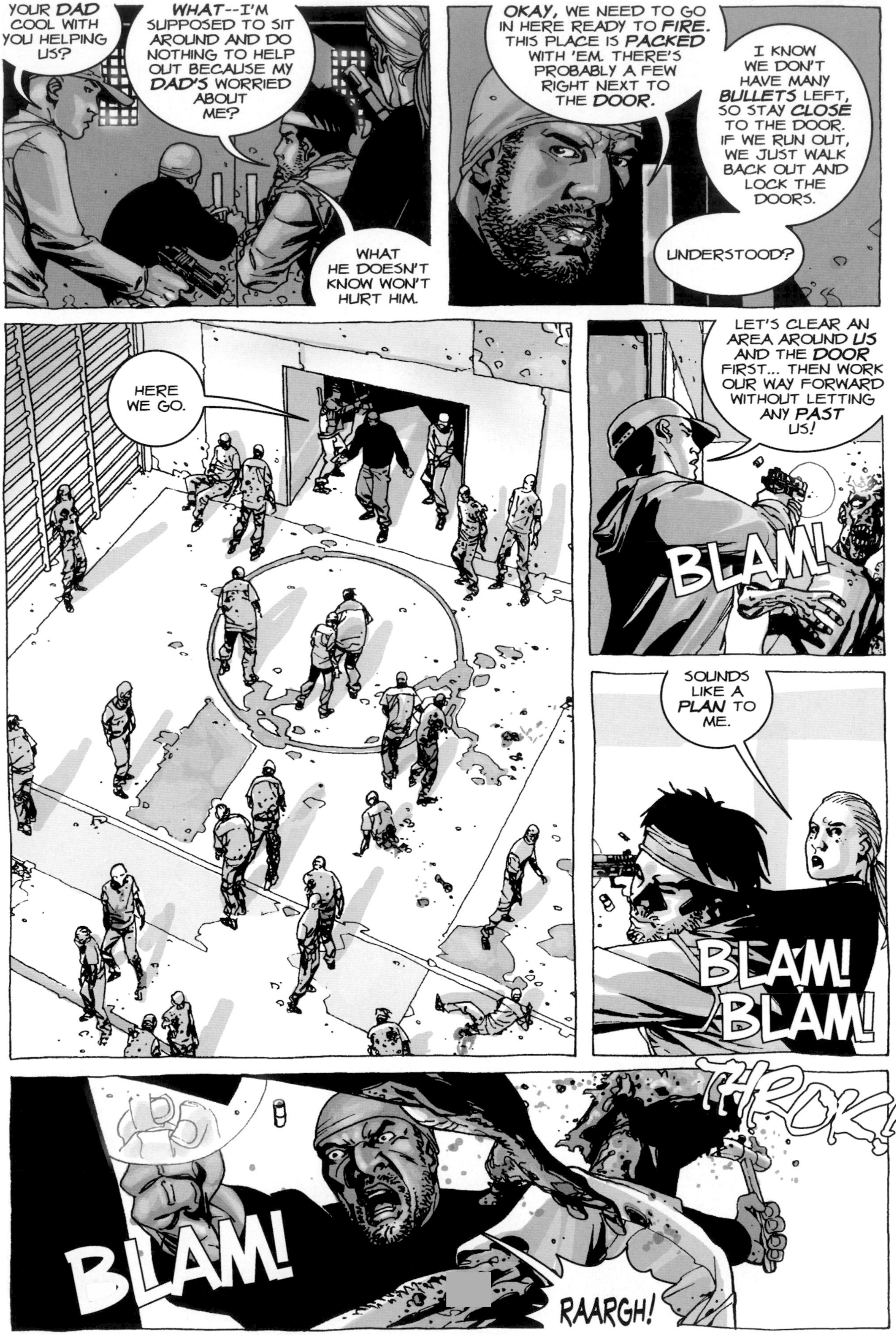
YOUR DAD COOL WITH YOU HELPING US?
WHAT--I'M SUPPOSED TO SIT AROUND AND DO NOTHING TO HELP OUT BECAUSE MY DAD'S WORRIED ABOUT ME?
WHAT HE DOESN'T KNOW WON'T HURT HIM.
OKAY, WE NEED TO GO IN HERE READY TO FIRE. THIS PLACE IS PACKED WITH 'EM. THERE'S PROBABLY A FEW RIGHT NEXT TO THE DOOR.
I KNOW WE DON'T HAVE MANY BULLETS LEFT, SO STAY CLOSE TO THE DOOR. IF WE RUN OUT, WE JUST WALK BACK OUT AND LOCK THE DOORS.
UNDERSTOOD?
HERE WE GO.
LET'S CLEAR AN AREA AROUND US AND THE DOOR FIRST... THEN WORK OUR WAY FORWARD WITHOUT LETTING ANY PAST US!
BLAM!
SOUNDS LIKE A PLAN TO ME.
BLAM! BLAM!
THROK!
BLAM!
RAARGH!

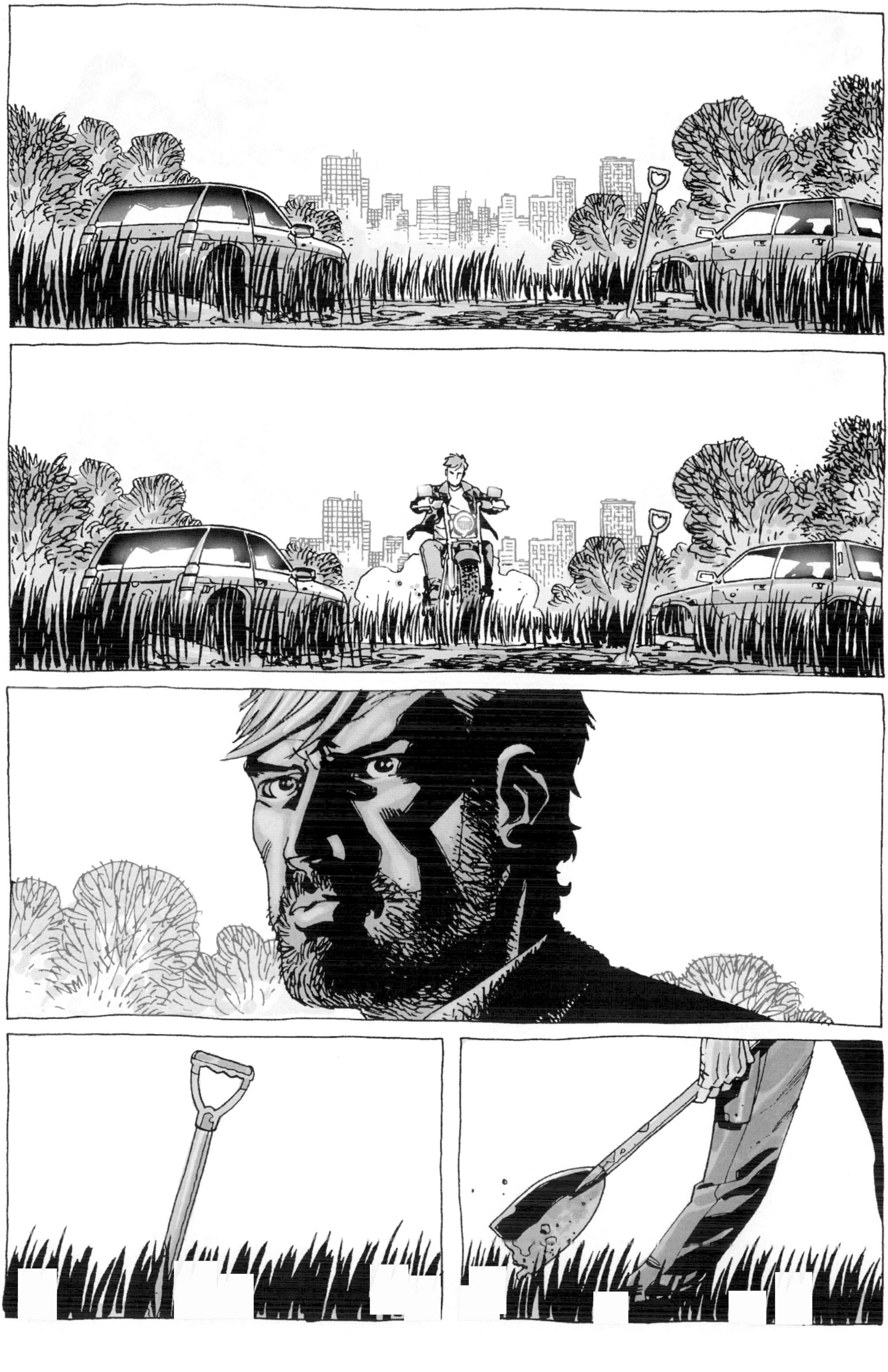

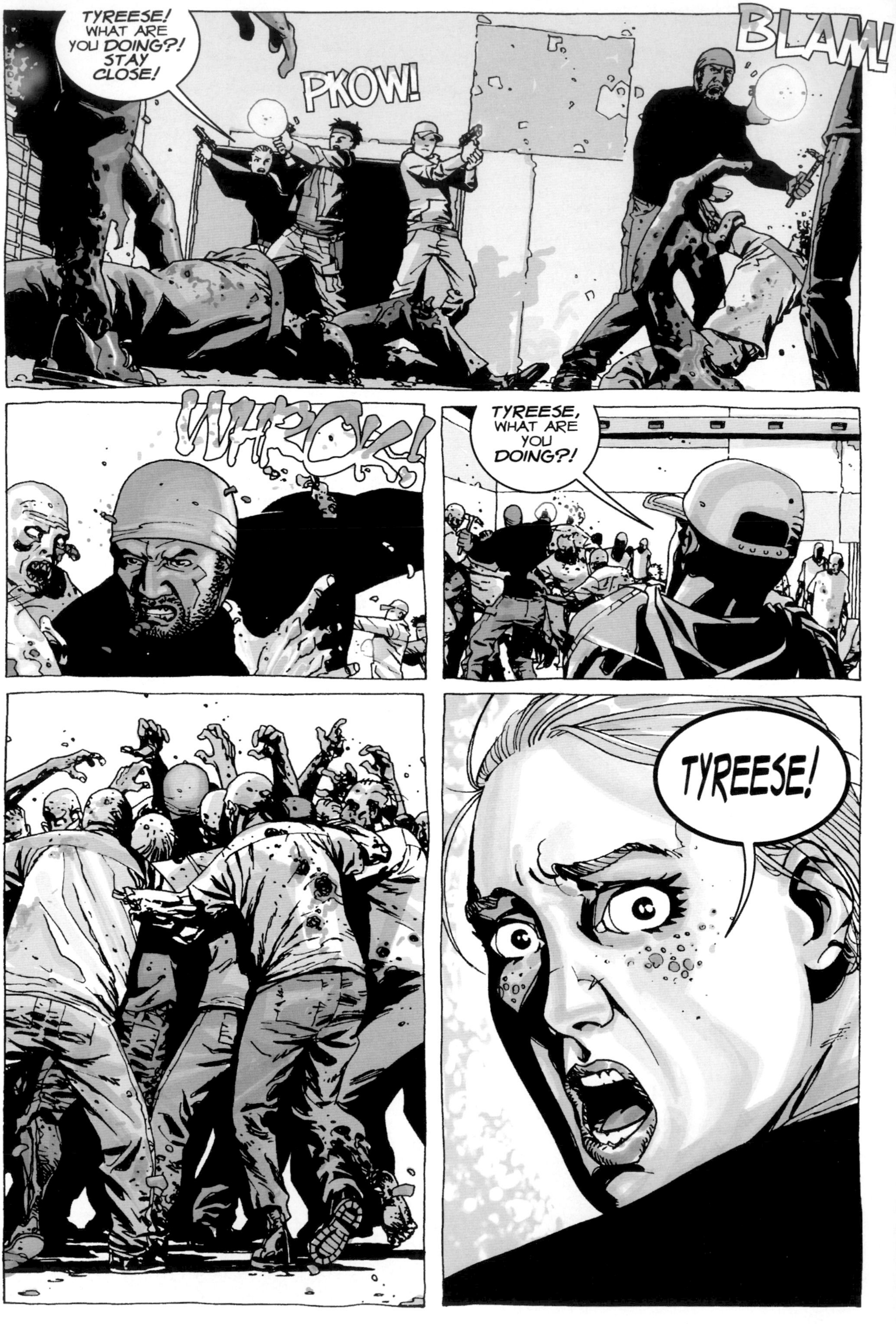
TYREESE! WHAT ARE YOU DOING?! STAY CLOSE!
PKOW!
BLAM!
TYREESE, WHAT ARE YOU DOING?!
TYREESE!

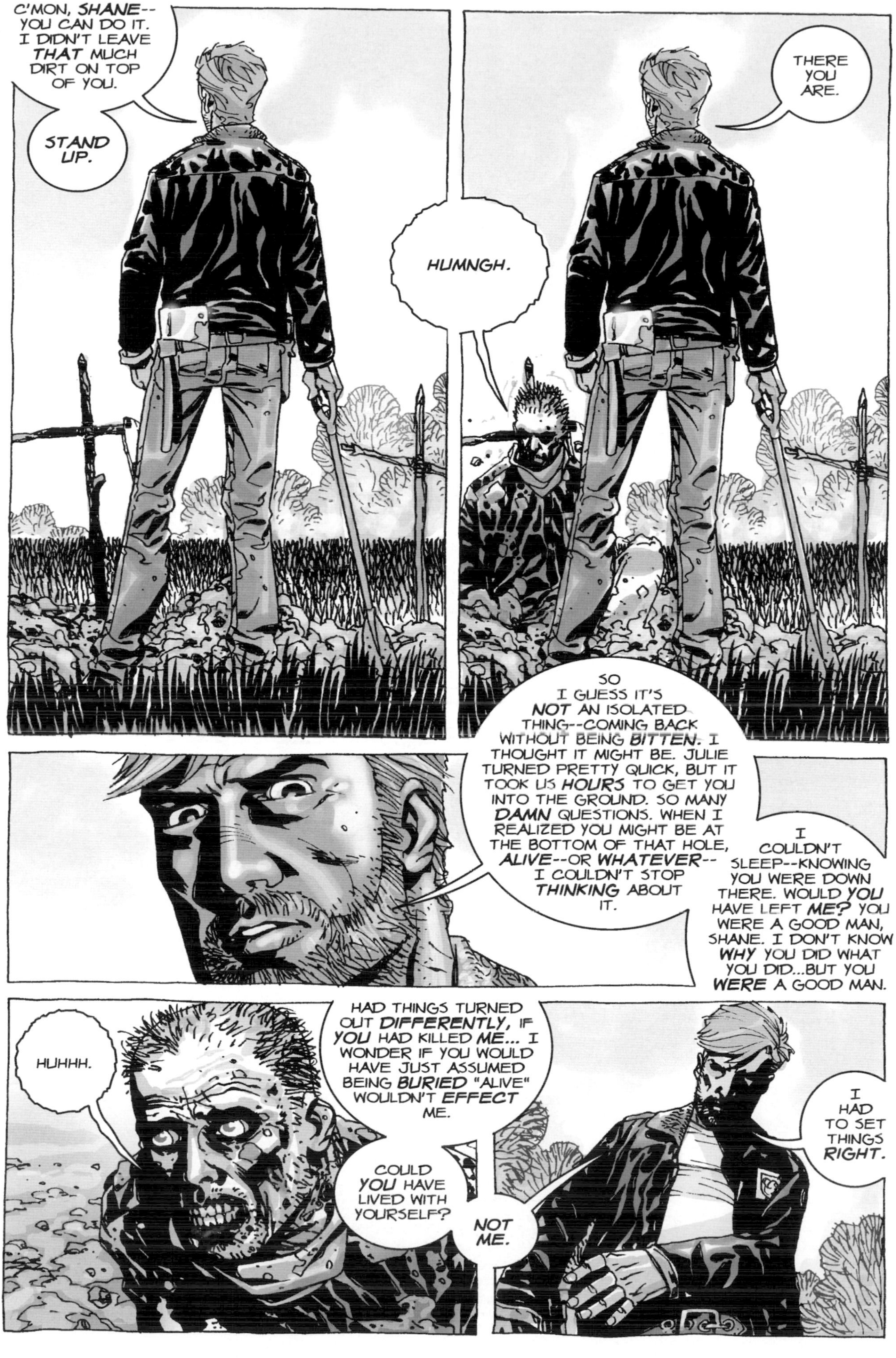
C'MON, SHANE-- YOU CAN DO IT. I DIDN'T LEAVE THAT MUCH DIRT ON TOP OF YOU.
STAND UP.
HUMNGH.
THERE YOU ARE.
SO I GUESS IT'S NOT AN ISOLATED THING--COMING BACK WITHOUT BEING BITTEN. I THOUGHT IT MIGHT BE. JULIE TURNED PRETTY QUICK, BUT IT TOOK US HOURS TO GET YOU INTO THE GROUND. SO MANY DAMN QUESTIONS. WHEN I REALIZED YOU MIGHT BE AT THE BOTTOM OF THAT HOLE, ALIVE--OR WHATEVER-- I COULDN'T STOP THINKING ABOUT IT.
I COULDN'T SLEEP--KNOWING YOU WERE DOWN THERE. WOULD YOU HAVE LEFT ME? YOU WERE A GOOD MAN, SHANE. I DON'T KNOW WHY YOU DID WHAT YOU DID...BUT YOU WERE A GOOD MAN.
HUHHH.
HAD THINGS TURNED OUT DIFFERENTLY, IF YOU HAD KILLED ME... I WONDER IF YOU WOULD HAVE JUST ASSUMED BEING BURIED "ALIVE" WOULDN'T EFFECT ME.
COULD YOU HAVE LIVED WITH YOURSELF?
NOT ME.
I HAD TO SET THINGS RIGHT.

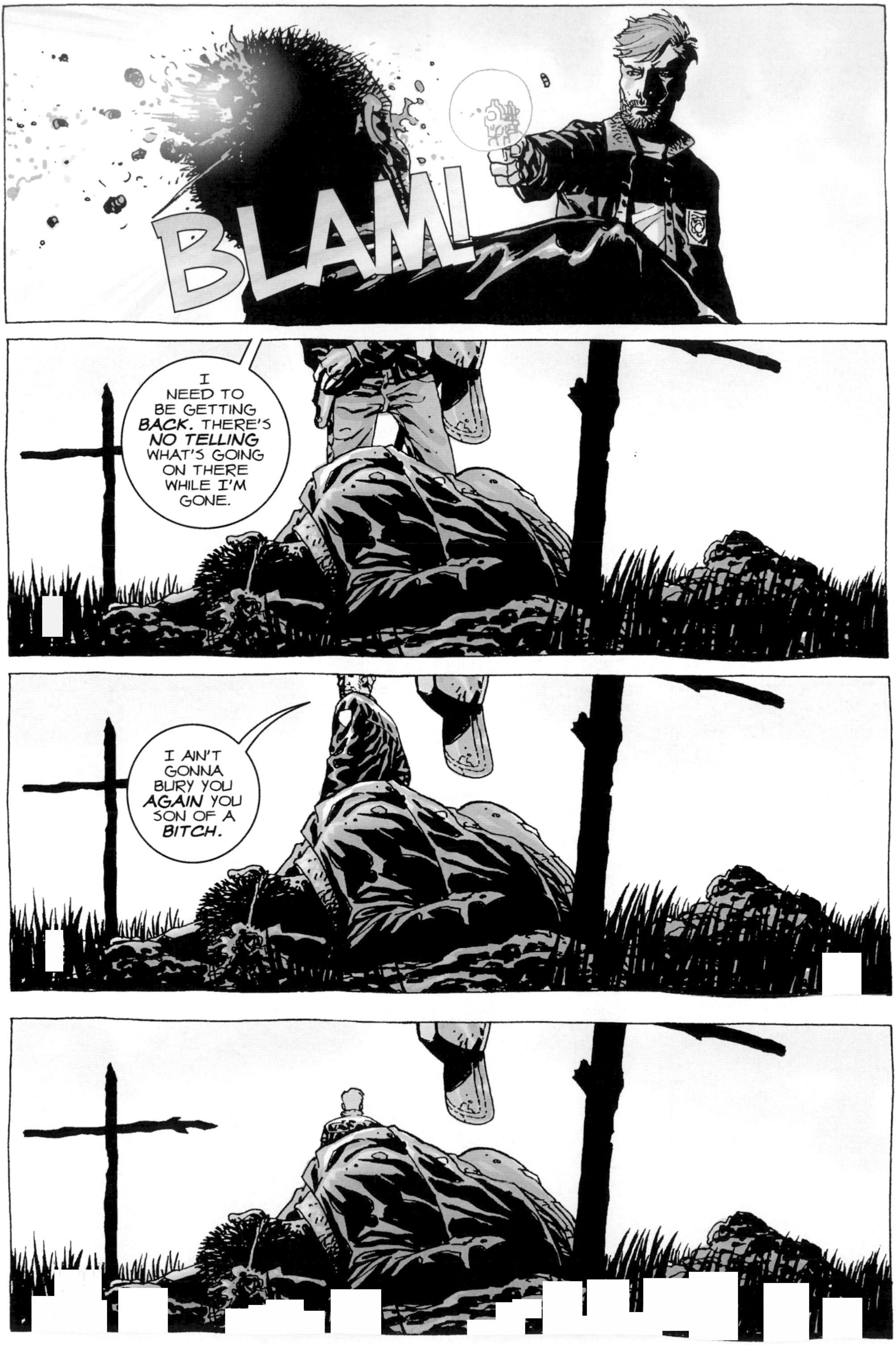
BLAM!
I NEED TO BE GETTING BACK. THERE'S NO TELLING WHAT'S GOING ON THERE WHILE I'M GONE.
I AIN'T GONNA BURY YOU AGAIN YOU SON OF A BITCH.

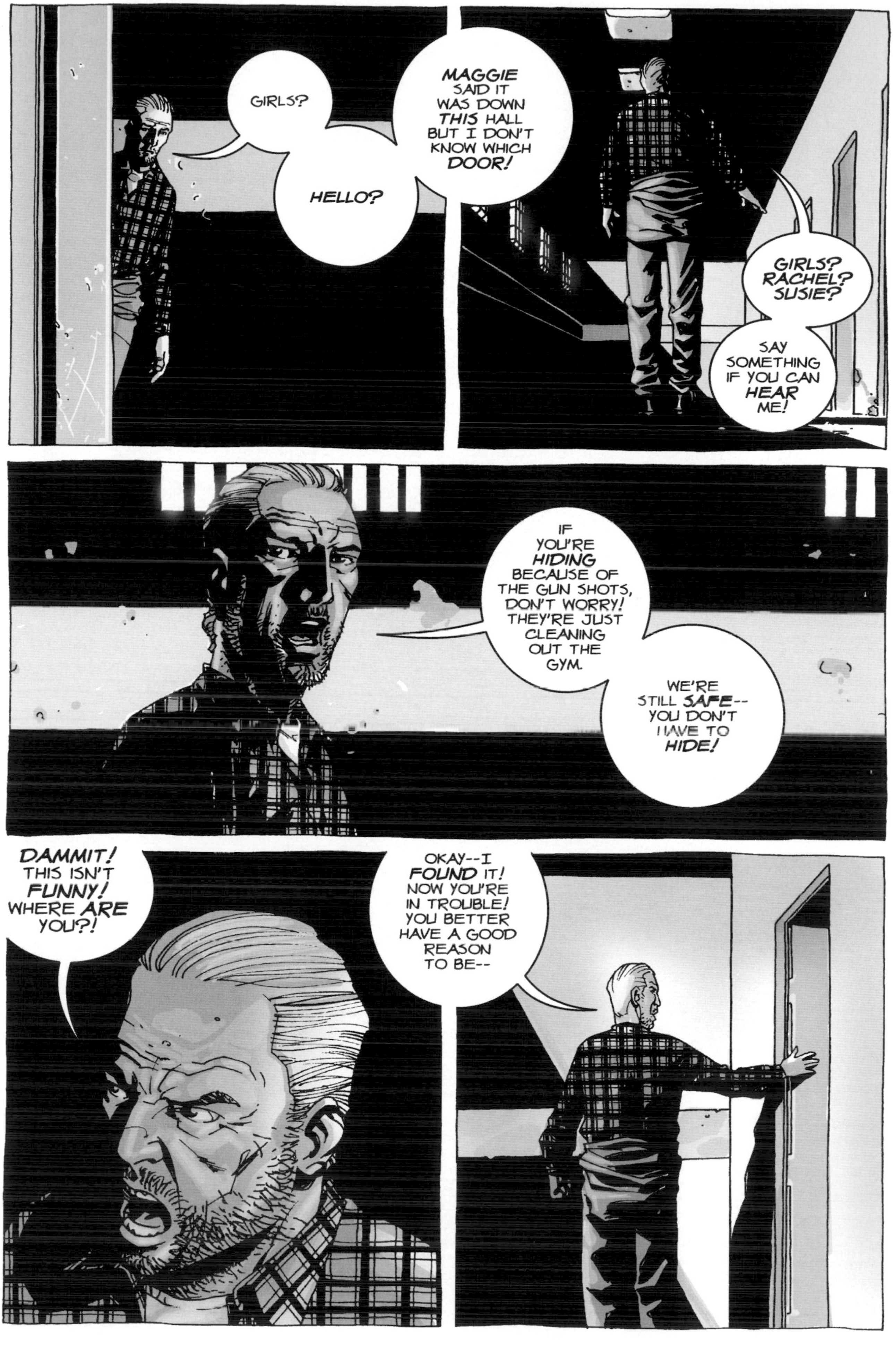
GIRLS?
HELLO?
MAGGIE SAID IT WAS DOWN THIS HALL BUT I DON'T KNOW WHICH DOOR!
GIRLS? RACHEL? SUSIE?
SAY SOMETHING IF YOU CAN HEAR ME!
IF YOU'RE HIDING BECAUSE OF THE GUN SHOTS, DON'T WORRY! THEY'RE JUST CLEANING OUT THE GYM.
WE'RE STILL SAFE-- YOU DON'T HAVE TO HIDE!
DAMMIT! THIS ISN'T FUNNY! WHERE ARE YOU?!
OKAY--I FOUND IT! NOW YOU'RE IN TROUBLE! YOU BETTER HAVE A GOOD REASON TO BE--

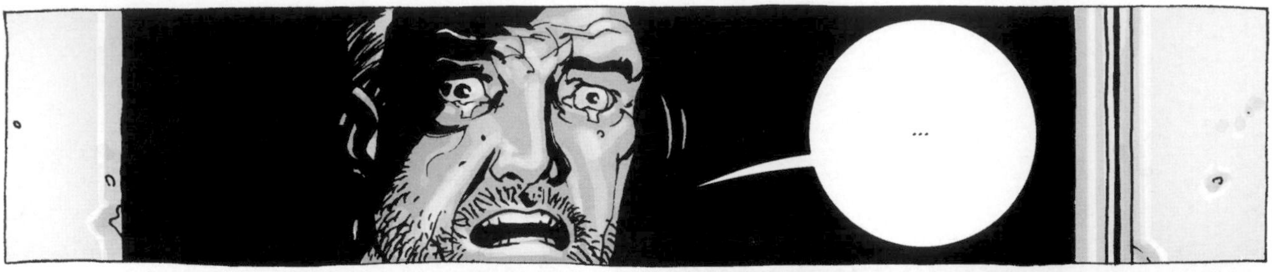
...
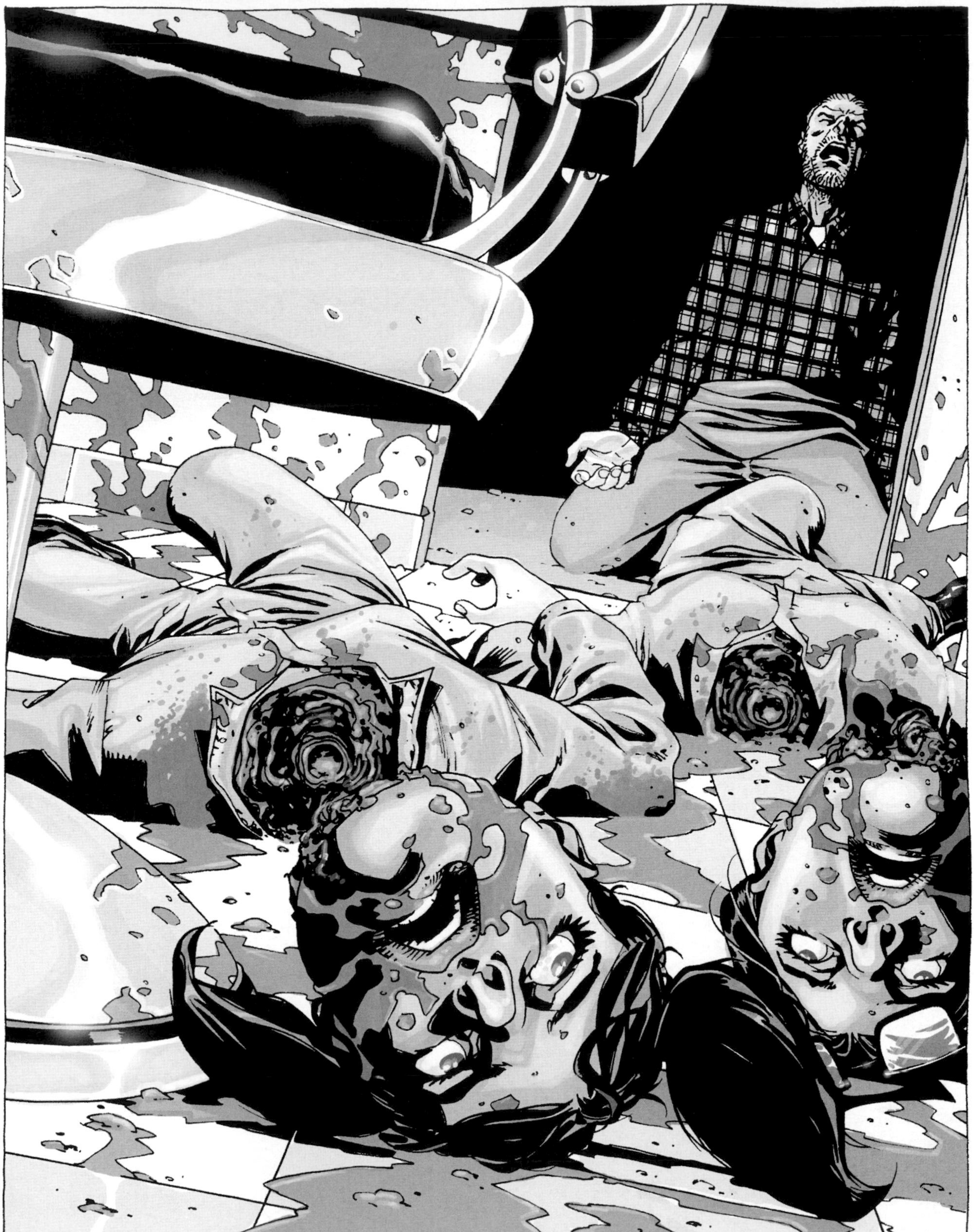

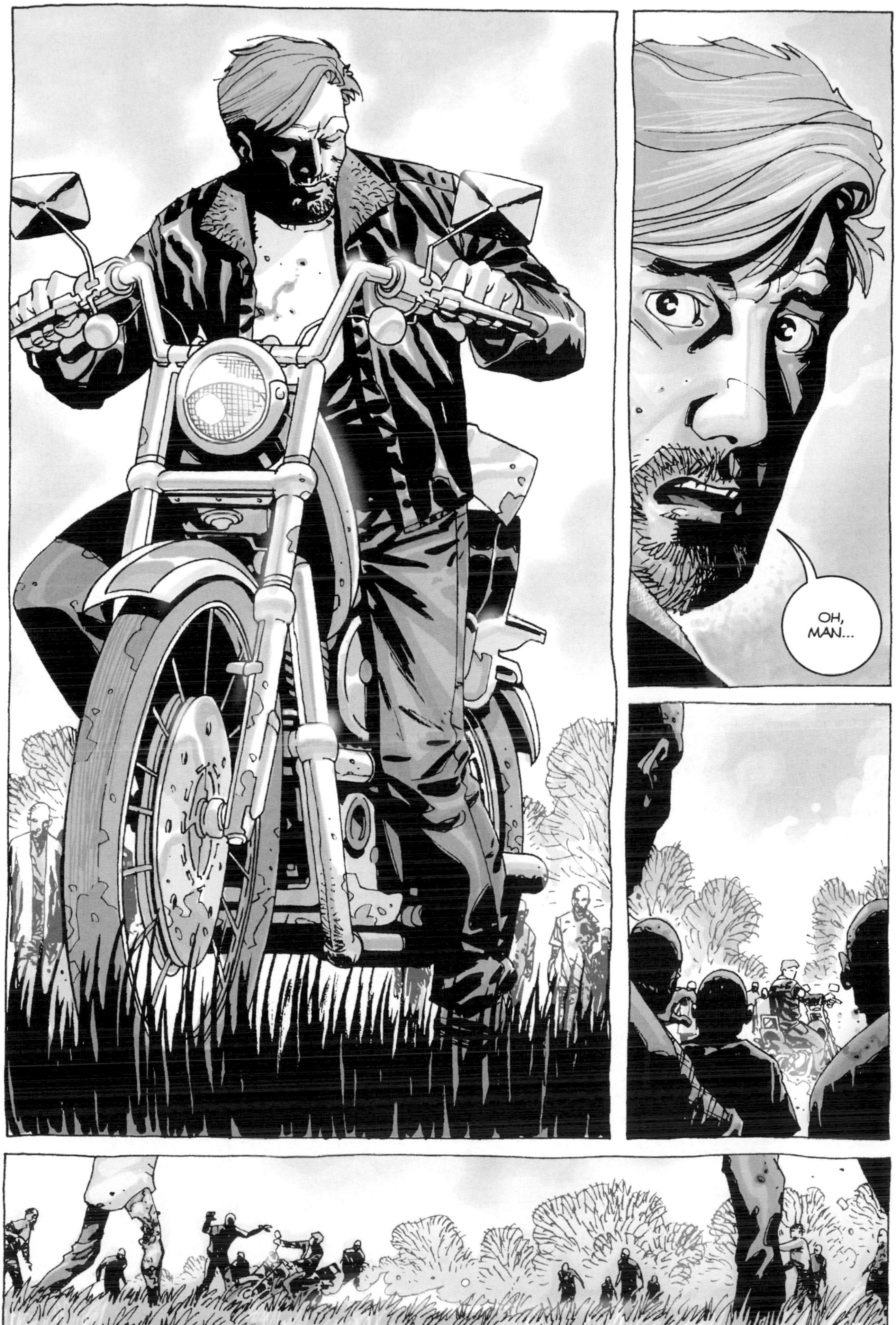
OH, MAN...

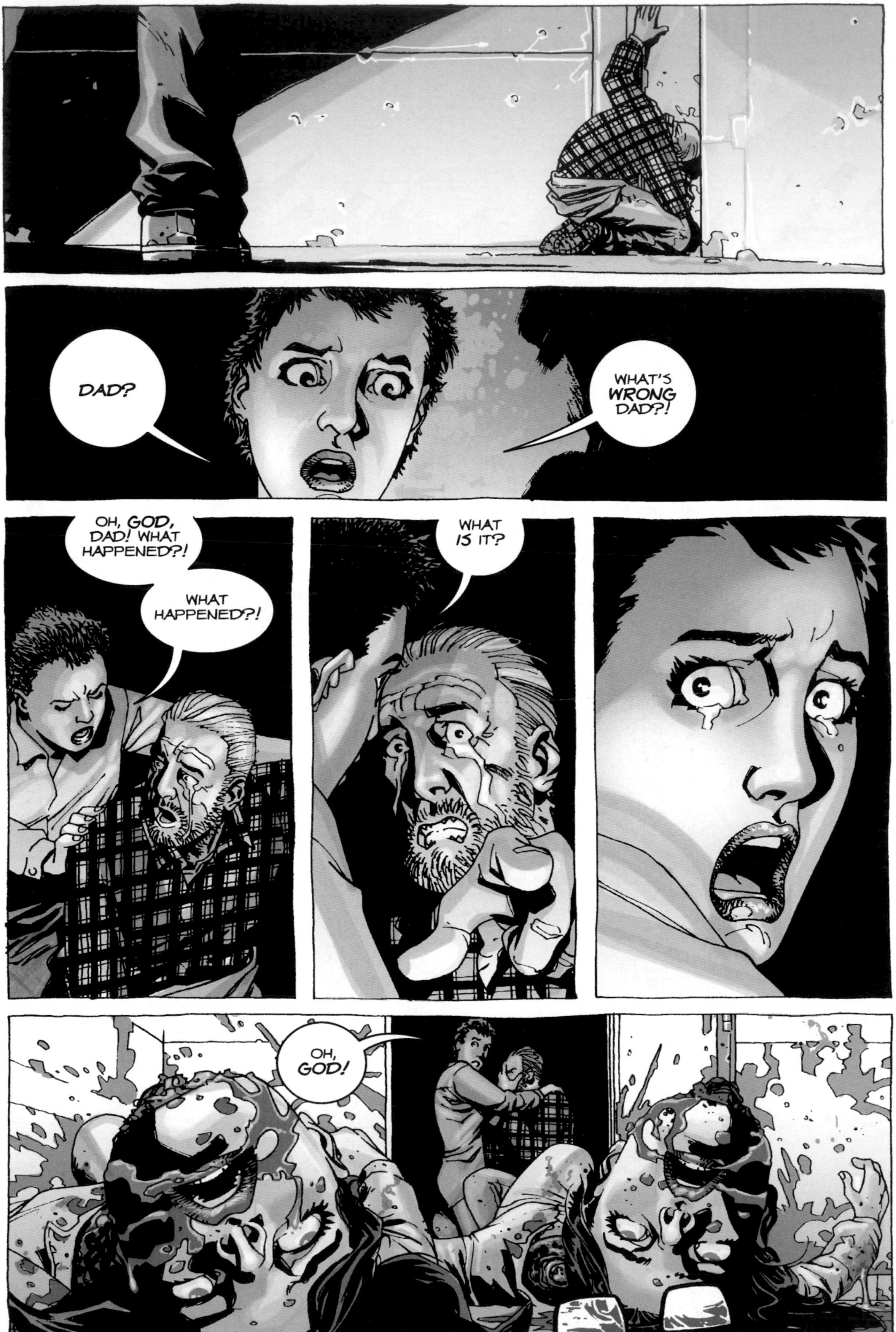
DAD?
WHAT'S WRONG DAD?!
OH, GOD, DAD! WHAT HAPPENED?!
WHAT HAPPENED?!
WHAT IS IT?
OH, GOD!

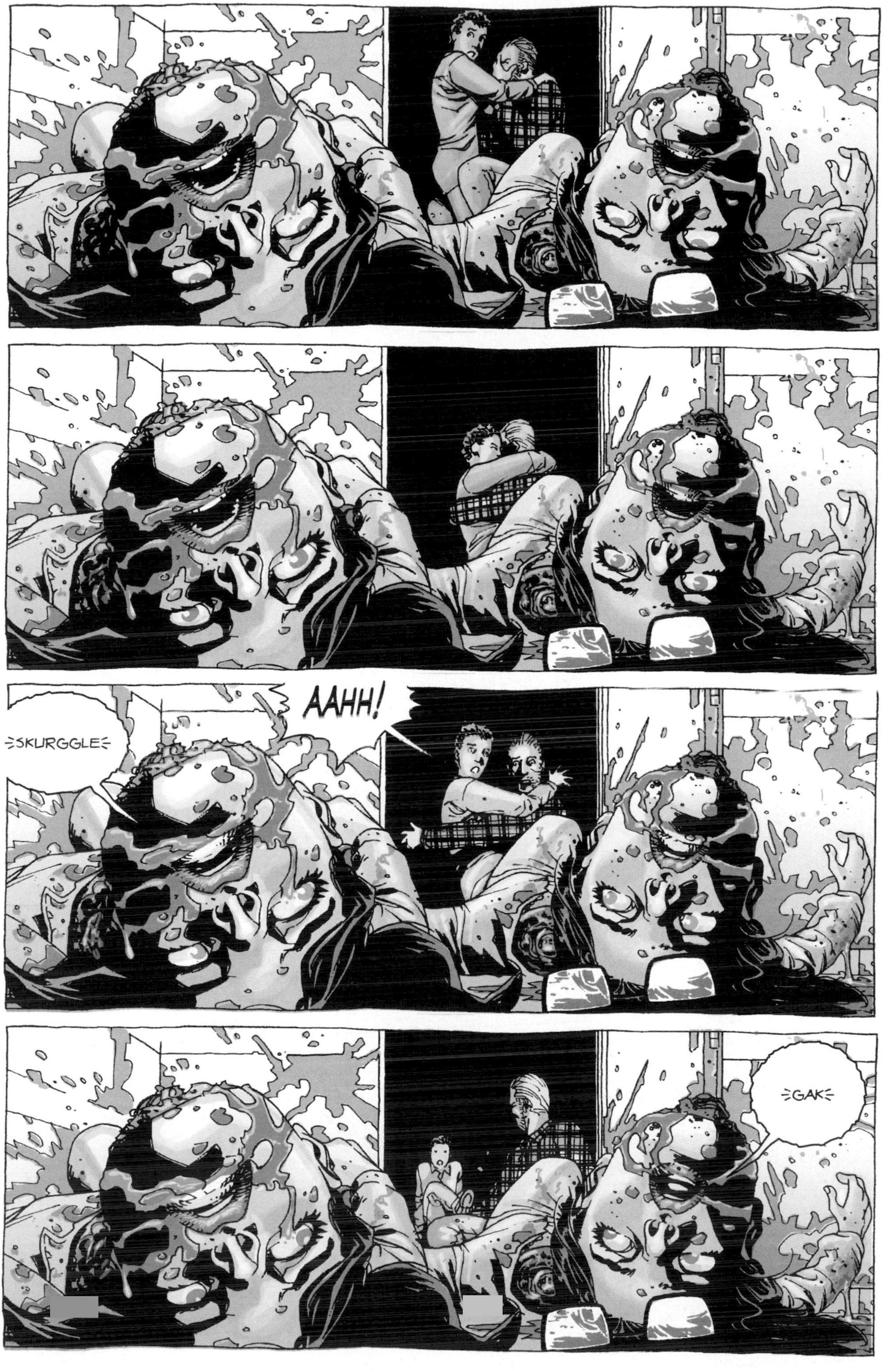
SKURGGLE
AAHH!
GAK

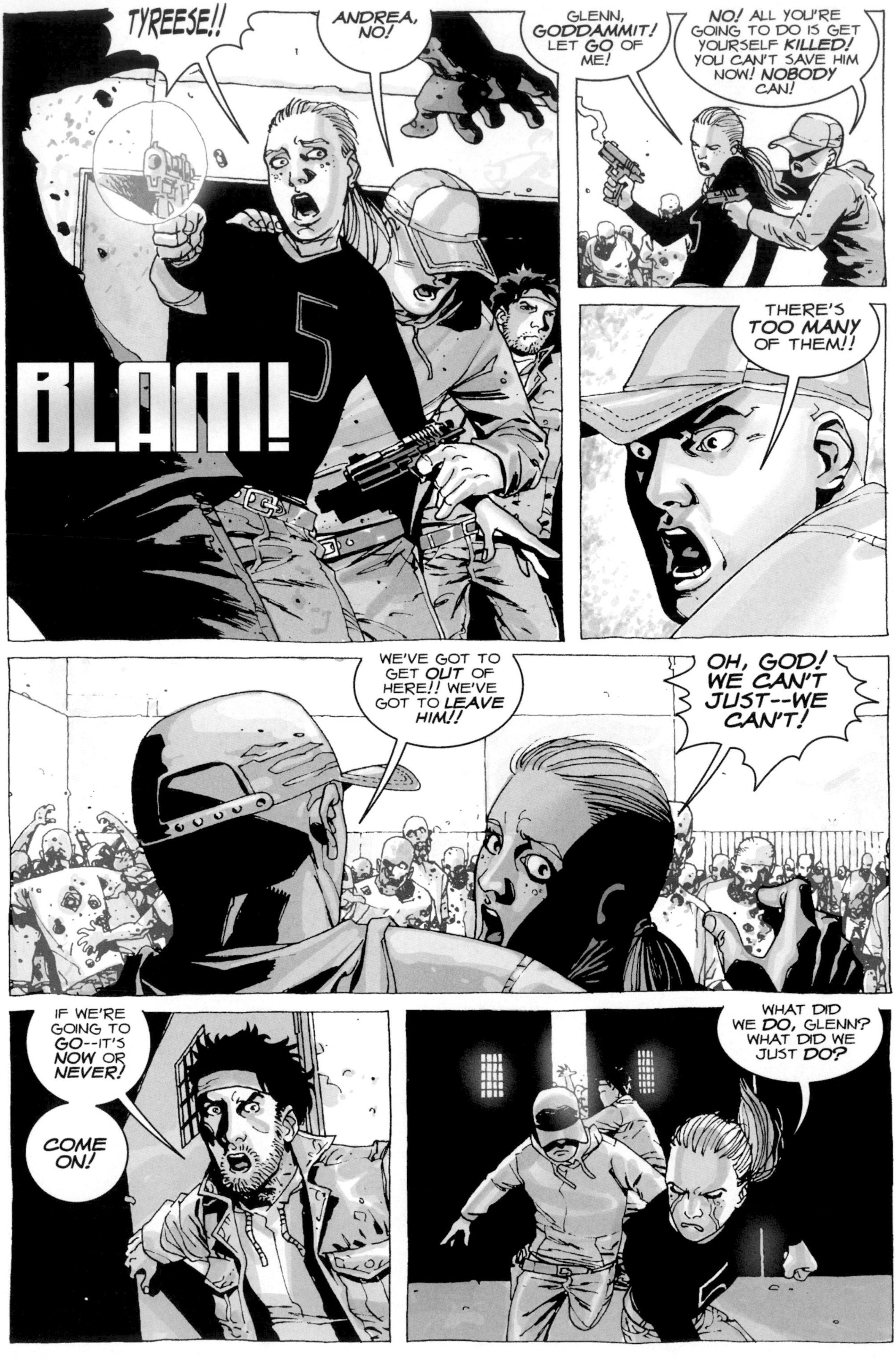
TYREESE!!
ANDREA, NO!
BLAM!
GLENN, GODDAMMIT! LET GO OF ME!
NO! ALL YOU'RE GOING TO DO IS GET YOURSELF KILLED! YOU CAN'T SAVE HIM NOW! NOBODY CAN!
THERE'S TOO MANY OF THEM!!
WE'VE GOT TO GET OUT OF HERE!! WE'VE GOT TO LEAVE HIM!!
OH, GOD! WE CAN'T JUST--WE CAN'T!
IF WE'RE GOING TO GO--IT'S NOW OR NEVER!
COME ON!
WHAT DID WE DO, GLENN? WHAT DID WE JUST DO?

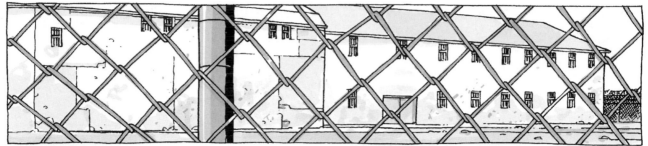

STILL WORRIED ABOUT RICK?

A *LITTLE*. I'M TRYING NOT TO *THINK* ABOUT IT, ACTUALLY.

SORRY.

SO IT WAS NICE OF DALE TO OFFER TO WATCH THE KIDS SO WE COULD CLEAN UP...

YEAH...

THIS IS *NICE* ISN'T IT? I STILL CAN'T GET OVER THE FACT THAT THIS PLACE STILL HAS *RUNNING WATER.*

I *SERIOUSLY* DOUBT THE WATER IS *TREATED* MUCH AT THIS POINT. IT'S STILL COMING TO US, BUT I DON'T THINK IT'S *CLEAN* ENOUGH TO DRINK WITHOUT BOILING.

UH-HUH.

IT DOESN'T *STINK*, THOUGH... SO I DON'T MIND SHOWERING IN--

AAAIIIEEEEK!!

I'M SORRY! I'M SORRY! I DIDN'T KNOW ANYONE WAS IN HERE! I SWEAR!

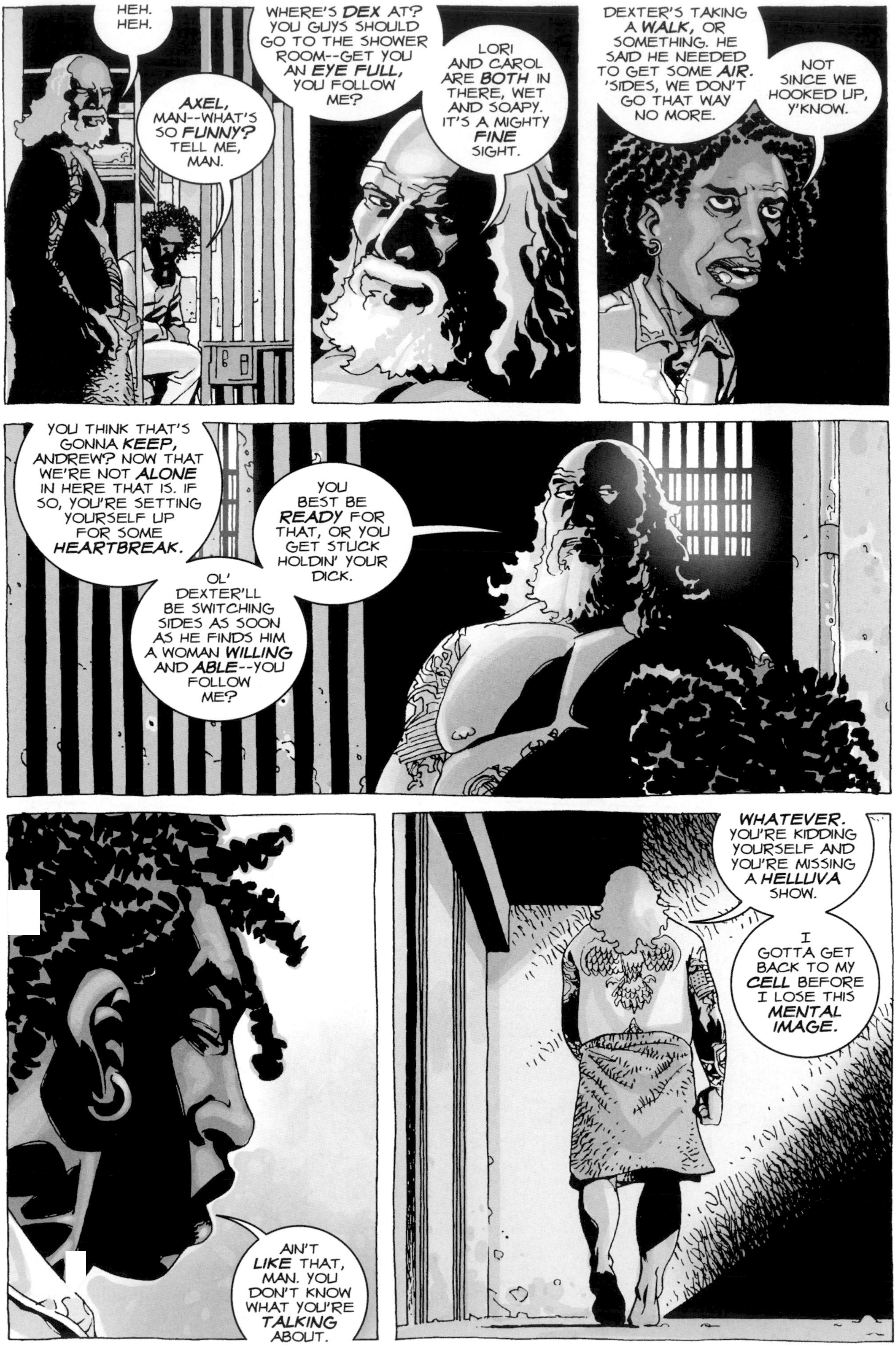

HEH. HEH.
AXEL, MAN--WHAT'S SO FUNNY? TELL ME, MAN.
WHERE'S DEX AT? YOU GUYS SHOULD GO TO THE SHOWER ROOM--GET YOU AN EYE FULL, YOU FOLLOW ME?
LORI AND CAROL ARE BOTH IN THERE, WET AND SOAPY. IT'S A MIGHTY FINE SIGHT.
DEXTER'S TAKING A WALK, OR SOMETHING. HE SAID HE NEEDED TO GET SOME AIR. 'SIDES, WE DON'T GO THAT WAY NO MORE.
NOT SINCE WE HOOKED UP, Y'KNOW.
YOU THINK THAT'S GONNA KEEP, ANDREW? NOW THAT WE'RE NOT ALONE IN HERE THAT IS. IF SO, YOU'RE SETTING YOURSELF UP FOR SOME HEARTBREAK.
OL' DEXTER'LL BE SWITCHING SIDES AS SOON AS HE FINDS HIM A WOMAN WILLING AND ABLE--YOU FOLLOW ME?
YOU BEST BE READY FOR THAT, OR YOU GET STUCK HOLDIN' YOUR DICK.
AIN'T LIKE THAT, MAN. YOU DON'T KNOW WHAT YOU'RE TALKING ABOUT.
WHATEVER. YOU'RE KIDDING YOURSELF AND YOU'RE MISSING A HELLUVA SHOW.
I GOTTA GET BACK TO MY CELL BEFORE I LOSE THIS MENTAL IMAGE.

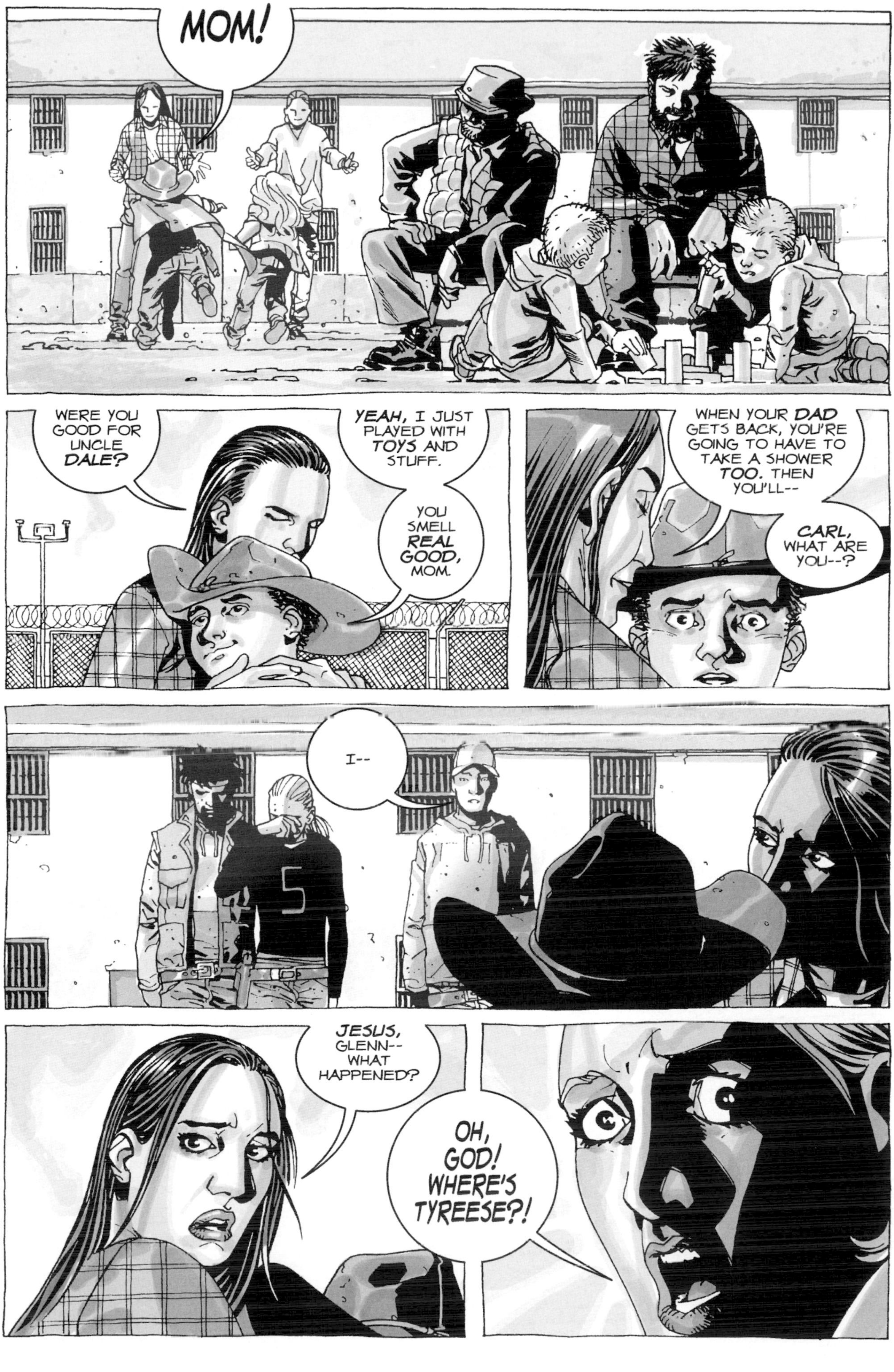
MOM!
WERE YOU GOOD FOR UNCLE DALE?
YEAH, I JUST PLAYED WITH TOYS AND STUFF.
YOU SMELL REAL GOOD, MOM.
WHEN YOUR DAD GETS BACK, YOU'RE GOING TO HAVE TO TAKE A SHOWER TOO. THEN YOU'LL--
CARL, WHAT ARE YOU--?
I--
JESUS, GLENN-- WHAT HAPPENED?
OH, GOD! WHERE'S TYREESE?!

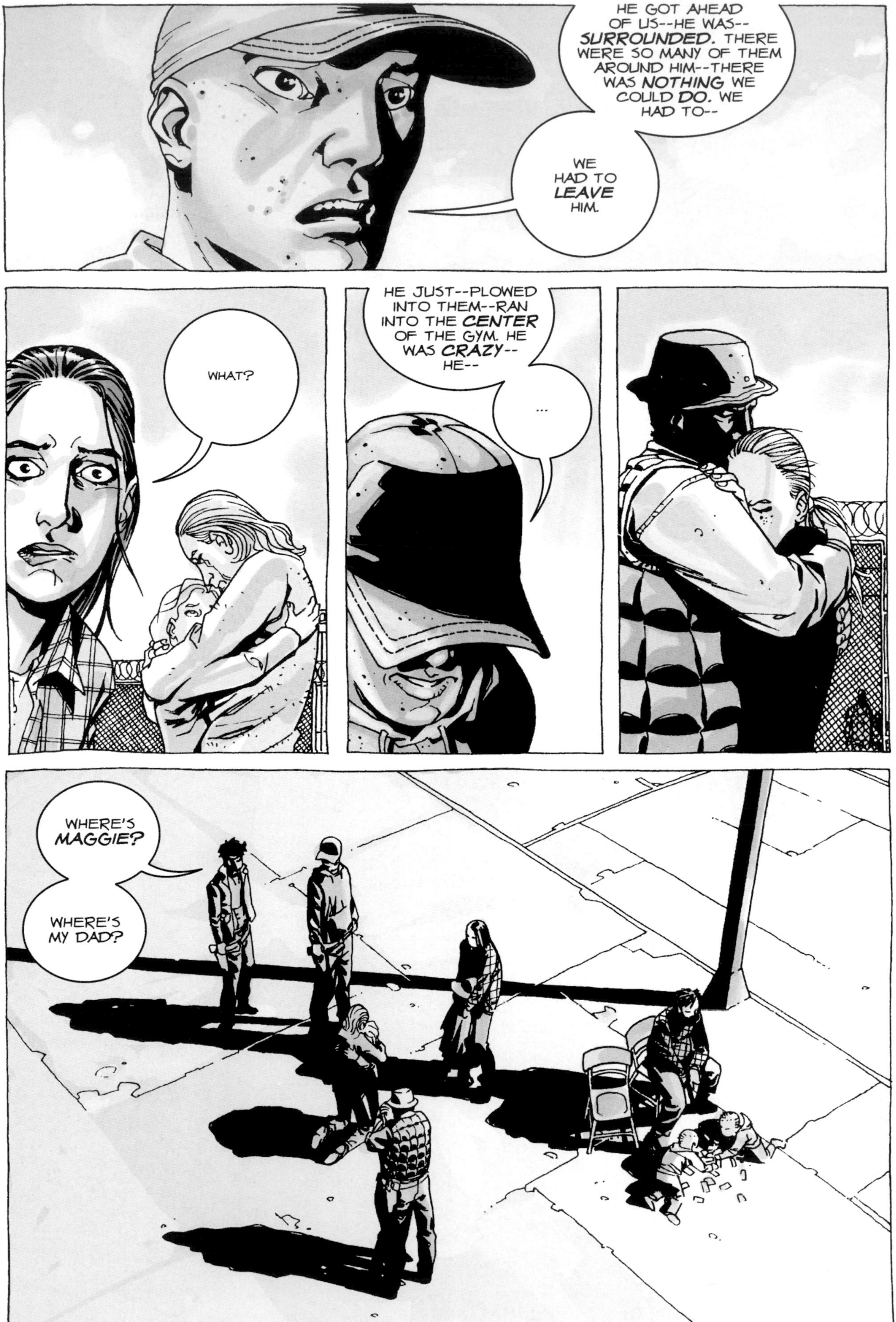

HE GOT AHEAD OF US--HE WAS-- SURROUNDED. THERE WERE SO MANY OF THEM AROUND HIM--THERE WAS NOTHING WE COULD DO. WE HAD TO--
WE HAD TO LEAVE HIM.
WHAT?
HE JUST--PLOWED INTO THEM--RAN INTO THE CENTER OF THE GYM. HE WAS CRAZY-- HE--
...
WHERE'S MAGGIE?
WHERE'S MY DAD?

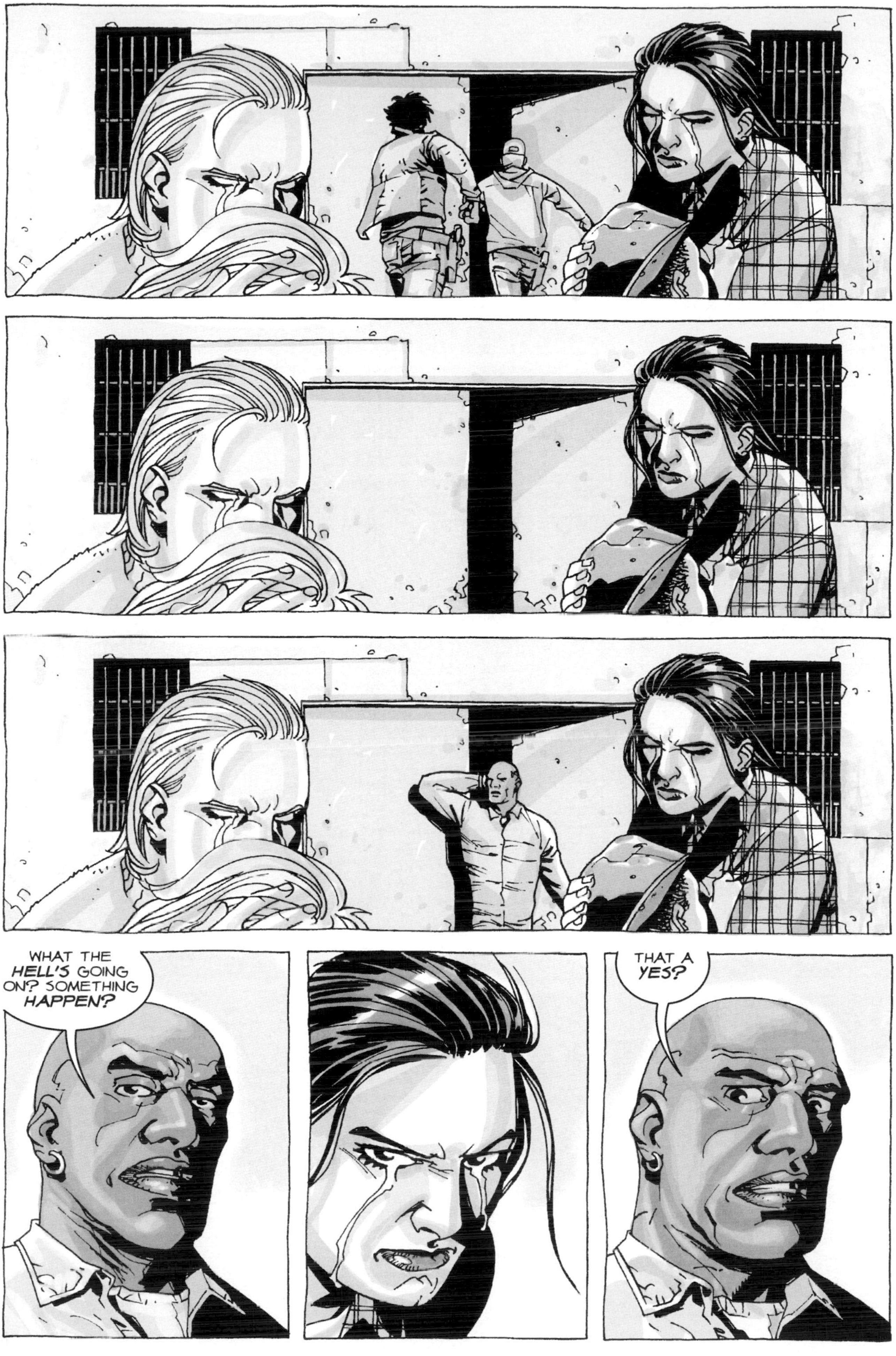
WHAT THE HELL'S GOING ON? SOMETHING HAPPEN?
THAT A YES?

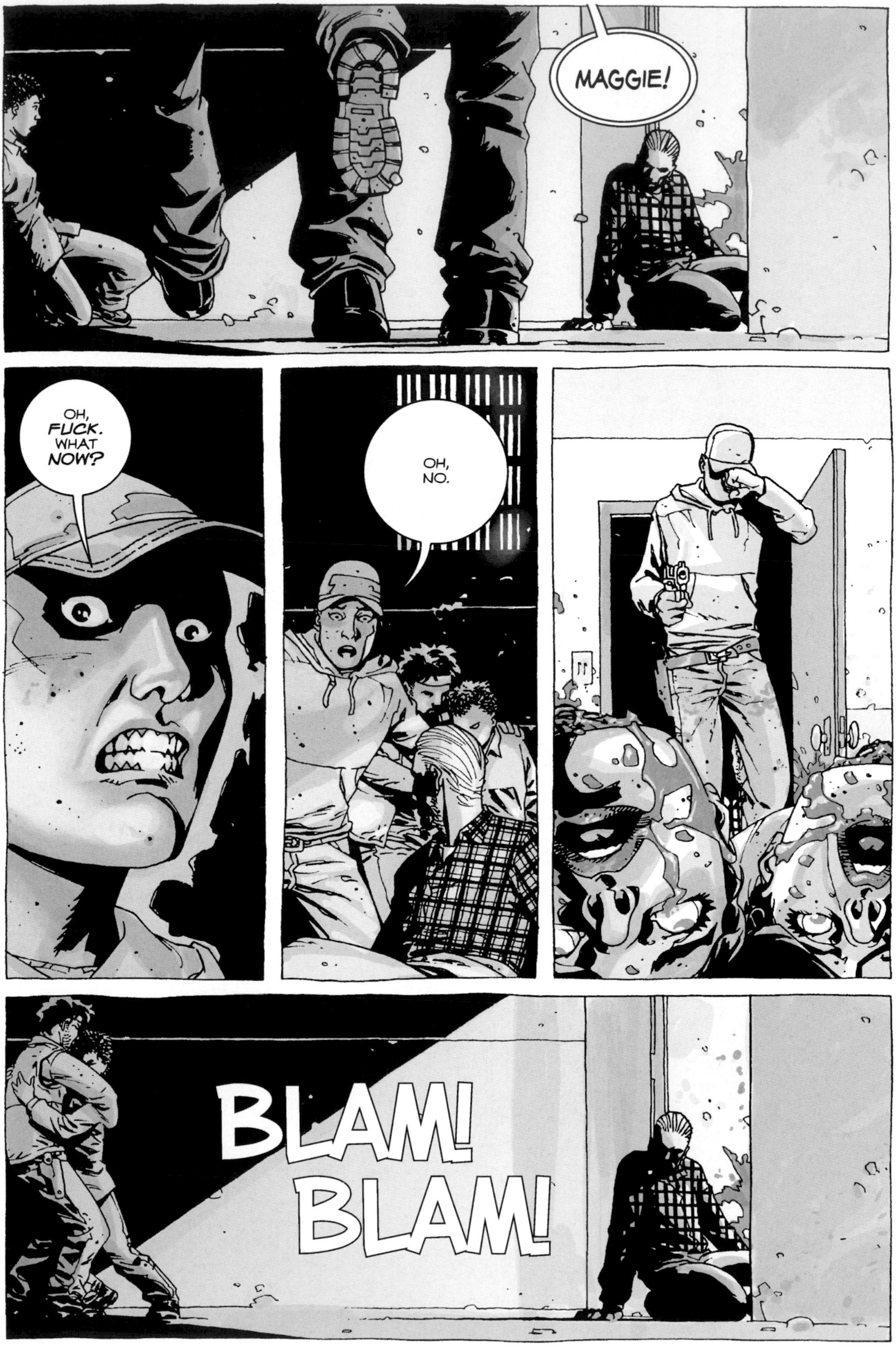
MAGGIE!
OH, FUCK. WHAT NOW?
OH, NO.
BLAM! BLAM!

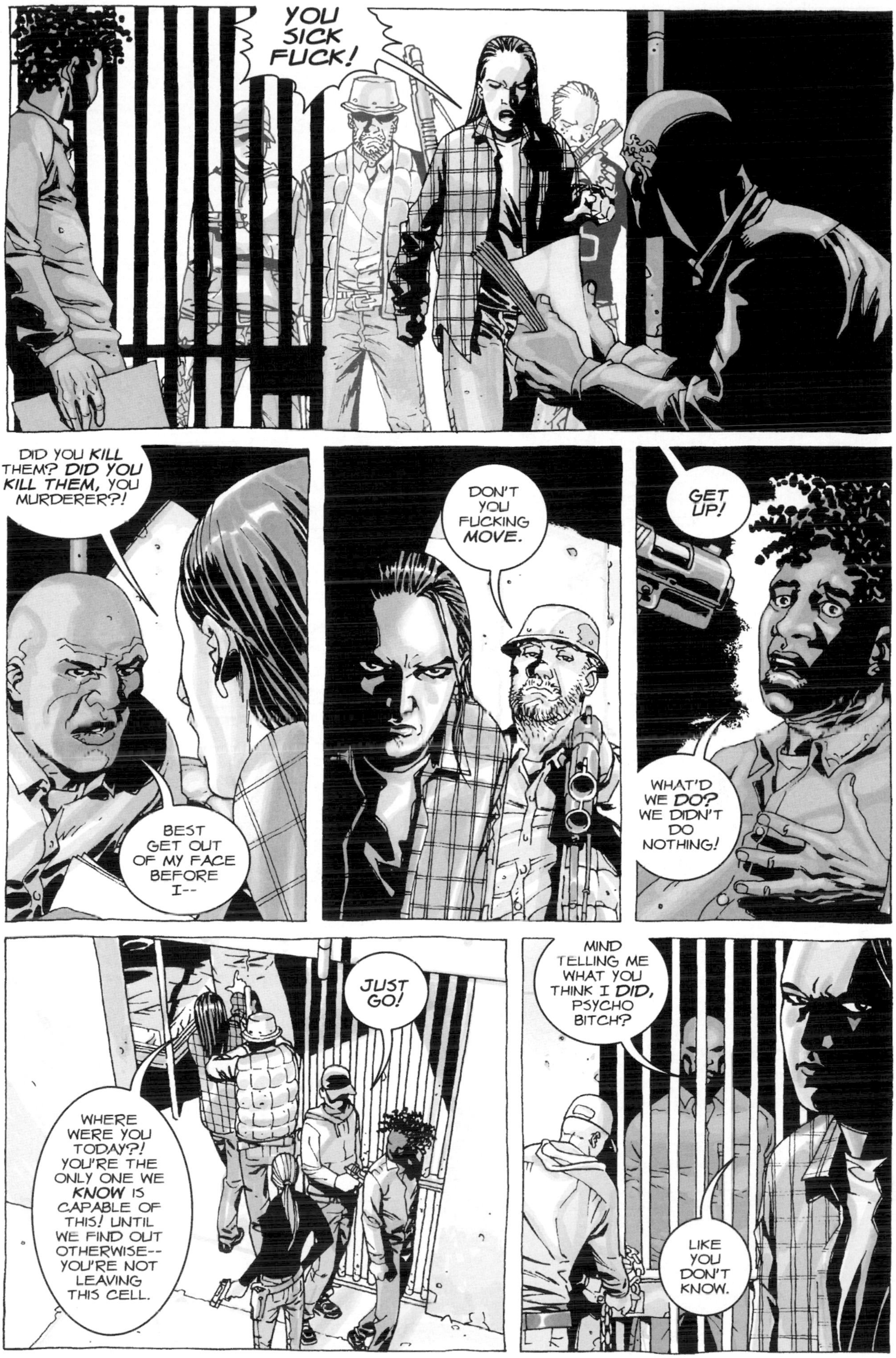
YOU SICK FUCK!
DID YOU KILL THEM? DID YOU KILL THEM, YOU MURDERER?!
BEST GET OUT OF MY FACE BEFORE I--
DON'T YOU FUCKING MOVE.
GET UP!
WHAT'D WE DO? WE DIDN'T DO NOTHING!
JUST GO!
WHERE WERE YOU TODAY?! YOU'RE THE ONLY ONE WE KNOW IS CAPABLE OF THIS! UNTIL WE FIND OUT OTHERWISE-- YOU'RE NOT LEAVING THIS CELL.
MIND TELLING ME WHAT YOU THINK I DID, PSYCHO BITCH?
LIKE YOU DON'T KNOW.

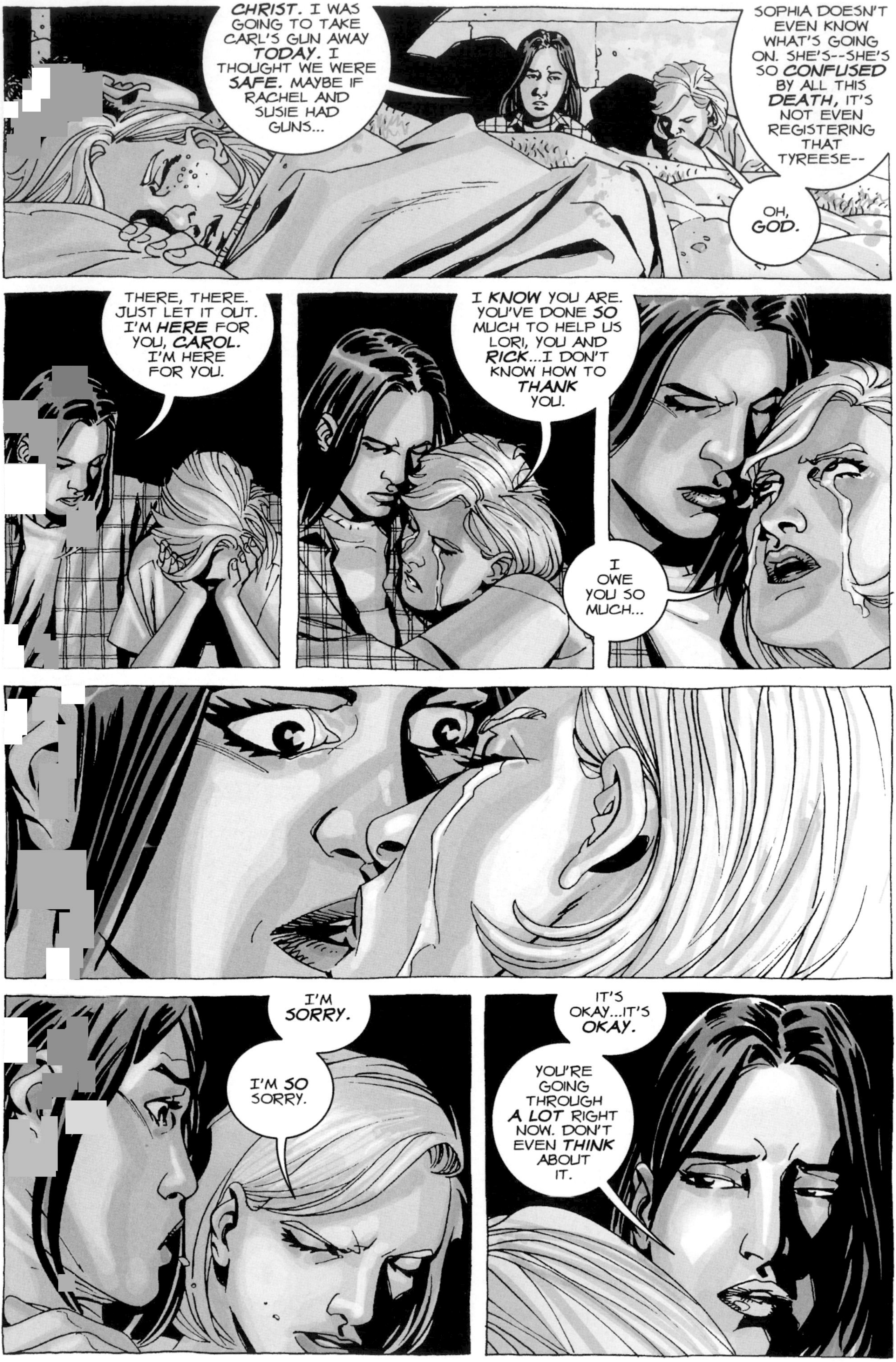
CHRIST. I WAS GOING TO TAKE CARL'S GUN AWAY TODAY. I THOUGHT WE WERE SAFE. MAYBE IF RACHEL AND SUSIE HAD GUNS...
SOPHIA DOESN'T EVEN KNOW WHAT'S GOING ON. SHE'S--SHE'S SO CONFUSED BY ALL THIS DEATH, IT'S NOT EVEN REGISTERING THAT TYREESE--
OH, GOD.
THERE, THERE. JUST LET IT OUT. I'M HERE FOR YOU, CAROL. I'M HERE FOR YOU.
I KNOW YOU ARE. YOU'VE DONE SO MUCH TO HELP US LORI, YOU AND RICK...I DON'T KNOW HOW TO THANK YOU.
I OWE YOU SO MUCH...
I'M SORRY.
I'M SO SORRY.
IT'S OKAY...IT'S OKAY.
YOU'RE GOING THROUGH A LOT RIGHT NOW. DON'T EVEN THINK ABOUT IT.

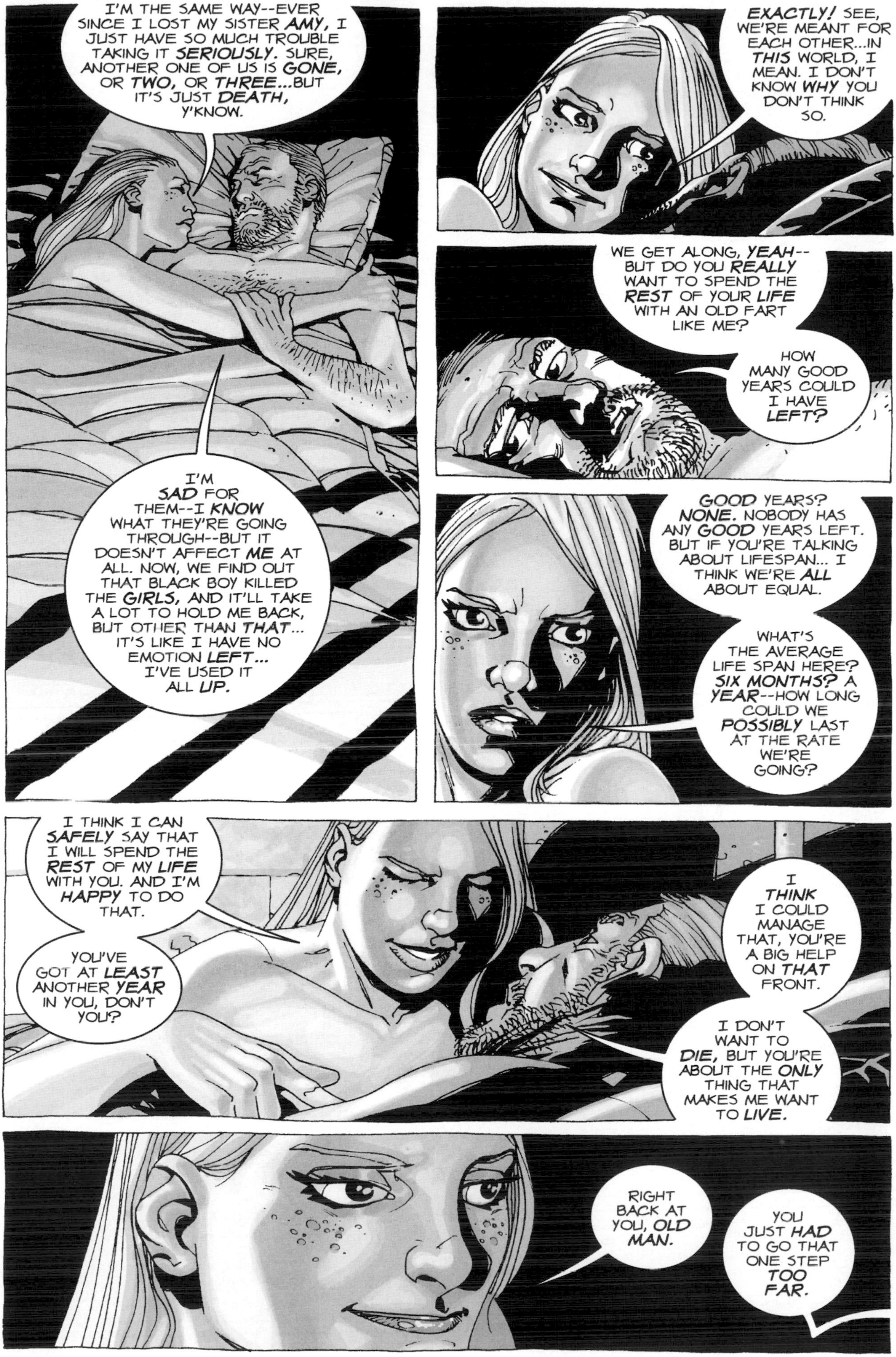
I'M THE SAME WAY--EVER SINCE I LOST MY SISTER AMY, I JUST HAVE SO MUCH TROUBLE TAKING IT SERIOUSLY. SURE, ANOTHER ONE OF US IS GONE, OR TWO, OR THREE...BUT IT'S JUST DEATH, Y'KNOW.
I'M SAD FOR THEM--I KNOW WHAT THEY'RE GOING THROUGH--BUT IT DOESN'T AFFECT ME AT ALL. NOW, WE FIND OUT THAT BLACK BOY KILLED THE GIRLS, AND IT'LL TAKE A LOT TO HOLD ME BACK, BUT OTHER THAN THAT... IT'S LIKE I HAVE NO EMOTION LEFT... I'VE USED IT ALL UP.
EXACTLY! SEE, WE'RE MEANT FOR EACH OTHER...IN THIS WORLD, I MEAN. I DON'T KNOW WHY YOU DON'T THINK SO.
WE GET ALONG, YEAH-- BUT DO YOU REALLY WANT TO SPEND THE REST OF YOUR LIFE WITH AN OLD FART LIKE ME?
HOW MANY GOOD YEARS COULD I HAVE LEFT?
GOOD YEARS? NONE. NOBODY HAS ANY GOOD YEARS LEFT. BUT IF YOU'RE TALKING ABOUT LIFESPAN... I THINK WE'RE ALL ABOUT EQUAL.
WHAT'S THE AVERAGE LIFE SPAN HERE? SIX MONTHS? A YEAR--HOW LONG COULD WE POSSIBLY LAST AT THE RATE WE'RE GOING?
I THINK I CAN SAFELY SAY THAT I WILL SPEND THE REST OF MY LIFE WITH YOU. AND I'M HAPPY TO DO THAT.
YOU'VE GOT AT LEAST ANOTHER YEAR IN YOU, DON'T YOU?
I THINK I COULD MANAGE THAT, YOU'RE A BIG HELP ON THAT FRONT.
I DON'T WANT TO DIE, BUT YOU'RE ABOUT THE ONLY THING THAT MAKES ME WANT TO LIVE.
RIGHT BACK AT YOU, OLD MAN.
YOU JUST HAD TO GO THAT ONE STEP TOO FAR.

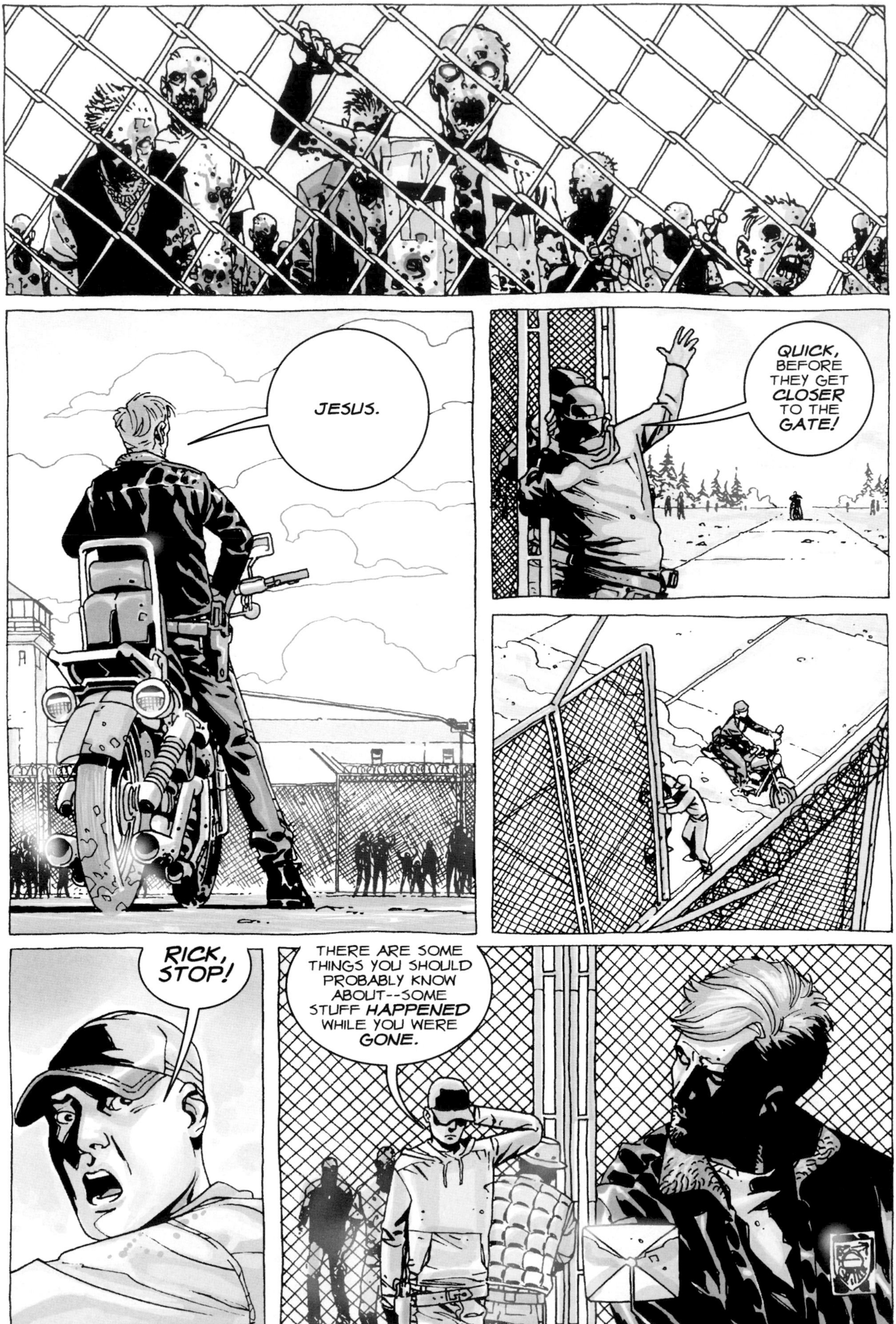

JESUS.
QUICK, BEFORE THEY GET CLOSER TO THE GATE!
RICK, STOP!
THERE ARE SOME THINGS YOU SHOULD PROBABLY KNOW ABOUT--SOME STUFF HAPPENED WHILE YOU WERE GONE.

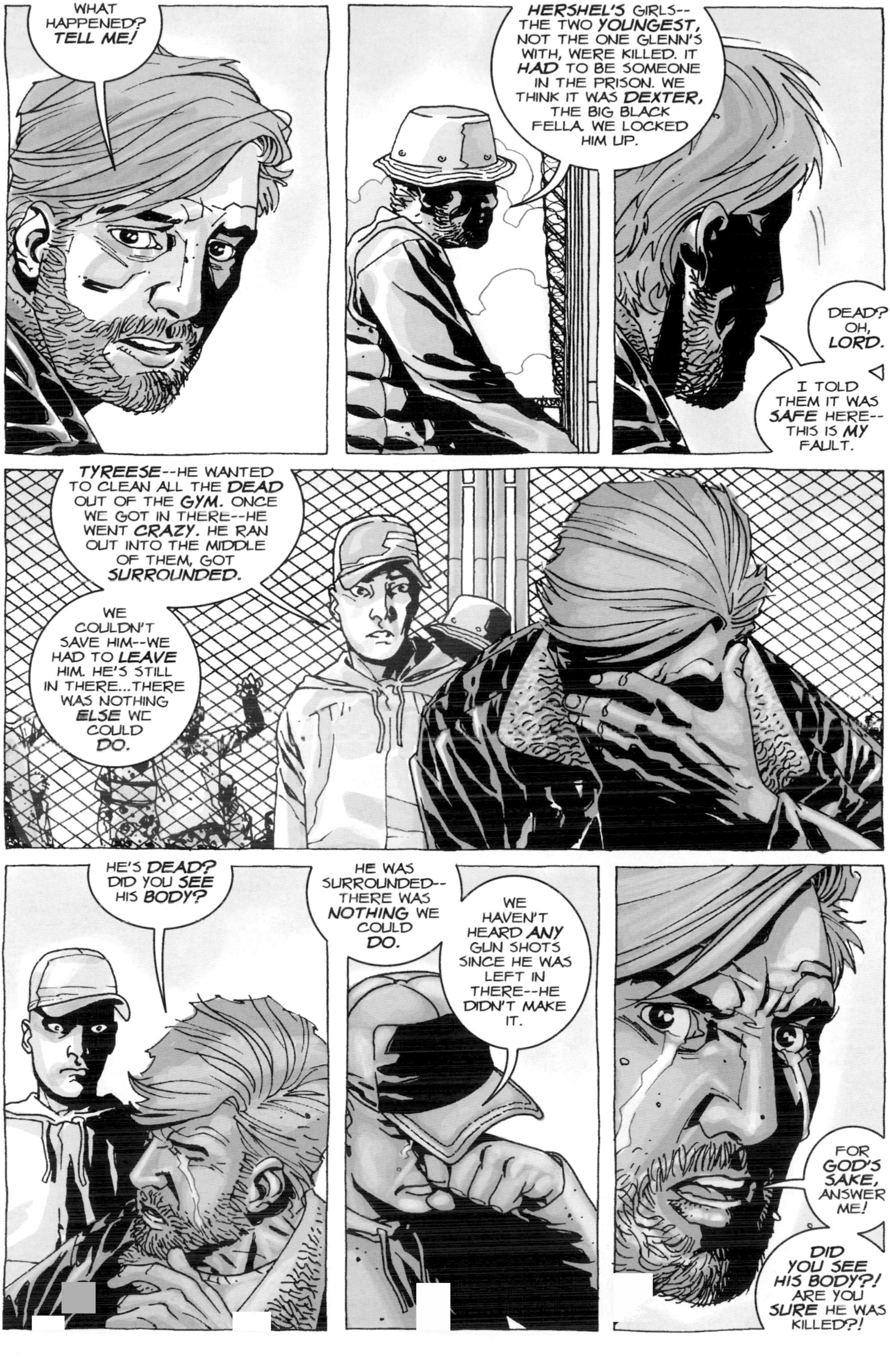
WHAT HAPPENED? TELL ME!
HERSHEL'S GIRLS-- THE TWO YOUNGEST, NOT THE ONE GLENN'S WITH, WERE KILLED. IT HAD TO BE SOMEONE IN THE PRISON. WE THINK IT WAS DEXTER, THE BIG BLACK FELLA. WE LOCKED HIM UP.
DEAD? OH, LORD.
I TOLD THEM IT WAS SAFE HERE-- THIS IS MY FAULT.
TYREESE--HE WANTED TO CLEAN ALL THE DEAD OUT OF THE GYM. ONCE WE GOT IN THERE--HE WENT CRAZY. HE RAN OUT INTO THE MIDDLE OF THEM, GOT SURROUNDED.
WE COULDN'T SAVE HIM--WE HAD TO LEAVE HIM. HE'S STILL IN THERE...THERE WAS NOTHING ELSE WE COULD DO.
HE'S DEAD? DID YOU SEE HIS BODY?
HE WAS SURROUNDED-- THERE WAS NOTHING WE COULD DO.
WE HAVEN'T HEARD ANY GUN SHOTS SINCE HE WAS LEFT IN THERE--HE DIDN'T MAKE IT.
FOR GOD'S SAKE, ANSWER ME!
DID YOU SEE HIS BODY?! ARE YOU SURE HE WAS KILLED?!

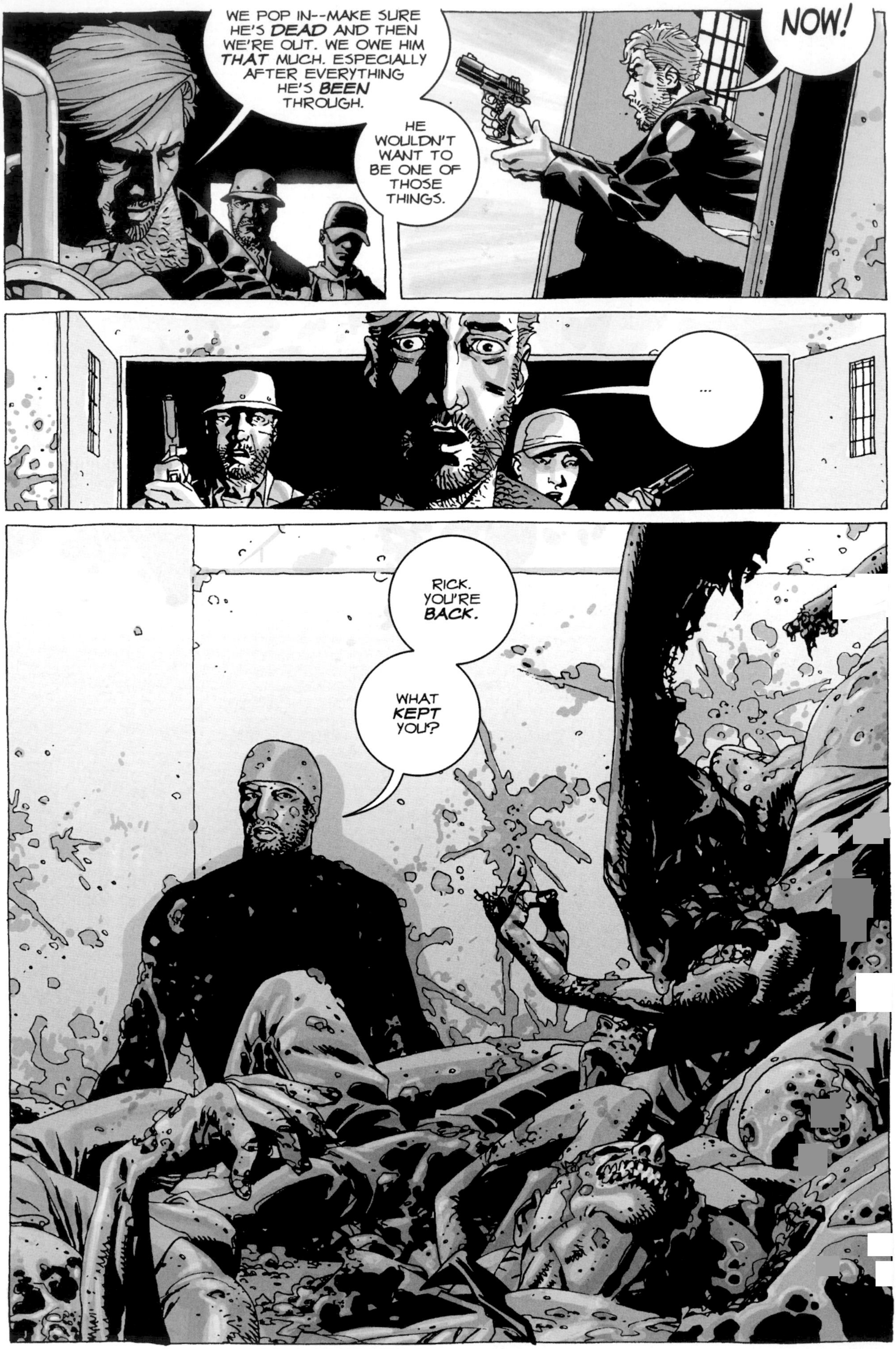
WE POP IN--MAKE SURE HE'S DEAD AND THEN WE'RE OUT. WE OWE HIM THAT MUCH. ESPECIALLY AFTER EVERYTHING HE'S BEEN THROUGH.
HE WOULDN'T WANT TO BE ONE OF THOSE THINGS.
NOW!
...
RICK. YOU'RE BACK.
WHAT KEPT YOU?

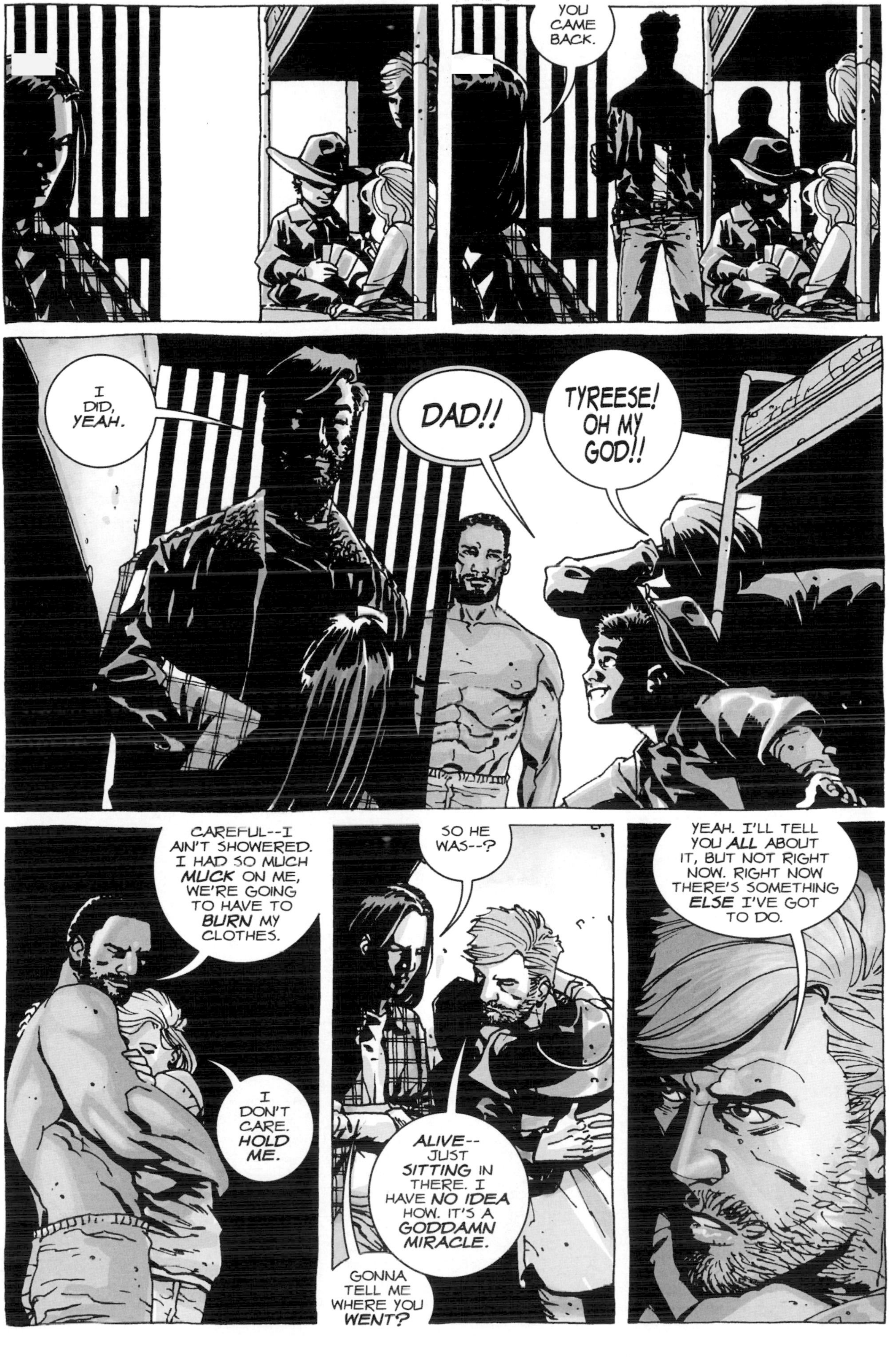
YOU CAME BACK.
I DID, YEAH.
DAD!!
TYREESE! OH MY GOD!!
CAREFUL--I AIN'T SHOWERED. I HAD SO MUCH MUCK ON ME, WE'RE GOING TO HAVE TO BURN MY CLOTHES.
I DON'T CARE. HOLD ME.
SO HE WAS--?
ALIVE--JUST SITTING IN THERE. I HAVE NO IDEA HOW. IT'S A GODDAMN MIRACLE.
GONNA TELL ME WHERE YOU WENT?
YEAH. I'LL TELL YOU ALL ABOUT IT, BUT NOT RIGHT NOW. RIGHT NOW THERE'S SOMETHING ELSE I'VE GOT TO DO.

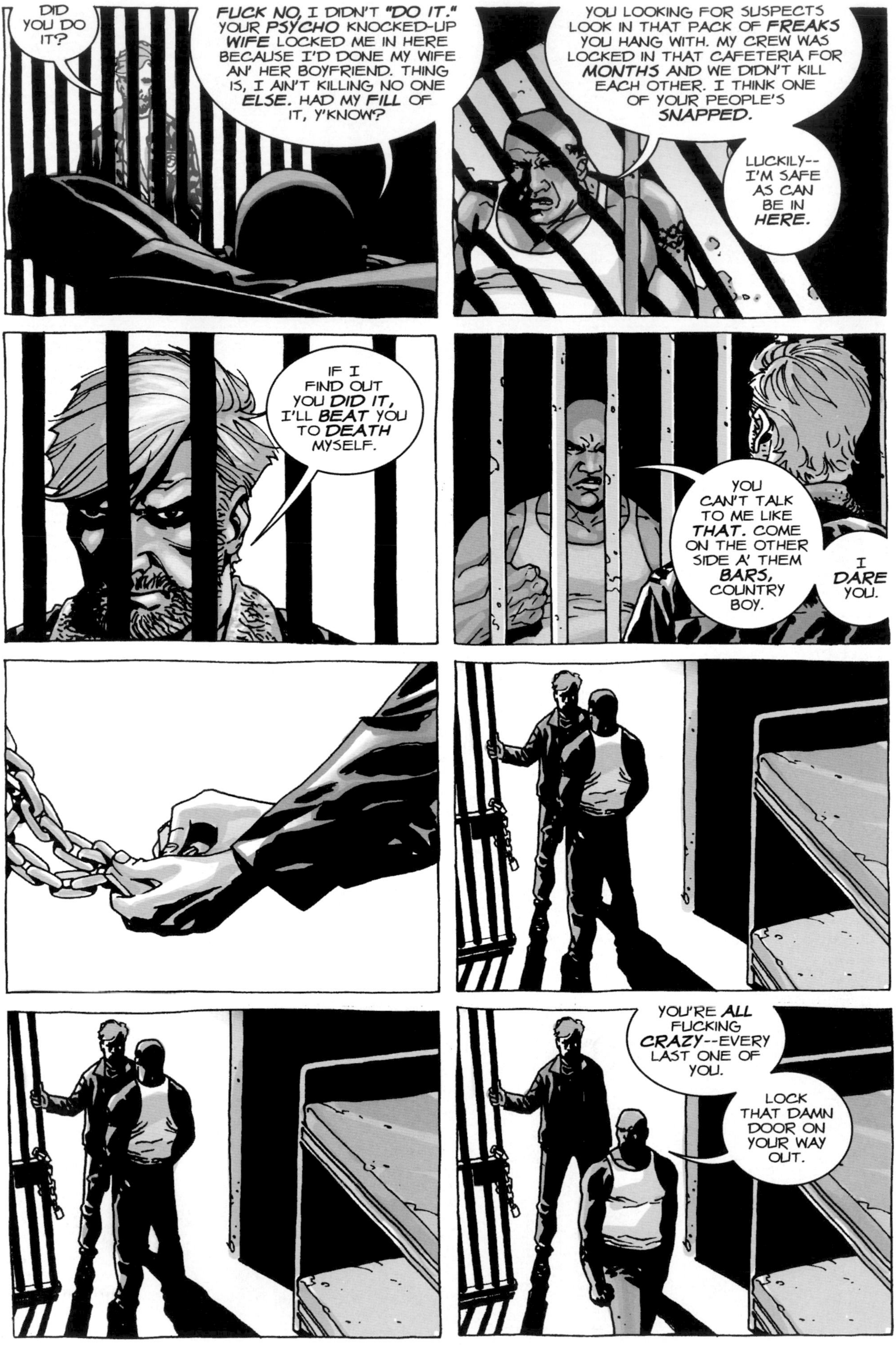
DID YOU DO IT?
FUCK NO, I DIDN'T "DO IT." YOUR PSYCHO KNOCKED-UP WIFE LOCKED ME IN HERE BECAUSE I'D DONE MY WIFE AN' HER BOYFRIEND. THING IS, I AIN'T KILLING NO ONE ELSE. HAD MY FILL OF IT, Y'KNOW?
YOU LOOKING FOR SUSPECTS LOOK IN THAT PACK OF FREAKS YOU HANG WITH. MY CREW WAS LOCKED IN THAT CAFETERIA FOR MONTHS AND WE DIDN'T KILL EACH OTHER. I THINK ONE OF YOUR PEOPLE'S SNAPPED.
LUCKILY-- I'M SAFE AS CAN BE IN HERE.
IF I FIND OUT YOU DID IT, I'LL BEAT YOU TO DEATH MYSELF.
YOU CAN'T TALK TO ME LIKE THAT. COME ON THE OTHER SIDE A' THEM BARS, COUNTRY BOY.
I DARE YOU.
YOU'RE ALL FUCKING CRAZY--EVERY LAST ONE OF YOU.
LOCK THAT DAMN DOOR ON YOUR WAY OUT.

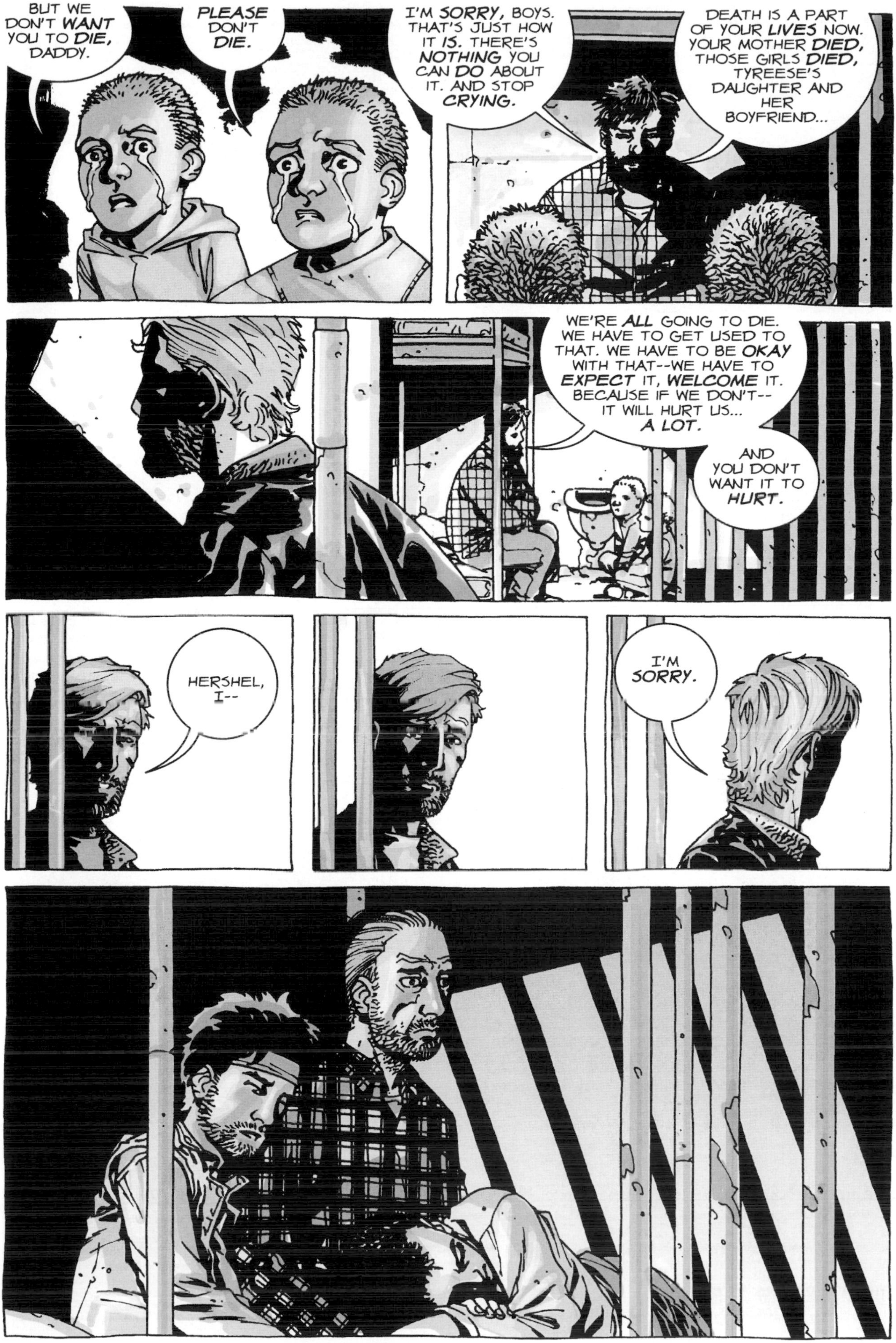

BUT WE DON'T WANT YOU TO DIE, DADDY.
PLEASE DON'T DIE.
I'M SORRY, BOYS. THAT'S JUST HOW IT IS. THERE'S NOTHING YOU CAN DO ABOUT IT. AND STOP CRYING.
DEATH IS A PART OF YOUR LIVES NOW. YOUR MOTHER DIED, THOSE GIRLS DIED, TYREESE'S DAUGHTER AND HER BOYFRIEND...
WE'RE ALL GOING TO DIE. WE HAVE TO GET USED TO THAT. WE HAVE TO BE OKAY WITH THAT--WE HAVE TO EXPECT IT, WELCOME IT. BECAUSE IF WE DON'T--IT WILL HURT US... A LOT.
AND YOU DON'T WANT IT TO HURT.
HERSHEL, I--
I'M SORRY.

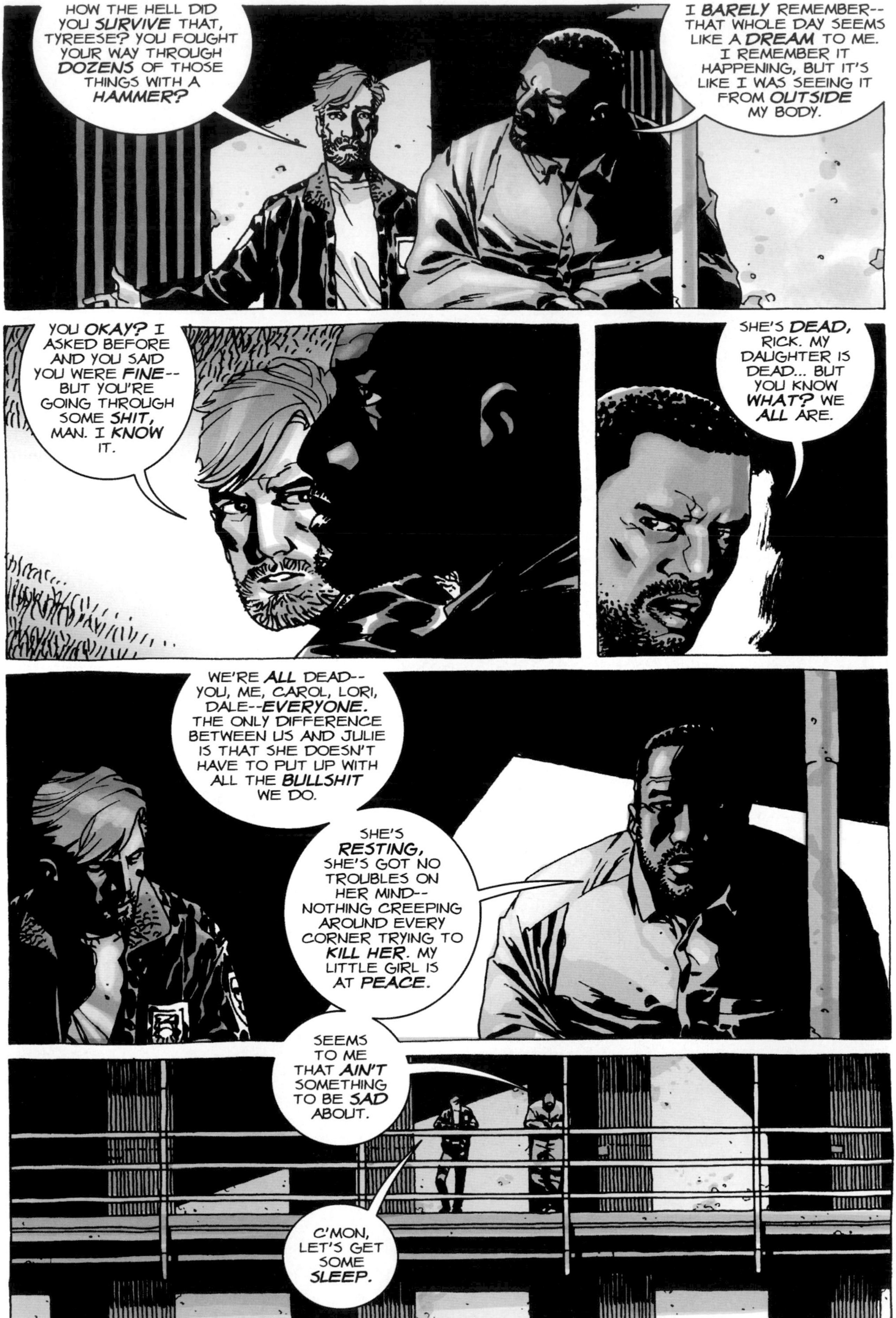
HOW THE HELL DID YOU SURVIVE THAT, TYREESE? YOU FOUGHT YOUR WAY THROUGH DOZENS OF THOSE THINGS WITH A HAMMER?
I BARELY REMEMBER-- THAT WHOLE DAY SEEMS LIKE A DREAM TO ME. I REMEMBER IT HAPPENING, BUT IT'S LIKE I WAS SEEING IT FROM OUTSIDE MY BODY.
YOU OKAY? I ASKED BEFORE AND YOU SAID YOU WERE FINE-- BUT YOU'RE GOING THROUGH SOME SHIT, MAN. I KNOW IT.
SHE'S DEAD, RICK. MY DAUGHTER IS DEAD... BUT YOU KNOW WHAT? WE ALL ARE.
WE'RE ALL DEAD-- YOU, ME, CAROL, LORI, DALE--EVERYONE. THE ONLY DIFFERENCE BETWEEN US AND JULIE IS THAT SHE DOESN'T HAVE TO PUT UP WITH ALL THE BULLSHIT WE DO.
SHE'S RESTING, SHE'S GOT NO TROUBLES ON HER MIND-- NOTHING CREEPING AROUND EVERY CORNER TRYING TO KILL HER. MY LITTLE GIRL IS AT PEACE.
SEEMS TO ME THAT AIN'T SOMETHING TO BE SAD ABOUT.
C'MON, LET'S GET SOME SLEEP.

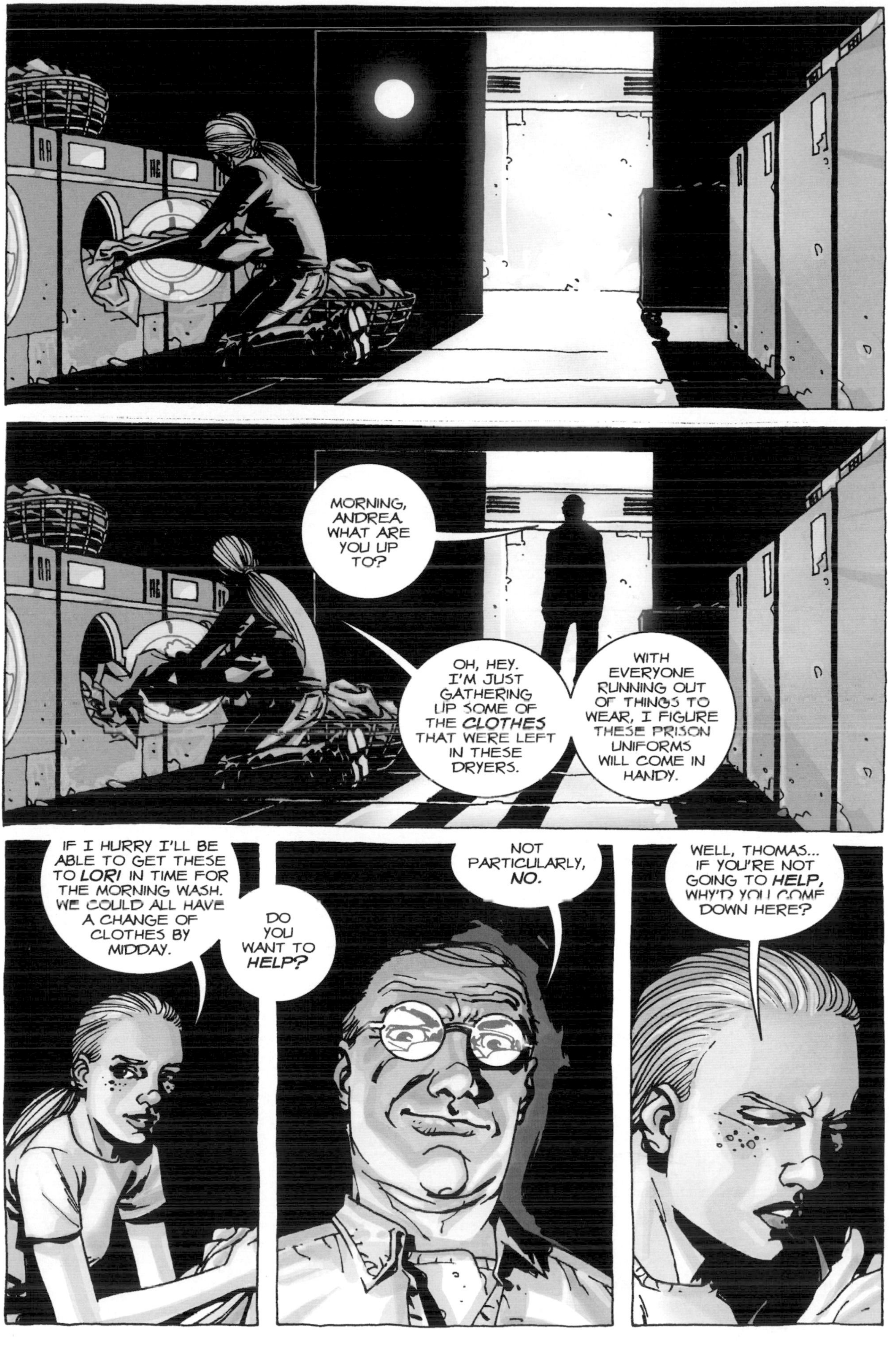

MORNING, ANDREA WHAT ARE YOU UP TO?
OH, HEY. I'M JUST GATHERING UP SOME OF THE CLOTHES THAT WERE LEFT IN THESE DRYERS.
WITH EVERYONE RUNNING OUT OF THINGS TO WEAR, I FIGURE THESE PRISON UNIFORMS WILL COME IN HANDY.
IF I HURRY I'LL BE ABLE TO GET THESE TO LORI IN TIME FOR THE MORNING WASH. WE COULD ALL HAVE A CHANGE OF CLOTHES BY MIDDAY.
DO YOU WANT TO HELP?
NOT PARTICULARLY, NO.
WELL, THOMAS... IF YOU'RE NOT GOING TO HELP, WHY'D YOU COME DOWN HERE?

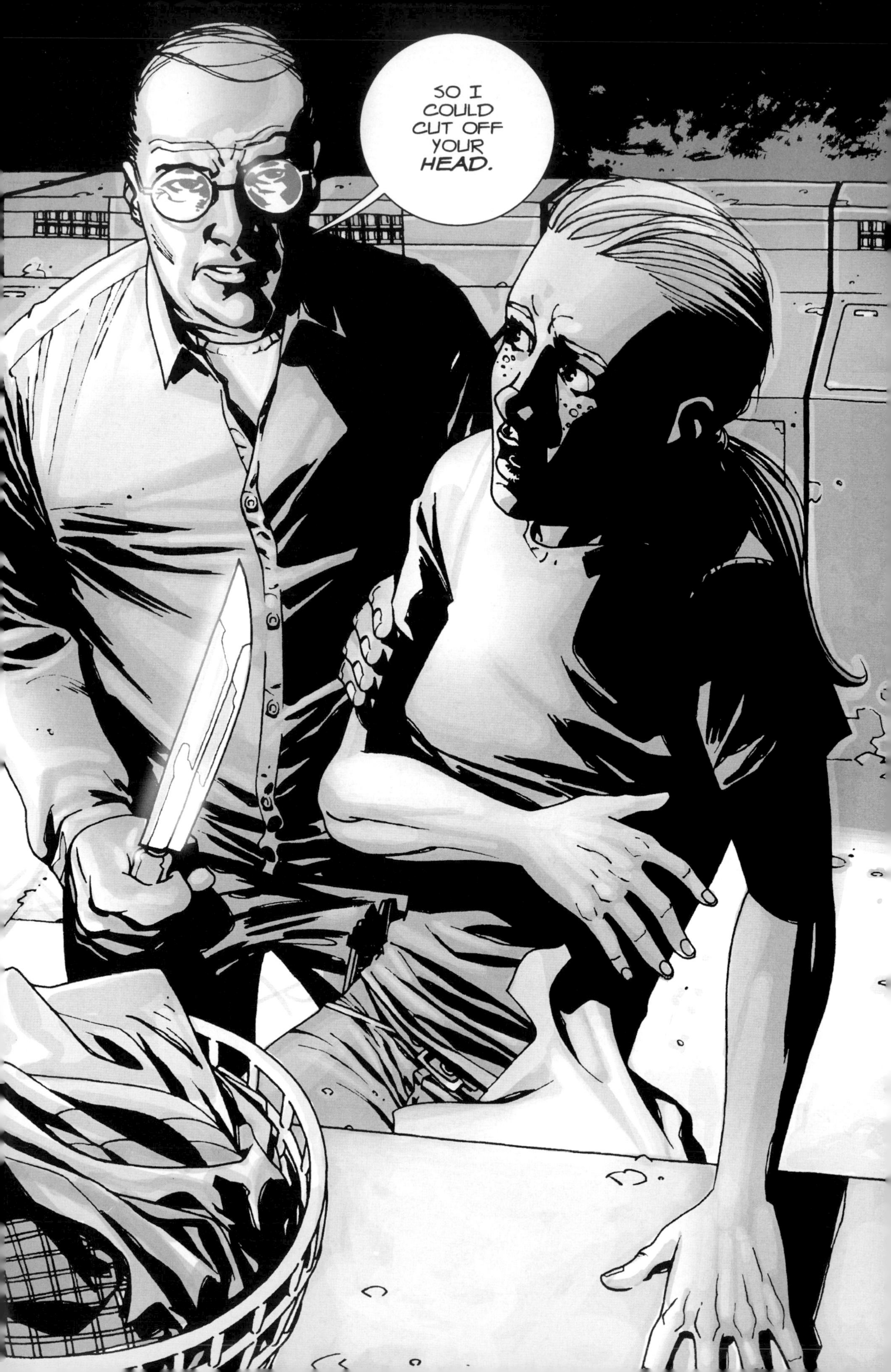
SO I COULD CUT OFF YOUR HEAD.

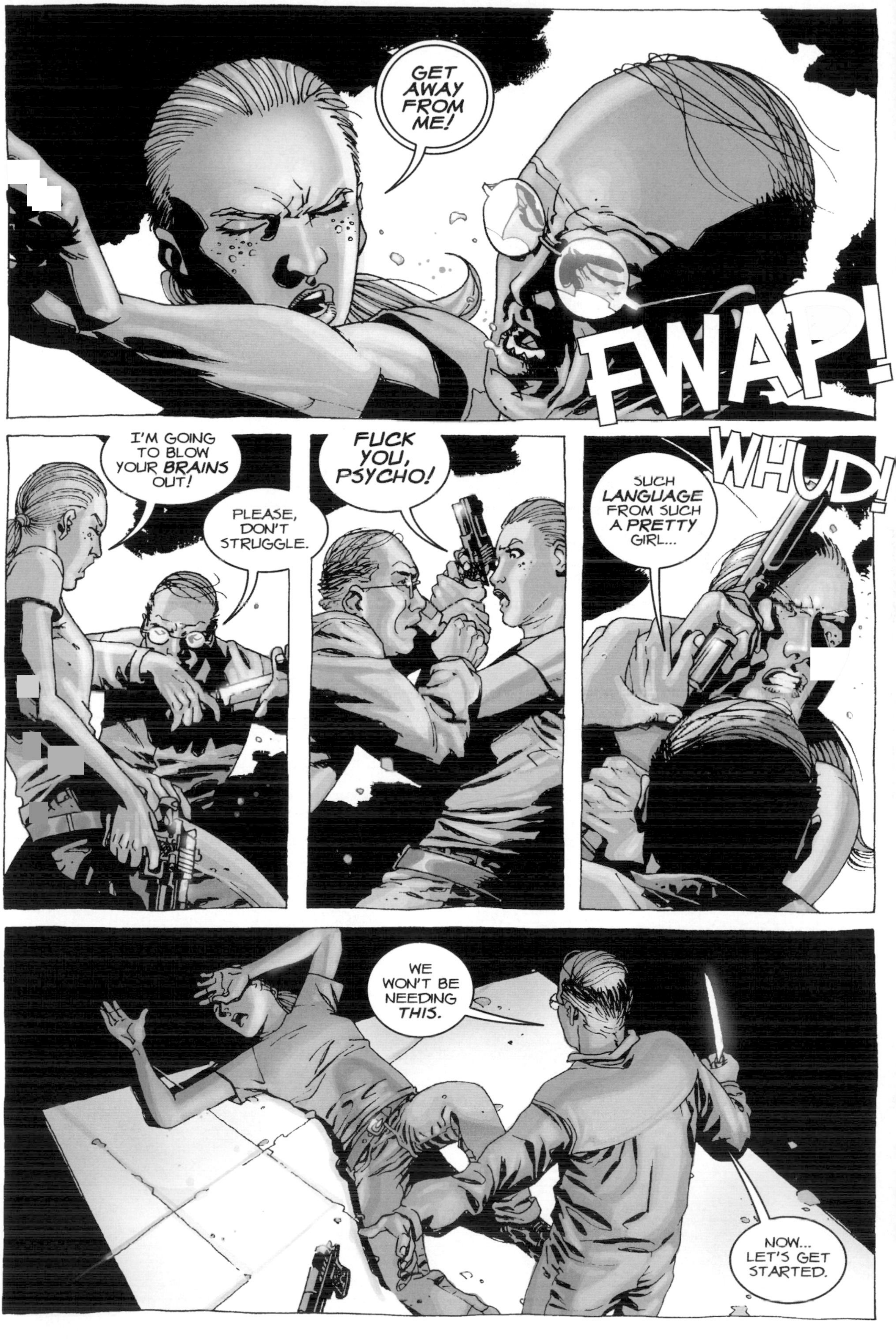
GET AWAY FROM ME!
FWAP!
I'M GOING TO BLOW YOUR BRAINS OUT!
PLEASE, DON'T STRUGGLE.
FUCK YOU, PSYCHO!
SUCH LANGUAGE FROM SUCH A PRETTY GIRL...
WHUD!
WE WON'T BE NEEDING THIS.
NOW... LET'S GET STARTED.

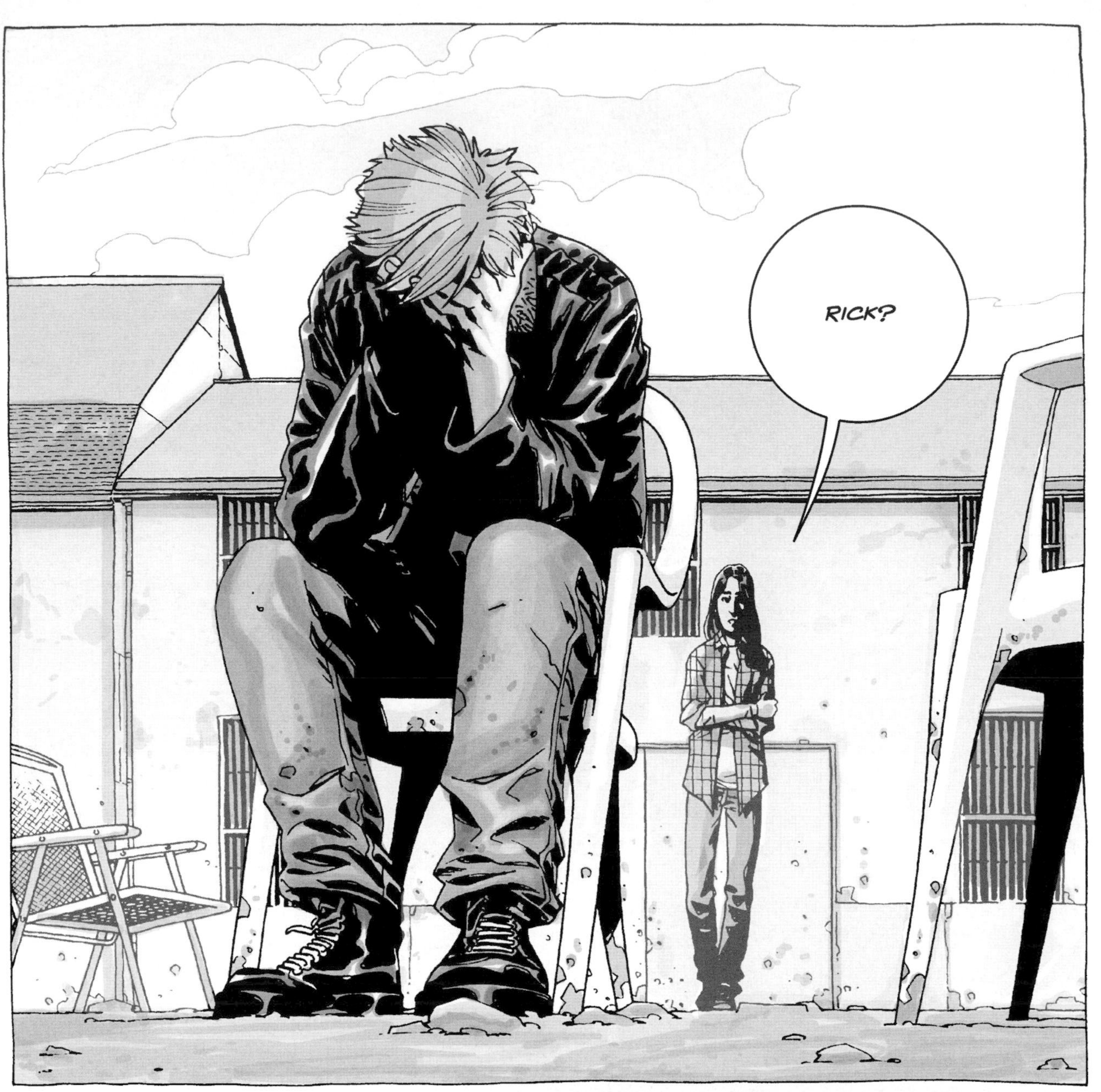
RICK?

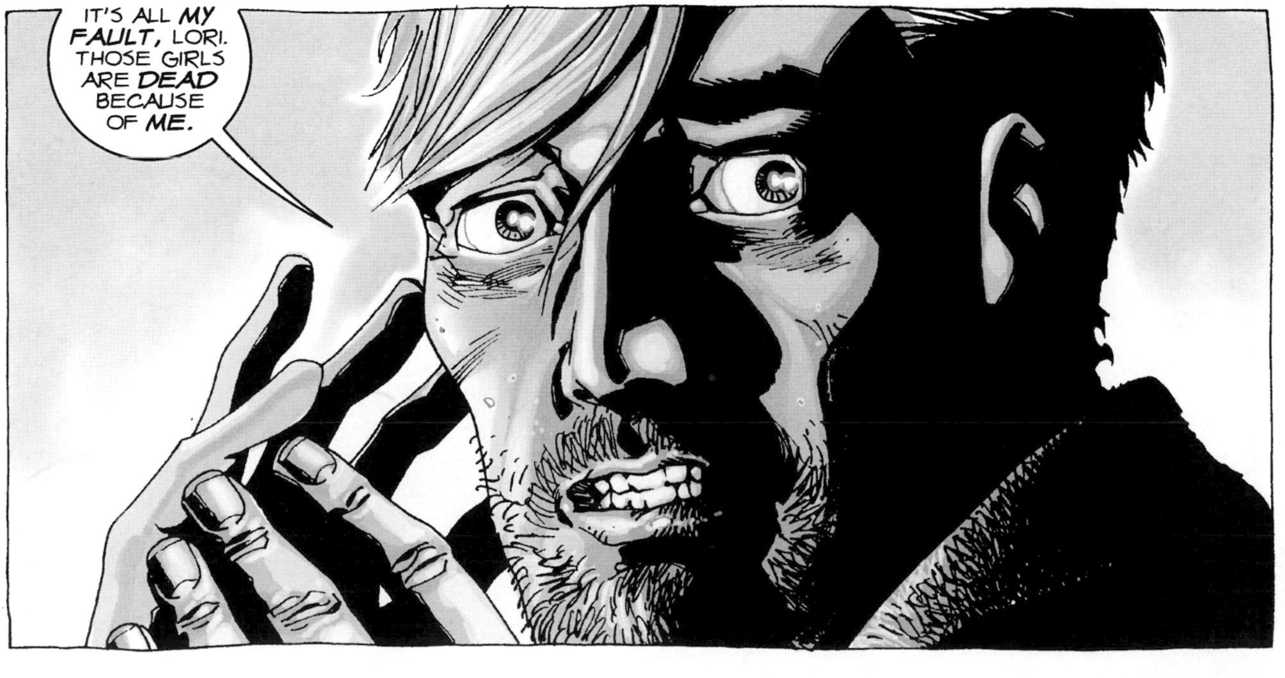
IT'S ALL MY FAULT, LORI. THOSE GIRLS ARE DEAD BECAUSE OF ME.

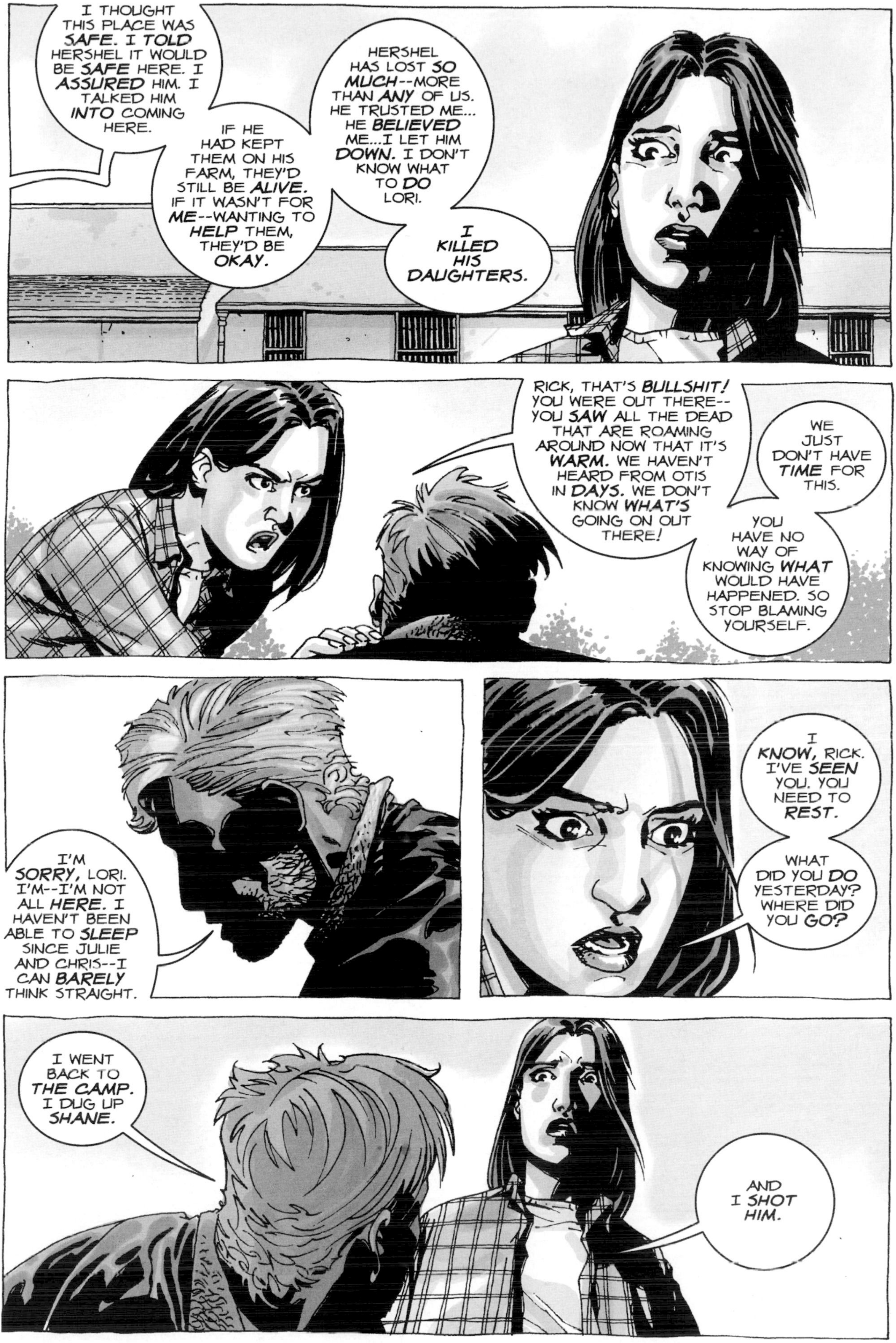
I THOUGHT THIS PLACE WAS SAFE. I TOLD HERSHEL IT WOULD BE SAFE HERE. I ASSURED HIM. I TALKED HIM INTO COMING HERE.
IF HE HAD KEPT THEM ON HIS FARM, THEY'D STILL BE ALIVE. IF IT WASN'T FOR ME--WANTING TO HELP THEM, THEY'D BE OKAY.
HERSHEL HAS LOST SO MUCH--MORE THAN ANY OF US. HE TRUSTED ME... HE BELIEVED ME...I LET HIM DOWN. I DON'T KNOW WHAT TO DO LORI.
I KILLED HIS DAUGHTERS.
RICK, THAT'S BULLSHIT! YOU WERE OUT THERE-- YOU SAW ALL THE DEAD THAT ARE ROAMING AROUND NOW THAT IT'S WARM. WE HAVEN'T HEARD FROM OTIS IN DAYS. WE DON'T KNOW WHAT'S GOING ON OUT THERE!
WE JUST DON'T HAVE TIME FOR THIS.
YOU HAVE NO WAY OF KNOWING WHAT WOULD HAVE HAPPENED. SO STOP BLAMING YOURSELF.
I'M SORRY, LORI. I'M--I'M NOT ALL HERE. I HAVEN'T BEEN ABLE TO SLEEP SINCE JULIE AND CHRIS--I CAN BARELY THINK STRAIGHT.
I KNOW, RICK. I'VE SEEN YOU. YOU NEED TO REST.
WHAT DID YOU DO YESTERDAY? WHERE DID YOU GO?
I WENT BACK TO THE CAMP. I DUG UP SHANE.
AND I SHOT HIM.

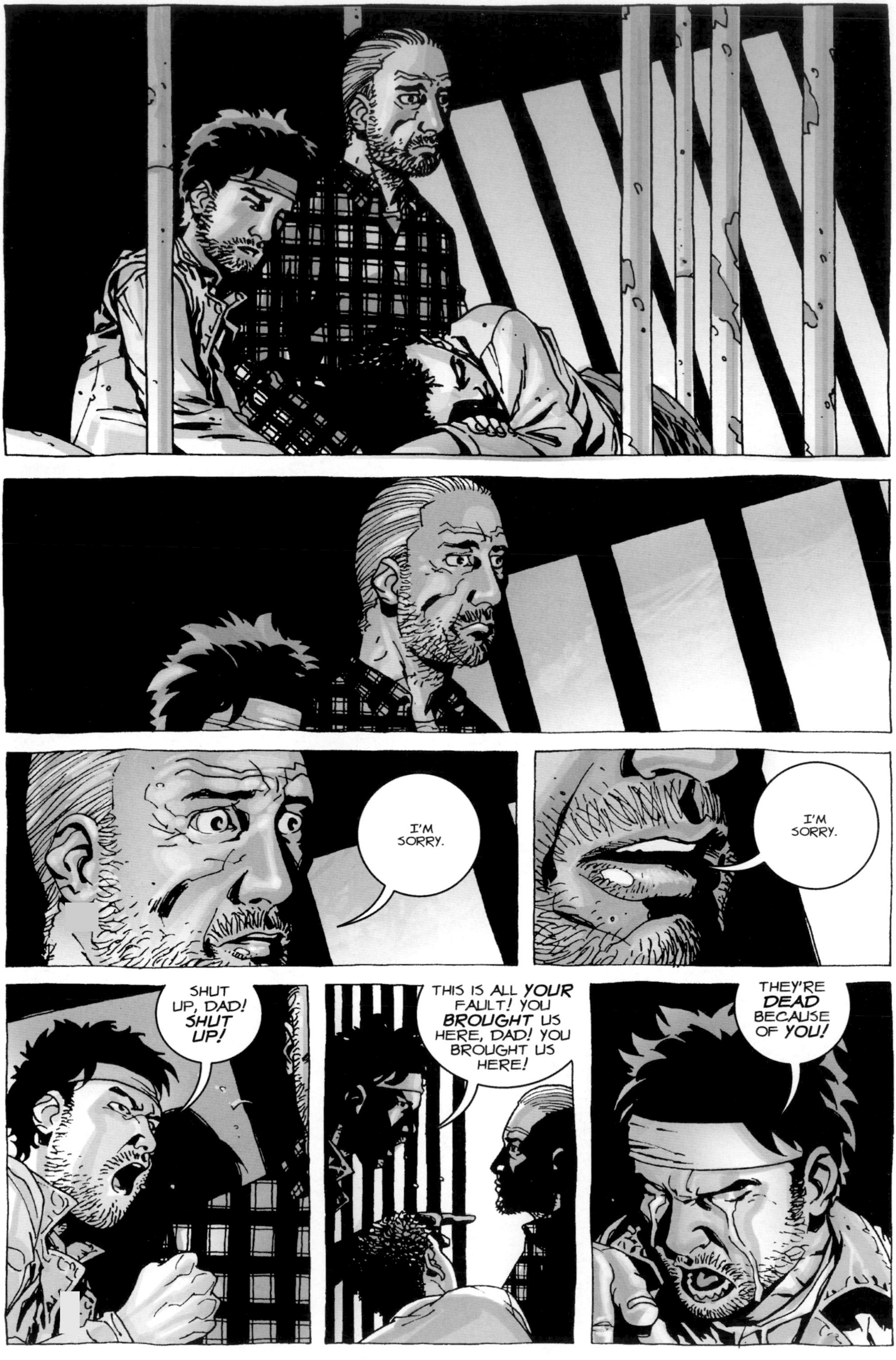

I'M SORRY.
I'M SORRY.
SHUT UP, DAD! SHUT UP!
THIS IS ALL YOUR FAULT! YOU BROUGHT US HERE, DAD! YOU BROUGHT US HERE!
THEY'RE DEAD BECAUSE OF YOU!

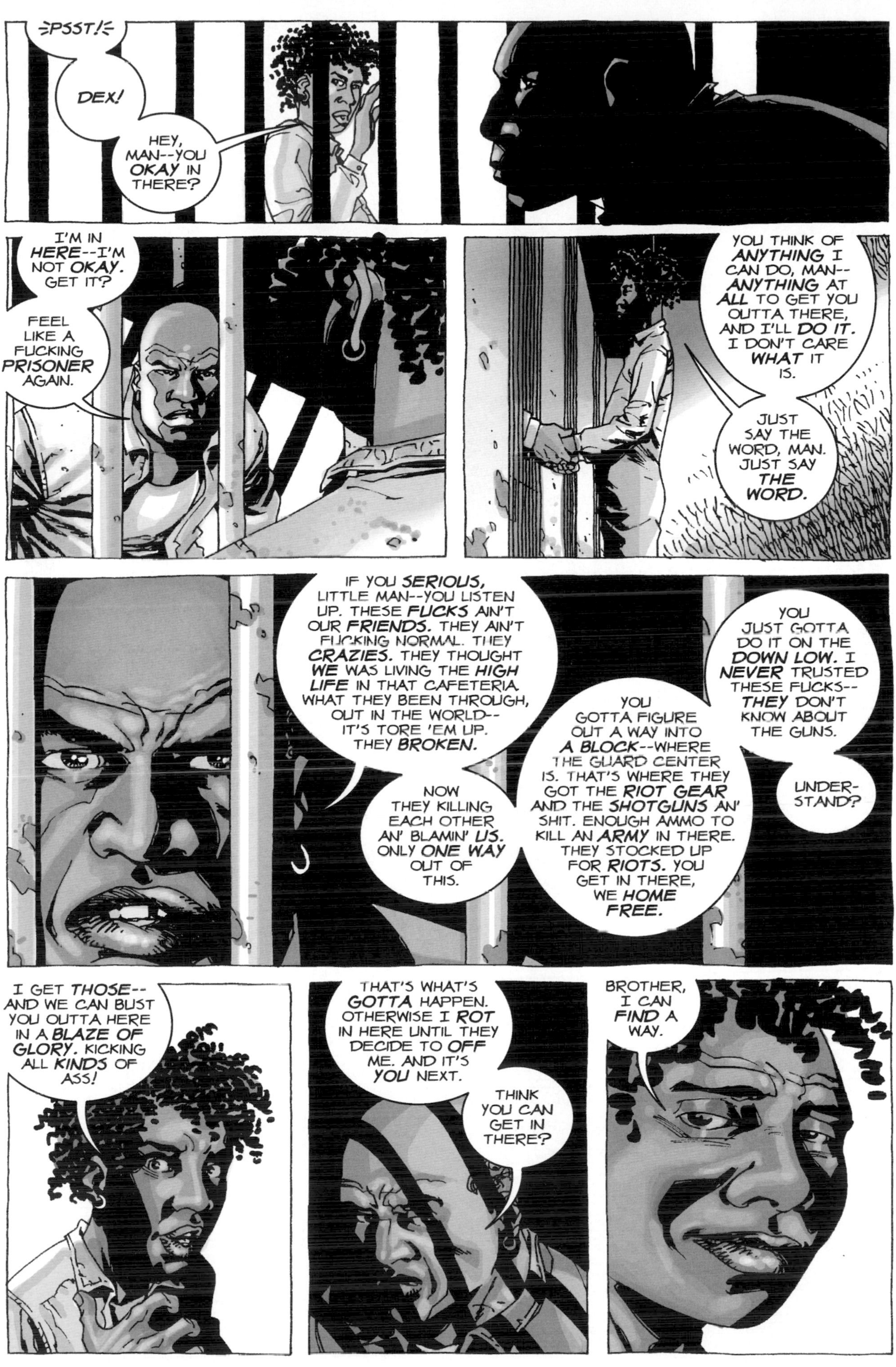
PSST!
DEX!
HEY, MAN--YOU OKAY IN THERE?
I'M IN HERE--I'M NOT OKAY. GET IT?
FEEL LIKE A FUCKING PRISONER AGAIN.
YOU THINK OF ANYTHING I CAN DO, MAN--ANYTHING AT ALL TO GET YOU OUTTA THERE, AND I'LL DO IT. I DON'T CARE WHAT IT IS.
JUST SAY THE WORD, MAN. JUST SAY THE WORD.
IF YOU SERIOUS, LITTLE MAN--YOU LISTEN UP. THESE FUCKS AIN'T OUR FRIENDS. THEY AIN'T FUCKING NORMAL. THEY CRAZIES. THEY THOUGHT WE WAS LIVING THE HIGH LIFE IN THAT CAFETERIA. WHAT THEY BEEN THROUGH, OUT IN THE WORLD-- IT'S TORE 'EM UP. THEY BROKEN.
NOW THEY KILLING EACH OTHER AN' BLAMIN' US. ONLY ONE WAY OUT OF THIS.
YOU GOTTA FIGURE OUT A WAY INTO A BLOCK--WHERE THE GUARD CENTER IS. THAT'S WHERE THEY GOT THE RIOT GEAR AND THE SHOTGUNS AN' SHIT. ENOUGH AMMO TO KILL AN ARMY IN THERE. THEY STOCKED UP FOR RIOTS. YOU GET IN THERE, WE HOME FREE.
YOU JUST GOTTA DO IT ON THE DOWN LOW. I NEVER TRUSTED THESE FUCKS-- THEY DON'T KNOW ABOUT THE GUNS.
UNDER-STAND?
I GET THOSE-- AND WE CAN BUST YOU OUTTA HERE IN A BLAZE OF GLORY. KICKING ALL KINDS OF ASS!
THAT'S WHAT'S GOTTA HAPPEN. OTHERWISE I ROT IN HERE UNTIL THEY DECIDE TO OFF ME. AND IT'S YOU NEXT.
THINK YOU CAN GET IN THERE?
BROTHER, I CAN FIND A WAY.

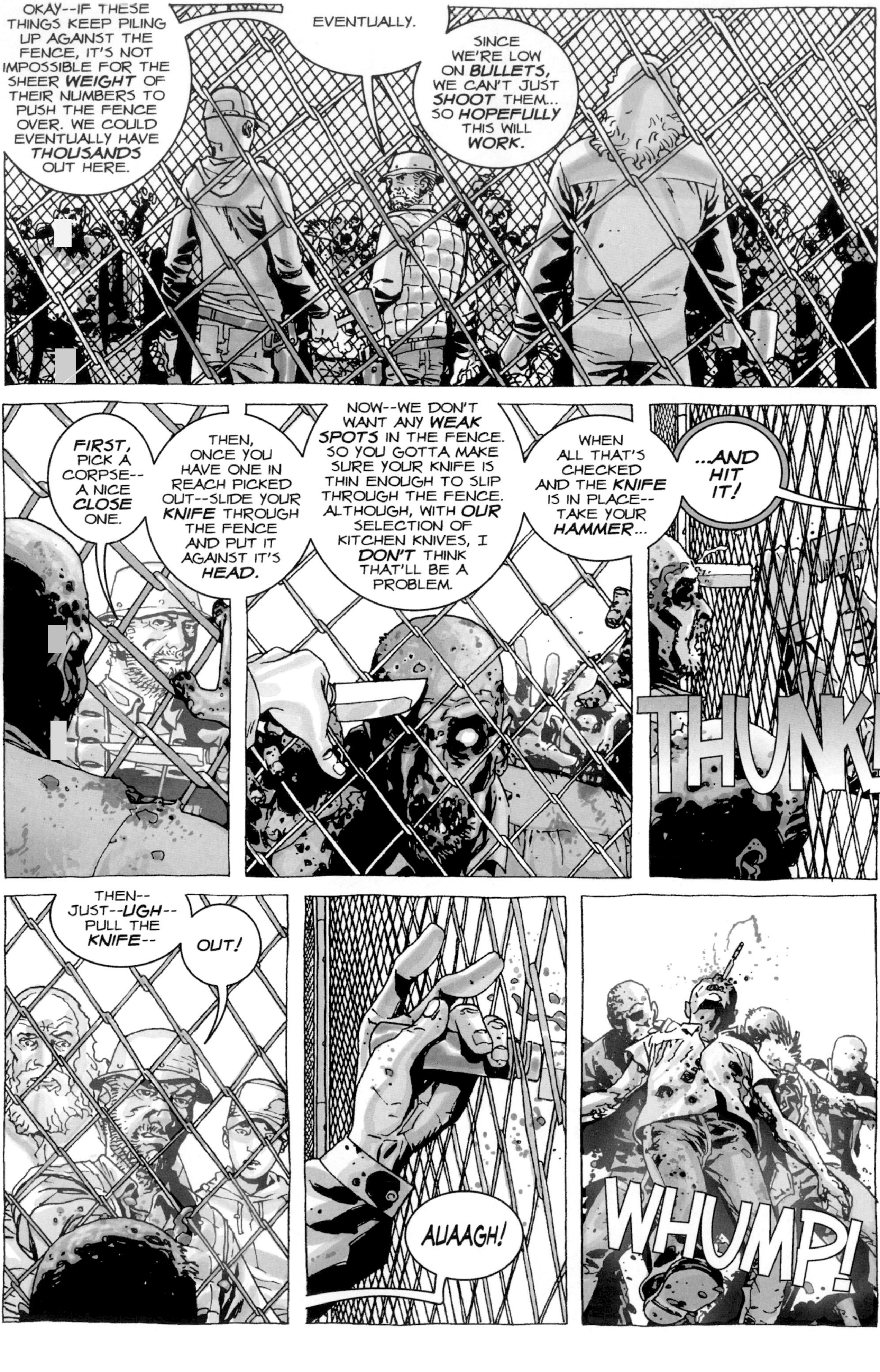
OKAY--IF THESE THINGS KEEP PILING UP AGAINST THE FENCE, IT'S NOT IMPOSSIBLE FOR THE SHEER WEIGHT OF THEIR NUMBERS TO PUSH THE FENCE OVER. WE COULD EVENTUALLY HAVE THOUSANDS OUT HERE.
EVENTUALLY.
SINCE WE'RE LOW ON BULLETS, WE CAN'T JUST SHOOT THEM... SO HOPEFULLY THIS WILL WORK.
FIRST, PICK A CORPSE-- A NICE CLOSE ONE.
THEN, ONCE YOU HAVE ONE IN REACH PICKED OUT--SLIDE YOUR KNIFE THROUGH THE FENCE AND PUT IT AGAINST IT'S HEAD.
NOW--WE DON'T WANT ANY WEAK SPOTS IN THE FENCE. SO YOU GOTTA MAKE SURE YOUR KNIFE IS THIN ENOUGH TO SLIP THROUGH THE FENCE. ALTHOUGH, WITH OUR SELECTION OF KITCHEN KNIVES, I DON'T THINK THAT'LL BE A PROBLEM.
WHEN ALL THAT'S CHECKED AND THE KNIFE IS IN PLACE-- TAKE YOUR HAMMER...
...AND HIT IT!
THUNK!
THEN-- JUST--UGH-- PULL THE KNIFE--
OUT!
AUAAGH!
WHUMP!

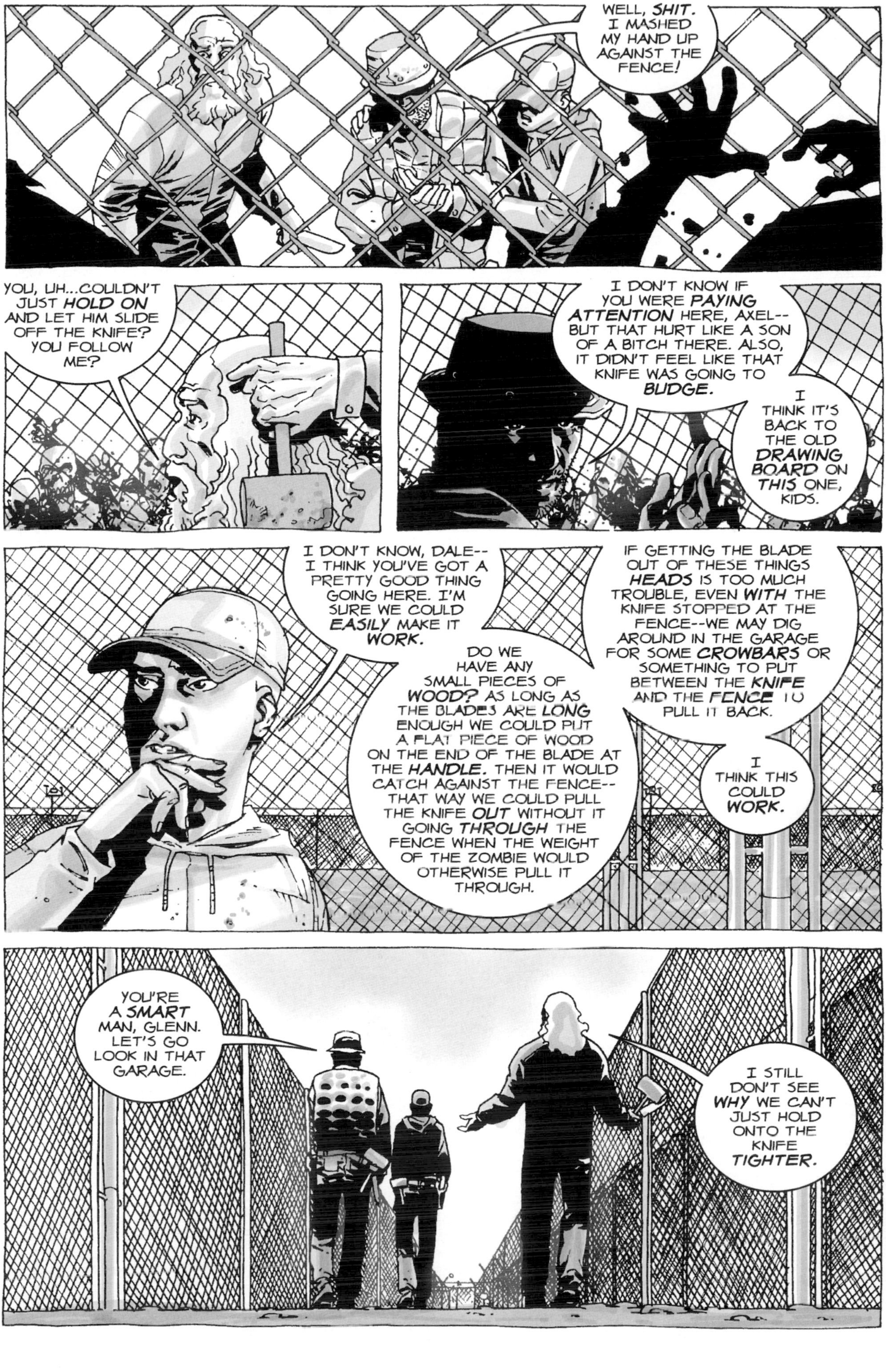
WELL, SHIT. I MASHED MY HAND UP AGAINST THE FENCE!
YOU, UH...COULDN'T JUST HOLD ON AND LET HIM SLIDE OFF THE KNIFE? YOU FOLLOW ME?
I DON'T KNOW IF YOU WERE PAYING ATTENTION HERE, AXEL-- BUT THAT HURT LIKE A SON OF A BITCH THERE. ALSO, IT DIDN'T FEEL LIKE THAT KNIFE WAS GOING TO BUDGE.
I THINK IT'S BACK TO THE OLD DRAWING BOARD ON THIS ONE, KIDS.
I DON'T KNOW, DALE-- I THINK YOU'VE GOT A PRETTY GOOD THING GOING HERE. I'M SURE WE COULD EASILY MAKE IT WORK.
DO WE HAVE ANY SMALL PIECES OF WOOD? AS LONG AS THE BLADES ARE LONG ENOUGH WE COULD PUT A FLAT PIECE OF WOOD ON THE END OF THE BLADE AT THE HANDLE. THEN IT WOULD CATCH AGAINST THE FENCE-- THAT WAY WE COULD PULL THE KNIFE OUT WITHOUT IT GOING THROUGH THE FENCE WHEN THE WEIGHT OF THE ZOMBIE WOULD OTHERWISE PULL IT THROUGH.
IF GETTING THE BLADE OUT OF THESE THINGS HEADS IS TOO MUCH TROUBLE, EVEN WITH THE KNIFE STOPPED AT THE FENCE--WE MAY DIG AROUND IN THE GARAGE FOR SOME CROWBARS OR SOMETHING TO PUT BETWEEN THE KNIFE AND THE FENCE TO PULL IT BACK.
I THINK THIS COULD WORK.
YOU'RE A SMART MAN, GLENN. LET'S GO LOOK IN THAT GARAGE.
I STILL DON'T SEE WHY WE CAN'T JUST HOLD ONTO THE KNIFE TIGHTER.

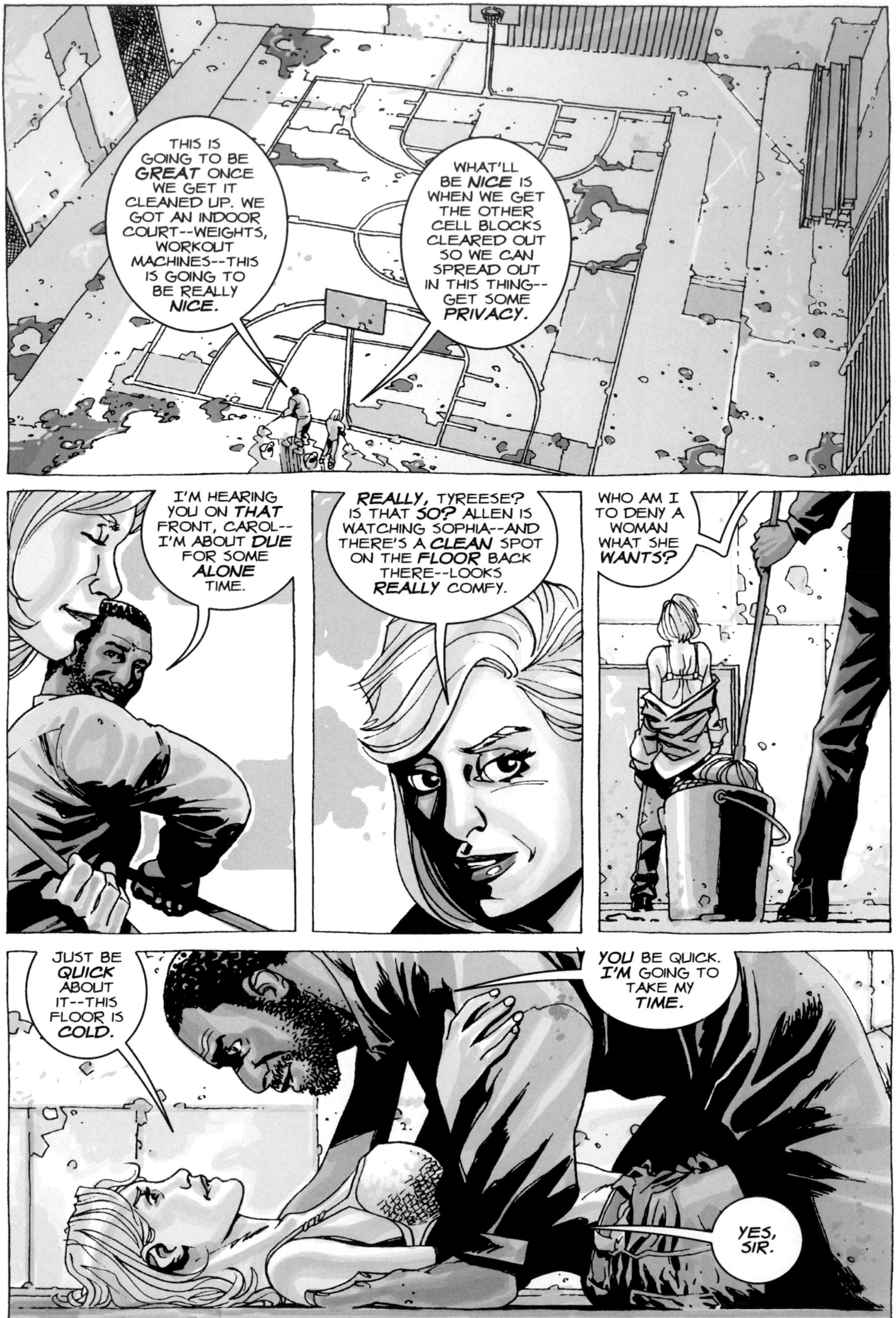

THIS IS GOING TO BE GREAT ONCE WE GET IT CLEANED UP. WE GOT AN INDOOR COURT--WEIGHTS, WORKOUT MACHINES--THIS IS GOING TO BE REALLY NICE.
WHAT'LL BE NICE IS WHEN WE GET THE OTHER CELL BLOCKS CLEARED OUT SO WE CAN SPREAD OUT IN THIS THING--GET SOME PRIVACY.
I'M HEARING YOU ON THAT FRONT, CAROL--I'M ABOUT DUE FOR SOME ALONE TIME.
REALLY, TYREESE? IS THAT SO? ALLEN IS WATCHING SOPHIA--AND THERE'S A CLEAN SPOT ON THE FLOOR BACK THERE--LOOKS REALLY COMFY.
WHO AM I TO DENY A WOMAN WHAT SHE WANTS?
JUST BE QUICK ABOUT IT--THIS FLOOR IS COLD.
YOU BE QUICK. I'M GOING TO TAKE MY TIME.
YES, SIR.

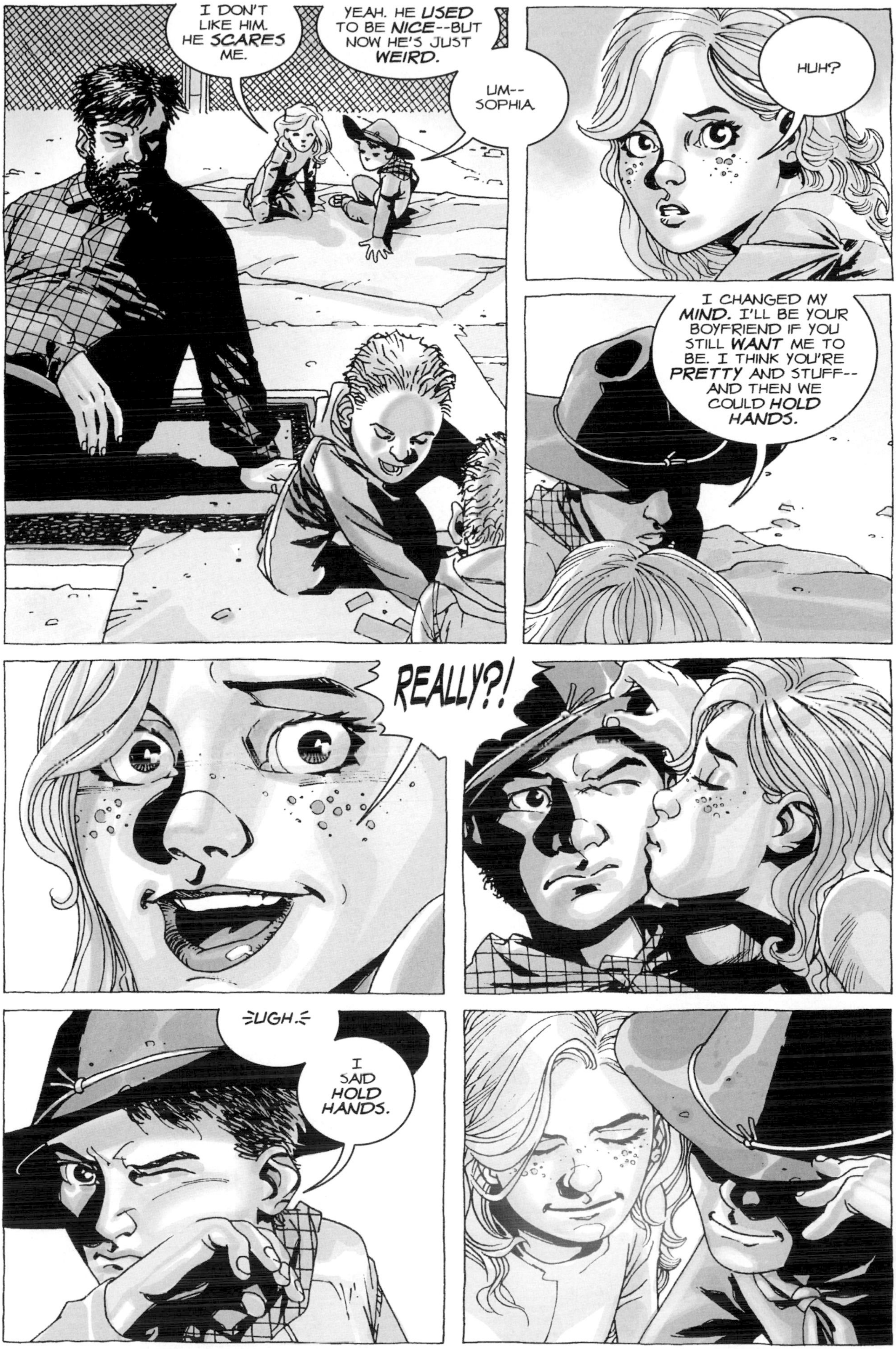
I DON'T LIKE HIM. HE SCARES ME.
YEAH. HE USED TO BE NICE--BUT NOW HE'S JUST WEIRD.
UM-- SOPHIA.
HUH?
I CHANGED MY MIND. I'LL BE YOUR BOYFRIEND IF YOU STILL WANT ME TO BE. I THINK YOU'RE PRETTY AND STUFF-- AND THEN WE COULD HOLD HANDS.
REALLY?!
UGH.
I SAID HOLD HANDS.

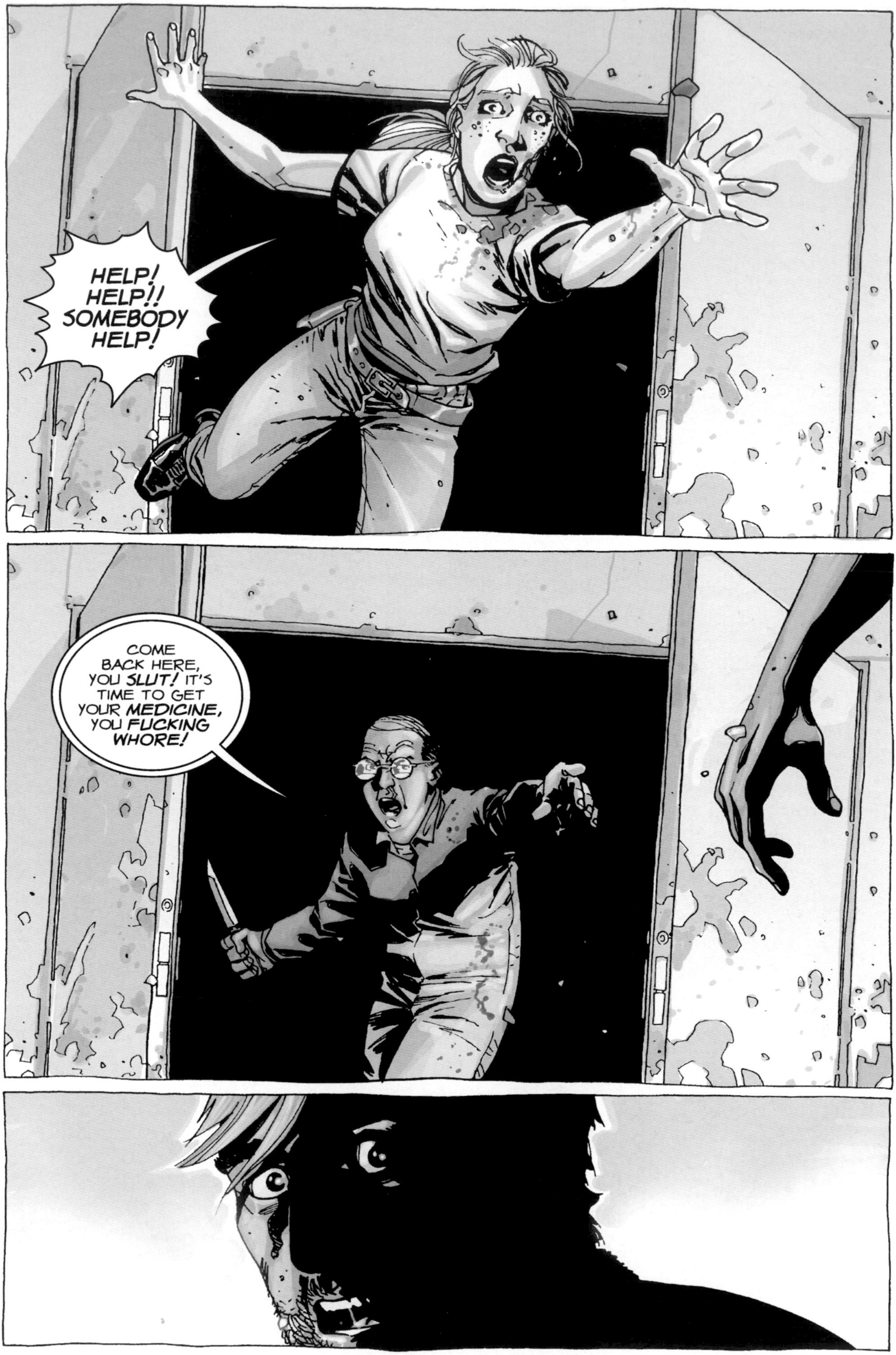
HELP! HELP!! SOMEBODY HELP!
COME BACK HERE, YOU SLUT! IT'S TIME TO GET YOUR MEDICINE, YOU FUCKING WHORE!

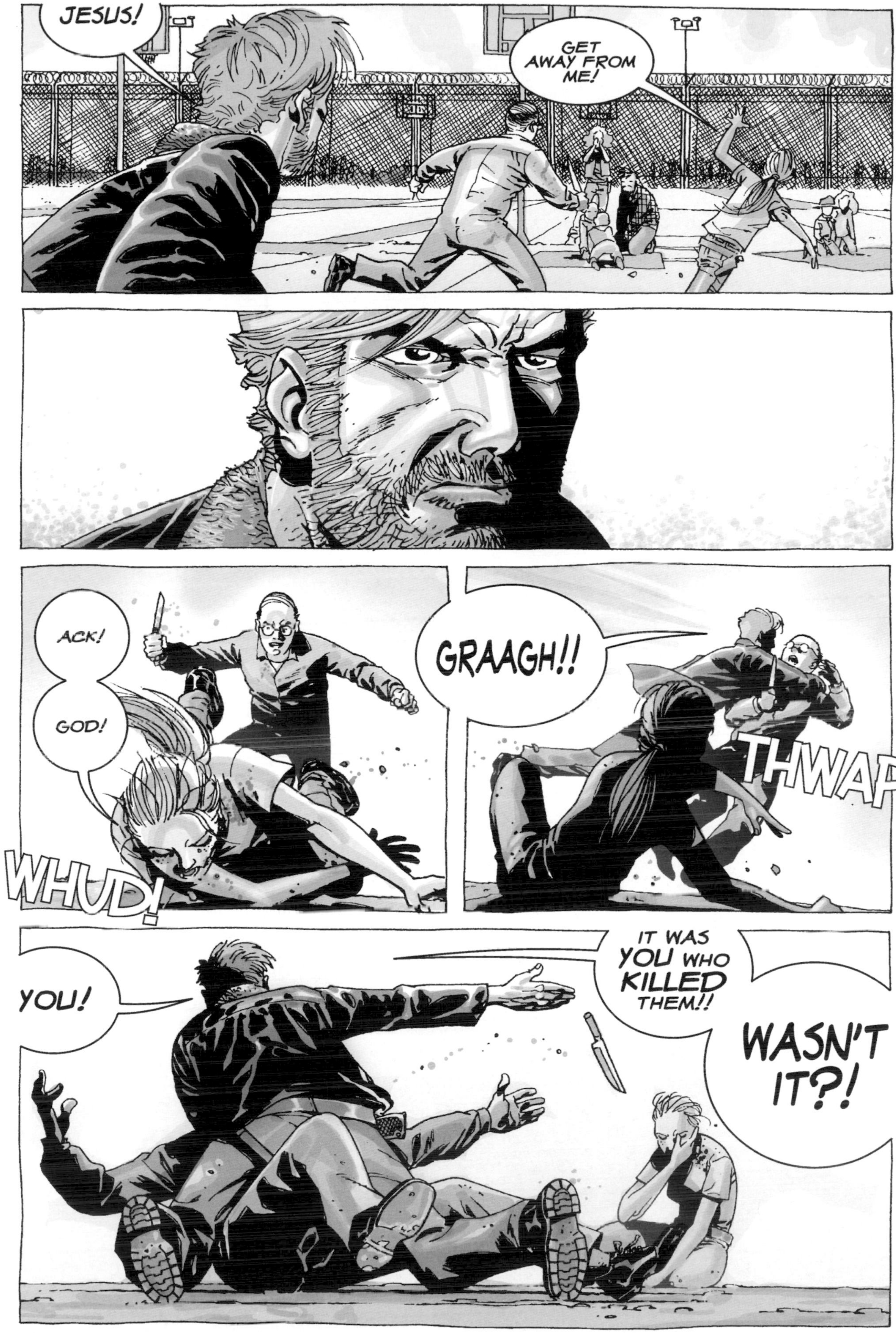
JESUS!
GET AWAY FROM ME!
ACK!
GOD!
WHUD!
GRAAGH!!
THWAP!
YOU!
IT WAS YOU WHO KILLED THEM!!
WASN'T IT?!

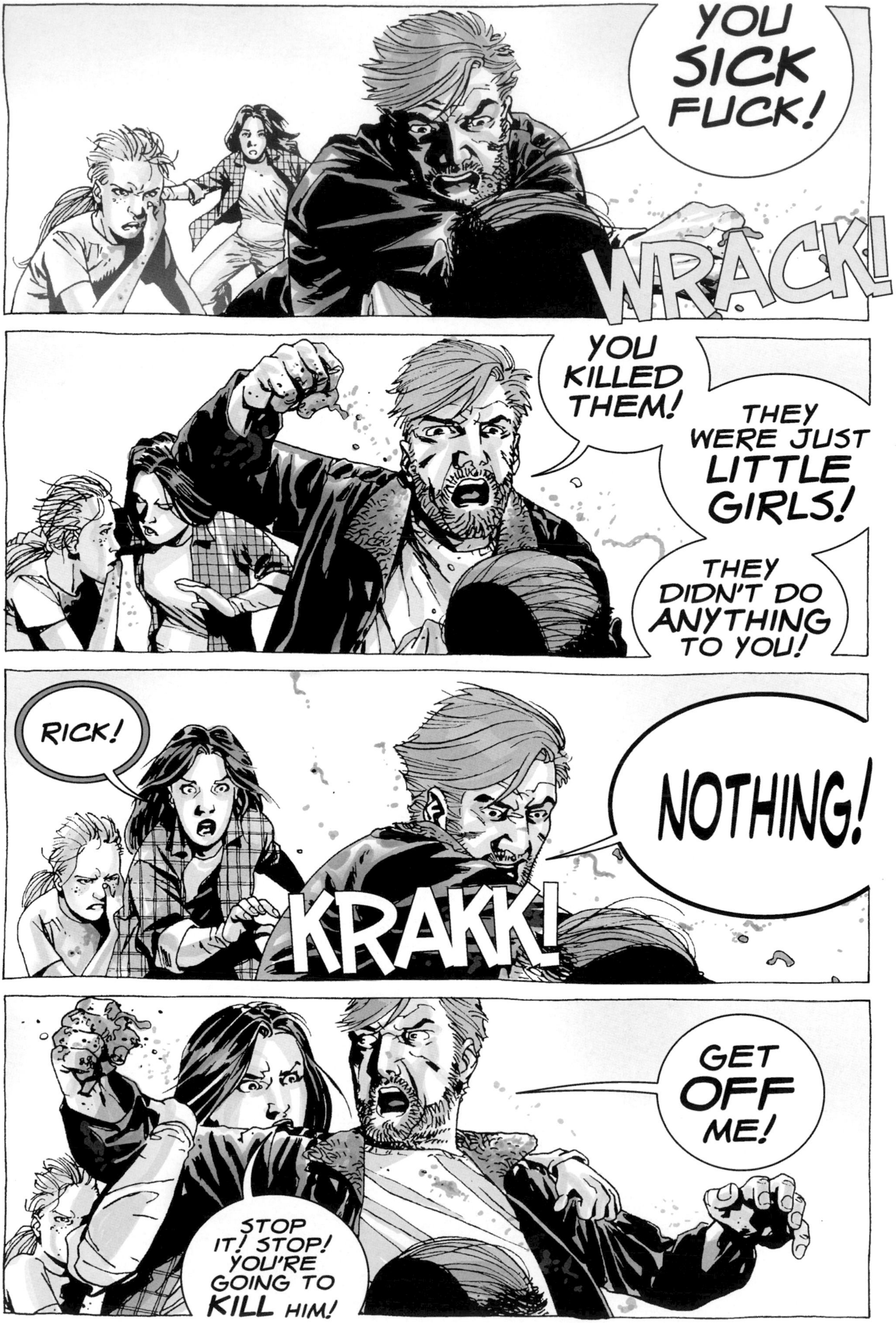
YOU SICK FUCK!
WRACK!
YOU KILLED THEM!
THEY WERE JUST LITTLE GIRLS!
THEY DIDN'T DO ANYTHING TO YOU!
RICK!
NOTHING!
KRAKK!
GET OFF ME!
STOP IT! STOP! YOU'RE GOING TO KILL HIM!

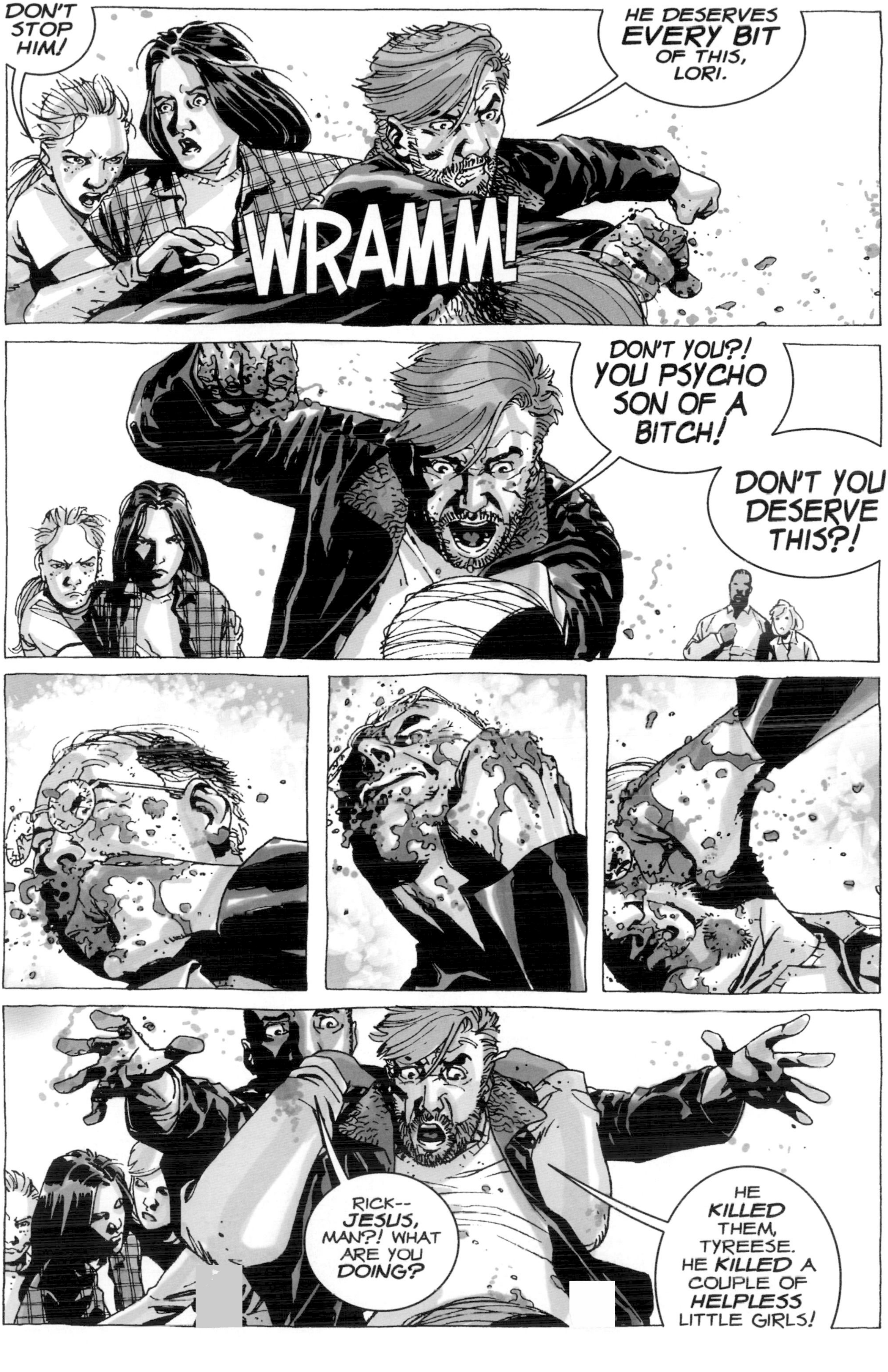
DON'T STOP HIM!
HE DESERVES EVERY BIT OF THIS, LORI.
WRAMM!
DON'T YOU?! YOU PSYCHO SON OF A BITCH!
DON'T YOU DESERVE THIS?!
RICK-- JESUS, MAN?! WHAT ARE YOU DOING?
HE KILLED THEM, TYREESE. HE KILLED A COUPLE OF HELPLESS LITTLE GIRLS!

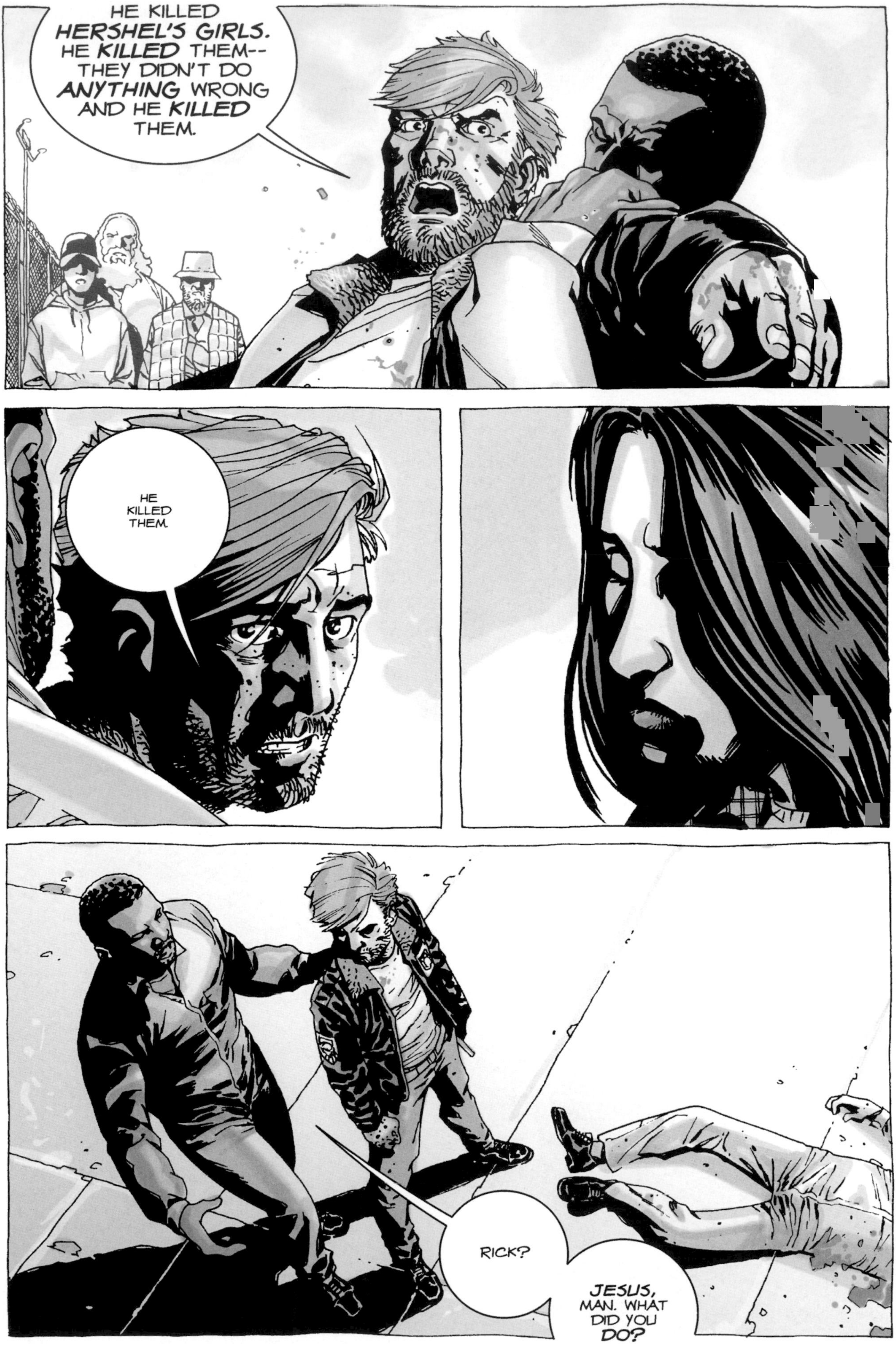
HE KILLED HERSHEL'S GIRLS. HE KILLED THEM-- THEY DIDN'T DO ANYTHING WRONG AND HE KILLED THEM.
HE KILLED THEM.
RICK?
JESUS, MAN. WHAT DID YOU DO?

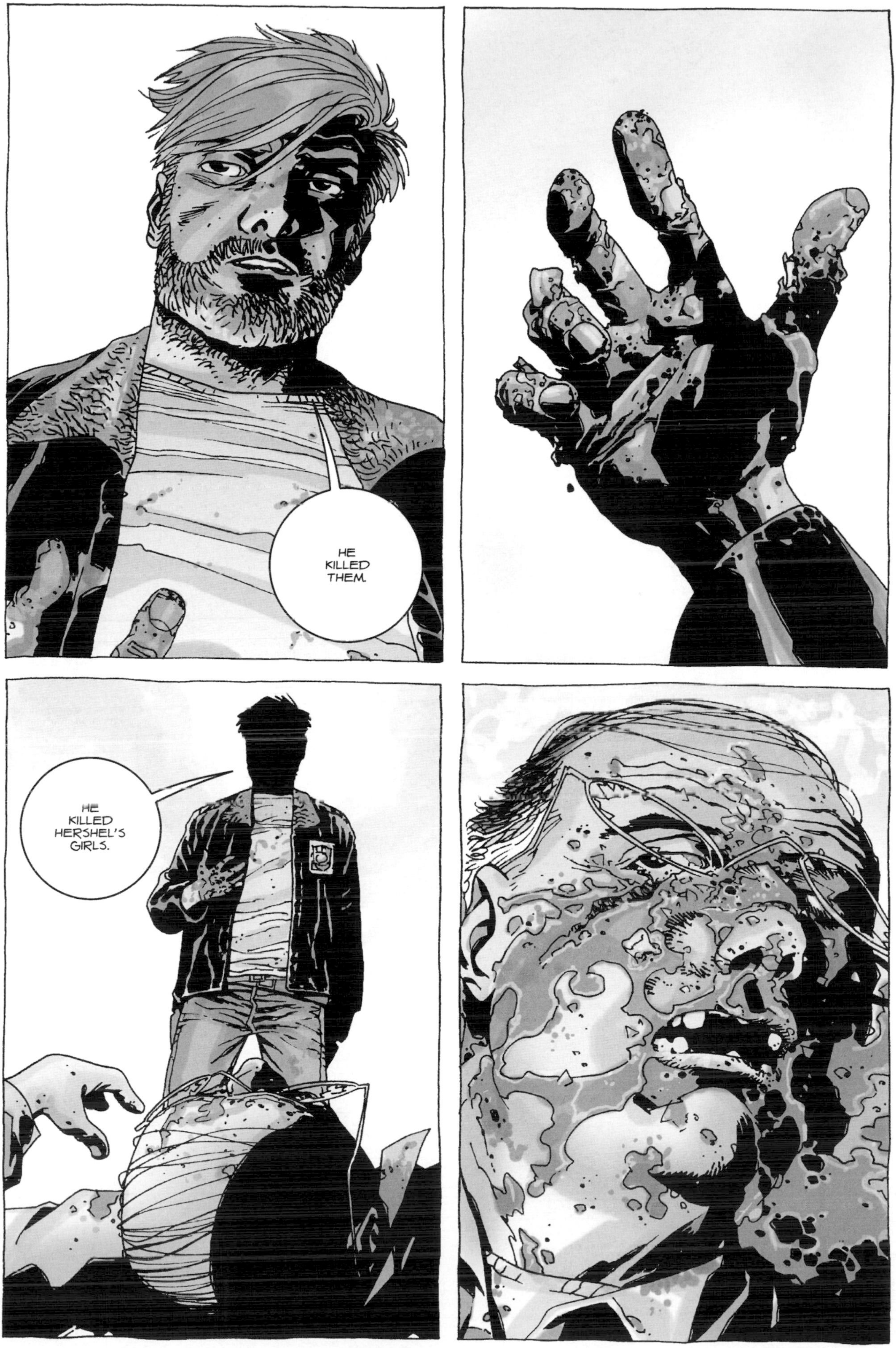
HE KILLED THEM.
HE KILLED HERSHEL'S GIRLS.

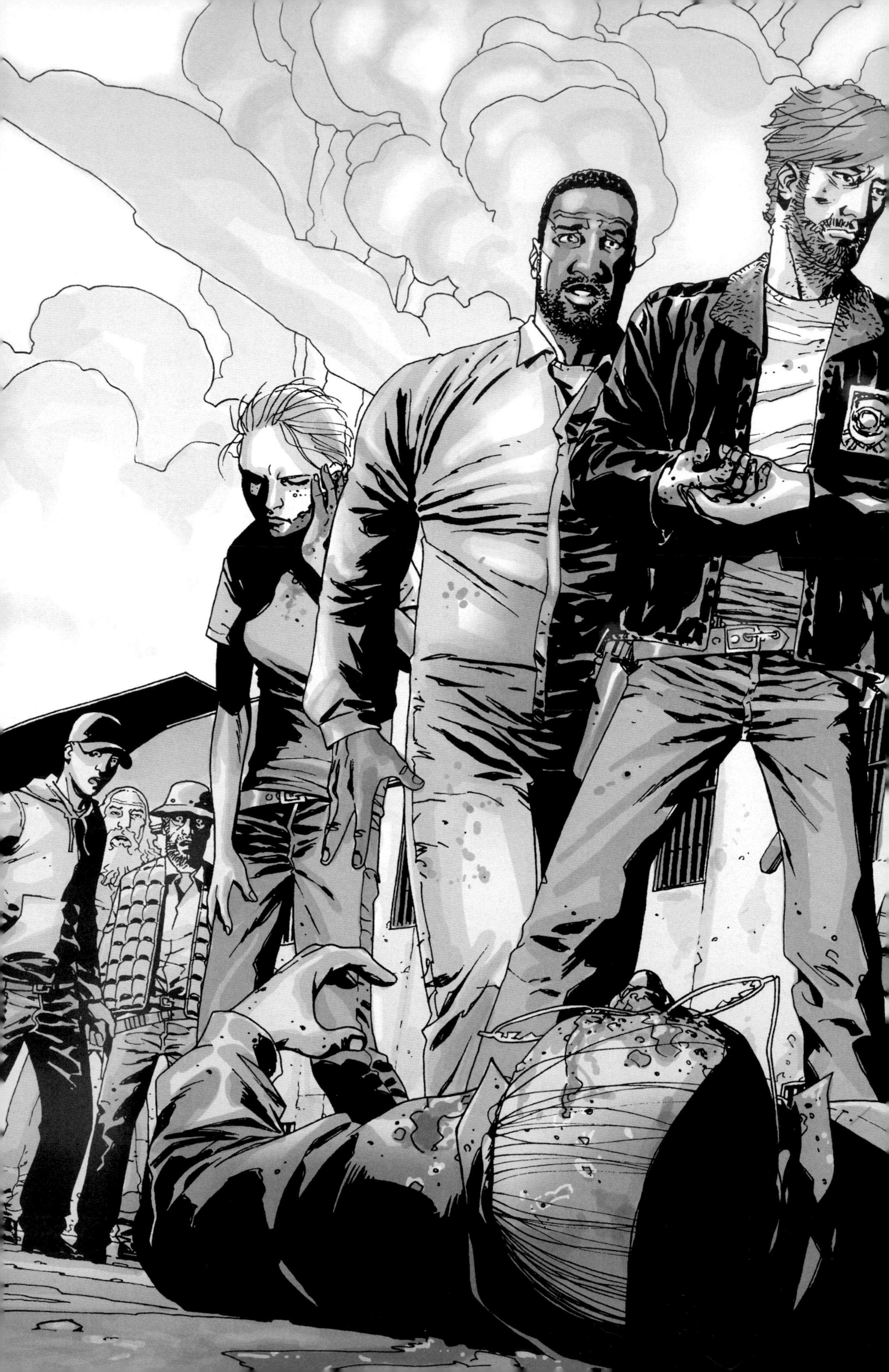

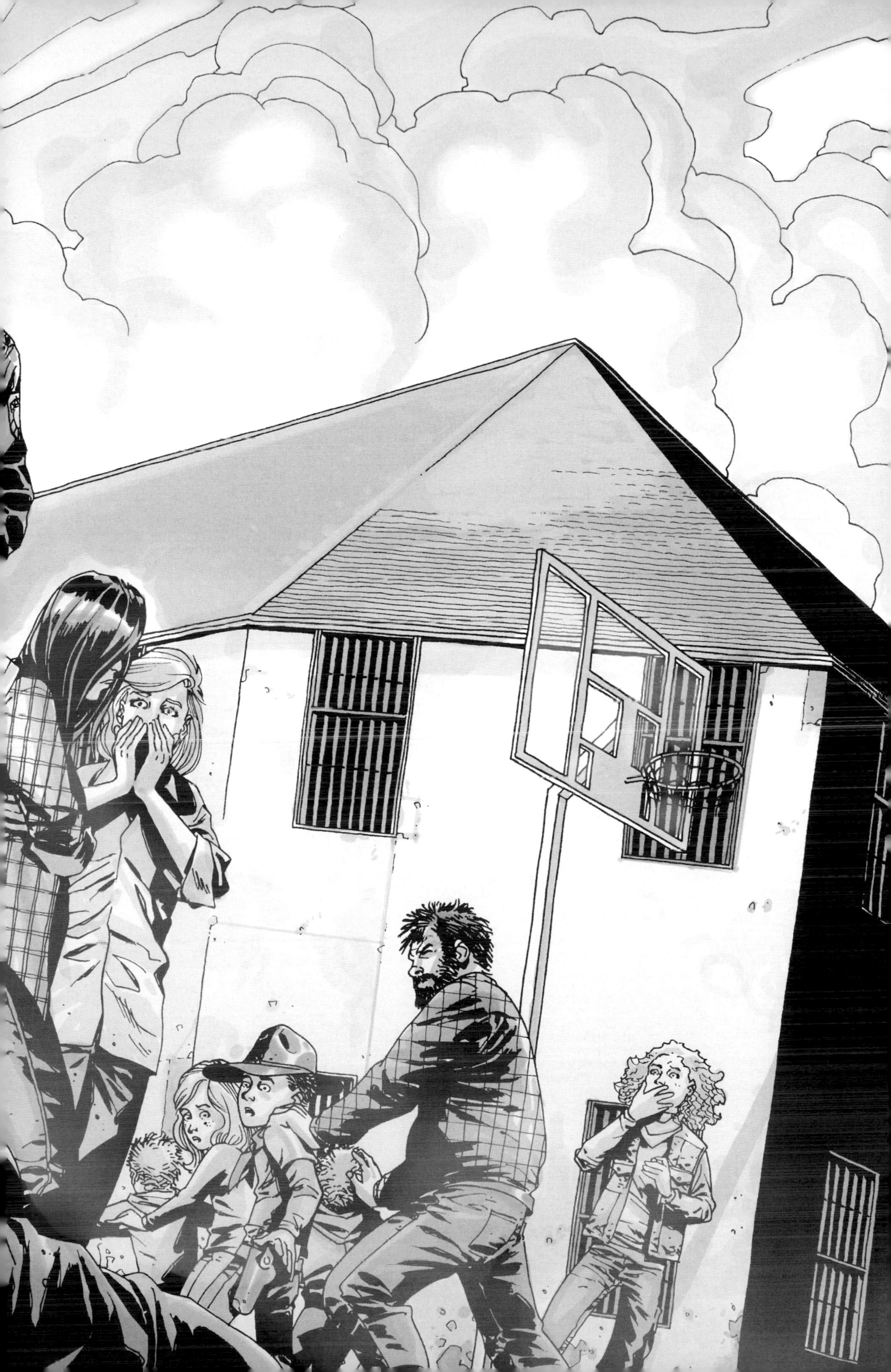

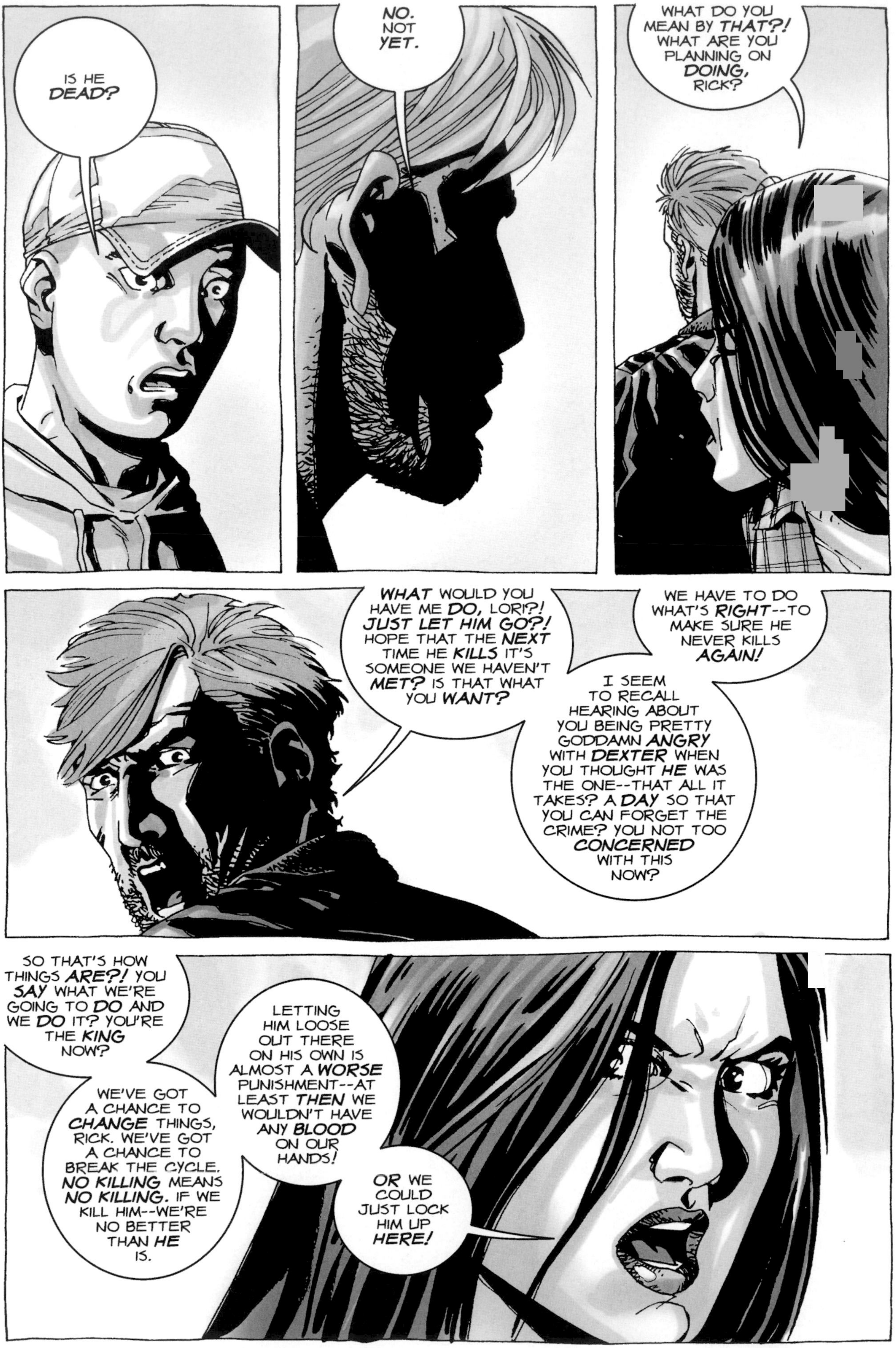
IS HE DEAD?
NO. NOT YET.
WHAT DO YOU MEAN BY THAT?! WHAT ARE YOU PLANNING ON DOING, RICK?
WHAT WOULD YOU HAVE ME DO, LORI?! JUST LET HIM GO?! HOPE THAT THE NEXT TIME HE KILLS IT'S SOMEONE WE HAVEN'T MET? IS THAT WHAT YOU WANT?
WE HAVE TO DO WHAT'S RIGHT--TO MAKE SURE HE NEVER KILLS AGAIN!
I SEEM TO RECALL HEARING ABOUT YOU BEING PRETTY GODDAMN ANGRY WITH DEXTER WHEN YOU THOUGHT HE WAS THE ONE--THAT ALL IT TAKES? A DAY SO THAT YOU CAN FORGET THE CRIME? YOU NOT TOO CONCERNED WITH THIS NOW?
SO THAT'S HOW THINGS ARE?! YOU SAY WHAT WE'RE GOING TO DO AND WE DO IT? YOU'RE THE KING NOW?
WE'VE GOT A CHANCE TO CHANGE THINGS, RICK. WE'VE GOT A CHANCE TO BREAK THE CYCLE. NO KILLING MEANS NO KILLING. IF WE KILL HIM--WE'RE NO BETTER THAN HE IS.
LETTING HIM LOOSE OUT THERE ON HIS OWN IS ALMOST A WORSE PUNISHMENT--AT LEAST THEN WE WOULDN'T HAVE ANY BLOOD ON OUR HANDS!
OR WE COULD JUST LOCK HIM UP HERE!

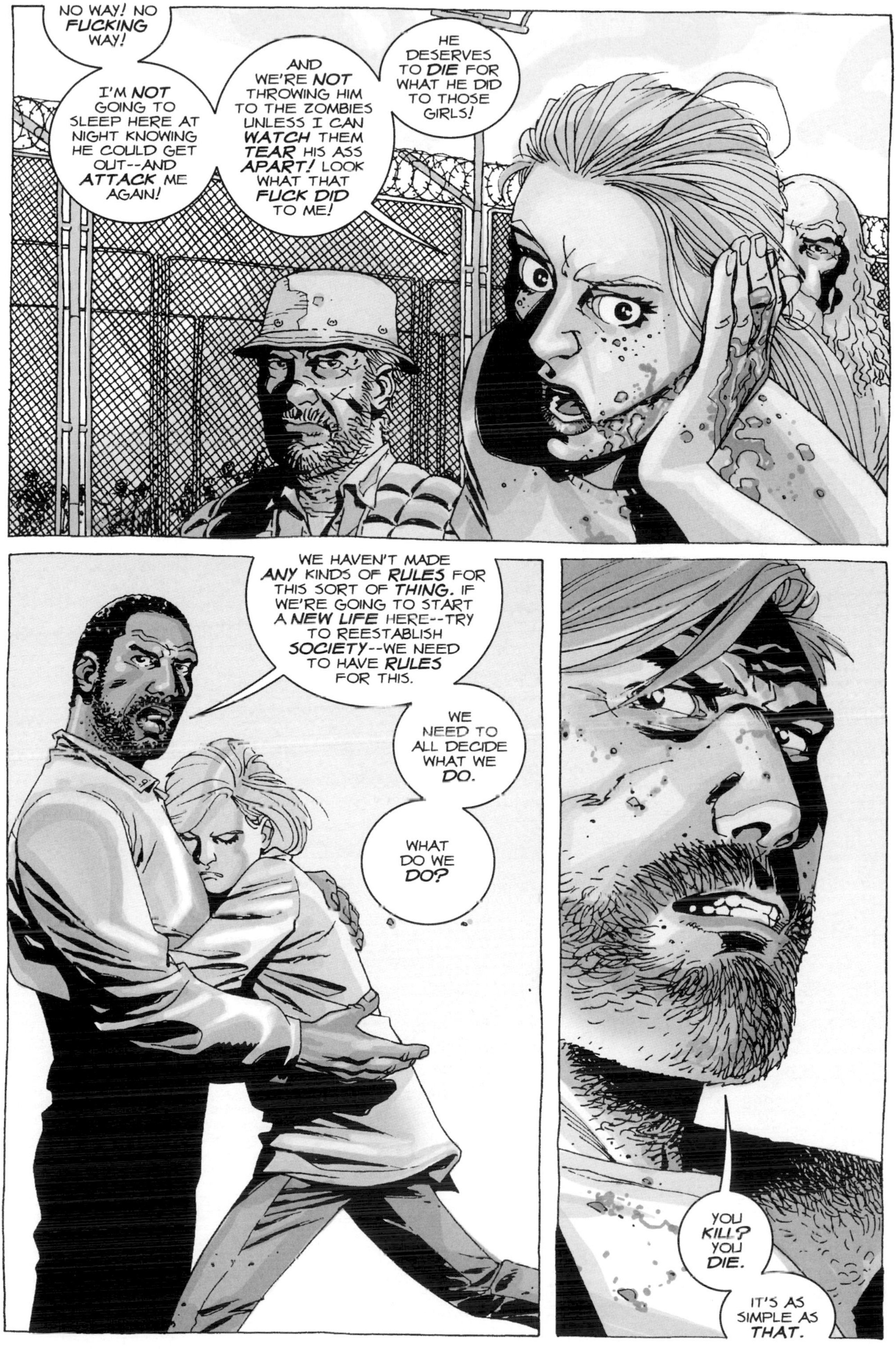

NO WAY! NO FUCKING WAY!
I'M NOT GOING TO SLEEP HERE AT NIGHT KNOWING HE COULD GET OUT--AND ATTACK ME AGAIN!
AND WE'RE NOT THROWING HIM TO THE ZOMBIES UNLESS I CAN WATCH THEM TEAR HIS ASS APART! LOOK WHAT THAT FUCK DID TO ME!
HE DESERVES TO DIE FOR WHAT HE DID TO THOSE GIRLS!
WE HAVEN'T MADE ANY KINDS OF RULES FOR THIS SORT OF THING. IF WE'RE GOING TO START A NEW LIFE HERE--TRY TO REESTABLISH SOCIETY--WE NEED TO HAVE RULES FOR THIS.
WE NEED TO ALL DECIDE WHAT WE DO.
WHAT DO WE DO?
YOU KILL? YOU DIE.
IT'S AS SIMPLE AS THAT.

THAT WORKS FOR **ME**.

HE WAS **SO**... HE WAS...

NICE.

SO THAT'S **IT**? YOU'RE JUST MAKING THE DECISION FOR **ALL OF US** THEN?!

I'M JUST MAKING SURE WE DO WHAT'S **RIGHT**, LORI. I WAS PUT IN CHARGE AFTER WE LEFT ATLANTA.

HONEY, **LISTEN** TO ME. I'M A **COP**--I'VE BEEN **TRAINED** TO MAKE DECISIONS LIKE THIS. I'M THE **ONLY** ONE HERE IN A POSITION OF **AUTHORITY**.

I'M MAKING THE CHOICE THAT'S **BEST** FOR **ALL** OF US. THAT'S WHAT YOU ALL **LOOK UP** TO ME FOR. THAT'S WHY **EVERYONE** COMES TO ME FOR **ADVICE** AND **GUIDANCE**.

I'M IN CHARGE.

LISTEN TO **YOURSELF**. YOU'RE MY **HUSBAND**, YOU PRICK--NOT MY **FATHER**!

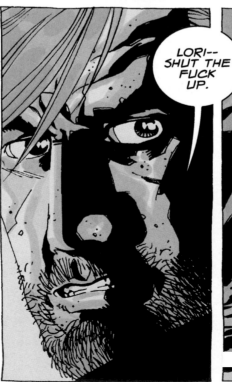

LORI-- SHUT THE FUCK UP.

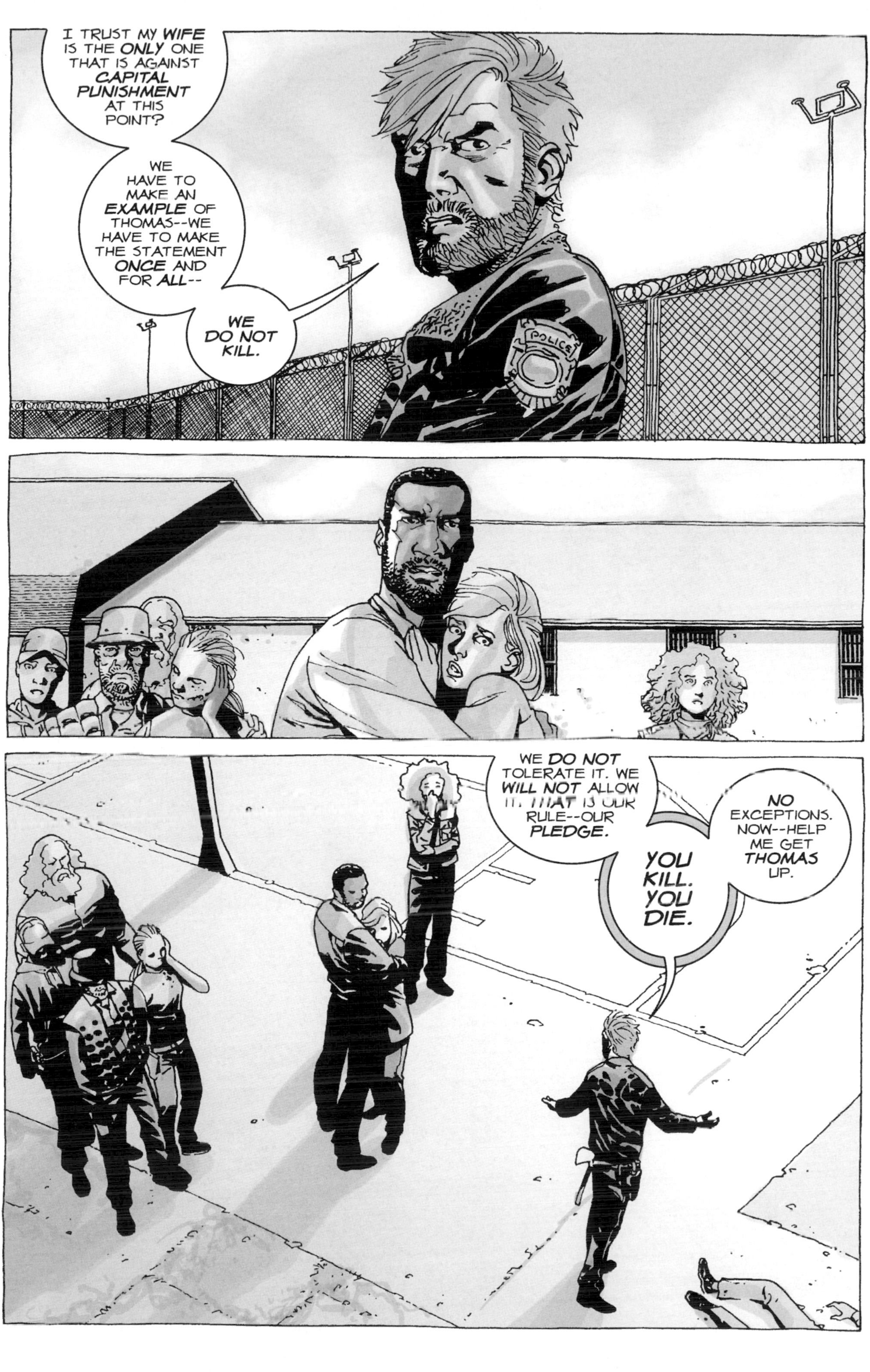
I TRUST MY WIFE IS THE ONLY ONE THAT IS AGAINST CAPITAL PUNISHMENT AT THIS POINT?
WE HAVE TO MAKE AN EXAMPLE OF THOMAS--WE HAVE TO MAKE THE STATEMENT ONCE AND FOR ALL--
WE DO NOT KILL.
POLICE
WE DO NOT TOLERATE IT. WE WILL NOT ALLOW IT. THAT IS OUR RULE--OUR PLEDGE.
YOU KILL. YOU DIE.
NO EXCEPTIONS. NOW--HELP ME GET THOMAS UP.

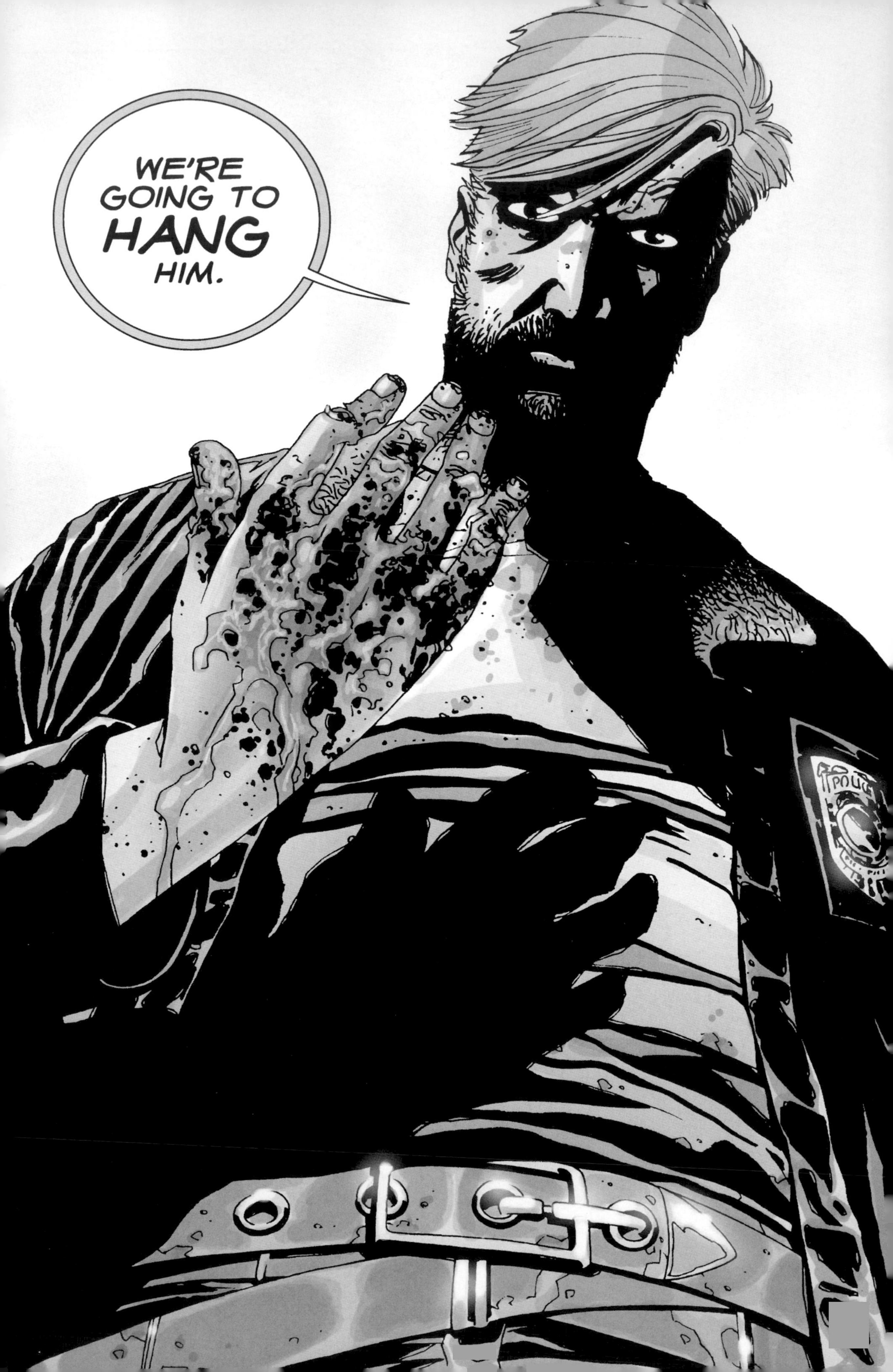
WE'RE GOING TO HANG HIM.

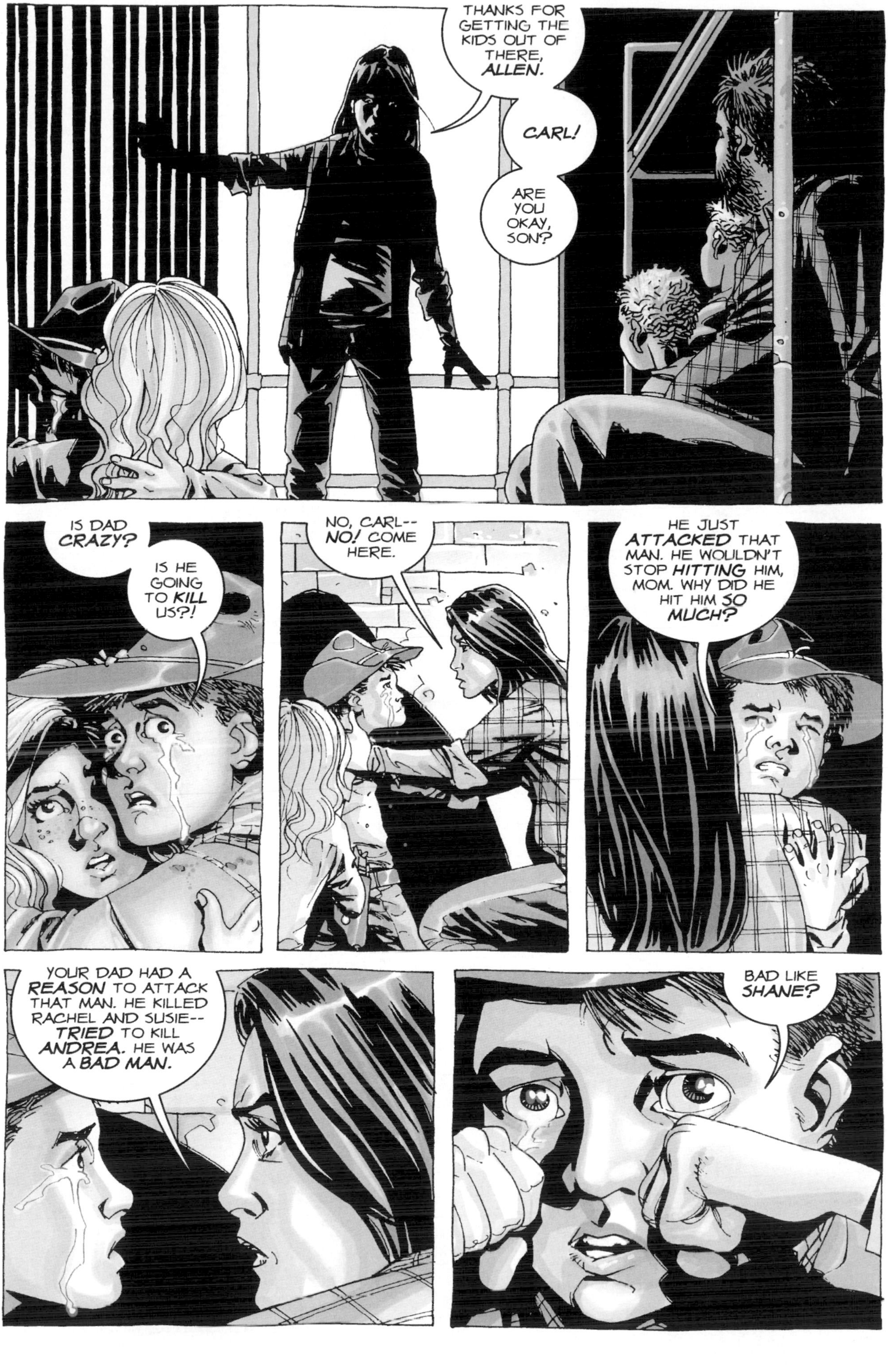
THANKS FOR GETTING THE KIDS OUT OF THERE, ALLEN.
CARL!
ARE YOU OKAY, SON?
IS DAD CRAZY?
IS HE GOING TO KILL US?!
NO, CARL-- NO! COME HERE.
HE JUST ATTACKED THAT MAN. HE WOULDN'T STOP HITTING HIM, MOM. WHY DID HE HIT HIM SO MUCH?
YOUR DAD HAD A REASON TO ATTACK THAT MAN. HE KILLED RACHEL AND SUSIE-- TRIED TO KILL ANDREA. HE WAS A BAD MAN.
BAD LIKE SHANE?

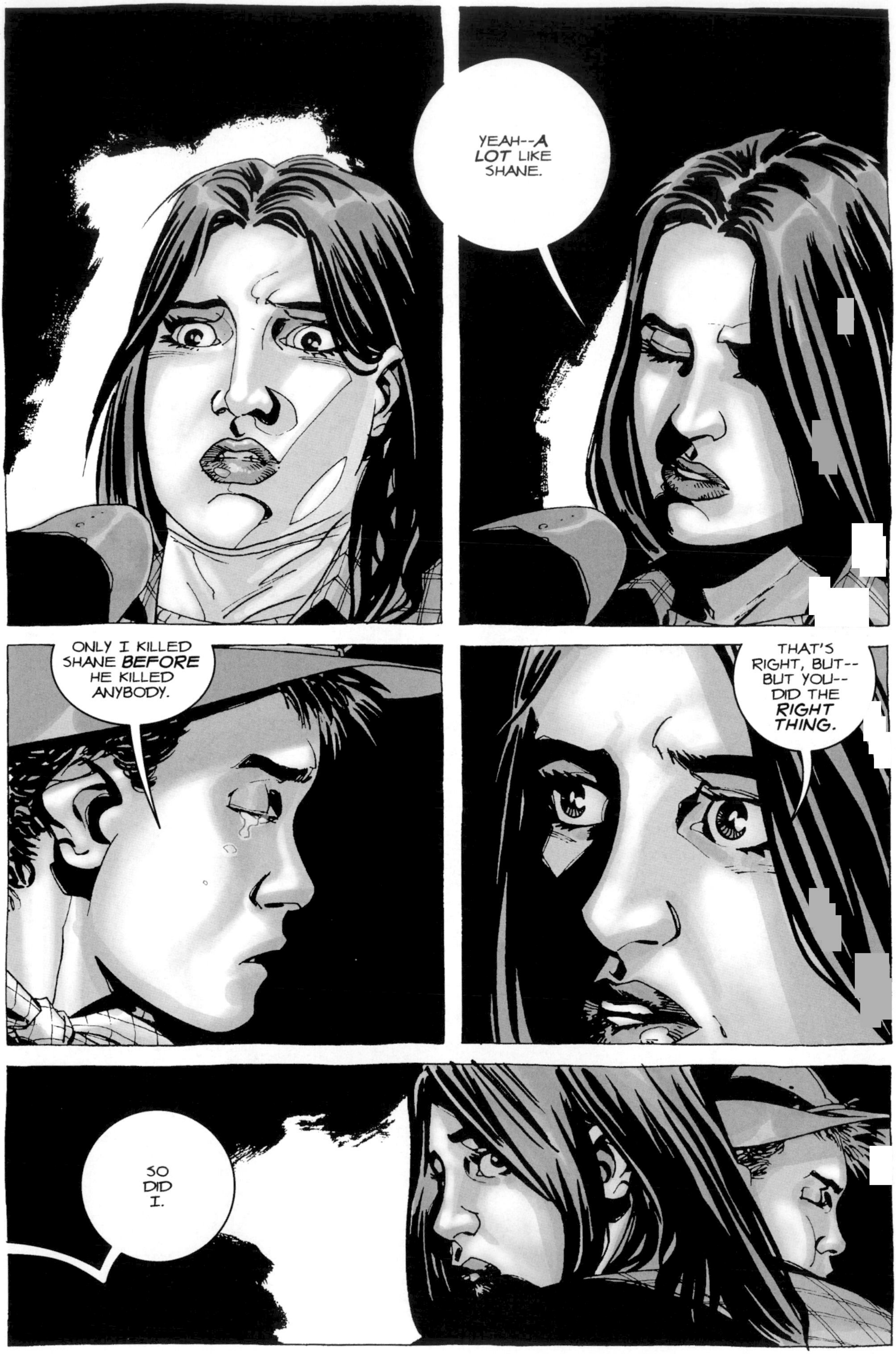
YEAH--A LOT LIKE SHANE.
ONLY I KILLED SHANE BEFORE HE KILLED ANYBODY.
THAT'S RIGHT, BUT-- BUT YOU-- DID THE RIGHT THING.
SO DID I.

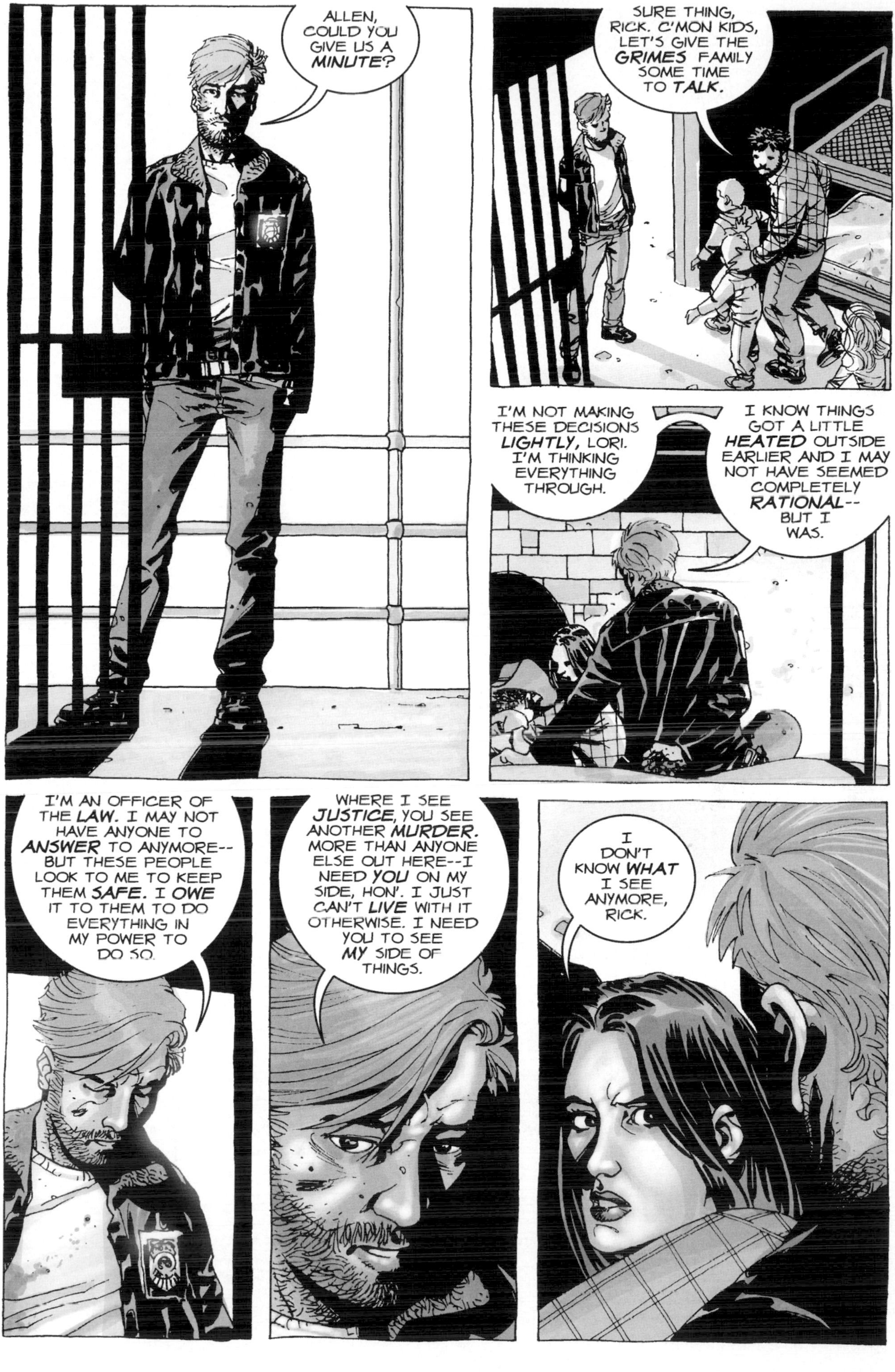
ALLEN, COULD YOU GIVE US A MINUTE?
SURE THING, RICK. C'MON KIDS, LET'S GIVE THE GRIMES FAMILY SOME TIME TO TALK.
I'M NOT MAKING THESE DECISIONS LIGHTLY, LORI. I'M THINKING EVERYTHING THROUGH.
I KNOW THINGS GOT A LITTLE HEATED OUTSIDE EARLIER AND I MAY NOT HAVE SEEMED COMPLETELY RATIONAL-- BUT I WAS.
I'M AN OFFICER OF THE LAW. I MAY NOT HAVE ANYONE TO ANSWER TO ANYMORE-- BUT THESE PEOPLE LOOK TO ME TO KEEP THEM SAFE. I OWE IT TO THEM TO DO EVERYTHING IN MY POWER TO DO SO.
WHERE I SEE JUSTICE, YOU SEE ANOTHER MURDER. MORE THAN ANYONE ELSE OUT HERE--I NEED YOU ON MY SIDE, HON'. I JUST CAN'T LIVE WITH IT OTHERWISE. I NEED YOU TO SEE MY SIDE OF THINGS.
I DON'T KNOW WHAT I SEE ANYMORE, RICK.

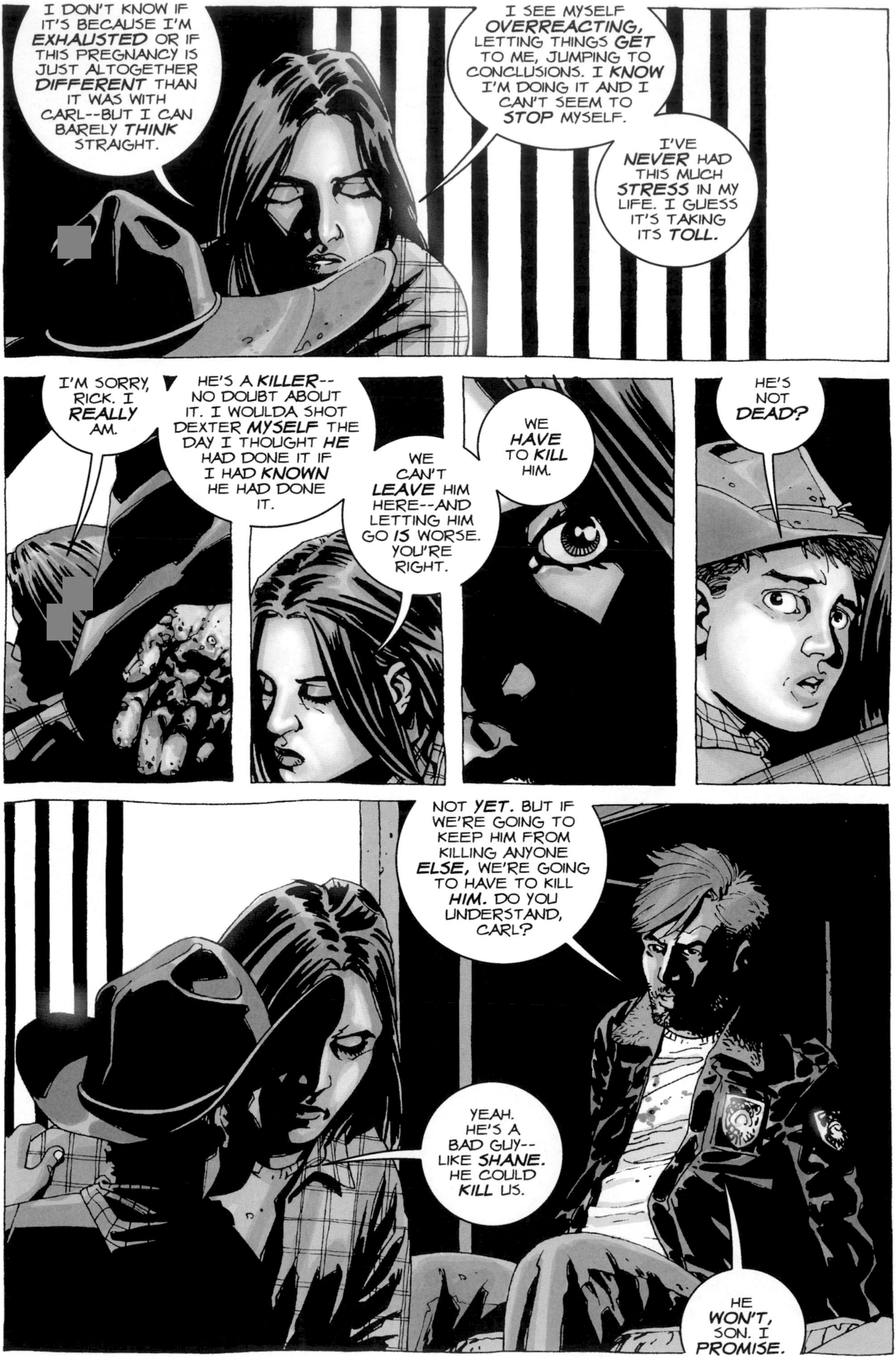
I DON'T KNOW IF IT'S BECAUSE I'M EXHAUSTED OR IF THIS PREGNANCY IS JUST ALTOGETHER DIFFERENT THAN IT WAS WITH CARL--BUT I CAN BARELY THINK STRAIGHT.
I SEE MYSELF OVERREACTING, LETTING THINGS GET TO ME, JUMPING TO CONCLUSIONS. I KNOW I'M DOING IT AND I CAN'T SEEM TO STOP MYSELF.
I'VE NEVER HAD THIS MUCH STRESS IN MY LIFE. I GUESS IT'S TAKING ITS TOLL.
I'M SORRY, RICK. I REALLY AM.
HE'S A KILLER-- NO DOUBT ABOUT IT. I WOULDA SHOT DEXTER MYSELF THE DAY I THOUGHT HE HAD DONE IT IF I HAD KNOWN HE HAD DONE IT.
WE CAN'T LEAVE HIM HERE--AND LETTING HIM GO IS WORSE. YOU'RE RIGHT.
WE HAVE TO KILL HIM.
HE'S NOT DEAD?
NOT YET. BUT IF WE'RE GOING TO KEEP HIM FROM KILLING ANYONE ELSE, WE'RE GOING TO HAVE TO KILL HIM. DO YOU UNDERSTAND, CARL?
YEAH. HE'S A BAD GUY-- LIKE SHANE. HE COULD KILL US.
HE WON'T, SON. I PROMISE.

OKAY--YOU SIT RIGHT THERE. I STILL HAVE THE **FIRST AID** KIT FROM THE **RV.** LET ME GET IT.

HERSHEL'D PROBABLY DO A BETTER JOB PATCHING YOU UP BUT I DON'T THINK HE'S **READY** TO HELP **ANYONE** AFTER WHAT HE JUST WENT THROUGH.

I'M NOT IN TOO GOOD A MOOD **EITHER**--THAT FUCKER **DID** JUST TRY TO **KILL** ME.

JESUS! THIS **FUCKING** HURTS!

LOOK FORWARD--LET ME MAKE SURE I CAN STOP THIS BLEEDING. I THINK MOST OF IT'S **STOPPED** ALREADY. THIS'LL BE **MOSTLY** CLEAN UP.

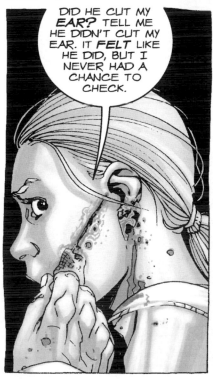

DID HE CUT MY **EAR?** TELL ME HE DIDN'T CUT MY EAR. IT **FELT** LIKE HE DID, BUT I NEVER HAD A CHANCE TO CHECK.

YOUR LOBE IS **GONE**--BUT YOU'LL STILL BE ABLE TO **HEAR.**

I COULDN'T CARE **LESS** ABOUT HEARING. I DON'T WANT TO LOOK LIKE A **FREAK.**

YOU'VE GOT NOTHING TO WORRY ABOUT. YOU'LL BE AS PRETTY AS **EVER,** AS SOON AS WE CLEAN YOU UP.

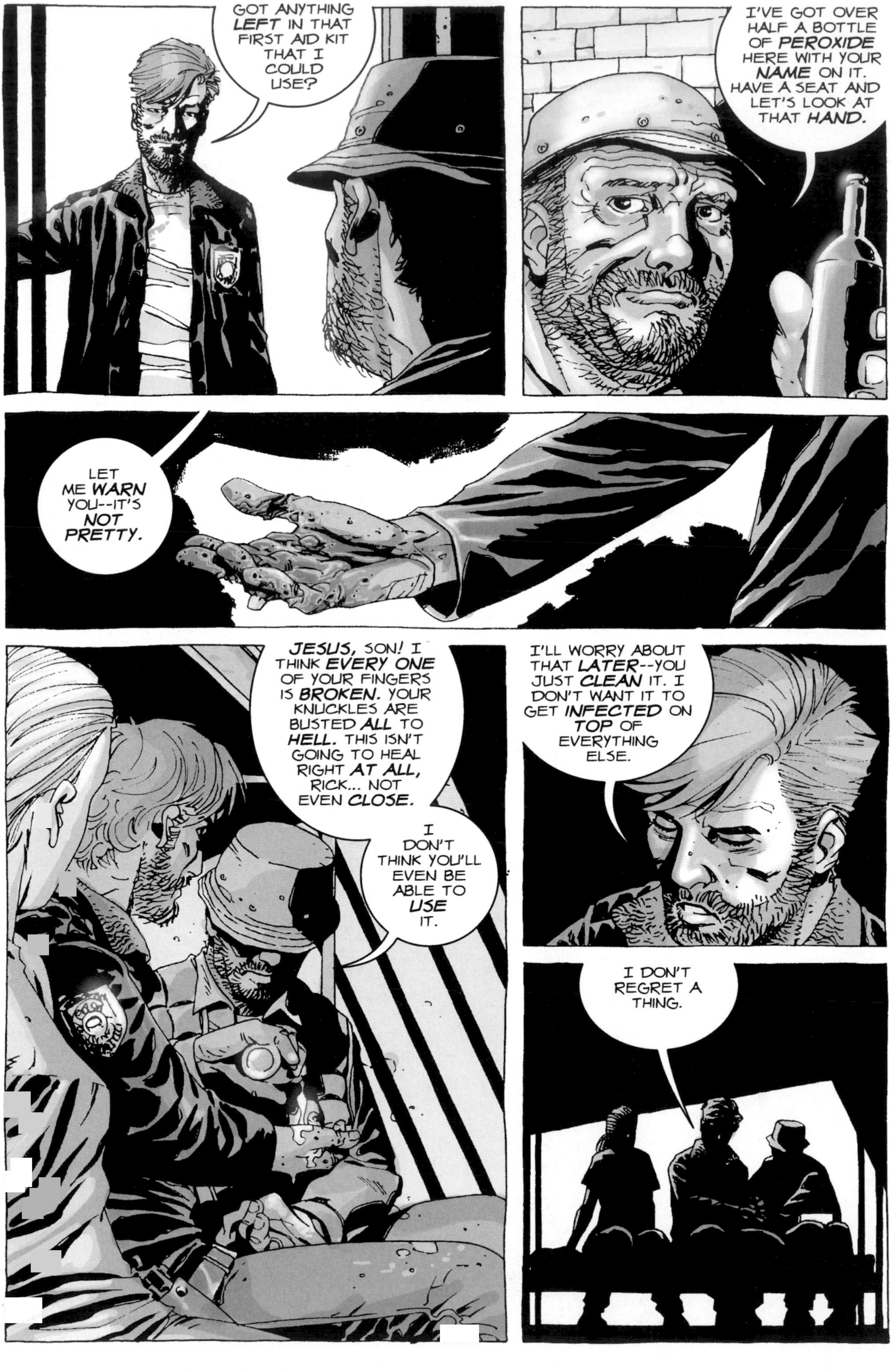
GOT ANYTHING LEFT IN THAT FIRST AID KIT THAT I COULD USE?
I'VE GOT OVER HALF A BOTTLE OF PEROXIDE HERE WITH YOUR NAME ON IT. HAVE A SEAT AND LET'S LOOK AT THAT HAND.
LET ME WARN YOU--IT'S NOT PRETTY.
JESUS, SON! I THINK EVERY ONE OF YOUR FINGERS IS BROKEN. YOUR KNUCKLES ARE BUSTED ALL TO HELL. THIS ISN'T GOING TO HEAL RIGHT AT ALL, RICK... NOT EVEN CLOSE.
I DON'T THINK YOU'LL EVEN BE ABLE TO USE IT.
I'LL WORRY ABOUT THAT LATER--YOU JUST CLEAN IT. I DON'T WANT IT TO GET INFECTED ON TOP OF EVERYTHING ELSE.
I DON'T REGRET A THING.

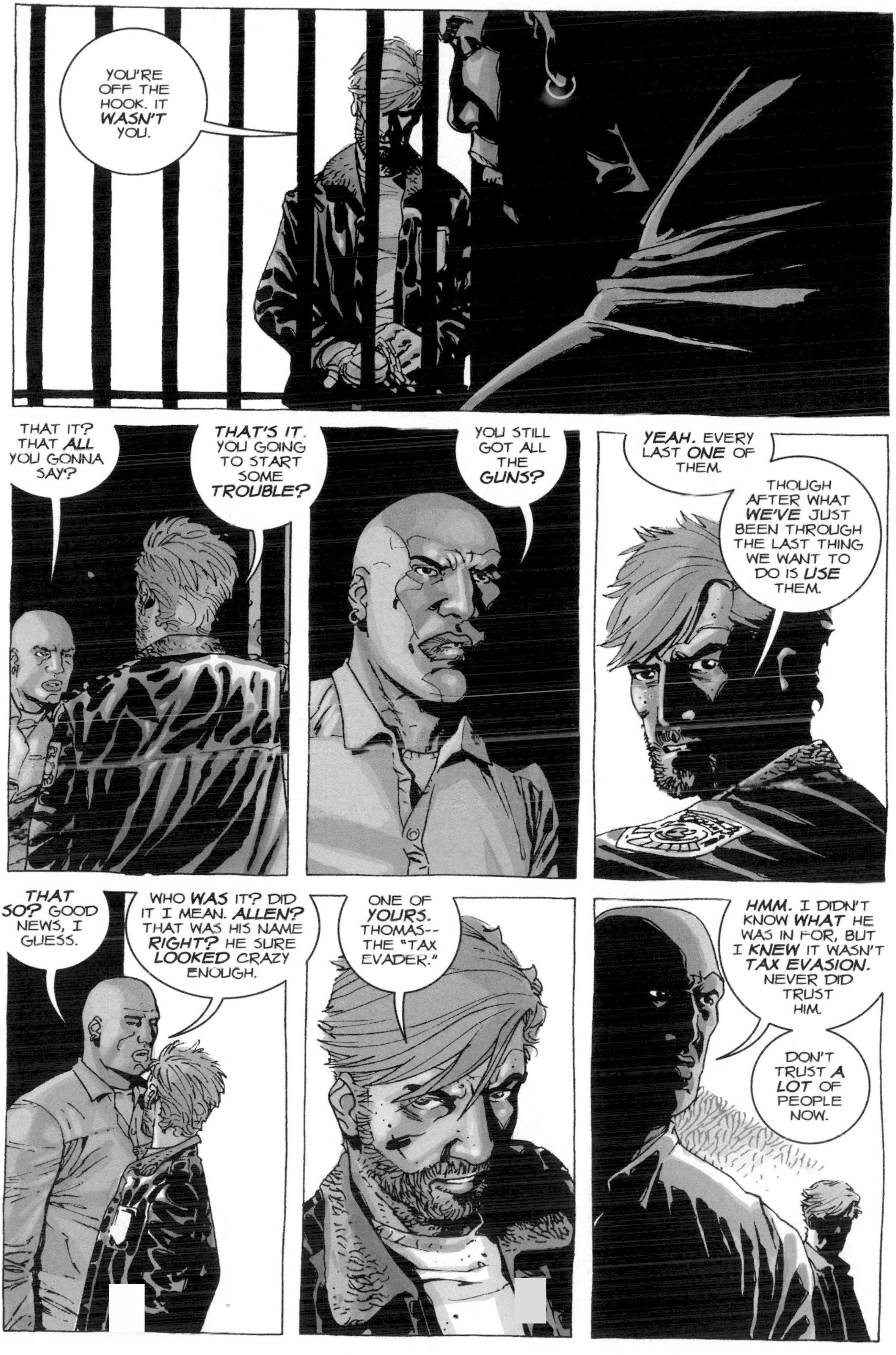
YOU'RE OFF THE HOOK. IT WASN'T YOU.
THAT IT? THAT ALL YOU GONNA SAY?
THAT'S IT. YOU GOING TO START SOME TROUBLE?
YOU STILL GOT ALL THE GUNS?
YEAH. EVERY LAST ONE OF THEM.
THOUGH AFTER WHAT WE'VE JUST BEEN THROUGH THE LAST THING WE WANT TO DO IS USE THEM.
THAT SO? GOOD NEWS, I GUESS.
WHO WAS IT? DID IT I MEAN. ALLEN? THAT WAS HIS NAME RIGHT? HE SURE LOOKED CRAZY ENOUGH.
ONE OF YOURS. THOMAS-- THE "TAX EVADER."
HMM. I DIDN'T KNOW WHAT HE WAS IN FOR, BUT I KNEW IT WASN'T TAX EVASION. NEVER DID TRUST HIM.
DON'T TRUST A LOT OF PEOPLE NOW.

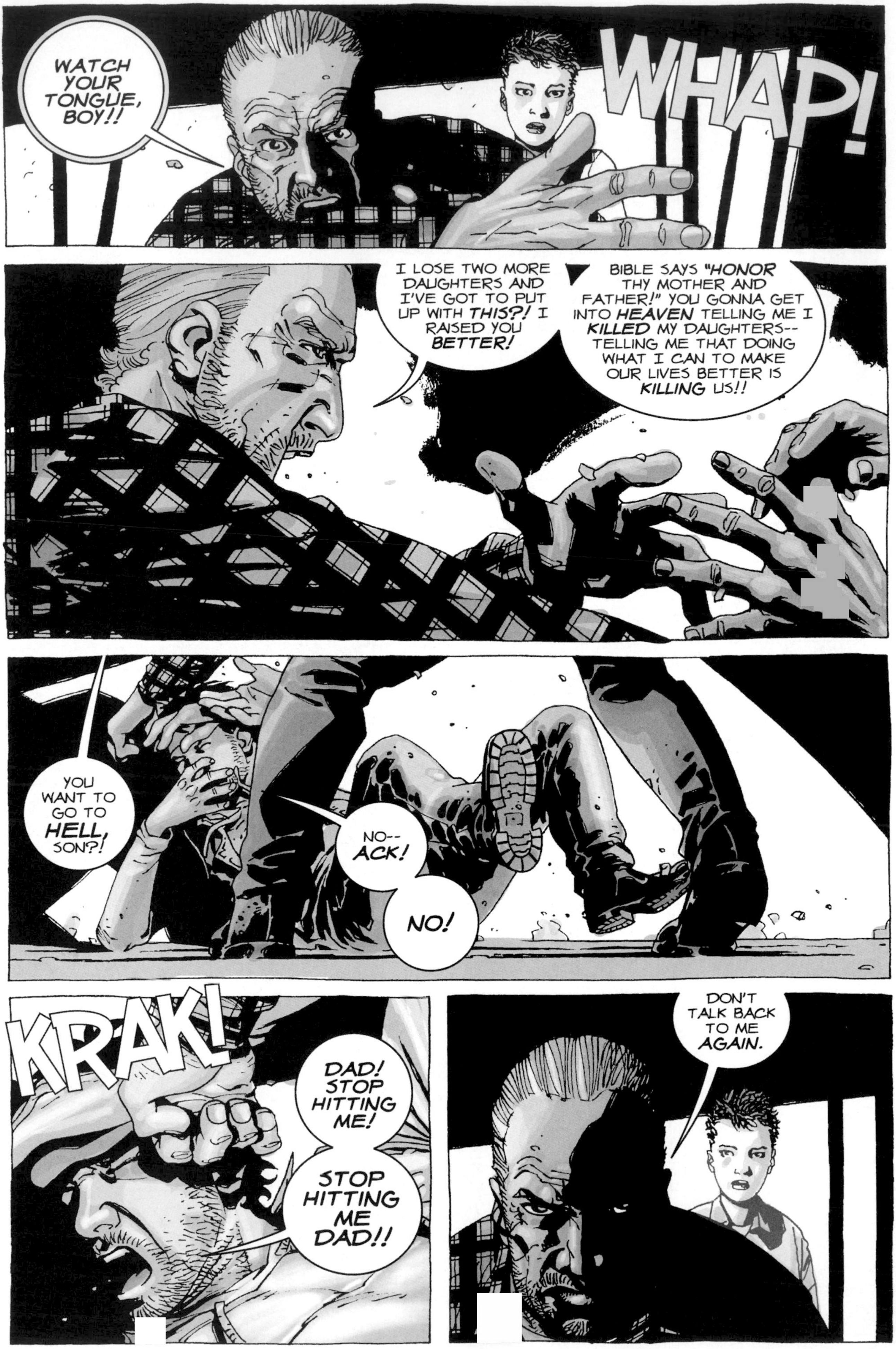
WATCH YOUR TONGUE, BOY!!
WHAP!
I LOSE TWO MORE DAUGHTERS AND I'VE GOT TO PUT UP WITH THIS?! I RAISED YOU BETTER!
BIBLE SAYS "HONOR THY MOTHER AND FATHER!" YOU GONNA GET INTO HEAVEN TELLING ME I KILLED MY DAUGHTERS-- TELLING ME THAT DOING WHAT I CAN TO MAKE OUR LIVES BETTER IS KILLING US!!
YOU WANT TO GO TO HELL, SON?!
NO-- ACK!
NO!
KRAK!
DAD! STOP HITTING ME!
STOP HITTING ME DAD!!
DON'T TALK BACK TO ME AGAIN.

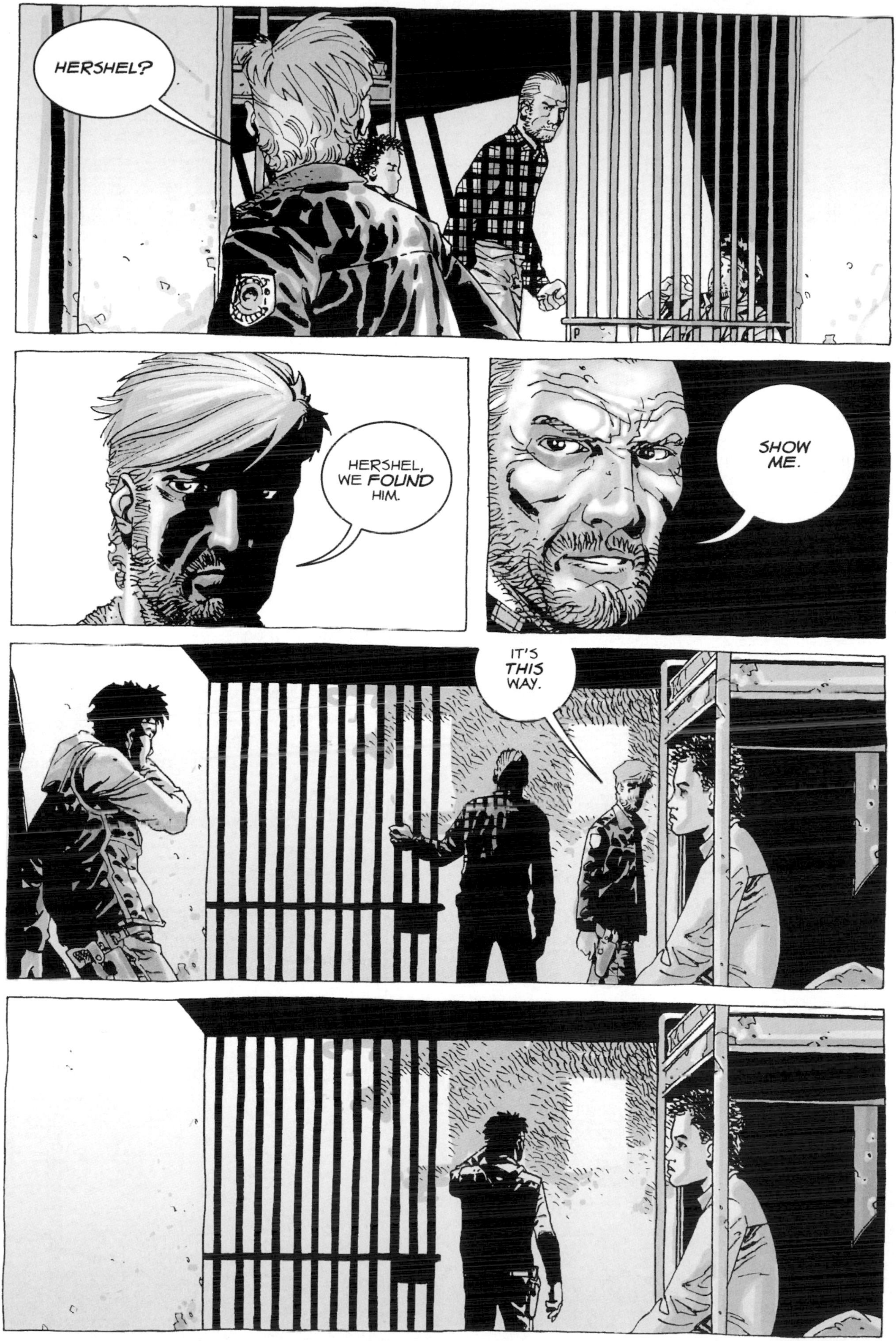
HERSHEL?
HERSHEL, WE FOUND HIM.
SHOW ME.
IT'S THIS WAY.

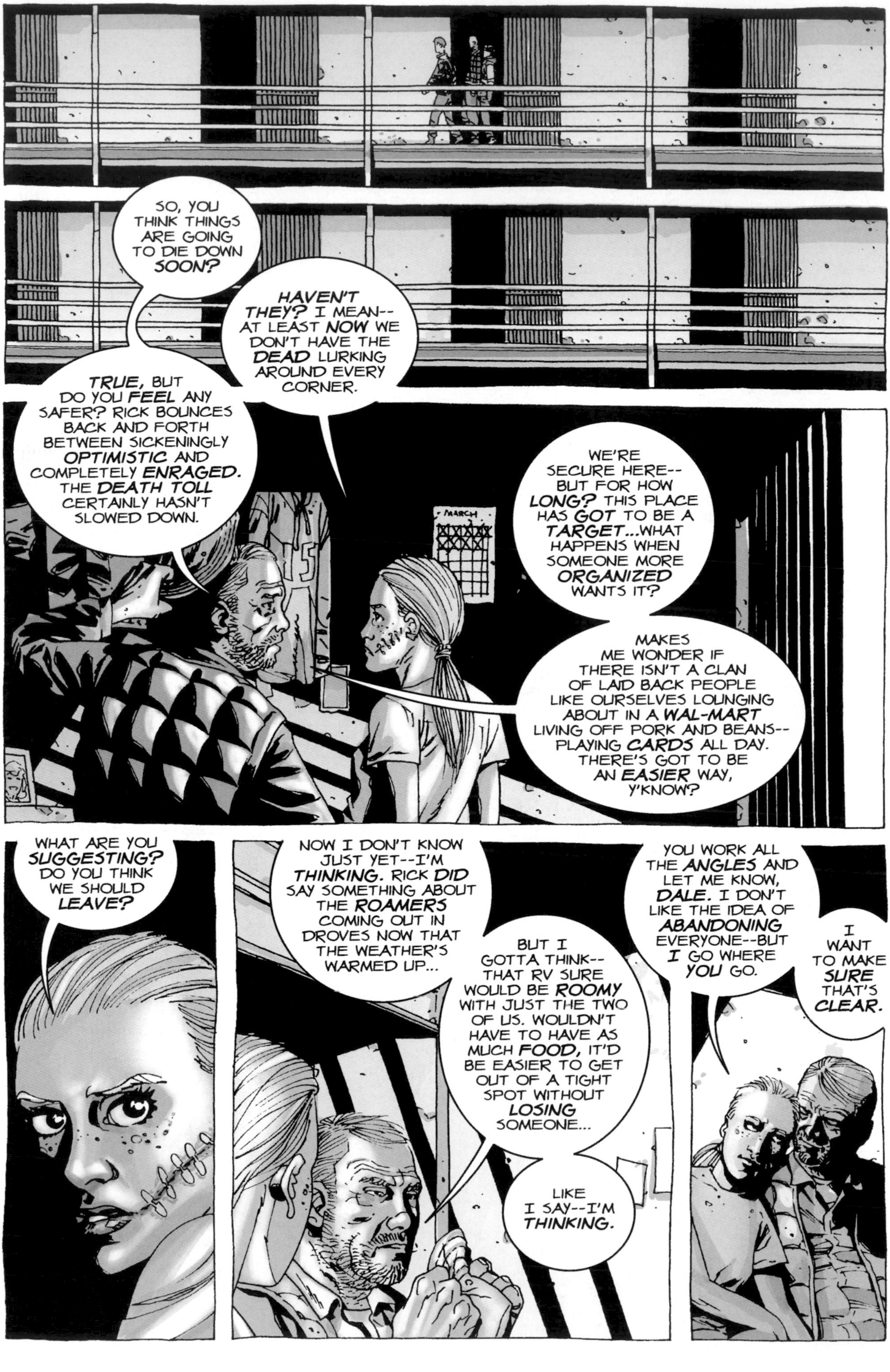
SO, YOU THINK THINGS ARE GOING TO DIE DOWN SOON?
HAVEN'T THEY? I MEAN-- AT LEAST NOW WE DON'T HAVE THE DEAD LURKING AROUND EVERY CORNER.
TRUE, BUT DO YOU FEEL ANY SAFER? RICK BOUNCES BACK AND FORTH BETWEEN SICKENINGLY OPTIMISTIC AND COMPLETELY ENRAGED. THE DEATH TOLL CERTAINLY HASN'T SLOWED DOWN.
MARCH
WE'RE SECURE HERE-- BUT FOR HOW LONG? THIS PLACE HAS GOT TO BE A TARGET...WHAT HAPPENS WHEN SOMEONE MORE ORGANIZED WANTS IT?
MAKES ME WONDER IF THERE ISN'T A CLAN OF LAID BACK PEOPLE LIKE OURSELVES LOUNGING ABOUT IN A WAL-MART LIVING OFF PORK AND BEANS-- PLAYING CARDS ALL DAY. THERE'S GOT TO BE AN EASIER WAY, Y'KNOW?
WHAT ARE YOU SUGGESTING? DO YOU THINK WE SHOULD LEAVE?
NOW I DON'T KNOW JUST YET--I'M THINKING. RICK DID SAY SOMETHING ABOUT THE ROAMERS COMING OUT IN DROVES NOW THAT THE WEATHER'S WARMED UP...
BUT I GOTTA THINK-- THAT RV SURE WOULD BE ROOMY WITH JUST THE TWO OF US. WOULDN'T HAVE TO HAVE AS MUCH FOOD, IT'D BE EASIER TO GET OUT OF A TIGHT SPOT WITHOUT LOSING SOMEONE...
LIKE I SAY--I'M THINKING.
YOU WORK ALL THE ANGLES AND LET ME KNOW, DALE. I DON'T LIKE THE IDEA OF ABANDONING EVERYONE--BUT I GO WHERE YOU GO.
I WANT TO MAKE SURE THAT'S CLEAR.

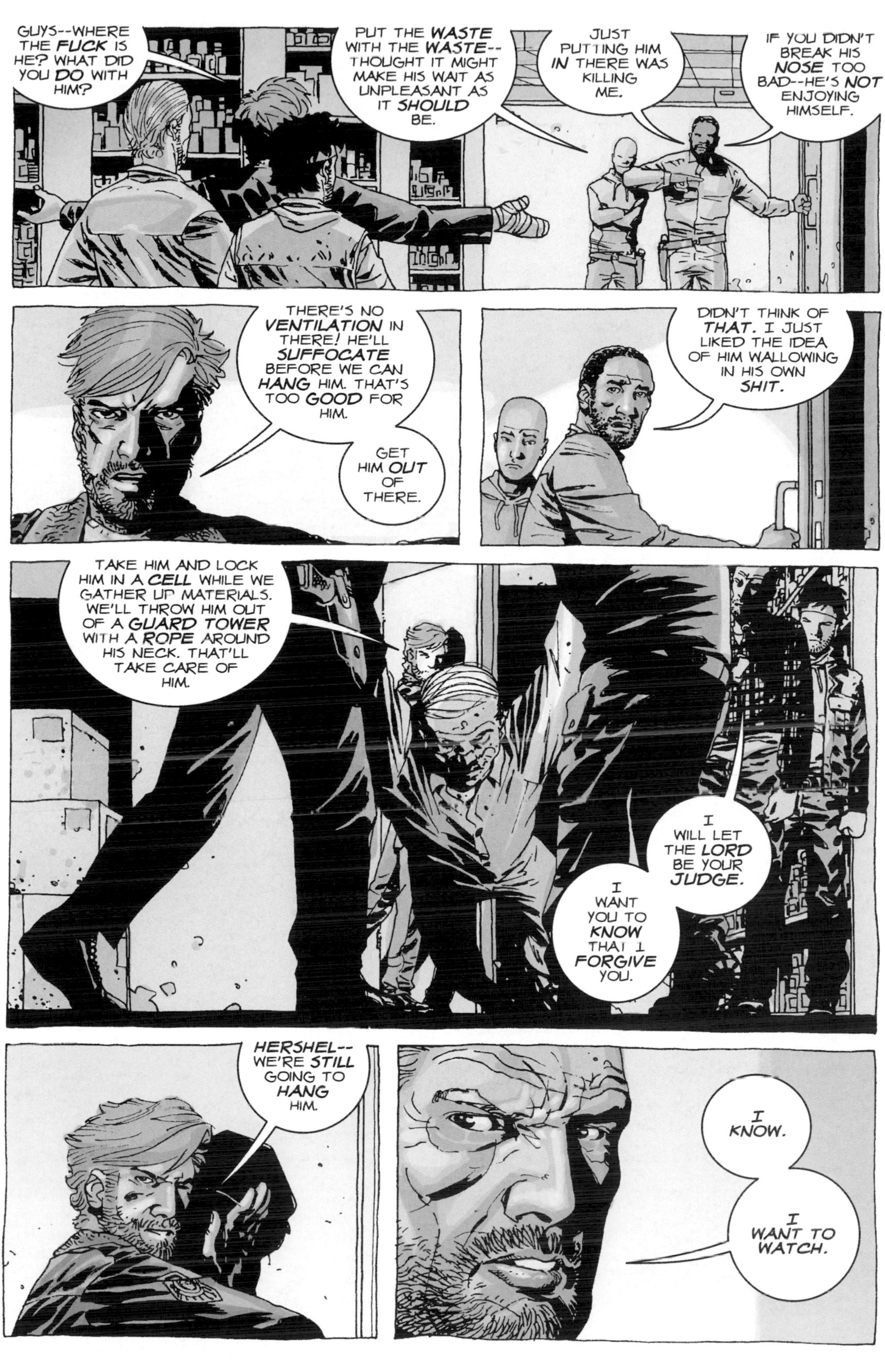
GUYS--WHERE THE FUCK IS HE? WHAT DID YOU DO WITH HIM?
PUT THE WASTE WITH THE WASTE--THOUGHT IT MIGHT MAKE HIS WAIT AS UNPLEASANT AS IT SHOULD BE.
JUST PUTTING HIM IN THERE WAS KILLING ME.
IF YOU DIDN'T BREAK HIS NOSE TOO BAD--HE'S NOT ENJOYING HIMSELF.
THERE'S NO VENTILATION IN THERE! HE'LL SUFFOCATE BEFORE WE CAN HANG HIM. THAT'S TOO GOOD FOR HIM.
GET HIM OUT OF THERE.
DIDN'T THINK OF THAT. I JUST LIKED THE IDEA OF HIM WALLOWING IN HIS OWN SHIT.
TAKE HIM AND LOCK HIM IN A CELL WHILE WE GATHER UP MATERIALS. WE'LL THROW HIM OUT OF A GUARD TOWER WITH A ROPE AROUND HIS NECK. THAT'LL TAKE CARE OF HIM.
I WANT YOU TO KNOW THAT I FORGIVE YOU.
I WILL LET THE LORD BE YOUR JUDGE.
HERSHEL--WE'RE STILL GOING TO HANG HIM.
I KNOW.
I WANT TO WATCH.

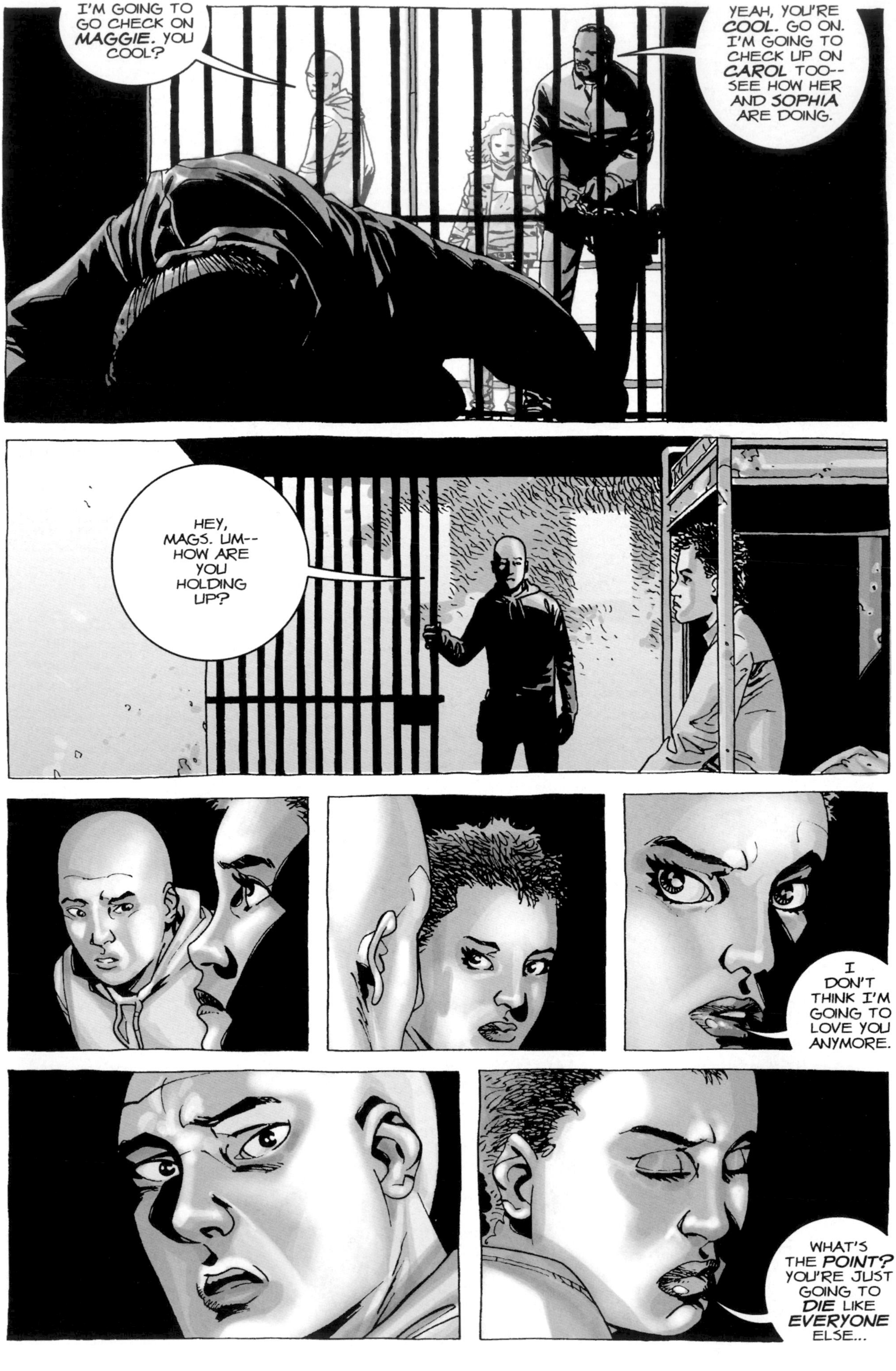
I'M GOING TO GO CHECK ON MAGGIE. YOU COOL?
YEAH, YOU'RE COOL. GO ON. I'M GOING TO CHECK UP ON CAROL TOO-- SEE HOW HER AND SOPHIA ARE DOING.
HEY, MAGS. UM-- HOW ARE YOU HOLDING UP?
I DON'T THINK I'M GOING TO LOVE YOU ANYMORE.
WHAT'S THE POINT? YOU'RE JUST GOING TO DIE LIKE EVERYONE ELSE...

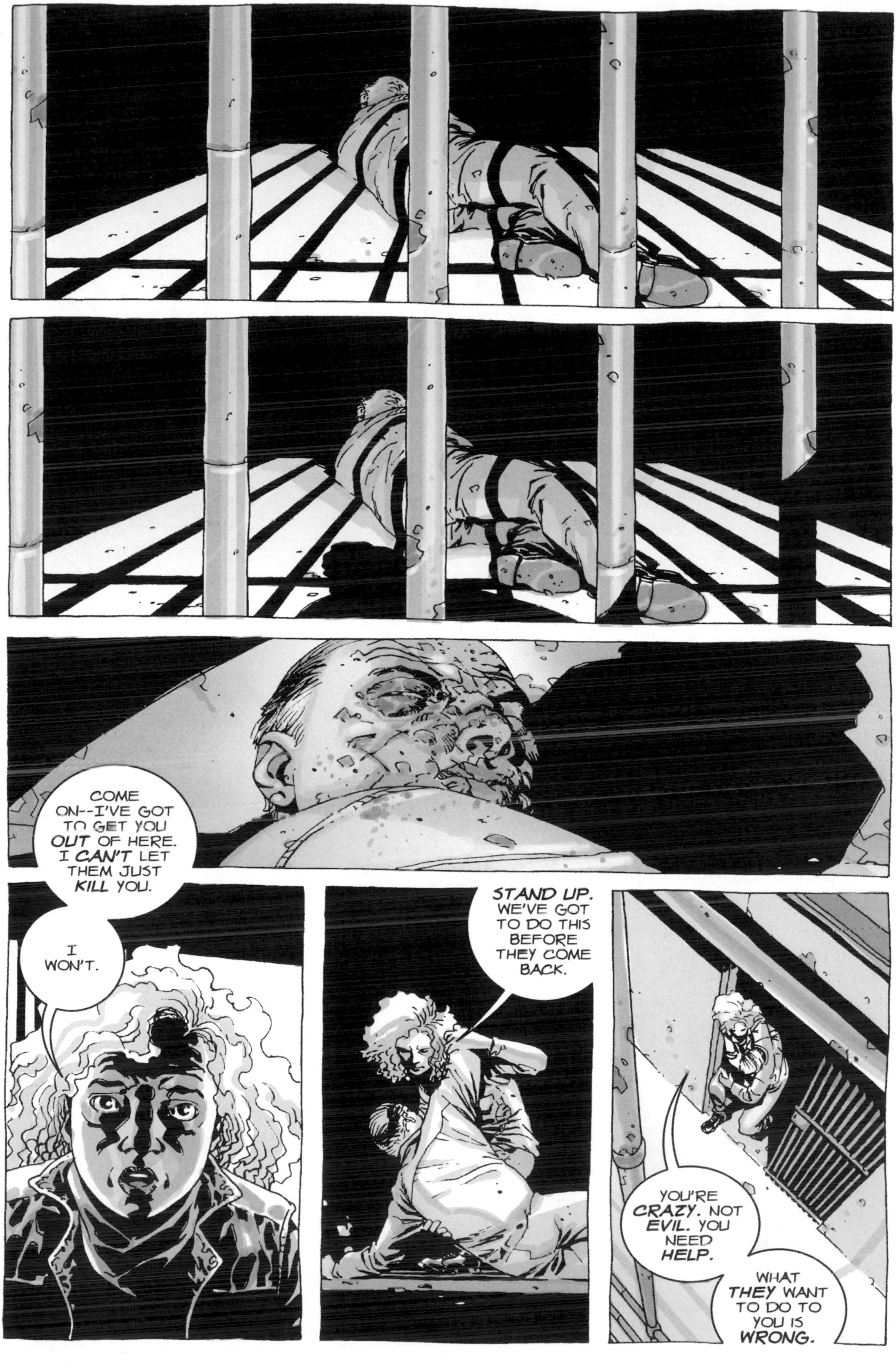
COME ON--I'VE GOT TO GET YOU OUT OF HERE. I CAN'T LET THEM JUST KILL YOU.
I WON'T.
STAND UP. WE'VE GOT TO DO THIS BEFORE THEY COME BACK.
YOU'RE CRAZY. NOT EVIL. YOU NEED HELP.
WHAT THEY WANT TO DO TO YOU IS WRONG.

=HUAKK!=

MRPHG RUAGH PHROAR!

WHUD!

HELP ME! SOMEBODY HELP!

HURGH! HUMPH!

WRAMM!

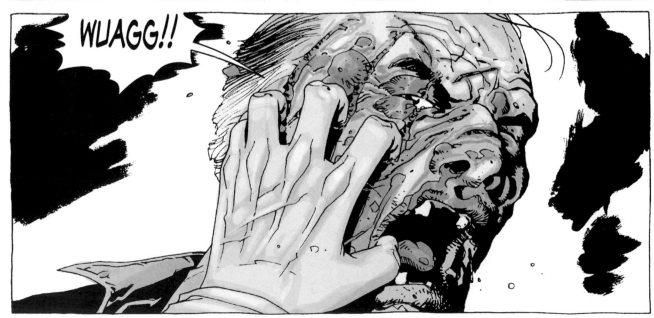

WUAGG!!

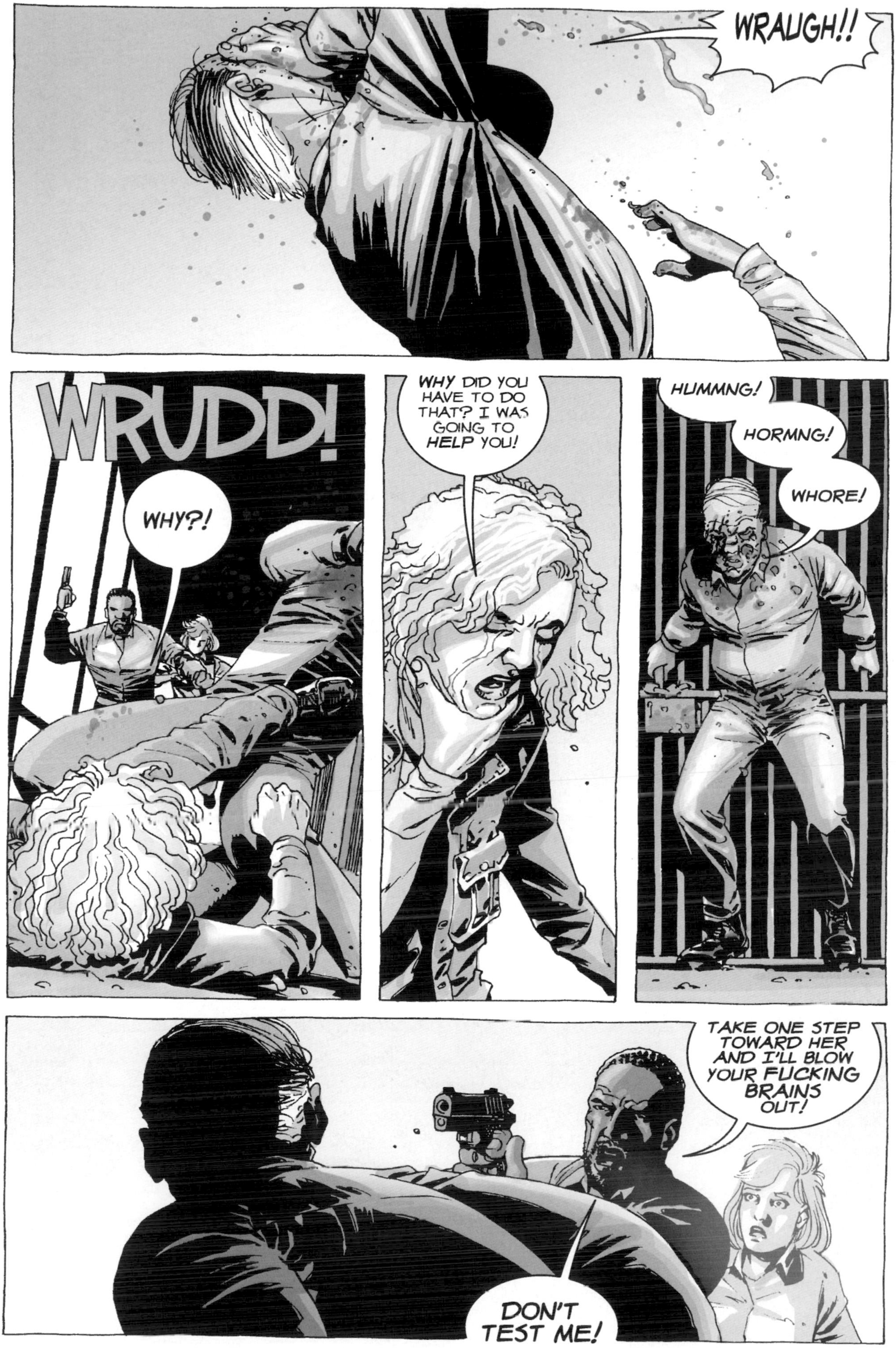
WRAUGH!!
WRUDD!
WHY?!
WHY DID YOU HAVE TO DO THAT? I WAS GOING TO HELP YOU!
HUMMNG!
HORMNG!
WHORE!
TAKE ONE STEP TOWARD HER AND I'LL BLOW YOUR FUCKING BRAINS OUT!
DON'T TEST ME!

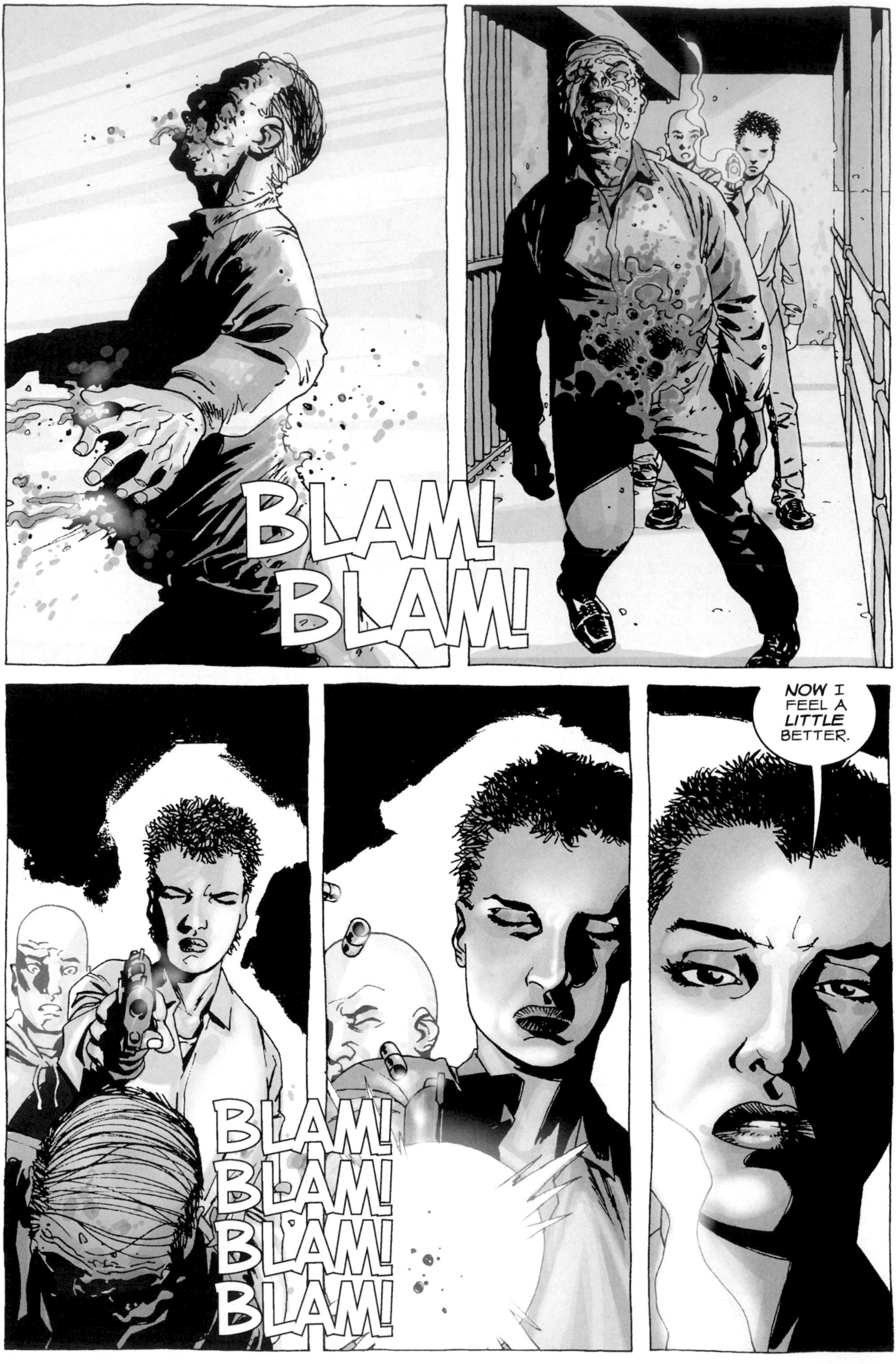

BLAM!
BLAM!
BLAM!
BLAM!
BLAM!
BLAM!
NOW I FEEL A LITTLE BETTER.

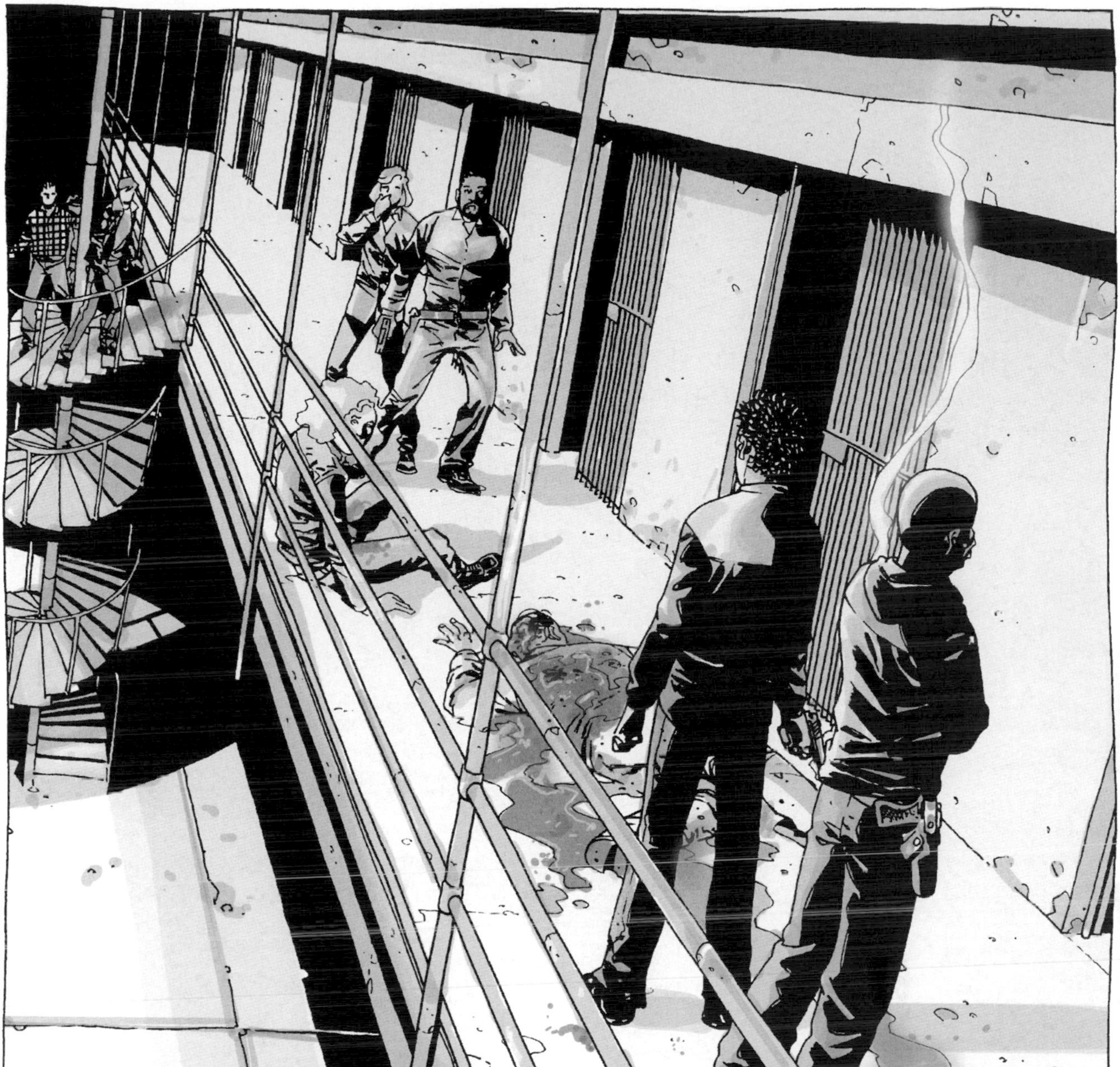
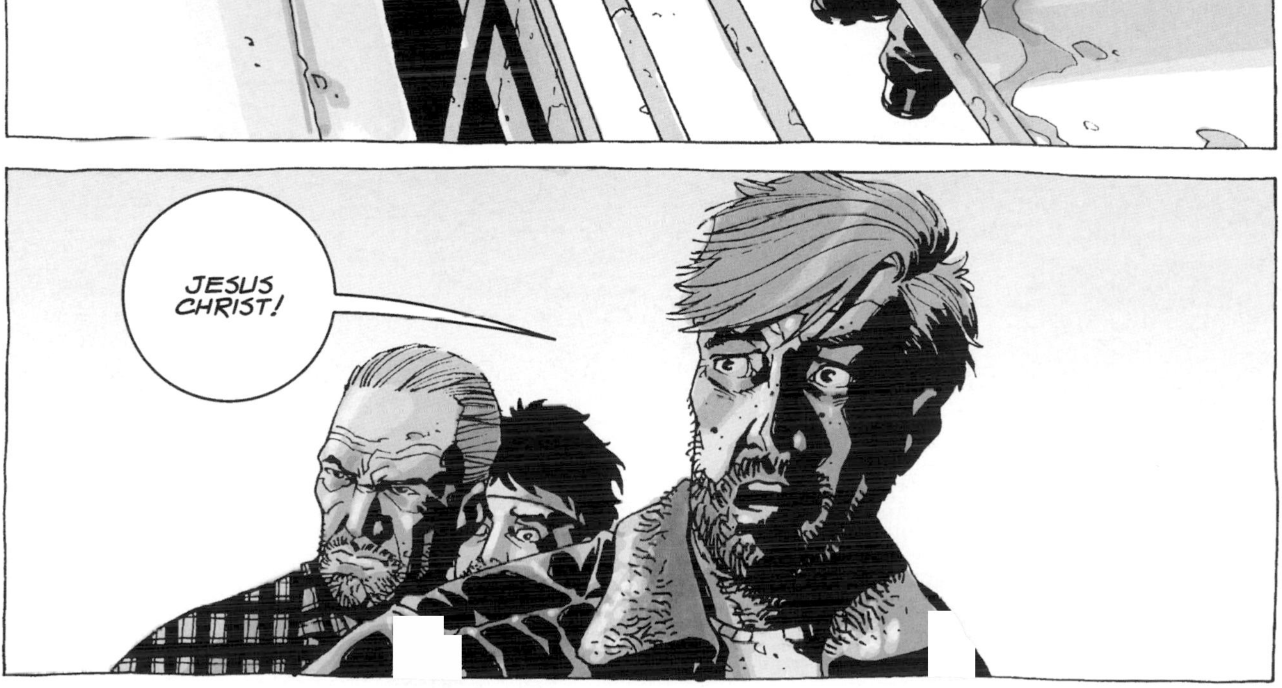
JESUS CHRIST!

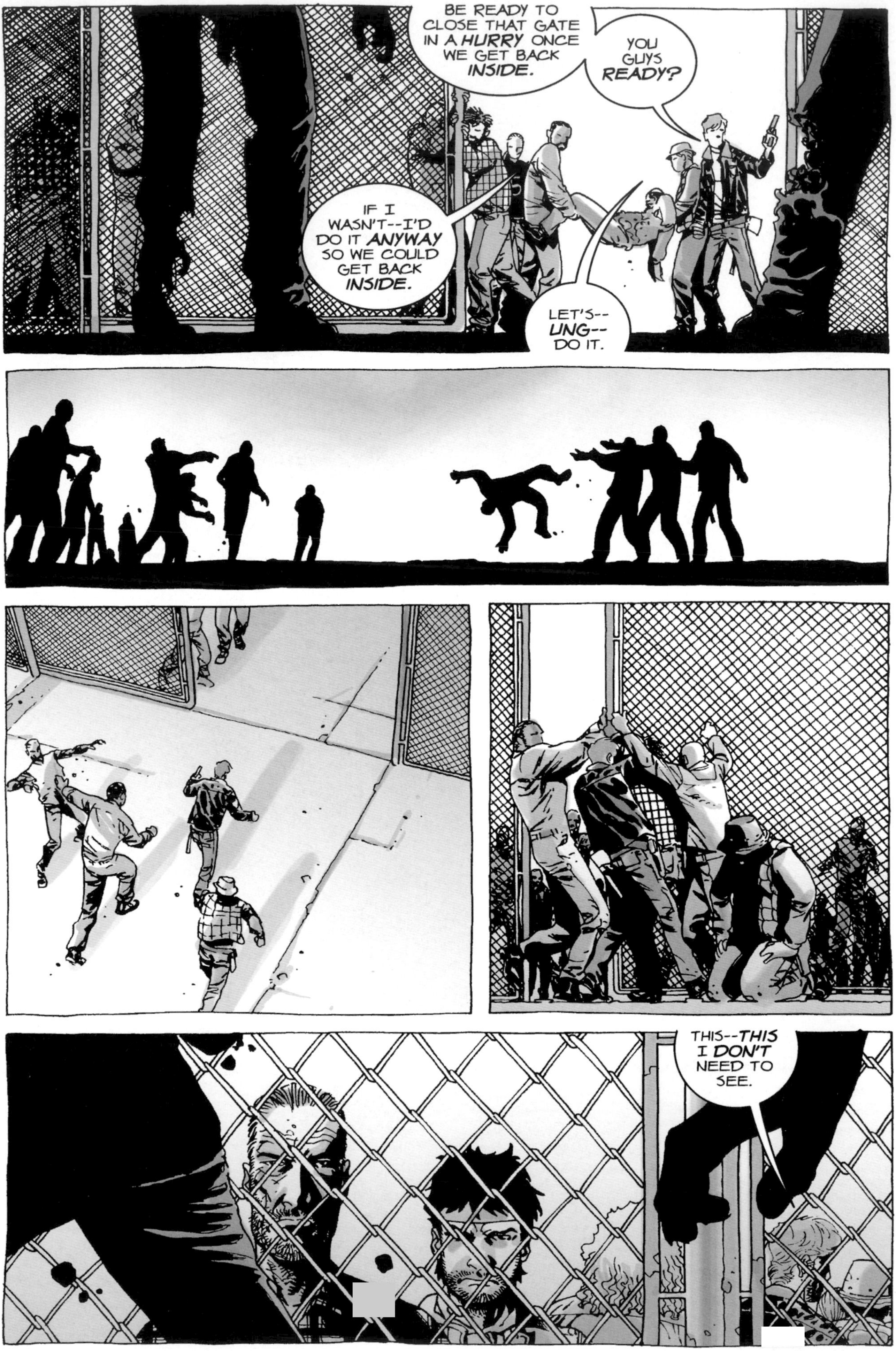
BE READY TO CLOSE THAT GATE IN A *HURRY* ONCE WE GET BACK *INSIDE.*
YOU GUYS *READY?*
IF I WASN'T--I'D DO IT *ANYWAY* SO WE COULD GET BACK *INSIDE.*
LET'S-- *UNG--* DO IT.
THIS--*THIS* I *DON'T* NEED TO SEE.

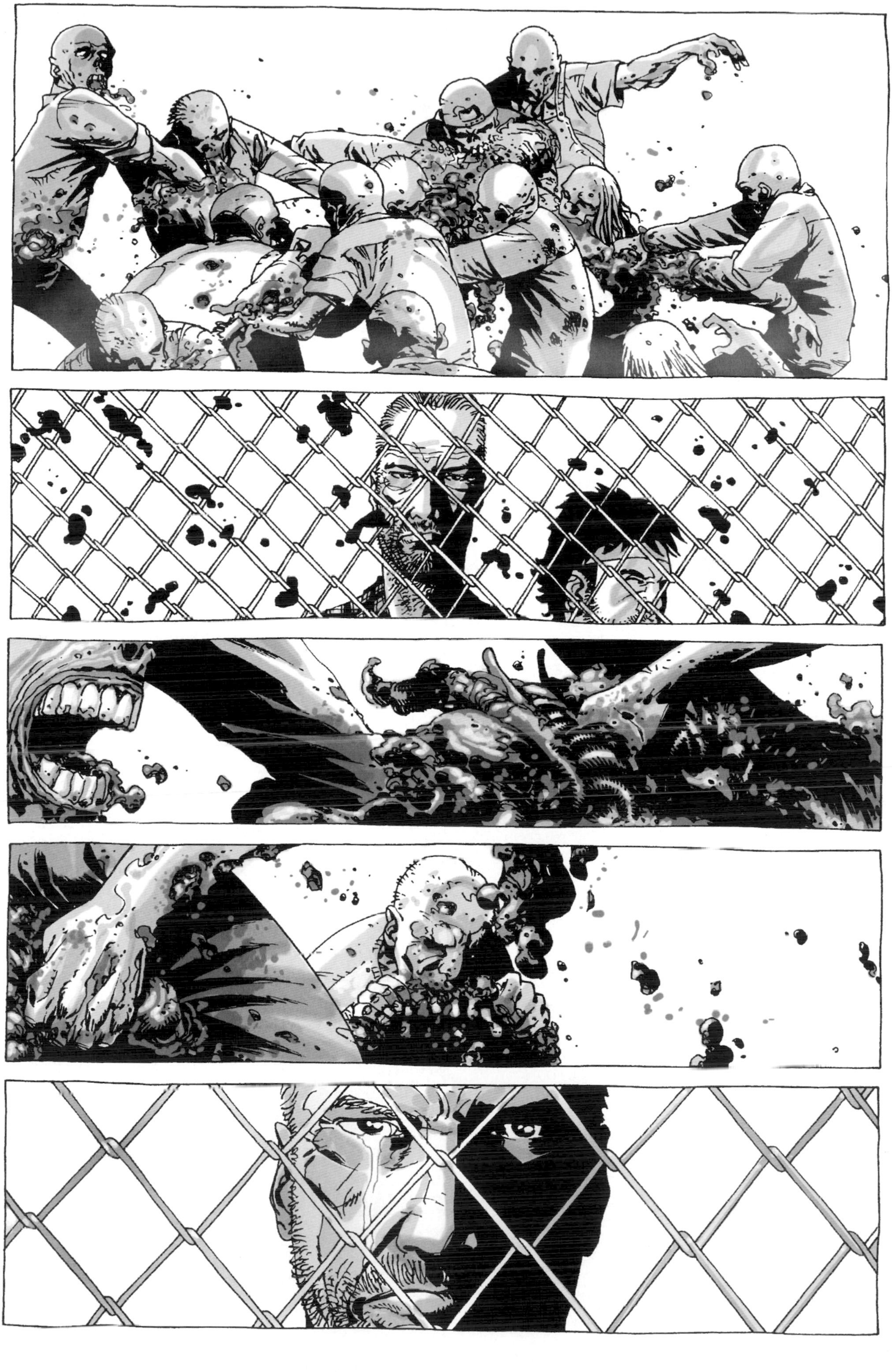

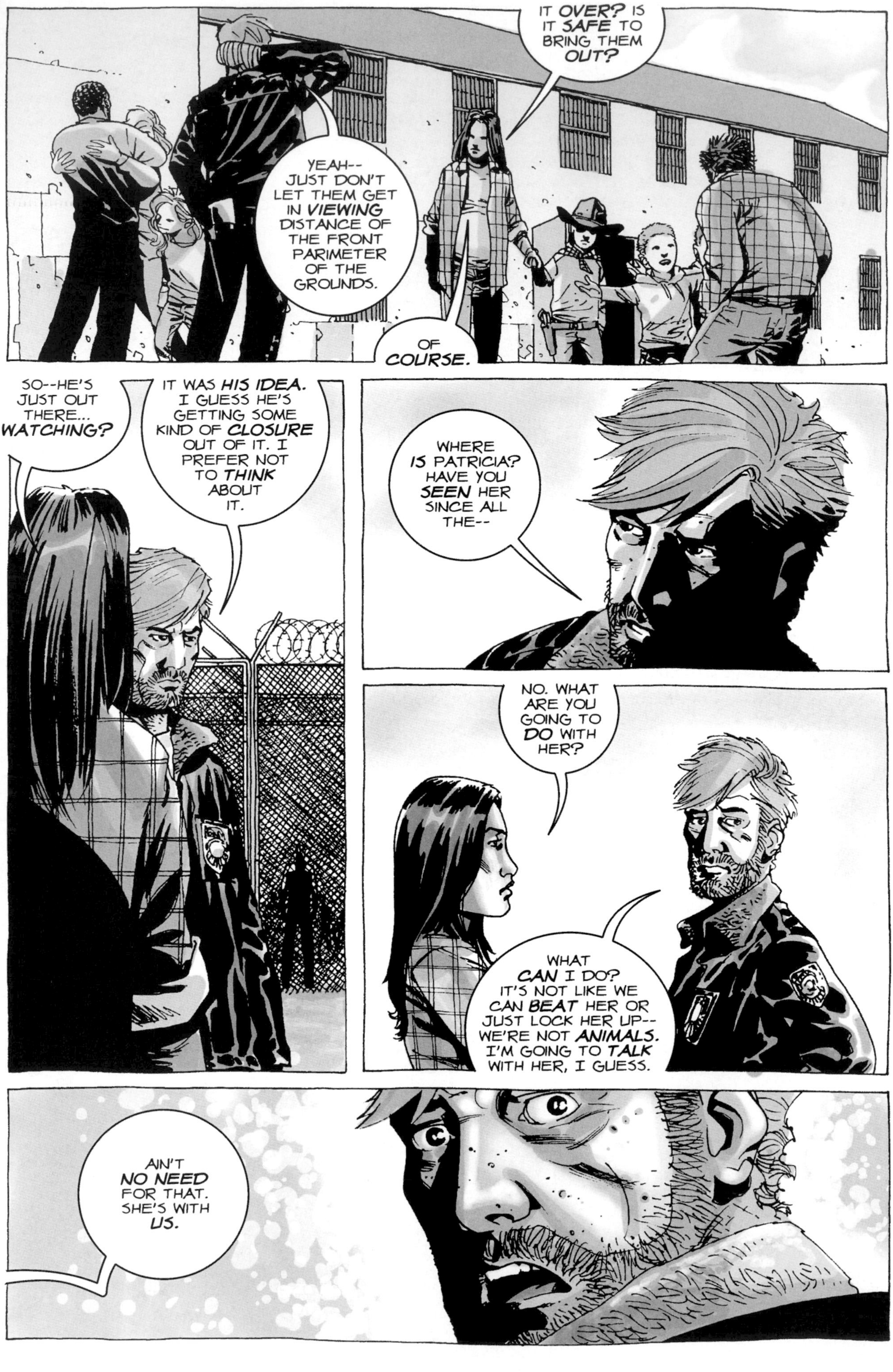
IT OVER? IS IT SAFE TO BRING THEM OUT?
YEAH-- JUST DON'T LET THEM GET IN VIEWING DISTANCE OF THE FRONT PARIMETER OF THE GROUNDS.
OF COURSE.
SO--HE'S JUST OUT THERE... WATCHING?
IT WAS HIS IDEA. I GUESS HE'S GETTING SOME KIND OF CLOSURE OUT OF IT. I PREFER NOT TO THINK ABOUT IT.
WHERE IS PATRICIA? HAVE YOU SEEN HER SINCE ALL THE--
NO. WHAT ARE YOU GOING TO DO WITH HER?
WHAT CAN I DO? IT'S NOT LIKE WE CAN BEAT HER OR JUST LOCK HER UP-- WE'RE NOT ANIMALS. I'M GOING TO TALK WITH HER, I GUESS.
AIN'T NO NEED FOR THAT. SHE'S WITH US.

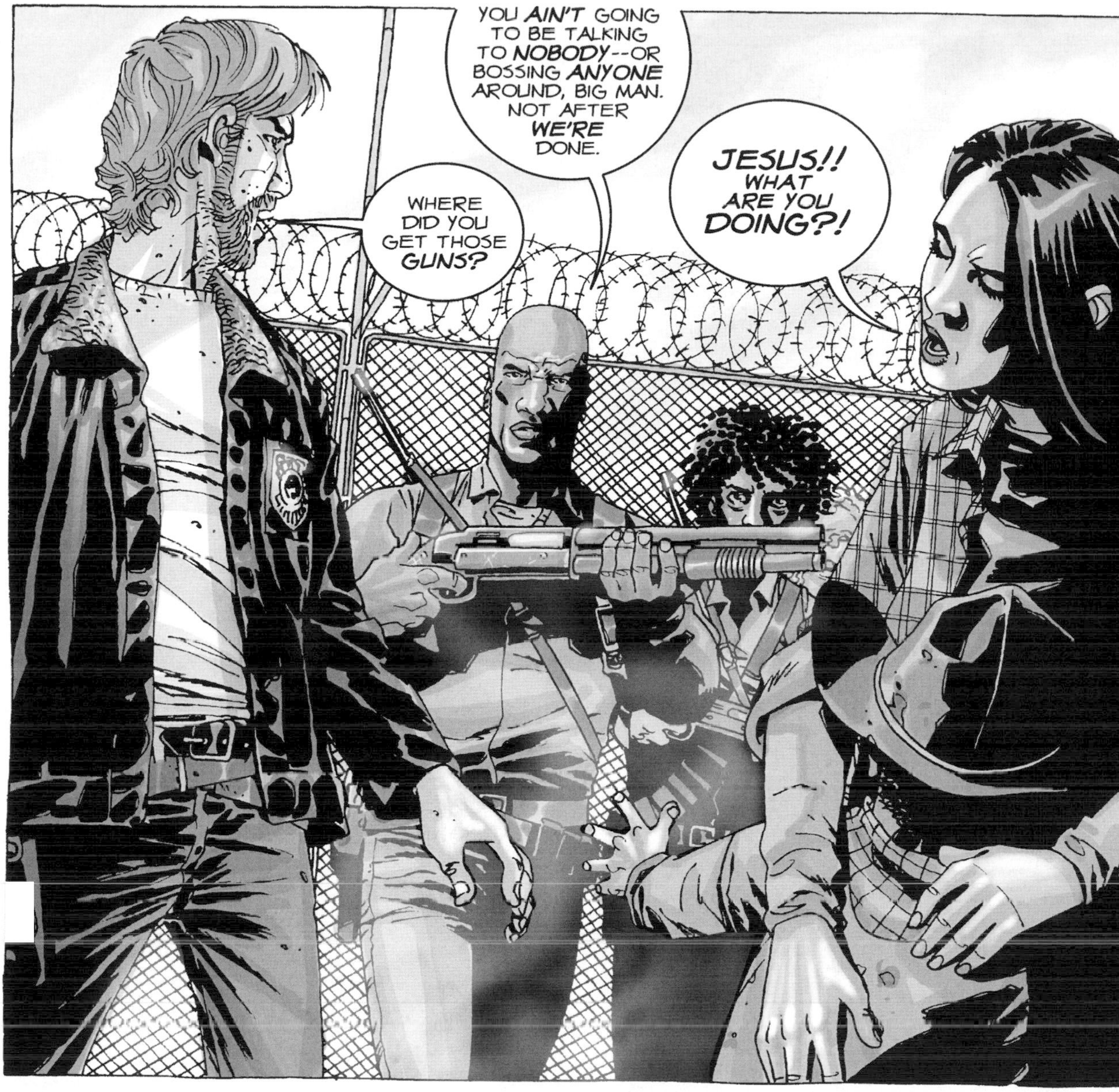
WHERE DID YOU GET THOSE GUNS?
YOU AIN'T GOING TO BE TALKING TO NOBODY--OR BOSSING ANYONE AROUND, BIG MAN. NOT AFTER WE'RE DONE.
JESUS!! WHAT ARE YOU DOING?!

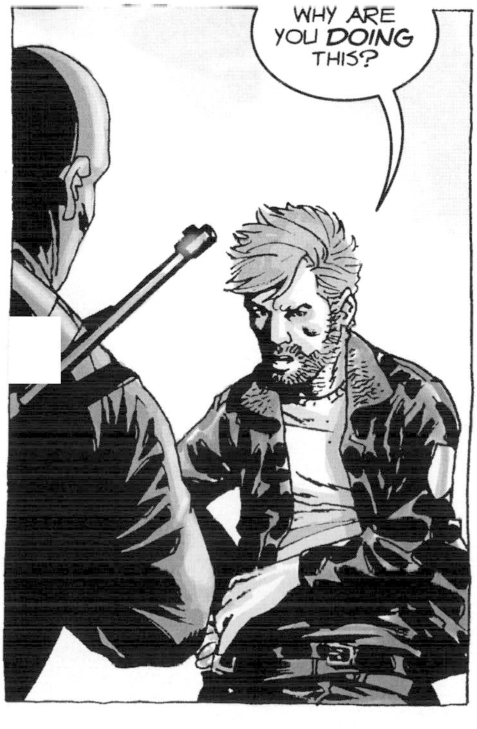
WHY ARE YOU DOING THIS?

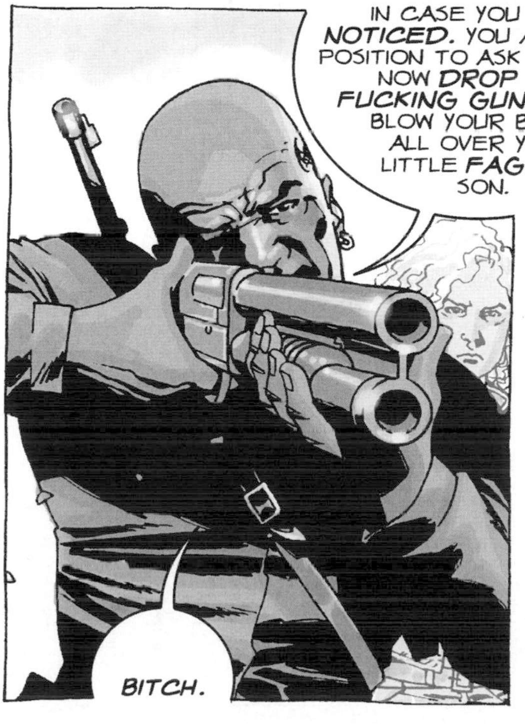
IN CASE YOU AIN'T NOTICED. YOU AIN'T IN A POSITION TO ASK ME SHIT. NOW DROP THAT FUCKING GUN OR I'LL BLOW YOUR BRAINS ALL OVER YOUR LITTLE FAGGOT SON.
BITCH.

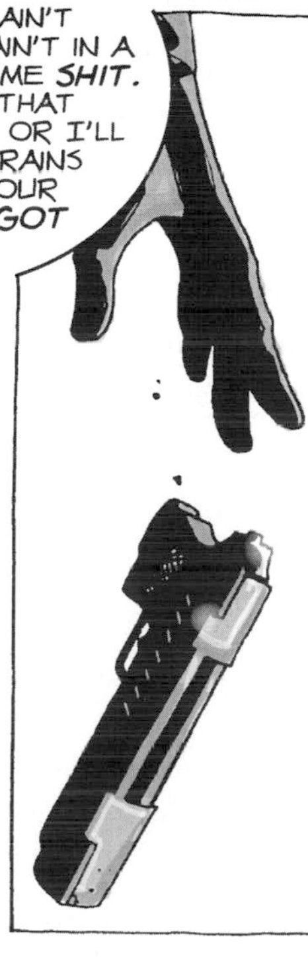

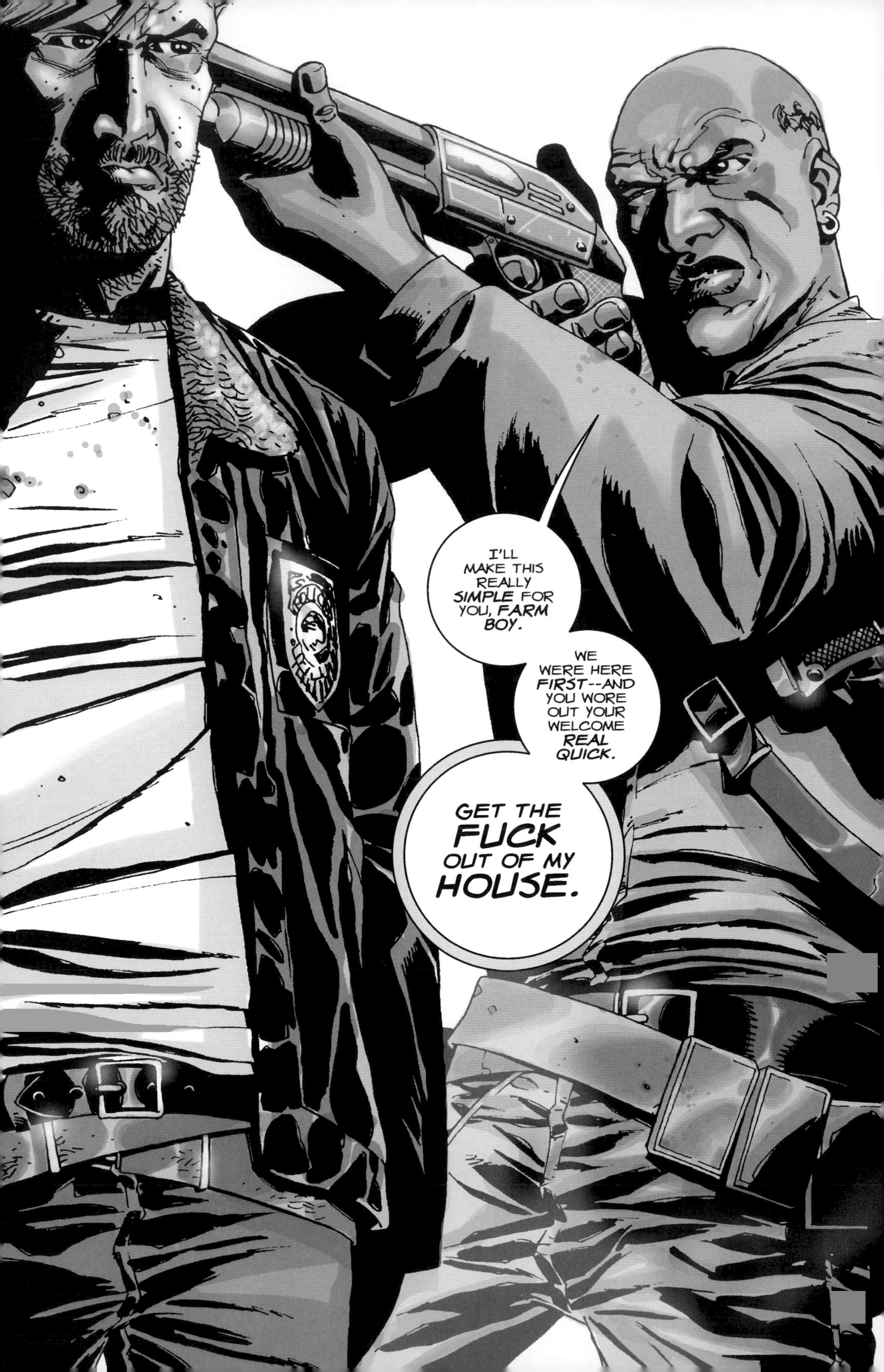

I'LL MAKE THIS REALLY SIMPLE FOR YOU, FARM BOY.
WE WERE HERE FIRST--AND YOU WORE OUT YOUR WELCOME REAL QUICK.
GET THE FUCK OUT OF MY HOUSE.

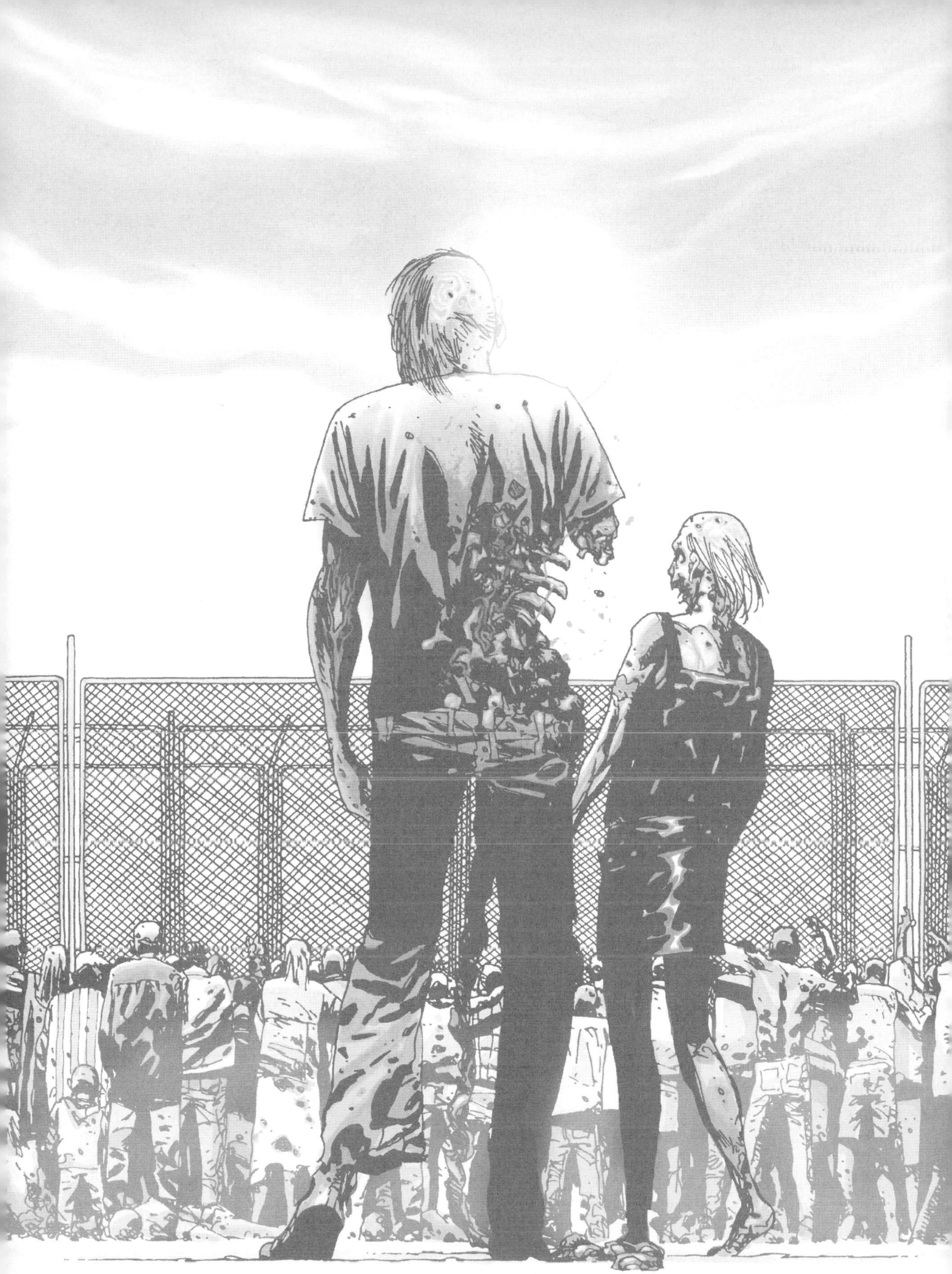

Chapter Four:
The Heart's Desire

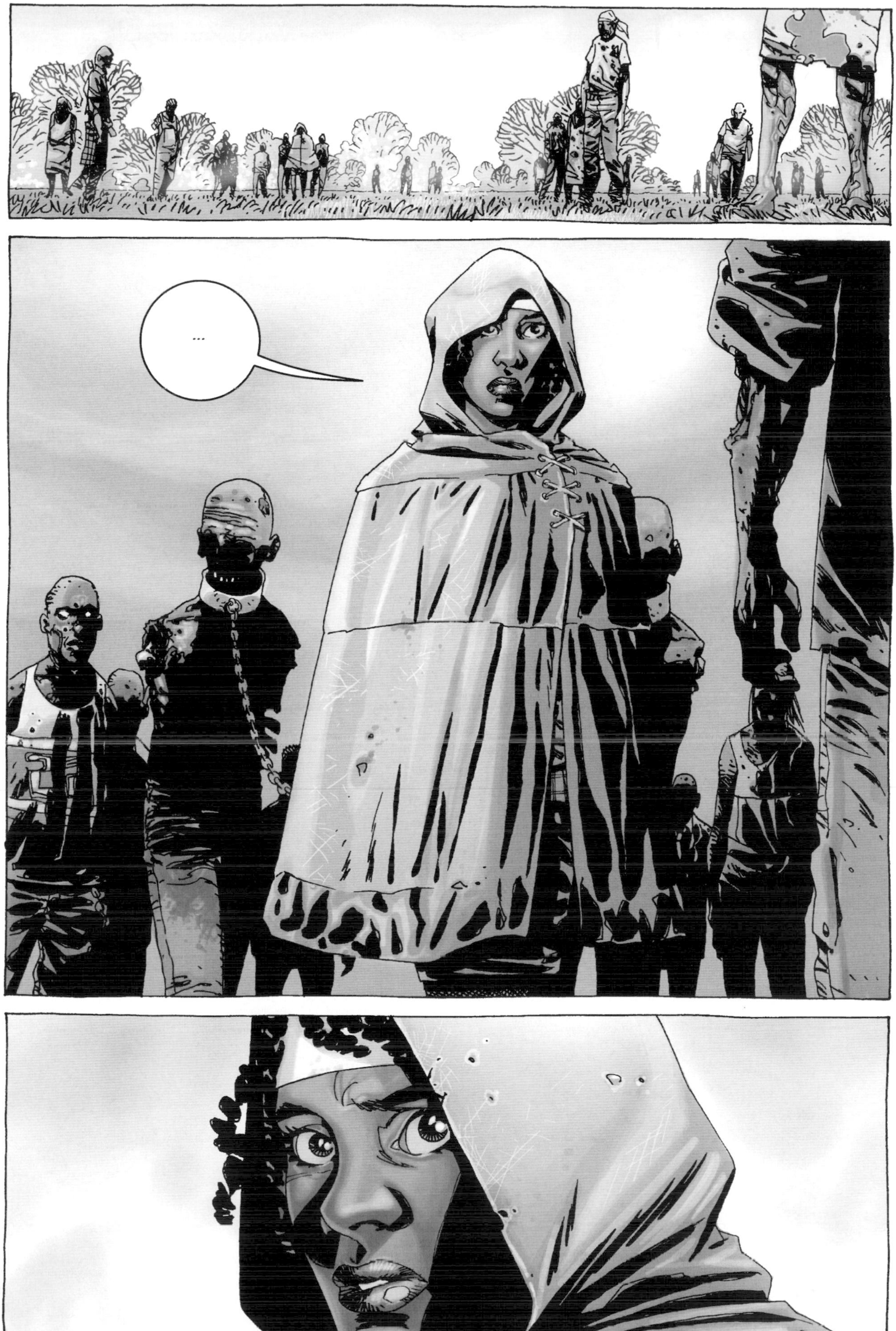
...

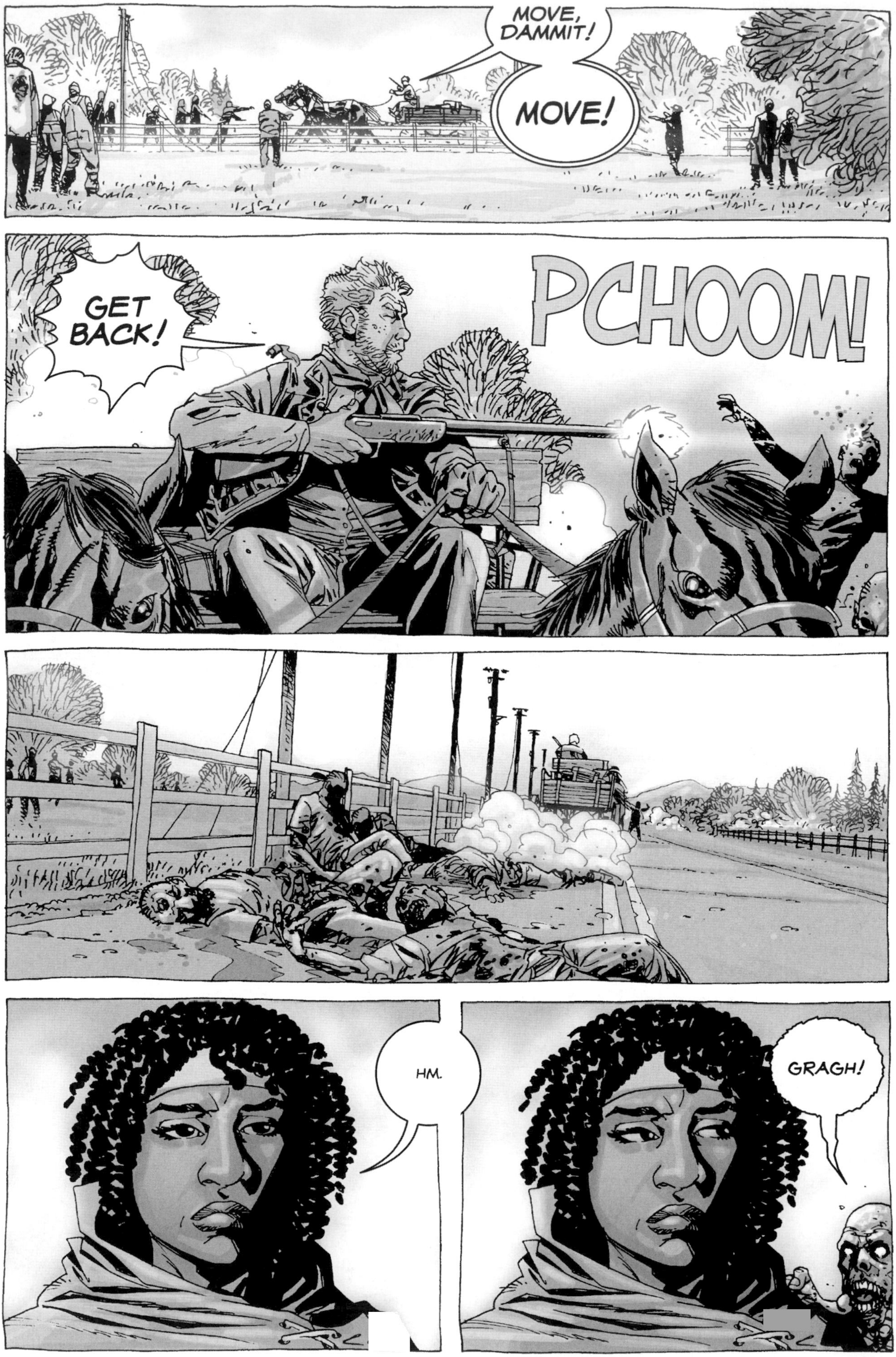
MOVE, DAMMIT!
MOVE!
GET BACK!
PCHOOM!
HM.
GRAGH!

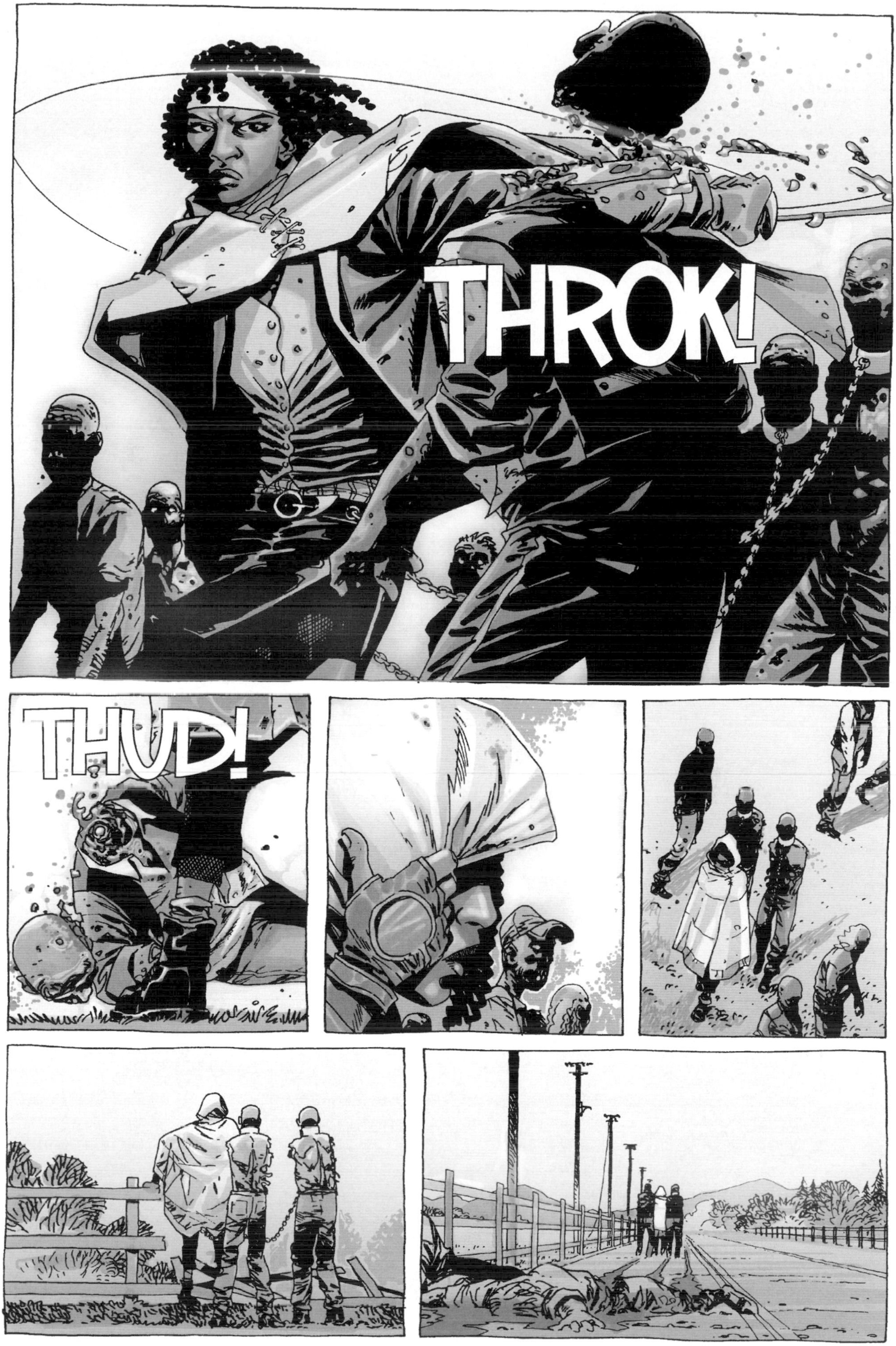
THROK!
THUD!

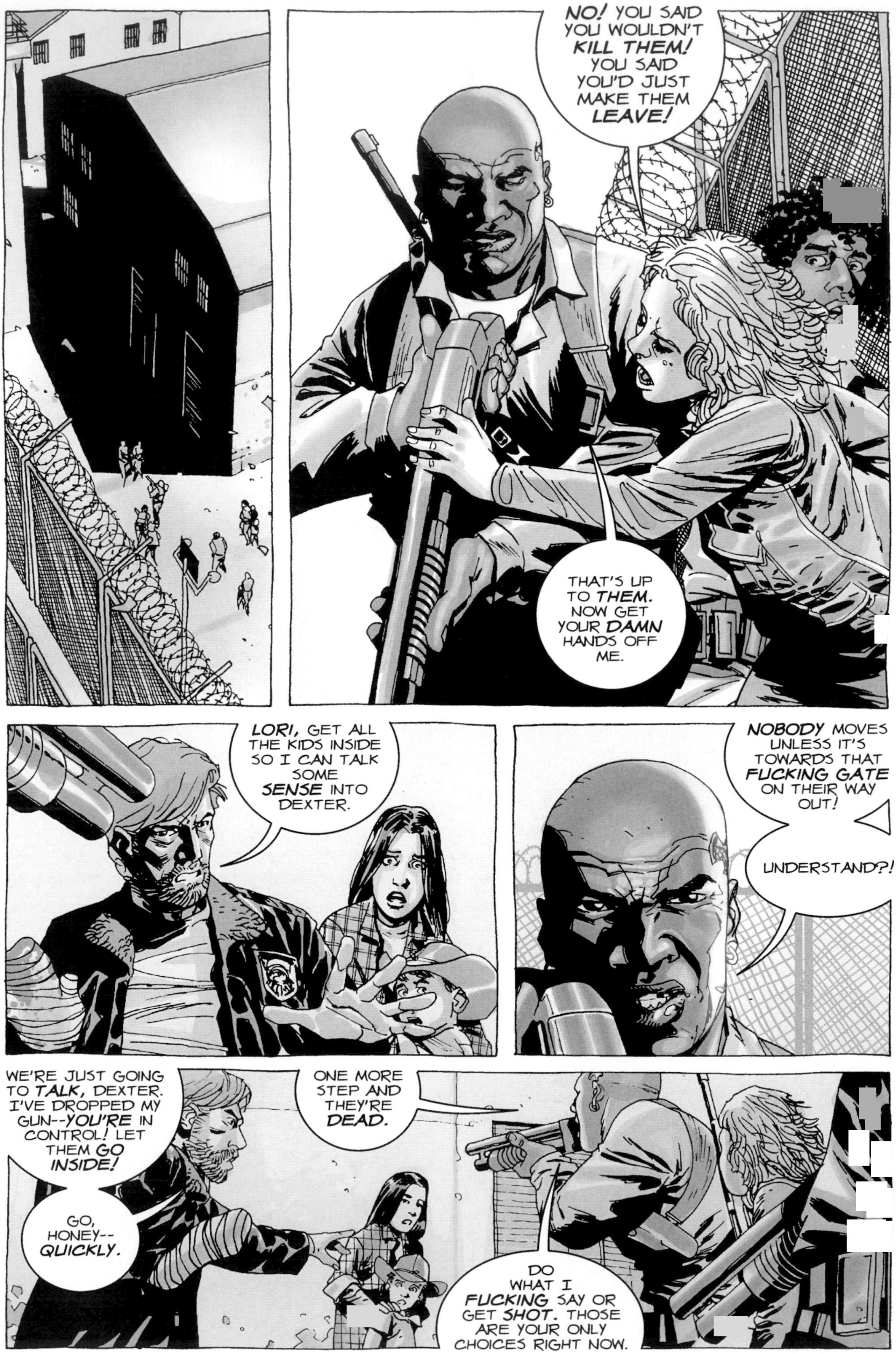

NO! YOU SAID YOU WOULDN'T KILL THEM! YOU SAID YOU'D JUST MAKE THEM LEAVE!
THAT'S UP TO THEM. NOW GET YOUR DAMN HANDS OFF ME.
LORI, GET ALL THE KIDS INSIDE SO I CAN TALK SOME SENSE INTO DEXTER.
NOBODY MOVES UNLESS IT'S TOWARDS THAT FUCKING GATE ON THEIR WAY OUT!
UNDERSTAND?!
WE'RE JUST GOING TO TALK, DEXTER. I'VE DROPPED MY GUN--YOU'RE IN CONTROL! LET THEM GO INSIDE!
ONE MORE STEP AND THEY'RE DEAD.
GO, HONEY--QUICKLY.
DO WHAT I FUCKING SAY OR GET SHOT. THOSE ARE YOUR ONLY CHOICES RIGHT NOW.

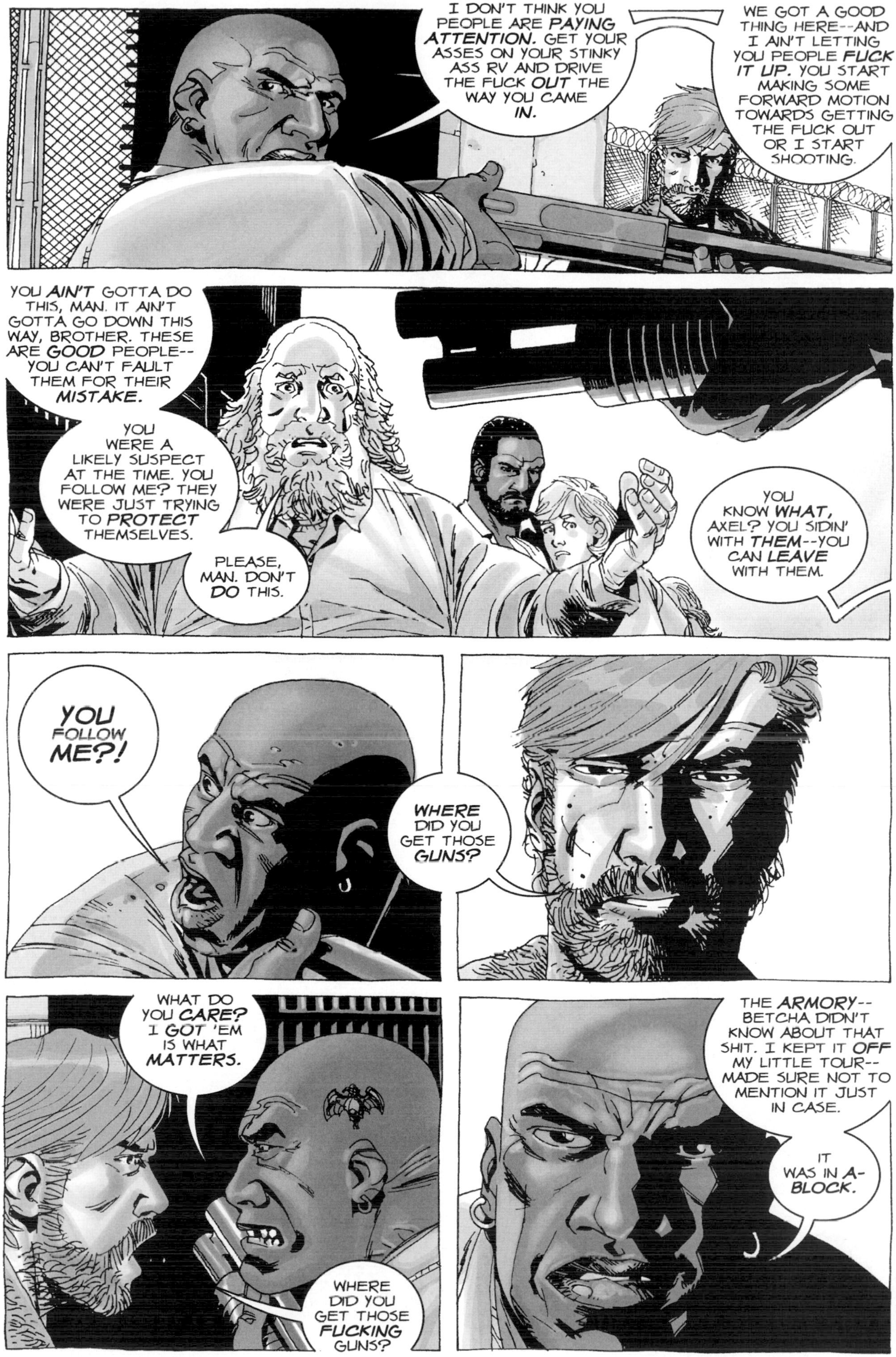
I DON'T THINK YOU PEOPLE ARE PAYING ATTENTION. GET YOUR ASSES ON YOUR STINKY ASS RV AND DRIVE THE FUCK OUT THE WAY YOU CAME IN.
WE GOT A GOOD THING HERE--AND I AIN'T LETTING YOU PEOPLE FUCK IT UP. YOU START MAKING SOME FORWARD MOTION TOWARDS GETTING THE FUCK OUT OR I START SHOOTING.
YOU AIN'T GOTTA DO THIS, MAN. IT AIN'T GOTTA GO DOWN THIS WAY, BROTHER. THESE ARE GOOD PEOPLE-- YOU CAN'T FAULT THEM FOR THEIR MISTAKE.
YOU WERE A LIKELY SUSPECT AT THE TIME. YOU FOLLOW ME? THEY WERE JUST TRYING TO PROTECT THEMSELVES.
PLEASE, MAN. DON'T DO THIS.
YOU KNOW WHAT, AXEL? YOU SIDIN' WITH THEM--YOU CAN LEAVE WITH THEM.
YOU FOLLOW ME?!
WHERE DID YOU GET THOSE GUNS?
WHAT DO YOU CARE? I GOT 'EM IS WHAT MATTERS.
WHERE DID YOU GET THOSE FUCKING GUNS?
THE ARMORY-- BETCHA DIDN'T KNOW ABOUT THAT SHIT. I KEPT IT OFF MY LITTLE TOUR-- MADE SURE NOT TO MENTION IT JUST IN CASE.
IT WAS IN A-BLOCK.

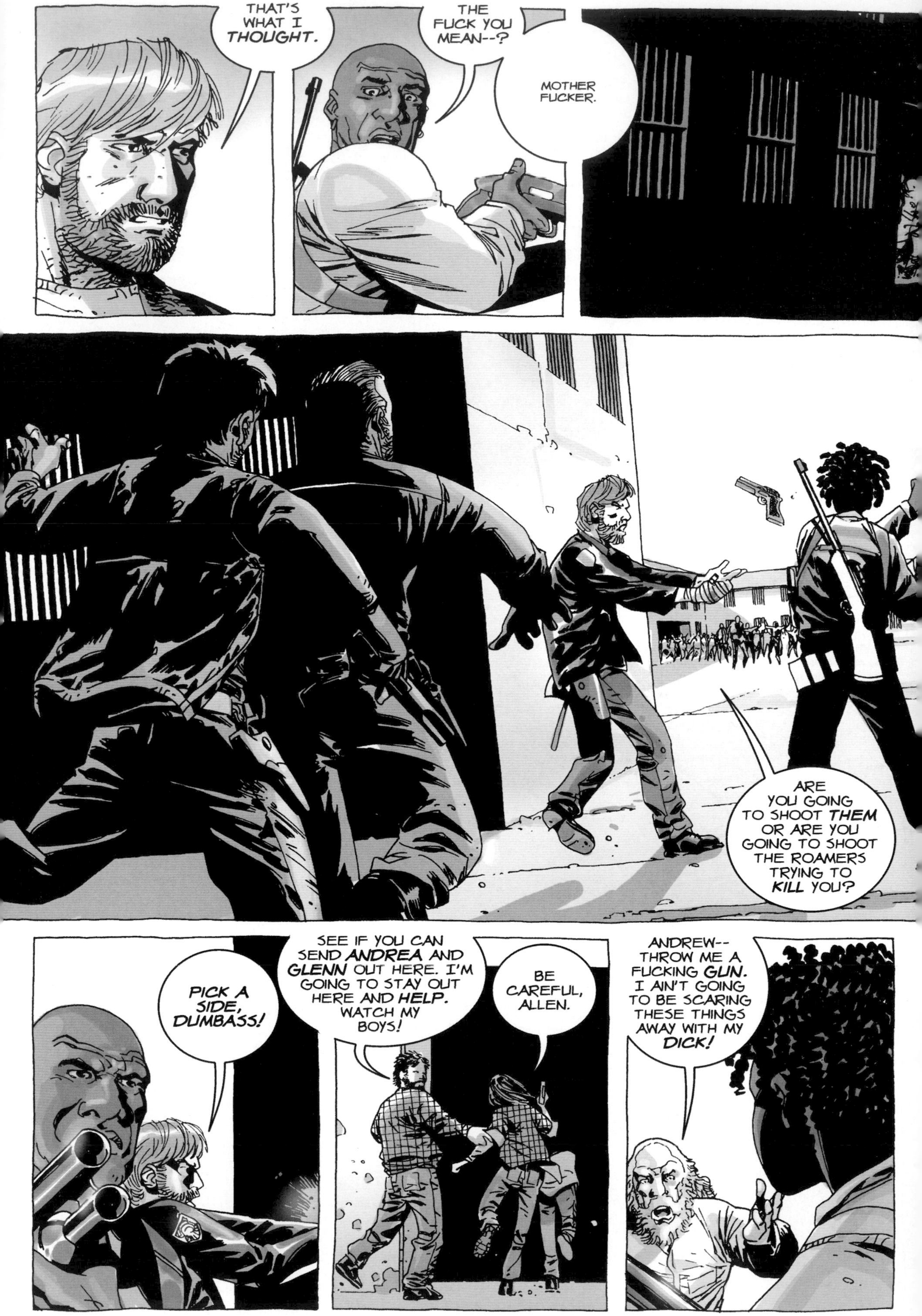
THAT'S WHAT I THOUGHT.
THE FUCK YOU MEAN--?
MOTHER FUCKER.
ARE YOU GOING TO SHOOT THEM OR ARE YOU GOING TO SHOOT THE ROAMERS TRYING TO KILL YOU?
PICK A SIDE, DUMBASS!
SEE IF YOU CAN SEND ANDREA AND GLENN OUT HERE. I'M GOING TO STAY OUT HERE AND HELP. WATCH MY BOYS!
BE CAREFUL, ALLEN.
ANDREW-- THROW ME A FUCKING GUN. I AIN'T GOING TO BE SCARING THESE THINGS AWAY WITH MY DICK!

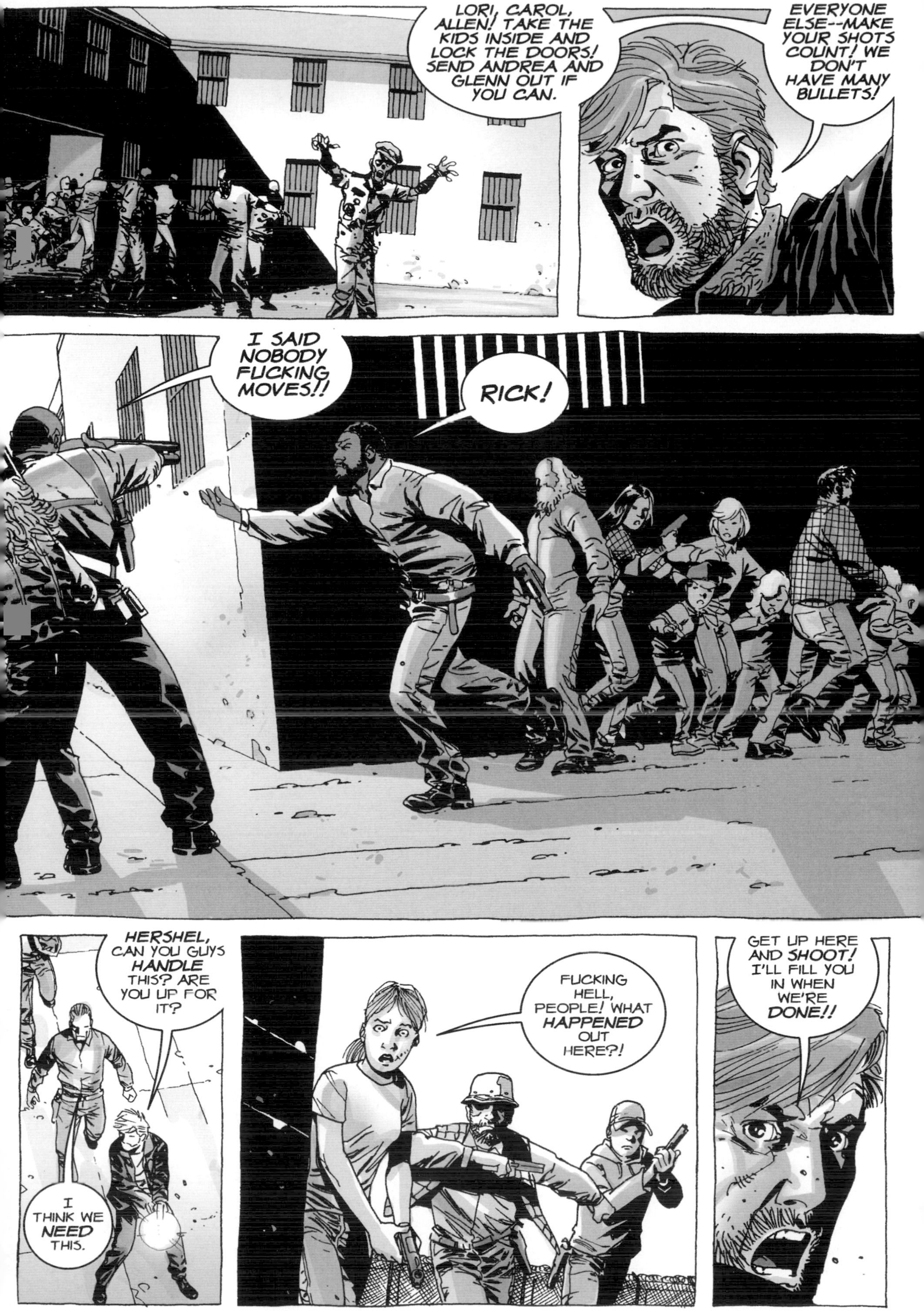
LORI, CAROL, ALLEN! TAKE THE KIDS INSIDE AND LOCK THE DOORS! SEND ANDREA AND GLENN OUT IF YOU CAN.
EVERYONE ELSE--MAKE YOUR SHOTS COUNT! WE DON'T HAVE MANY BULLETS!
I SAID NOBODY FUCKING MOVES!!
RICK!
HERSHEL, CAN YOU GUYS HANDLE THIS? ARE YOU UP FOR IT?
I THINK WE NEED THIS.
FUCKING HELL, PEOPLE! WHAT HAPPENED OUT HERE?!
GET UP HERE AND SHOOT! I'LL FILL YOU IN WHEN WE'RE DONE!!

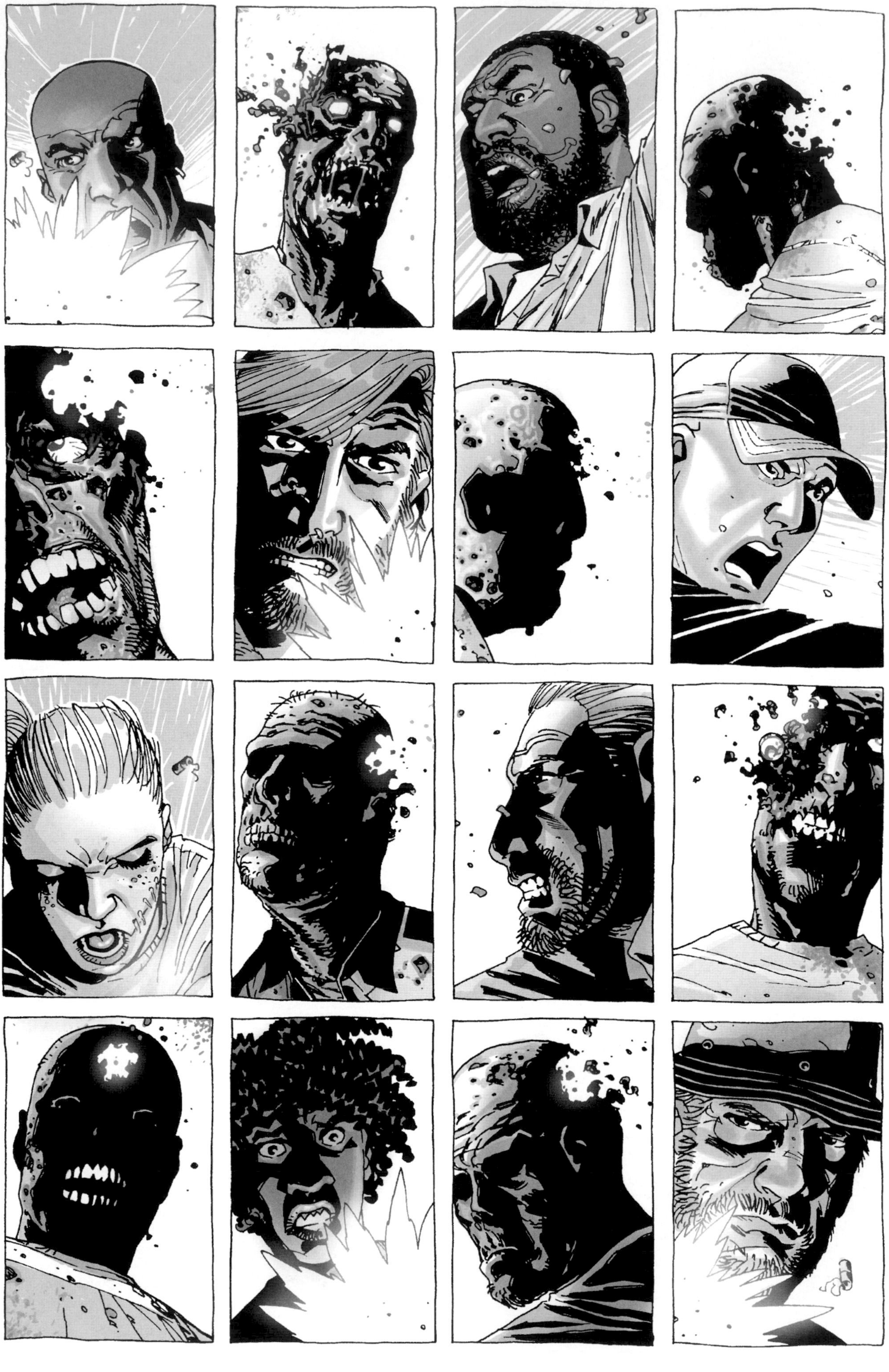

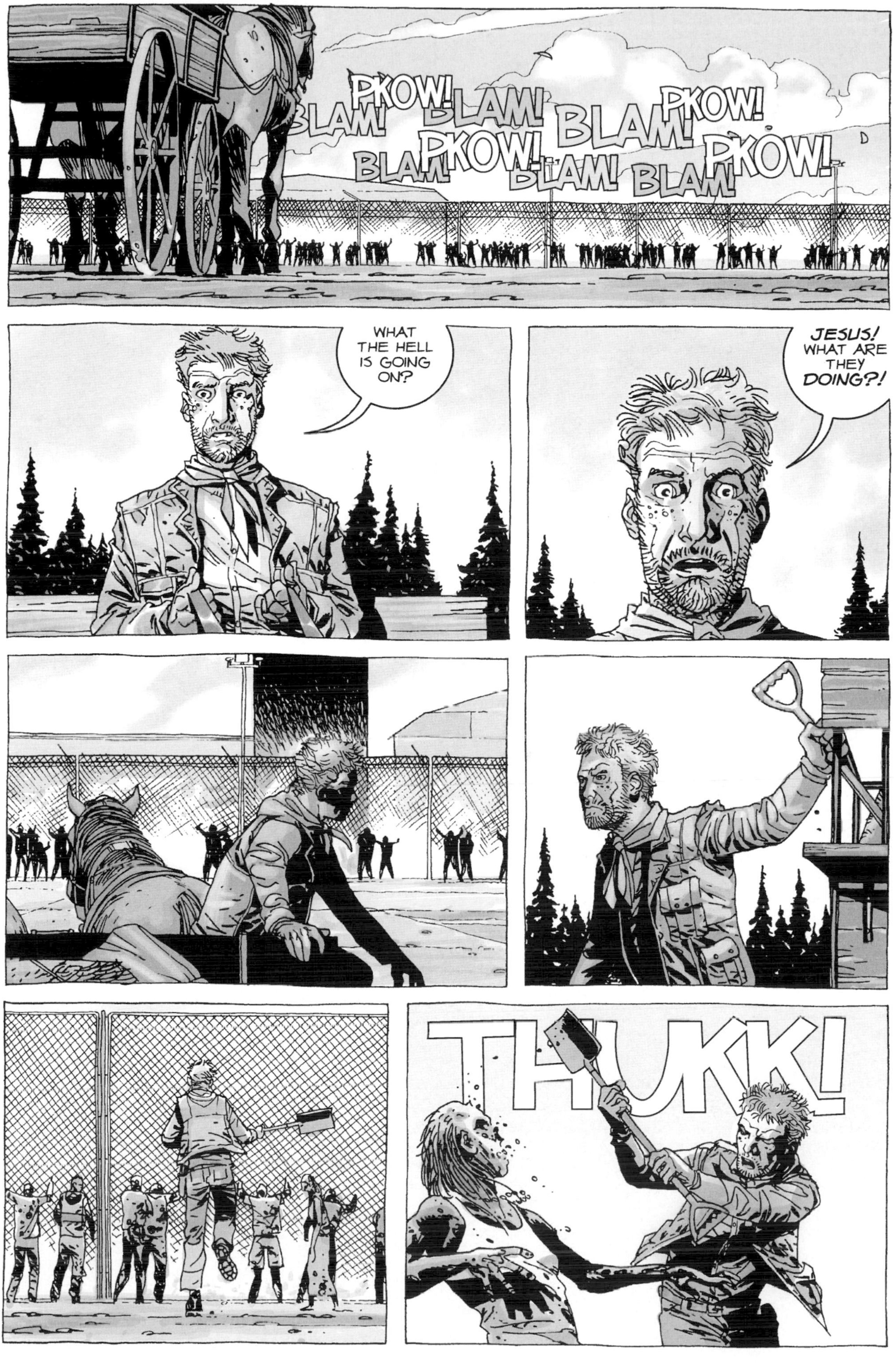

PKOW! BLAM! BLAM! BLAM! PKOW! BLAM! PKOW! BLAM! BLAM! PKOW!
WHAT THE HELL IS GOING ON?
JESUS! WHAT ARE THEY DOING?!
THUKK!

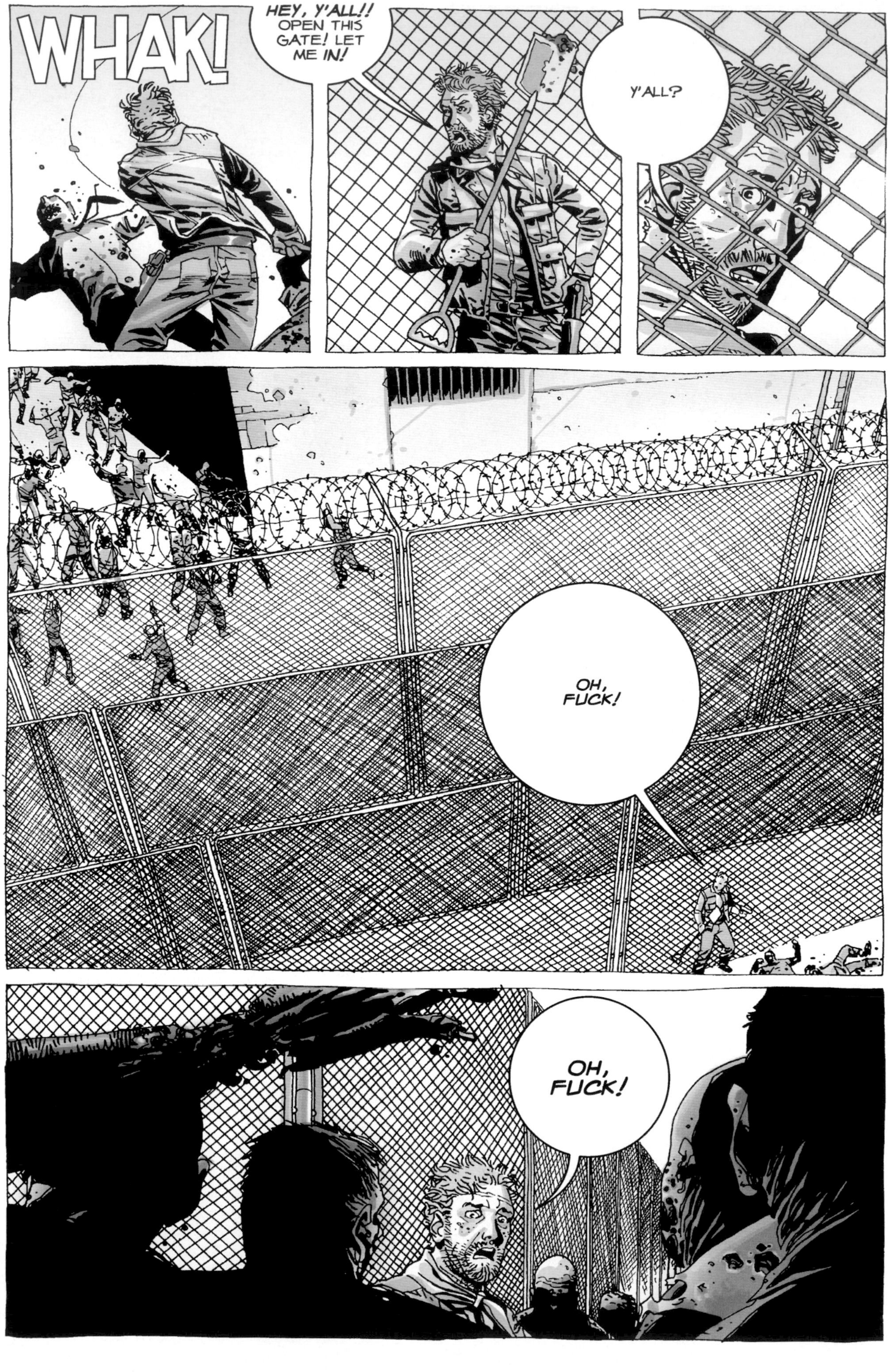
WHAK!
HEY, Y'ALL!! OPEN THIS GATE! LET ME IN!
Y'ALL?
OH, FUCK!
OH, FUCK!

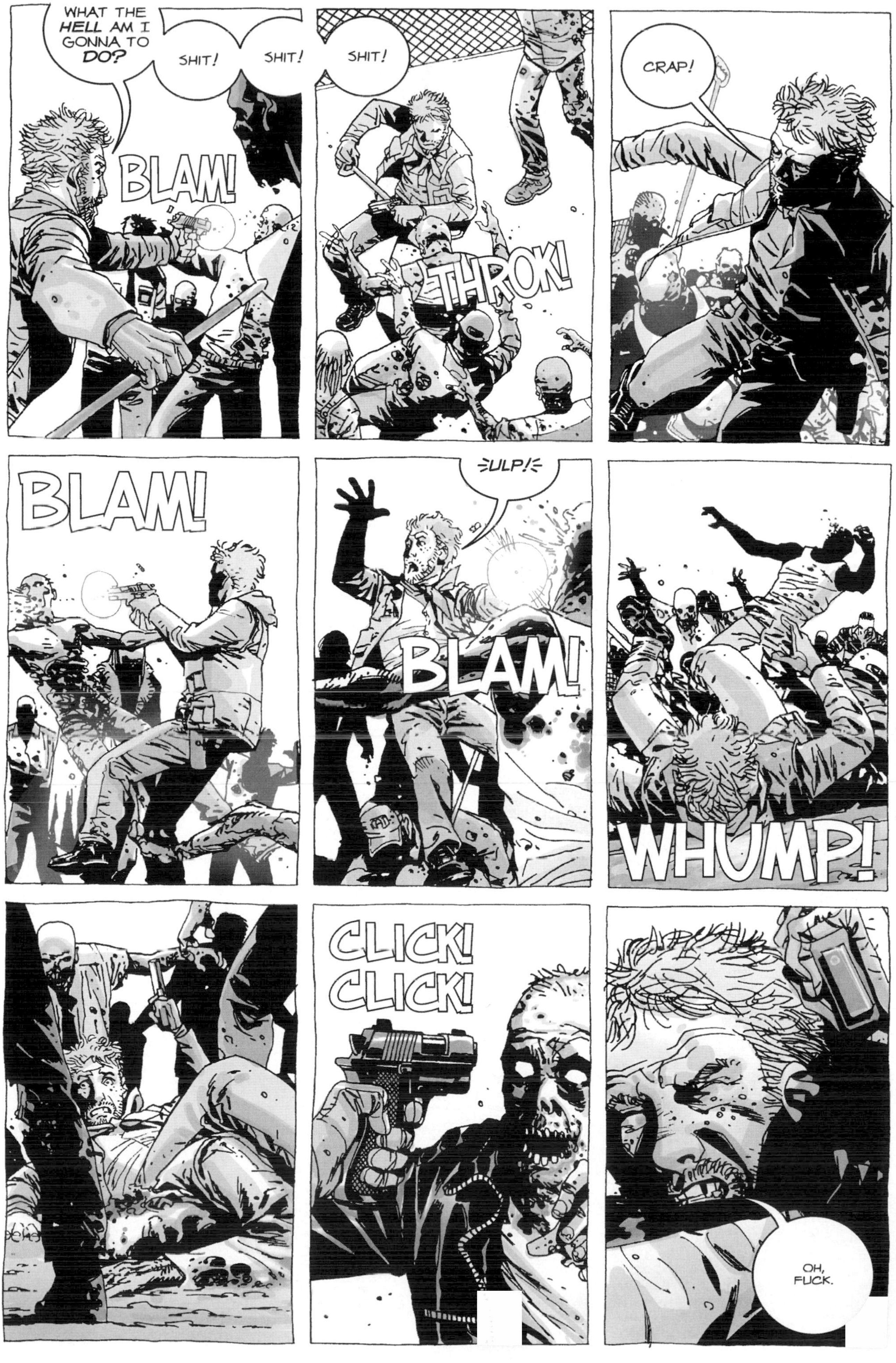
WHAT THE HELL AM I GONNA TO DO?
SHIT!
SHIT!
BLAM!
SHIT!
THROK!
CRAP!
BLAM!
ULP!
BLAM!
WHUMP!
CLICK! CLICK!
OH, FUCK.

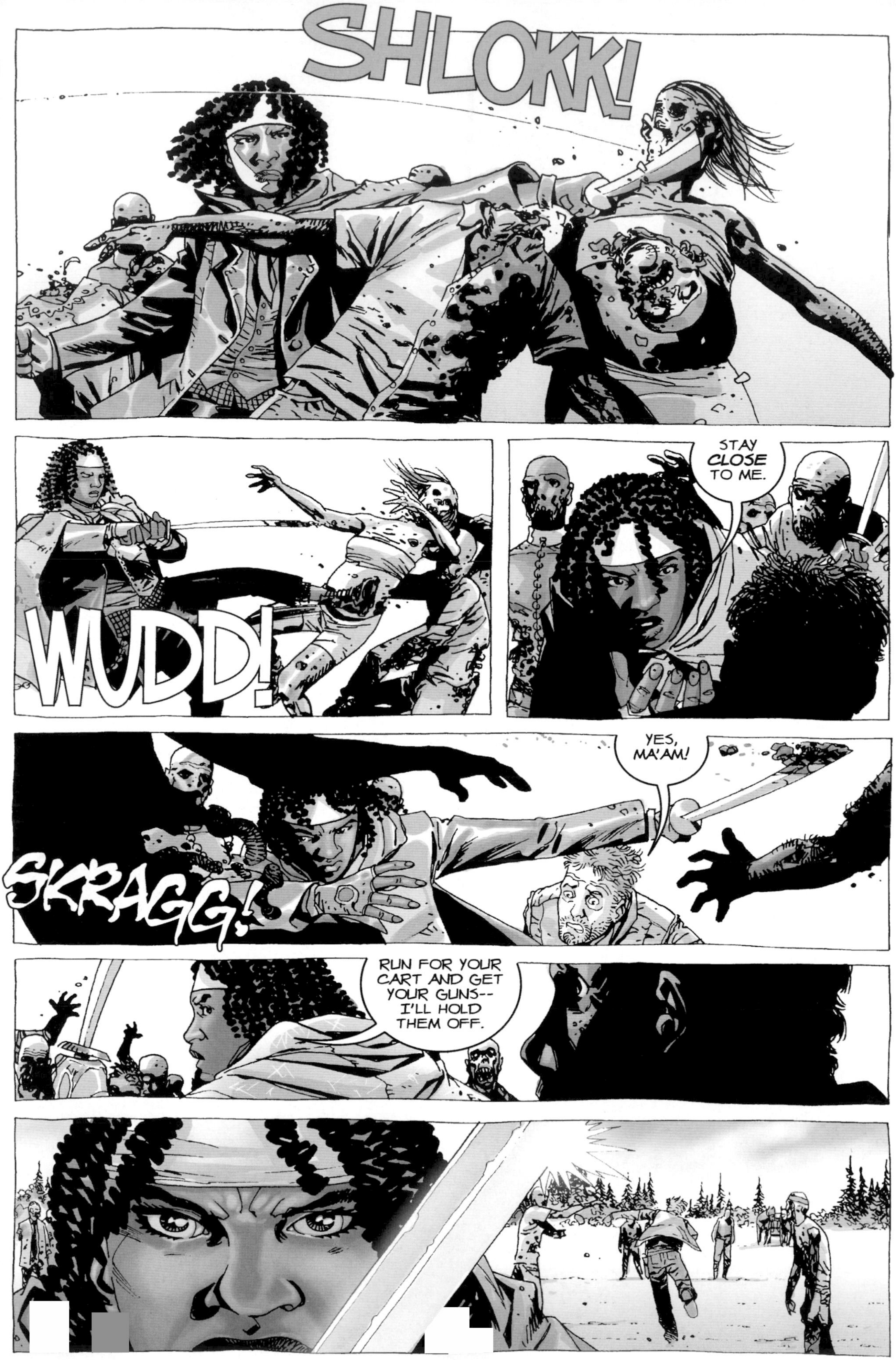
SHLOKK!
WUDD!
STAY CLOSE TO ME.
YES, MA'AM!
SKRAGG!
RUN FOR YOUR CART AND GET YOUR GUNS-- I'LL HOLD THEM OFF.

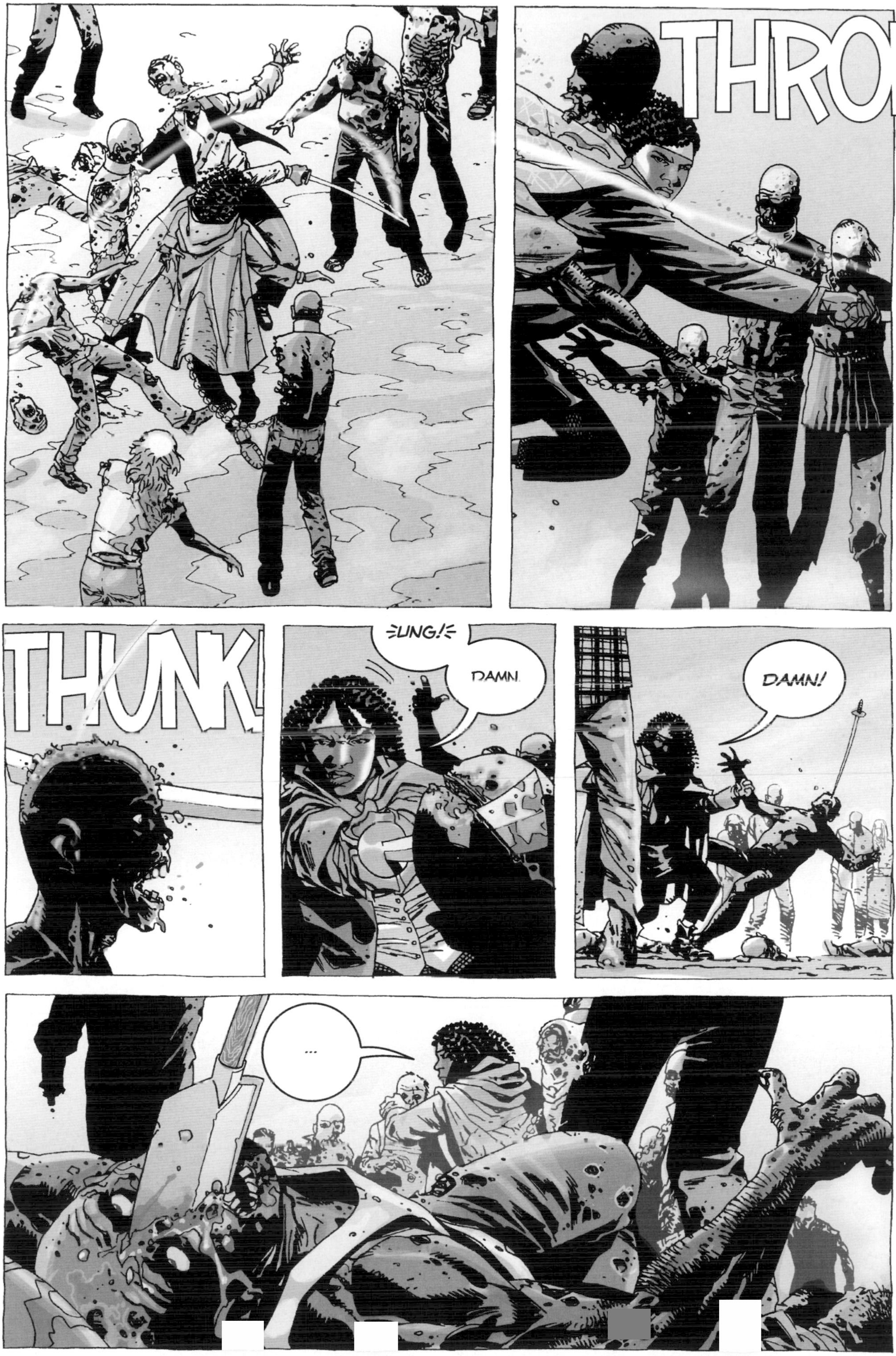
THROK
THUNK!
UNG!
DAMN.
DAMN!
...

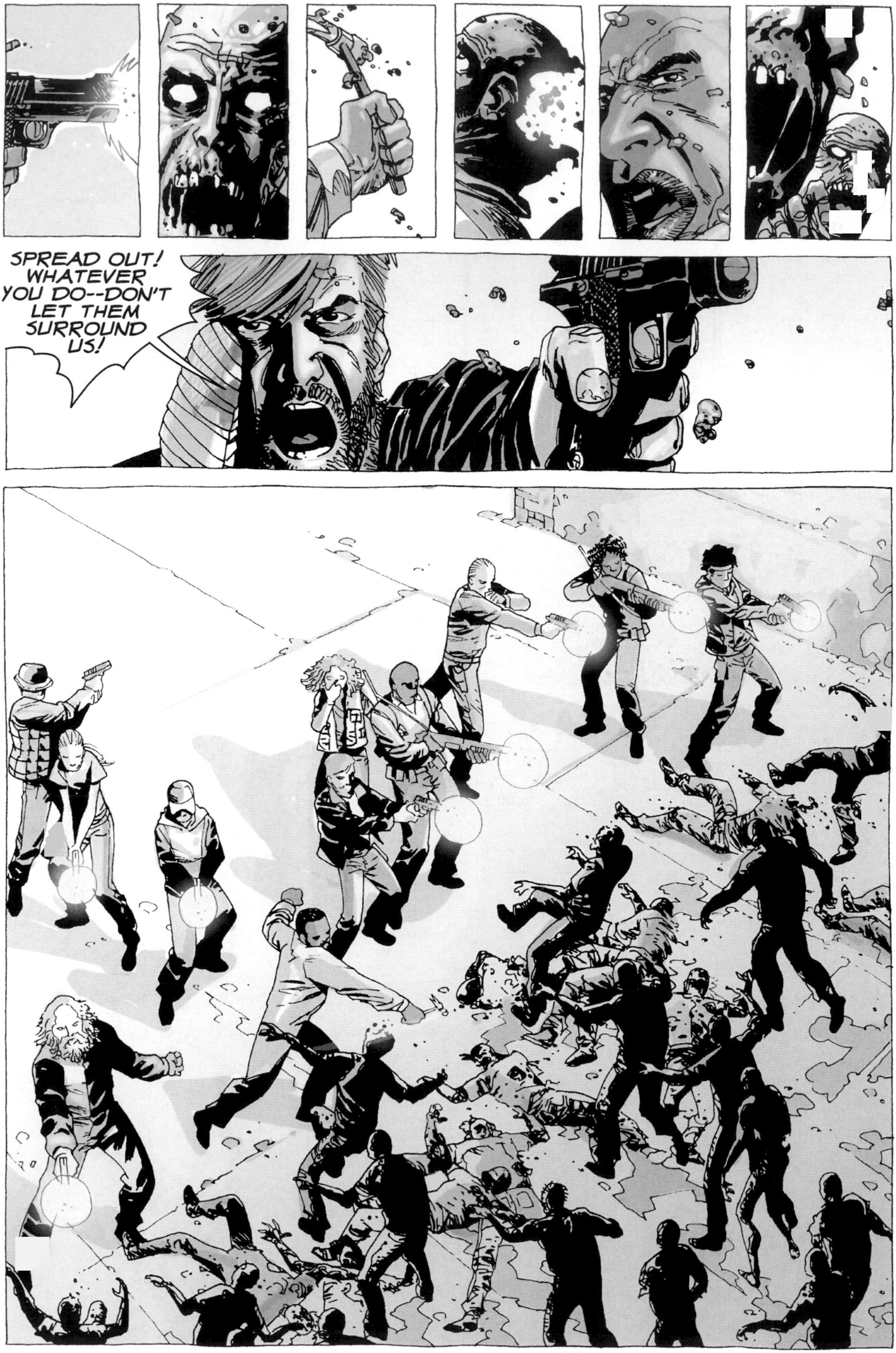
SPREAD OUT! WHATEVER YOU DO--DON'T LET THEM SURROUND US!

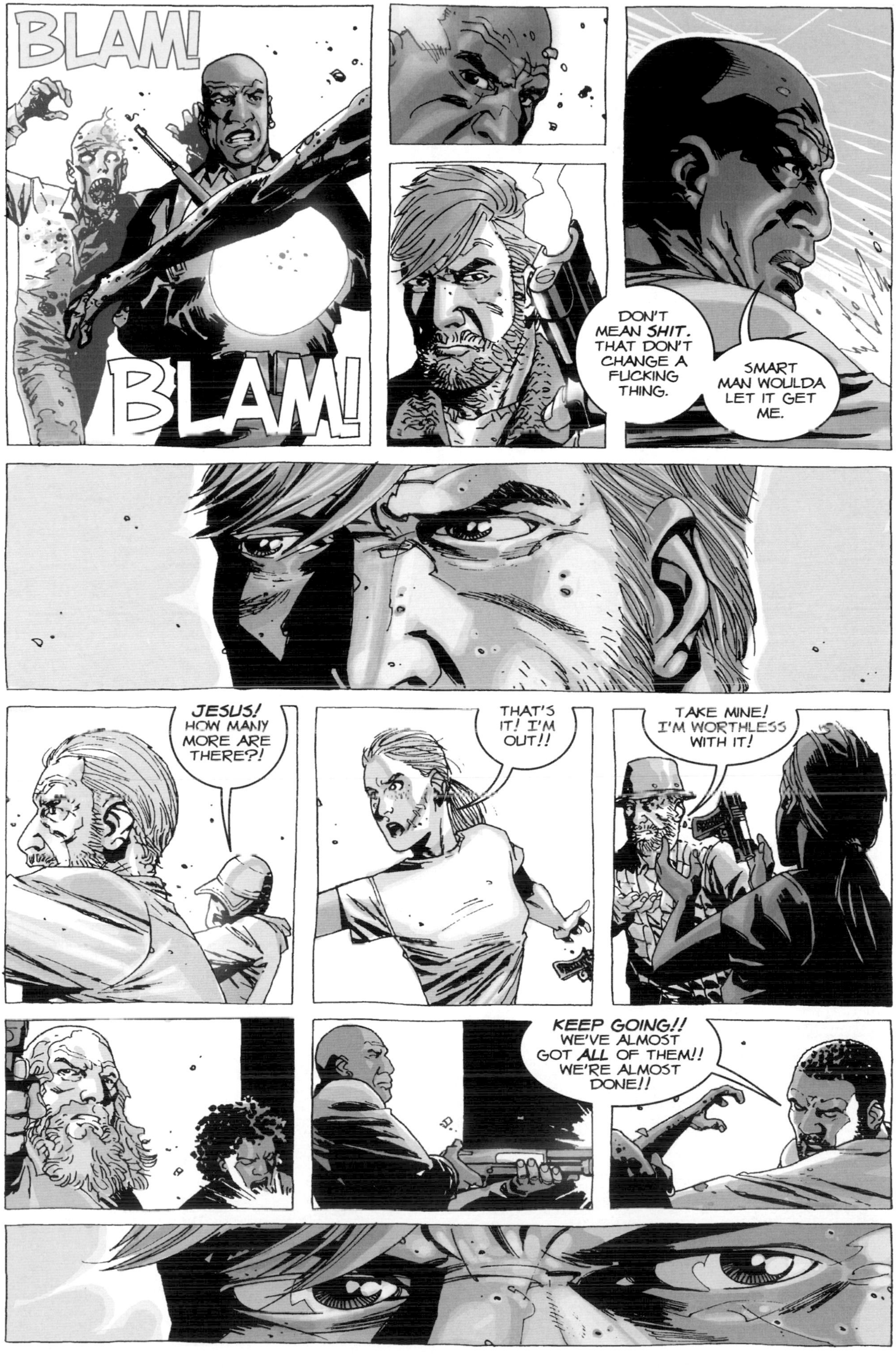
BLAM!
BLAM!
DON'T MEAN SHIT. THAT DON'T CHANGE A FUCKING THING.
SMART MAN WOULDA LET IT GET ME.
JESUS! HOW MANY MORE ARE THERE?!
THAT'S IT! I'M OUT!!
TAKE MINE! I'M WORTHLESS WITH IT!
KEEP GOING!! WE'VE ALMOST GOT ALL OF THEM!! WE'RE ALMOST DONE!!

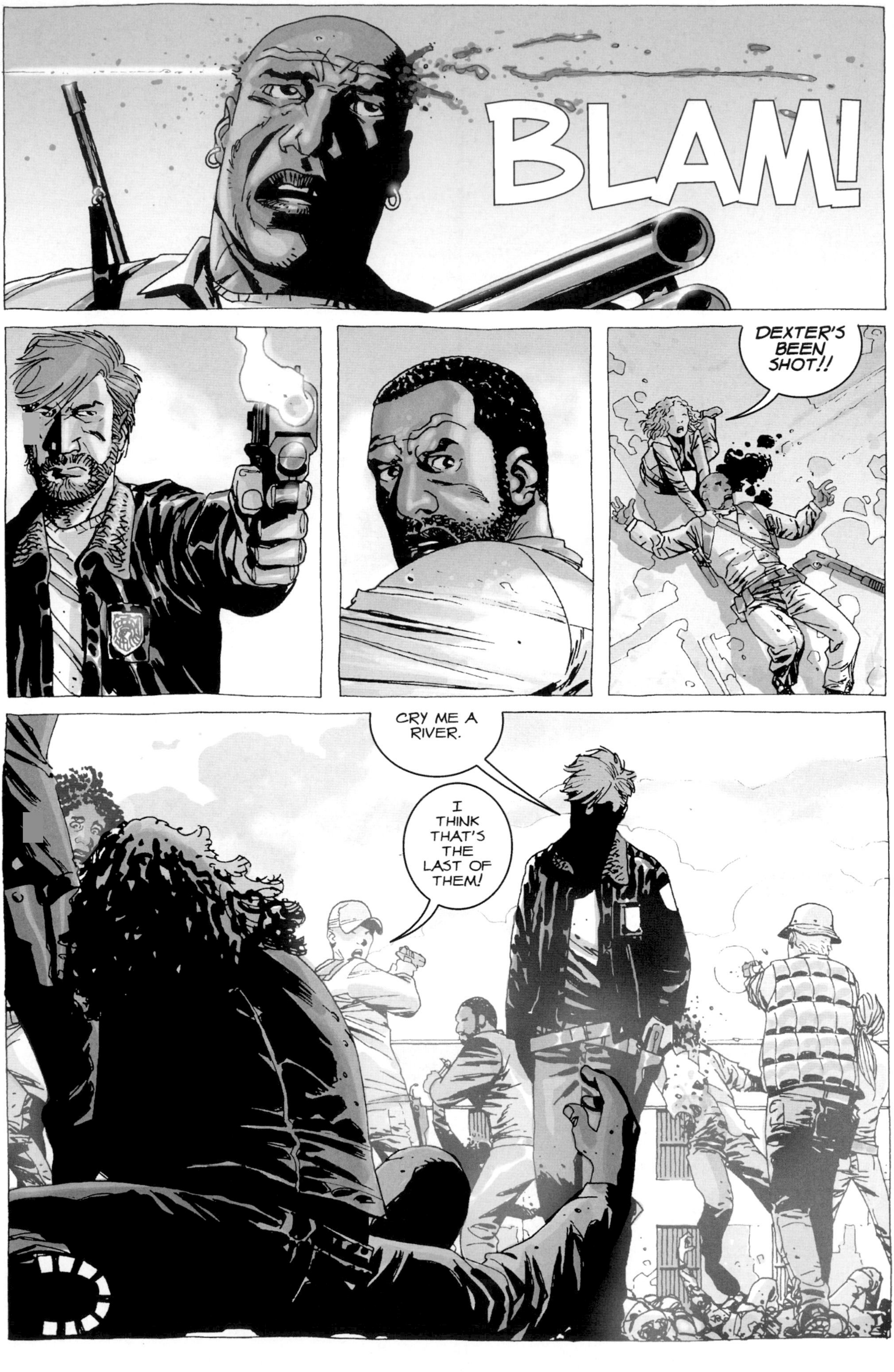
BLAM!
DEXTER'S BEEN SHOT!!
CRY ME A RIVER.
I THINK THAT'S THE LAST OF THEM!

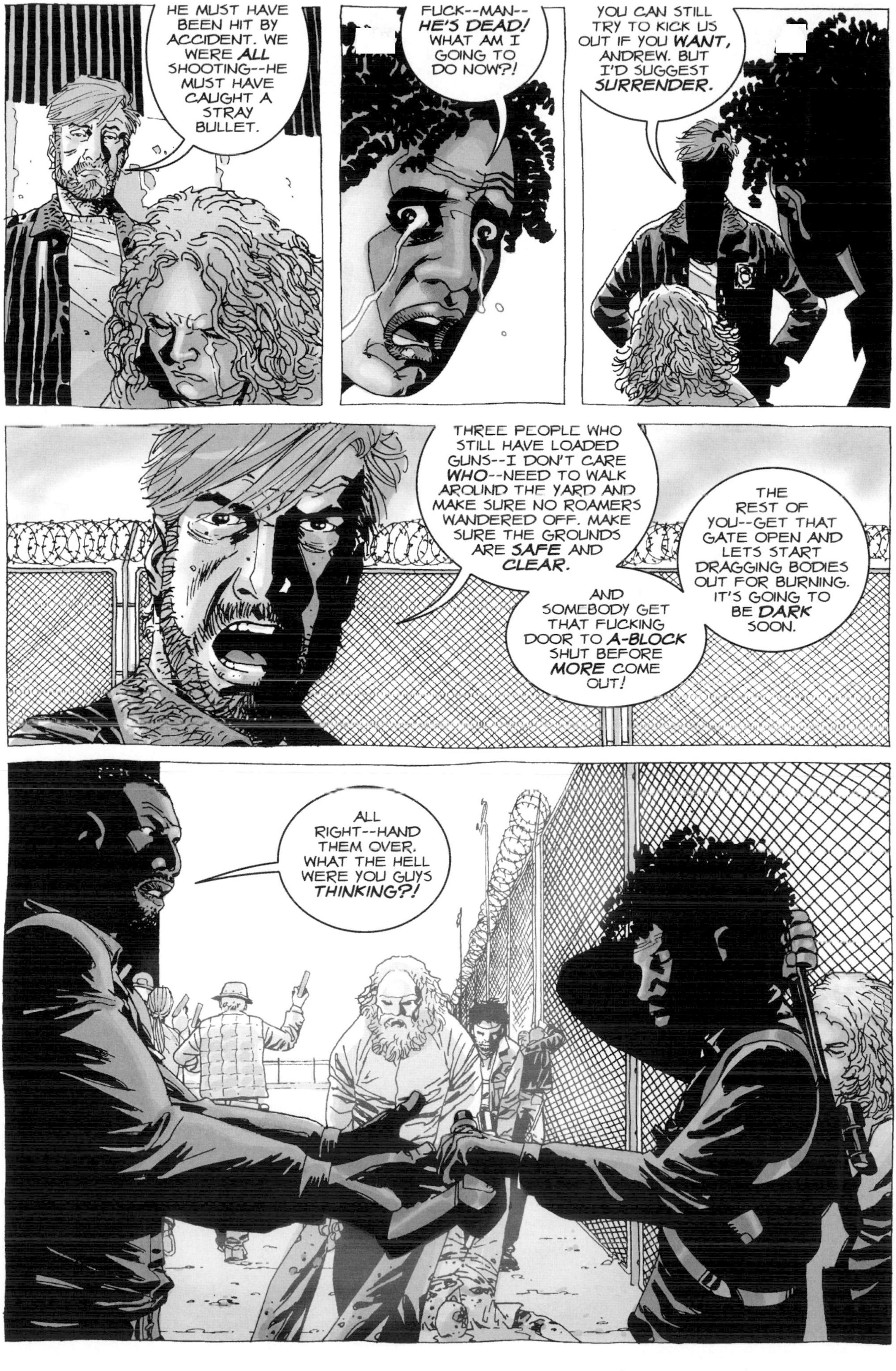
HE MUST HAVE BEEN HIT BY ACCIDENT. WE WERE ALL SHOOTING--HE MUST HAVE CAUGHT A STRAY BULLET.
FUCK--MAN-- HE'S DEAD! WHAT AM I GOING TO DO NOW?!
YOU CAN STILL TRY TO KICK US OUT IF YOU WANT, ANDREW. BUT I'D SUGGEST SURRENDER.
THREE PEOPLE WHO STILL HAVE LOADED GUNS--I DON'T CARE WHO--NEED TO WALK AROUND THE YARD AND MAKE SURE NO ROAMERS WANDERED OFF. MAKE SURE THE GROUNDS ARE SAFE AND CLEAR.
AND SOMEBODY GET THAT FUCKING DOOR TO A-BLOCK SHUT BEFORE MORE COME OUT!
THE REST OF YOU--GET THAT GATE OPEN AND LETS START DRAGGING BODIES OUT FOR BURNING. IT'S GOING TO BE DARK SOON.
ALL RIGHT--HAND THEM OVER. WHAT THE HELL WERE YOU GUYS THINKING?!

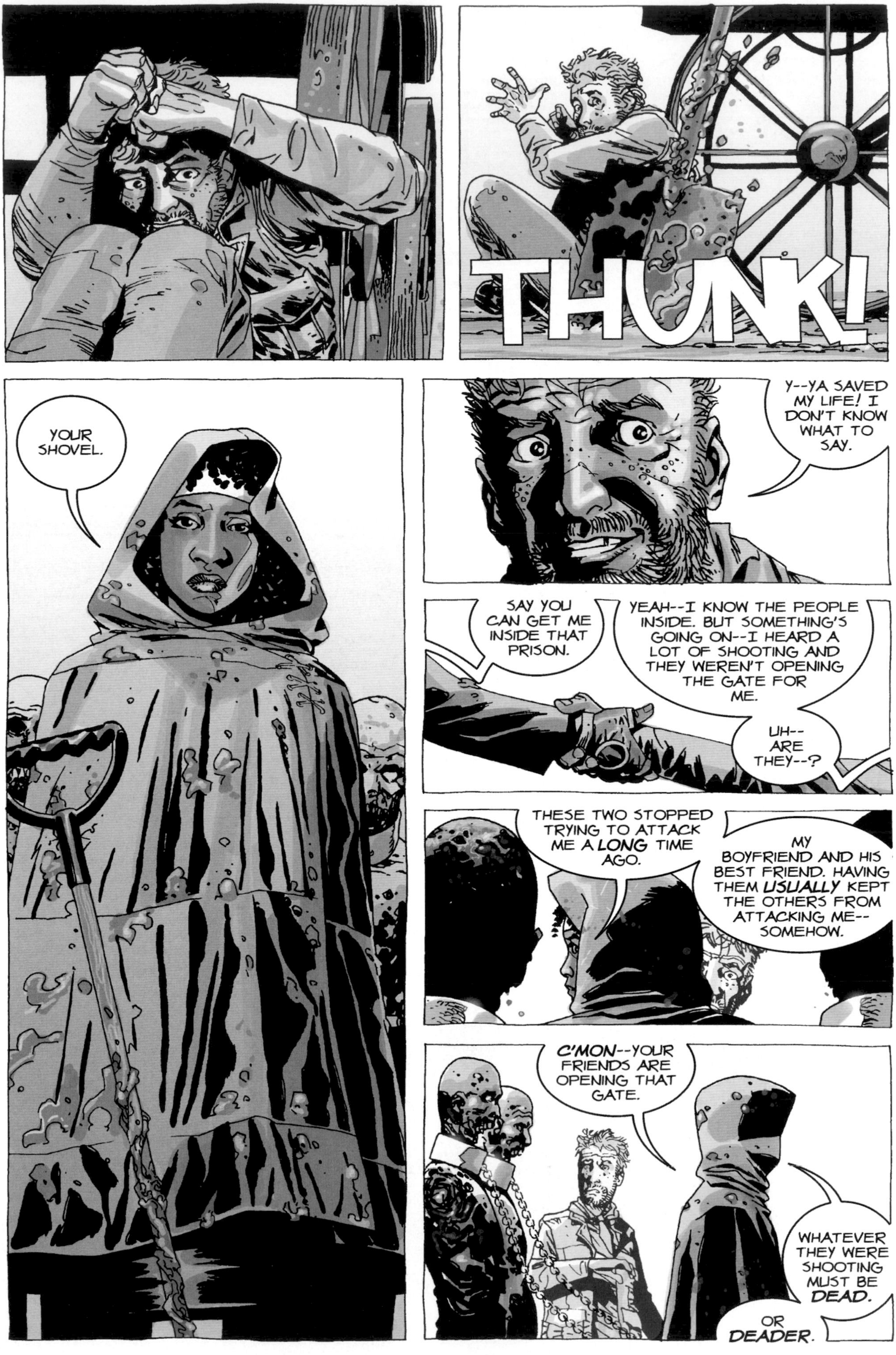
THUNK!
YOUR SHOVEL.
Y--YA SAVED MY LIFE! I DON'T KNOW WHAT TO SAY.
SAY YOU CAN GET ME INSIDE THAT PRISON.
YEAH--I KNOW THE PEOPLE INSIDE. BUT SOMETHING'S GOING ON--I HEARD A LOT OF SHOOTING AND THEY WEREN'T OPENING THE GATE FOR ME.
UH-- ARE THEY--?
THESE TWO STOPPED TRYING TO ATTACK ME A LONG TIME AGO.
MY BOYFRIEND AND HIS BEST FRIEND. HAVING THEM USUALLY KEPT THE OTHERS FROM ATTACKING ME-- SOMEHOW.
C'MON--YOUR FRIENDS ARE OPENING THAT GATE.
WHATEVER THEY WERE SHOOTING MUST BE DEAD.
OR DEADER.

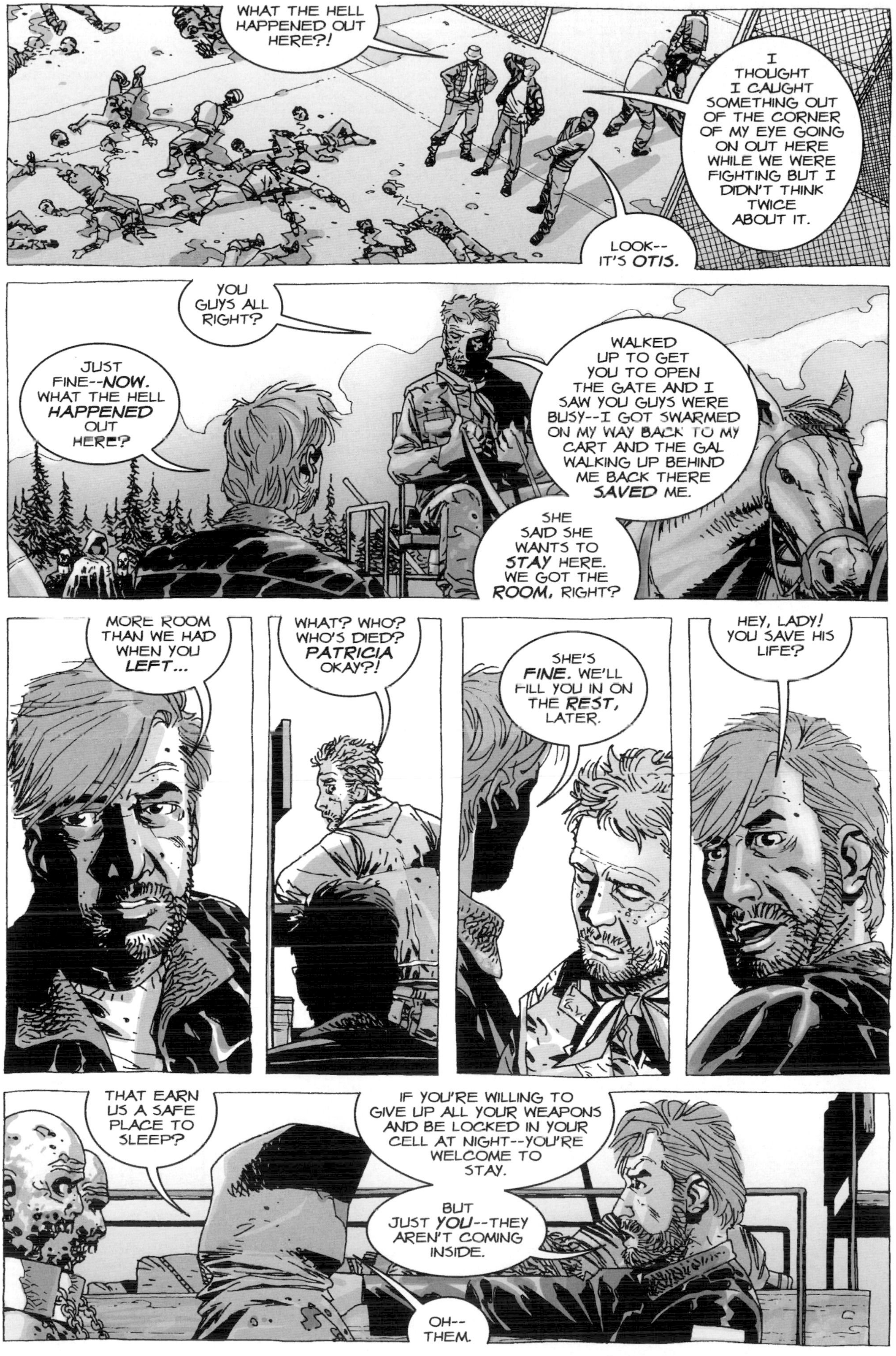

WHAT THE HELL HAPPENED OUT HERE?!
I THOUGHT I CAUGHT SOMETHING OUT OF THE CORNER OF MY EYE GOING ON OUT HERE WHILE WE WERE FIGHTING BUT I DIDN'T THINK TWICE ABOUT IT.
LOOK-- IT'S OTIS.
YOU GUYS ALL RIGHT?
JUST FINE--NOW. WHAT THE HELL HAPPENED OUT HERE?
WALKED UP TO GET YOU TO OPEN THE GATE AND I SAW YOU GUYS WERE BUSY--I GOT SWARMED ON MY WAY BACK TO MY CART AND THE GAL WALKING UP BEHIND ME BACK THERE SAVED ME.
SHE SAID SHE WANTS TO STAY HERE. WE GOT THE ROOM, RIGHT?
MORE ROOM THAN WE HAD WHEN YOU LEFT...
WHAT? WHO? WHO'S DIED? PATRICIA OKAY?!
SHE'S FINE. WE'LL FILL YOU IN ON THE REST, LATER.
HEY, LADY! YOU SAVE HIS LIFE?
THAT EARN US A SAFE PLACE TO SLEEP?
IF YOU'RE WILLING TO GIVE UP ALL YOUR WEAPONS AND BE LOCKED IN YOUR CELL AT NIGHT--YOU'RE WELCOME TO STAY.
BUT JUST YOU--THEY AREN'T COMING INSIDE.
OH-- THEM.

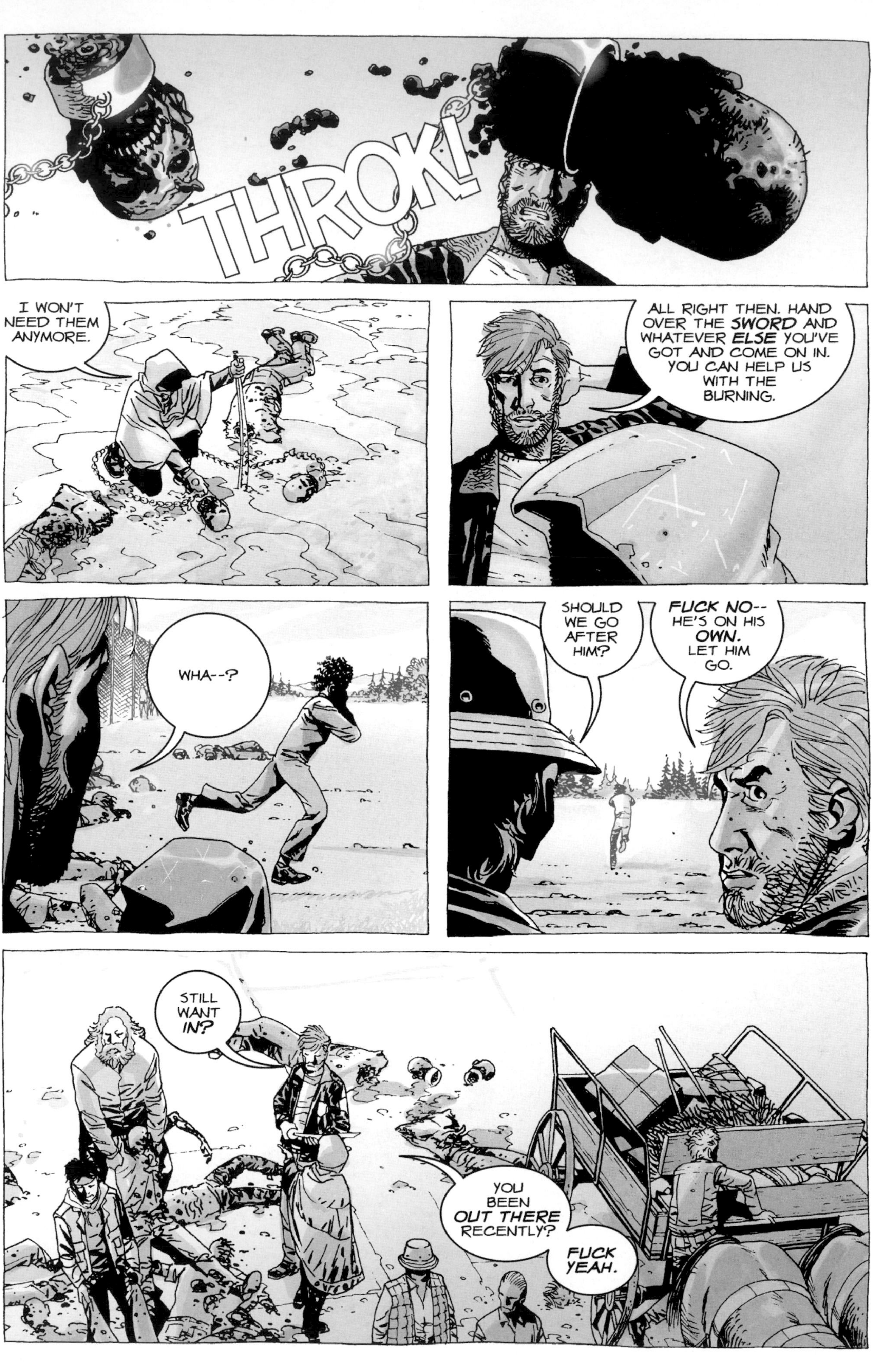

THROK!
I WON'T NEED THEM ANYMORE.
ALL RIGHT THEN. HAND OVER THE SWORD AND WHATEVER ELSE YOU'VE GOT AND COME ON IN. YOU CAN HELP US WITH THE BURNING.
WHA--?
SHOULD WE GO AFTER HIM?
FUCK NO-- HE'S ON HIS OWN. LET HIM GO.
STILL WANT IN?
YOU BEEN OUT THERE RECENTLY?
FUCK YEAH.

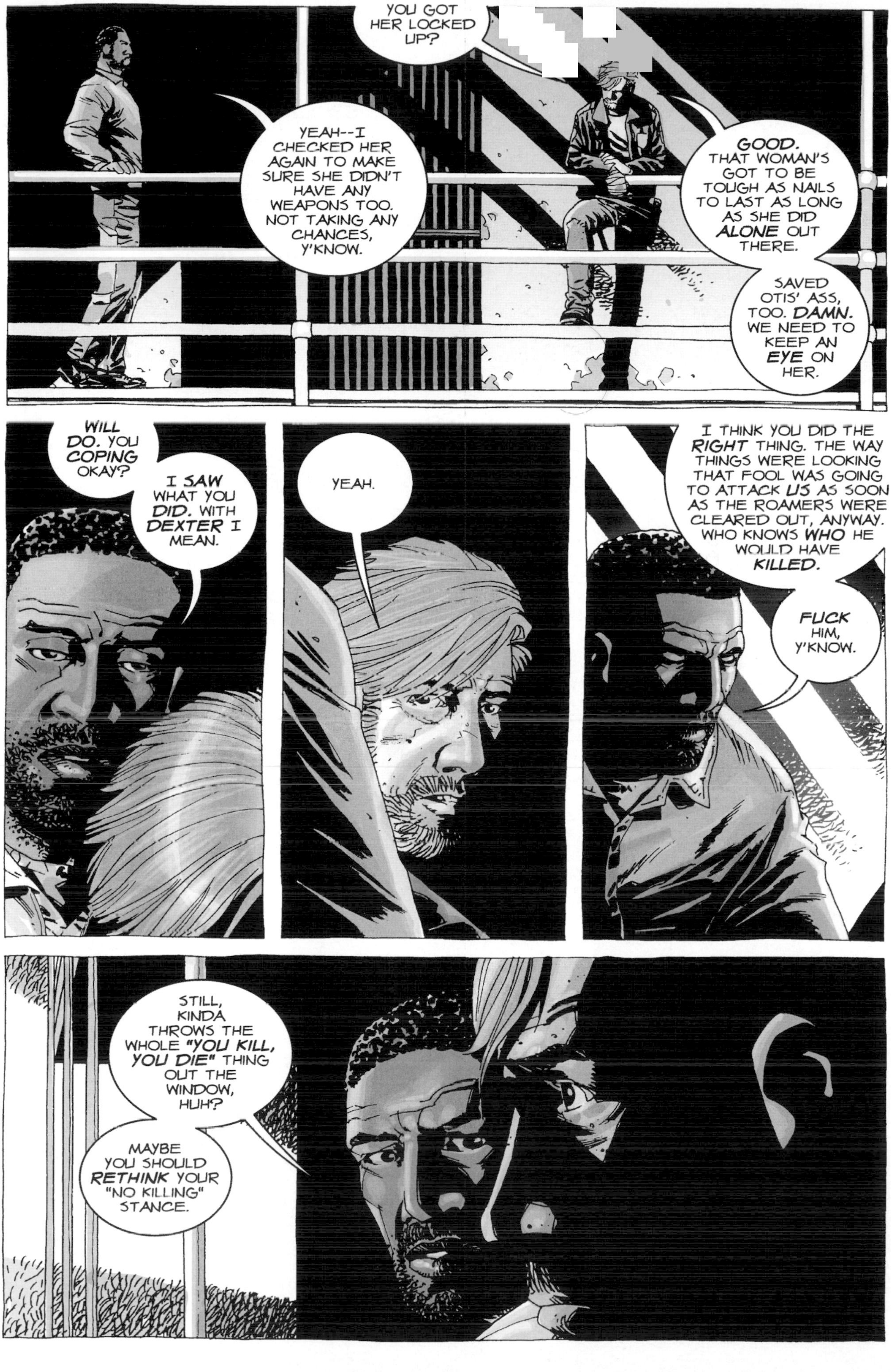
YOU GOT HER LOCKED UP?
YEAH--I CHECKED HER AGAIN TO MAKE SURE SHE DIDN'T HAVE ANY WEAPONS TOO. NOT TAKING ANY CHANCES, Y'KNOW.
GOOD. THAT WOMAN'S GOT TO BE TOUGH AS NAILS TO LAST AS LONG AS SHE DID ALONE OUT THERE.
SAVED OTIS' ASS, TOO. DAMN. WE NEED TO KEEP AN EYE ON HER.
WILL DO. YOU COPING OKAY?
I SAW WHAT YOU DID. WITH DEXTER I MEAN.
YEAH.
I THINK YOU DID THE RIGHT THING. THE WAY THINGS WERE LOOKING THAT FOOL WAS GOING TO ATTACK US AS SOON AS THE ROAMERS WERE CLEARED OUT, ANYWAY. WHO KNOWS WHO HE WOULD HAVE KILLED.
FUCK HIM, Y'KNOW.
STILL, KINDA THROWS THE WHOLE "YOU KILL, YOU DIE" THING OUT THE WINDOW, HUH?
MAYBE YOU SHOULD RETHINK YOUR "NO KILLING" STANCE.

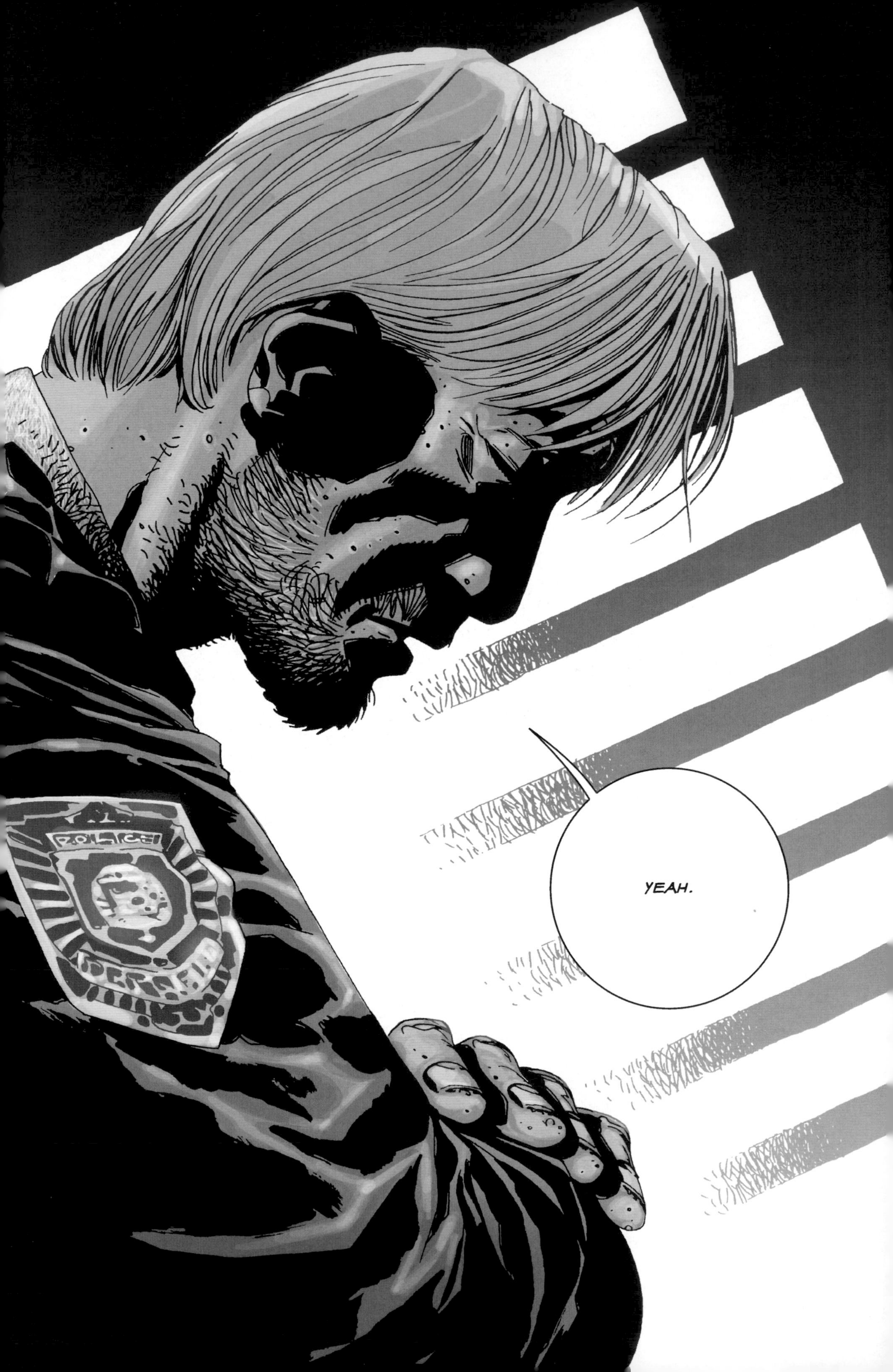
YEAH.

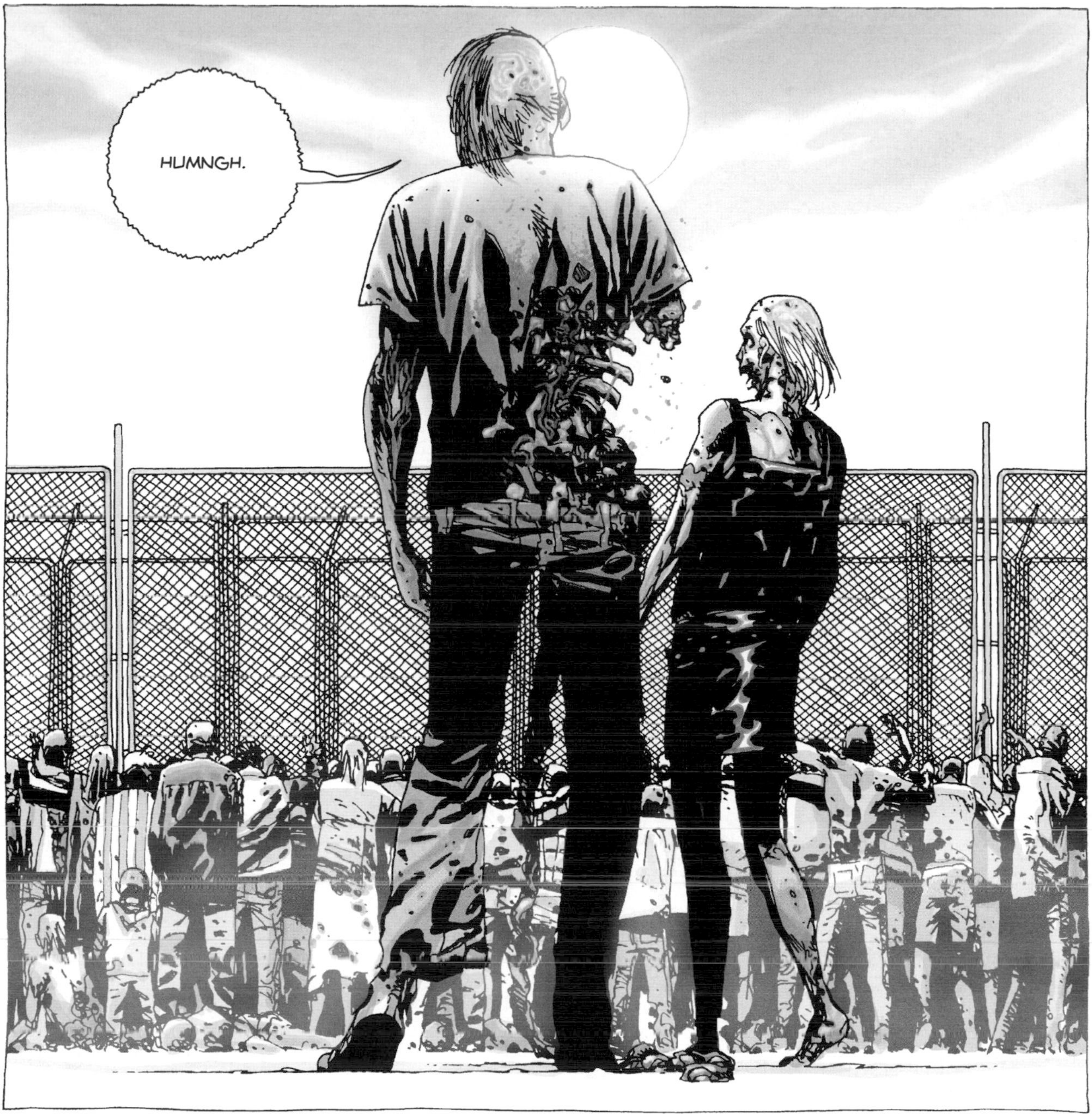
HUMNGH.

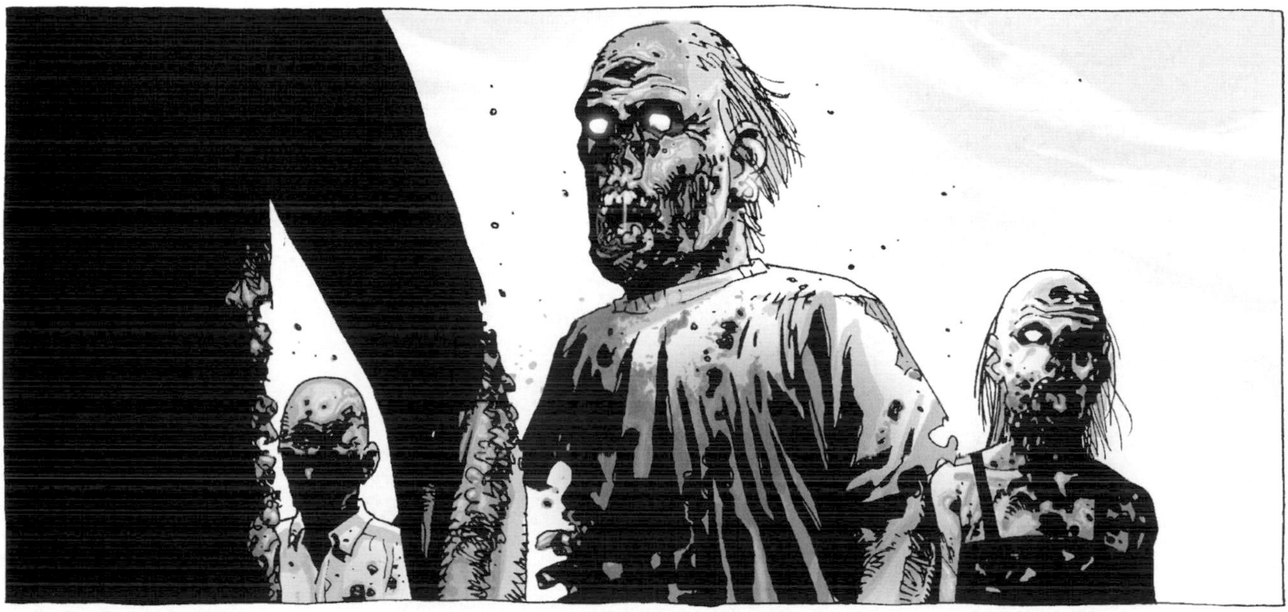

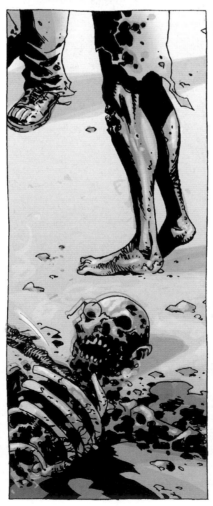

GUH.

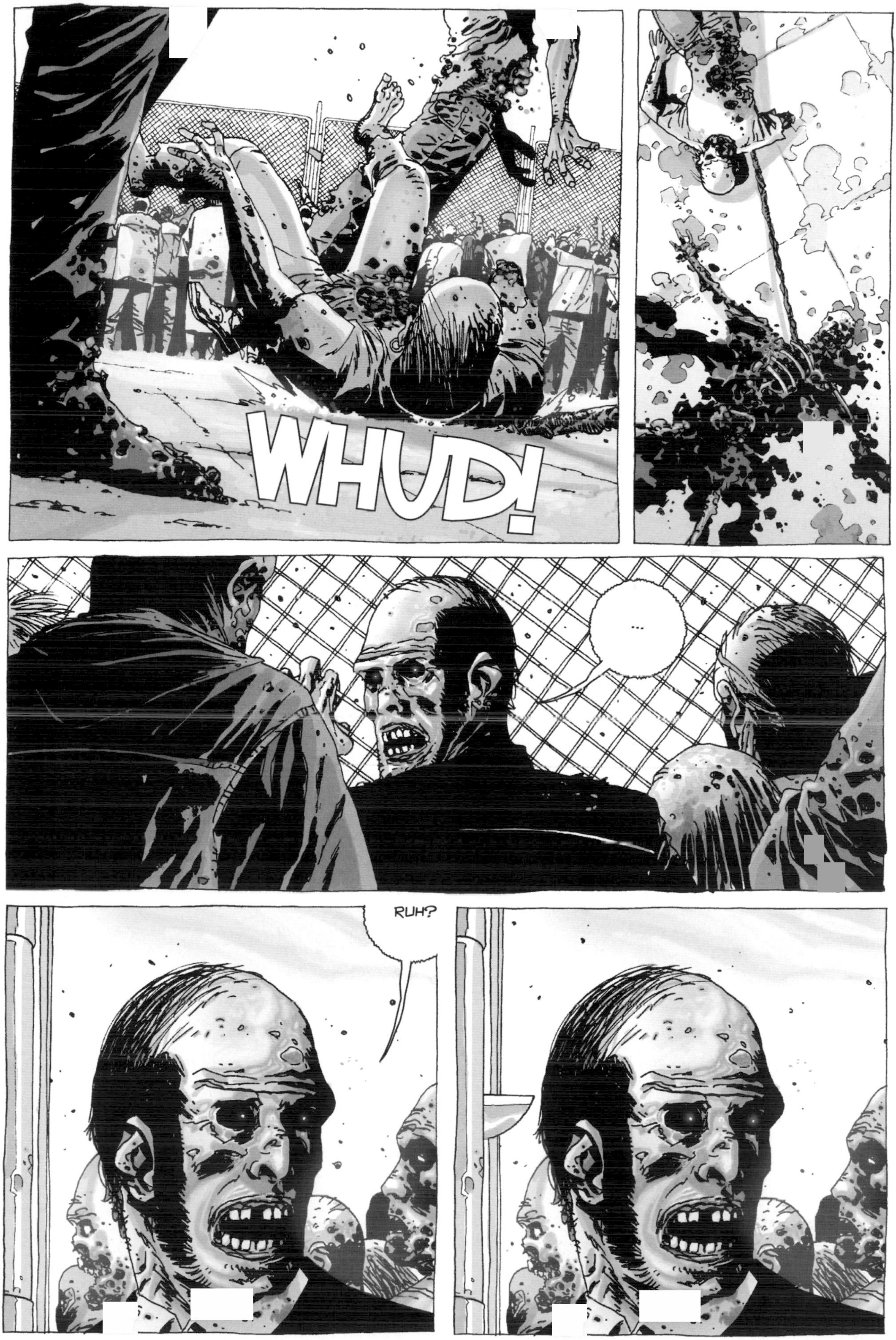
WHUD!
...
RUH?

THUNK!!

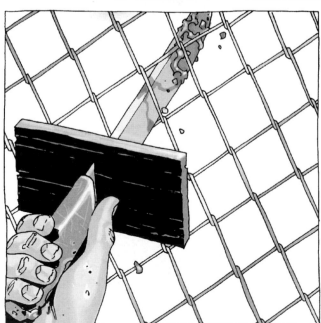

WOW.

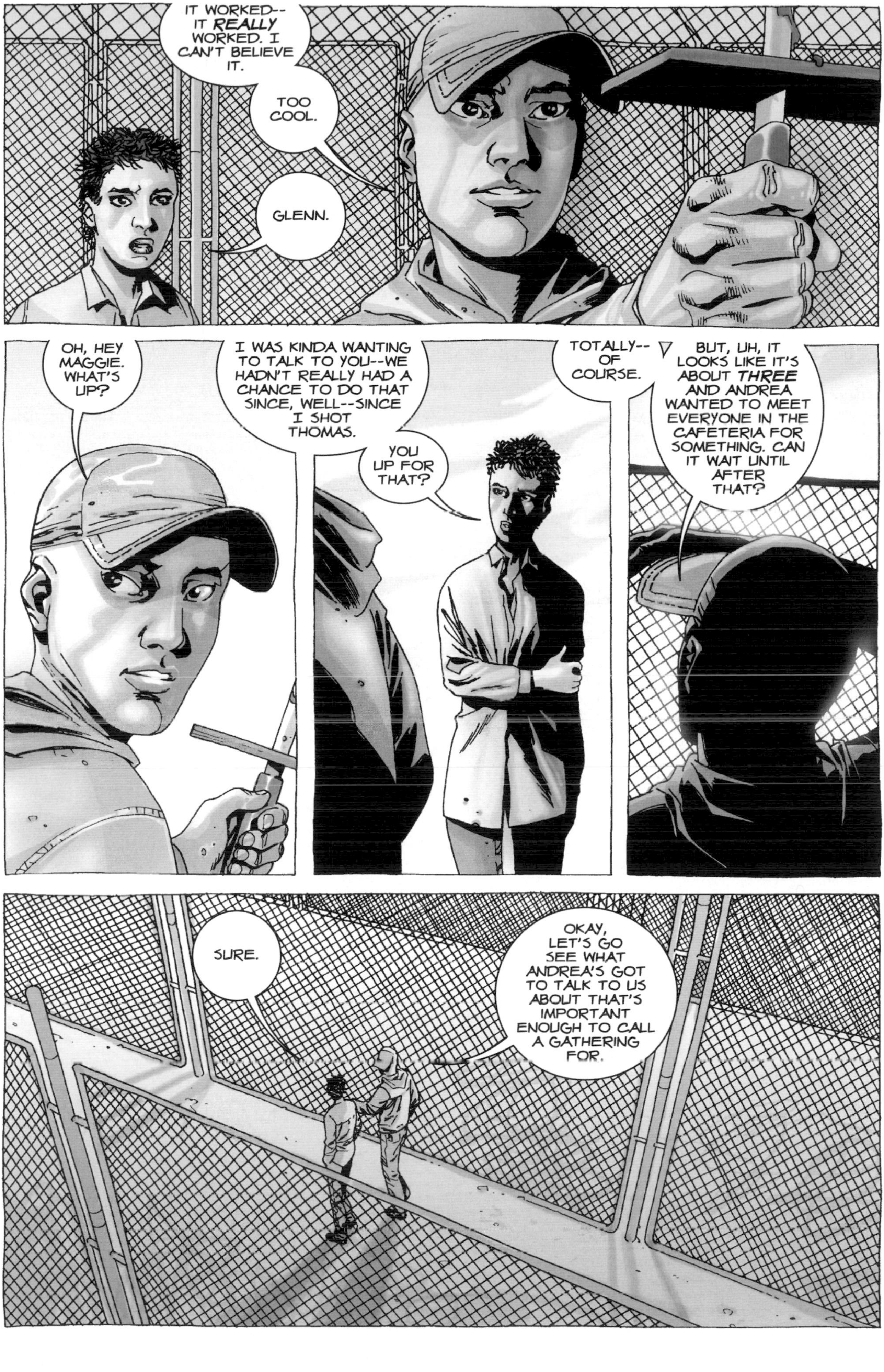
IT WORKED-- IT REALLY WORKED. I CAN'T BELIEVE IT.
TOO COOL.
GLENN.
OH, HEY MAGGIE. WHAT'S UP?
I WAS KINDA WANTING TO TALK TO YOU--WE HADN'T REALLY HAD A CHANCE TO DO THAT SINCE, WELL--SINCE I SHOT THOMAS.
YOU UP FOR THAT?
TOTALLY-- OF COURSE.
BUT, UH, IT LOOKS LIKE IT'S ABOUT THREE AND ANDREA WANTED TO MEET EVERYONE IN THE CAFETERIA FOR SOMETHING. CAN IT WAIT UNTIL AFTER THAT?
SURE.
OKAY, LET'S GO SEE WHAT ANDREA'S GOT TO TALK TO US ABOUT THAT'S IMPORTANT ENOUGH TO CALL A GATHERING FOR.

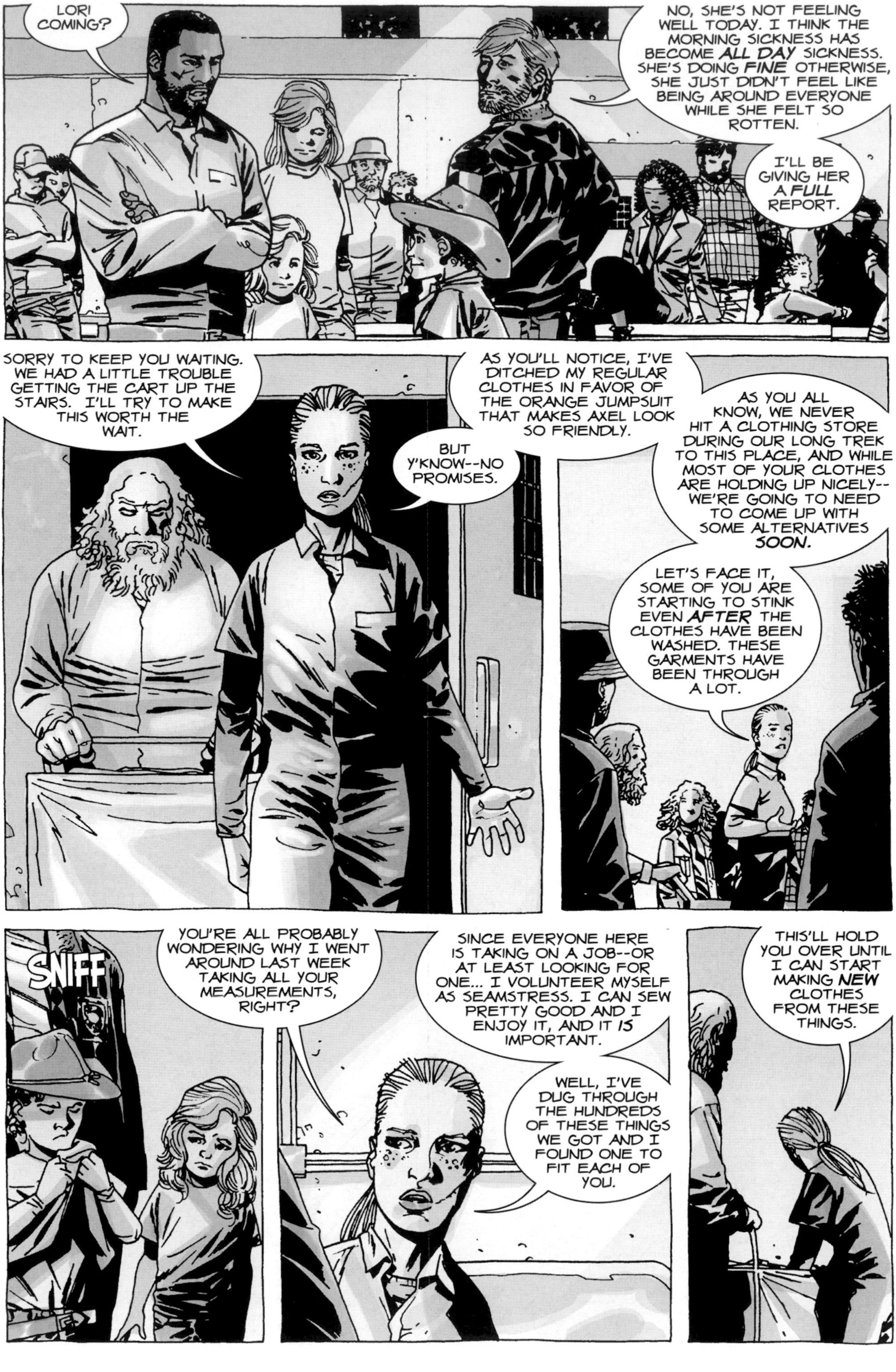
LORI COMING?
NO, SHE'S NOT FEELING WELL TODAY. I THINK THE MORNING SICKNESS HAS BECOME ALL DAY SICKNESS. SHE'S DOING FINE OTHERWISE, SHE JUST DIDN'T FEEL LIKE BEING AROUND EVERYONE WHILE SHE FELT SO ROTTEN.
I'LL BE GIVING HER A FULL REPORT.
SORRY TO KEEP YOU WAITING. WE HAD A LITTLE TROUBLE GETTING THE CART UP THE STAIRS. I'LL TRY TO MAKE THIS WORTH THE WAIT.
BUT Y'KNOW--NO PROMISES.
AS YOU'LL NOTICE, I'VE DITCHED MY REGULAR CLOTHES IN FAVOR OF THE ORANGE JUMPSUIT THAT MAKES AXEL LOOK SO FRIENDLY.
AS YOU ALL KNOW, WE NEVER HIT A CLOTHING STORE DURING OUR LONG TREK TO THIS PLACE, AND WHILE MOST OF YOUR CLOTHES ARE HOLDING UP NICELY-- WE'RE GOING TO NEED TO COME UP WITH SOME ALTERNATIVES SOON.
LET'S FACE IT, SOME OF YOU ARE STARTING TO STINK EVEN AFTER THE CLOTHES HAVE BEEN WASHED. THESE GARMENTS HAVE BEEN THROUGH A LOT.
SNIFF
YOU'RE ALL PROBABLY WONDERING WHY I WENT AROUND LAST WEEK TAKING ALL YOUR MEASUREMENTS, RIGHT?
SINCE EVERYONE HERE IS TAKING ON A JOB--OR AT LEAST LOOKING FOR ONE... I VOLUNTEER MYSELF AS SEAMSTRESS. I CAN SEW PRETTY GOOD AND I ENJOY IT, AND IT IS IMPORTANT.
WELL, I'VE DUG THROUGH THE HUNDREDS OF THESE THINGS WE GOT AND I FOUND ONE TO FIT EACH OF YOU.
THIS'LL HOLD YOU OVER UNTIL I CAN START MAKING NEW CLOTHES FROM THESE THINGS.

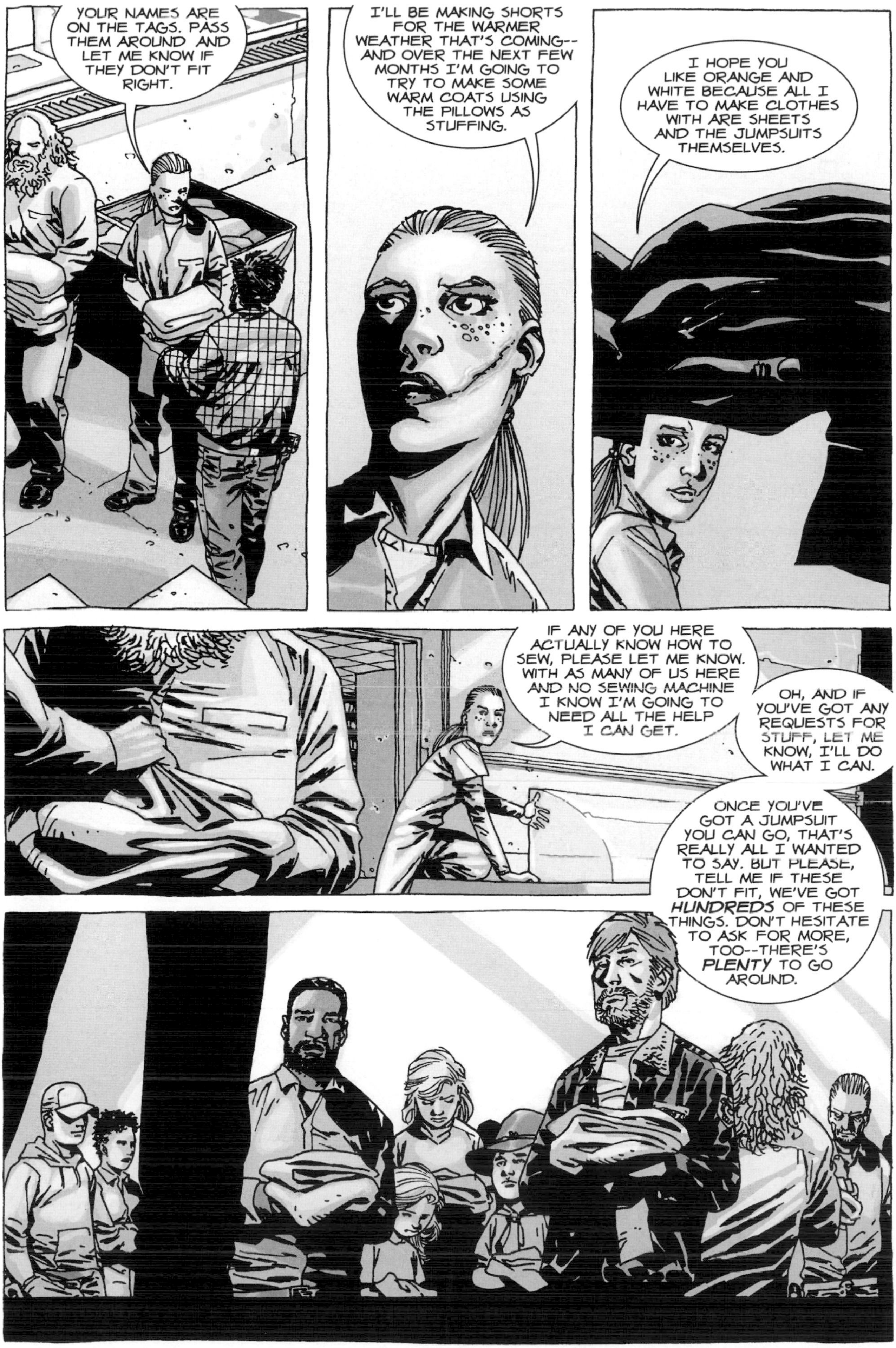
YOUR NAMES ARE ON THE TAGS. PASS THEM AROUND AND LET ME KNOW IF THEY DON'T FIT RIGHT.
I'LL BE MAKING SHORTS FOR THE WARMER WEATHER THAT'S COMING-- AND OVER THE NEXT FEW MONTHS I'M GOING TO TRY TO MAKE SOME WARM COATS USING THE PILLOWS AS STUFFING.
I HOPE YOU LIKE ORANGE AND WHITE BECAUSE ALL I HAVE TO MAKE CLOTHES WITH ARE SHEETS AND THE JUMPSUITS THEMSELVES.
IF ANY OF YOU HERE ACTUALLY KNOW HOW TO SEW, PLEASE LET ME KNOW. WITH AS MANY OF US HERE AND NO SEWING MACHINE I KNOW I'M GOING TO NEED ALL THE HELP I CAN GET.
OH, AND IF YOU'VE GOT ANY REQUESTS FOR STUFF, LET ME KNOW, I'LL DO WHAT I CAN.
ONCE YOU'VE GOT A JUMPSUIT YOU CAN GO, THAT'S REALLY ALL I WANTED TO SAY. BUT PLEASE, TELL ME IF THESE DON'T FIT, WE'VE GOT *HUNDREDS* OF THESE THINGS. DON'T HESITATE TO ASK FOR MORE, TOO--THERE'S *PLENTY* TO GO AROUND.

LORI-- ARE YOU FEELING BETTER?

NO.

I DON'T KNOW HOW I *CAN*. I CAN'T GET IT OUT OF MY HEAD, RICK, I CAN'T STOP *DWELLING* ON IT. THOSE MONSTERS OUTSIDE ARE ONE THING BUT ANY OF THE PEOPLE IN HERE *WITH* US COULD CAUSE US JUST AS MUCH HARM ANY TIME.

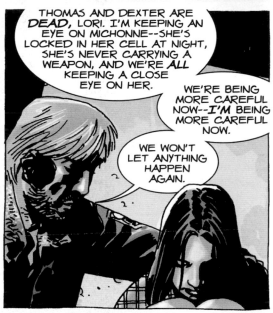

THOMAS AND DEXTER ARE *DEAD*, LORI. I'M KEEPING AN EYE ON MICHONNE--SHE'S LOCKED IN HER CELL AT NIGHT, SHE'S NEVER CARRYING A WEAPON, AND WE'RE *ALL* KEEPING A CLOSE EYE ON HER.

WE'RE BEING MORE CAREFUL NOW--*I'M* BEING MORE CAREFUL NOW.

WE WON'T LET ANYTHING HAPPEN AGAIN.

BUT AXEL IS STILL HERE--AND PATRICIA, SHE--THERE'S NO TELLING WHAT *SHE* COULD DO NEXT.

AXEL IS HARMLESS, BUT WE'RE NOT IGNORING HIM, AND PATRICIA IS JUST INCREDIBLY NAÏVE, OR STUPID... I DON'T THINK SHE'D--

LORI... YOU'RE *SHAKING*.

I KNOW, RICK.

I KNOW.

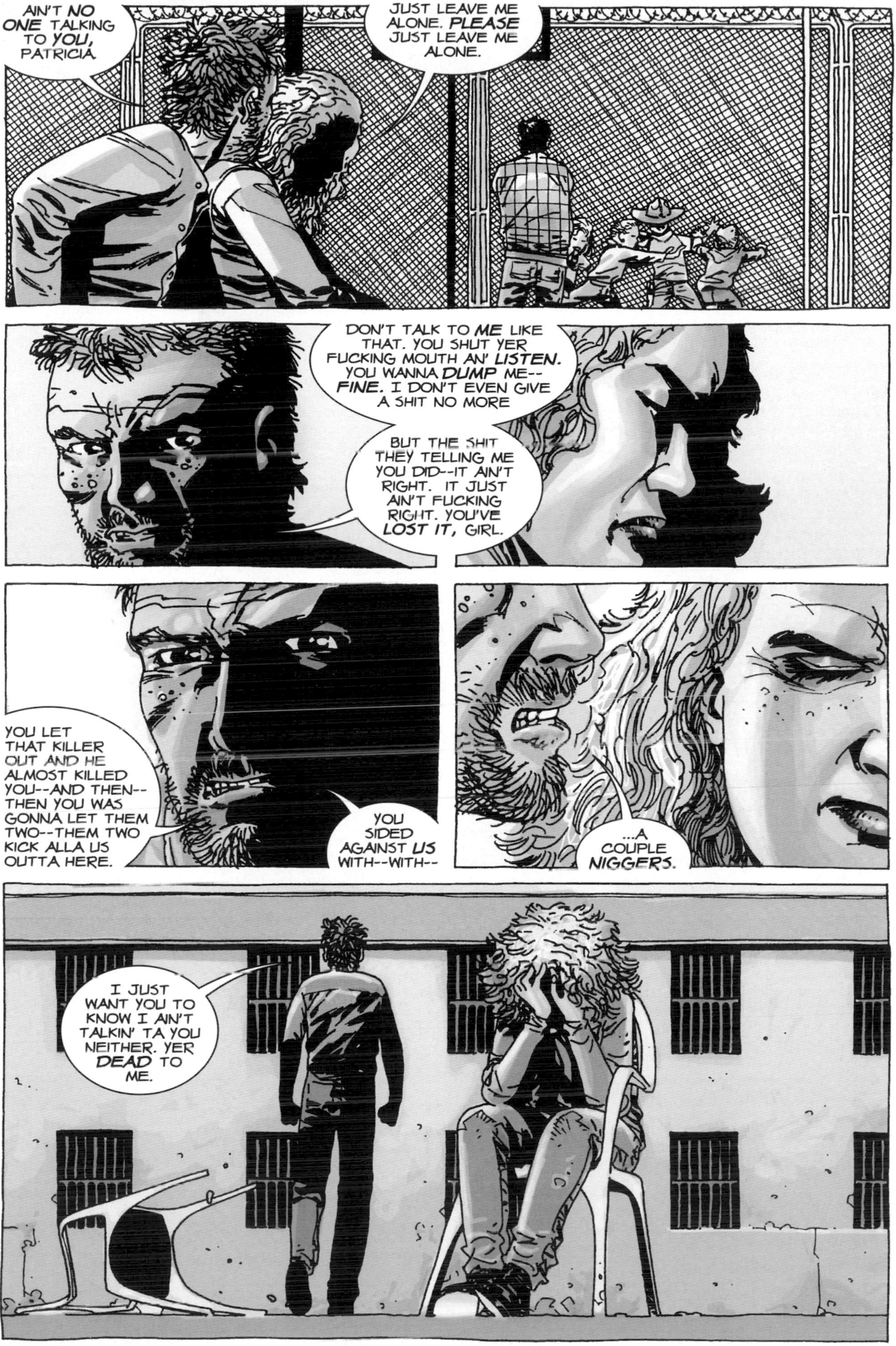
AIN'T NO ONE TALKING TO YOU, PATRICIA.
JUST LEAVE ME ALONE. PLEASE JUST LEAVE ME ALONE.
DON'T TALK TO ME LIKE THAT. YOU SHUT YER FUCKING MOUTH AN' LISTEN. YOU WANNA DUMP ME-- FINE. I DON'T EVEN GIVE A SHIT NO MORE
BUT THE SHIT THEY TELLING ME YOU DID--IT AIN'T RIGHT. IT JUST AIN'T FUCKING RIGHT. YOU'VE LOST IT, GIRL.
YOU LET THAT KILLER OUT AND HE ALMOST KILLED YOU--AND THEN-- THEN YOU WAS GONNA LET THEM TWO--THEM TWO KICK ALLA US OUTTA HERE.
YOU SIDED AGAINST US WITH--WITH--
...A COUPLE NIGGERS.
I JUST WANT YOU TO KNOW I AIN'T TALKIN' TA YOU NEITHER. YER DEAD TO ME.

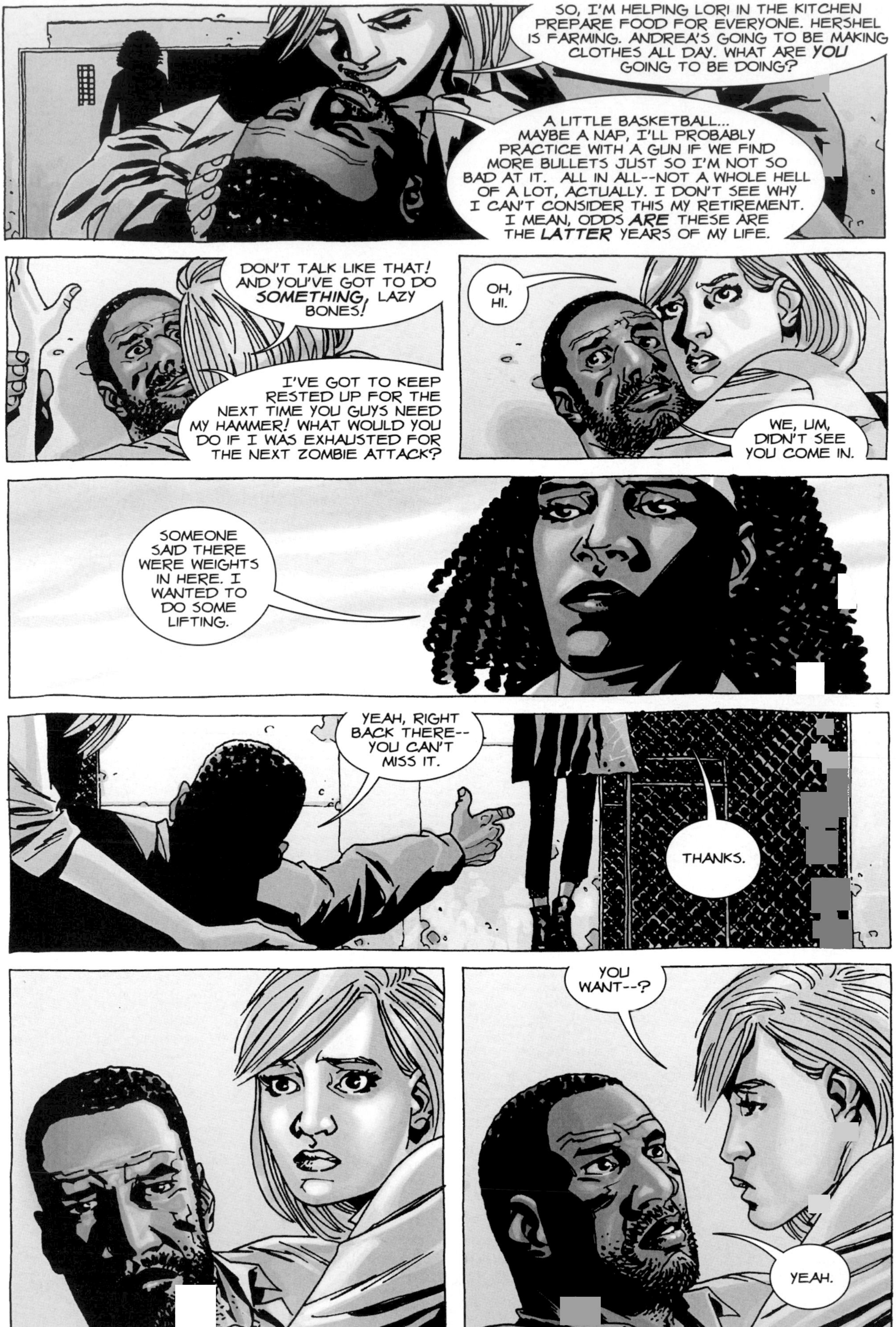
SO, I'M HELPING LORI IN THE KITCHEN PREPARE FOOD FOR EVERYONE. HERSHEL IS FARMING. ANDREA'S GOING TO BE MAKING CLOTHES ALL DAY. WHAT ARE *YOU* GOING TO BE DOING?
A LITTLE BASKETBALL... MAYBE A NAP, I'LL PROBABLY PRACTICE WITH A GUN IF WE FIND MORE BULLETS JUST SO I'M NOT SO BAD AT IT. ALL IN ALL--NOT A WHOLE HELL OF A LOT, ACTUALLY. I DON'T SEE WHY I CAN'T CONSIDER THIS MY RETIREMENT. I MEAN, ODDS *ARE* THESE ARE THE *LATTER* YEARS OF MY LIFE.
DON'T TALK LIKE THAT! AND YOU'VE GOT TO DO *SOMETHING,* LAZY BONES!
I'VE GOT TO KEEP RESTED UP FOR THE NEXT TIME YOU GUYS NEED MY HAMMER! WHAT WOULD YOU DO IF I WAS EXHAUSTED FOR THE NEXT ZOMBIE ATTACK?
OH, HI.
WE, UM, DIDN'T SEE YOU COME IN.
SOMEONE SAID THERE WERE WEIGHTS IN HERE. I WANTED TO DO SOME LIFTING.
YEAH, RIGHT BACK THERE-- YOU CAN'T MISS IT.
THANKS.
YOU WANT--?
YEAH.

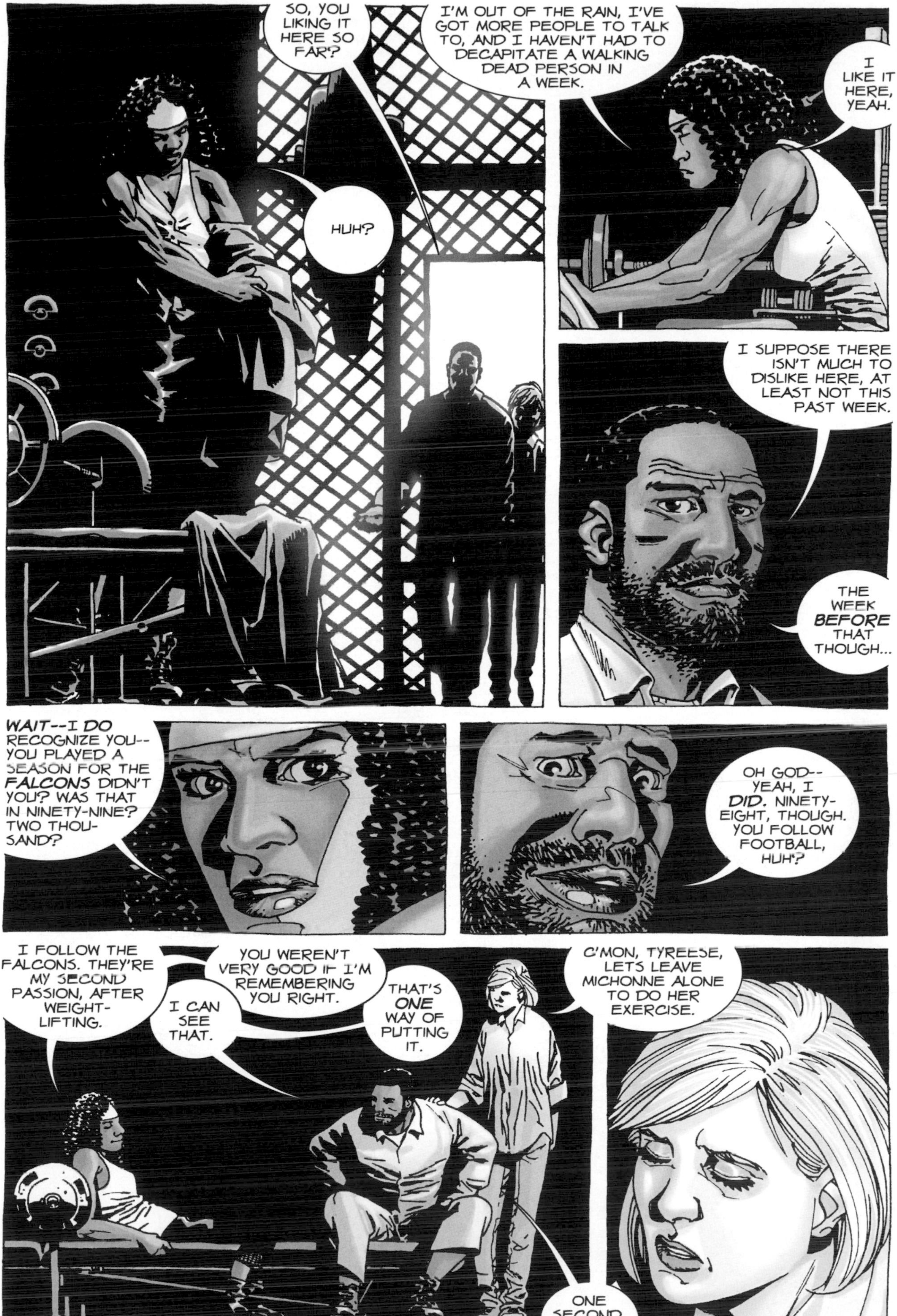

SO, YOU LIKING IT HERE SO FAR?
HUH?
I'M OUT OF THE RAIN, I'VE GOT MORE PEOPLE TO TALK TO, AND I HAVEN'T HAD TO DECAPITATE A WALKING DEAD PERSON IN A WEEK.
I LIKE IT HERE, YEAH.
I SUPPOSE THERE ISN'T MUCH TO DISLIKE HERE, AT LEAST NOT THIS PAST WEEK.
THE WEEK BEFORE THAT THOUGH...
WAIT--I DO RECOGNIZE YOU--YOU PLAYED A SEASON FOR THE FALCONS DIDN'T YOU? WAS THAT IN NINETY-NINE? TWO THOUSAND?
OH GOD--YEAH, I DID. NINETY-EIGHT, THOUGH. YOU FOLLOW FOOTBALL, HUH?
I FOLLOW THE FALCONS. THEY'RE MY SECOND PASSION, AFTER WEIGHT-LIFTING.
I CAN SEE THAT.
YOU WEREN'T VERY GOOD IF I'M REMEMBERING YOU RIGHT.
THAT'S ONE WAY OF PUTTING IT.
C'MON, TYREESE, LETS LEAVE MICHONNE ALONE TO DO HER EXERCISE.
ONE SECOND, CAROL.

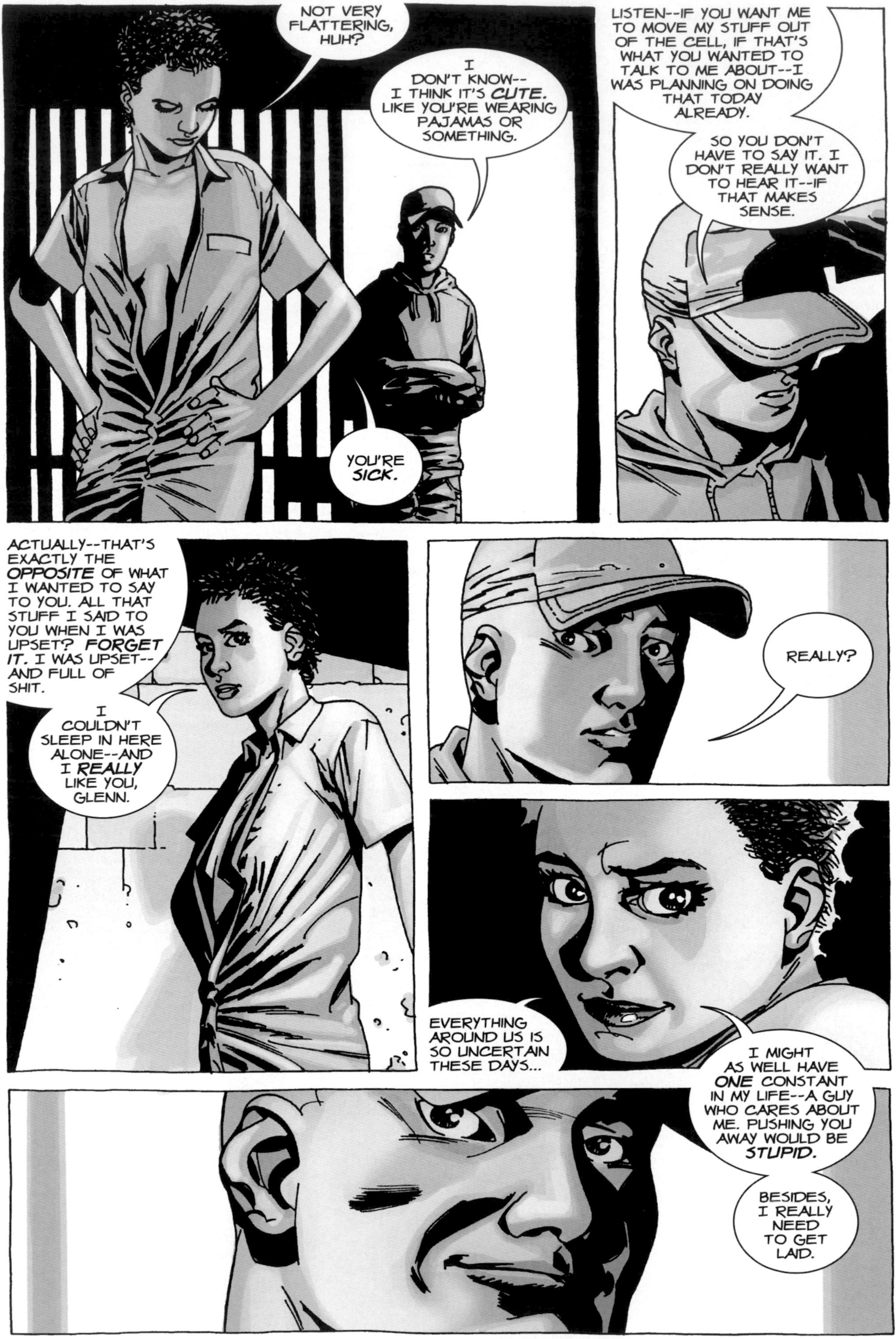
NOT VERY FLATTERING, HUH?
I DON'T KNOW-- I THINK IT'S CUTE. LIKE YOU'RE WEARING PAJAMAS OR SOMETHING.
YOU'RE SICK.
LISTEN--IF YOU WANT ME TO MOVE MY STUFF OUT OF THE CELL, IF THAT'S WHAT YOU WANTED TO TALK TO ME ABOUT--I WAS PLANNING ON DOING THAT TODAY ALREADY.
SO YOU DON'T HAVE TO SAY IT. I DON'T REALLY WANT TO HEAR IT--IF THAT MAKES SENSE.
ACTUALLY--THAT'S EXACTLY THE OPPOSITE OF WHAT I WANTED TO SAY TO YOU. ALL THAT STUFF I SAID TO YOU WHEN I WAS UPSET? FORGET IT. I WAS UPSET-- AND FULL OF SHIT.
I COULDN'T SLEEP IN HERE ALONE--AND I REALLY LIKE YOU, GLENN.
REALLY?
EVERYTHING AROUND US IS SO UNCERTAIN THESE DAYS...
I MIGHT AS WELL HAVE ONE CONSTANT IN MY LIFE--A GUY WHO CARES ABOUT ME. PUSHING YOU AWAY WOULD BE STUPID.
BESIDES, I REALLY NEED TO GET LAID.

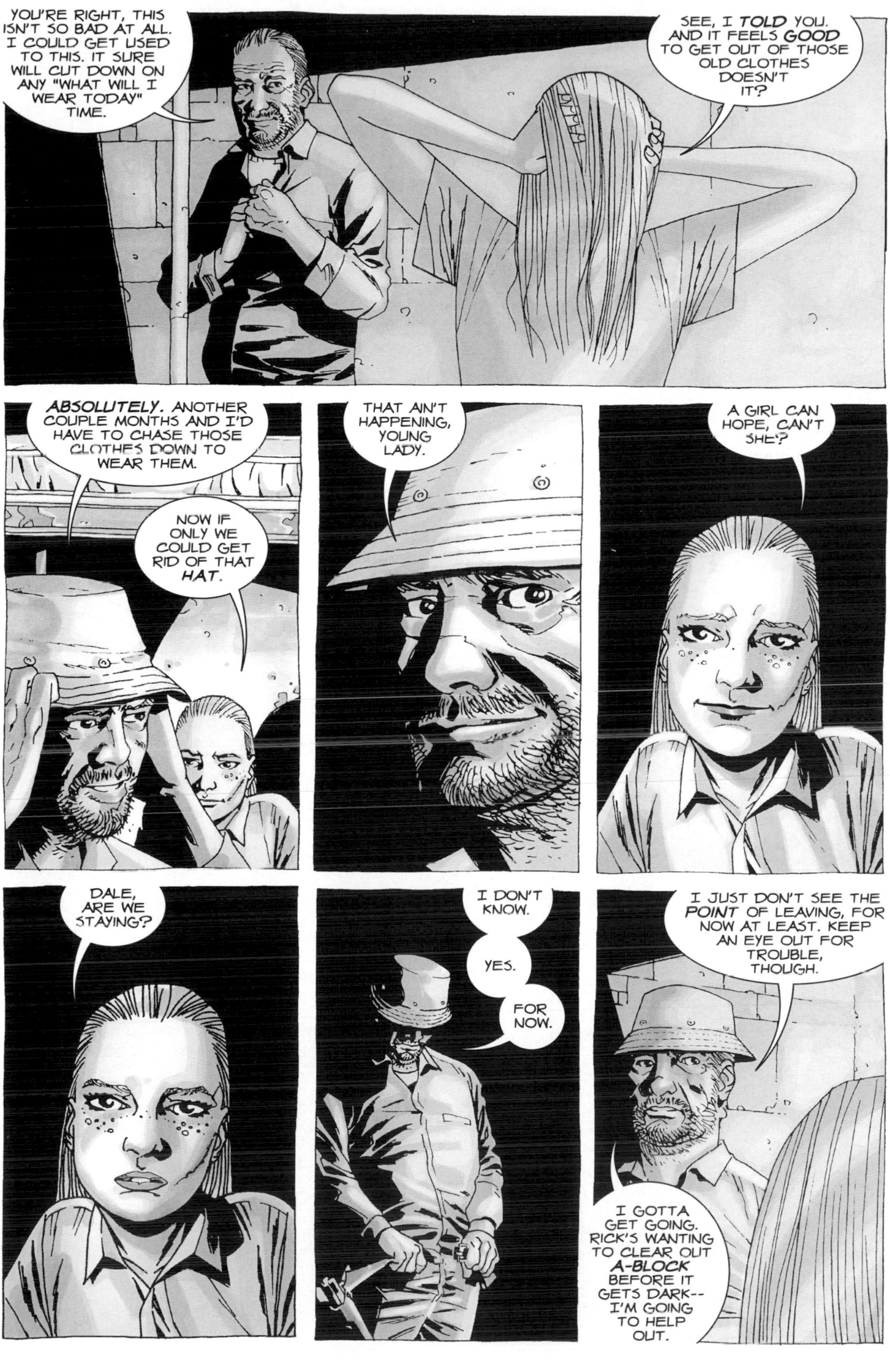
YOU'RE RIGHT, THIS ISN'T SO BAD AT ALL. I COULD GET USED TO THIS. IT SURE WILL CUT DOWN ON ANY "WHAT WILL I WEAR TODAY" TIME.
SEE, I TOLD YOU. AND IT FEELS GOOD TO GET OUT OF THOSE OLD CLOTHES DOESN'T IT?
ABSOLUTELY. ANOTHER COUPLE MONTHS AND I'D HAVE TO CHASE THOSE CLOTHES DOWN TO WEAR THEM.
NOW IF ONLY WE COULD GET RID OF THAT HAT.
THAT AIN'T HAPPENING, YOUNG LADY.
A GIRL CAN HOPE, CAN'T SHE?
DALE, ARE WE STAYING?
I DON'T KNOW.
YES.
FOR NOW.
I JUST DON'T SEE THE POINT OF LEAVING, FOR NOW AT LEAST. KEEP AN EYE OUT FOR TROUBLE, THOUGH.
I GOTTA GET GOING. RICK'S WANTING TO CLEAR OUT A-BLOCK BEFORE IT GETS DARK-- I'M GOING TO HELP OUT.

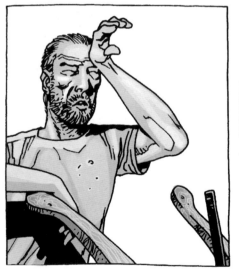

HURRY UP THERE, WILL YOU?

WHOA, WHOA--CALM DOWN THERE, BUDDY. I'M JUST LOOKING FORWARD TO SOME FRESH PRODUCE. YOU FOLLOW ME?

AFTER EATING ALL THE CANNED STUFF... YOU SEE?

LOOK, YOU CAN *NOT* LIKE ME HOWEVER MUCH YOU WANT--BUT I DIDN'T KNOW HIM AND I FOR *DAMN* SURE DIDN'T *LIKE* HIM.

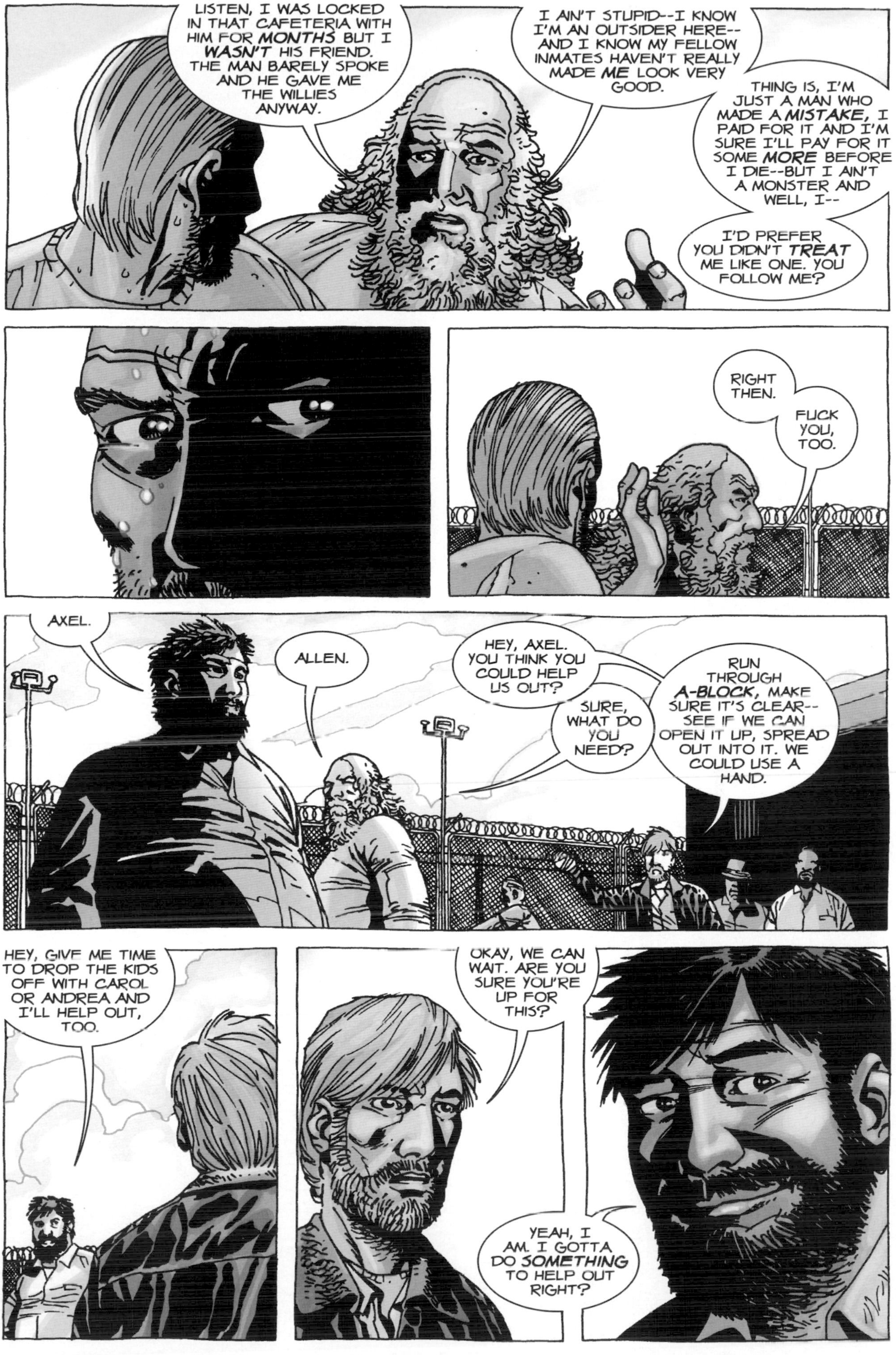
LISTEN, I WAS LOCKED IN THAT CAFETERIA WITH HIM FOR MONTHS BUT I WASN'T HIS FRIEND. THE MAN BARELY SPOKE AND HE GAVE ME THE WILLIES ANYWAY.
I AIN'T STUPID--I KNOW I'M AN OUTSIDER HERE-- AND I KNOW MY FELLOW INMATES HAVEN'T REALLY MADE ME LOOK VERY GOOD.
THING IS, I'M JUST A MAN WHO MADE A MISTAKE, I PAID FOR IT AND I'M SURE I'LL PAY FOR IT SOME MORE BEFORE I DIE--BUT I AIN'T A MONSTER AND WELL, I--
I'D PREFER YOU DIDN'T TREAT ME LIKE ONE. YOU FOLLOW ME?
RIGHT THEN.
FUCK YOU, TOO.
AXEL.
ALLEN.
HEY, AXEL. YOU THINK YOU COULD HELP US OUT?
SURE, WHAT DO YOU NEED?
RUN THROUGH A-BLOCK, MAKE SURE IT'S CLEAR-- SEE IF WE CAN OPEN IT UP, SPREAD OUT INTO IT. WE COULD USE A HAND.
HEY, GIVE ME TIME TO DROP THE KIDS OFF WITH CAROL OR ANDREA AND I'LL HELP OUT, TOO.
OKAY, WE CAN WAIT. ARE YOU SURE YOU'RE UP FOR THIS?
YEAH, I AM. I GOTTA DO SOMETHING TO HELP OUT RIGHT?

OKAY, HOPEFULLY MOST OF THE ROAMERS FLOODED OUT WHEN DEXTER AND ANDREW LET THEM LOOSE. IF THAT'S THE CASE, AND ALL WE'VE GOT IN HERE ARE LURKERS... THIS SHOULD BE EASY-- LIKE IT WAS WITH C-BLOCK WHEN WE FIRST GOT HERE.

I GOT THIS ONE.

ALLEN-- NO!

WHAT? THIS IS WHAT WE'RE HERE FOR RIGHT?

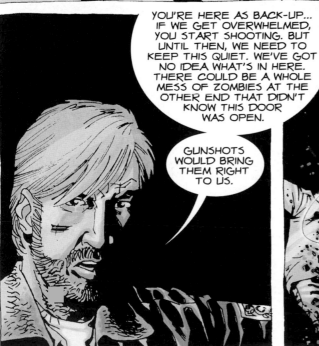

YOU'RE HERE AS BACK-UP... IF WE GET OVERWHELMED, YOU START SHOOTING. BUT UNTIL THEN, WE NEED TO KEEP THIS QUIET. WE'VE GOT NO IDEA WHAT'S IN HERE. THERE COULD BE A WHOLE MESS OF ZOMBIES AT THE OTHER END THAT DIDN'T KNOW THIS DOOR WAS OPEN.

GUNSHOTS WOULD BRING THEM RIGHT TO US.

OH.

WHACK!

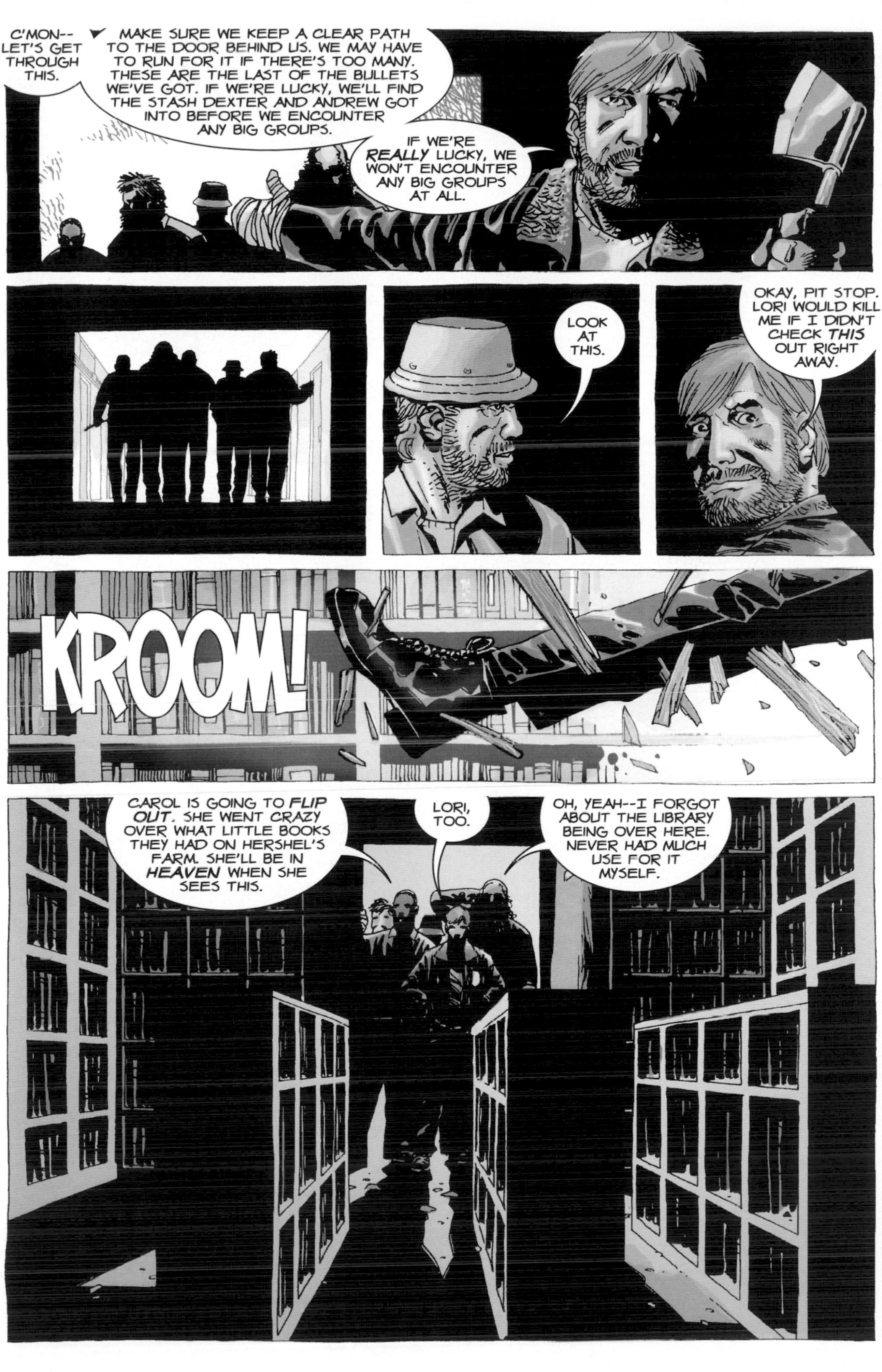
C'MON-- LET'S GET THROUGH THIS.
MAKE SURE WE KEEP A CLEAR PATH TO THE DOOR BEHIND US. WE MAY HAVE TO RUN FOR IT IF THERE'S TOO MANY. THESE ARE THE LAST OF THE BULLETS WE'VE GOT. IF WE'RE LUCKY, WE'LL FIND THE STASH DEXTER AND ANDREW GOT INTO BEFORE WE ENCOUNTER ANY BIG GROUPS.
IF WE'RE REALLY LUCKY, WE WON'T ENCOUNTER ANY BIG GROUPS AT ALL.
LOOK AT THIS.
OKAY, PIT STOP. LORI WOULD KILL ME IF I DIDN'T CHECK THIS OUT RIGHT AWAY.
KROOM!
CAROL IS GOING TO FLIP OUT. SHE WENT CRAZY OVER WHAT LITTLE BOOKS THEY HAD ON HERSHEL'S FARM. SHE'LL BE IN HEAVEN WHEN SHE SEES THIS.
LORI, TOO.
OH, YEAH--I FORGOT ABOUT THE LIBRARY BEING OVER HERE. NEVER HAD MUCH USE FOR IT MYSELF.

UH, GUYS.

IS THAT THING MOVING?

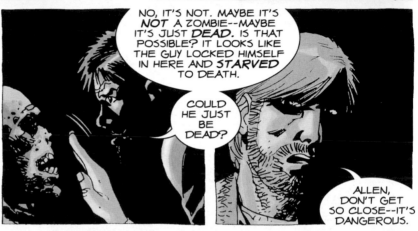

NO, IT'S NOT. MAYBE IT'S *NOT* A ZOMBIE--MAYBE IT'S JUST *DEAD*. IS THAT POSSIBLE? IT LOOKS LIKE THE GUY LOCKED HIMSELF IN HERE AND *STARVED* TO DEATH.

COULD HE JUST BE DEAD?

ALLEN, DON'T GET SO CLOSE--IT'S DANGEROUS.

AAAGH!

GRAH!!

OH, JESUS!!

WHUMP!

BLAM! BLAM!

LIBRARY.

OKAY, I'M NOT HEARING ANY MOANING OR ECHOES OR ANYTHING... SO MOST OF THE ROAMERS MUST HAVE FILED OUT OF THIS PLACE AND GOTTEN SHOT.

SO WE'LL DO THIS QUICKER IF WE SPLIT UP. TYREESE AND DALE, YOU GUYS HEAD UP THAT WAY. I'LL KEEP ALLEN AND AXEL WITH ME.

SOUNDS LIKE A PLAN.

JUST *SCREAM* IF YOU NEED HELP.

YOU DO THE SAME.

STAY ALERT, THERE'RE NOT AS MANY WINDOWS BACK HERE SO IT'S GETTING DARKER.

IF IT GETS TOO BAD, WE'LL GO BACK AND GET DALE'S FLASH-LIGHT.

HOLD UP, GUYS-- I'M STILL A BIT WINDED FROM THE LIBRARIAN BACK THERE.

JUST GIVE ME A MINUTE.

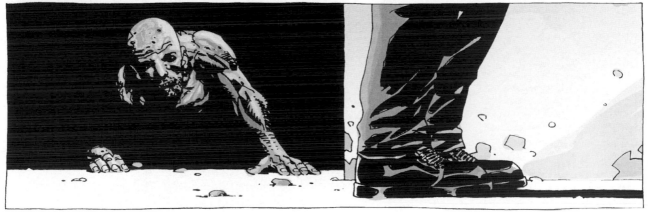

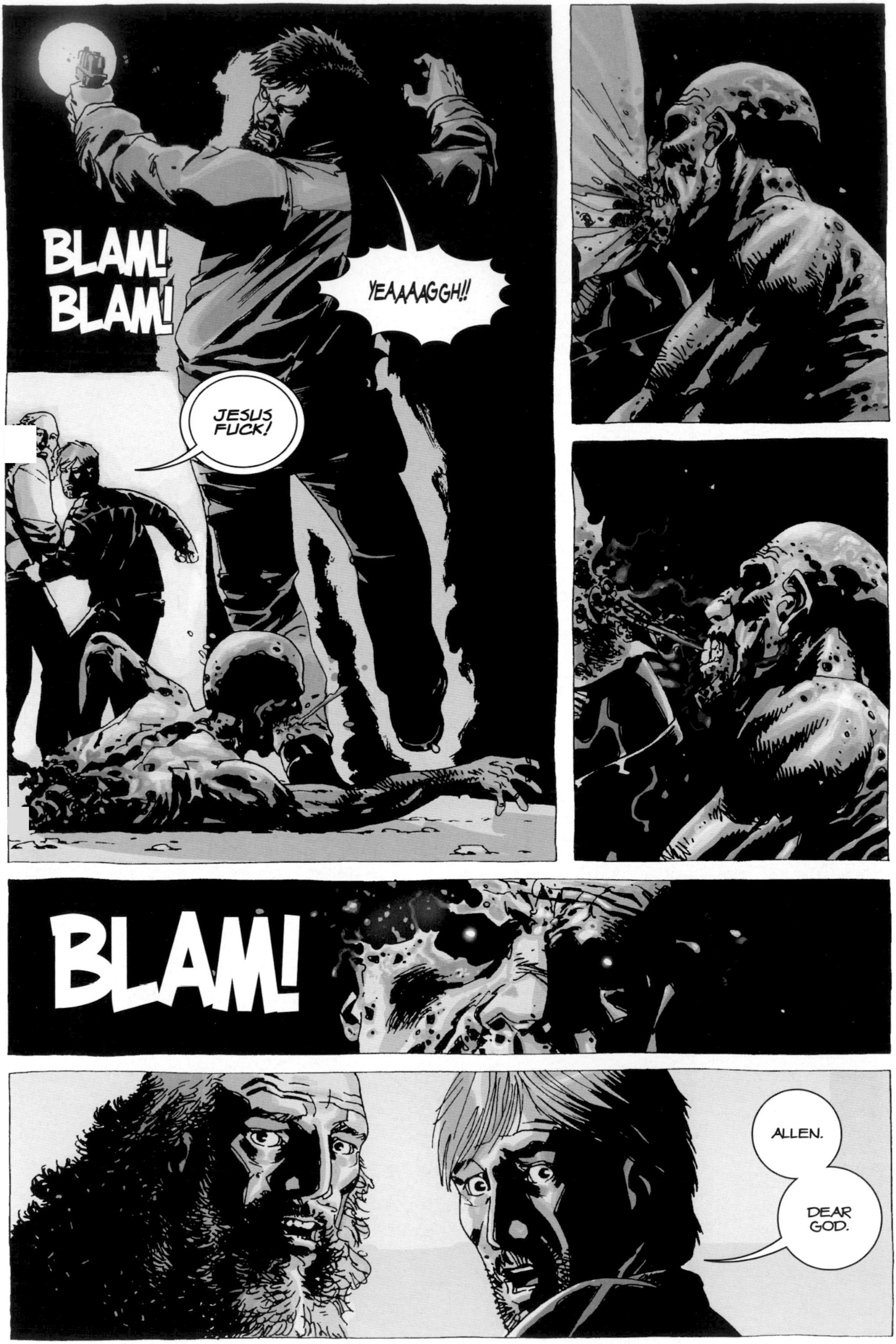
BLAM! BLAM!
YEAAAAGGH!!
JESUS FUCK!
BLAM!
ALLEN.
DEAR GOD.

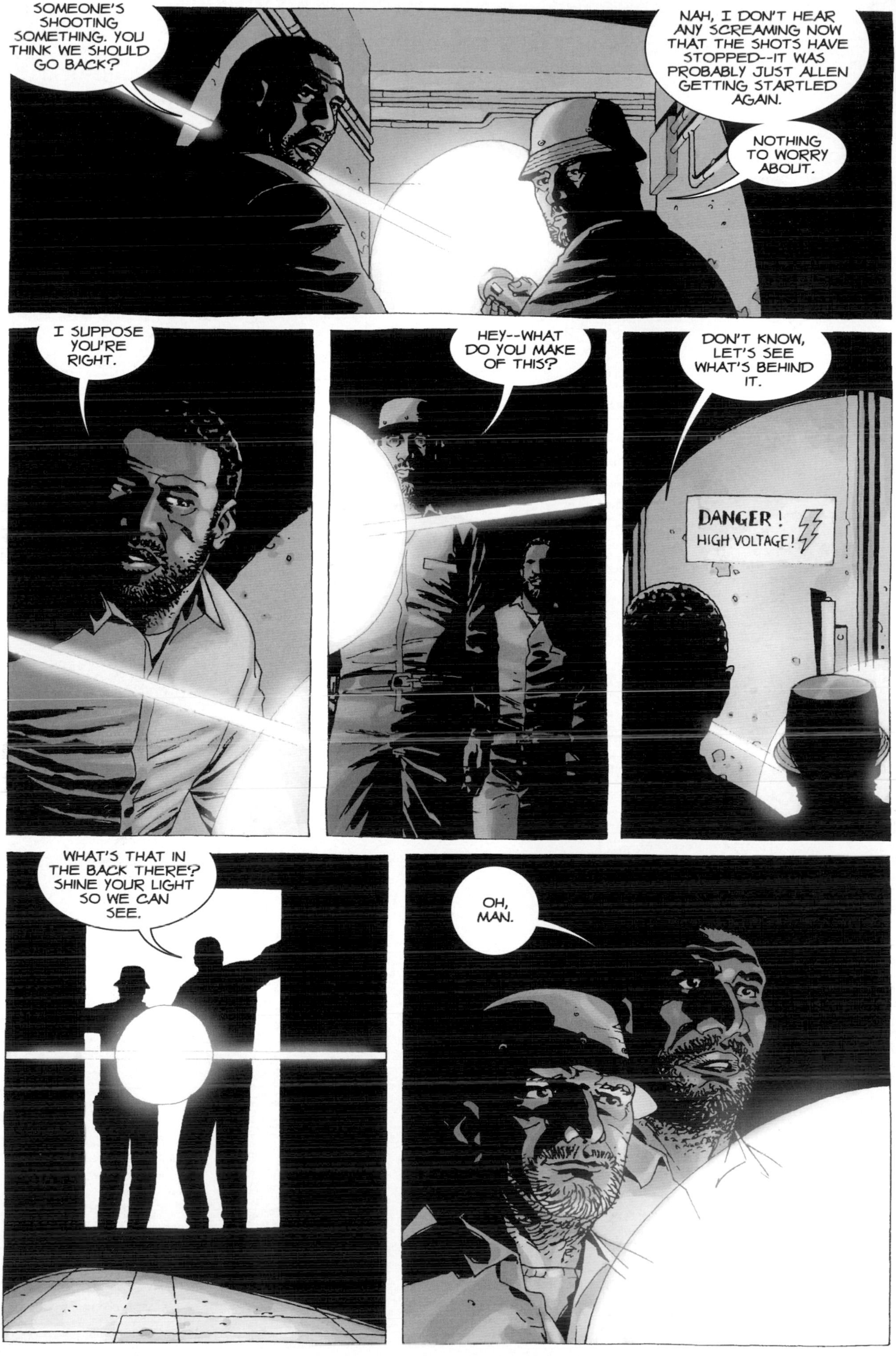
SOMEONE'S SHOOTING SOMETHING. YOU THINK WE SHOULD GO BACK?
NAH, I DON'T HEAR ANY SCREAMING NOW THAT THE SHOTS HAVE STOPPED--IT WAS PROBABLY JUST ALLEN GETTING STARTLED AGAIN.
NOTHING TO WORRY ABOUT.
I SUPPOSE YOU'RE RIGHT.
HEY--WHAT DO YOU MAKE OF THIS?
DON'T KNOW, LET'S SEE WHAT'S BEHIND IT.
DANGER ! HIGH VOLTAGE!
WHAT'S THAT IN THE BACK THERE? SHINE YOUR LIGHT SO WE CAN SEE.
OH, MAN.

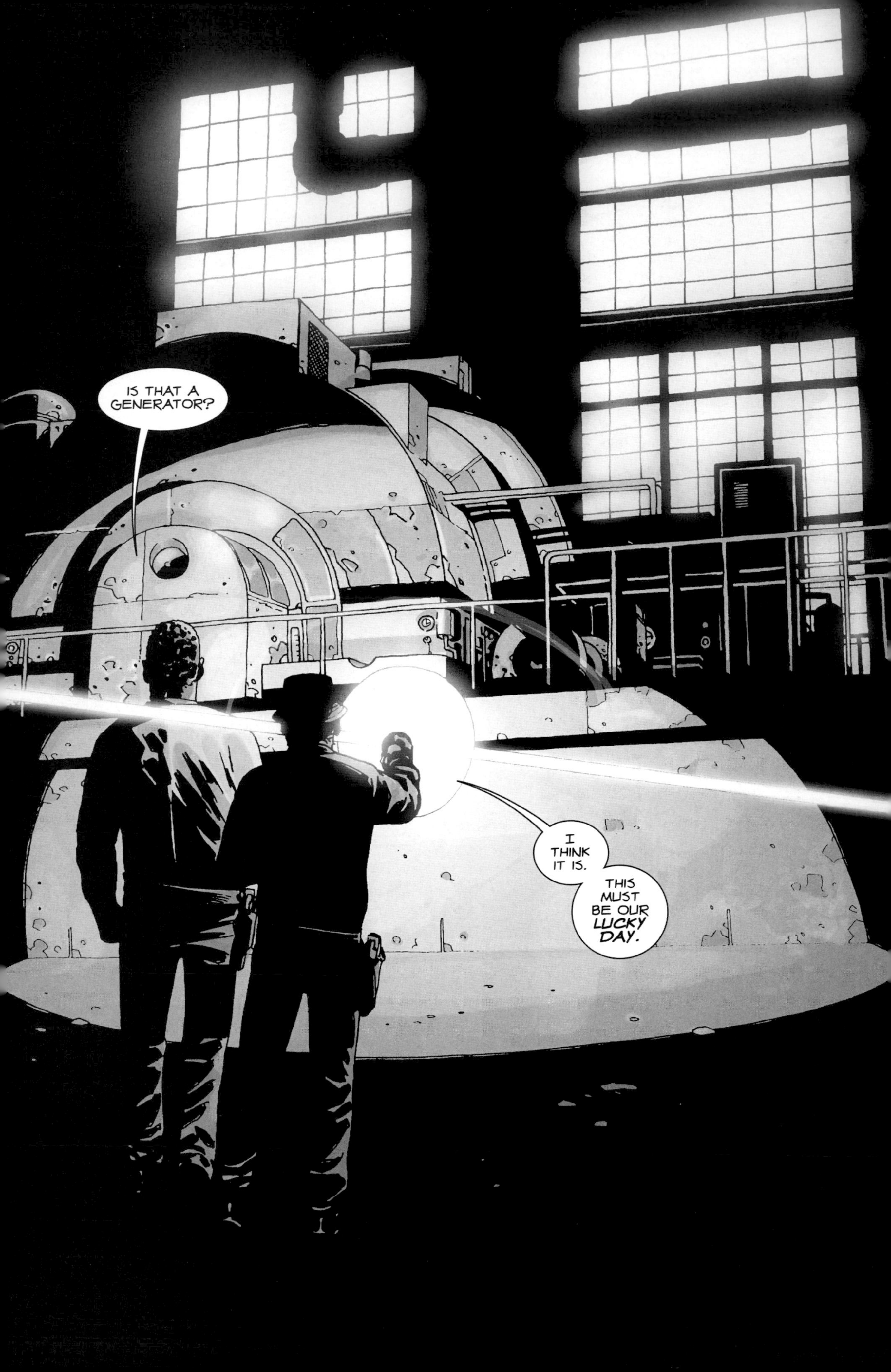
IS THAT A GENERATOR?
I THINK IT IS.
THIS MUST BE OUR LUCKY DAY.

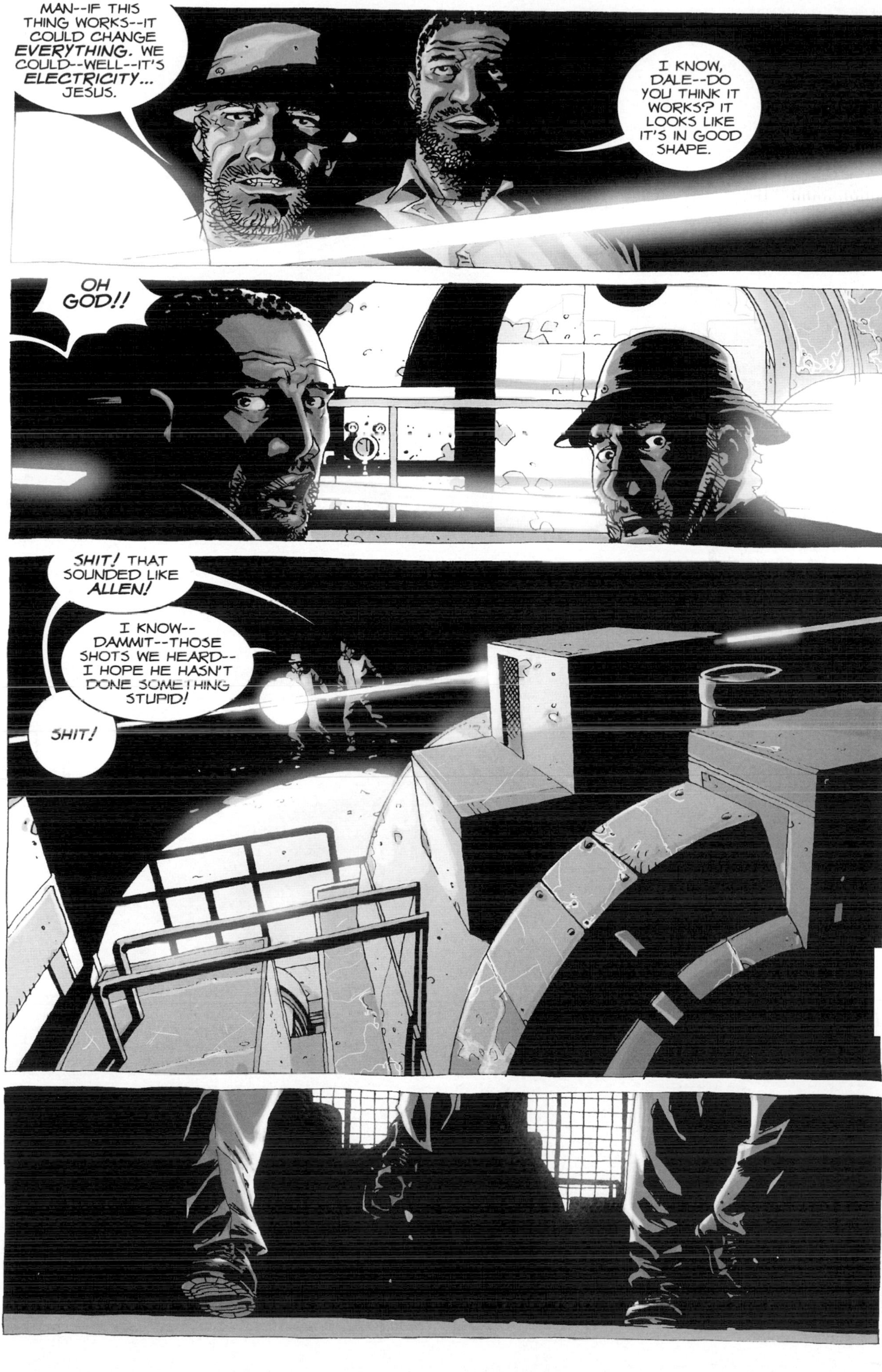
MAN--IF THIS THING WORKS--IT COULD CHANGE EVERYTHING. WE COULD--WELL--IT'S ELECTRICITY... JESUS.
I KNOW, DALE--DO YOU THINK IT WORKS? IT LOOKS LIKE IT'S IN GOOD SHAPE.
OH GOD!!
SHIT! THAT SOUNDED LIKE ALLEN!
I KNOW--DAMMIT--THOSE SHOTS WE HEARD--I HOPE HE HASN'T DONE SOMETHING STUPID!
SHIT!

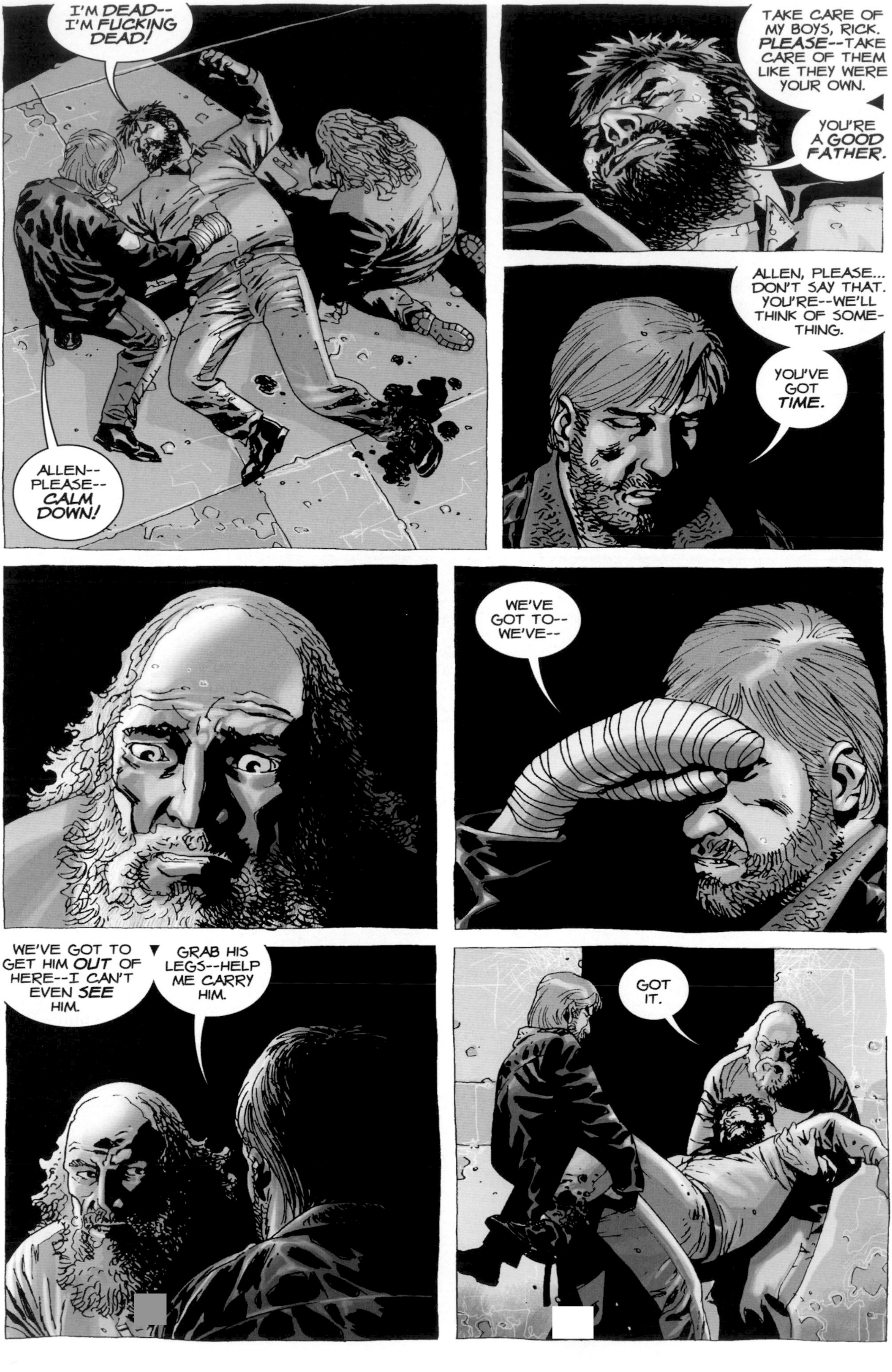
I'M DEAD-- I'M FUCKING DEAD!
ALLEN-- PLEASE-- CALM DOWN!
TAKE CARE OF MY BOYS, RICK. PLEASE--TAKE CARE OF THEM LIKE THEY WERE YOUR OWN.
YOU'RE A GOOD FATHER.
ALLEN, PLEASE... DON'T SAY THAT. YOU'RE--WE'LL THINK OF SOME-THING.
YOU'VE GOT TIME.
WE'VE GOT TO-- WE'VE--
WE'VE GOT TO GET HIM OUT OF HERE--I CAN'T EVEN SEE HIM.
GRAB HIS LEGS--HELP ME CARRY HIM.
GOT IT.

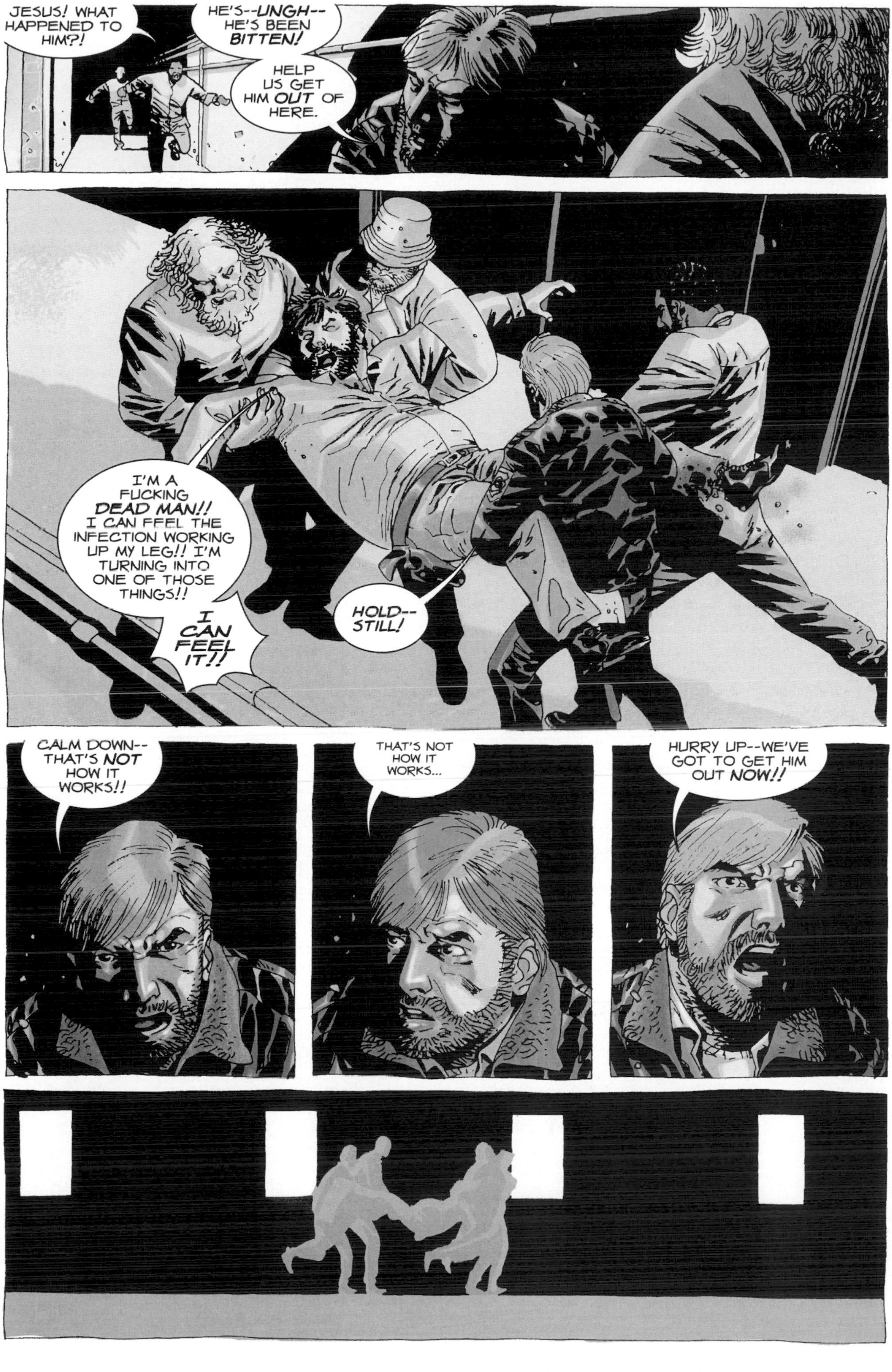
JESUS! WHAT HAPPENED TO HIM?!
HE'S--UNGH--HE'S BEEN BITTEN!
HELP US GET HIM OUT OF HERE.
I'M A FUCKING DEAD MAN!! I CAN FEEL THE INFECTION WORKING UP MY LEG!! I'M TURNING INTO ONE OF THOSE THINGS!!
I CAN FEEL IT!!
HOLD--STILL!
CALM DOWN--THAT'S NOT HOW IT WORKS!!
THAT'S NOT HOW IT WORKS...
HURRY UP--WE'VE GOT TO GET HIM OUT NOW!!

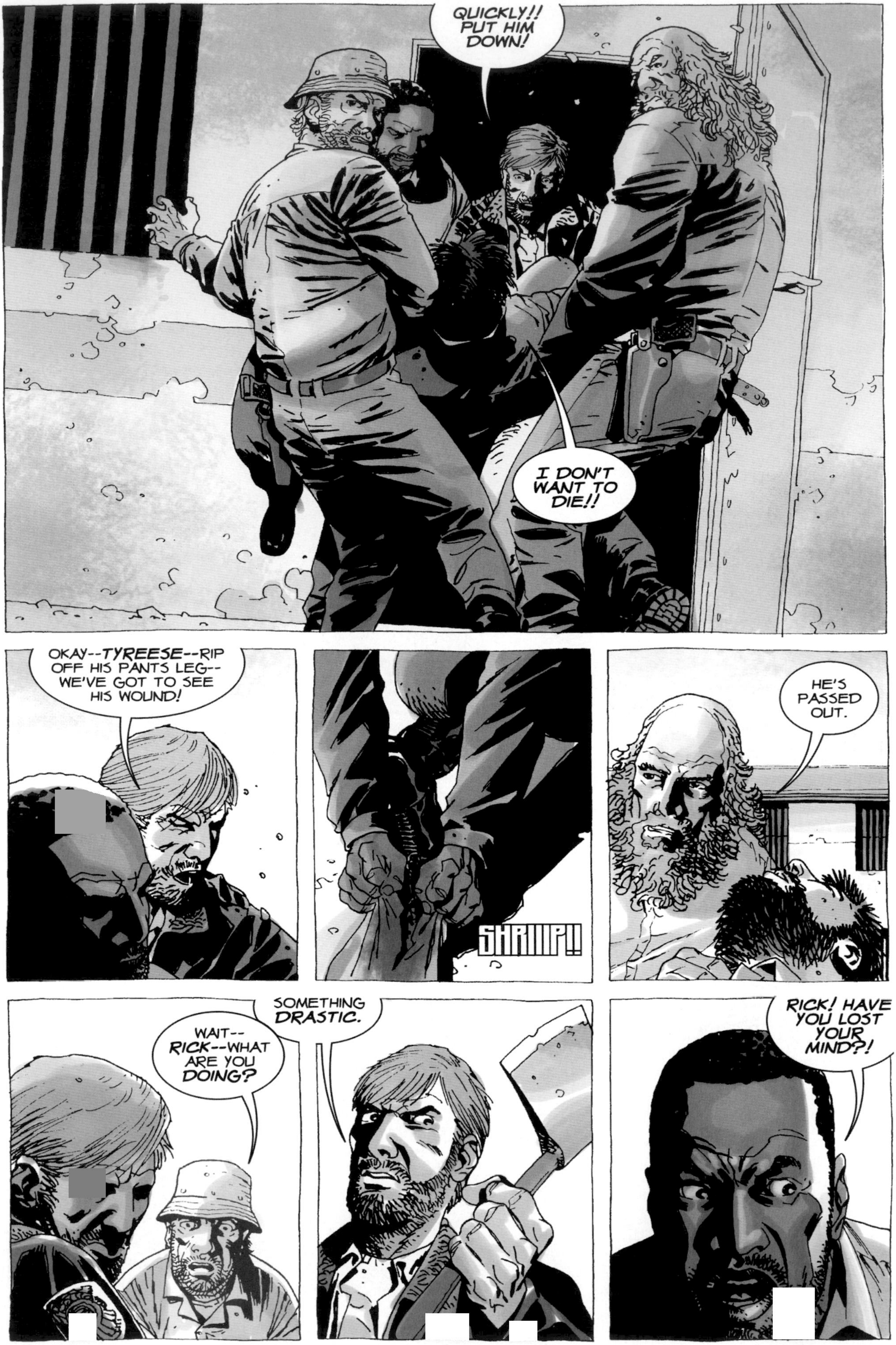
QUICKLY!! PUT HIM DOWN!
I DON'T WANT TO DIE!!
OKAY--TYREESE--RIP OFF HIS PANTS LEG-- WE'VE GOT TO SEE HIS WOUND!
SHRIIIP!!
HE'S PASSED OUT.
WAIT-- RICK--WHAT ARE YOU DOING?
SOMETHING DRASTIC.
RICK! HAVE YOU LOST YOUR MIND?!

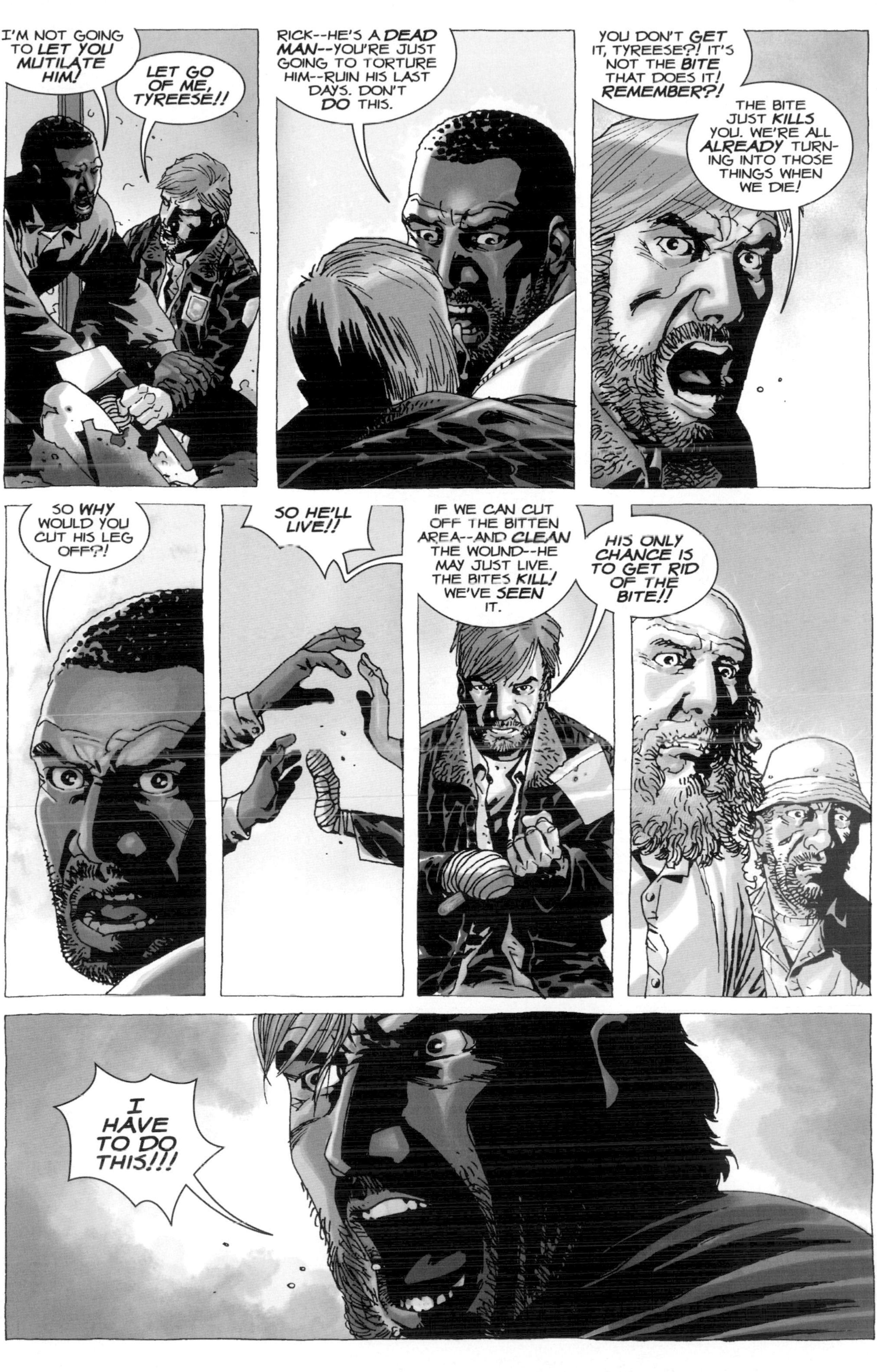

I'M NOT GOING TO LET YOU MUTILATE HIM!
LET GO OF ME, TYREESE!!
RICK--HE'S A DEAD MAN--YOU'RE JUST GOING TO TORTURE HIM--RUIN HIS LAST DAYS. DON'T DO THIS.
YOU DON'T GET IT, TYREESE?! IT'S NOT THE BITE THAT DOES IT! REMEMBER?!
THE BITE JUST KILLS YOU. WE'RE ALL ALREADY TURNING INTO THOSE THINGS WHEN WE DIE!
SO WHY WOULD YOU CUT HIS LEG OFF?!
SO HE'LL LIVE!!
IF WE CAN CUT OFF THE BITTEN AREA--AND CLEAN THE WOUND--HE MAY JUST LIVE. THE BITES KILL! WE'VE SEEN IT.
HIS ONLY CHANCE IS TO GET RID OF THE BITE!!
I HAVE TO DO THIS!!!

DO IT.

I DON'T KNOW...

JUST DO IT.

THUNK!!

THUNK!

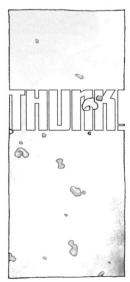

THUNK!

THUNK!

THUNK!

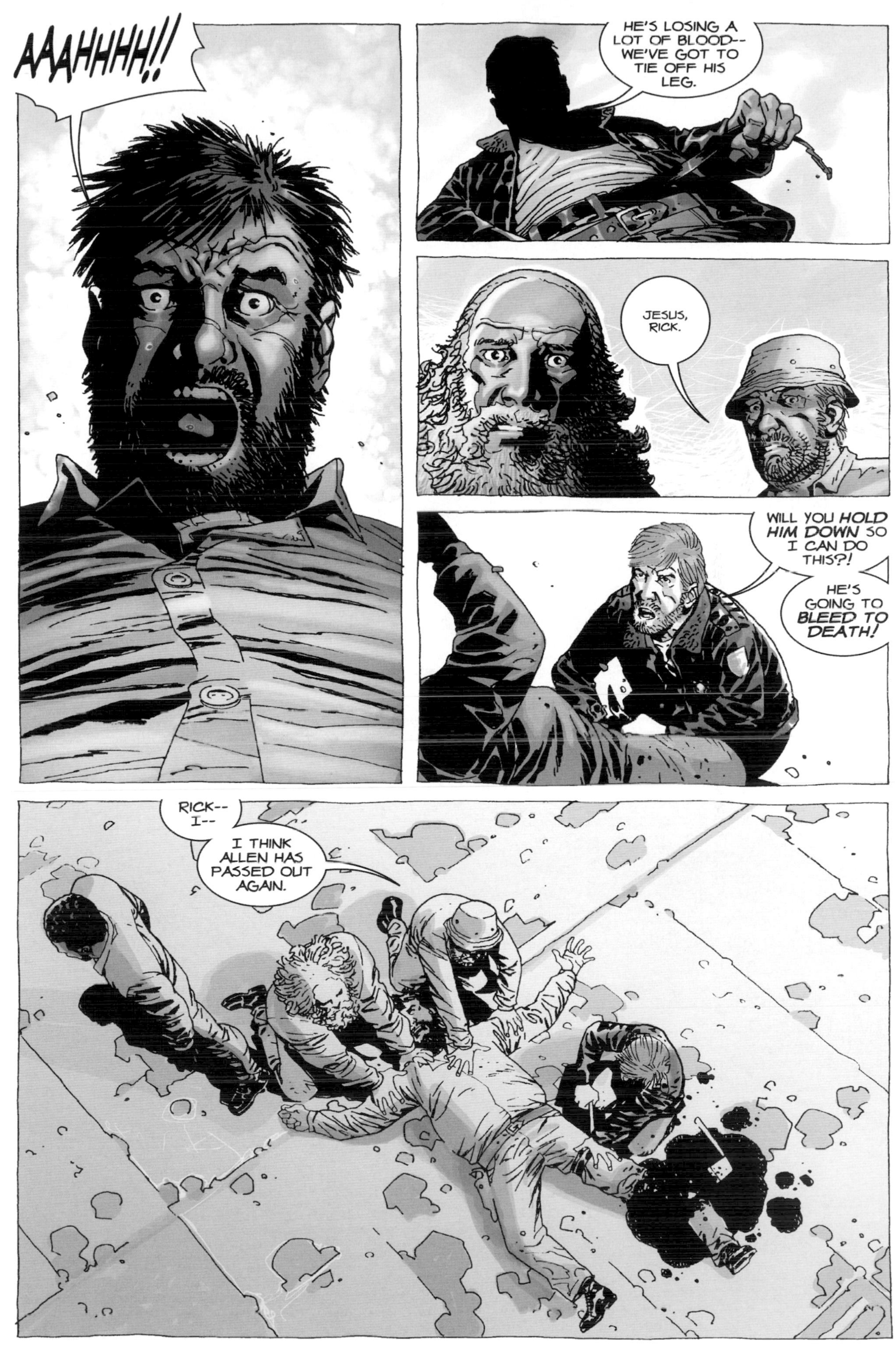
AAAHHHH!!
HE'S LOSING A LOT OF BLOOD-- WE'VE GOT TO TIE OFF HIS LEG.
JESUS, RICK.
WILL YOU HOLD HIM DOWN SO I CAN DO THIS?!
HE'S GOING TO BLEED TO DEATH!
RICK-- I--
I THINK ALLEN HAS PASSED OUT AGAIN.

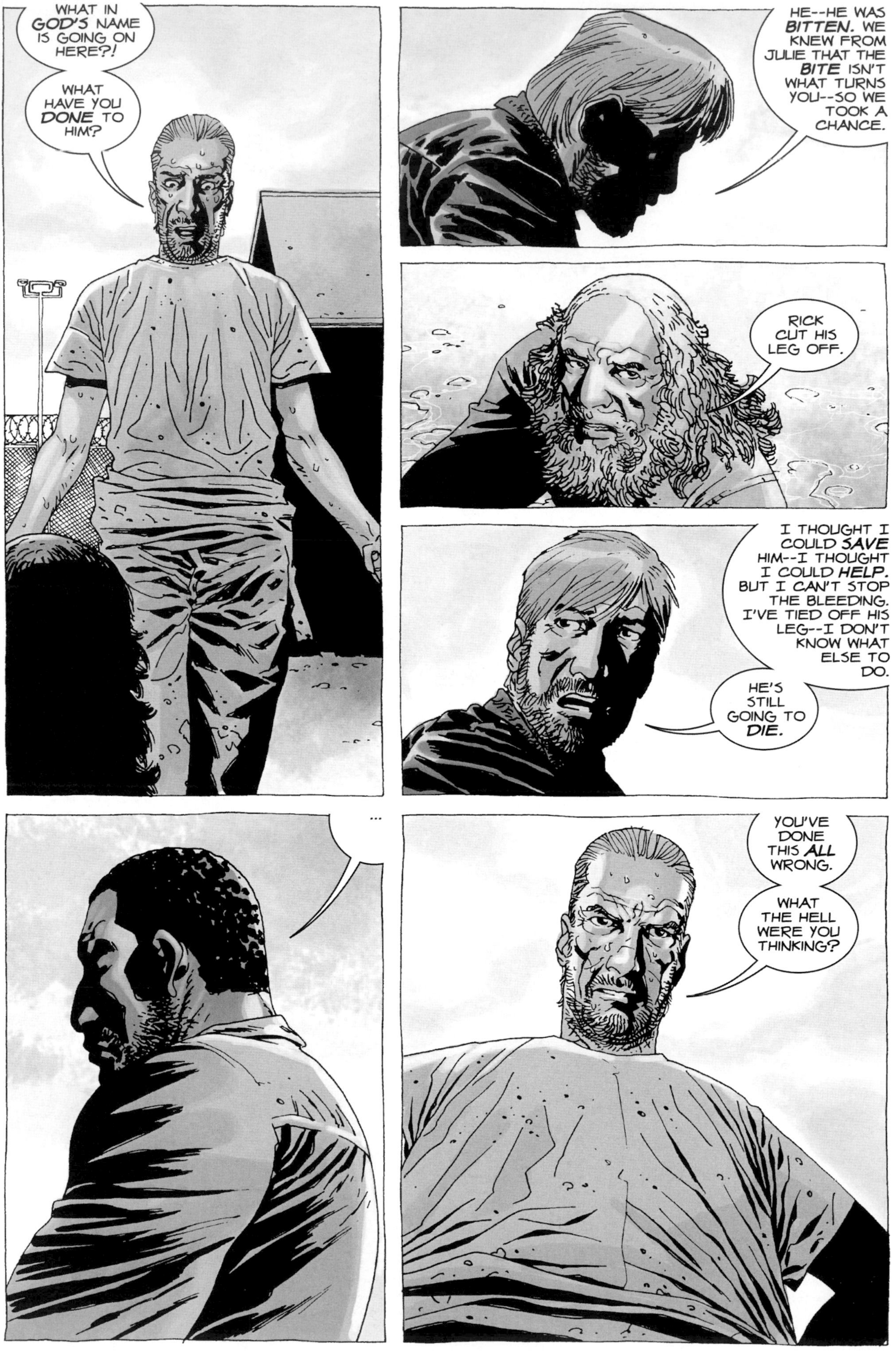
WHAT IN GOD'S NAME IS GOING ON HERE?!
WHAT HAVE YOU DONE TO HIM?
HE--HE WAS BITTEN. WE KNEW FROM JULIE THAT THE BITE ISN'T WHAT TURNS YOU--SO WE TOOK A CHANCE.
RICK CUT HIS LEG OFF.
I THOUGHT I COULD SAVE HIM--I THOUGHT I COULD HELP. BUT I CAN'T STOP THE BLEEDING. I'VE TIED OFF HIS LEG--I DON'T KNOW WHAT ELSE TO DO.
HE'S STILL GOING TO DIE.
...
YOU'VE DONE THIS ALL WRONG.
WHAT THE HELL WERE YOU THINKING?

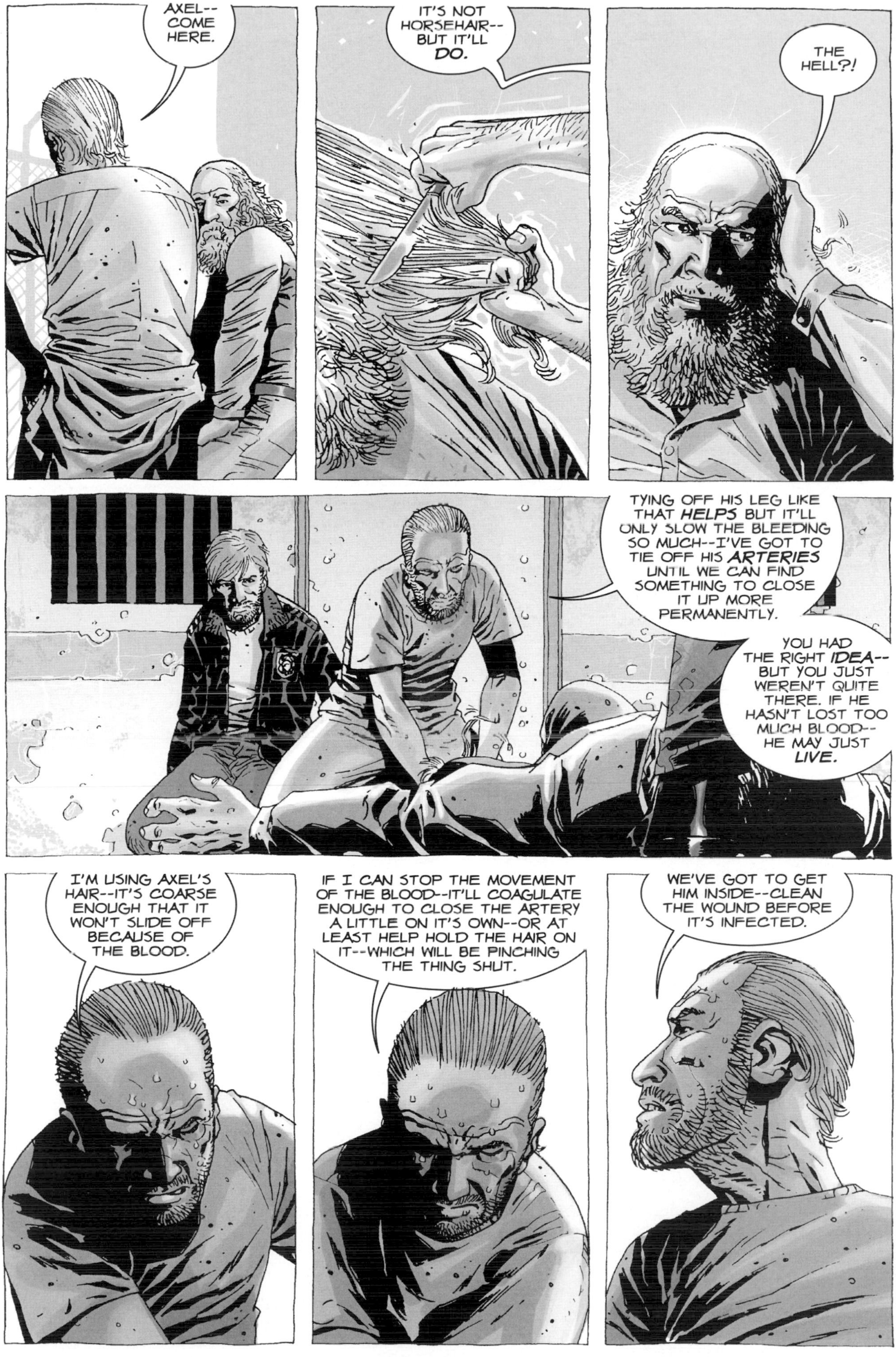
AXEL-- COME HERE.
IT'S NOT HORSEHAIR-- BUT IT'LL DO.
THE HELL?!
TYING OFF HIS LEG LIKE THAT HELPS BUT IT'LL ONLY SLOW THE BLEEDING SO MUCH--I'VE GOT TO TIE OFF HIS ARTERIES UNTIL WE CAN FIND SOMETHING TO CLOSE IT UP MORE PERMANENTLY.
YOU HAD THE RIGHT IDEA-- BUT YOU JUST WEREN'T QUITE THERE. IF HE HASN'T LOST TOO MUCH BLOOD-- HE MAY JUST LIVE.
I'M USING AXEL'S HAIR--IT'S COARSE ENOUGH THAT IT WON'T SLIDE OFF BECAUSE OF THE BLOOD.
IF I CAN STOP THE MOVEMENT OF THE BLOOD--IT'LL COAGULATE ENOUGH TO CLOSE THE ARTERY A LITTLE ON IT'S OWN--OR AT LEAST HELP HOLD THE HAIR ON IT--WHICH WILL BE PINCHING THE THING SHUT.
WE'VE GOT TO GET HIM INSIDE--CLEAN THE WOUND BEFORE IT'S INFECTED.

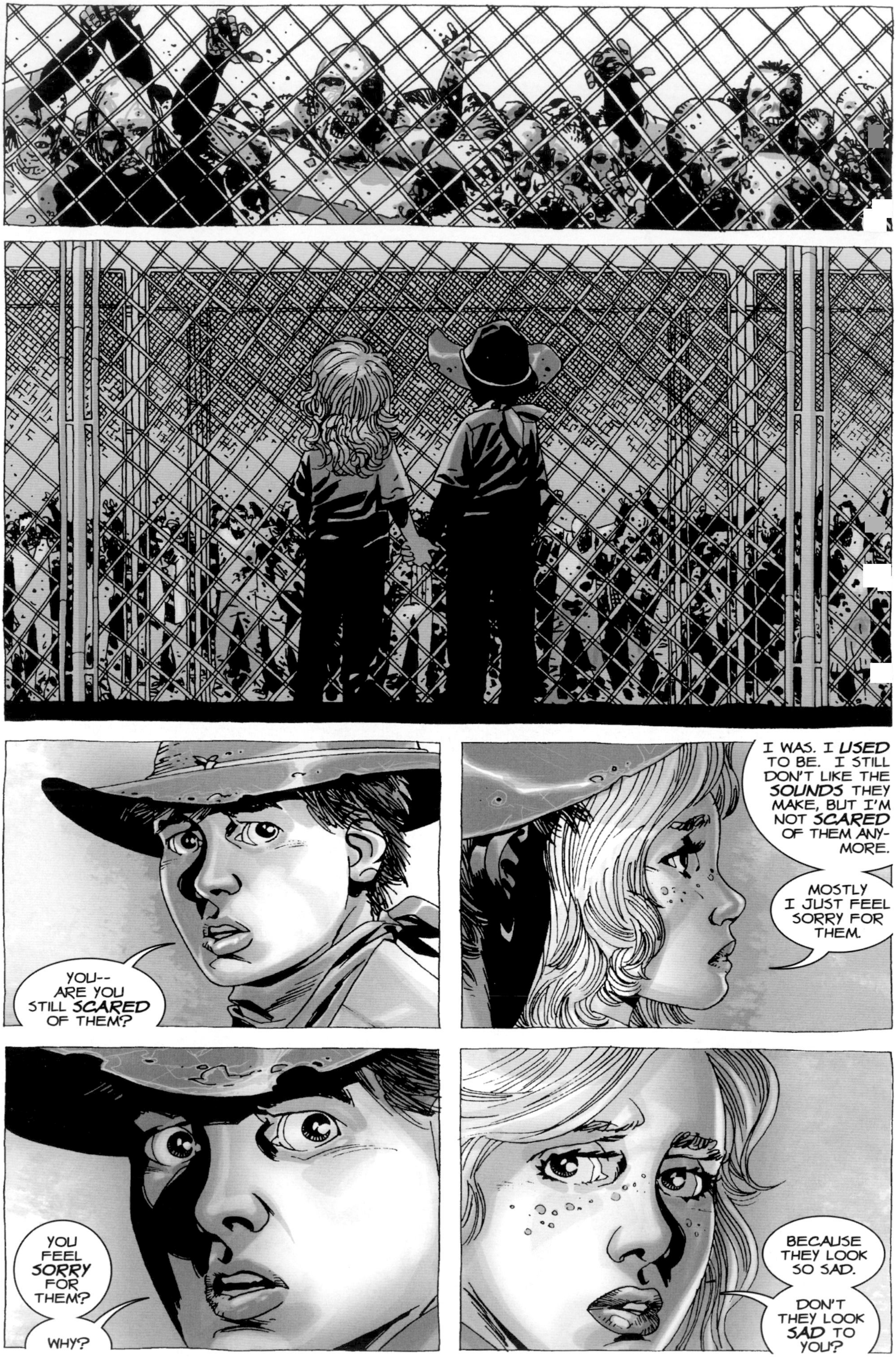
YOU-- ARE YOU STILL SCARED OF THEM?
I WAS. I USED TO BE. I STILL DON'T LIKE THE SOUNDS THEY MAKE, BUT I'M NOT SCARED OF THEM ANY-MORE.
MOSTLY I JUST FEEL SORRY FOR THEM.
YOU FEEL SORRY FOR THEM?
WHY?
BECAUSE THEY LOOK SO SAD.
DON'T THEY LOOK SAD TO YOU?

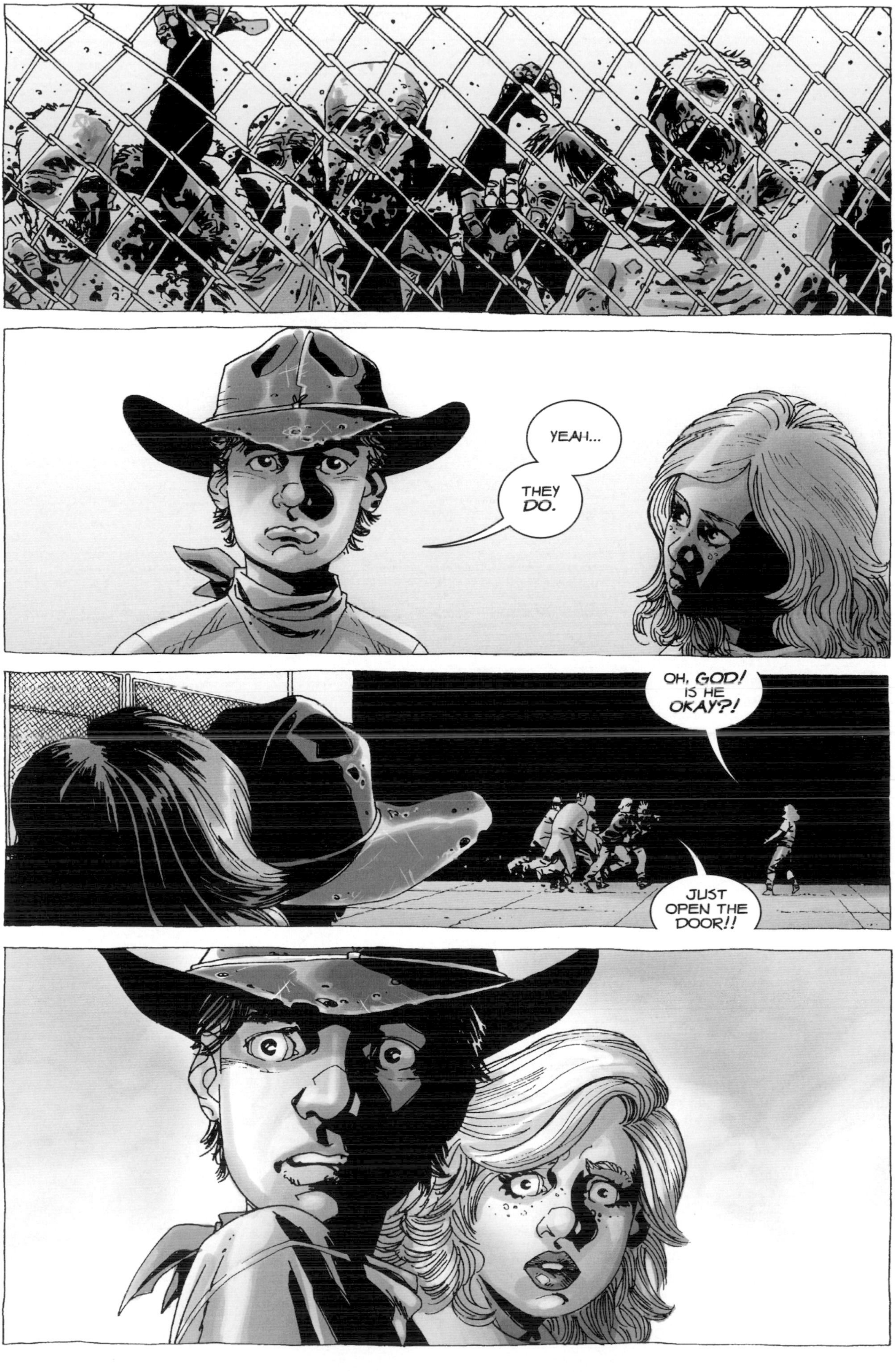
YEAH...
THEY DO.
OH, GOD! IS HE OKAY?!
JUST OPEN THE DOOR!!

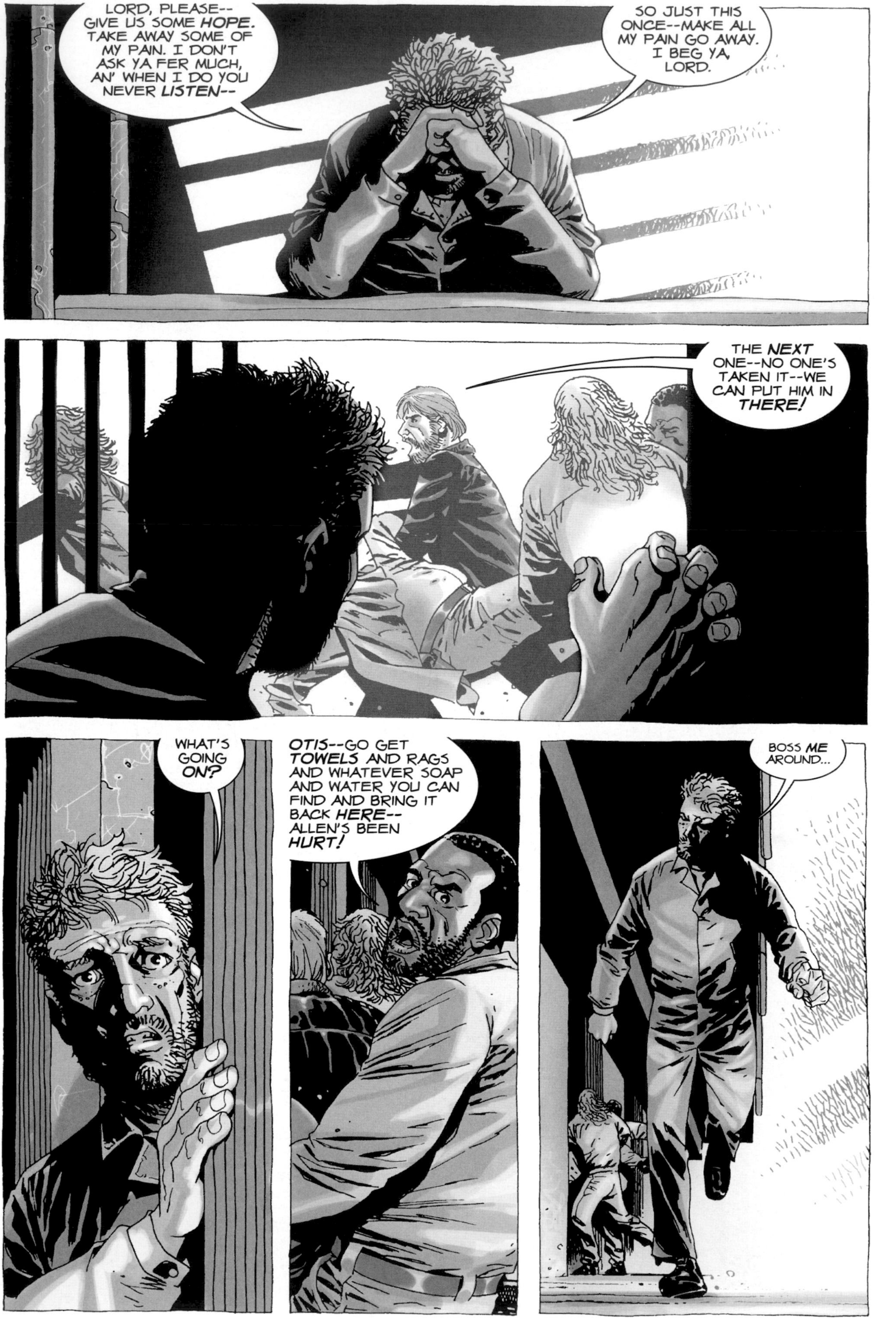

LORD, PLEASE-- GIVE US SOME HOPE. TAKE AWAY SOME OF MY PAIN. I DON'T ASK YA FER MUCH, AN' WHEN I DO YOU NEVER LISTEN--
SO JUST THIS ONCE--MAKE ALL MY PAIN GO AWAY. I BEG YA, LORD.
THE NEXT ONE--NO ONE'S TAKEN IT--WE CAN PUT HIM IN THERE!
WHAT'S GOING ON?
OTIS--GO GET TOWELS AND RAGS AND WHATEVER SOAP AND WATER YOU CAN FIND AND BRING IT BACK HERE-- ALLEN'S BEEN HURT!
BOSS ME AROUND...

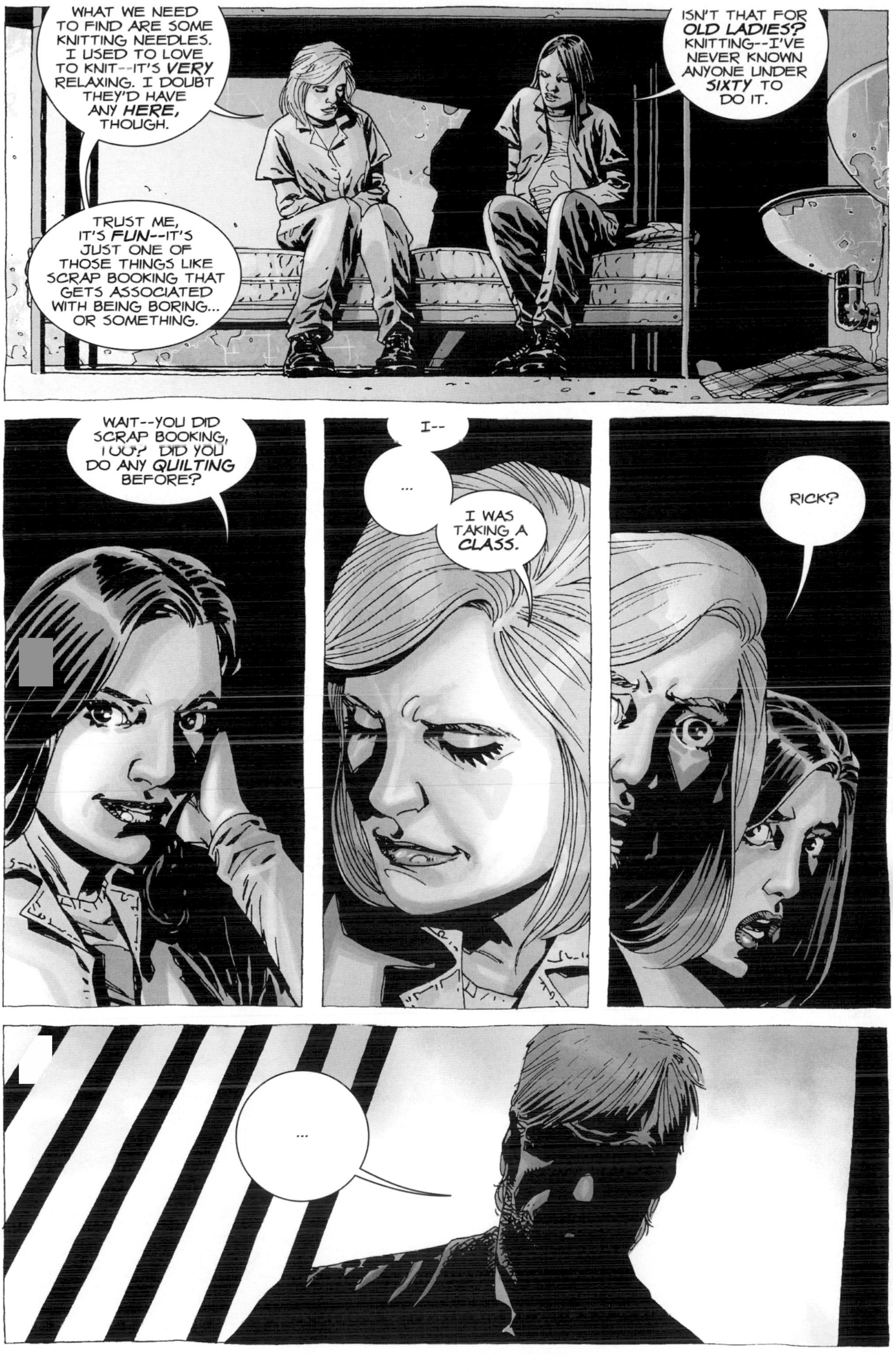
WHAT WE NEED TO FIND ARE SOME KNITTING NEEDLES. I USED TO LOVE TO KNIT--IT'S *VERY* RELAXING. I DOUBT THEY'D HAVE ANY *HERE,* THOUGH.
TRUST ME, IT'S *FUN*--IT'S JUST ONE OF THOSE THINGS LIKE SCRAP BOOKING THAT GETS ASSOCIATED WITH BEING BORING... OR SOMETHING.
ISN'T THAT FOR *OLD LADIES?* KNITTING--I'VE NEVER KNOWN ANYONE UNDER *SIXTY* TO DO IT.
WAIT--YOU DID SCRAP BOOKING, TOO? DID YOU DO ANY *QUILTING* BEFORE?
I--
...
I WAS TAKING A *CLASS.*
RICK?
...

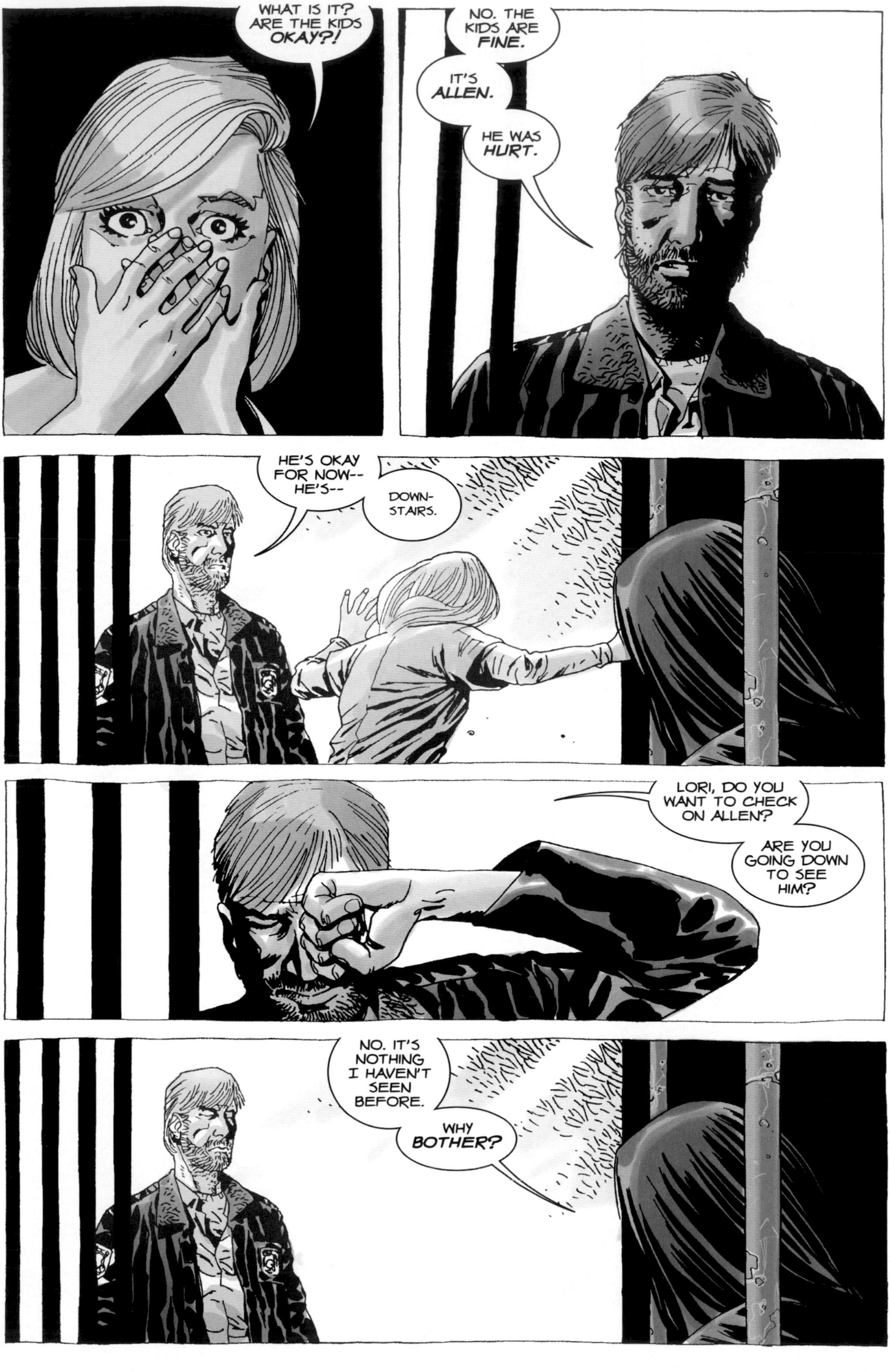

WHAT IS IT? ARE THE KIDS OKAY?!
NO. THE KIDS ARE FINE.
IT'S ALLEN.
HE WAS HURT.
HE'S OKAY FOR NOW-- HE'S--
DOWN-STAIRS.
LORI, DO YOU WANT TO CHECK ON ALLEN?
ARE YOU GOING DOWN TO SEE HIM?
NO. IT'S NOTHING I HAVEN'T SEEN BEFORE.
WHY BOTHER?

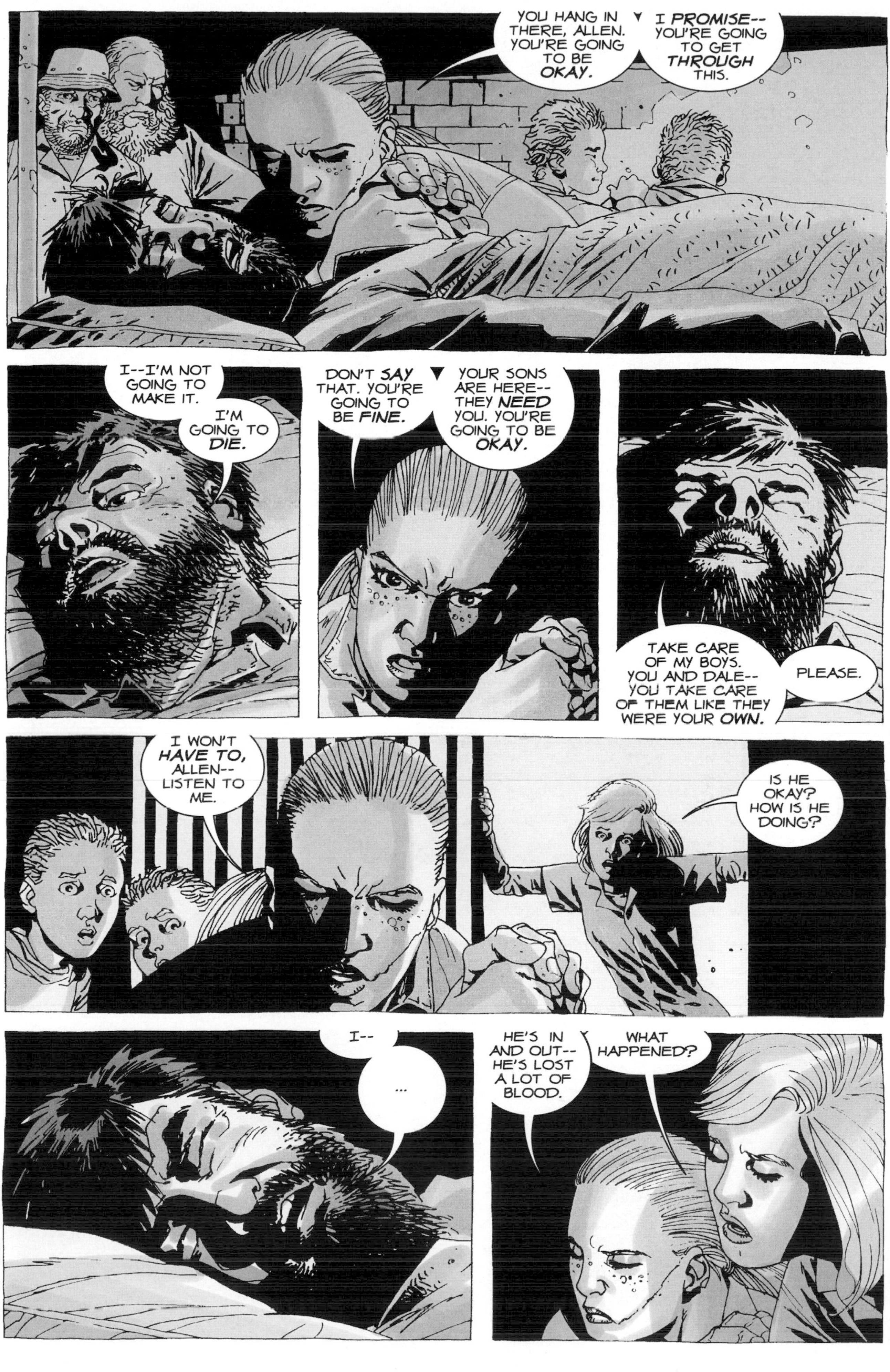
YOU HANG IN THERE, ALLEN. YOU'RE GOING TO BE OKAY.
I PROMISE-- YOU'RE GOING TO GET THROUGH THIS.
I--I'M NOT GOING TO MAKE IT.
I'M GOING TO DIE.
DON'T SAY THAT. YOU'RE GOING TO BE FINE.
YOUR SONS ARE HERE-- THEY NEED YOU. YOU'RE GOING TO BE OKAY.
TAKE CARE OF MY BOYS. YOU AND DALE-- YOU TAKE CARE OF THEM LIKE THEY WERE YOUR OWN.
PLEASE.
I WON'T HAVE TO, ALLEN-- LISTEN TO ME.
IS HE OKAY? HOW IS HE DOING?
I--
...
HE'S IN AND OUT-- HE'S LOST A LOT OF BLOOD.
WHAT HAPPENED?

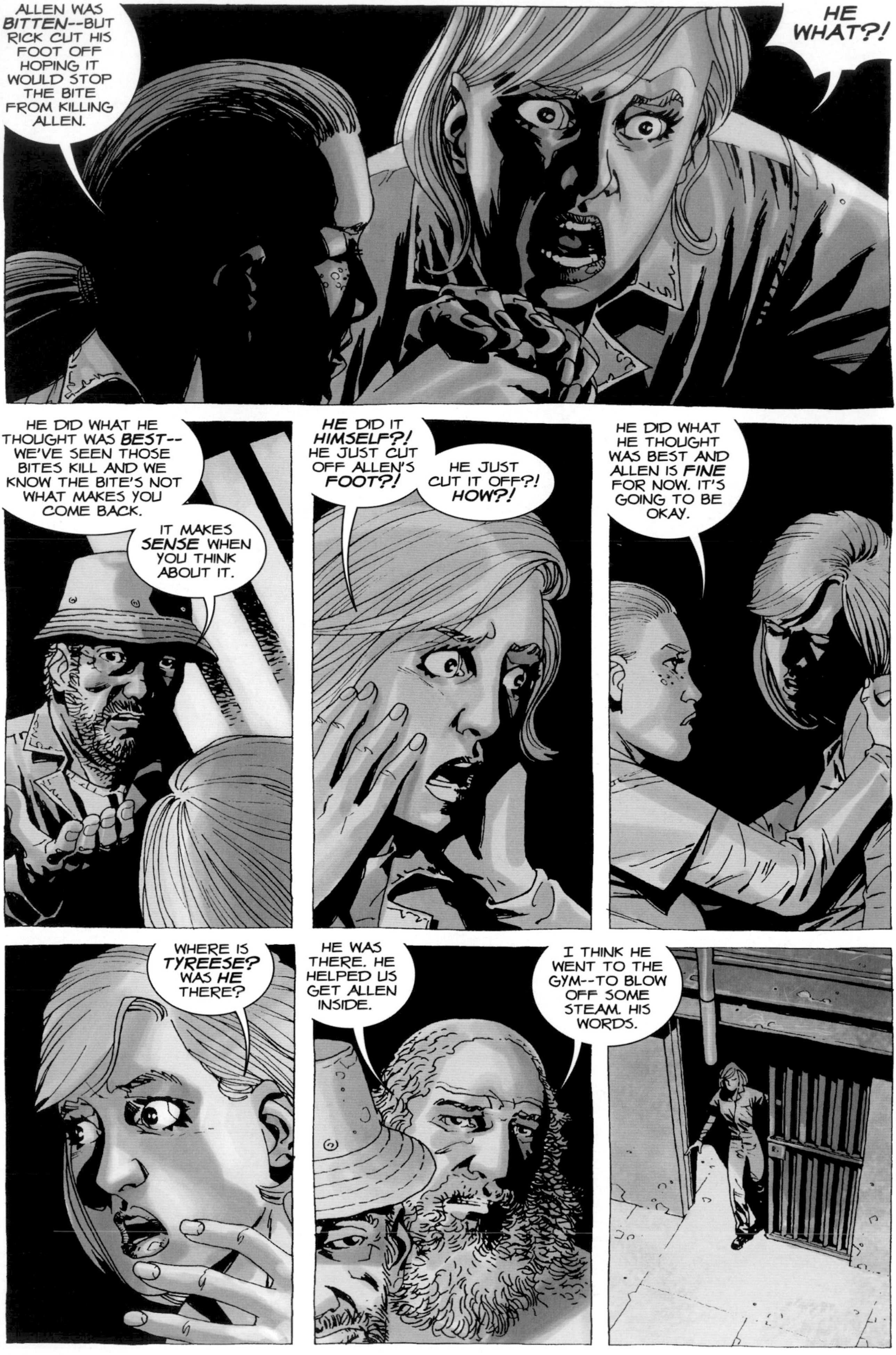
ALLEN WAS BITTEN--BUT RICK CUT HIS FOOT OFF HOPING IT WOULD STOP THE BITE FROM KILLING ALLEN.
HE WHAT?!
HE DID WHAT HE THOUGHT WAS BEST--WE'VE SEEN THOSE BITES KILL AND WE KNOW THE BITE'S NOT WHAT MAKES YOU COME BACK.
IT MAKES SENSE WHEN YOU THINK ABOUT IT.
HE DID IT HIMSELF?! HE JUST CUT OFF ALLEN'S FOOT?!
HE JUST CUT IT OFF?! HOW?!
HE DID WHAT HE THOUGHT WAS BEST AND ALLEN IS FINE FOR NOW. IT'S GOING TO BE OKAY.
WHERE IS TYREESE? WAS HE THERE?
HE WAS THERE. HE HELPED US GET ALLEN INSIDE.
I THINK HE WENT TO THE GYM--TO BLOW OFF SOME STEAM. HIS WORDS.

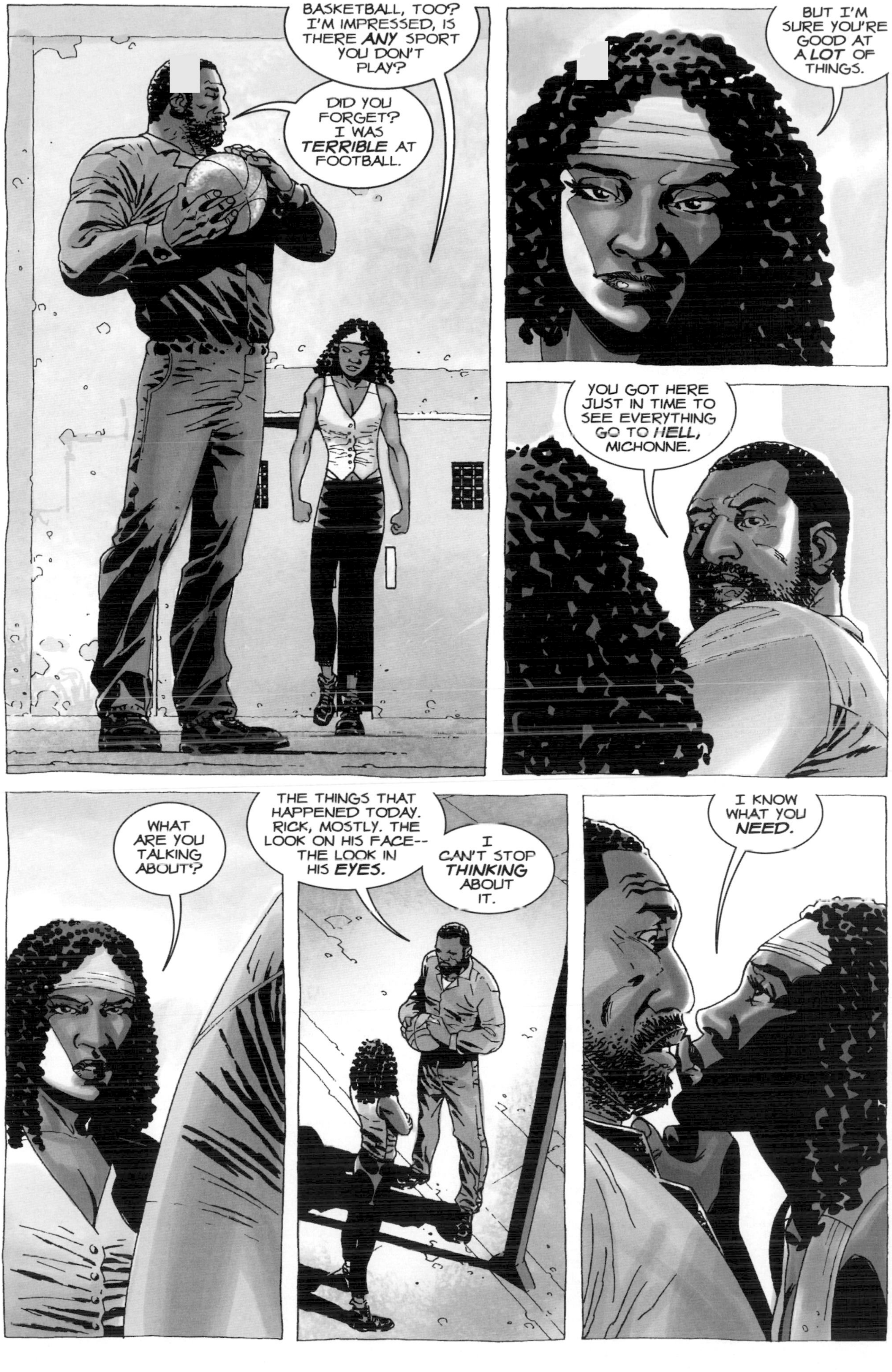
BASKETBALL, TOO? I'M IMPRESSED, IS THERE ANY SPORT YOU DON'T PLAY?
DID YOU FORGET? I WAS TERRIBLE AT FOOTBALL.
BUT I'M SURE YOU'RE GOOD AT A LOT OF THINGS.
YOU GOT HERE JUST IN TIME TO SEE EVERYTHING GO TO HELL, MICHONNE.
WHAT ARE YOU TALKING ABOUT?
THE THINGS THAT HAPPENED TODAY. RICK, MOSTLY. THE LOOK ON HIS FACE-- THE LOOK IN HIS EYES.
I CAN'T STOP THINKING ABOUT IT.
I KNOW WHAT YOU NEED.

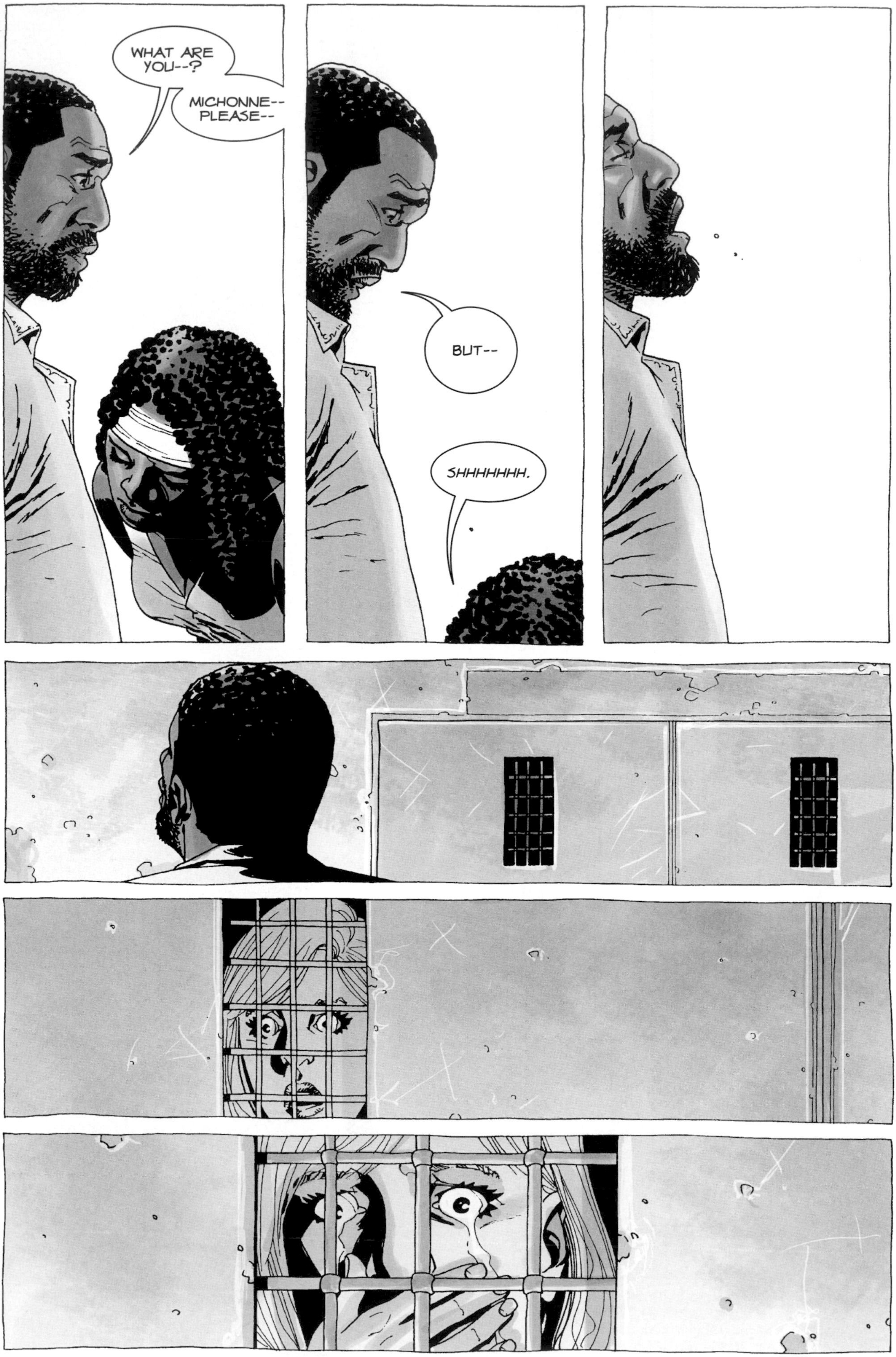
WHAT ARE YOU--?
MICHONNE-- PLEASE--
BUT--
SHHHHHHH.

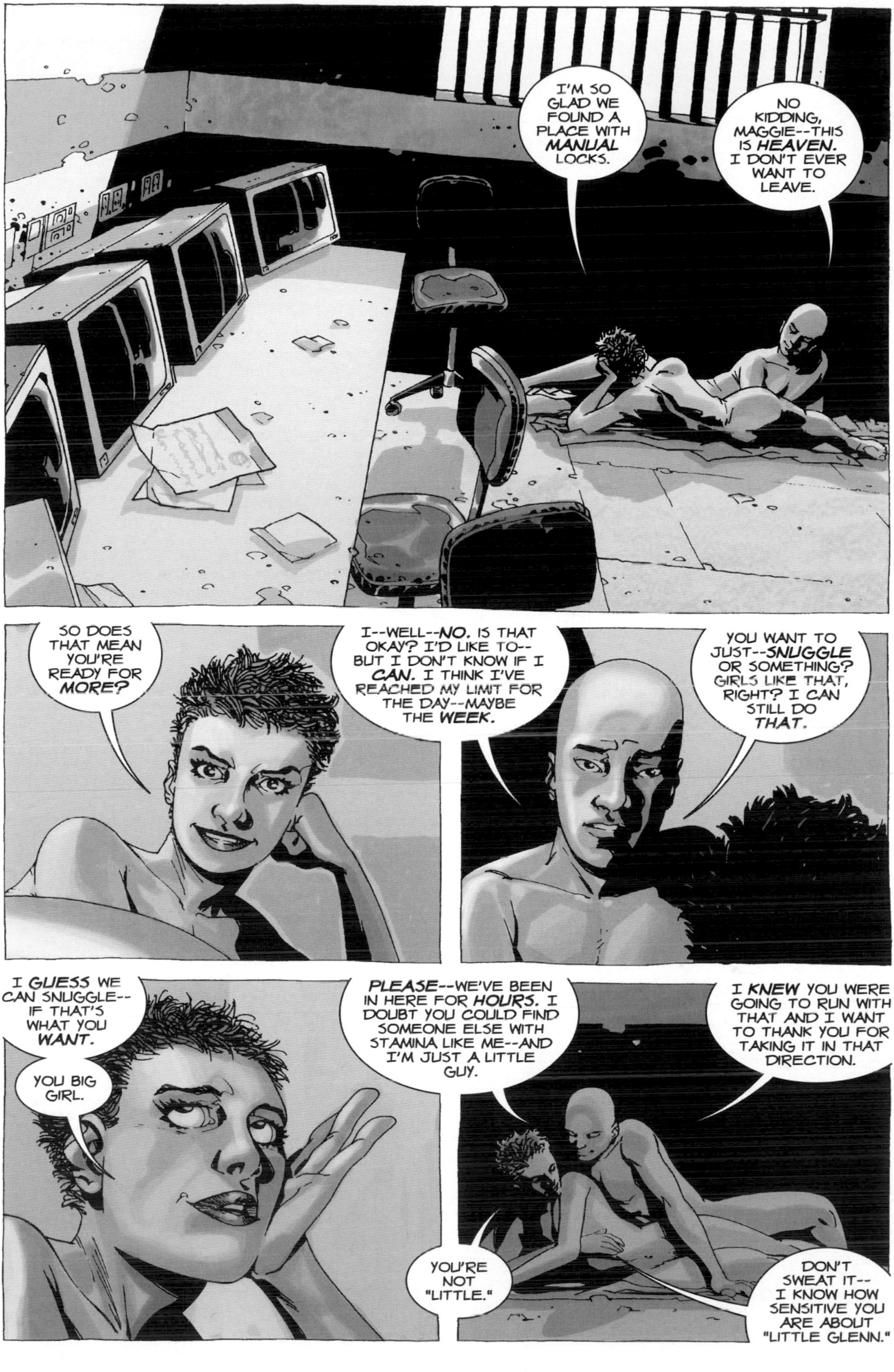
I'M SO GLAD WE FOUND A PLACE WITH MANUAL LOCKS.
NO KIDDING, MAGGIE--THIS IS HEAVEN. I DON'T EVER WANT TO LEAVE.
SO DOES THAT MEAN YOU'RE READY FOR MORE?
I--WELL--NO. IS THAT OKAY? I'D LIKE TO-- BUT I DON'T KNOW IF I CAN. I THINK I'VE REACHED MY LIMIT FOR THE DAY--MAYBE THE WEEK.
YOU WANT TO JUST--SNUGGLE OR SOMETHING? GIRLS LIKE THAT, RIGHT? I CAN STILL DO THAT.
I GUESS WE CAN SNUGGLE-- IF THAT'S WHAT YOU WANT.
YOU BIG GIRL.
PLEASE--WE'VE BEEN IN HERE FOR HOURS. I DOUBT YOU COULD FIND SOMEONE ELSE WITH STAMINA LIKE ME--AND I'M JUST A LITTLE GUY.
I KNEW YOU WERE GOING TO RUN WITH THAT AND I WANT TO THANK YOU FOR TAKING IT IN THAT DIRECTION.
YOU'RE NOT "LITTLE."
DON'T SWEAT IT-- I KNOW HOW SENSITIVE YOU ARE ABOUT "LITTLE GLENN."

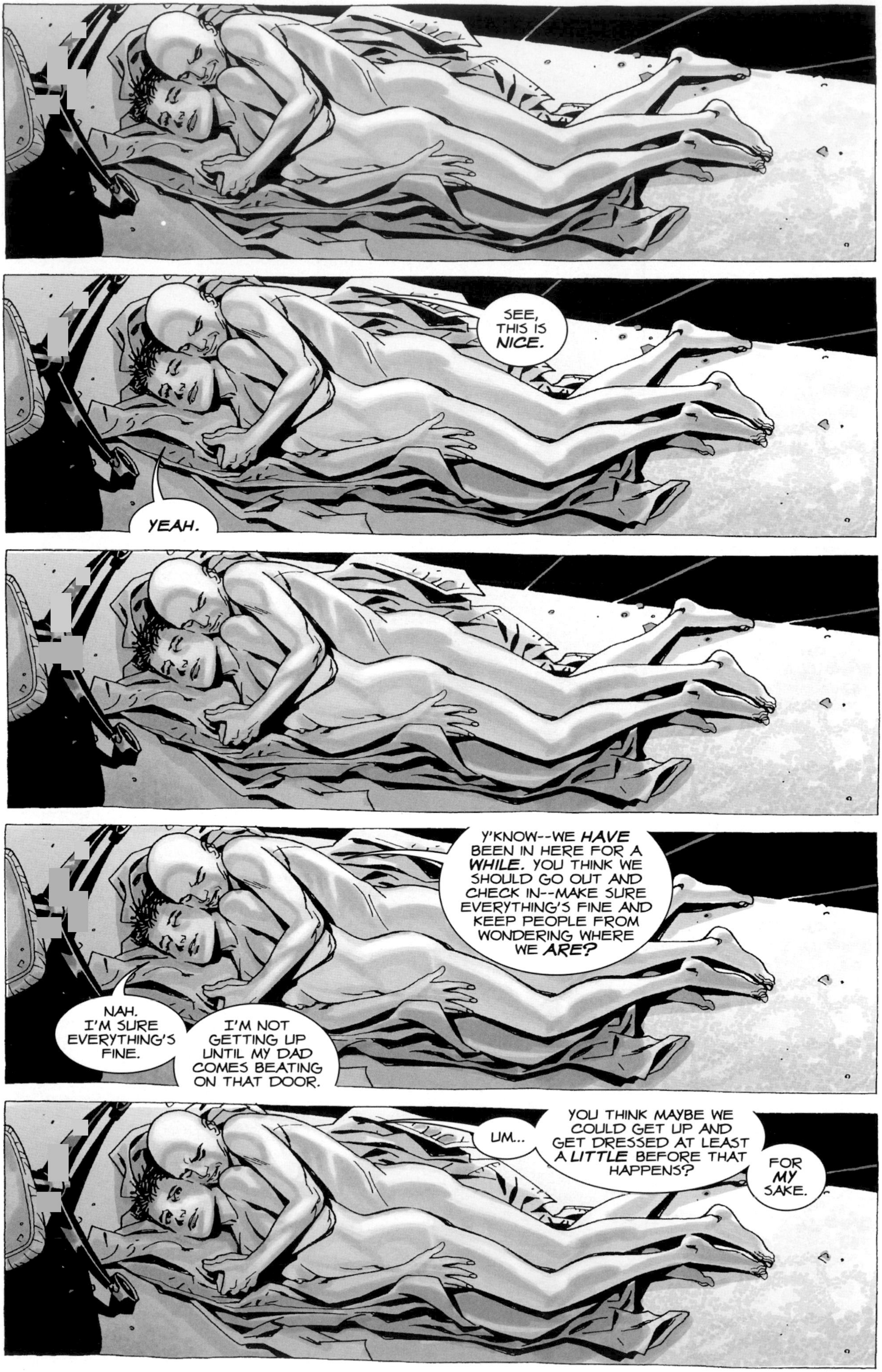
SEE, THIS IS NICE.
YEAH.
Y'KNOW--WE HAVE BEEN IN HERE FOR A WHILE. YOU THINK WE SHOULD GO OUT AND CHECK IN--MAKE SURE EVERYTHING'S FINE AND KEEP PEOPLE FROM WONDERING WHERE WE ARE?
NAH. I'M SURE EVERYTHING'S FINE.
I'M NOT GETTING UP UNTIL MY DAD COMES BEATING ON THAT DOOR.
UM...
YOU THINK MAYBE WE COULD GET UP AND GET DRESSED AT LEAST A LITTLE BEFORE THAT HAPPENS?
FOR MY SAKE.

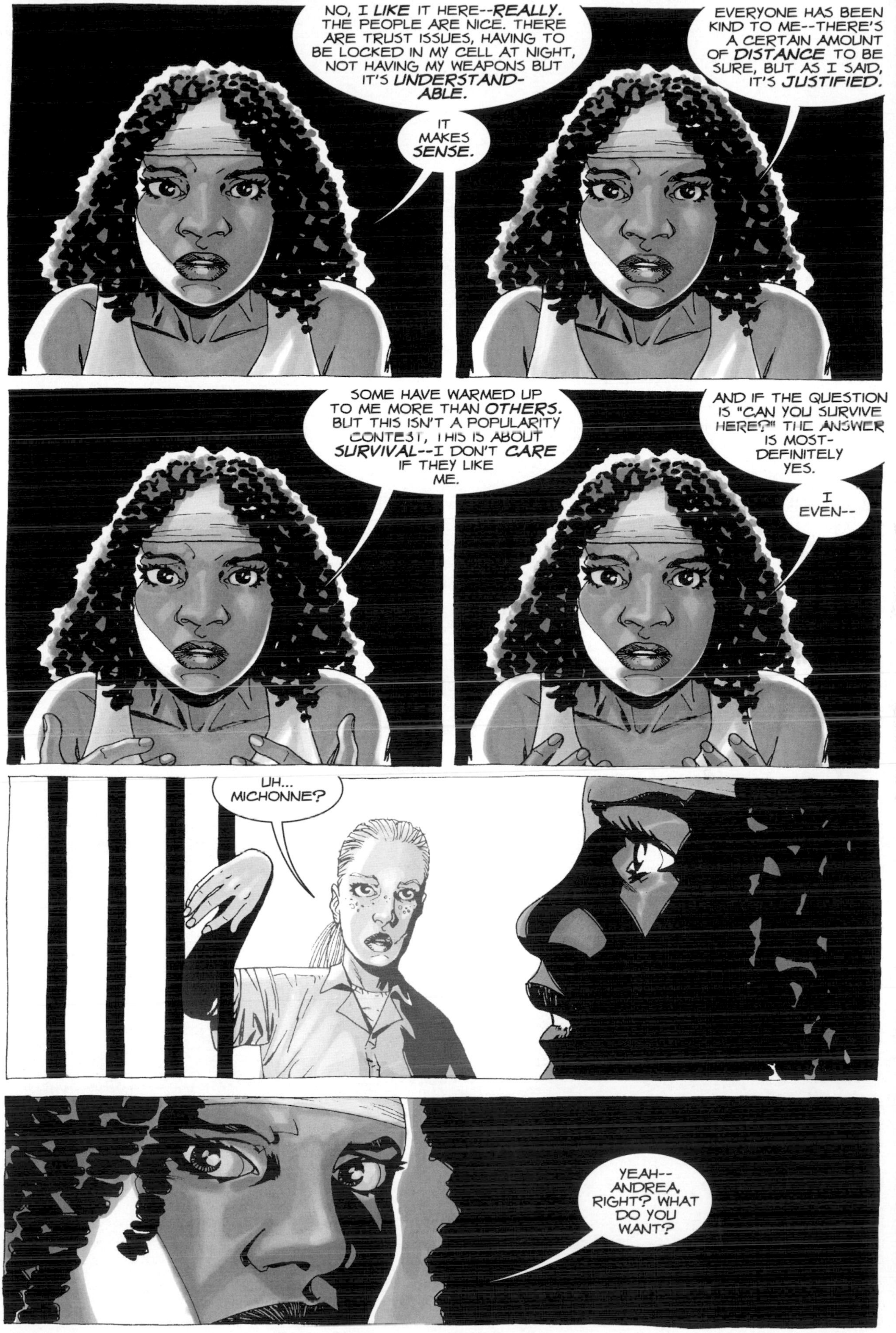
NO, I LIKE IT HERE--REALLY. THE PEOPLE ARE NICE. THERE ARE TRUST ISSUES, HAVING TO BE LOCKED IN MY CELL AT NIGHT, NOT HAVING MY WEAPONS BUT IT'S UNDERSTAND-ABLE.
IT MAKES SENSE.
EVERYONE HAS BEEN KIND TO ME--THERE'S A CERTAIN AMOUNT OF DISTANCE TO BE SURE, BUT AS I SAID, IT'S JUSTIFIED.
SOME HAVE WARMED UP TO ME MORE THAN OTHERS. BUT THIS ISN'T A POPULARITY CONTEST, THIS IS ABOUT SURVIVAL--I DON'T CARE IF THEY LIKE ME.
AND IF THE QUESTION IS "CAN YOU SURVIVE HERE?" THE ANSWER IS MOST-DEFINITELY YES.
I EVEN--
UH... MICHONNE?
YEAH-- ANDREA, RIGHT? WHAT DO YOU WANT?

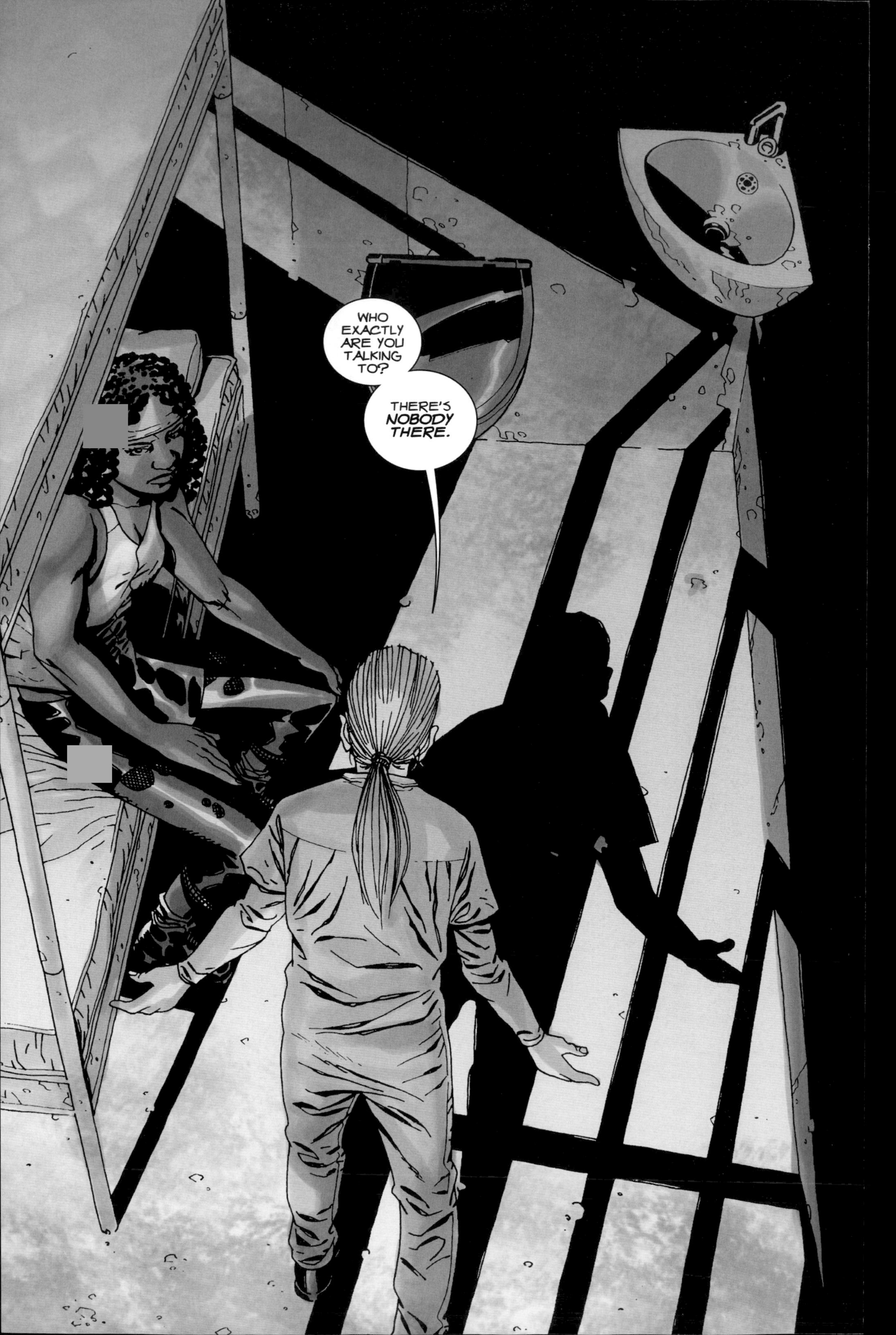
WHO EXACTLY ARE YOU TALKING TO?
THERE'S ***NOBODY*** *THERE.*

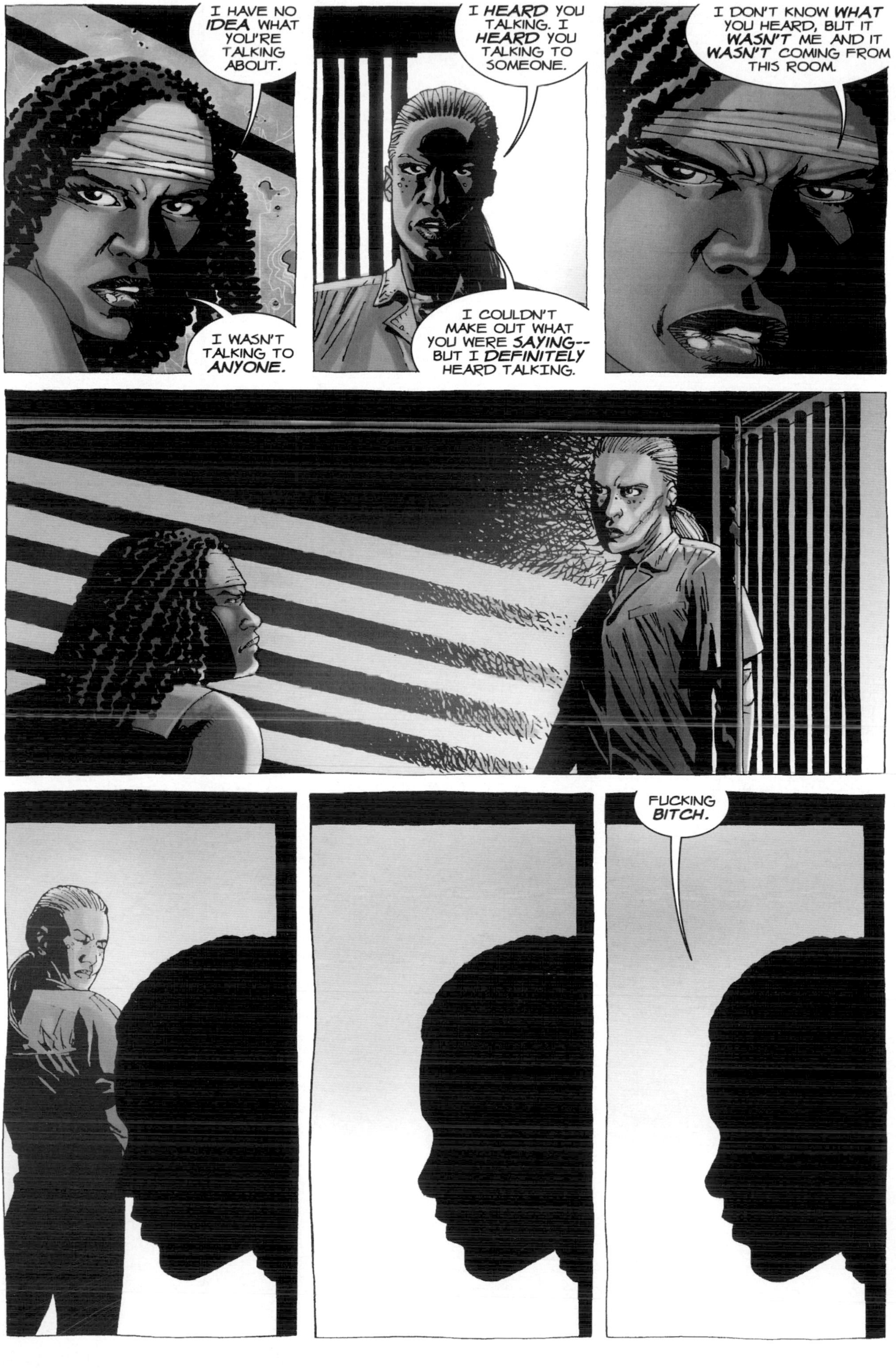
I HAVE NO IDEA WHAT YOU'RE TALKING ABOUT.
I WASN'T TALKING TO ANYONE.
I HEARD YOU TALKING. I HEARD YOU TALKING TO SOMEONE.
I COULDN'T MAKE OUT WHAT YOU WERE SAYING-- BUT I DEFINITELY HEARD TALKING.
I DON'T KNOW WHAT YOU HEARD, BUT IT WASN'T ME AND IT WASN'T COMING FROM THIS ROOM.
FUCKING BITCH.

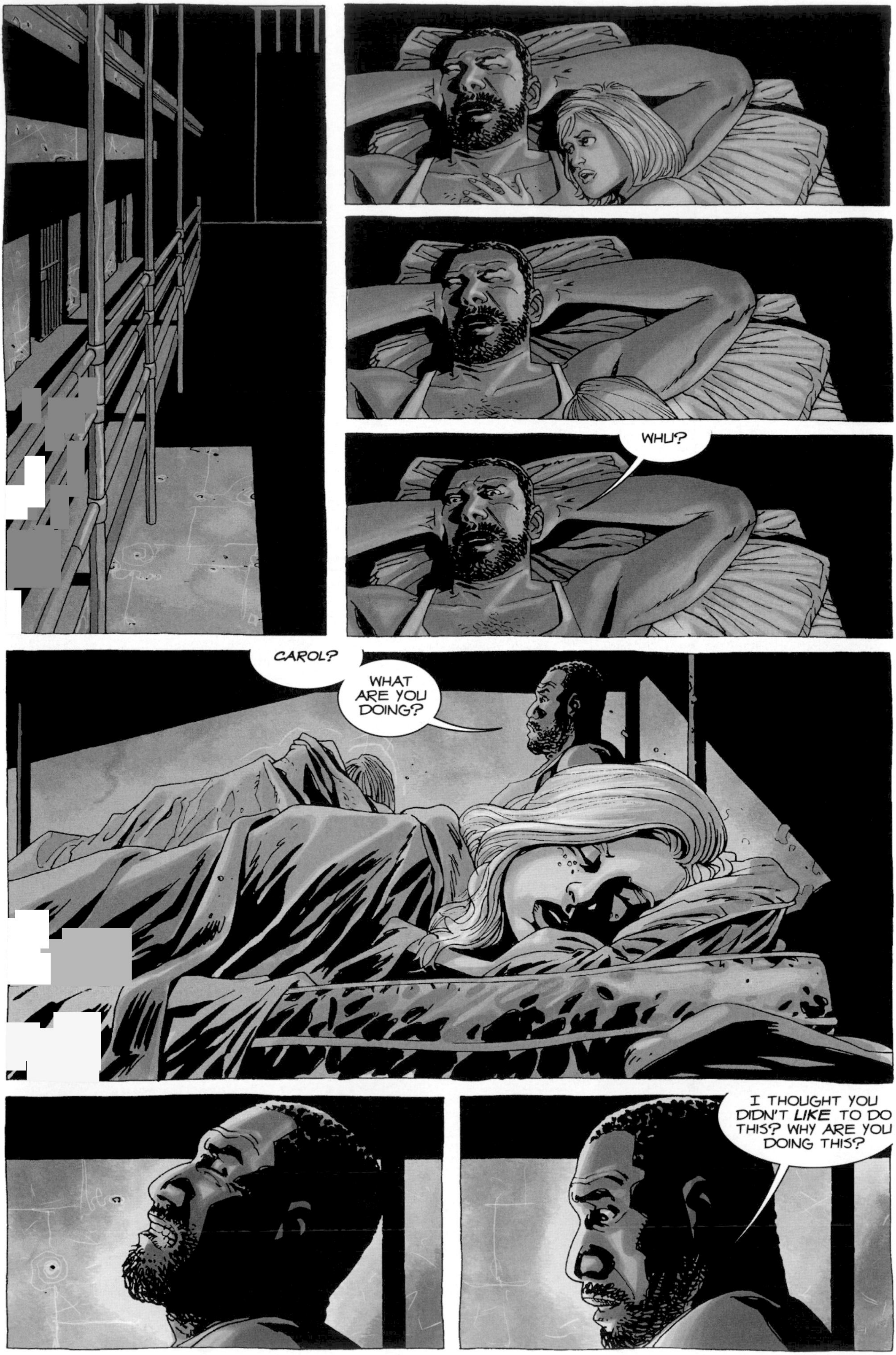
WHU?
CAROL?
WHAT ARE YOU DOING?
I THOUGHT YOU DIDN'T LIKE TO DO THIS? WHY ARE YOU DOING THIS?

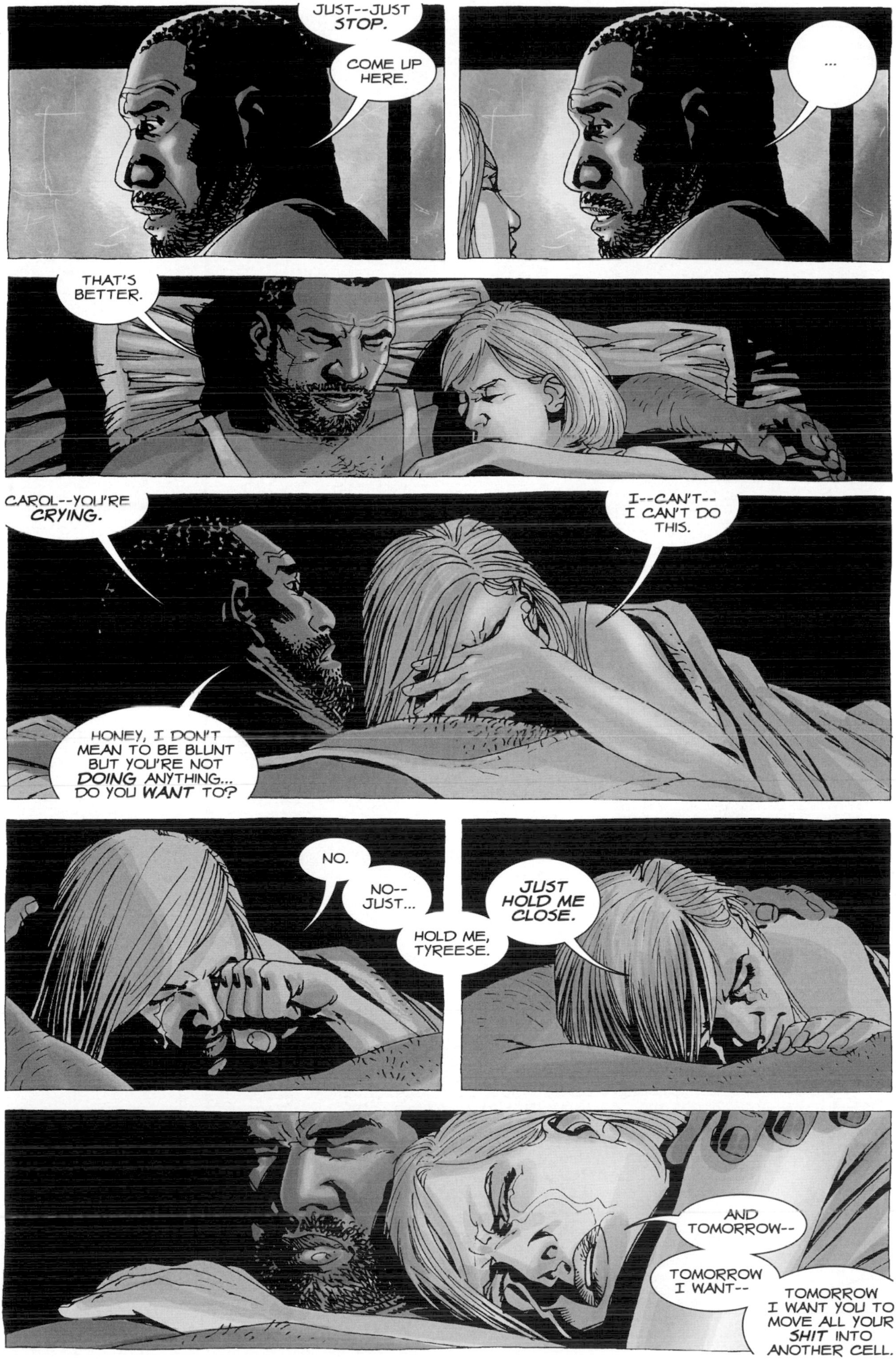
JUST--JUST STOP.
COME UP HERE.
...
THAT'S BETTER.
CAROL--YOU'RE CRYING.
I--CAN'T-- I CAN'T DO THIS.
HONEY, I DON'T MEAN TO BE BLUNT BUT YOU'RE NOT DOING ANYTHING... DO YOU WANT TO?
NO.
NO-- JUST...
HOLD ME, TYREESE.
JUST HOLD ME CLOSE.
AND TOMORROW--
TOMORROW I WANT--
TOMORROW I WANT YOU TO MOVE ALL YOUR SHIT INTO ANOTHER CELL.

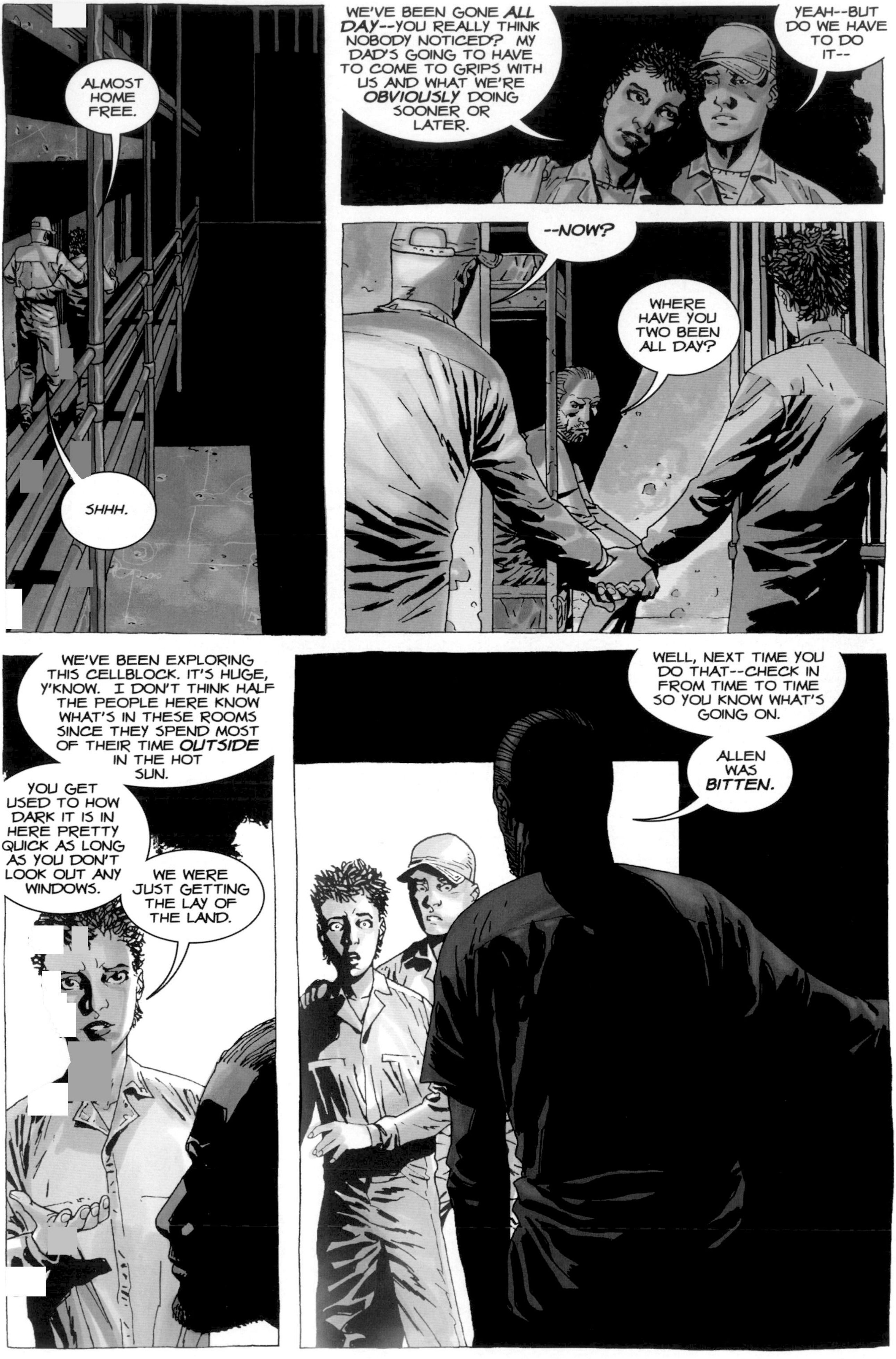
ALMOST HOME FREE.
SHHH.
WE'VE BEEN GONE ALL DAY--YOU REALLY THINK NOBODY NOTICED? MY DAD'S GOING TO HAVE TO COME TO GRIPS WITH US AND WHAT WE'RE OBVIOUSLY DOING SOONER OR LATER.
YEAH--BUT DO WE HAVE TO DO IT--
--NOW?
WHERE HAVE YOU TWO BEEN ALL DAY?
WE'VE BEEN EXPLORING THIS CELLBLOCK. IT'S HUGE, Y'KNOW. I DON'T THINK HALF THE PEOPLE HERE KNOW WHAT'S IN THESE ROOMS SINCE THEY SPEND MOST OF THEIR TIME OUTSIDE IN THE HOT SUN.
YOU GET USED TO HOW DARK IT IS IN HERE PRETTY QUICK AS LONG AS YOU DON'T LOOK OUT ANY WINDOWS.
WE WERE JUST GETTING THE LAY OF THE LAND.
WELL, NEXT TIME YOU DO THAT--CHECK IN FROM TIME TO TIME SO YOU KNOW WHAT'S GOING ON.
ALLEN WAS BITTEN.

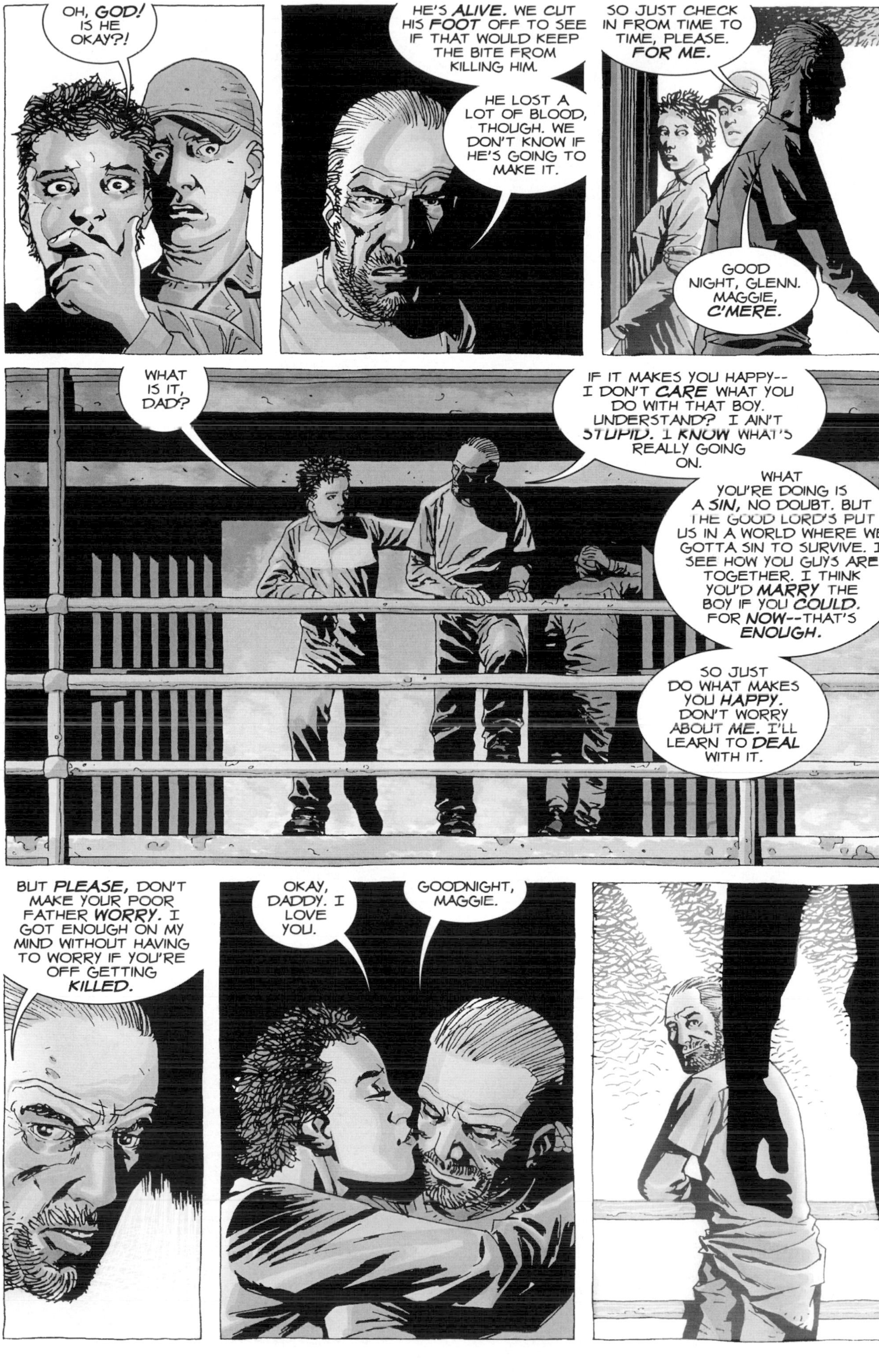
OH, GOD! IS HE OKAY?!
HE'S ALIVE. WE CUT HIS FOOT OFF TO SEE IF THAT WOULD KEEP THE BITE FROM KILLING HIM.
HE LOST A LOT OF BLOOD, THOUGH. WE DON'T KNOW IF HE'S GOING TO MAKE IT.
SO JUST CHECK IN FROM TIME TO TIME, PLEASE. FOR ME.
GOOD NIGHT, GLENN. MAGGIE, C'MERE.
WHAT IS IT, DAD?
IF IT MAKES YOU HAPPY-- I DON'T CARE WHAT YOU DO WITH THAT BOY. UNDERSTAND? I AIN'T STUPID. I KNOW WHAT'S REALLY GOING ON.
WHAT YOU'RE DOING IS A SIN, NO DOUBT. BUT THE GOOD LORD'S PUT US IN A WORLD WHERE WE GOTTA SIN TO SURVIVE. I SEE HOW YOU GUYS ARE TOGETHER. I THINK YOU'D MARRY THE BOY IF YOU COULD. FOR NOW--THAT'S ENOUGH.
SO JUST DO WHAT MAKES YOU HAPPY. DON'T WORRY ABOUT ME. I'LL LEARN TO DEAL WITH IT.
BUT PLEASE, DON'T MAKE YOUR POOR FATHER WORRY. I GOT ENOUGH ON MY MIND WITHOUT HAVING TO WORRY IF YOU'RE OFF GETTING KILLED.
OKAY, DADDY. I LOVE YOU.
GOODNIGHT, MAGGIE.

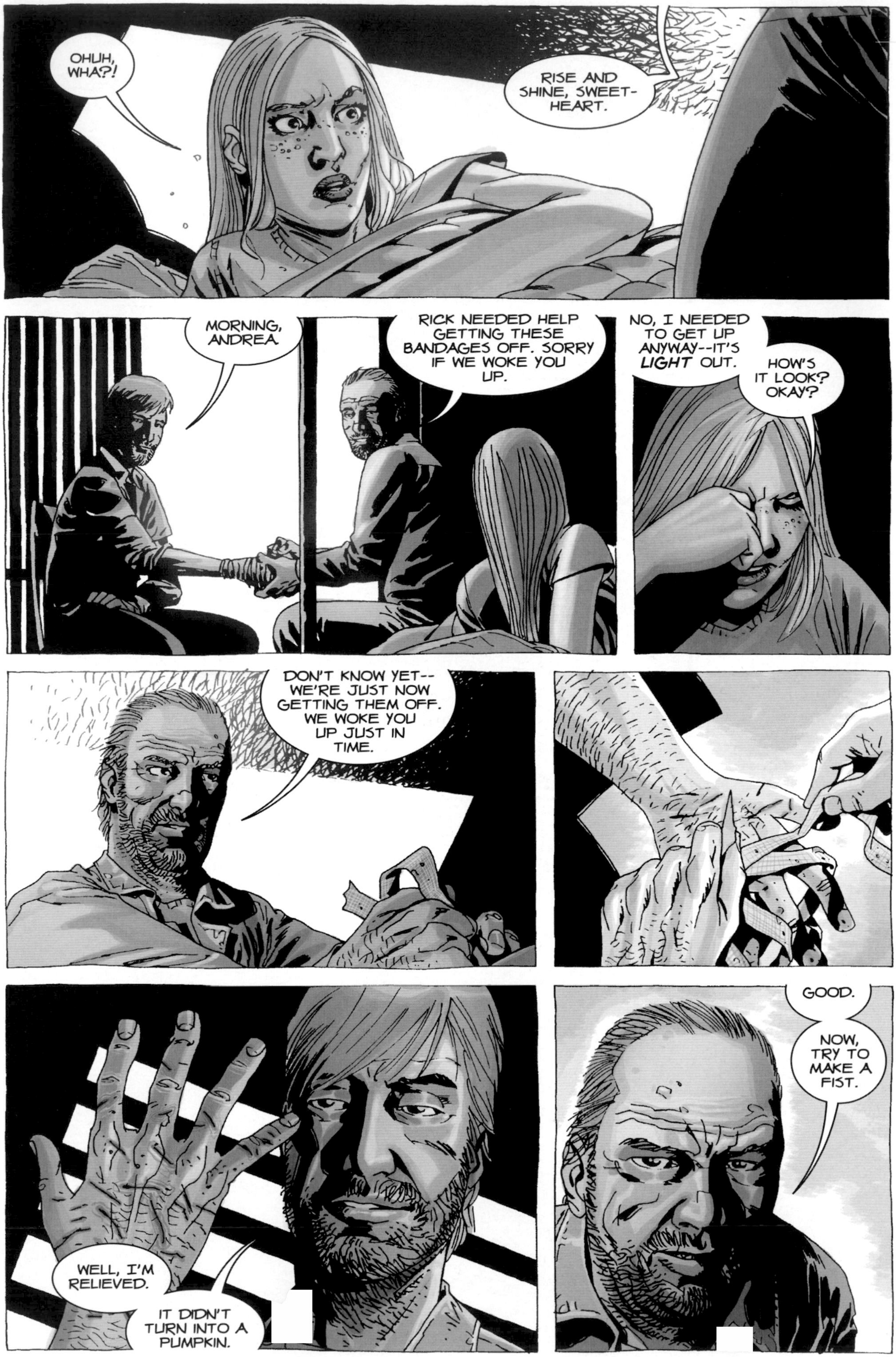
OHUH, WHA?!
RISE AND SHINE, SWEET-HEART.
MORNING, ANDREA.
RICK NEEDED HELP GETTING THESE BANDAGES OFF. SORRY IF WE WOKE YOU UP.
NO, I NEEDED TO GET UP ANYWAY--IT'S LIGHT OUT.
HOW'S IT LOOK? OKAY?
DON'T KNOW YET-- WE'RE JUST NOW GETTING THEM OFF. WE WOKE YOU UP JUST IN TIME.
WELL, I'M RELIEVED.
IT DIDN'T TURN INTO A PUMPKIN.
GOOD.
NOW, TRY TO MAKE A FIST.

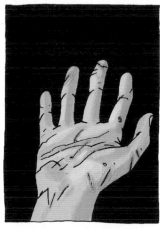

WELL, THAT'S SEEMS TO BE AS *GOOD* AS IT GETS.

FOR *NOW* AT LEAST--IT COULD STILL BE HEALING, AND THE MORE YOU *USE* YOUR HAND THE BETTER IT COULD GET.

IT'S NOT THE END OF THE WORLD.

OH, *REALLY?*

TELL *THAT* TO THE LIVING DEAD OUT *THERE.*

POOR CHOICE OF WORDS.

JUST DON'T BE TOO UPSET OVER THE HAND-- LIKE I SAY, IT SHOULD GET BETTER, WITH TIME. I MEAN, I'M JUST GUESSING HERE-- I'M NO *DOCTOR.*

UNDERSTOOD. WELL, WITH PRACTICE I SHOULD STILL BE ABLE TO FIRE A GUN.

WHAT MORE DO I *NEED* IN THIS DAY AND AGE?

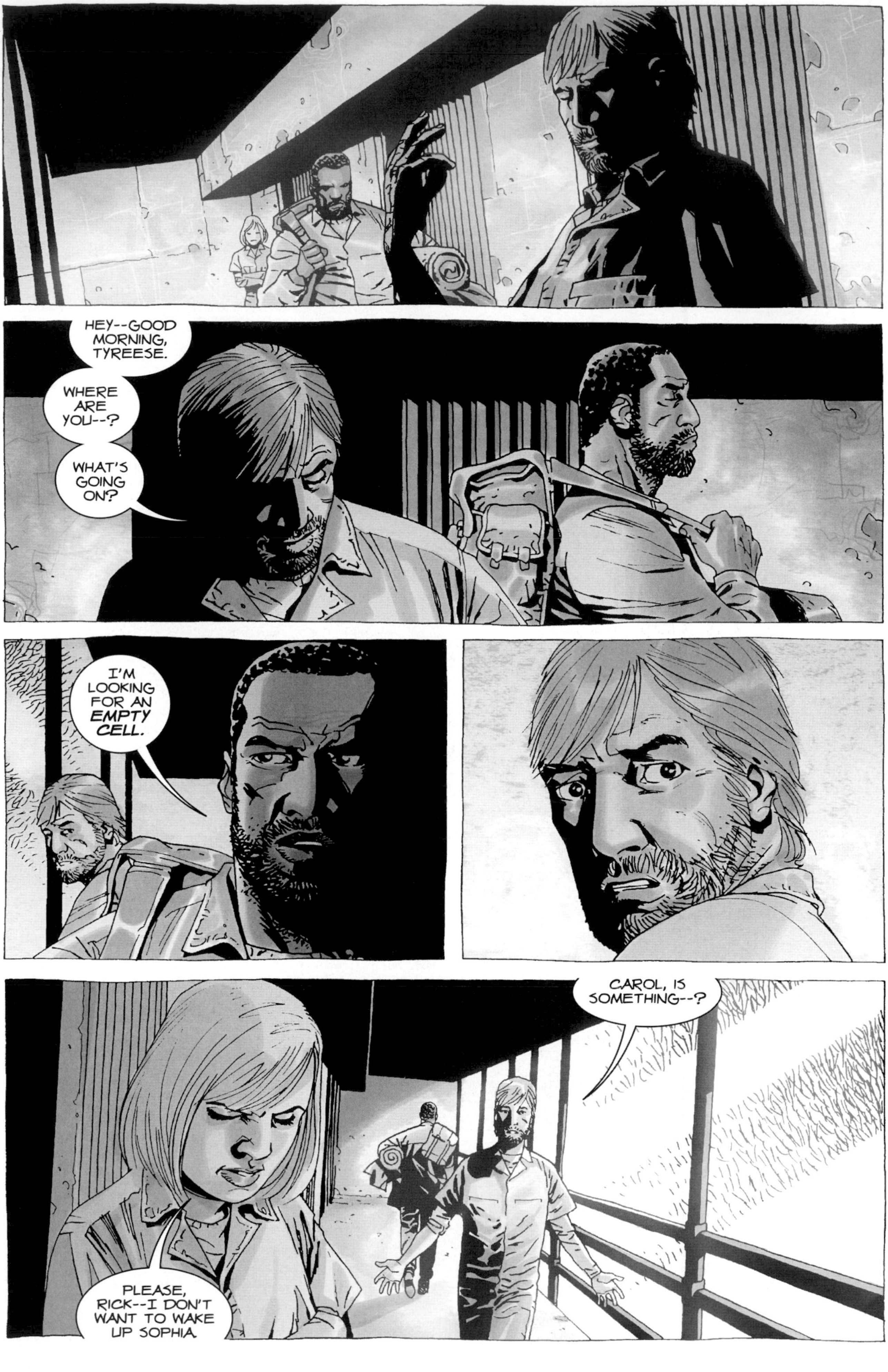
HEY--GOOD MORNING, TYREESE.
WHERE ARE YOU--?
WHAT'S GOING ON?
I'M LOOKING FOR AN *EMPTY CELL.*
CAROL, IS SOMETHING--?
PLEASE, RICK--I DON'T WANT TO WAKE UP SOPHIA.

SORRY--I'LL BE QUIET. I JUST WANTED TO MAKE SURE-- IS SOMETHING GOING ON WITH YOU TWO?

NOT ANYMORE.

WE BROKE UP. WE'RE NOT GOING TO BE TOGETHER ANYMORE.

IT'S OVER.

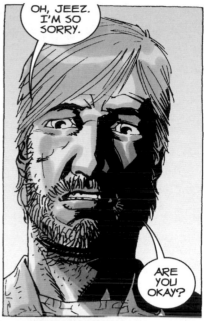

OH, JEEZ. I'M SO SORRY.

ARE YOU OKAY?

NO--I'M-- NOT!

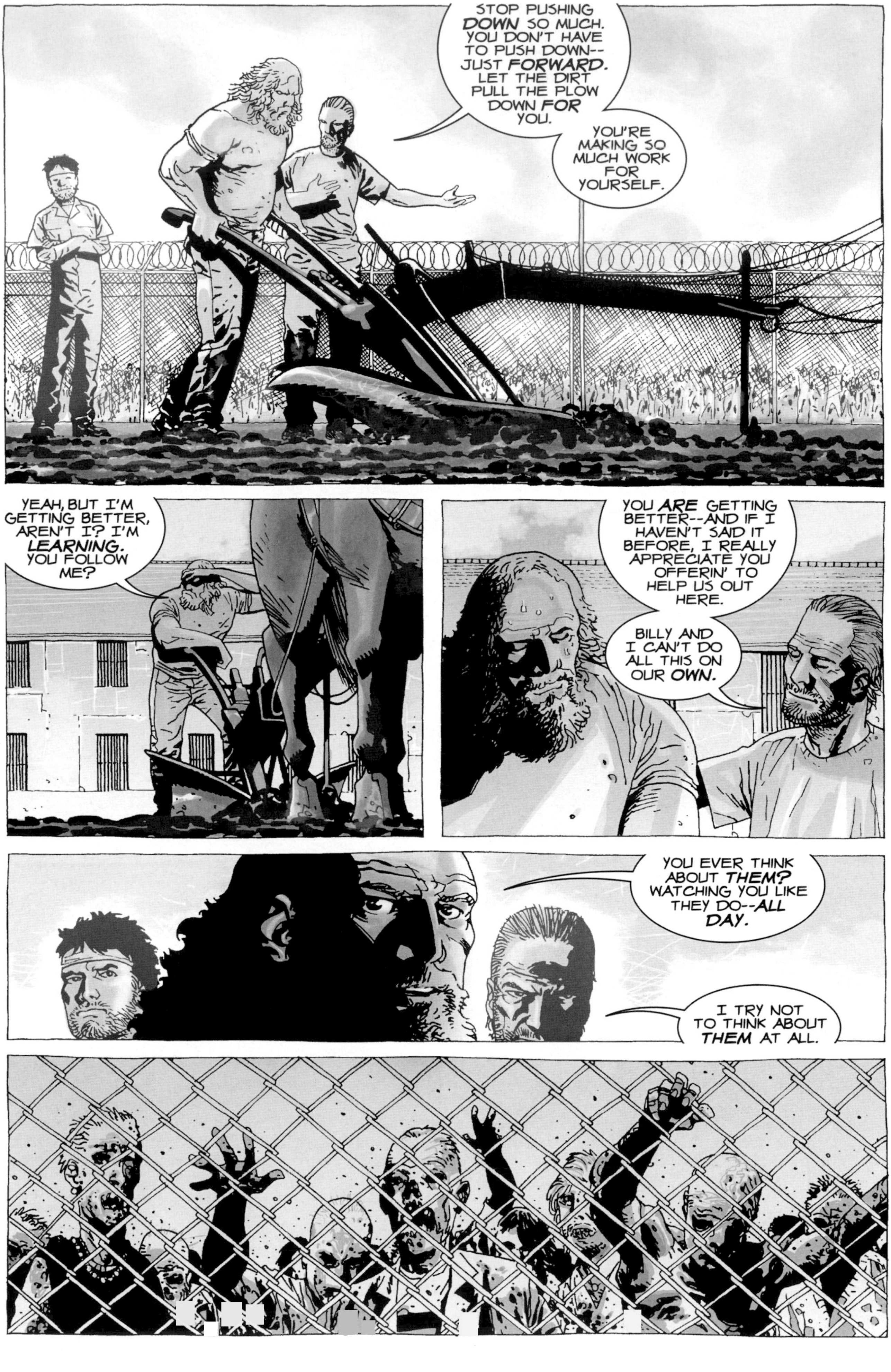
STOP PUSHING DOWN SO MUCH. YOU DON'T HAVE TO PUSH DOWN-- JUST FORWARD. LET THE DIRT PULL THE PLOW DOWN FOR YOU.
YOU'RE MAKING SO MUCH WORK FOR YOURSELF.
YEAH, BUT I'M GETTING BETTER, AREN'T I? I'M LEARNING. YOU FOLLOW ME?
YOU ARE GETTING BETTER--AND IF I HAVEN'T SAID IT BEFORE, I REALLY APPRECIATE YOU OFFERIN' TO HELP US OUT HERE.
BILLY AND I CAN'T DO ALL THIS ON OUR OWN.
YOU EVER THINK ABOUT THEM? WATCHING YOU LIKE THEY DO--ALL DAY.
I TRY NOT TO THINK ABOUT THEM AT ALL.

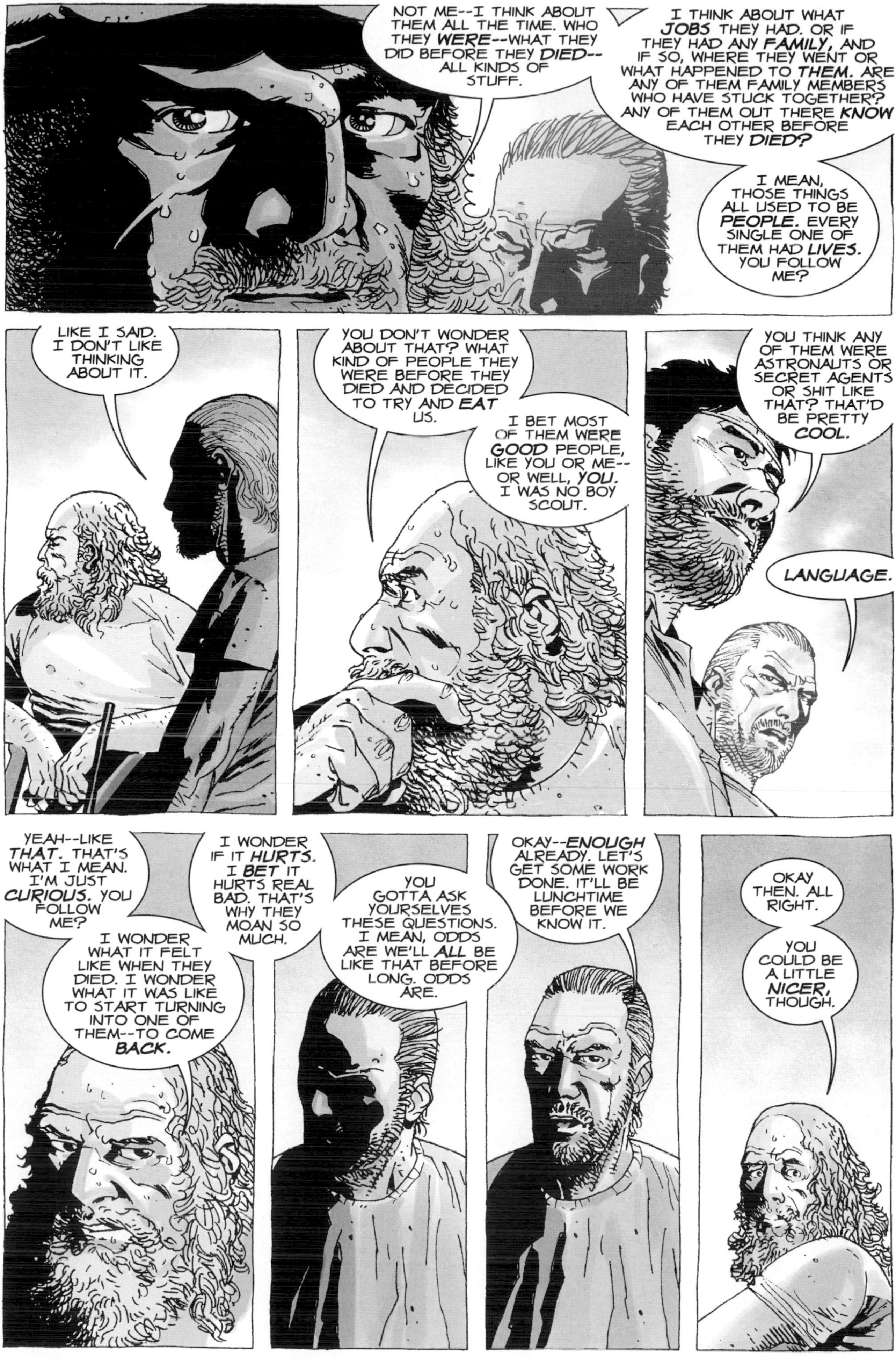
NOT ME--I THINK ABOUT THEM ALL THE TIME. WHO THEY WERE--WHAT THEY DID BEFORE THEY DIED--ALL KINDS OF STUFF.
I THINK ABOUT WHAT JOBS THEY HAD. OR IF THEY HAD ANY FAMILY, AND IF SO, WHERE THEY WENT OR WHAT HAPPENED TO THEM. ARE ANY OF THEM FAMILY MEMBERS WHO HAVE STUCK TOGETHER? ANY OF THEM OUT THERE KNOW EACH OTHER BEFORE THEY DIED?
I MEAN, THOSE THINGS ALL USED TO BE PEOPLE. EVERY SINGLE ONE OF THEM HAD LIVES. YOU FOLLOW ME?
LIKE I SAID. I DON'T LIKE THINKING ABOUT IT.
YOU DON'T WONDER ABOUT THAT? WHAT KIND OF PEOPLE THEY WERE BEFORE THEY DIED AND DECIDED TO TRY AND EAT US.
I BET MOST OF THEM WERE GOOD PEOPLE, LIKE YOU OR ME--OR WELL, YOU. I WAS NO BOY SCOUT.
YOU THINK ANY OF THEM WERE ASTRONAUTS OR SECRET AGENTS OR SHIT LIKE THAT? THAT'D BE PRETTY COOL.
LANGUAGE.
YEAH--LIKE THAT. THAT'S WHAT I MEAN. I'M JUST CURIOUS. YOU FOLLOW ME?
I WONDER WHAT IT FELT LIKE WHEN THEY DIED. I WONDER WHAT IT WAS LIKE TO START TURNING INTO ONE OF THEM--TO COME BACK.
I WONDER IF IT HURTS. I BET IT HURTS REAL BAD. THAT'S WHY THEY MOAN SO MUCH.
YOU GOTTA ASK YOURSELVES THESE QUESTIONS. I MEAN, ODDS ARE WE'LL ALL BE LIKE THAT BEFORE LONG. ODDS ARE.
OKAY--ENOUGH ALREADY. LET'S GET SOME WORK DONE. IT'LL BE LUNCHTIME BEFORE WE KNOW IT.
OKAY THEN. ALL RIGHT.
YOU COULD BE A LITTLE NICER, THOUGH.

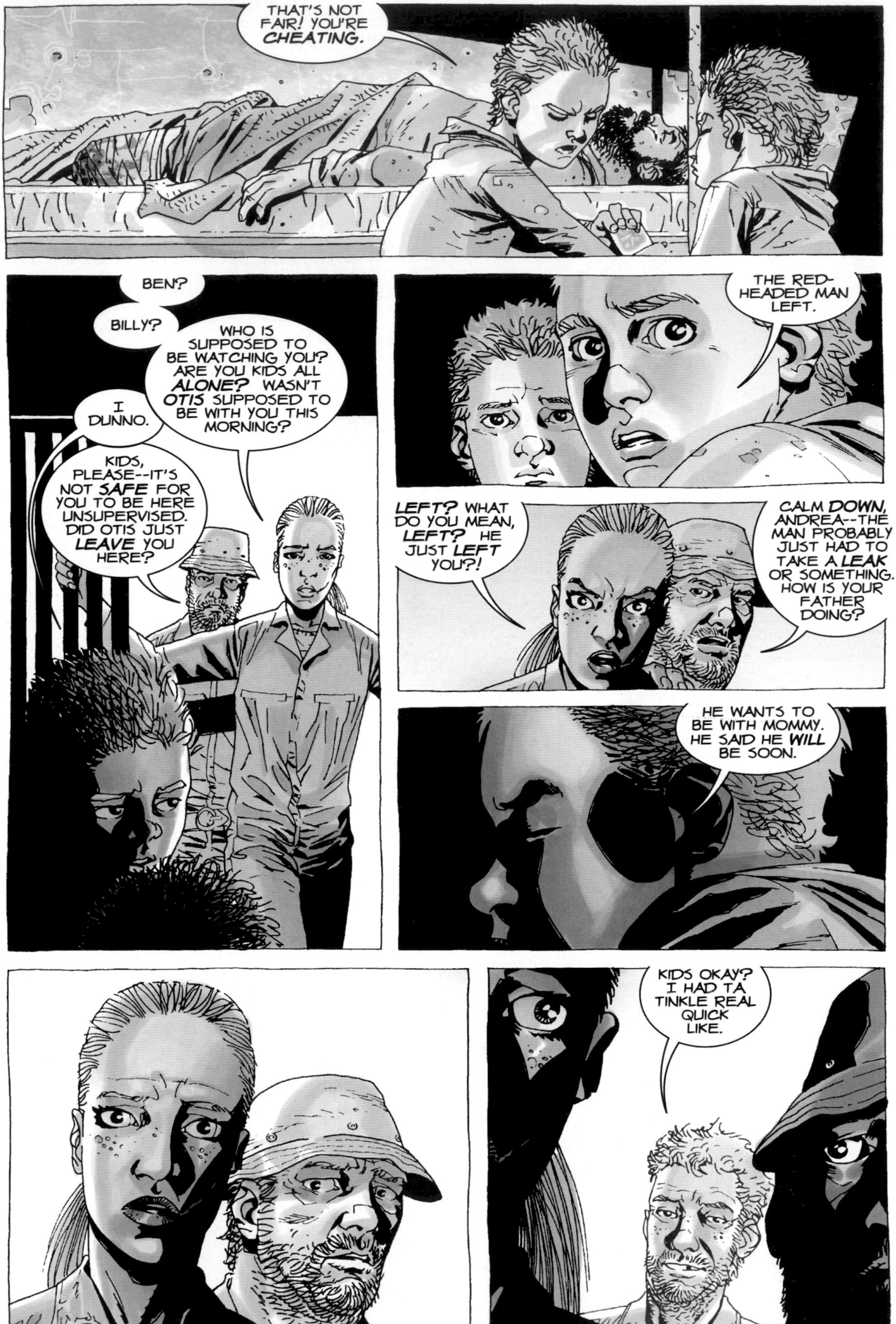
THAT'S NOT FAIR! YOU'RE CHEATING.
BEN?
BILLY?
WHO IS SUPPOSED TO BE WATCHING YOU? ARE YOU KIDS ALL ALONE? WASN'T OTIS SUPPOSED TO BE WITH YOU THIS MORNING?
I DUNNO.
KIDS, PLEASE--IT'S NOT SAFE FOR YOU TO BE HERE UNSUPERVISED. DID OTIS JUST LEAVE YOU HERE?
THE RED-HEADED MAN LEFT.
LEFT? WHAT DO YOU MEAN, LEFT? HE JUST LEFT YOU?!
CALM DOWN, ANDREA--THE MAN PROBABLY JUST HAD TO TAKE A LEAK OR SOMETHING. HOW IS YOUR FATHER DOING?
HE WANTS TO BE WITH MOMMY. HE SAID HE WILL BE SOON.
KIDS OKAY? I HAD TA TINKLE REAL QUICK LIKE.

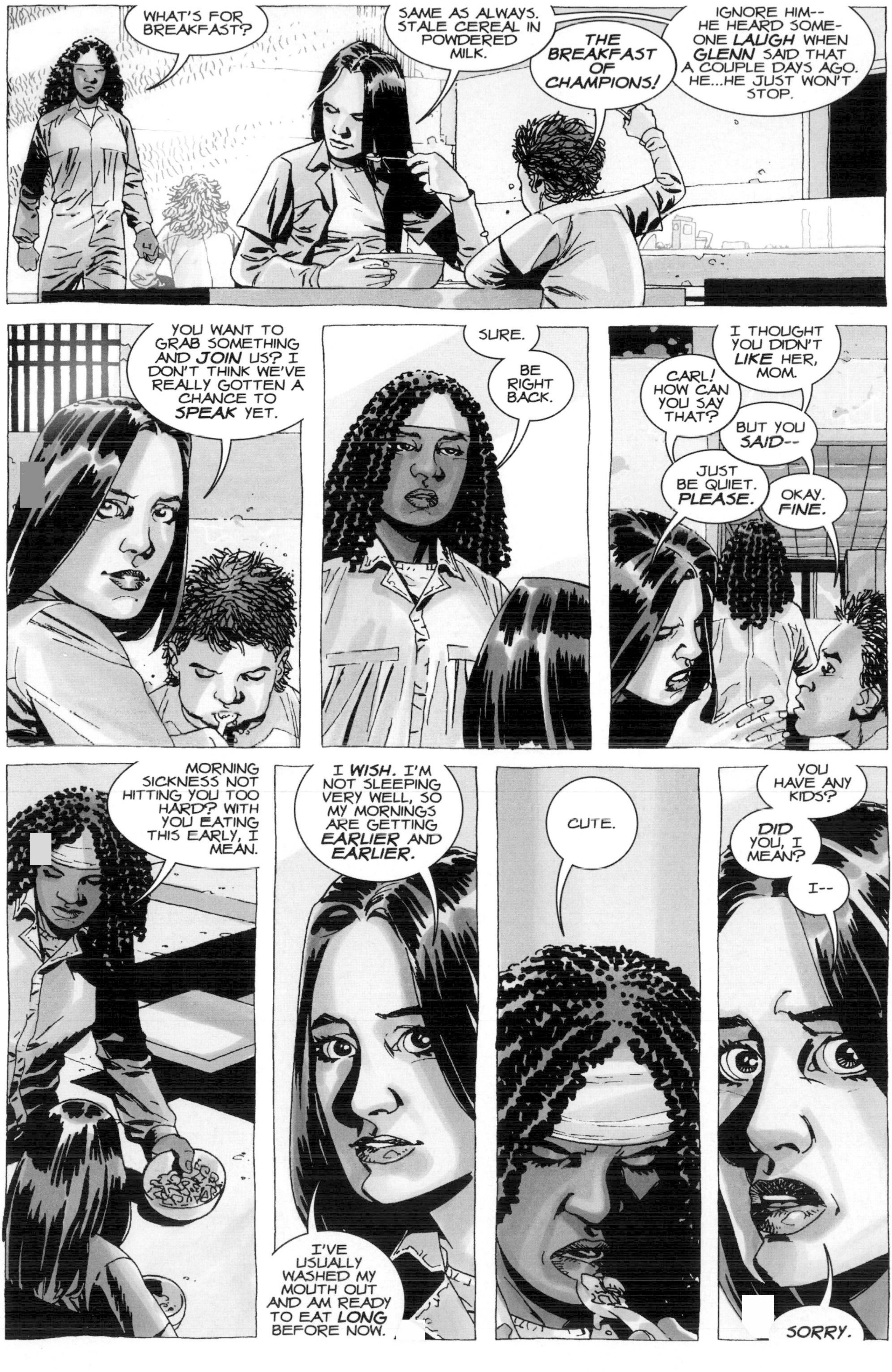
WHAT'S FOR BREAKFAST?
SAME AS ALWAYS. STALE CEREAL IN POWDERED MILK.
THE BREAKFAST OF CHAMPIONS!
IGNORE HIM-- HE HEARD SOME-ONE LAUGH WHEN GLENN SAID THAT A COUPLE DAYS AGO. HE...HE JUST WON'T STOP.
YOU WANT TO GRAB SOMETHING AND JOIN US? I DON'T THINK WE'VE REALLY GOTTEN A CHANCE TO SPEAK YET.
SURE.
BE RIGHT BACK.
I THOUGHT YOU DIDN'T LIKE HER, MOM.
CARL! HOW CAN YOU SAY THAT?
BUT YOU SAID--
JUST BE QUIET. PLEASE.
OKAY. FINE.
MORNING SICKNESS NOT HITTING YOU TOO HARD? WITH YOU EATING THIS EARLY, I MEAN.
I WISH. I'M NOT SLEEPING VERY WELL, SO MY MORNINGS ARE GETTING EARLIER AND EARLIER.
I'VE USUALLY WASHED MY MOUTH OUT AND AM READY TO EAT LONG BEFORE NOW.
CUTE.
YOU HAVE ANY KIDS?
DID YOU, I MEAN?
I--
SORRY.

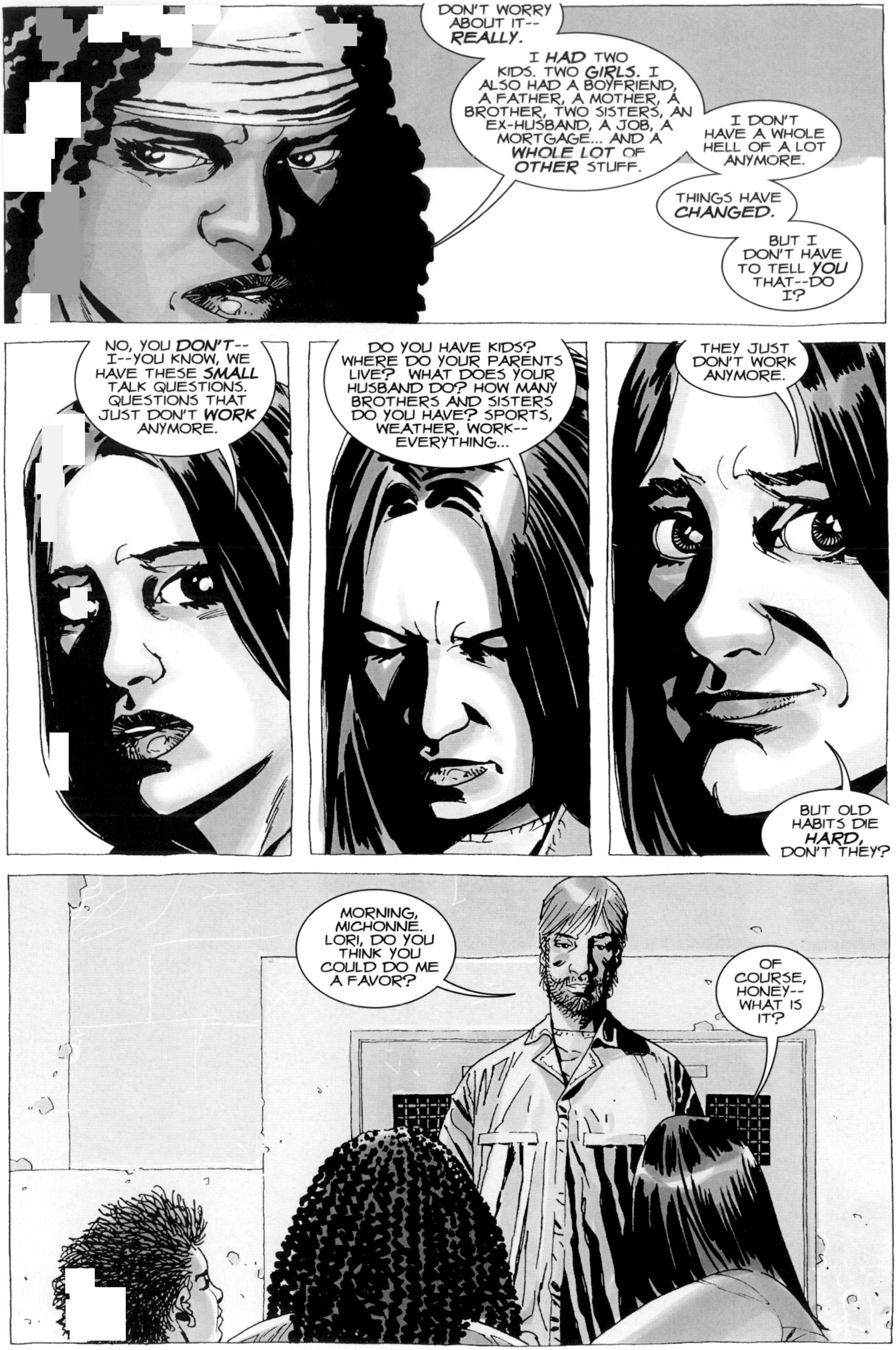
DON'T WORRY ABOUT IT-- REALLY.
I HAD TWO KIDS. TWO GIRLS. I ALSO HAD A BOYFRIEND, A FATHER, A MOTHER, A BROTHER, TWO SISTERS, AN EX-HUSBAND, A JOB, A MORTGAGE... AND A WHOLE LOT OF OTHER STUFF.
I DON'T HAVE A WHOLE HELL OF A LOT ANYMORE.
THINGS HAVE CHANGED.
BUT I DON'T HAVE TO TELL YOU THAT--DO I?
NO, YOU DON'T-- I--YOU KNOW, WE HAVE THESE SMALL TALK QUESTIONS. QUESTIONS THAT JUST DON'T WORK ANYMORE.
DO YOU HAVE KIDS? WHERE DO YOUR PARENTS LIVE? WHAT DOES YOUR HUSBAND DO? HOW MANY BROTHERS AND SISTERS DO YOU HAVE? SPORTS, WEATHER, WORK-- EVERYTHING...
THEY JUST DON'T WORK ANYMORE.
BUT OLD HABITS DIE HARD, DON'T THEY?
MORNING, MICHONNE. LORI, DO YOU THINK YOU COULD DO ME A FAVOR?
OF COURSE, HONEY-- WHAT IS IT?

IT SEEMS *TYREESE* AND *CAROL* HAVE BROKEN UP. I WAS GOING TO GO BACK OVER THERE AND GET *SOPHIA* SO YOU AND CAROL COULD TALK IN *PRIVATE*.

SHE DOESN'T *SEEM* TO BE TAKING IT TOO WELL. BUT THESE DAYS, WHO CAN REALLY TELL *NORMAL* UPSET FROM EVEN MORE UPSET ON TOP OF THAT?

WHAT I'M GETTING AT IS YOU TWO HAVE GOTTEN *CLOSE*. MAYBE *YOU* CAN TALK TO HER ABOUT THIS MORE THAN SOMEONE *ELSE* COULD.

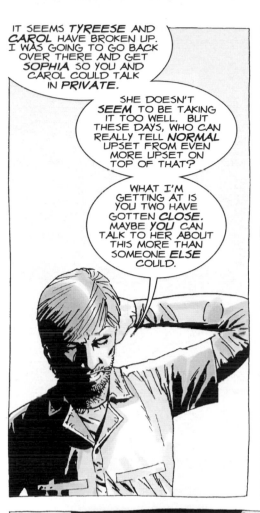

OH *GOD*-- I HAD NO IDEA. SURE, LET'S GO OVER THERE RIGHT NOW.

I'M *STILL* EATING.

MICHONNE, IS THERE ANY WAY I COULD ASK YOU TO WATCH CARL WHILE WE--?

I WAS ACTUALLY ON MY WAY OUT. *SORRY.*

HEY GUYS, COULD YOU WATCH CARL FOR A MINUTE?

OF COURSE.

THANKS SO MUCH, GLENN.

HOW WORRIED ABOUT HER ARE YOU?

YOU TOLD ME HOW CAROL WAS WHEN SHE THOUGHT TYREESE WAS *DEAD*--WELL, SHE SEEMS *WORSE* THAN YOU DESCRIBED, NOW. WHICH DOESN'T MAKE A WHOLE LOT OF *SENSE*.

SURE. I'VE *TALKED* TO PEOPLE BEFORE, Y'KNOW.

WHEN WE GET IN HERE I'M GOING TO ASK SOPHIA TO COME WITH ME TO SEE CARL-- YOU JUST START *TALKING.*

RIGHT. *SORRY.*

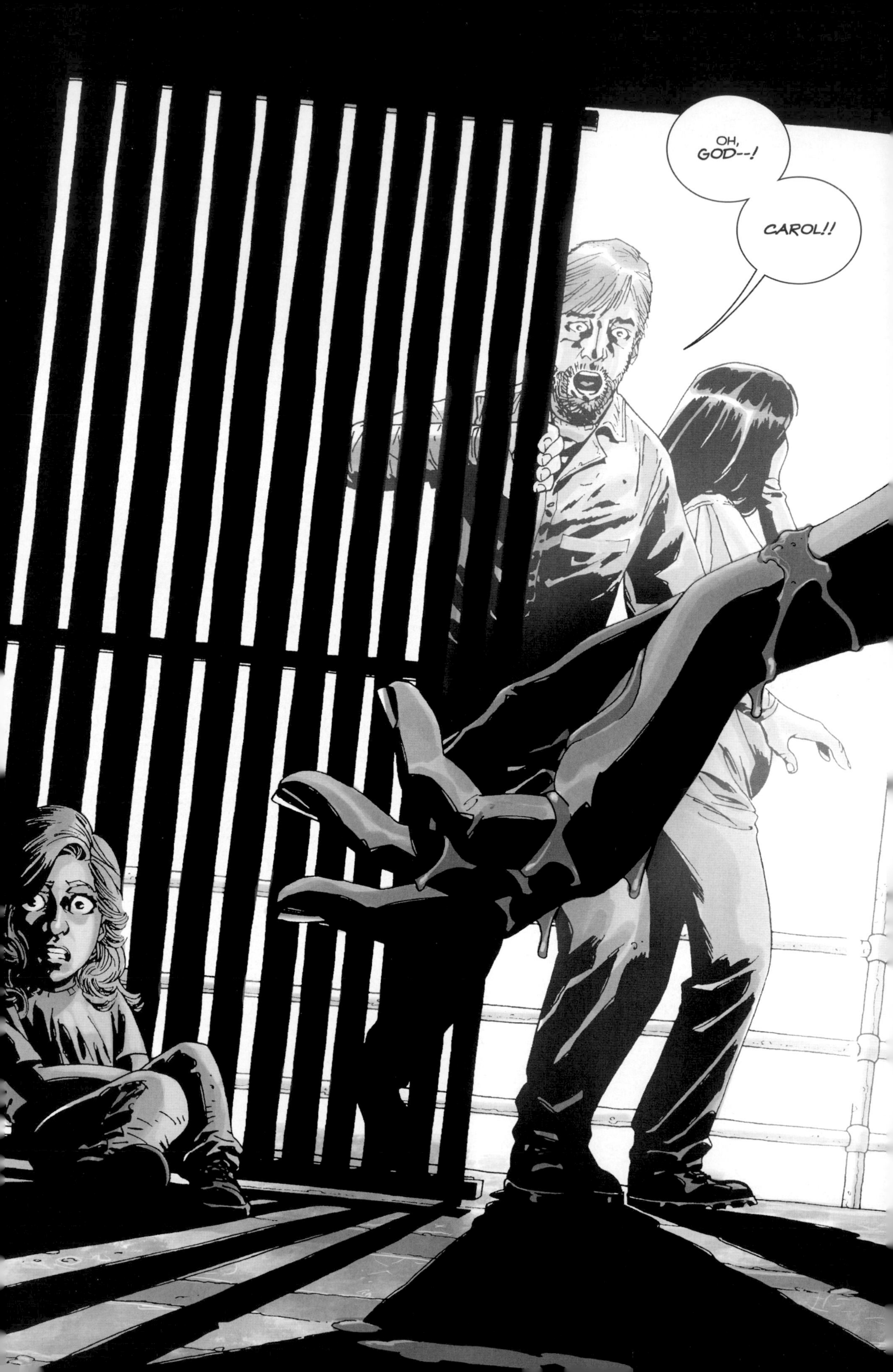
OH, GOD--!
CAROL!!

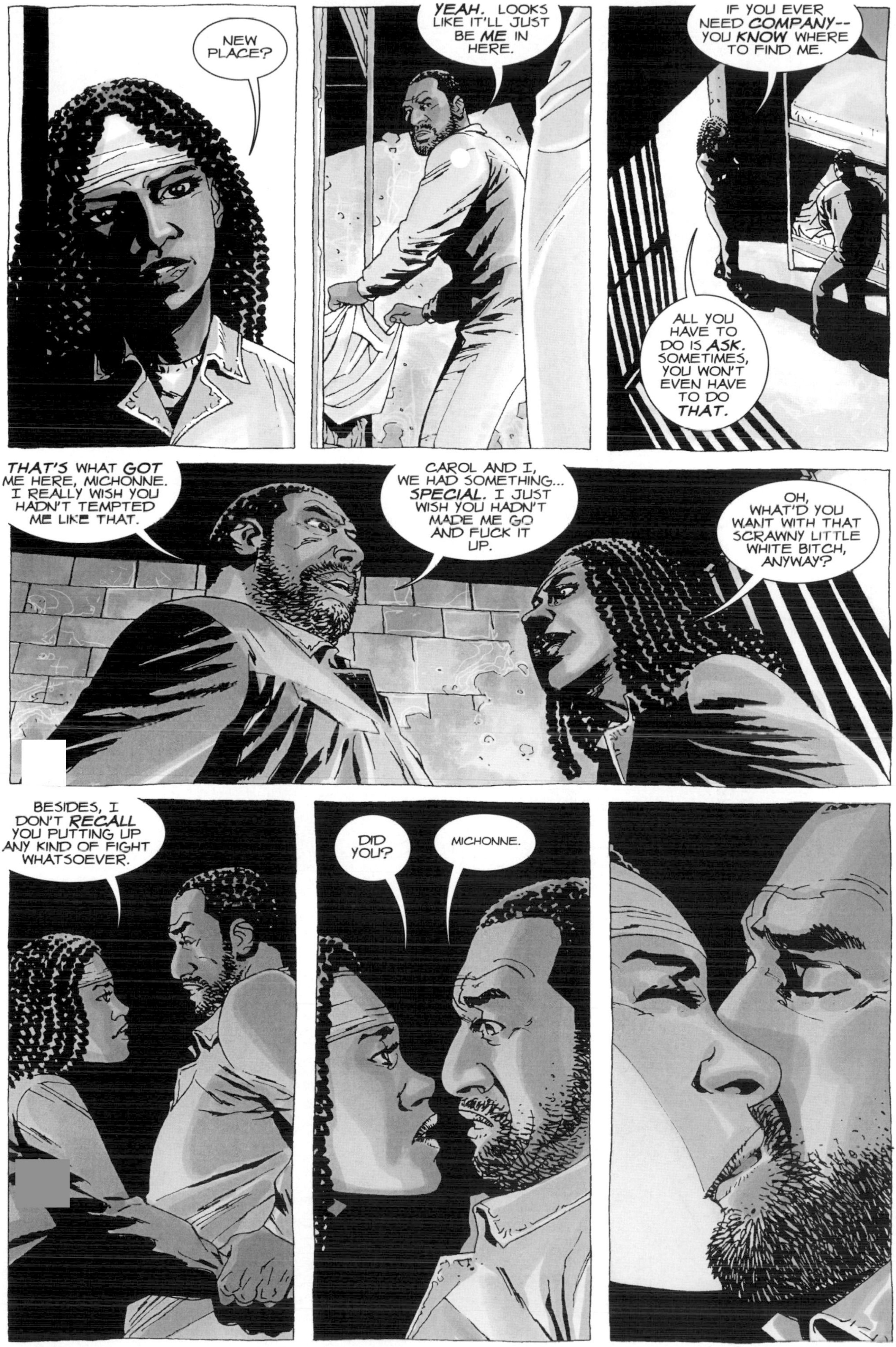
NEW PLACE?
YEAH. LOOKS LIKE IT'LL JUST BE ME IN HERE.
IF YOU EVER NEED COMPANY-- YOU KNOW WHERE TO FIND ME.
ALL YOU HAVE TO DO IS ASK. SOMETIMES, YOU WON'T EVEN HAVE TO DO THAT.
THAT'S WHAT GOT ME HERE, MICHONNE. I REALLY WISH YOU HADN'T TEMPTED ME LIKE THAT.
CAROL AND I, WE HAD SOMETHING... SPECIAL. I JUST WISH YOU HADN'T MADE ME GO AND FUCK IT UP.
OH, WHAT'D YOU WANT WITH THAT SCRAWNY LITTLE WHITE BITCH, ANYWAY?
BESIDES, I DON'T RECALL YOU PUTTING UP ANY KIND OF FIGHT WHATSOEVER.
DID YOU?
MICHONNE.

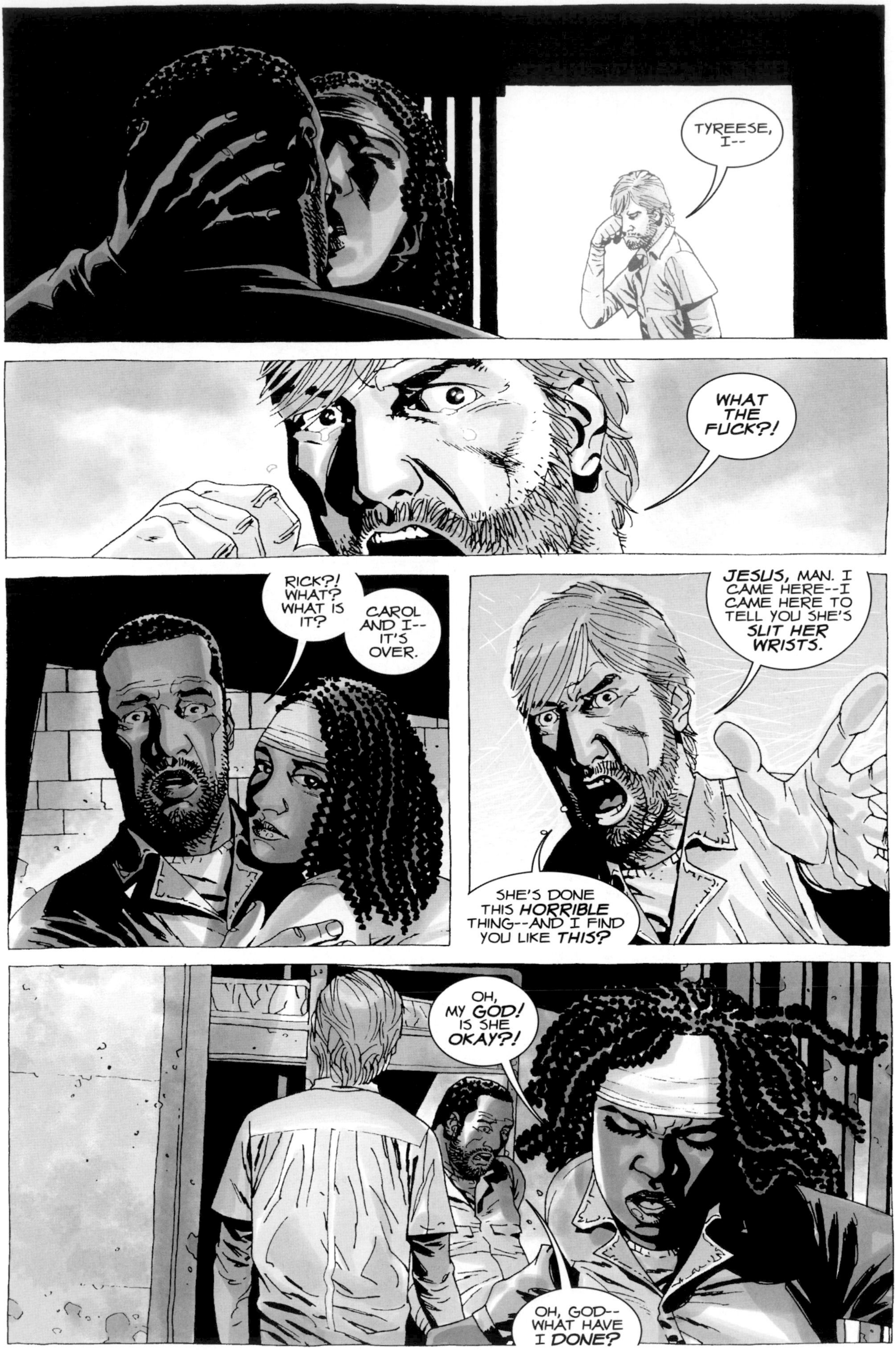
TYREESE, I--
WHAT THE FUCK?!
RICK?! WHAT? WHAT IS IT?
CAROL AND I-- IT'S OVER.
JESUS, MAN. I CAME HERE--I CAME HERE TO TELL YOU SHE'S SLIT HER WRISTS.
SHE'S DONE THIS HORRIBLE THING--AND I FIND YOU LIKE THIS?
OH, MY GOD! IS SHE OKAY?!
OH, GOD-- WHAT HAVE I DONE?

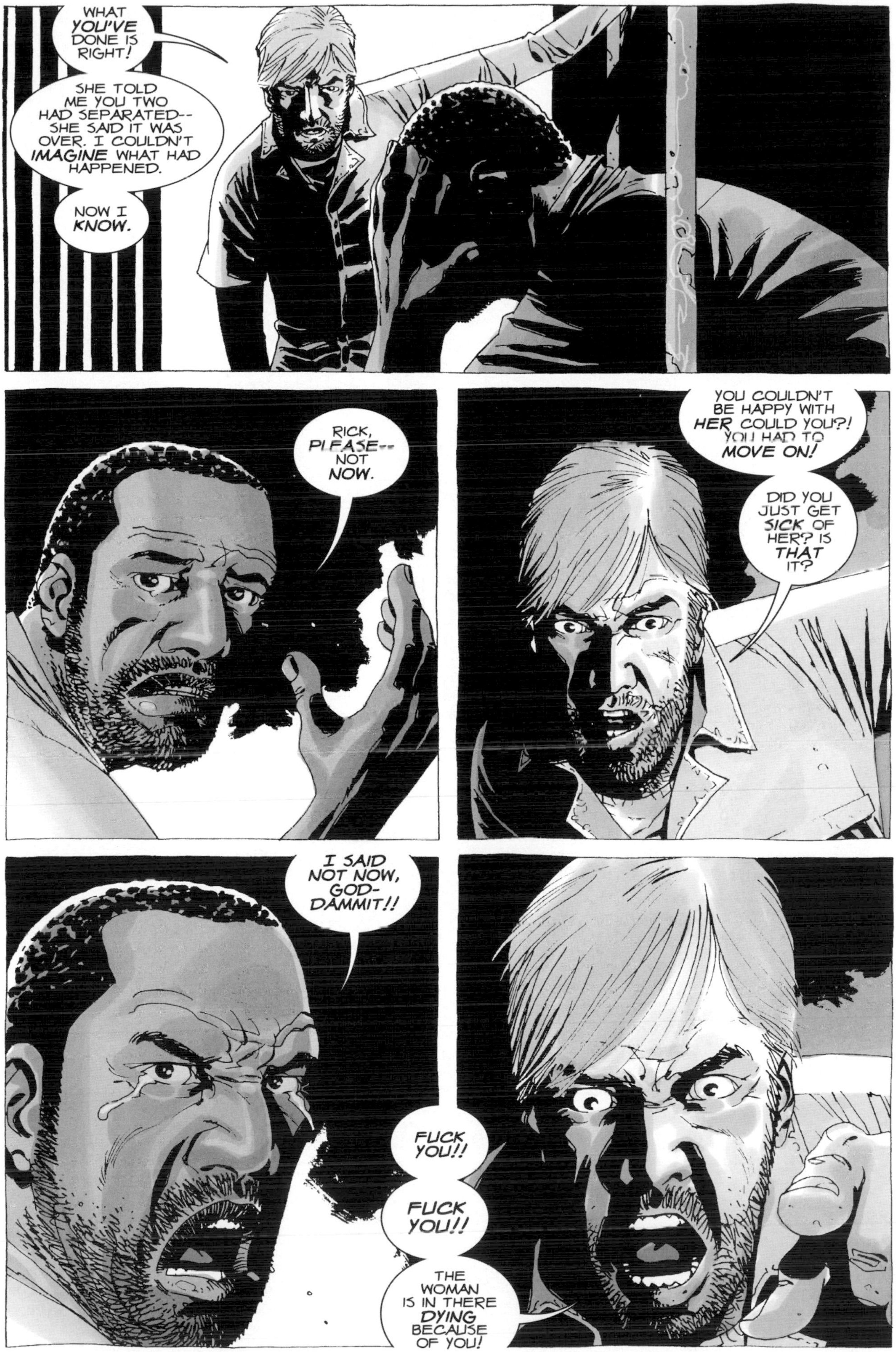
WHAT YOU'VE DONE IS RIGHT!
SHE TOLD ME YOU TWO HAD SEPARATED-- SHE SAID IT WAS OVER. I COULDN'T IMAGINE WHAT HAD HAPPENED.
NOW I KNOW.
RICK, PLEASE-- NOT NOW.
YOU COULDN'T BE HAPPY WITH HER COULD YOU?! YOU HAD TO MOVE ON!
DID YOU JUST GET SICK OF HER? IS THAT IT?
I SAID NOT NOW, GOD-DAMMIT!!
FUCK YOU!!
FUCK YOU!!
THE WOMAN IS IN THERE DYING BECAUSE OF YOU!

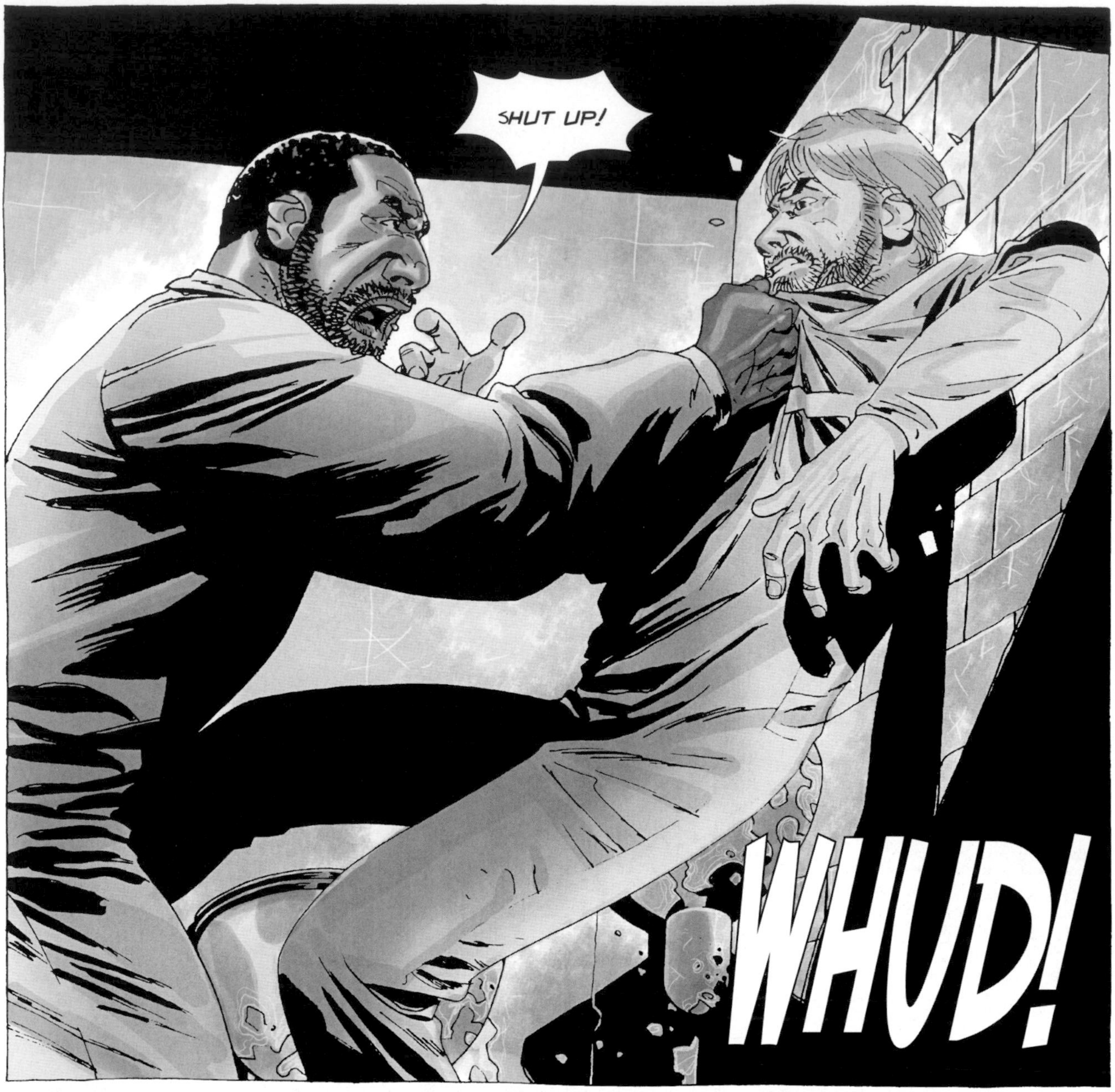
SHUT UP!
WHUD!

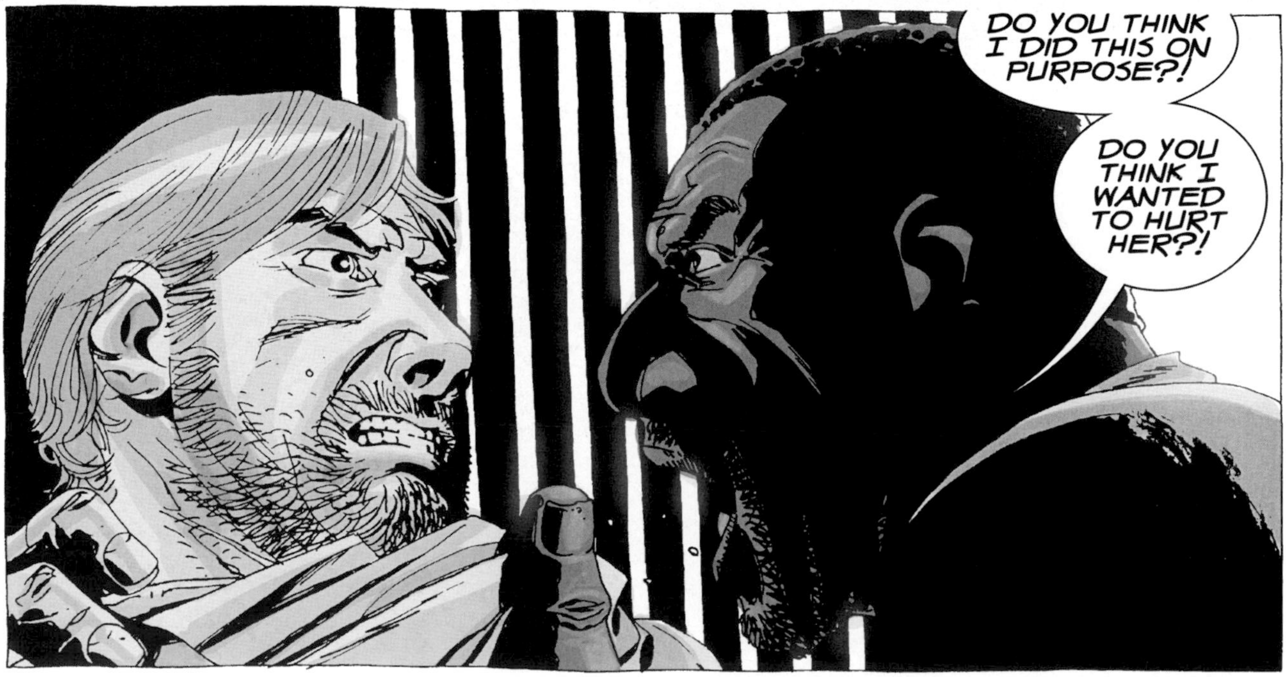
DO YOU THINK I DID THIS ON PURPOSE?!
DO YOU THINK I WANTED TO HURT HER?!

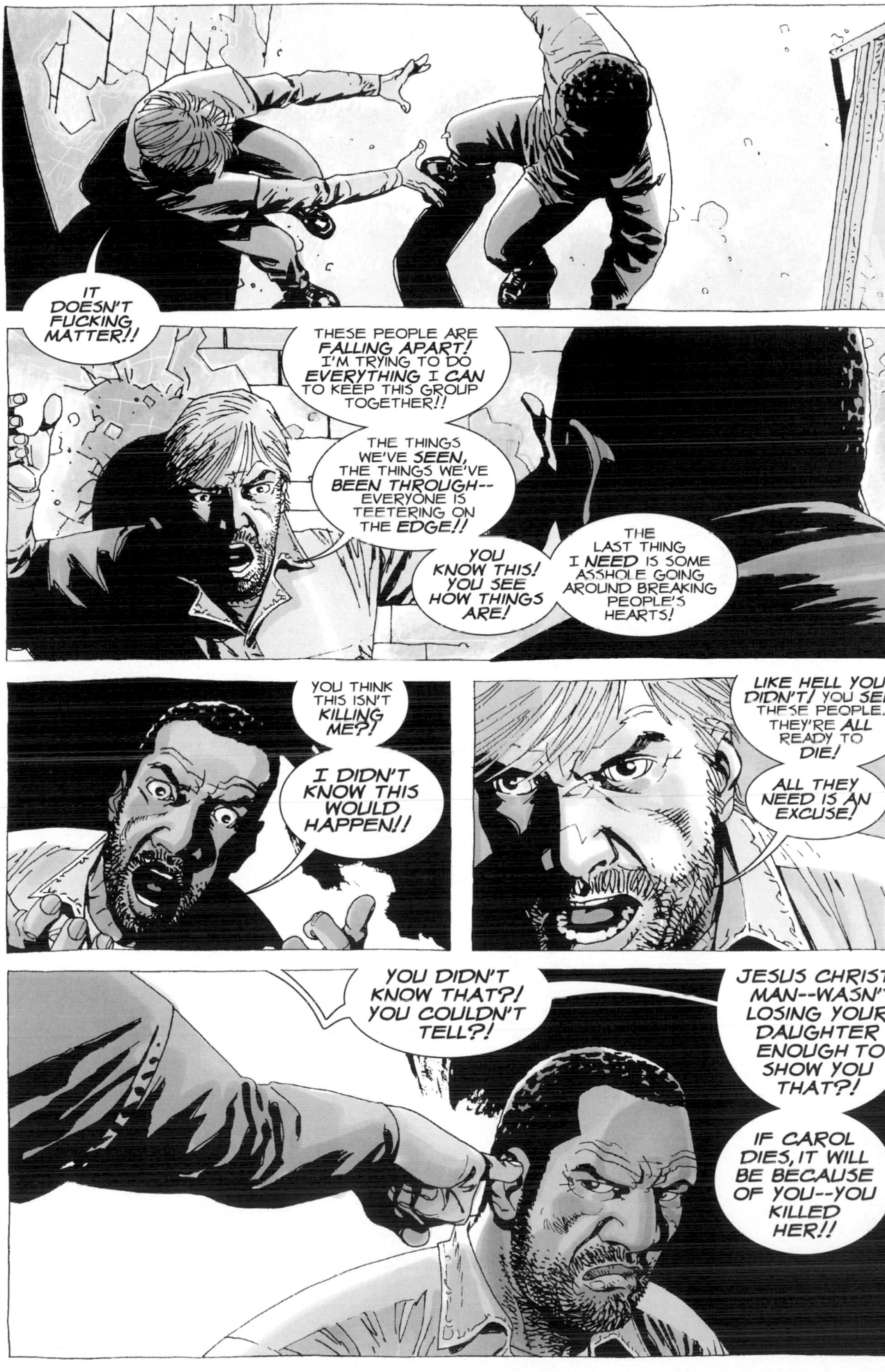
IT DOESN'T FUCKING MATTER!!
THESE PEOPLE ARE FALLING APART! I'M TRYING TO DO EVERYTHING I CAN TO KEEP THIS GROUP TOGETHER!!
THE THINGS WE'VE SEEN, THE THINGS WE'VE BEEN THROUGH-- EVERYONE IS TEETERING ON THE EDGE!!
YOU KNOW THIS! YOU SEE HOW THINGS ARE!
THE LAST THING I NEED IS SOME ASSHOLE GOING AROUND BREAKING PEOPLE'S HEARTS!
YOU THINK THIS ISN'T KILLING ME?!
I DIDN'T KNOW THIS WOULD HAPPEN!!
LIKE HELL YOU DIDN'T! YOU SEE THESE PEOPLE. THEY'RE ALL READY TO DIE!
ALL THEY NEED IS AN EXCUSE!
YOU DIDN'T KNOW THAT?! YOU COULDN'T TELL?!
JESUS CHRIST, MAN--WASN'T LOSING YOUR DAUGHTER ENOUGH TO SHOW YOU THAT?!
IF CAROL DIES, IT WILL BE BECAUSE OF YOU--YOU KILLED HER!!

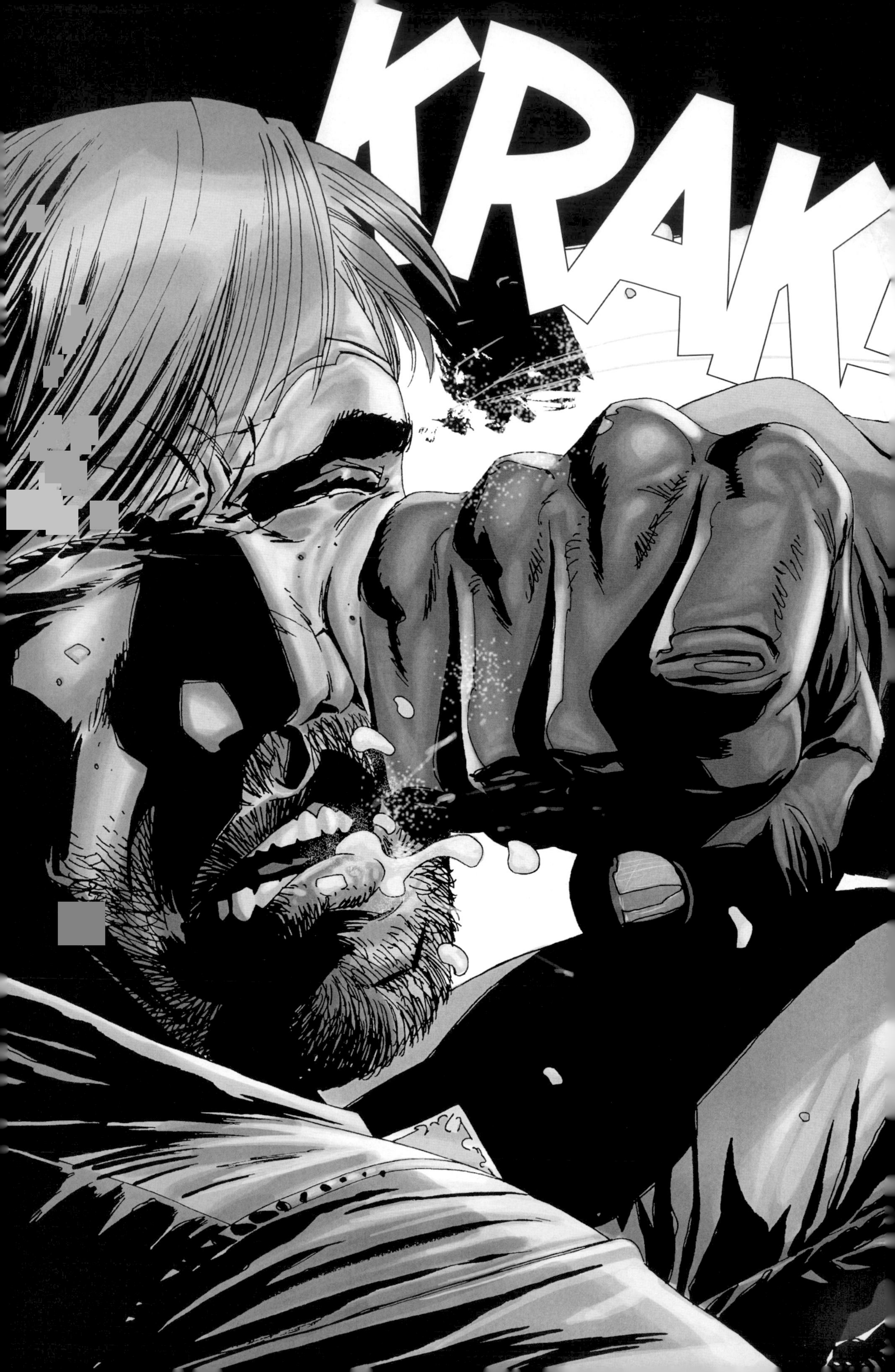
KRAK!

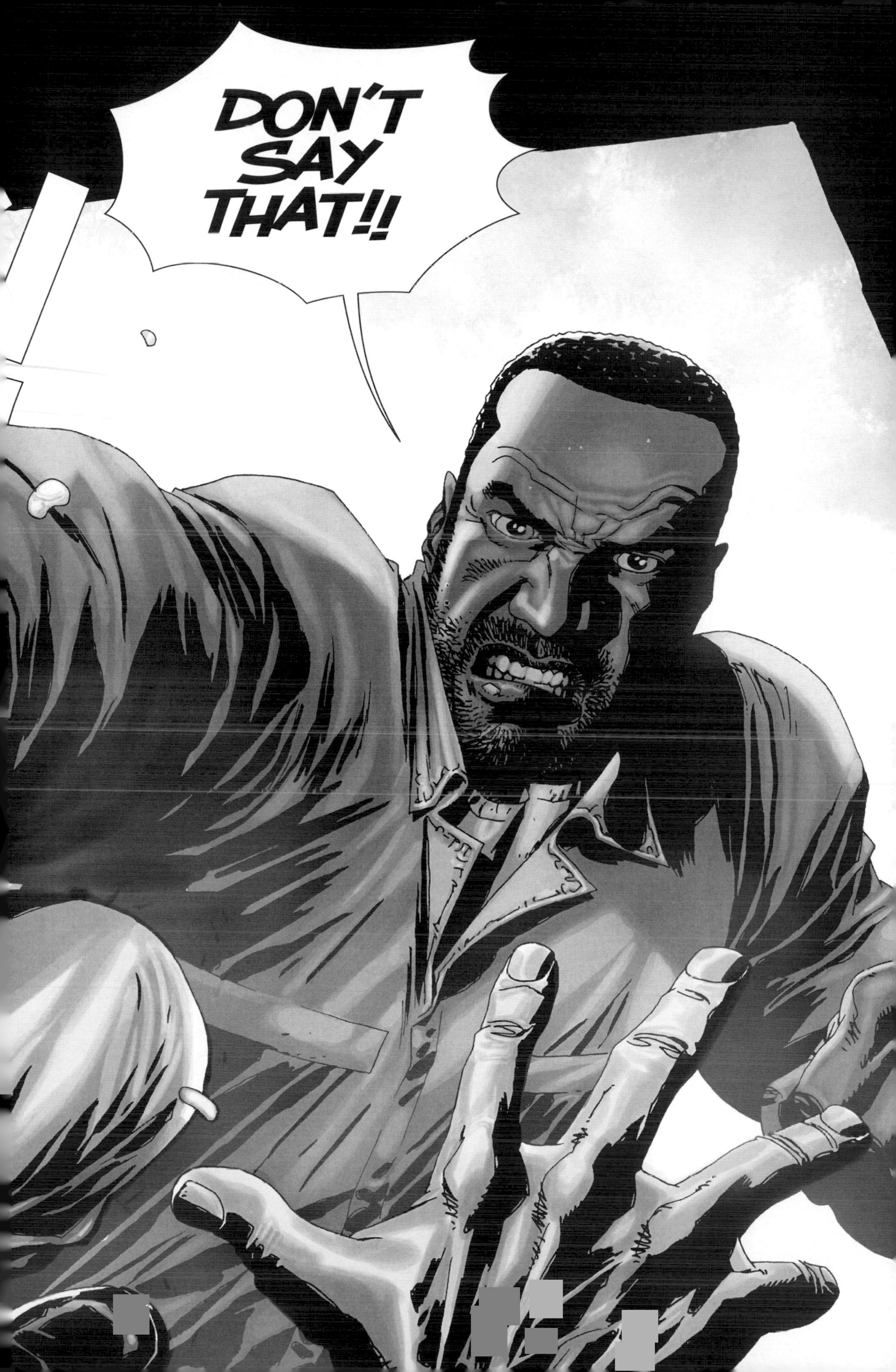
DON'T SAY THAT!!

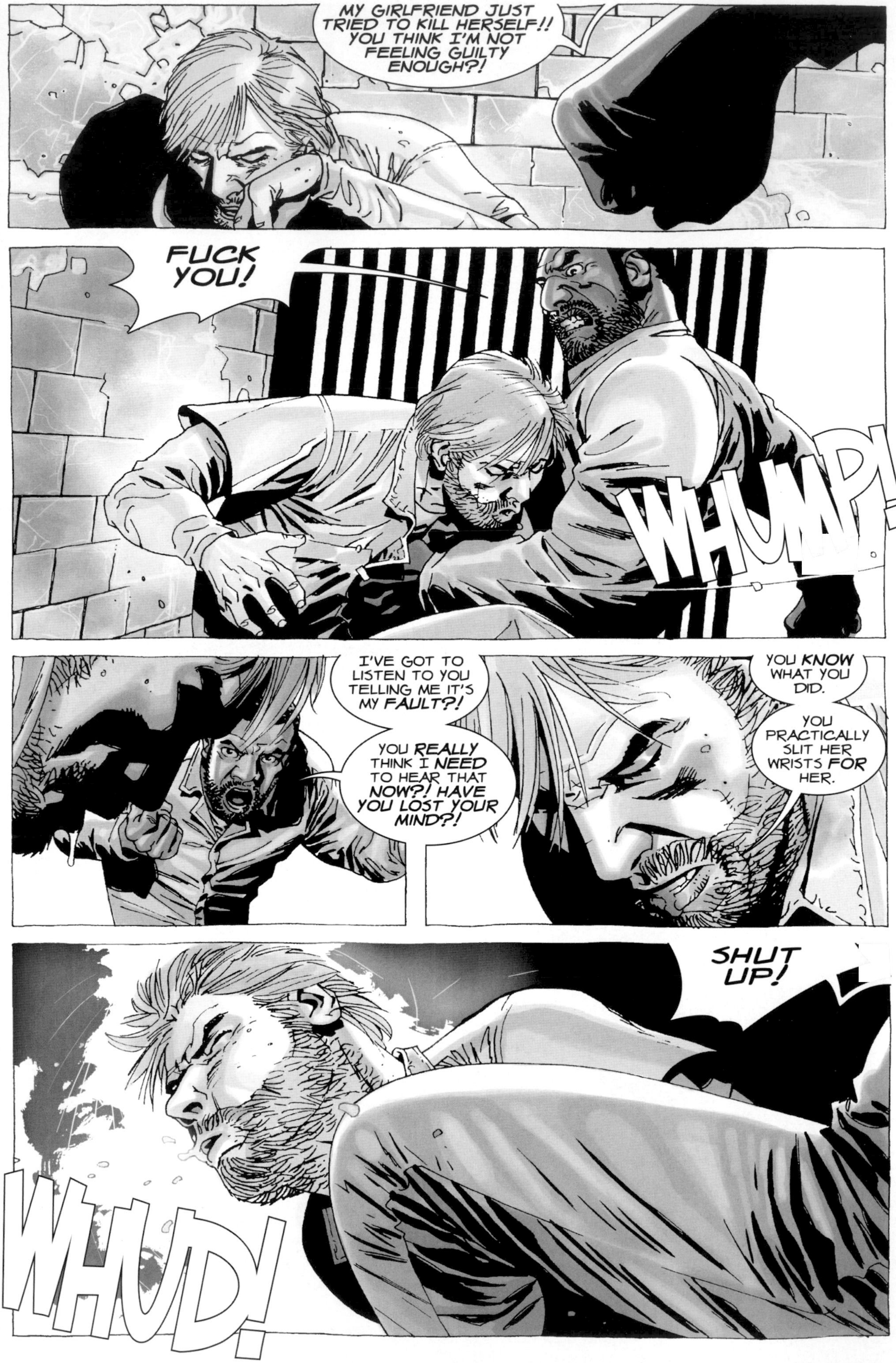
MY GIRLFRIEND JUST TRIED TO KILL HERSELF!! YOU THINK I'M NOT FEELING GUILTY ENOUGH?!
FUCK YOU!
WHUMP!
I'VE GOT TO LISTEN TO YOU TELLING ME IT'S MY FAULT?!
YOU REALLY THINK I NEED TO HEAR THAT NOW?! HAVE YOU LOST YOUR MIND?!
YOU KNOW WHAT YOU DID.
YOU PRACTICALLY SLIT HER WRISTS FOR HER.
SHUT UP!
WHUD!

I--

--DIDN'T--

--KILL HER!

I DIDN'T KILL HER.

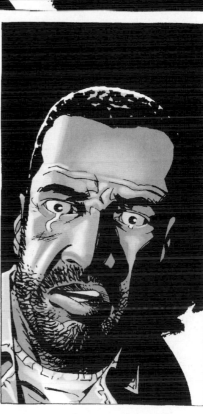

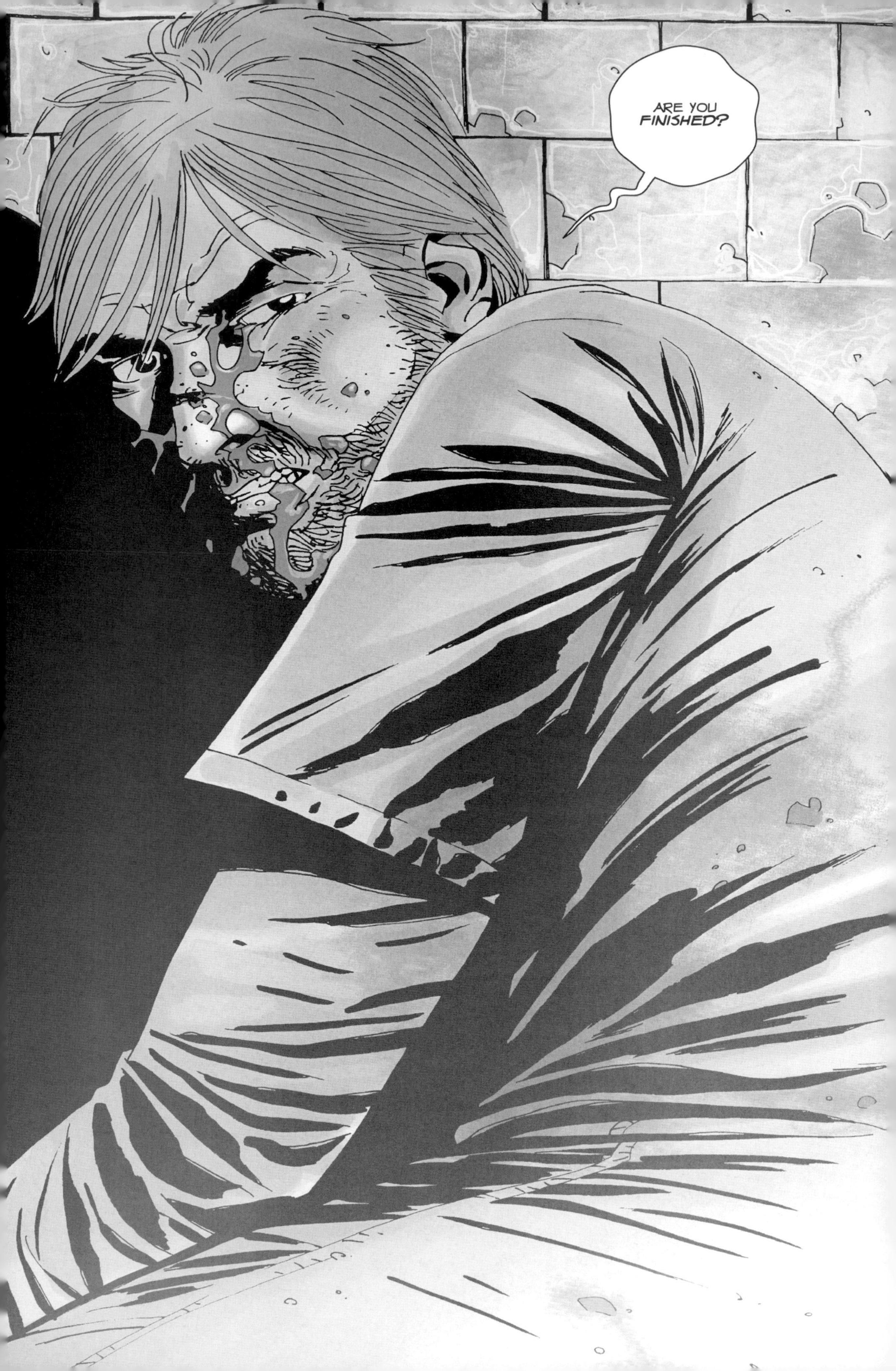
ARE YOU FINISHED?

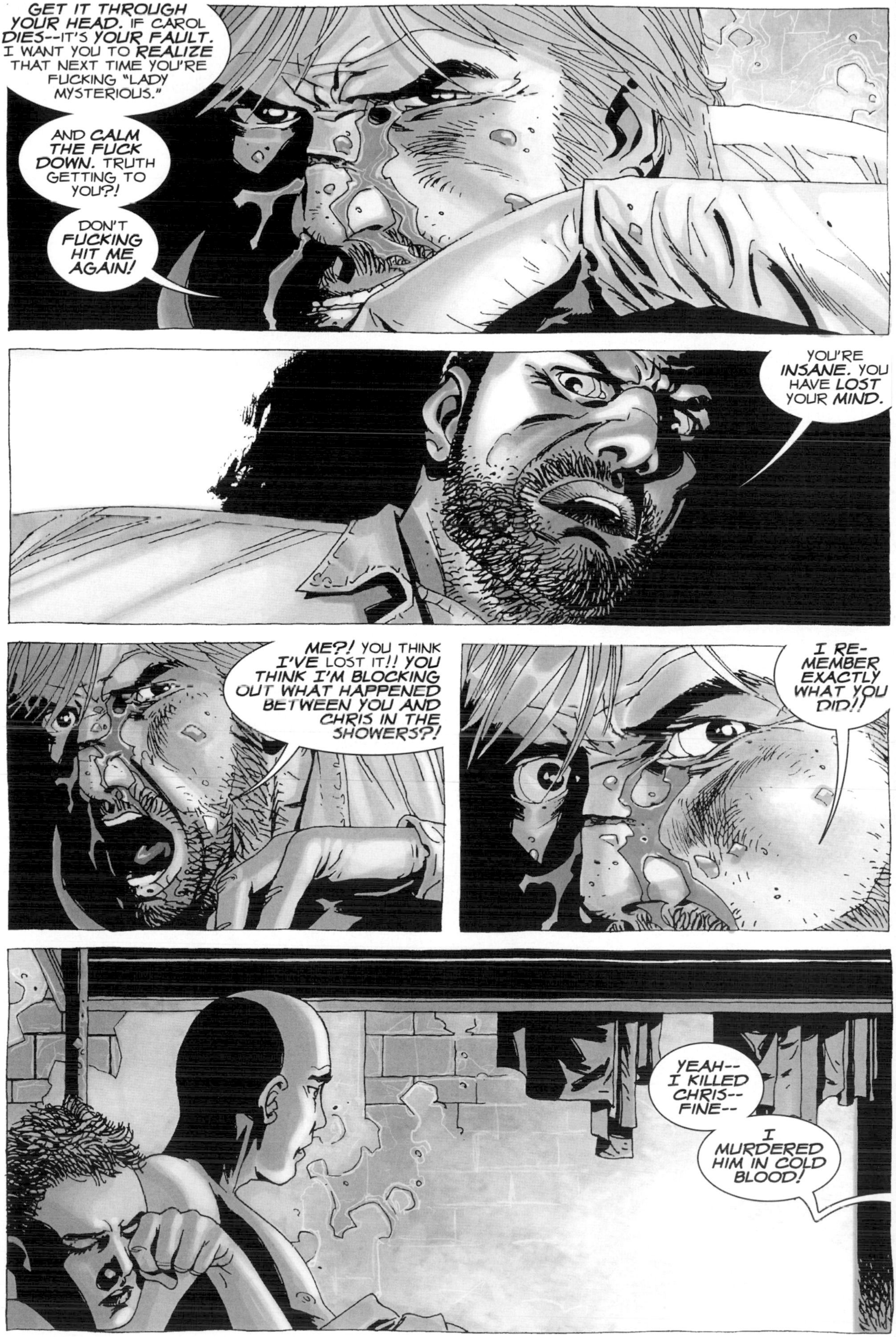
GET IT THROUGH YOUR HEAD. IF CAROL DIES--IT'S YOUR FAULT. I WANT YOU TO REALIZE THAT NEXT TIME YOU'RE FUCKING "LADY MYSTERIOUS."
AND CALM THE FUCK DOWN. TRUTH GETTING TO YOU?!
DON'T FUCKING HIT ME AGAIN!
YOU'RE INSANE. YOU HAVE LOST YOUR MIND.
ME?! YOU THINK I'VE LOST IT!! YOU THINK I'M BLOCKING OUT WHAT HAPPENED BETWEEN YOU AND CHRIS IN THE SHOWERS?!
I RE-MEMBER EXACTLY WHAT YOU DID!!
YEAH-- I KILLED CHRIS-- FINE--
I MURDERED HIM IN COLD BLOOD!

HE KILLED MY DAUGHTER! HE FUCKING SHOT HER DEAD! HE WAS TRYING TO COMMIT SUICIDE WITH HER AND AS FAR AS I'M CONCERNED I JUST FINISHED THE JOB!

AND I ENJOYED IT. AFTER ALL THESE MONTHS AND THE HELL WE'VE BEEN THROUGH--IT'S ALMOST THE ONLY THING I'VE ENJOYED!

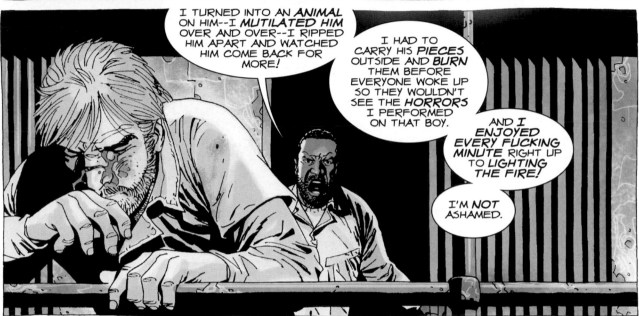

I TURNED INTO AN ANIMAL ON HIM--I MUTILATED HIM OVER AND OVER--I RIPPED HIM APART AND WATCHED HIM COME BACK FOR MORE!

I HAD TO CARRY HIS PIECES OUTSIDE AND BURN THEM BEFORE EVERYONE WOKE UP SO THEY WOULDN'T SEE THE HORRORS I PERFORMED ON THAT BOY.

AND I ENJOYED EVERY FUCKING MINUTE RIGHT UP TO LIGHTING THE FIRE!

I'M NOT ASHAMED.

I'M NOT ASHAMED!

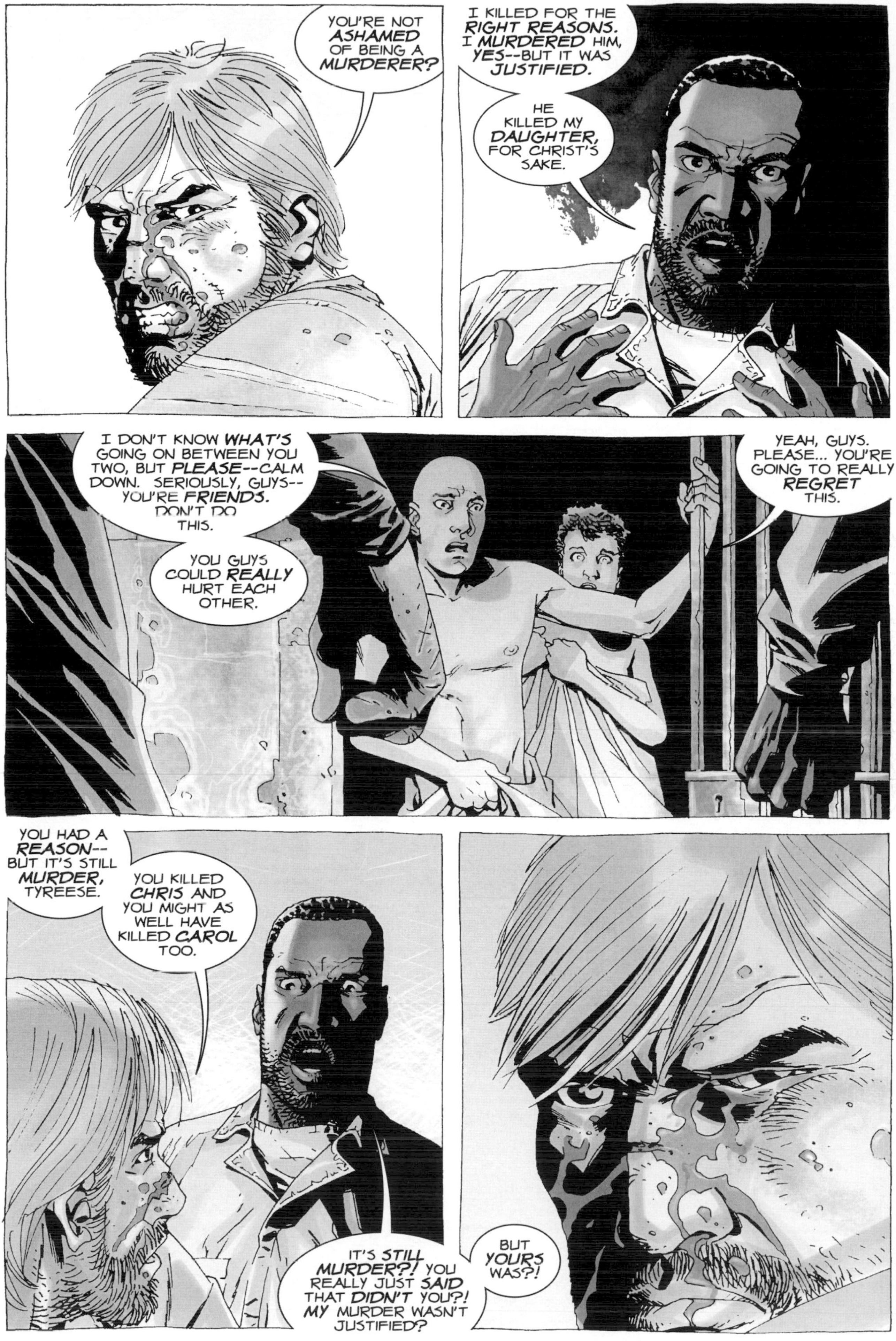
YOU'RE NOT ASHAMED OF BEING A MURDERER?
I KILLED FOR THE RIGHT REASONS. I MURDERED HIM, YES--BUT IT WAS JUSTIFIED.
HE KILLED MY DAUGHTER, FOR CHRIST'S SAKE.
I DON'T KNOW WHAT'S GOING ON BETWEEN YOU TWO, BUT PLEASE--CALM DOWN. SERIOUSLY, GUYS--YOU'RE FRIENDS. DON'T DO THIS.
YOU GUYS COULD REALLY HURT EACH OTHER.
YEAH, GUYS. PLEASE... YOU'RE GOING TO REALLY REGRET THIS.
YOU HAD A REASON--BUT IT'S STILL MURDER, TYREESE.
YOU KILLED CHRIS AND YOU MIGHT AS WELL HAVE KILLED CAROL TOO.
IT'S STILL MURDER?! YOU REALLY JUST SAID THAT DIDN'T YOU?! MY MURDER WASN'T JUSTIFIED?
BUT YOURS WAS?!

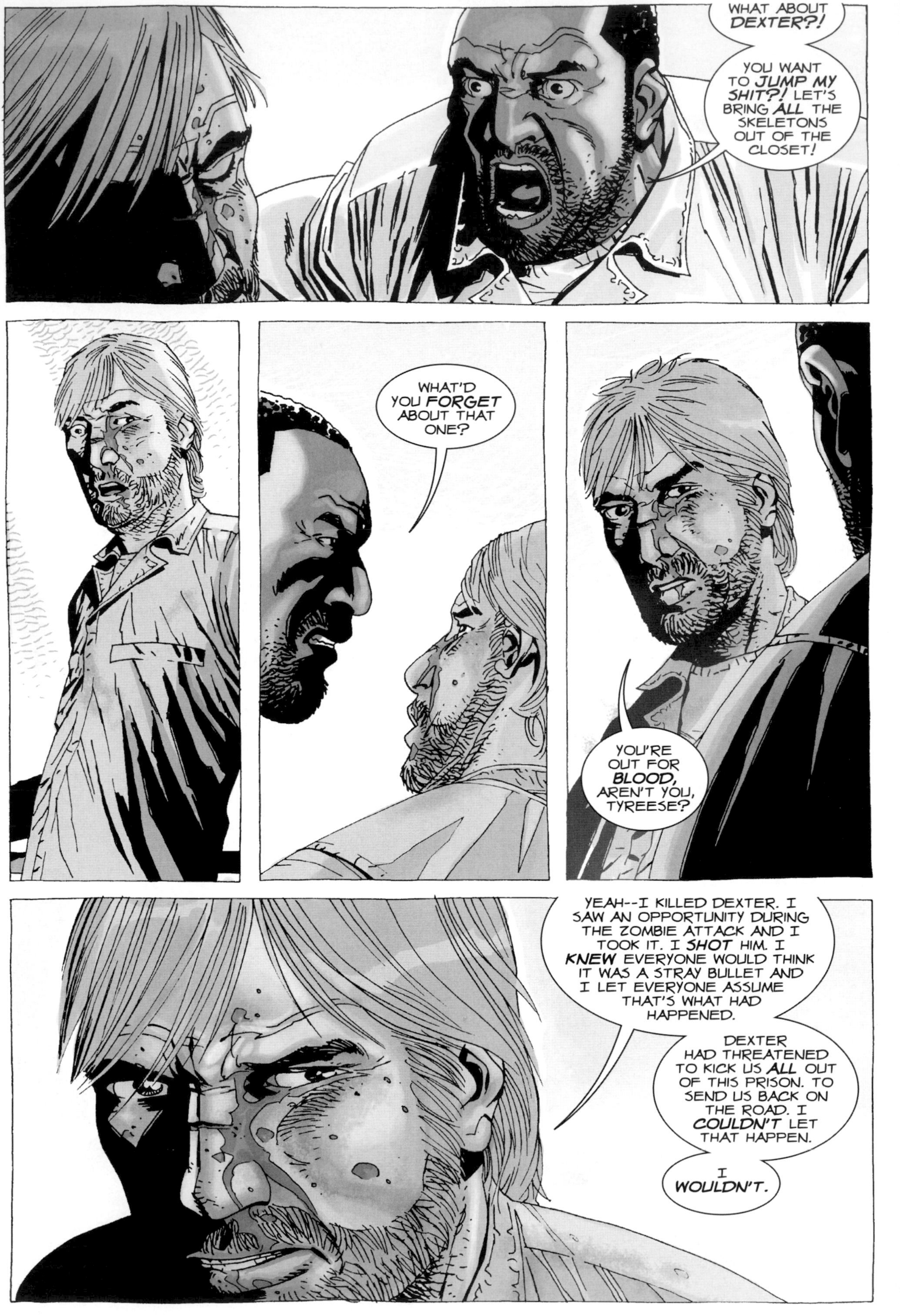

WHAT ABOUT DEXTER?!
YOU WANT TO JUMP MY SHIT?! LET'S BRING ALL THE SKELETONS OUT OF THE CLOSET!
WHAT'D YOU FORGET ABOUT THAT ONE?
YOU'RE OUT FOR BLOOD, AREN'T YOU, TYREESE?
YEAH--I KILLED DEXTER. I SAW AN OPPORTUNITY DURING THE ZOMBIE ATTACK AND I TOOK IT. I SHOT HIM. I KNEW EVERYONE WOULD THINK IT WAS A STRAY BULLET AND I LET EVERYONE ASSUME THAT'S WHAT HAD HAPPENED.
DEXTER HAD THREATENED TO KICK US ALL OUT OF THIS PRISON. TO SEND US BACK ON THE ROAD. I COULDN'T LET THAT HAPPEN.
I WOULDN'T.

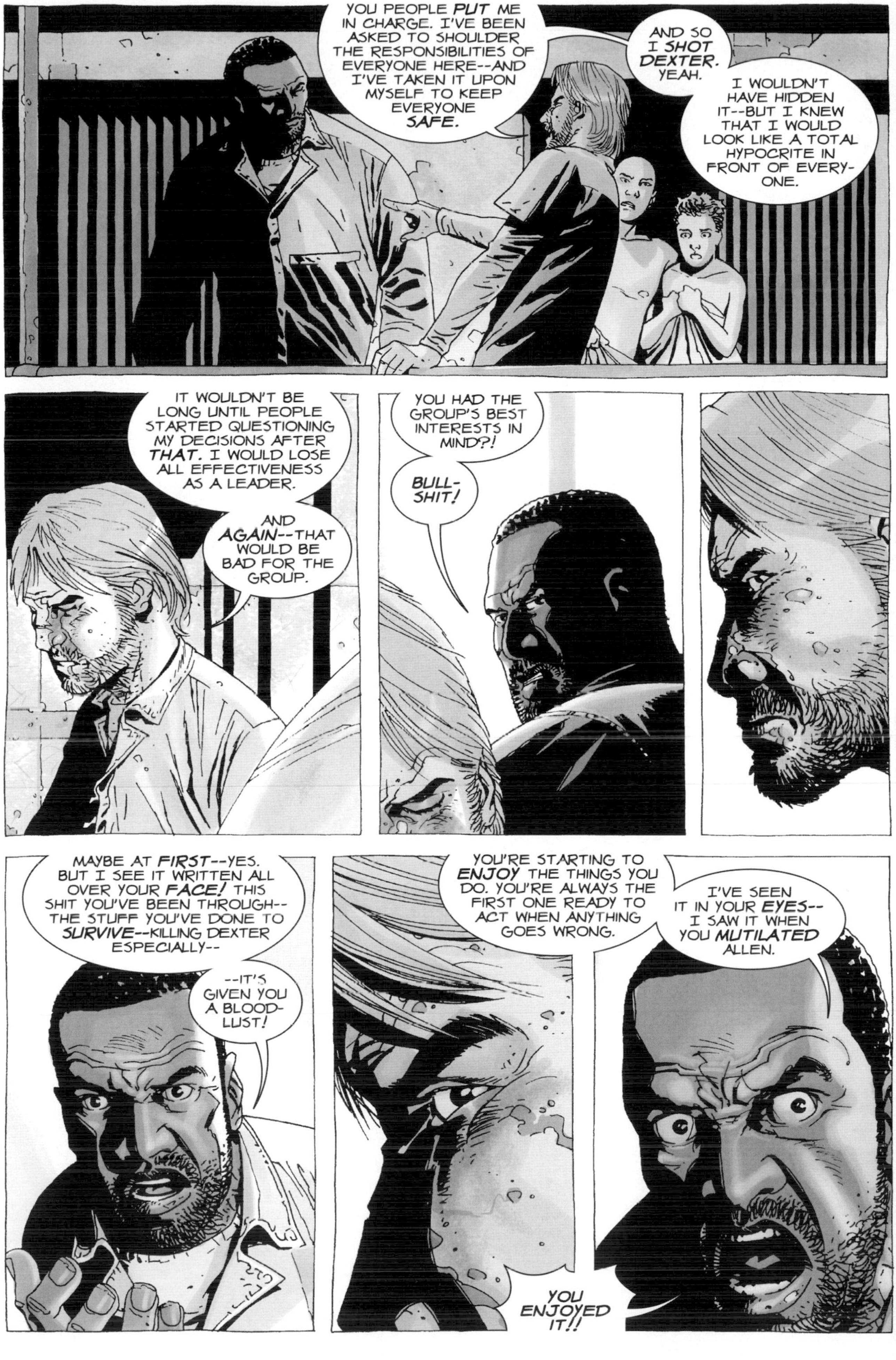
YOU PEOPLE PUT ME IN CHARGE. I'VE BEEN ASKED TO SHOULDER THE RESPONSIBILITIES OF EVERYONE HERE--AND I'VE TAKEN IT UPON MYSELF TO KEEP EVERYONE SAFE.
AND SO I SHOT DEXTER. YEAH.
I WOULDN'T HAVE HIDDEN IT--BUT I KNEW THAT I WOULD LOOK LIKE A TOTAL HYPOCRITE IN FRONT OF EVERY-ONE.
IT WOULDN'T BE LONG UNTIL PEOPLE STARTED QUESTIONING MY DECISIONS AFTER THAT. I WOULD LOSE ALL EFFECTIVENESS AS A LEADER.
AND AGAIN--THAT WOULD BE BAD FOR THE GROUP.
YOU HAD THE GROUP'S BEST INTERESTS IN MIND?!
BULL-SHIT!
MAYBE AT FIRST--YES. BUT I SEE IT WRITTEN ALL OVER YOUR FACE! THIS SHIT YOU'VE BEEN THROUGH--THE STUFF YOU'VE DONE TO SURVIVE--KILLING DEXTER ESPECIALLY--
--IT'S GIVEN YOU A BLOOD-LUST!
YOU'RE STARTING TO ENJOY THE THINGS YOU DO. YOU'RE ALWAYS THE FIRST ONE READY TO ACT WHEN ANYTHING GOES WRONG.
I'VE SEEN IT IN YOUR EYES--I SAW IT WHEN YOU MUTILATED ALLEN.
YOU ENJOYED IT!!

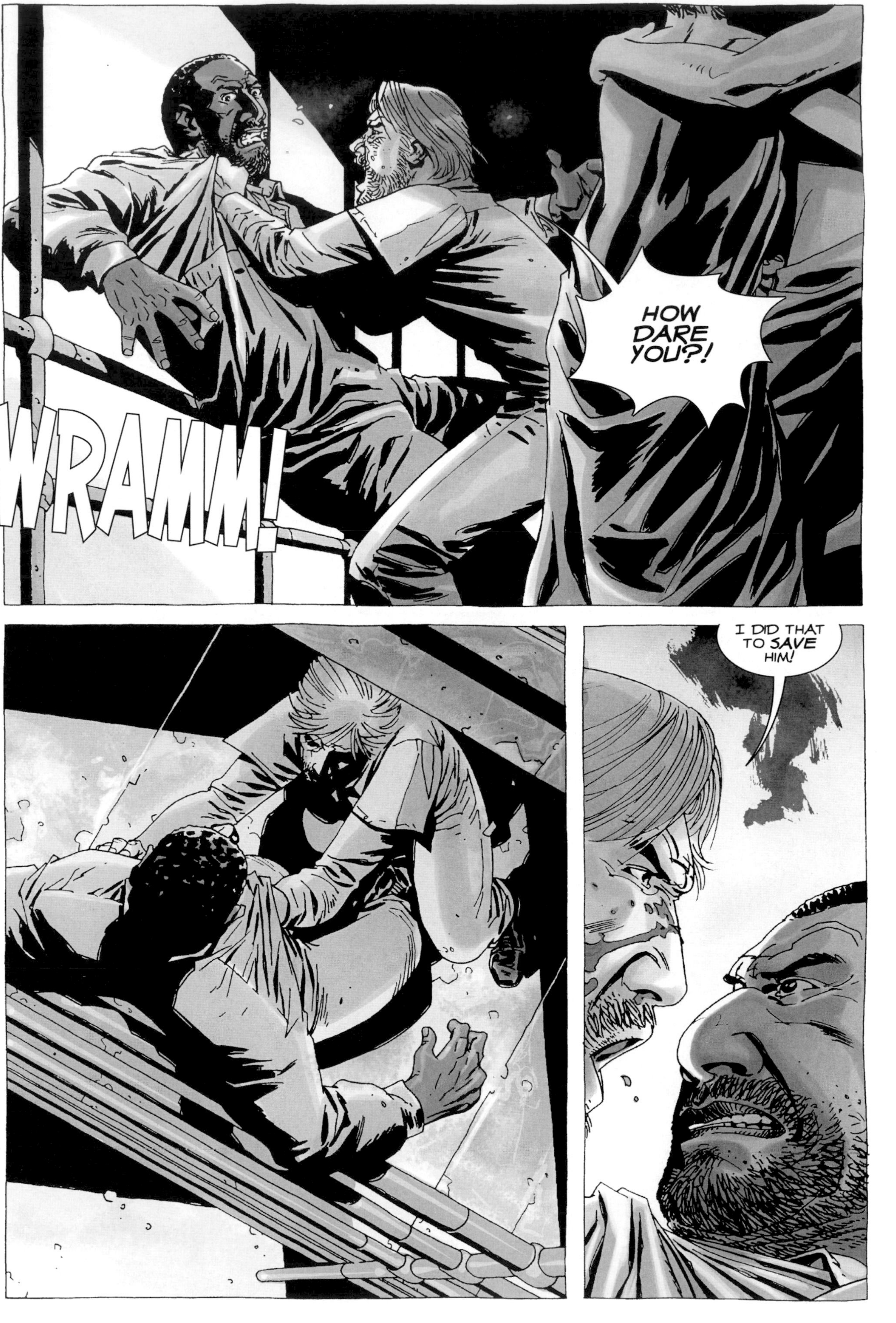
HOW DARE YOU?!
WRAMM!
I DID THAT TO SAVE HIM!

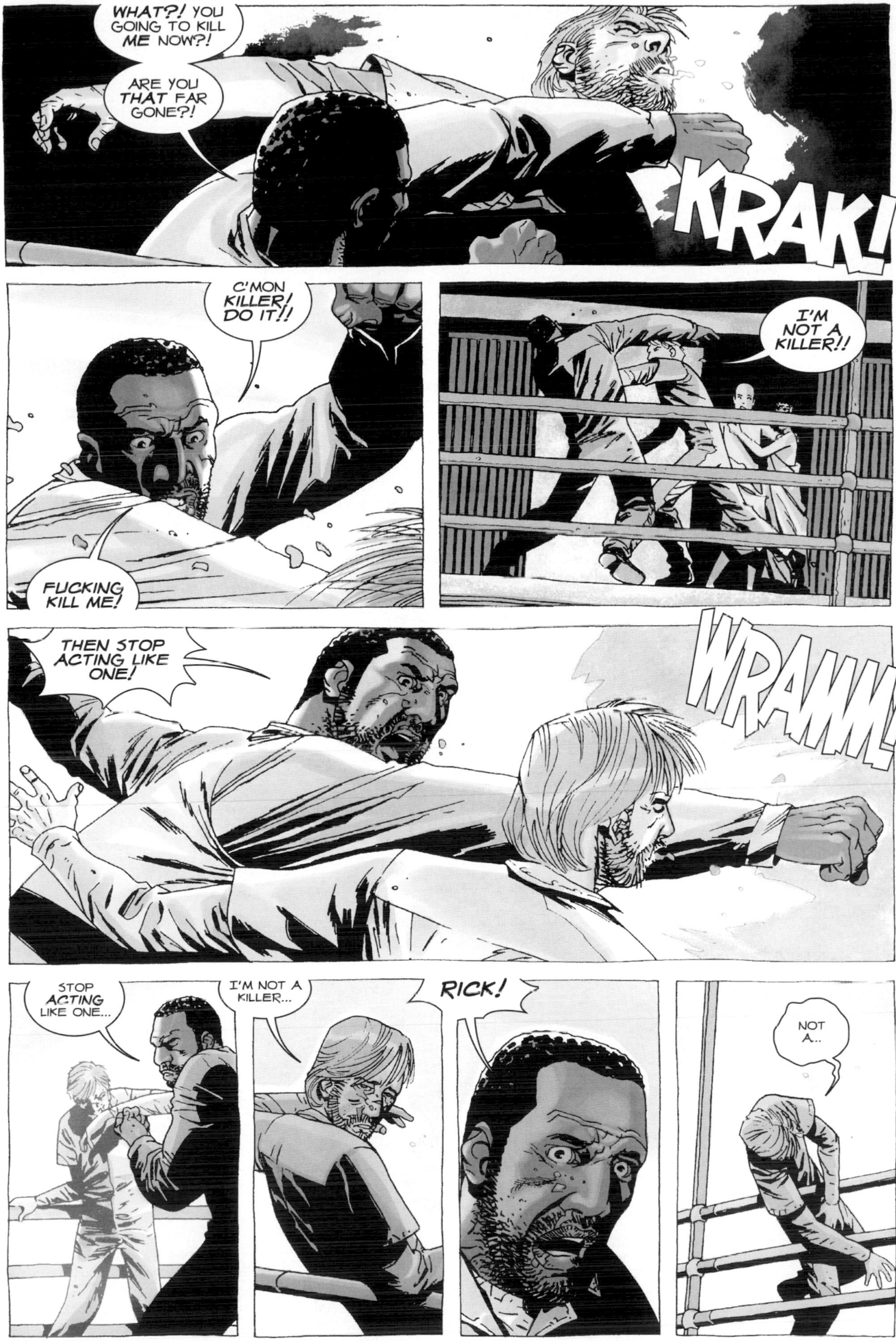
WHAT?! YOU GOING TO KILL ME NOW?!
ARE YOU THAT FAR GONE?!
KRAK!
C'MON KILLER! DO IT!!
FUCKING KILL ME!
I'M NOT A KILLER!!
THEN STOP ACTING LIKE ONE!
WRAMM!
STOP ACTING LIKE ONE...
I'M NOT A KILLER...
RICK!
NOT A...

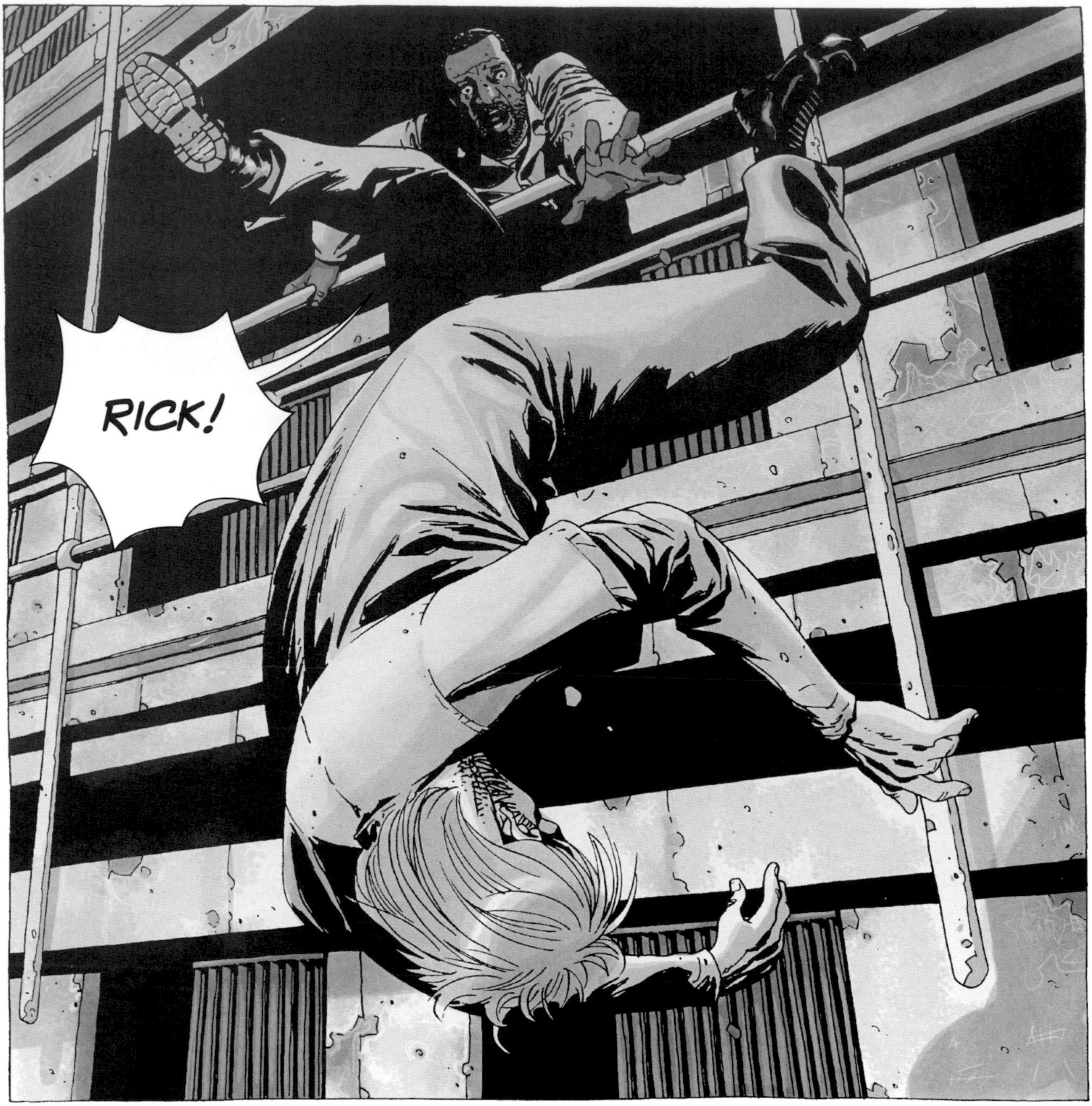
RICK!

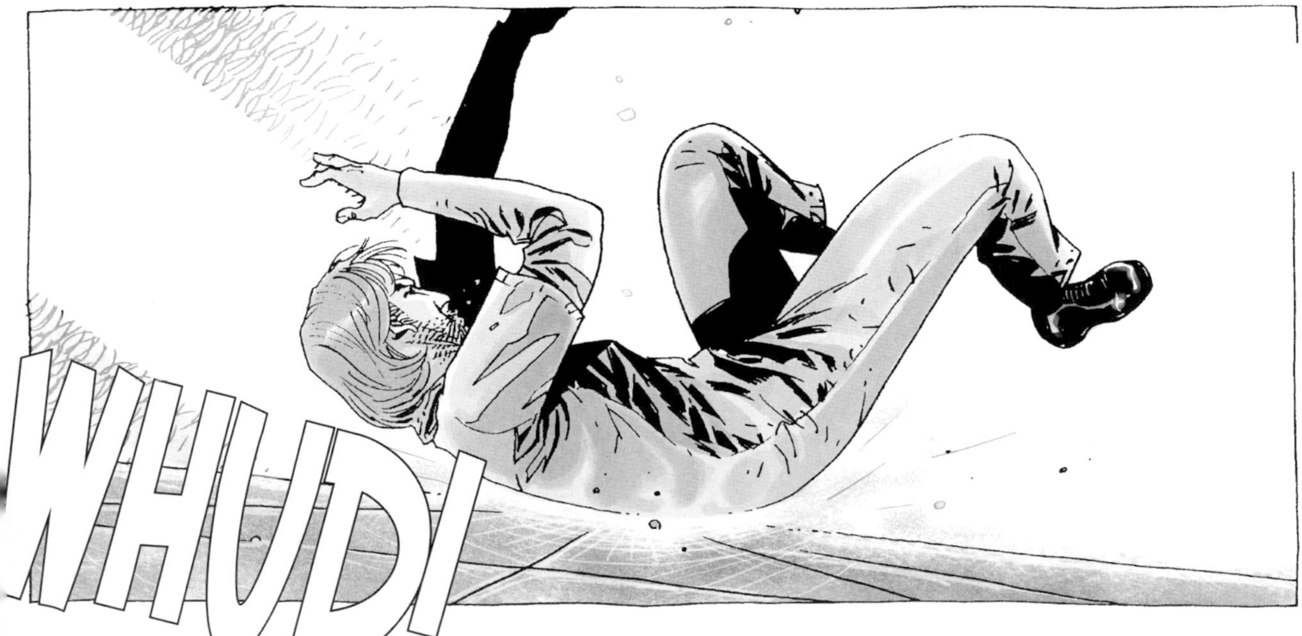
WHUD!

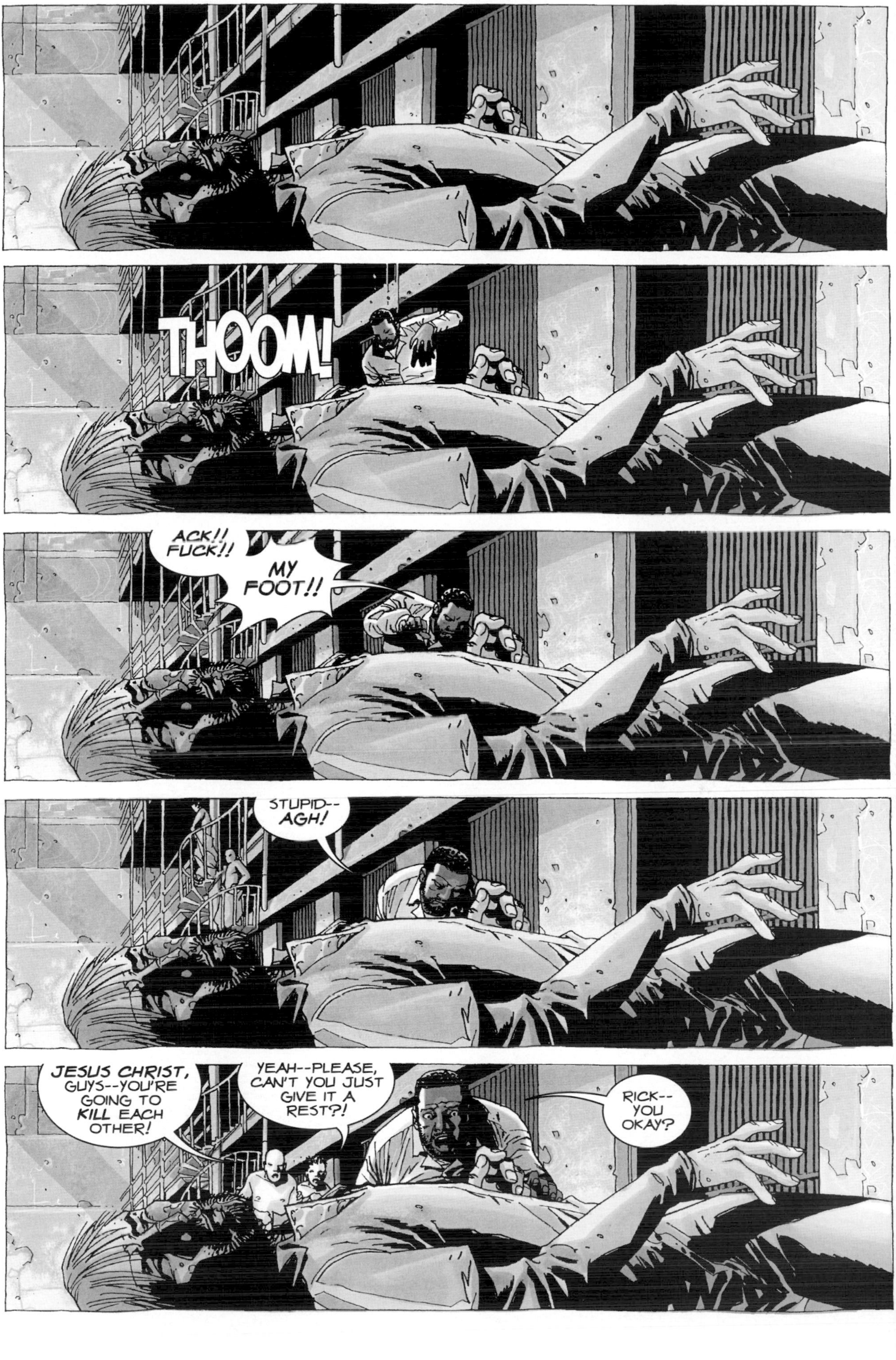
THOOM!
ACK!! FUCK!!
MY FOOT!!
STUPID-- AGH!
JESUS CHRIST, GUYS--YOU'RE GOING TO KILL EACH OTHER!
YEAH--PLEASE, CAN'T YOU JUST GIVE IT A REST?!
RICK-- YOU OKAY?

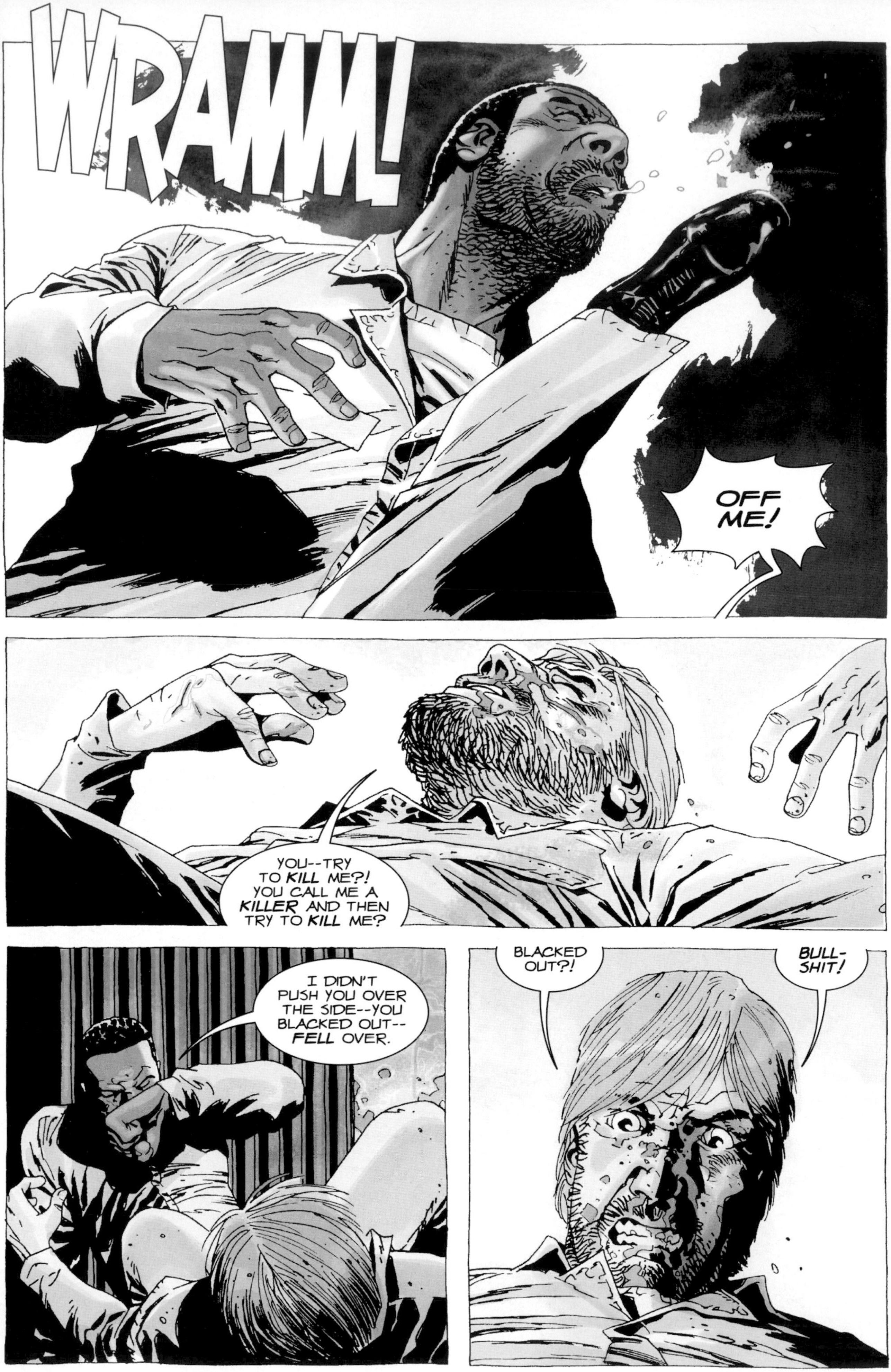
WRAMM!
OFF ME!
YOU--TRY TO KILL ME?! YOU CALL ME A KILLER AND THEN TRY TO KILL ME?
I DIDN'T PUSH YOU OVER THE SIDE--YOU BLACKED OUT-- FELL OVER.
BLACKED OUT?!
BULL-SHIT!

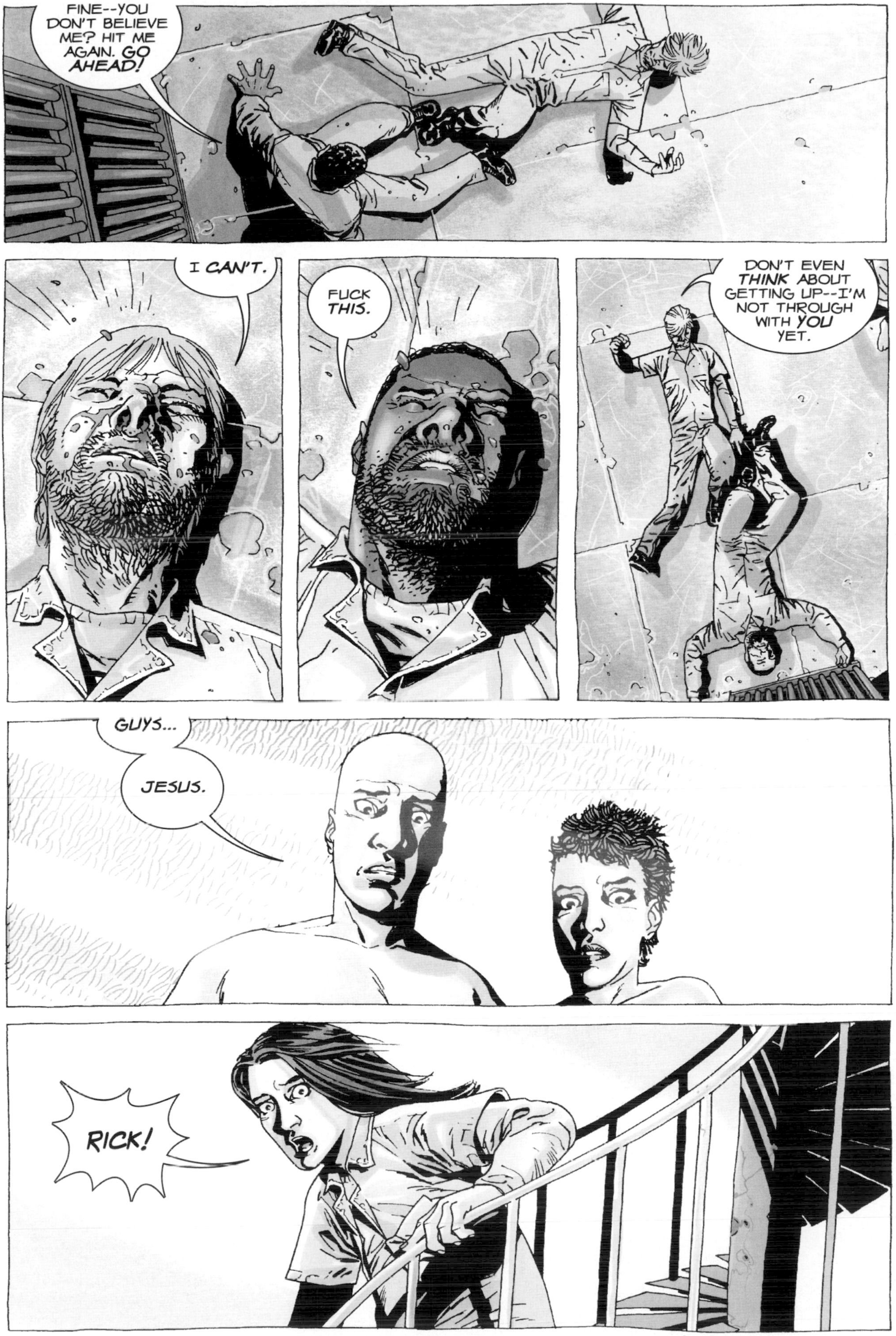
FINE--YOU DON'T BELIEVE ME? HIT ME AGAIN. GO AHEAD!
I CAN'T.
FUCK THIS.
DON'T EVEN THINK ABOUT GETTING UP--I'M NOT THROUGH WITH YOU YET.
GUYS...
JESUS.
RICK!

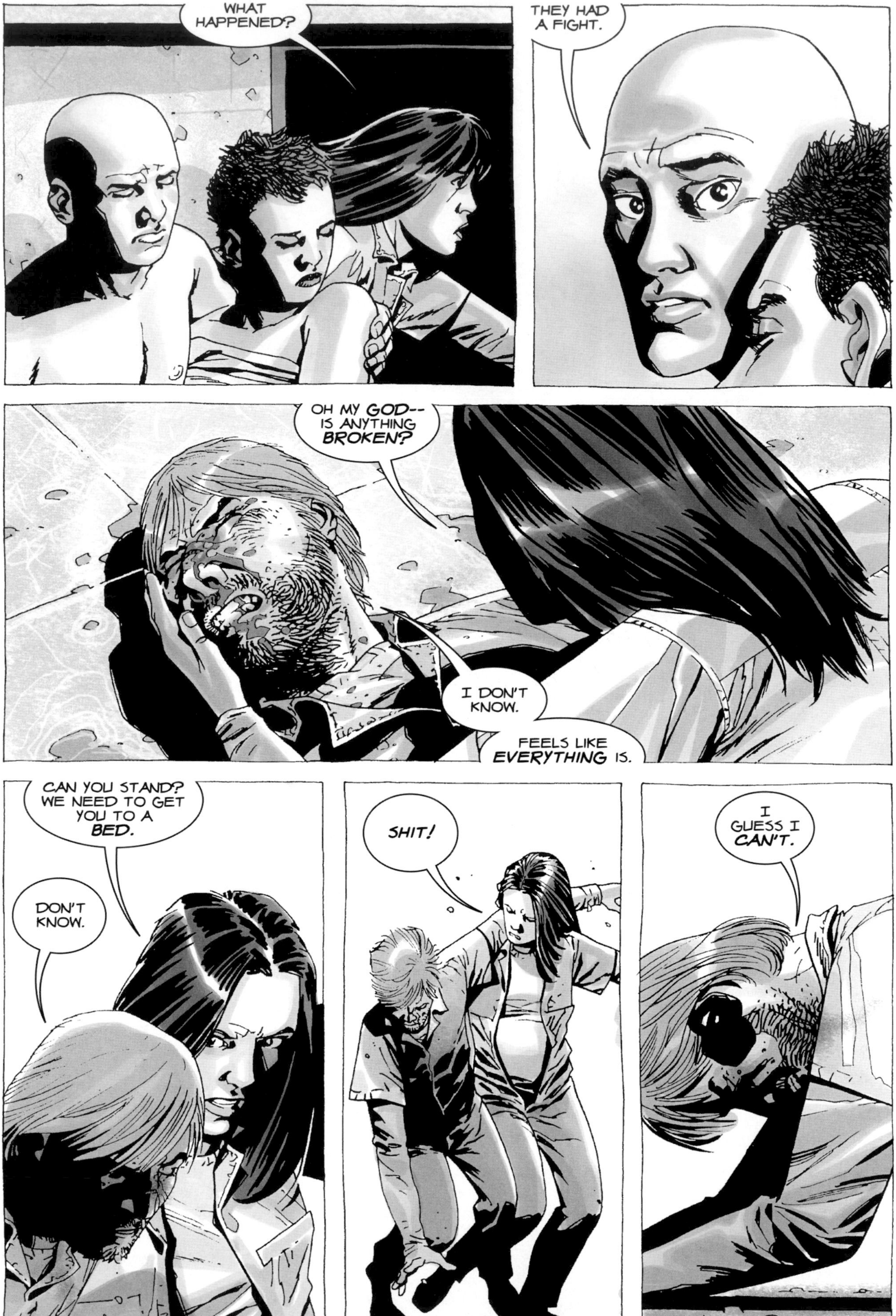
WHAT HAPPENED?
THEY HAD A FIGHT.
OH MY GOD-- IS ANYTHING BROKEN?
I DON'T KNOW.
FEELS LIKE EVERYTHING IS.
CAN YOU STAND? WE NEED TO GET YOU TO A BED.
DON'T KNOW.
SHIT!
I GUESS I CAN'T.

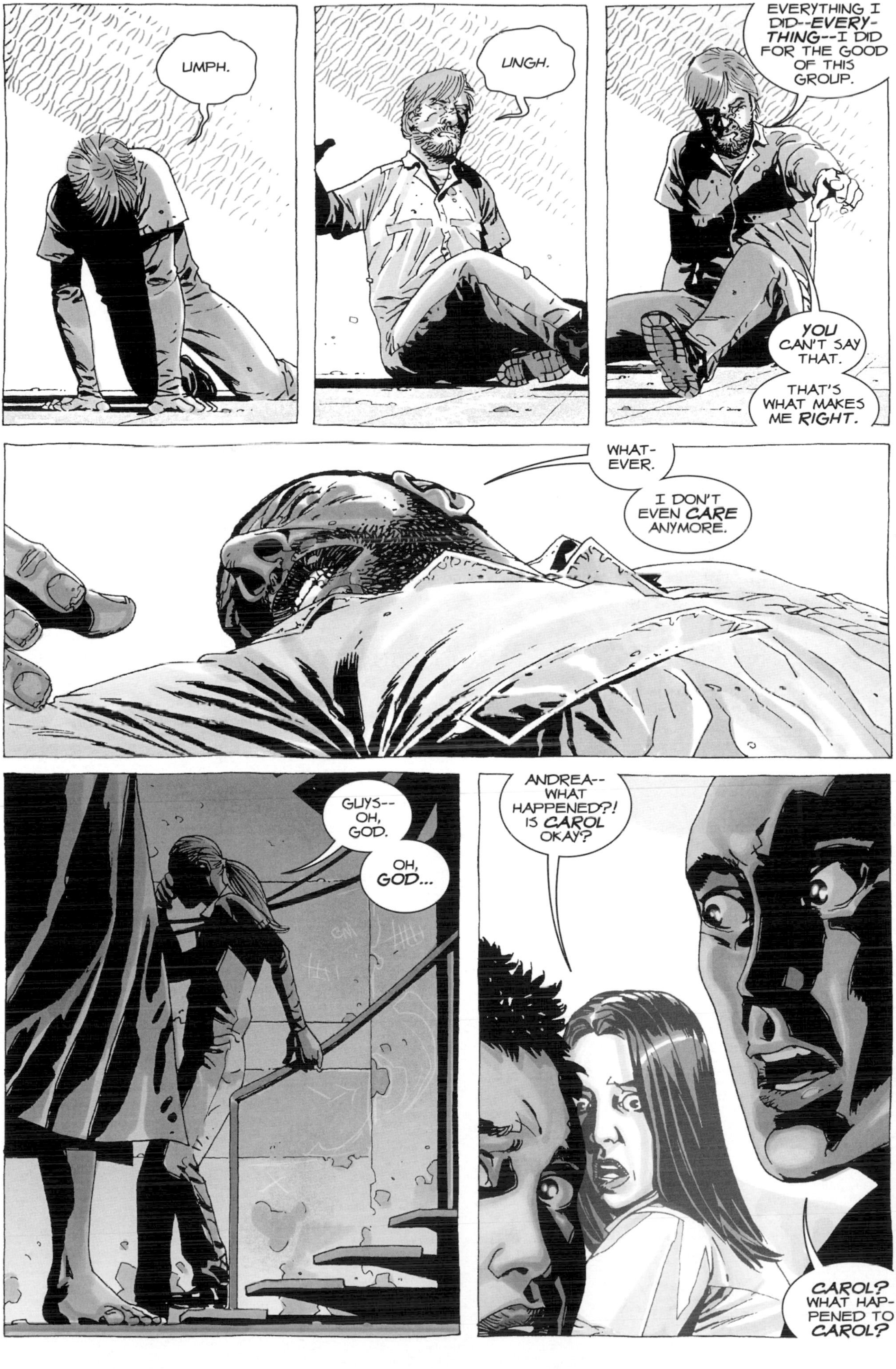
UMPH.
UNGH.
EVERYTHING I DID--EVERY-THING--I DID FOR THE GOOD OF THIS GROUP.
YOU CAN'T SAY THAT.
THAT'S WHAT MAKES ME RIGHT.
WHAT-EVER.
I DON'T EVEN CARE ANYMORE.
GUYS-- OH, GOD.
OH, GOD...
ANDREA-- WHAT HAPPENED?! IS CAROL OKAY?
CAROL? WHAT HAP-PENED TO CAROL?

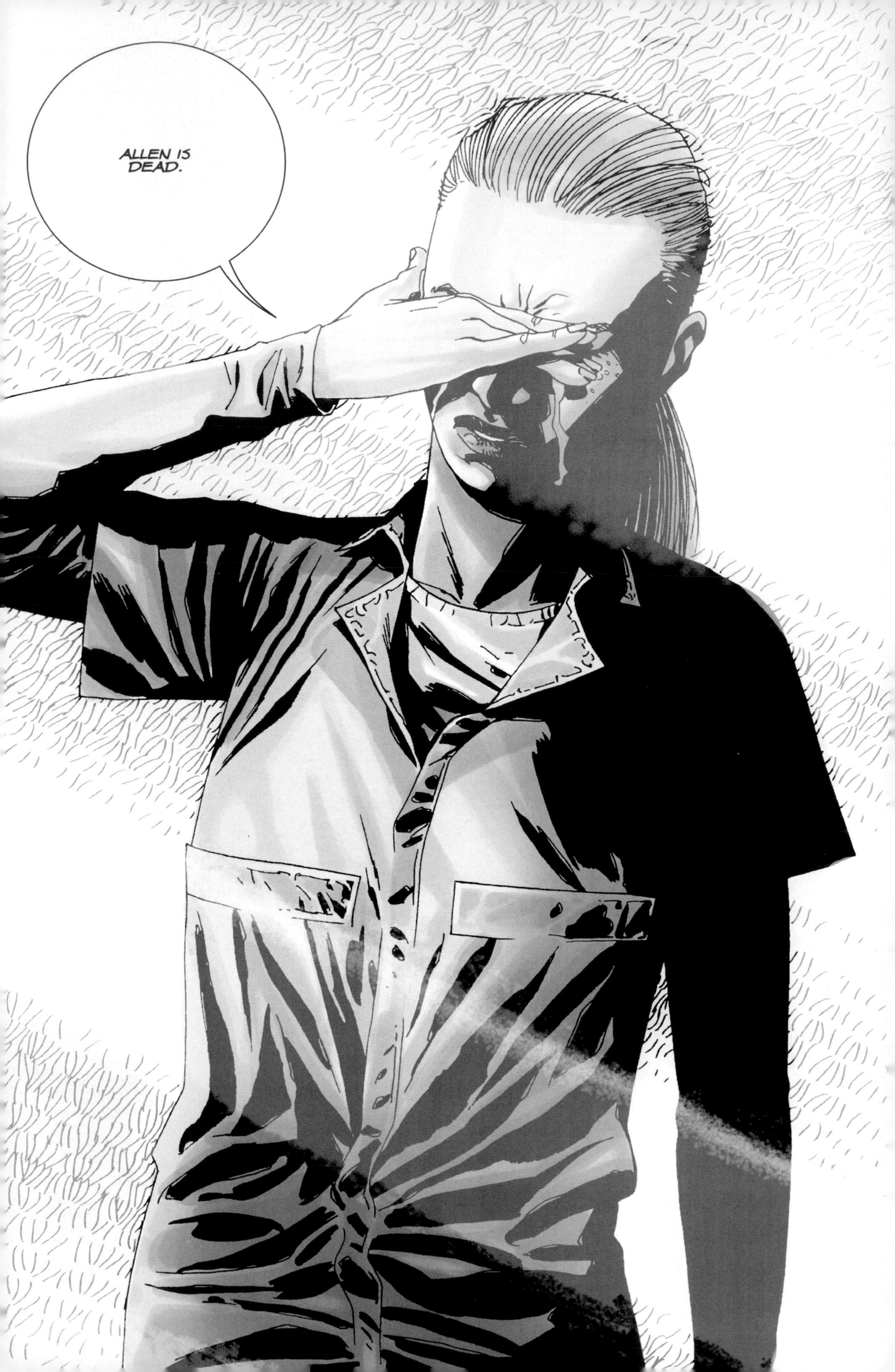
ALLEN IS DEAD.

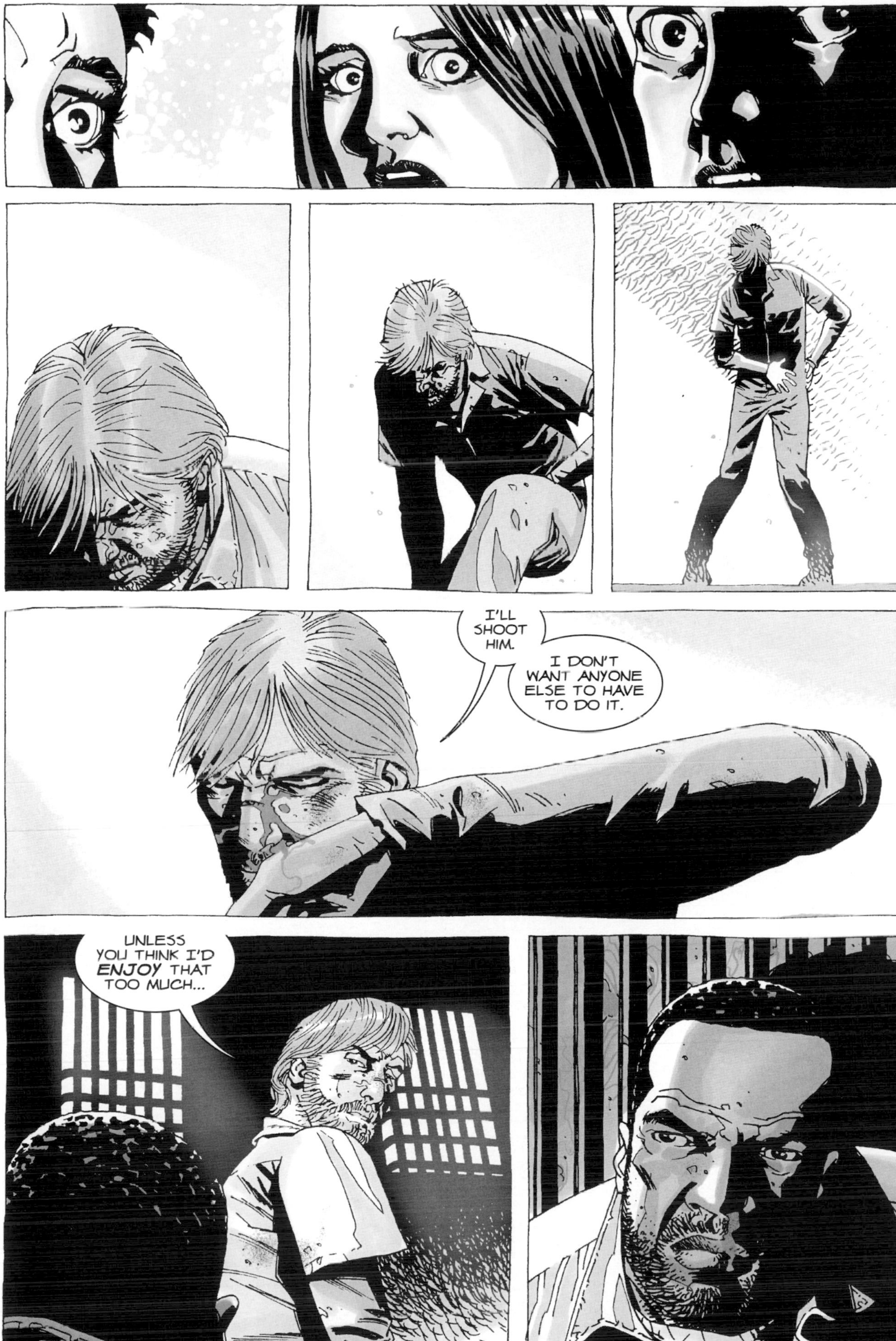
I'LL SHOOT HIM.
I DON'T WANT ANYONE ELSE TO HAVE TO DO IT.
UNLESS YOU THINK I'D *ENJOY* THAT TOO MUCH...

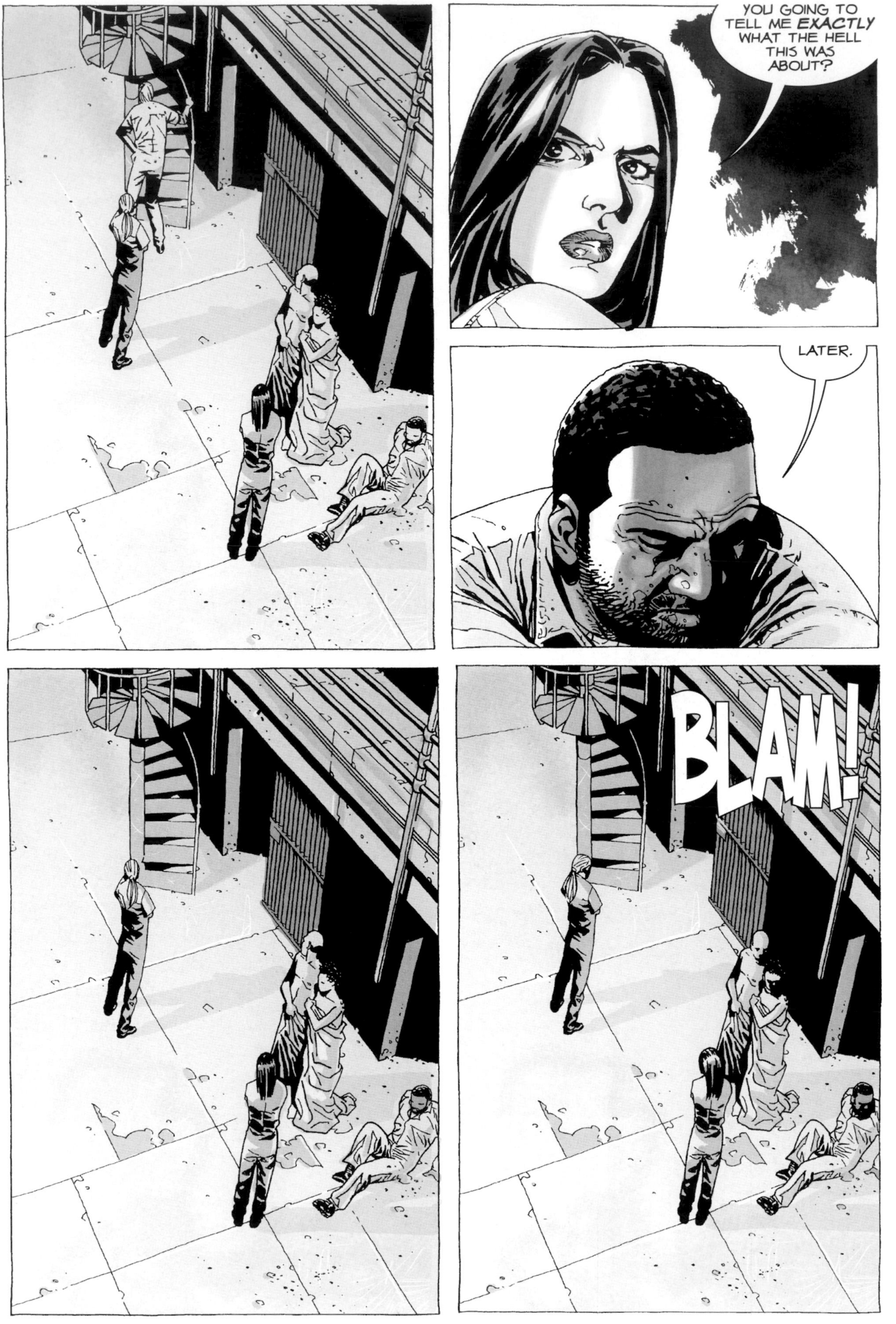
YOU GOING TO TELL ME EXACTLY WHAT THE HELL THIS WAS ABOUT?
LATER.
BLAM!

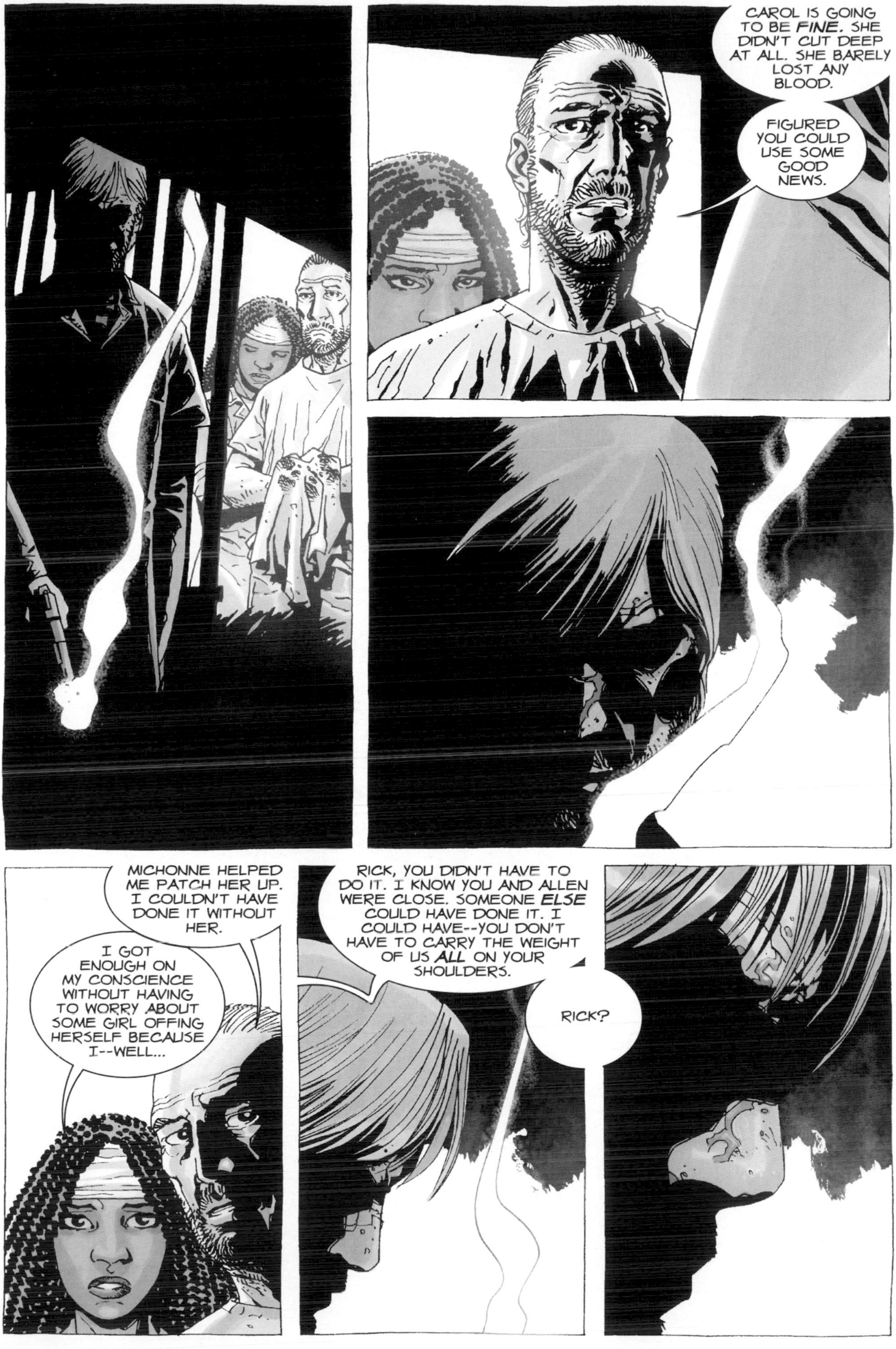
CAROL IS GOING TO BE FINE. SHE DIDN'T CUT DEEP AT ALL. SHE BARELY LOST ANY BLOOD.
FIGURED YOU COULD USE SOME GOOD NEWS.
MICHONNE HELPED ME PATCH HER UP. I COULDN'T HAVE DONE IT WITHOUT HER.
I GOT ENOUGH ON MY CONSCIENCE WITHOUT HAVING TO WORRY ABOUT SOME GIRL OFFING HERSELF BECAUSE I--WELL...
RICK, YOU DIDN'T HAVE TO DO IT. I KNOW YOU AND ALLEN WERE CLOSE. SOMEONE ELSE COULD HAVE DONE IT. I COULD HAVE--YOU DON'T HAVE TO CARRY THE WEIGHT OF US ALL ON YOUR SHOULDERS.
RICK?

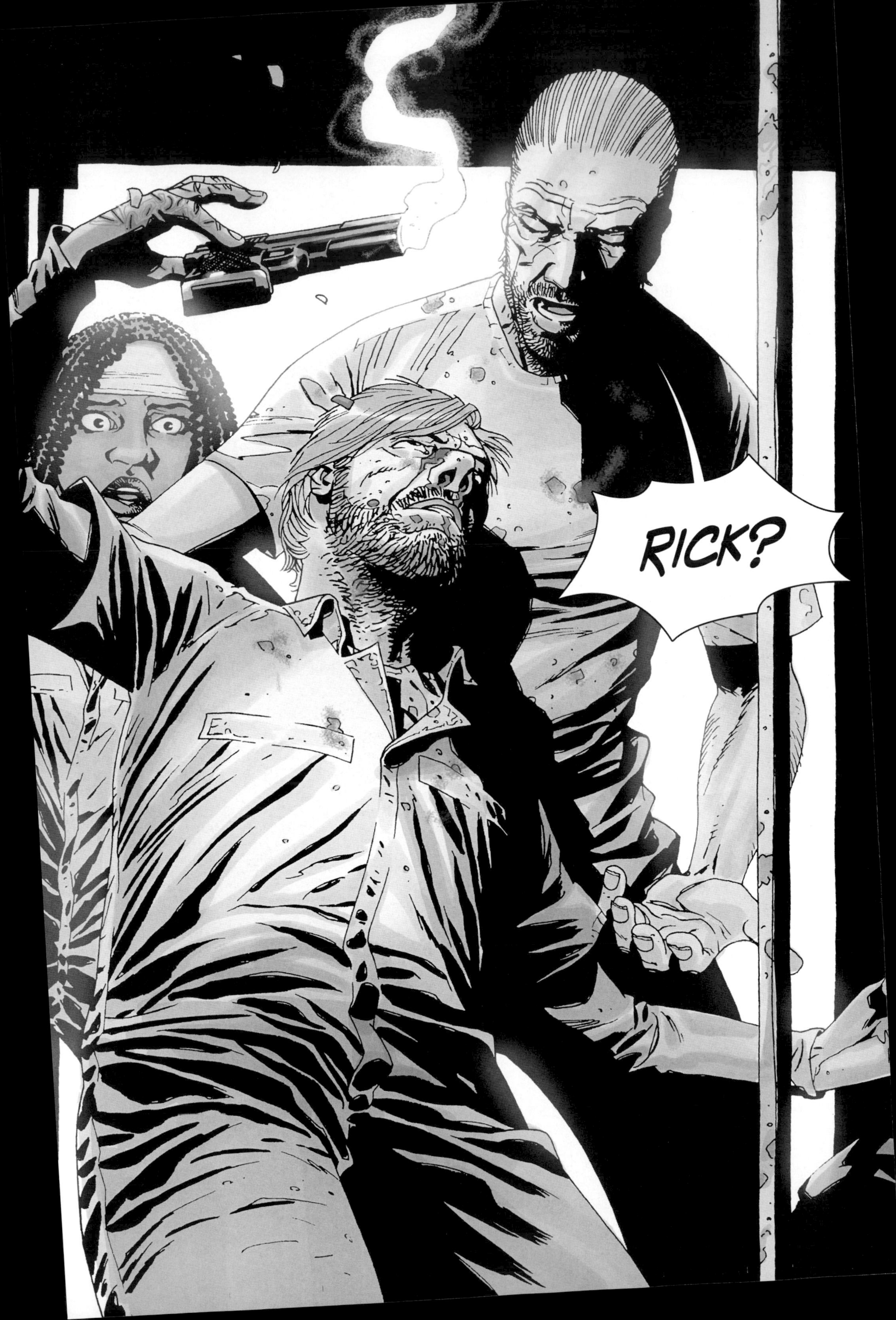
RICK?

RICK?

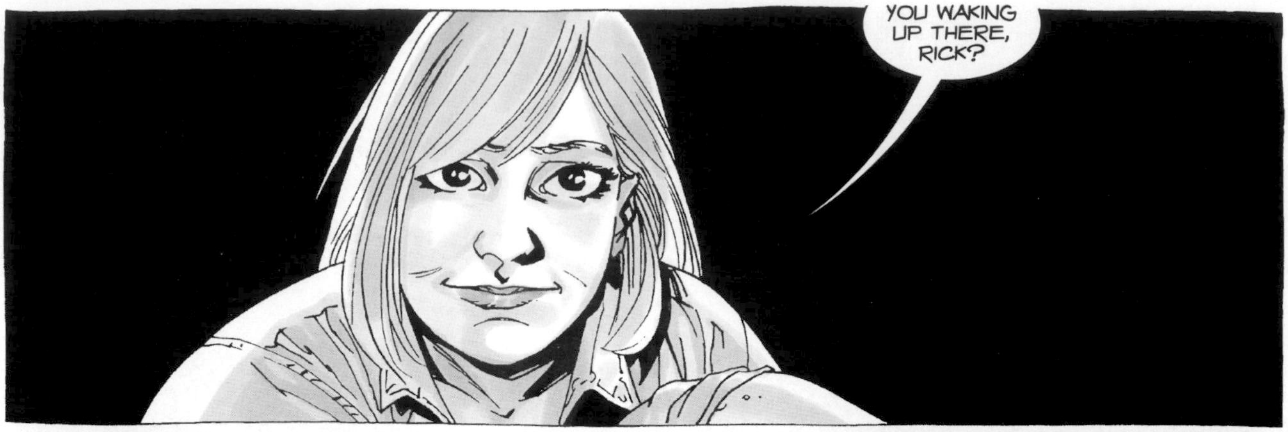
YOU WAKING UP THERE, RICK?

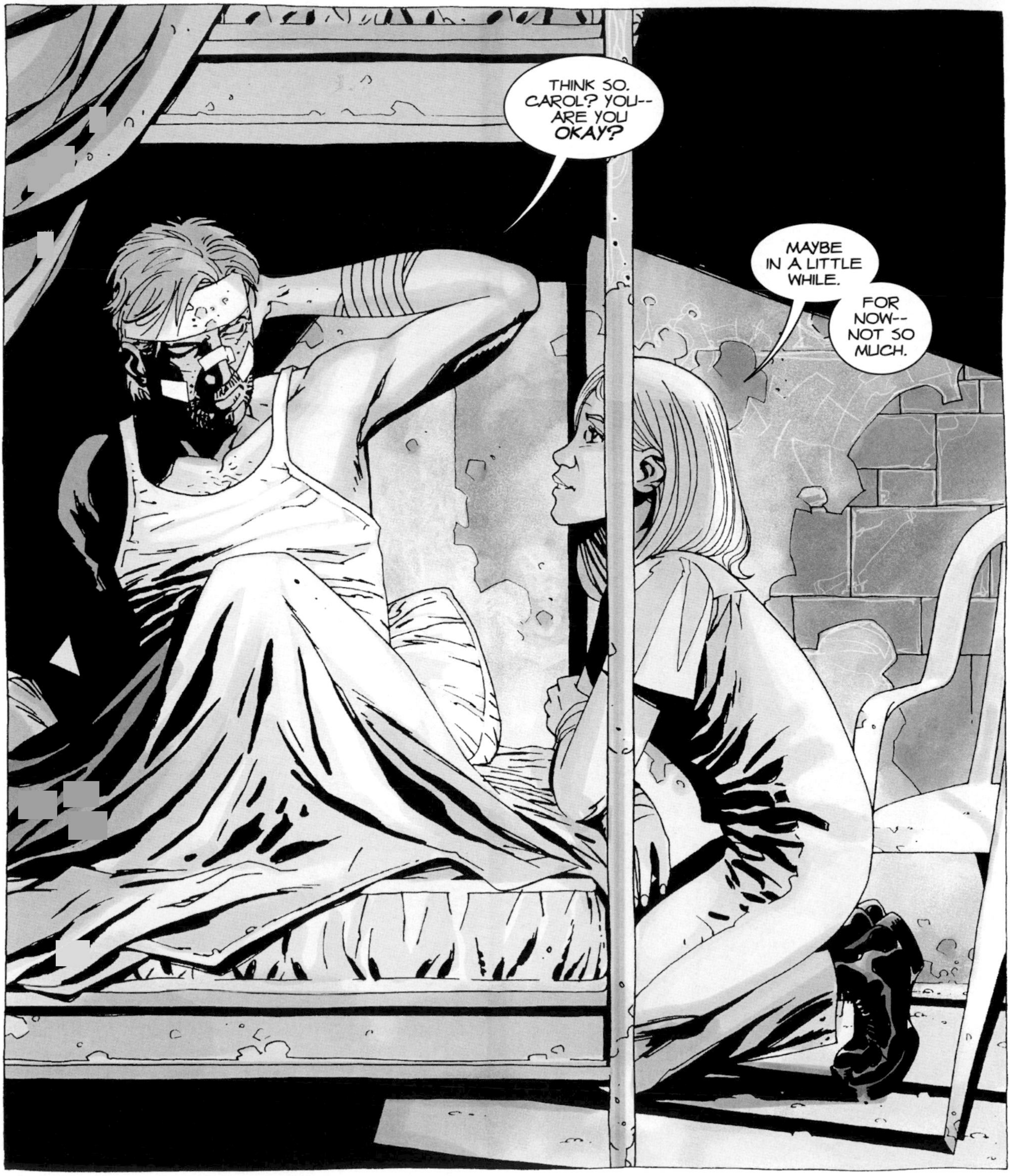
THINK SO. CAROL? YOU-- ARE YOU OKAY?
MAYBE IN A LITTLE WHILE.
FOR NOW-- NOT SO MUCH.

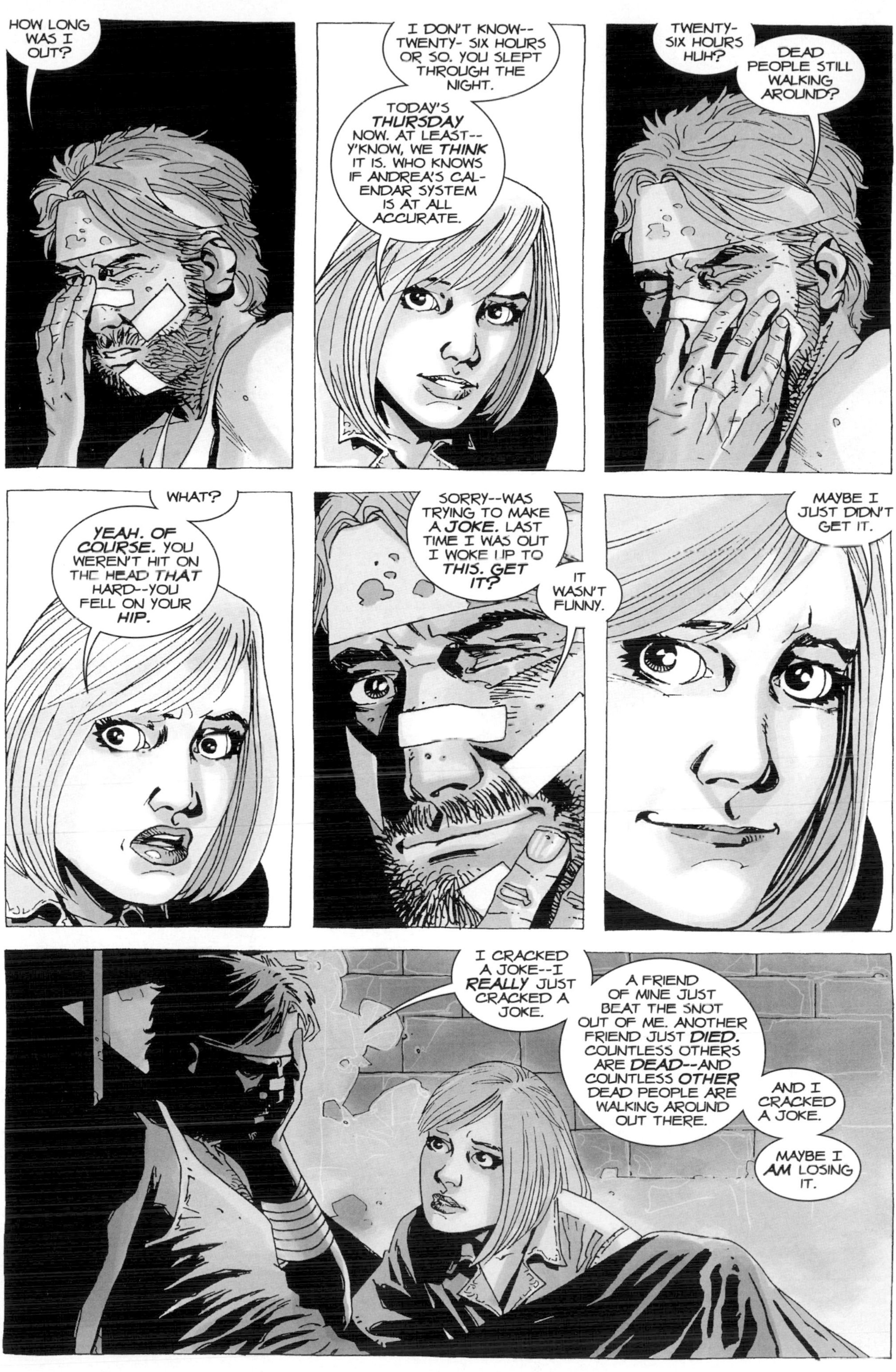
HOW LONG WAS I OUT?
I DON'T KNOW-- TWENTY- SIX HOURS OR SO. YOU SLEPT THROUGH THE NIGHT.
TODAY'S THURSDAY NOW. AT LEAST-- Y'KNOW, WE THINK IT IS. WHO KNOWS IF ANDREA'S CAL-ENDAR SYSTEM IS AT ALL ACCURATE.
TWENTY- SIX HOURS HUH?
DEAD PEOPLE STILL WALKING AROUND?
WHAT?
YEAH. OF COURSE. YOU WEREN'T HIT ON THE HEAD THAT HARD--YOU FELL ON YOUR HIP.
SORRY--WAS TRYING TO MAKE A JOKE. LAST TIME I WAS OUT I WOKE UP TO THIS. GET IT?
IT WASN'T FUNNY.
MAYBE I JUST DIDN'T GET IT.
I CRACKED A JOKE--I REALLY JUST CRACKED A JOKE.
A FRIEND OF MINE JUST BEAT THE SNOT OUT OF ME. ANOTHER FRIEND JUST DIED. COUNTLESS OTHERS ARE DEAD--AND COUNTLESS OTHER DEAD PEOPLE ARE WALKING AROUND OUT THERE.
AND I CRACKED A JOKE.
MAYBE I AM LOSING IT.

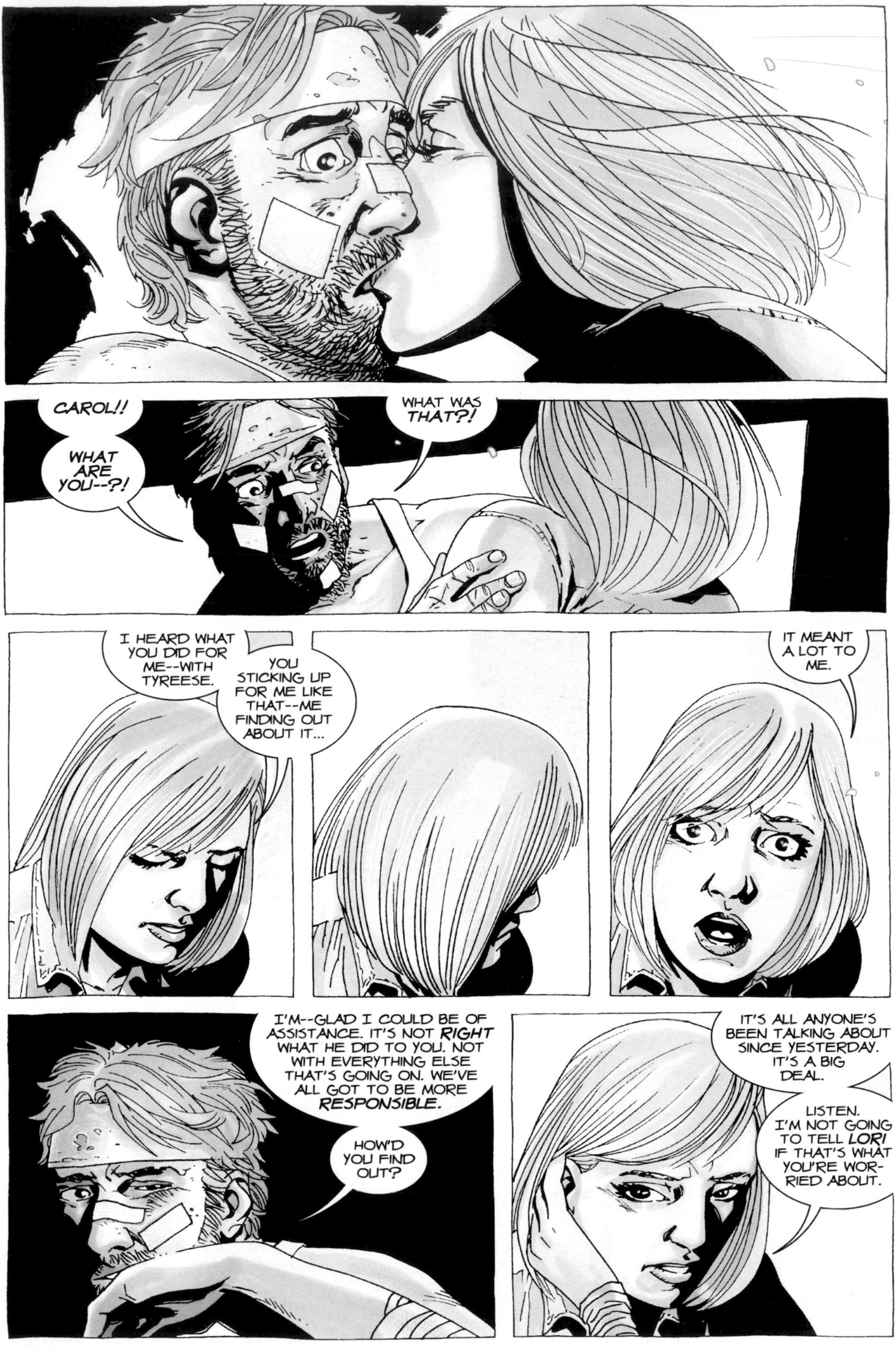
CAROL!!
WHAT ARE YOU--?!
WHAT WAS THAT?!
I HEARD WHAT YOU DID FOR ME--WITH TYREESE.
YOU STICKING UP FOR ME LIKE THAT--ME FINDING OUT ABOUT IT...
IT MEANT A LOT TO ME.
I'M--GLAD I COULD BE OF ASSISTANCE. IT'S NOT RIGHT WHAT HE DID TO YOU. NOT WITH EVERYTHING ELSE THAT'S GOING ON. WE'VE ALL GOT TO BE MORE RESPONSIBLE.
HOW'D YOU FIND OUT?
IT'S ALL ANYONE'S BEEN TALKING ABOUT SINCE YESTERDAY. IT'S A BIG DEAL.
LISTEN. I'M NOT GOING TO TELL LORI IF THAT'S WHAT YOU'RE WOR-RIED ABOUT.

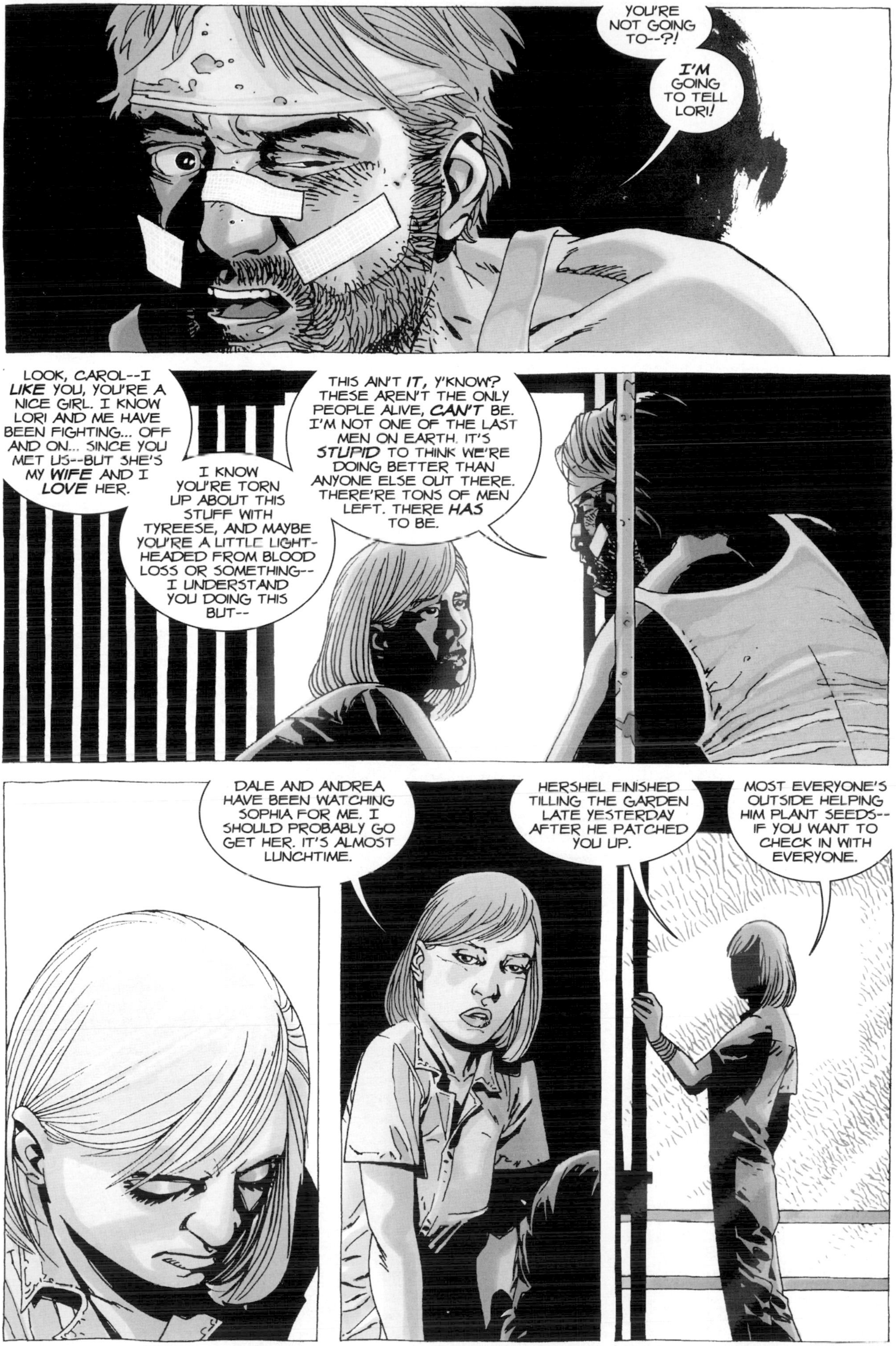
YOU'RE NOT GOING TO--?!
I'M GOING TO TELL LORI!
LOOK, CAROL--I LIKE YOU, YOU'RE A NICE GIRL. I KNOW LORI AND ME HAVE BEEN FIGHTING... OFF AND ON... SINCE YOU MET US--BUT SHE'S MY WIFE AND I LOVE HER.
I KNOW YOU'RE TORN UP ABOUT THIS STUFF WITH TYREESE, AND MAYBE YOU'RE A LITTLE LIGHT-HEADED FROM BLOOD LOSS OR SOMETHING--I UNDERSTAND YOU DOING THIS BUT--
THIS AIN'T IT, Y'KNOW? THESE AREN'T THE ONLY PEOPLE ALIVE, CAN'T BE. I'M NOT ONE OF THE LAST MEN ON EARTH. IT'S STUPID TO THINK WE'RE DOING BETTER THAN ANYONE ELSE OUT THERE. THERE'RE TONS OF MEN LEFT. THERE HAS TO BE.
DALE AND ANDREA HAVE BEEN WATCHING SOPHIA FOR ME. I SHOULD PROBABLY GO GET HER. IT'S ALMOST LUNCHTIME.
HERSHEL FINISHED TILLING THE GARDEN LATE YESTERDAY AFTER HE PATCHED YOU UP.
MOST EVERYONE'S OUTSIDE HELPING HIM PLANT SEEDS--IF YOU WANT TO CHECK IN WITH EVERYONE.

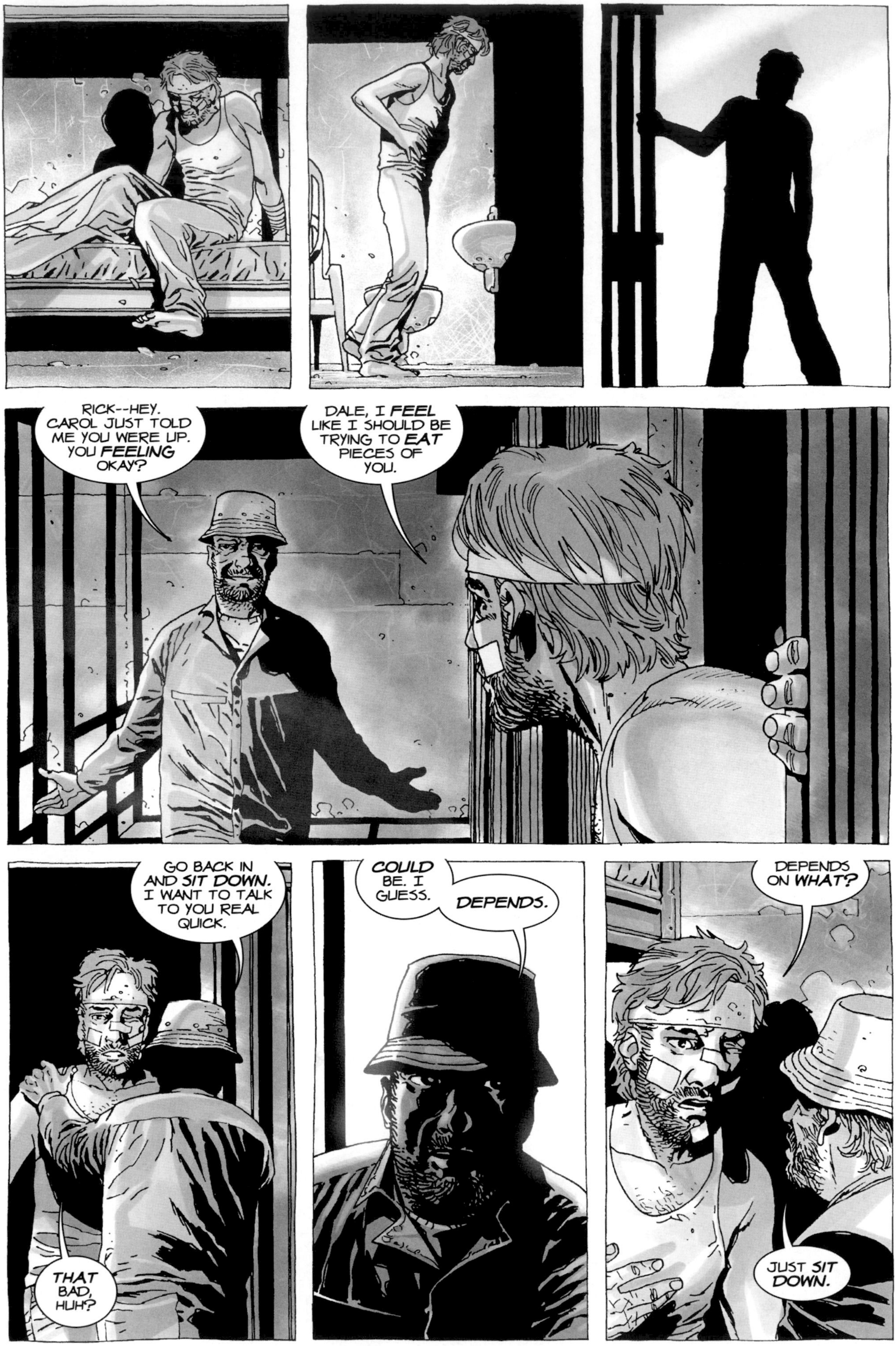

RICK--HEY. CAROL JUST TOLD ME YOU WERE UP. YOU FEELING OKAY?
DALE, I FEEL LIKE I SHOULD BE TRYING TO EAT PIECES OF YOU.
GO BACK IN AND SIT DOWN. I WANT TO TALK TO YOU REAL QUICK.
THAT BAD, HUH?
COULD BE. I GUESS.
DEPENDS.
DEPENDS ON WHAT?
JUST SIT DOWN.

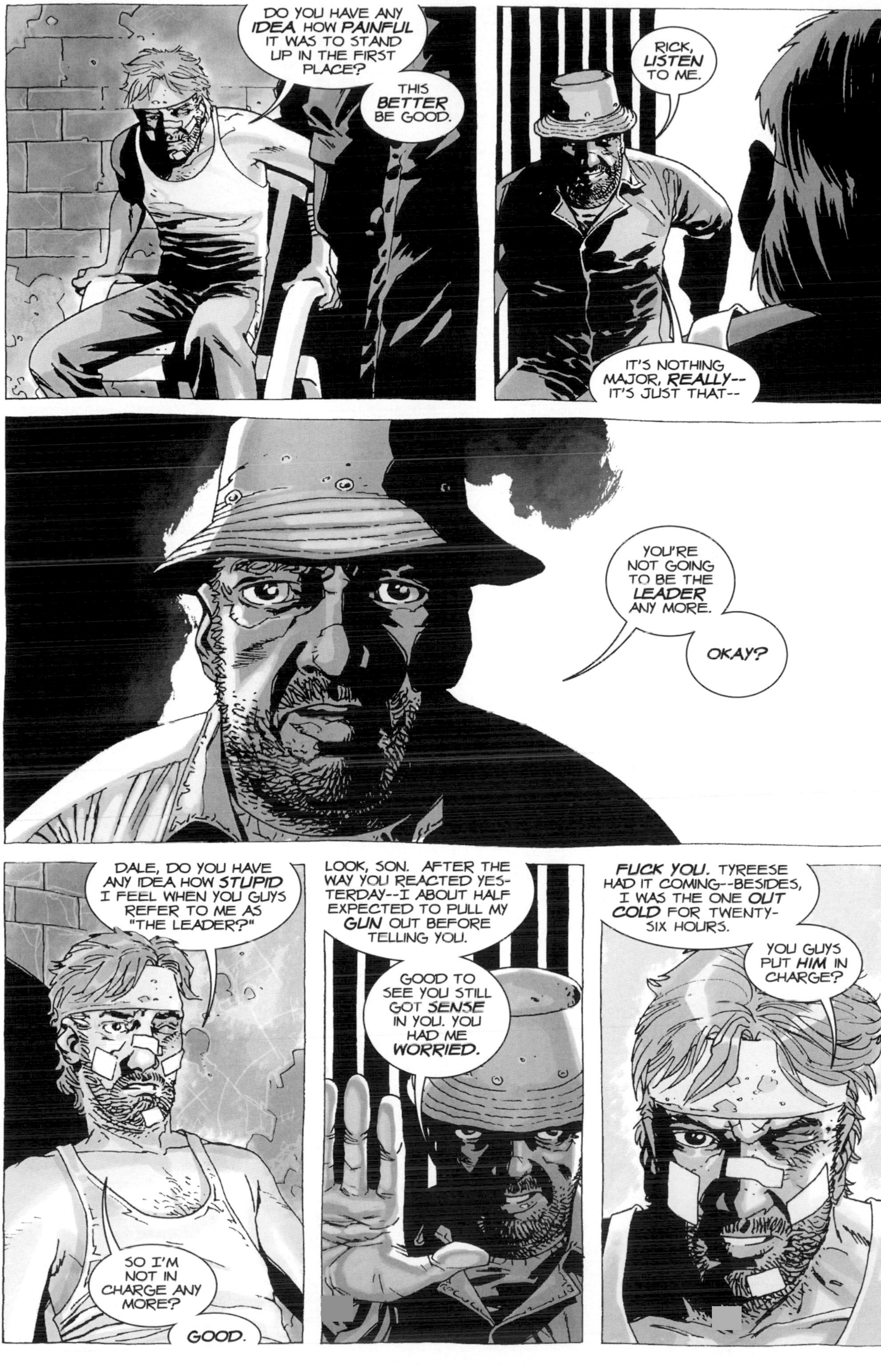
DO YOU HAVE ANY IDEA HOW PAINFUL IT WAS TO STAND UP IN THE FIRST PLACE?
THIS BETTER BE GOOD.
RICK, LISTEN TO ME.
IT'S NOTHING MAJOR, REALLY-- IT'S JUST THAT--
YOU'RE NOT GOING TO BE THE LEADER ANY MORE.
OKAY?
DALE, DO YOU HAVE ANY IDEA HOW STUPID I FEEL WHEN YOU GUYS REFER TO ME AS "THE LEADER?"
SO I'M NOT IN CHARGE ANY MORE?
GOOD.
LOOK, SON. AFTER THE WAY YOU REACTED YESTERDAY--I ABOUT HALF EXPECTED TO PULL MY GUN OUT BEFORE TELLING YOU.
GOOD TO SEE YOU STILL GOT SENSE IN YOU. YOU HAD ME WORRIED.
FUCK YOU. TYREESE HAD IT COMING--BESIDES, I WAS THE ONE OUT COLD FOR TWENTY-SIX HOURS.
YOU GUYS PUT HIM IN CHARGE?

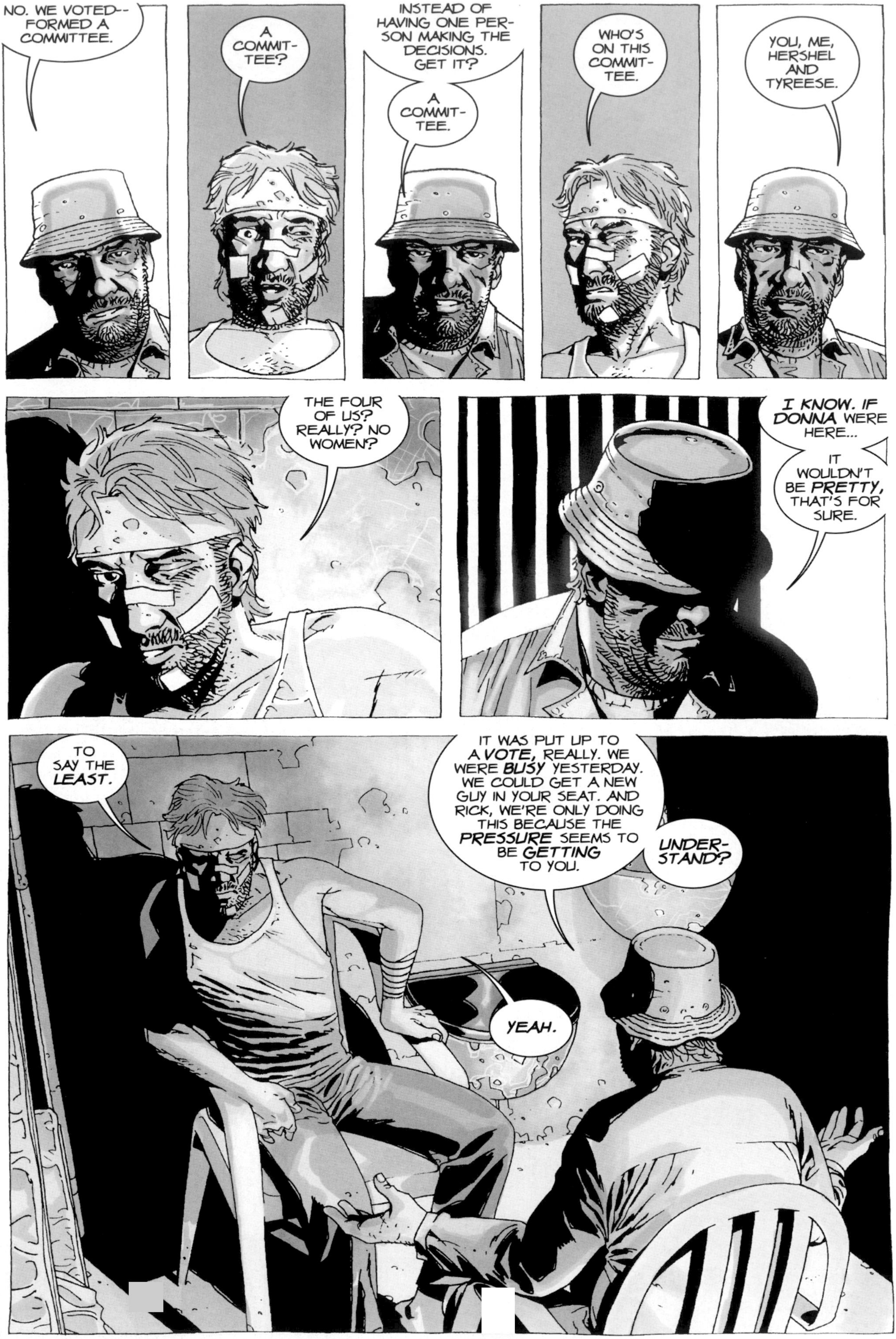
NO. WE VOTED-- FORMED A COMMITTEE.
A COMMIT-TEE?
INSTEAD OF HAVING ONE PERSON MAKING THE DECISIONS. GET IT?
A COMMIT-TEE.
WHO'S ON THIS COMMIT-TEE.
YOU, ME, HERSHEL AND TYREESE.
THE FOUR OF US? REALLY? NO WOMEN?
I KNOW. IF DONNA WERE HERE...
IT WOULDN'T BE PRETTY, THAT'S FOR SURE.
TO SAY THE LEAST.
IT WAS PUT UP TO A VOTE, REALLY. WE WERE BUSY YESTERDAY. WE COULD GET A NEW GUY IN YOUR SEAT. AND RICK, WE'RE ONLY DOING THIS BECAUSE THE PRESSURE SEEMS TO BE GETTING TO YOU.
UNDER-STAND?
YEAH.

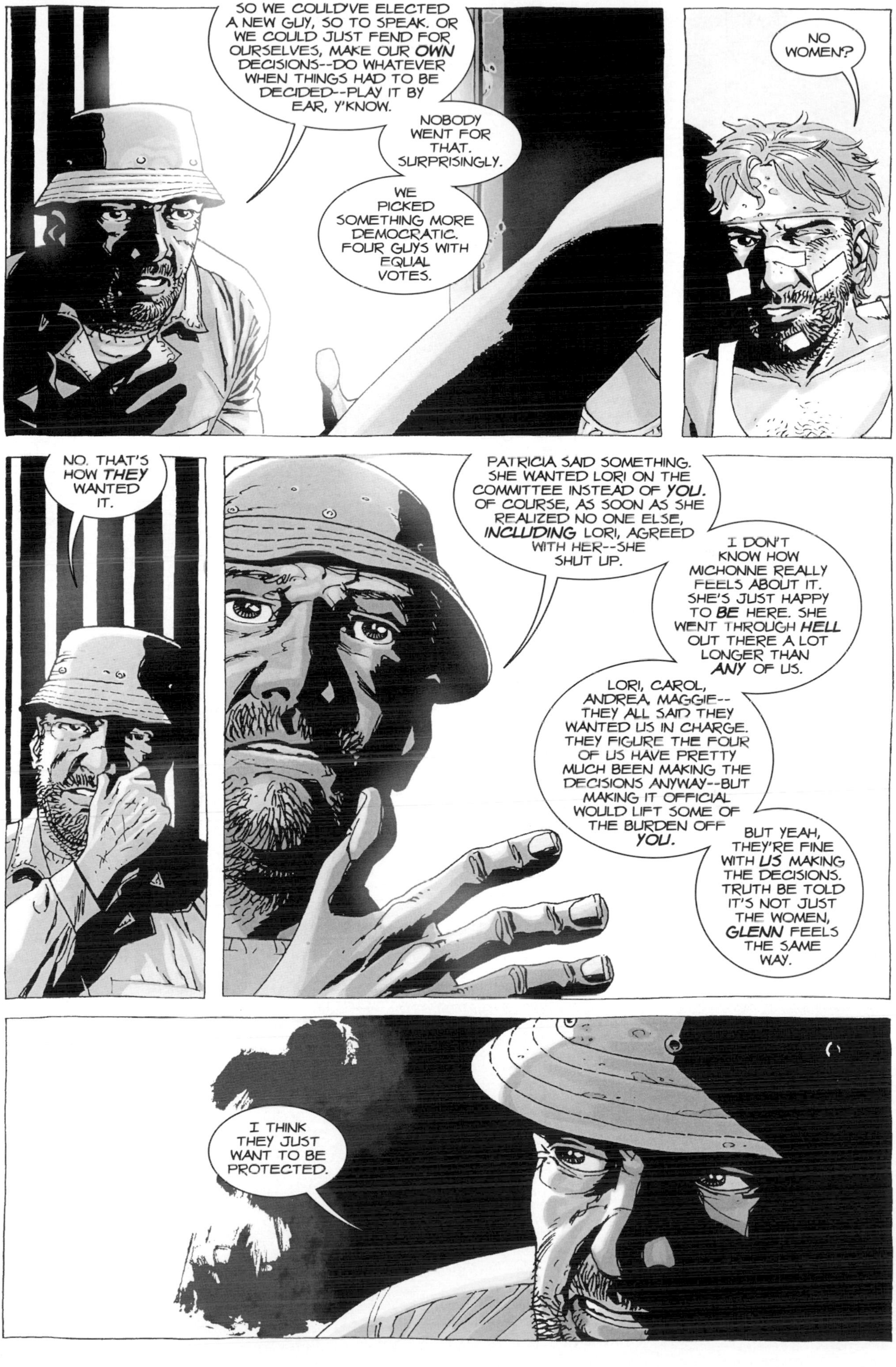
SO WE COULD'VE ELECTED A NEW GUY, SO TO SPEAK. OR WE COULD JUST FEND FOR OURSELVES, MAKE OUR OWN DECISIONS--DO WHATEVER WHEN THINGS HAD TO BE DECIDED--PLAY IT BY EAR, Y'KNOW.
NOBODY WENT FOR THAT. SURPRISINGLY.
WE PICKED SOMETHING MORE DEMOCRATIC. FOUR GUYS WITH EQUAL VOTES.
NO WOMEN?
NO. THAT'S HOW THEY WANTED IT.
PATRICIA SAID SOMETHING. SHE WANTED LORI ON THE COMMITTEE INSTEAD OF YOU. OF COURSE, AS SOON AS SHE REALIZED NO ONE ELSE, INCLUDING LORI, AGREED WITH HER--SHE SHUT UP.
I DON'T KNOW HOW MICHONNE REALLY FEELS ABOUT IT. SHE'S JUST HAPPY TO BE HERE. SHE WENT THROUGH HELL OUT THERE A LOT LONGER THAN ANY OF US.
LORI, CAROL, ANDREA, MAGGIE--THEY ALL SAID THEY WANTED US IN CHARGE. THEY FIGURE THE FOUR OF US HAVE PRETTY MUCH BEEN MAKING THE DECISIONS ANYWAY--BUT MAKING IT OFFICIAL WOULD LIFT SOME OF THE BURDEN OFF YOU.
BUT YEAH, THEY'RE FINE WITH US MAKING THE DECISIONS. TRUTH BE TOLD IT'S NOT JUST THE WOMEN, GLENN FEELS THE SAME WAY.
I THINK THEY JUST WANT TO BE PROTECTED.

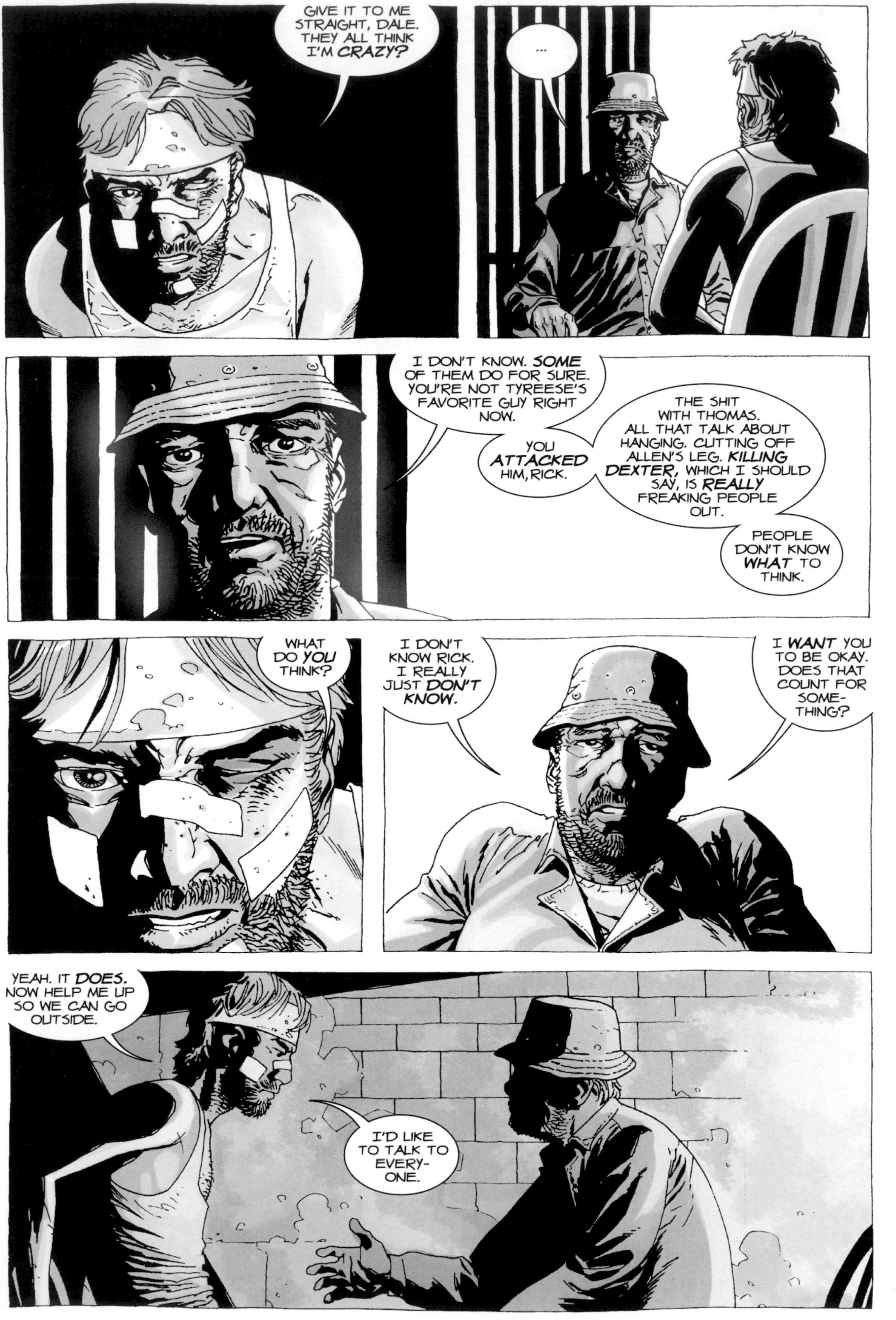
GIVE IT TO ME STRAIGHT, DALE. THEY ALL THINK I'M CRAZY?
...
I DON'T KNOW. SOME OF THEM DO FOR SURE. YOU'RE NOT TYREESE'S FAVORITE GUY RIGHT NOW.
YOU ATTACKED HIM, RICK.
THE SHIT WITH THOMAS. ALL THAT TALK ABOUT HANGING. CUTTING OFF ALLEN'S LEG. KILLING DEXTER, WHICH I SHOULD SAY, IS REALLY FREAKING PEOPLE OUT.
PEOPLE DON'T KNOW WHAT TO THINK.
WHAT DO YOU THINK?
I DON'T KNOW RICK. I REALLY JUST DON'T KNOW.
I WANT YOU TO BE OKAY. DOES THAT COUNT FOR SOME-THING?
YEAH. IT DOES. NOW HELP ME UP SO WE CAN GO OUTSIDE.
I'D LIKE TO TALK TO EVERY-ONE.

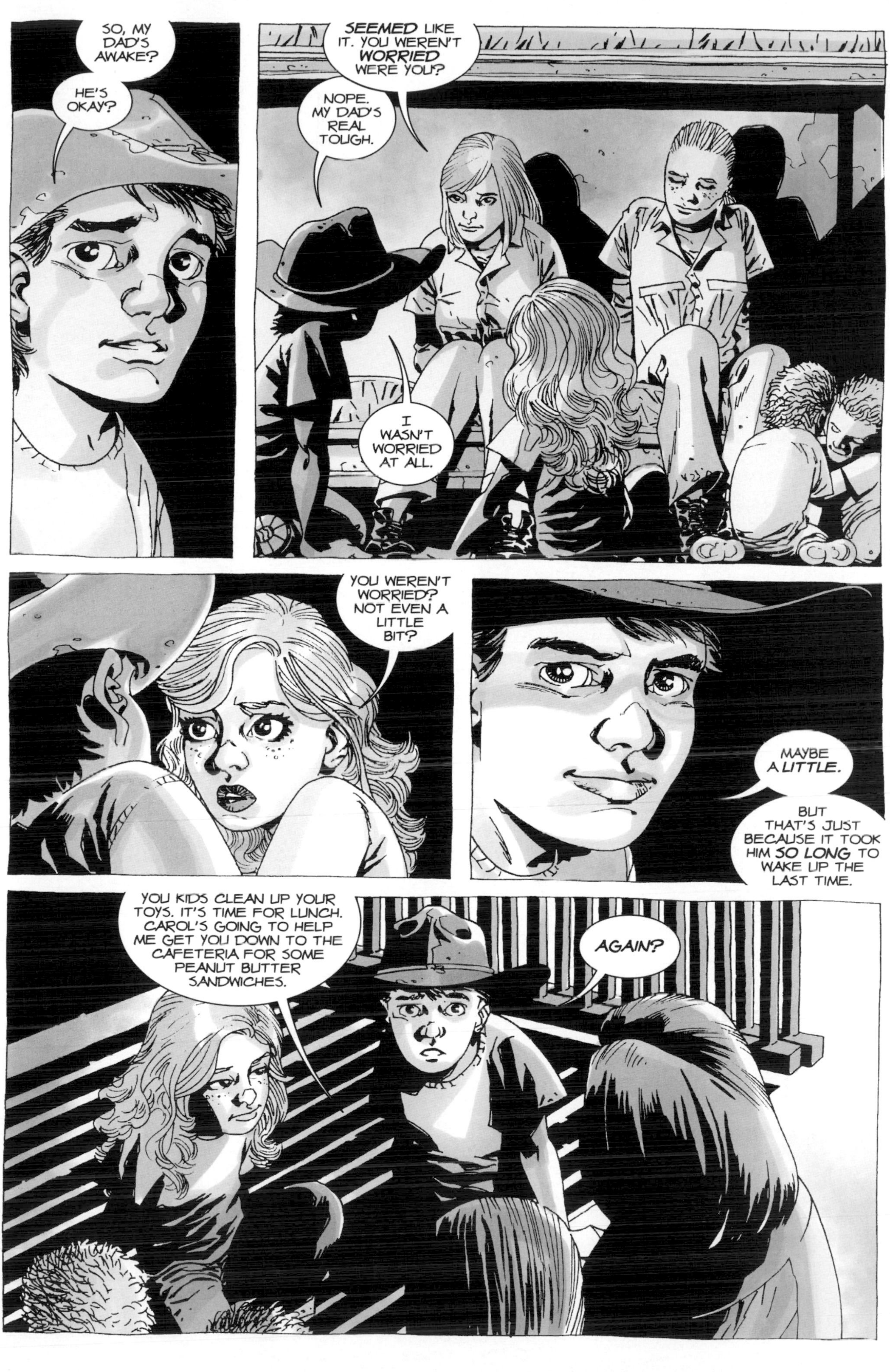
SO, MY DAD'S AWAKE?
HE'S OKAY?
SEEMED LIKE IT. YOU WEREN'T WORRIED WERE YOU?
NOPE. MY DAD'S REAL TOUGH.
I WASN'T WORRIED AT ALL.
YOU WEREN'T WORRIED? NOT EVEN A LITTLE BIT?
MAYBE A LITTLE.
BUT THAT'S JUST BECAUSE IT TOOK HIM SO LONG TO WAKE UP THE LAST TIME.
YOU KIDS CLEAN UP YOUR TOYS. IT'S TIME FOR LUNCH. CAROL'S GOING TO HELP ME GET YOU DOWN TO THE CAFETERIA FOR SOME PEANUT BUTTER SANDWICHES.
AGAIN?

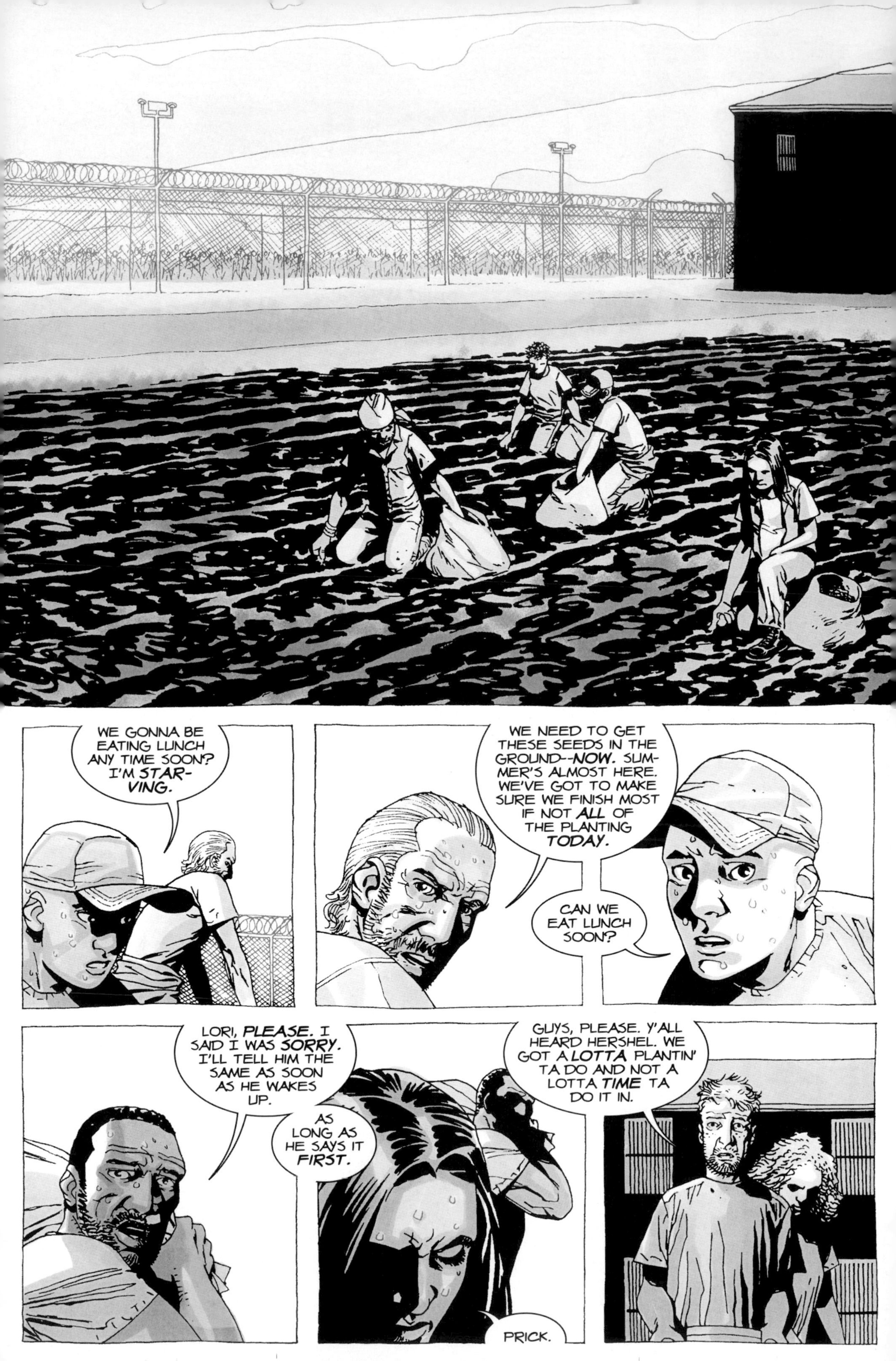
WE GONNA BE EATING LUNCH ANY TIME SOON? I'M STAR-VING.
WE NEED TO GET THESE SEEDS IN THE GROUND--NOW. SUMMER'S ALMOST HERE. WE'VE GOT TO MAKE SURE WE FINISH MOST IF NOT ALL OF THE PLANTING TODAY.
CAN WE EAT LUNCH SOON?
LORI, PLEASE. I SAID I WAS SORRY. I'LL TELL HIM THE SAME AS SOON AS HE WAKES UP.
AS LONG AS HE SAYS IT FIRST.
PRICK.
GUYS, PLEASE. Y'ALL HEARD HERSHEL. WE GOT A LOTTA PLANTIN' TA DO AND NOT A LOTTA TIME TA DO IT IN.

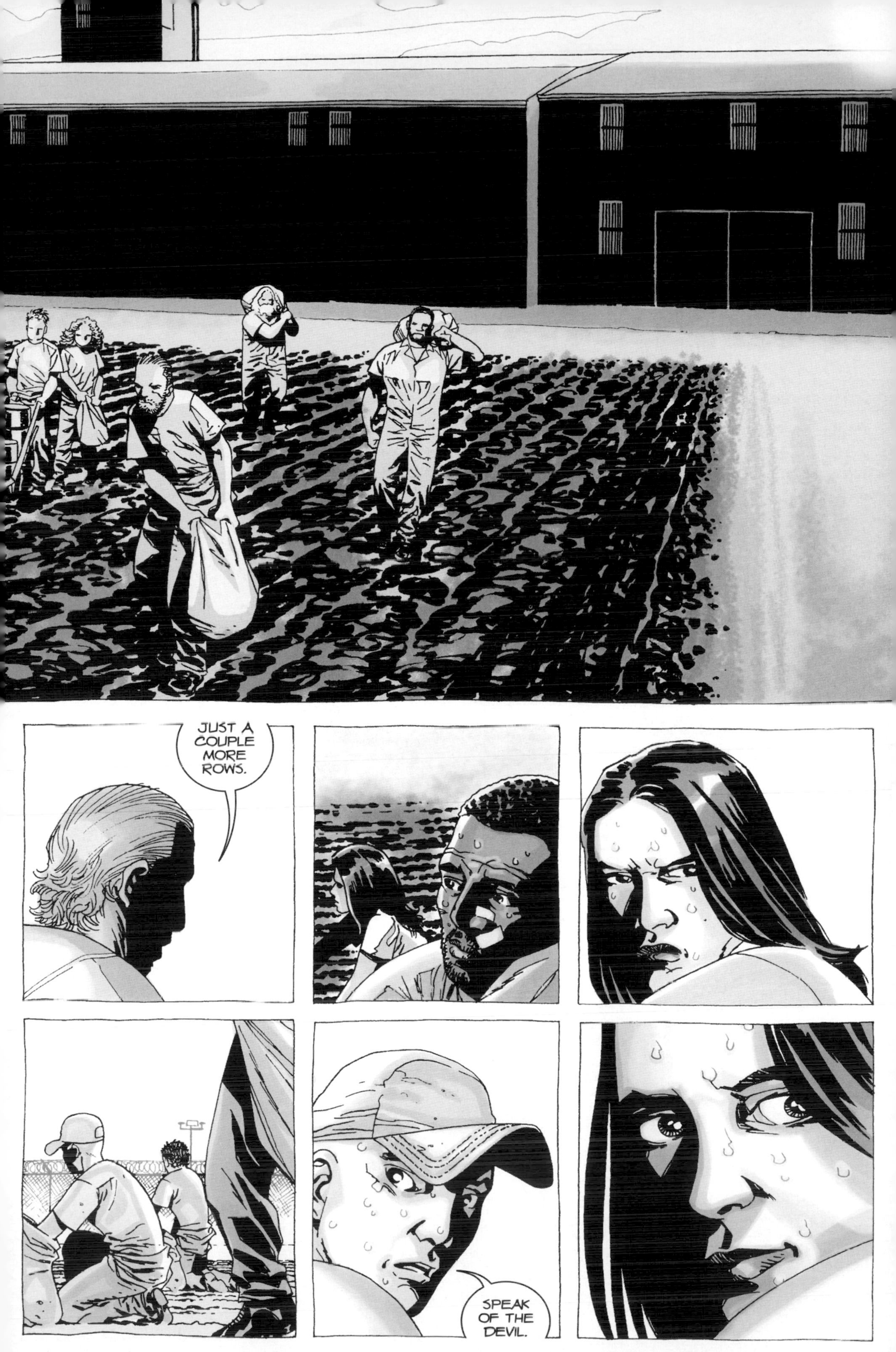
JUST A COUPLE MORE ROWS.
SPEAK OF THE DEVIL.

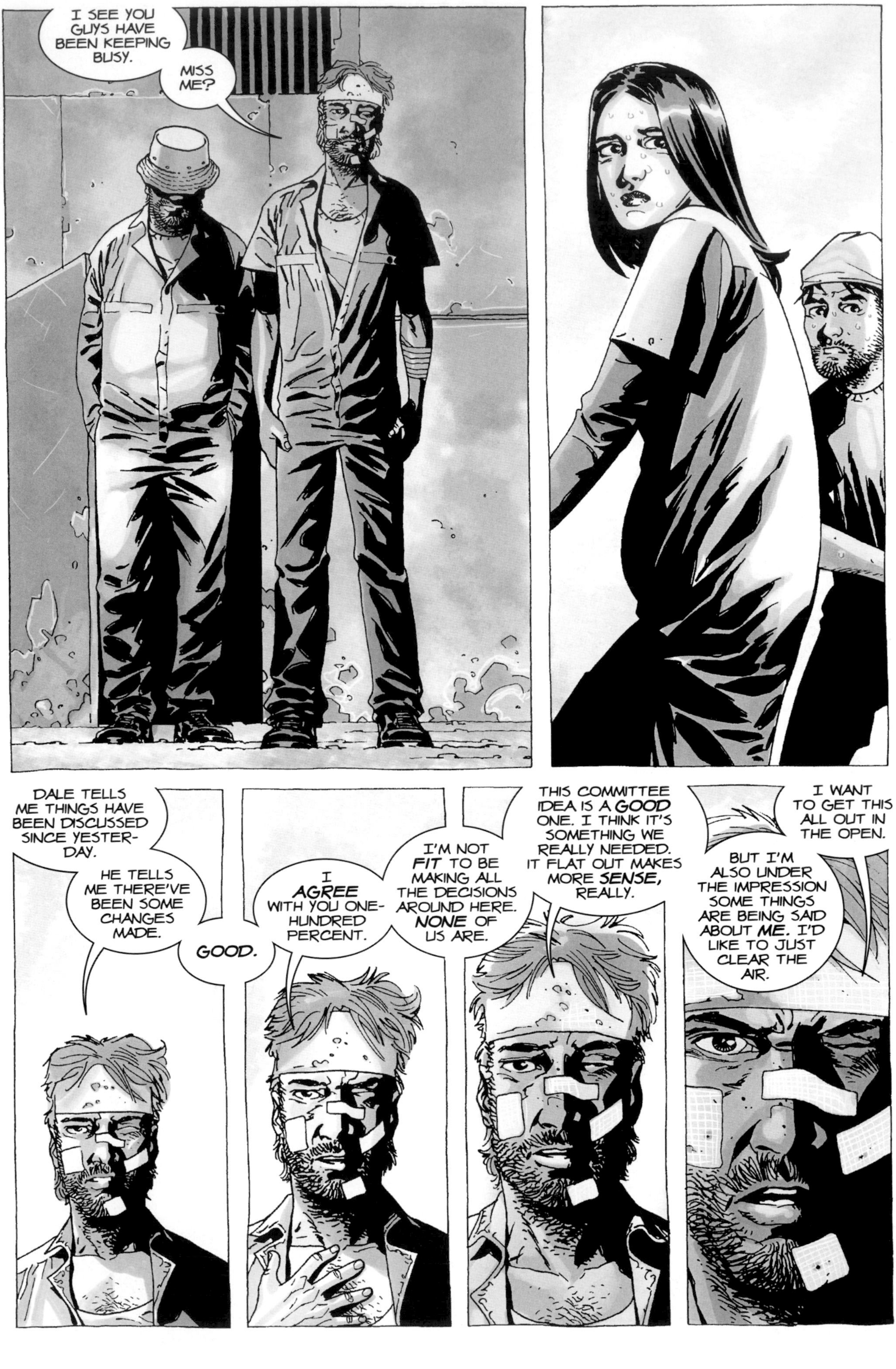

I SEE YOU GUYS HAVE BEEN KEEPING BUSY.
MISS ME?
DALE TELLS ME THINGS HAVE BEEN DISCUSSED SINCE YESTER-DAY.
HE TELLS ME THERE'VE BEEN SOME CHANGES MADE.
GOOD.
I **AGREE** WITH YOU ONE-HUNDRED PERCENT.
I'M NOT **FIT** TO BE MAKING ALL THE DECISIONS AROUND HERE. **NONE** OF US ARE.
THIS COMMITTEE IDEA IS A **GOOD** ONE. I THINK IT'S SOMETHING WE REALLY NEEDED. IT FLAT OUT MAKES MORE **SENSE,** REALLY.
I WANT TO GET THIS ALL OUT IN THE OPEN.
BUT I'M ALSO UNDER THE IMPRESSION SOME THINGS ARE BEING SAID ABOUT **ME.** I'D LIKE TO JUST CLEAR THE AIR.

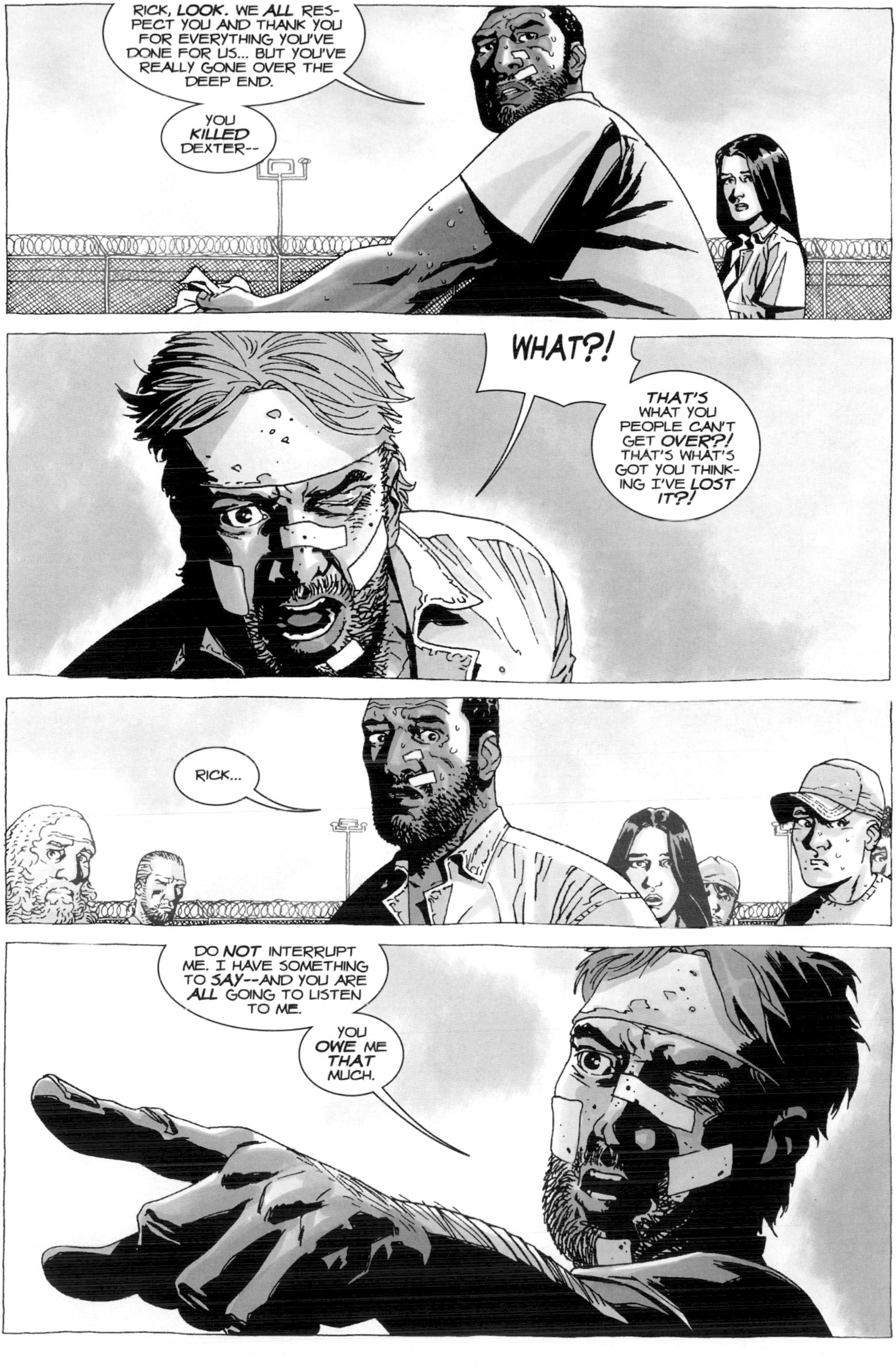
RICK, LOOK. WE ALL RESPECT YOU AND THANK YOU FOR EVERYTHING YOU'VE DONE FOR US... BUT YOU'VE REALLY GONE OVER THE DEEP END.
YOU KILLED DEXTER--
WHAT?!
THAT'S WHAT YOU PEOPLE CAN'T GET OVER?! THAT'S WHAT'S GOT YOU THINKING I'VE LOST IT?!
RICK...
DO NOT INTERRUPT ME. I HAVE SOMETHING TO SAY--AND YOU ARE ALL GOING TO LISTEN TO ME.
YOU OWE ME THAT MUCH.

I AM A *COP*--I KNOW THAT *TECHNICALLY* WHAT I DID WAS *WRONG*. I KNOW THE *LAWS*--I KNOW HOW THINGS *USED* TO BE.

THINGS HAVE *CHANGED!*

WE CAN'T JUST IGNORE THE *RULES*, RICK. WE'VE GOT TO RETAIN OUR *HUMANITY!*

THAT'S WHAT I'M *SAYING!*

I KILLED DEXTER TO PROTECT US *ALL*. HE WAS THREATENING TO KICK US OUT OF THIS PLACE, OUR *SANCTUARY*. HE WAS GOING TO FORCE US OUT INTO THE *WILD*. HOW HUMANE WOULD THINGS HAVE BEEN *OUT THERE?!* HOW MANY PEOPLE DID WE *LOSE* ON THE WAY *HERE?*

I SAW AN OPENING AND I *TOOK* IT. THERE WAS A LOT OF CONFUSION DURING THE ATTACK. I'LL *ADMIT*, I SHOULD HAVE COME CLEAN RIGHT AWAY-- AND EXPLAINED MYSELF RIGHT *THEN* AND THERE-- BUT I THOUGHT YOU PEOPLE MIGHT *PREFER* NOT TO KNOW JUST *HOW* SAVAGE WE'RE GOING TO HAVE TO *BE* FOR JUST A LITTLE WHILE LONGER.

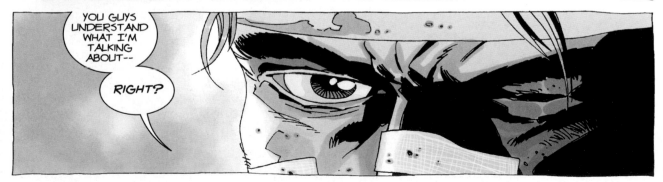

YOU GUYS UNDERSTAND WHAT I'M TALKING ABOUT--

RIGHT?

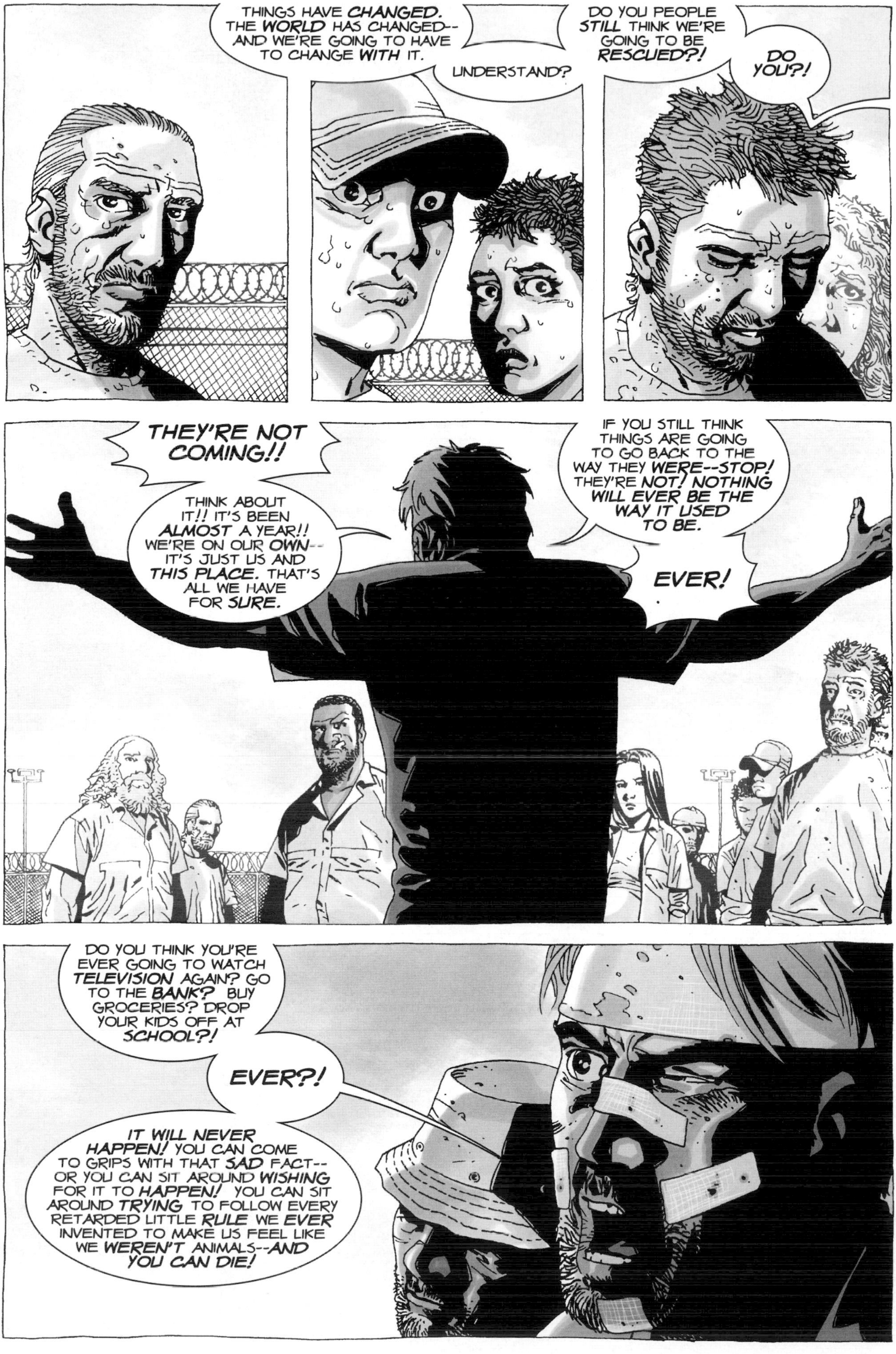
THINGS HAVE CHANGED. THE WORLD HAS CHANGED-- AND WE'RE GOING TO HAVE TO CHANGE WITH IT.
UNDERSTAND?
DO YOU PEOPLE STILL THINK WE'RE GOING TO BE RESCUED?!
DO YOU?!
THEY'RE NOT COMING!!
THINK ABOUT IT!! IT'S BEEN ALMOST A YEAR!! WE'RE ON OUR OWN-- IT'S JUST US AND THIS PLACE. THAT'S ALL WE HAVE FOR SURE.
IF YOU STILL THINK THINGS ARE GOING TO GO BACK TO THE WAY THEY WERE--STOP! THEY'RE NOT! NOTHING WILL EVER BE THE WAY IT USED TO BE.
EVER!
DO YOU THINK YOU'RE EVER GOING TO WATCH TELEVISION AGAIN? GO TO THE BANK? BUY GROCERIES? DROP YOUR KIDS OFF AT SCHOOL?!
EVER?!
IT WILL NEVER HAPPEN! YOU CAN COME TO GRIPS WITH THAT SAD FACT-- OR YOU CAN SIT AROUND WISHING FOR IT TO HAPPEN! YOU CAN SIT AROUND TRYING TO FOLLOW EVERY RETARDED LITTLE RULE WE EVER INVENTED TO MAKE US FEEL LIKE WE WEREN'T ANIMALS--AND YOU CAN DIE!

WE WILL *CHANGE!* WE WILL *EVOLVE.* WE'LL MAKE *NEW* RULES--WE'LL STILL BE *HUMANE* AND *KIND* AND WE'LL STILL *CARE* FOR EACH OTHER.

BUT WHEN THE TIME COMES-- WE *HAVE* TO BE PREPARED TO DO *WHATEVER* IT TAKES TO *KEEP* US *SAFE.*

WHAT-EVER IT TAKES!

"*YOU* KILL--YOU *DIE.*"

THAT WAS PROBABLY THE MOST NAIVE THING I'VE *EVER* SAID.

THE FACT IS--IN MOST CASES, *NOW,* THE WAY THINGS ARE--YOU KILL-- YOU *LIVE.*

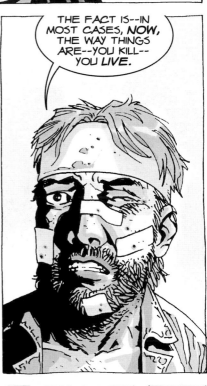

WE HAVE TO *ADAPT* TO THIS WORLD IF WE ARE GOING TO *SURVIVE.* HAVE I GONE A LITTLE *CRAZY? MAYBE*-- BUT SO HAS THE WORLD.

YOU DON'T WANT ME TO BE THE LEADER? FINE. I DON'T CARE. I'M *HAPPY* TO BE WITHOUT THE PRESSURE. I WILL TELL YOU THIS RIGHT NOW, THOUGH.

I WILL DO *WHATEVER* I HAVE TO DO TO KEEP US SAFE. *WHATEVER* IT IS--I WILL DO IT.

BUT YOU *HAVE* TO STOP THE *CHARADE*-- YOU'VE *GOT* TO STOP FOOLING YOURSELVES.

IF YOU WANT TO STOP BUTTING HEADS WITH ME--IF YOU WANT TO GET ON THE SAME PAGE WITH ME--*UNDER-STAND THAT.*

THIS IS IT. *THIS* IS OUR LIFE. WE'RE NOT *WAITING* HERE. WE'RE NOT BIDING OUR TIME--WAITING FOR WHAT COMES *NEXT.* OR WAITING TO BE *RES-CUED!*

THIS IS WHAT WE *HAVE!* THIS IS ALL WE'LL *EVER* HAVE.

IF YOU WANT TO MAKE THINGS BETTER, MAKE *THIS* PLACE BETTER. WE HAVE TO COME TO GRIPS WITH THAT.

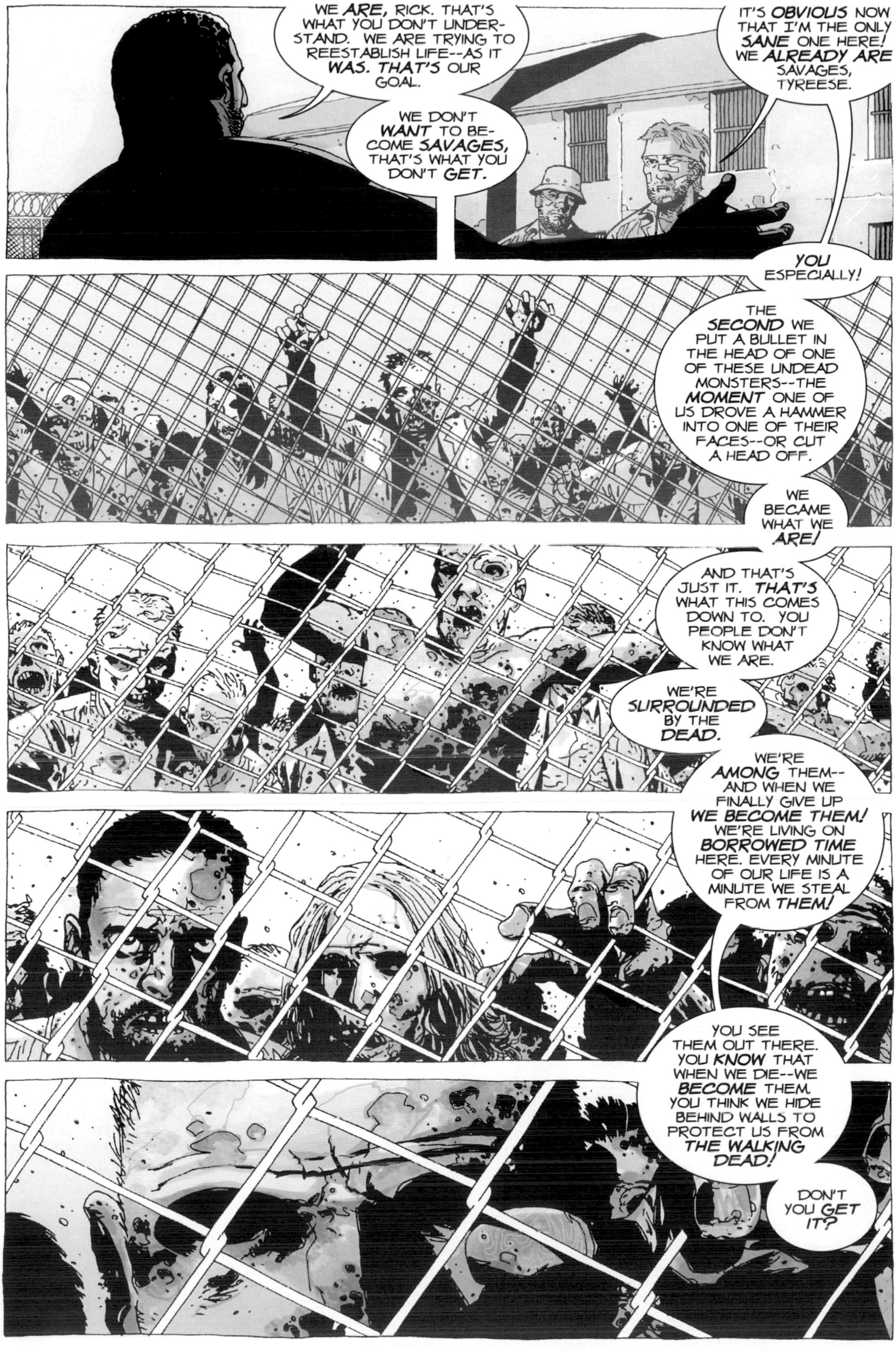

WE ARE, RICK. THAT'S WHAT YOU DON'T UNDER-STAND. WE ARE TRYING TO REESTABLISH LIFE--AS IT WAS. THAT'S OUR GOAL.
WE DON'T WANT TO BE-COME SAVAGES, THAT'S WHAT YOU DON'T GET.
IT'S OBVIOUS NOW THAT I'M THE ONLY SANE ONE HERE! WE ALREADY ARE SAVAGES, TYREESE.
YOU ESPECIALLY!
THE SECOND WE PUT A BULLET IN THE HEAD OF ONE OF THESE UNDEAD MONSTERS--THE MOMENT ONE OF US DROVE A HAMMER INTO ONE OF THEIR FACES--OR CUT A HEAD OFF.
WE BECAME WHAT WE ARE!
AND THAT'S JUST IT. THAT'S WHAT THIS COMES DOWN TO. YOU PEOPLE DON'T KNOW WHAT WE ARE.
WE'RE SURROUNDED BY THE DEAD.
WE'RE AMONG THEM-- AND WHEN WE FINALLY GIVE UP WE BECOME THEM! WE'RE LIVING ON BORROWED TIME HERE. EVERY MINUTE OF OUR LIFE IS A MINUTE WE STEAL FROM THEM!
YOU SEE THEM OUT THERE. YOU KNOW THAT WHEN WE DIE--WE BECOME THEM. YOU THINK WE HIDE BEHIND WALLS TO PROTECT US FROM THE WALKING DEAD!
DON'T YOU GET IT?

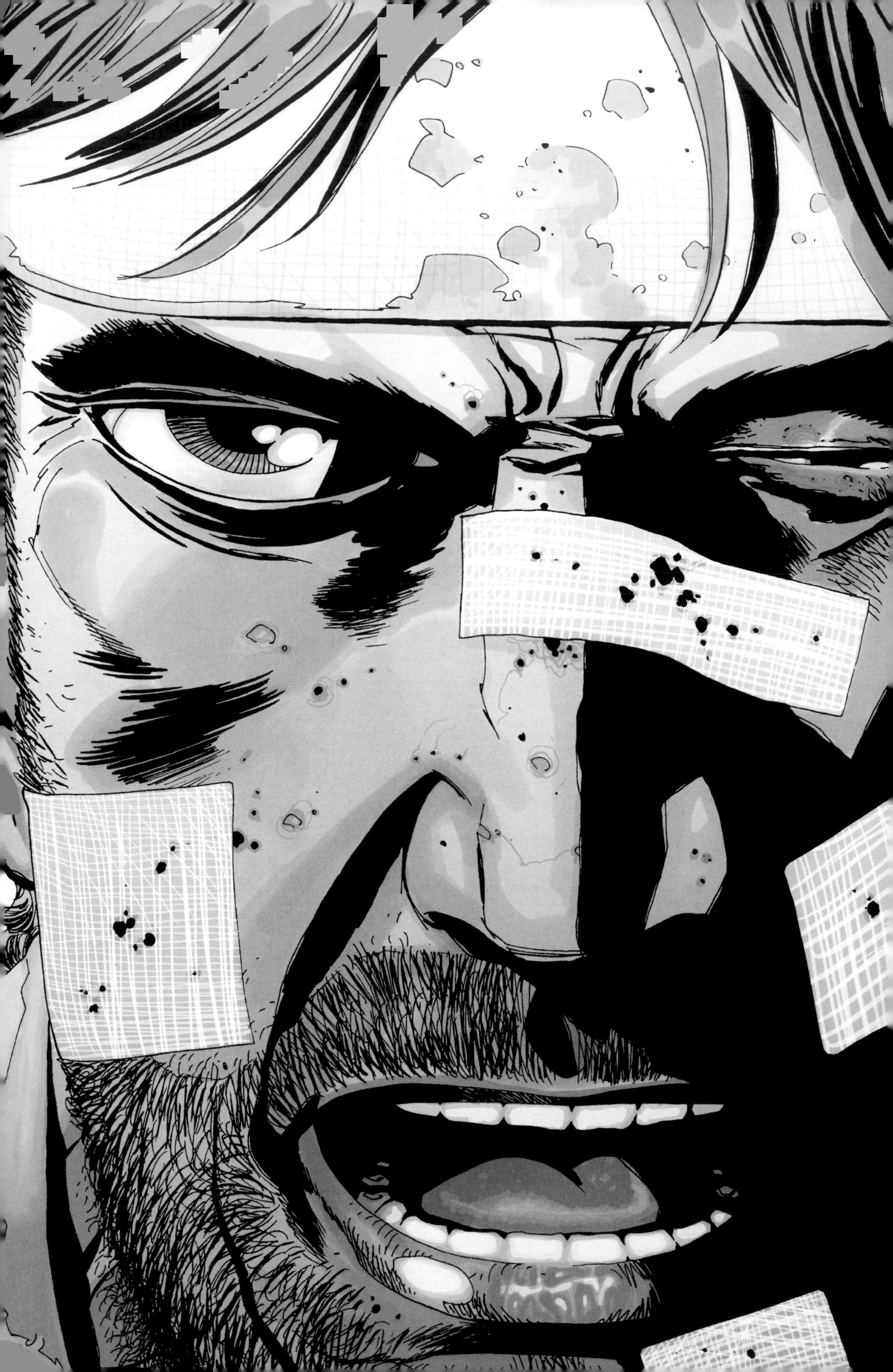

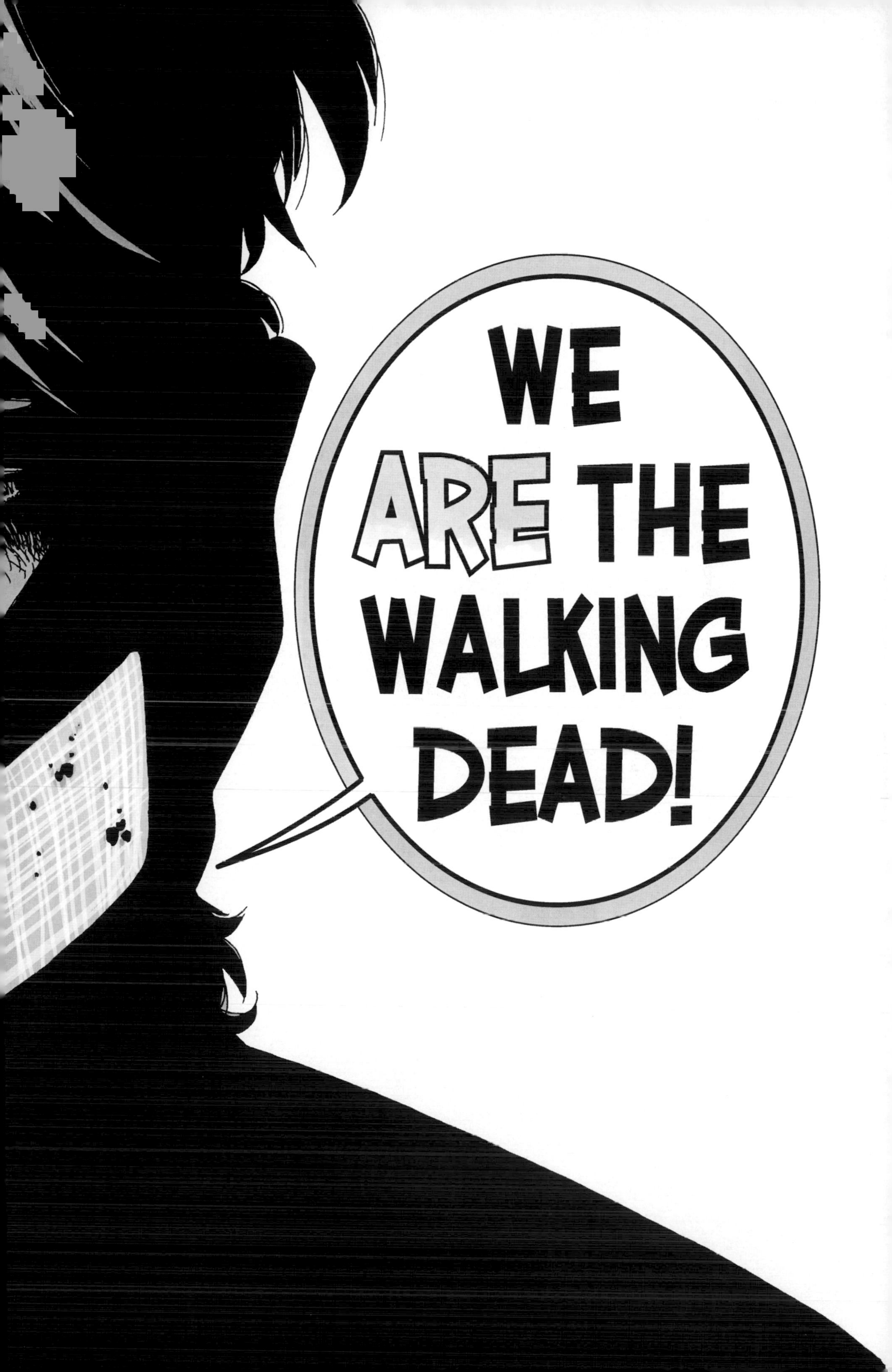
WE ARE THE WALKING DEAD!

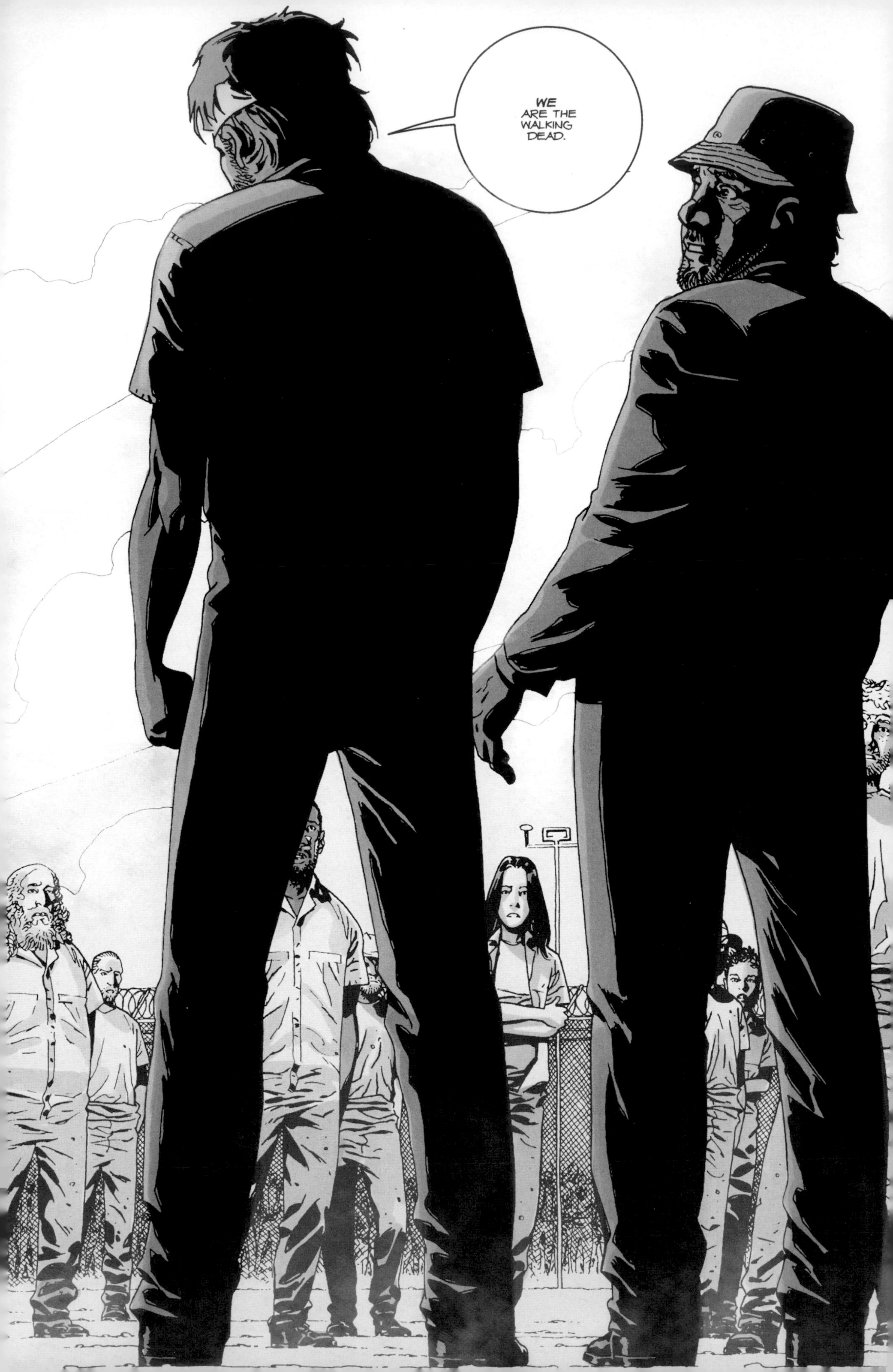
WE ARE THE WALKING DEAD.

to be continued...

Sketchbook

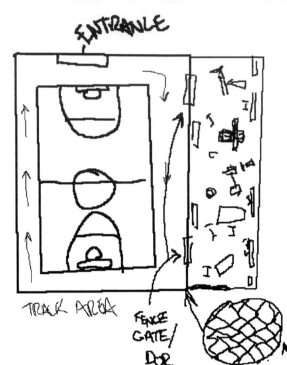

ENTRANCE

INDOOR GYM

TRACK AREA

FENCE GATE/ DOR

FENCE

Here we'll see an overhead layout of the prison gym. This was used in issue 15 or 16 for when Tyreese was left inside and later when they cleaned the place up. The weight room thing is right there next to it, see issue 20 when Michonne walked by Tyreese and Carol in the gym and then walked over to the weight room to do some lifting. See--these things are all mapped out!

Also on this page is a layout for page 17 of issue 18 (toward the end of what is chapter 3 of this book, actually, about 5 pages from the end). I thought my panel description was a little confusing so I made an even more confusing sketch for Charlie to go off of. As you can see by looking at the final page, Charlie did a bang-up job. He even added a nice little spiral staircase, which I get a real kick out of including in future scripts because Charlie admitted to me that he hates drawing the thing. What was he thinking?

CAN YOU MAKE OUT ANY OF THIS?

P B H I R C T M I G

JESUS CHRIST

Ah, Michonne.

I had the idea for Michonne long before work on the book started. The lone swordsman with the unarmed zombie pets was something I'd been itching to throw into the book for a long time. I've got big plans for her, so keep your eyes peeled for the Book Three hardcover, or run out to your local comic shop or book seller and grab a copy of The Walking Dead Volume 5 in paperback. She's a very important character in this series.

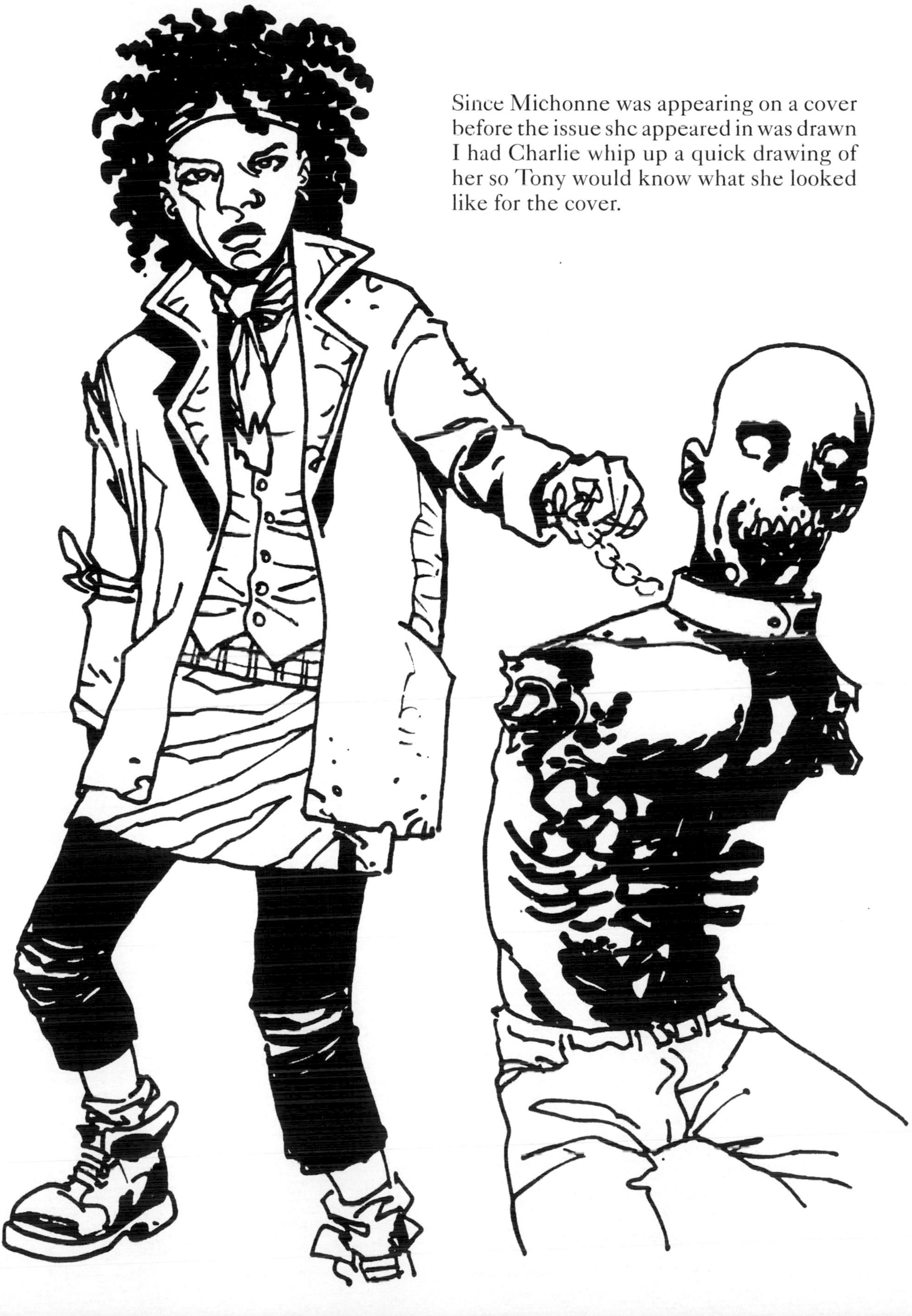

Since Michonne was appearing on a cover before the issue she appeared in was drawn I had Charlie whip up a quick drawing of her so Tony would know what she looked like for the cover.

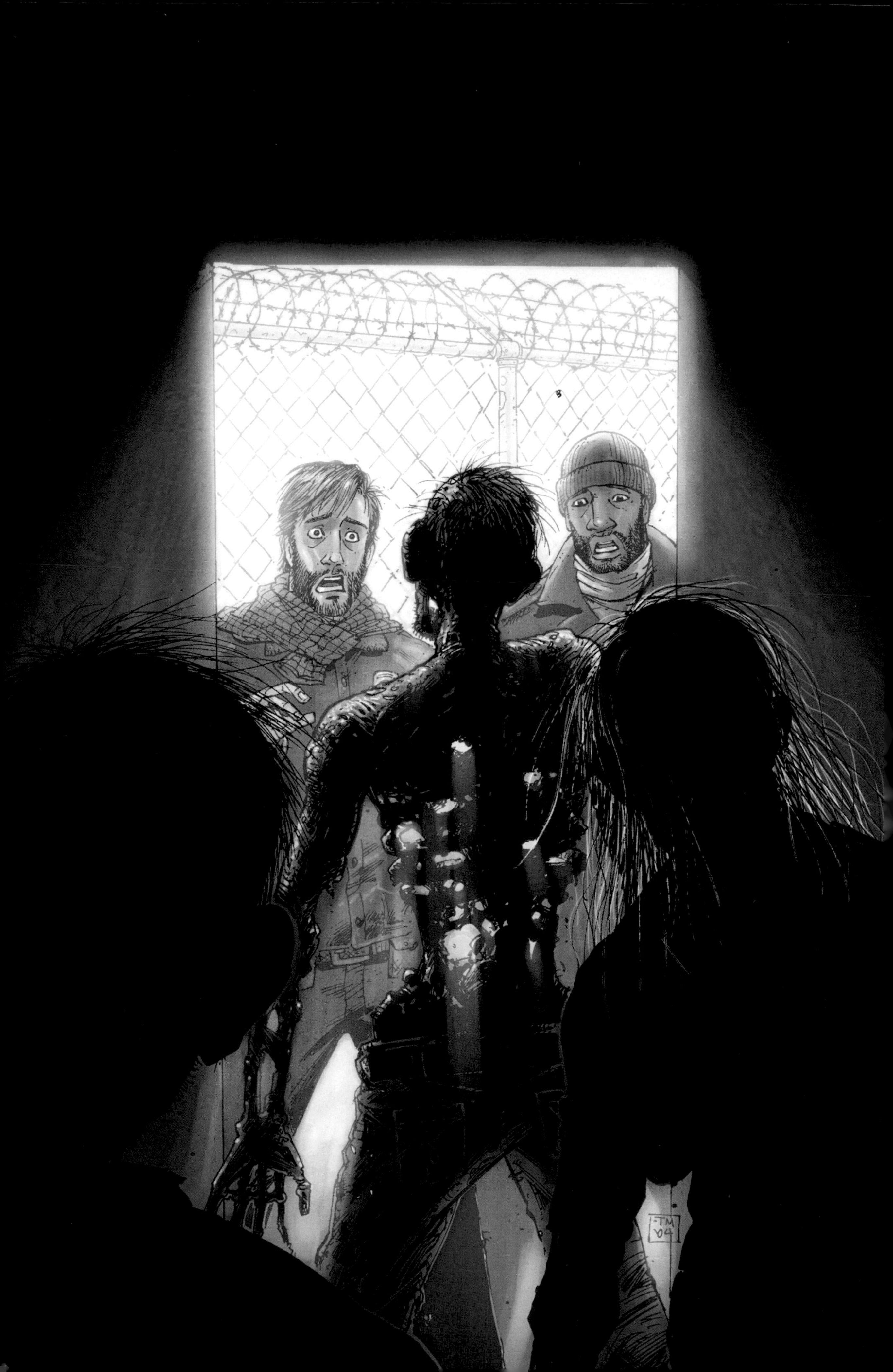

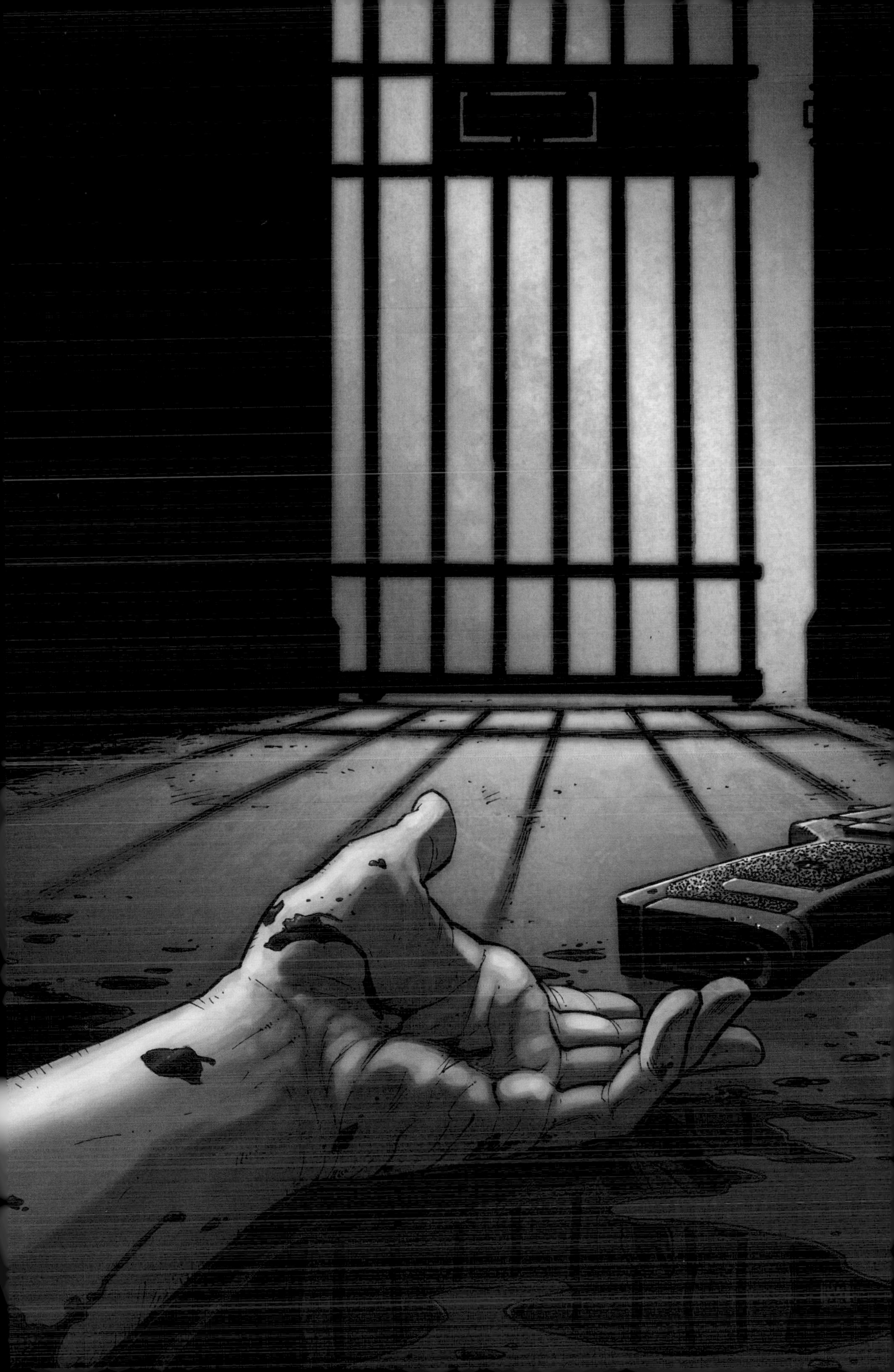

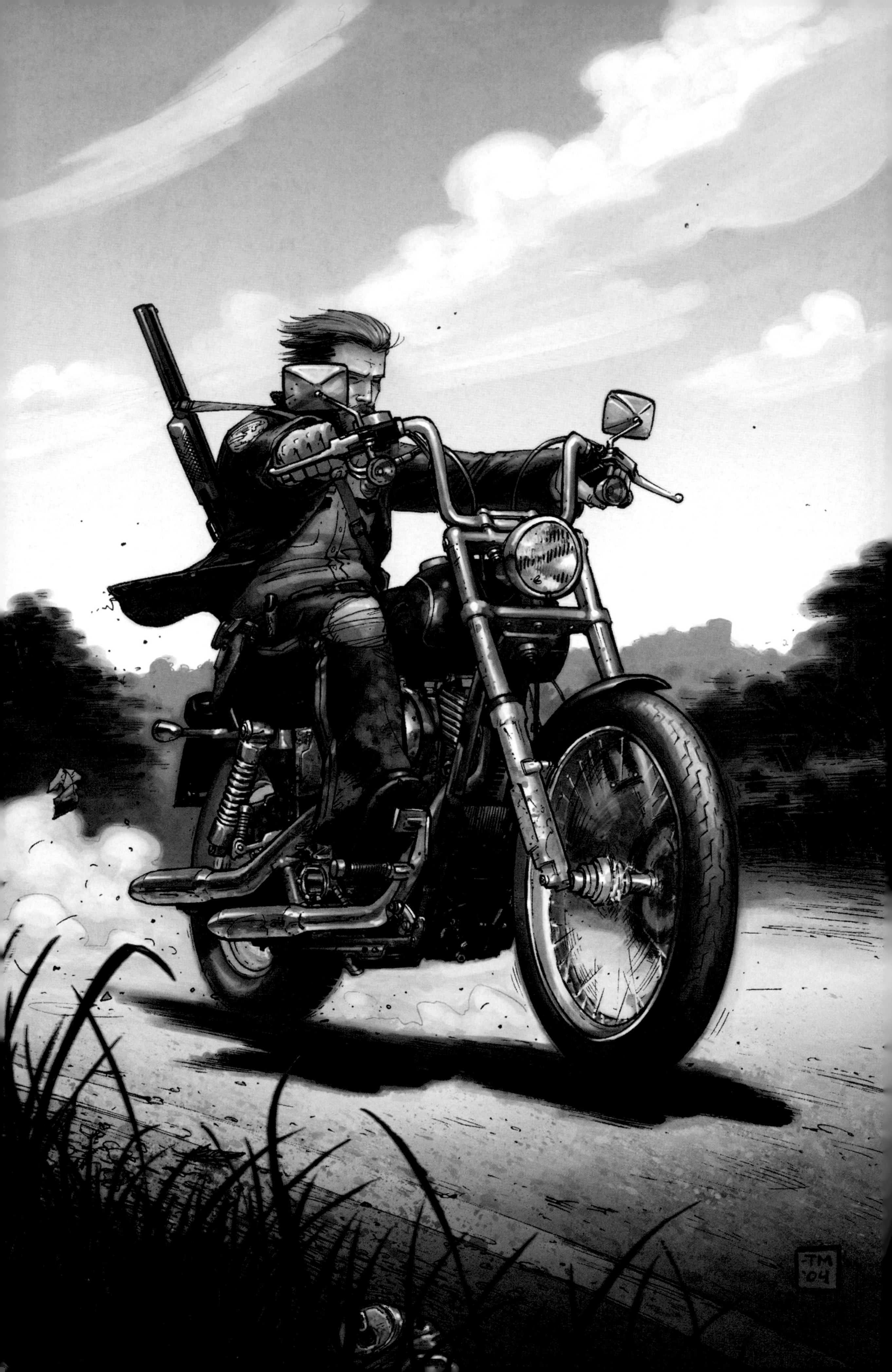
TM
'04

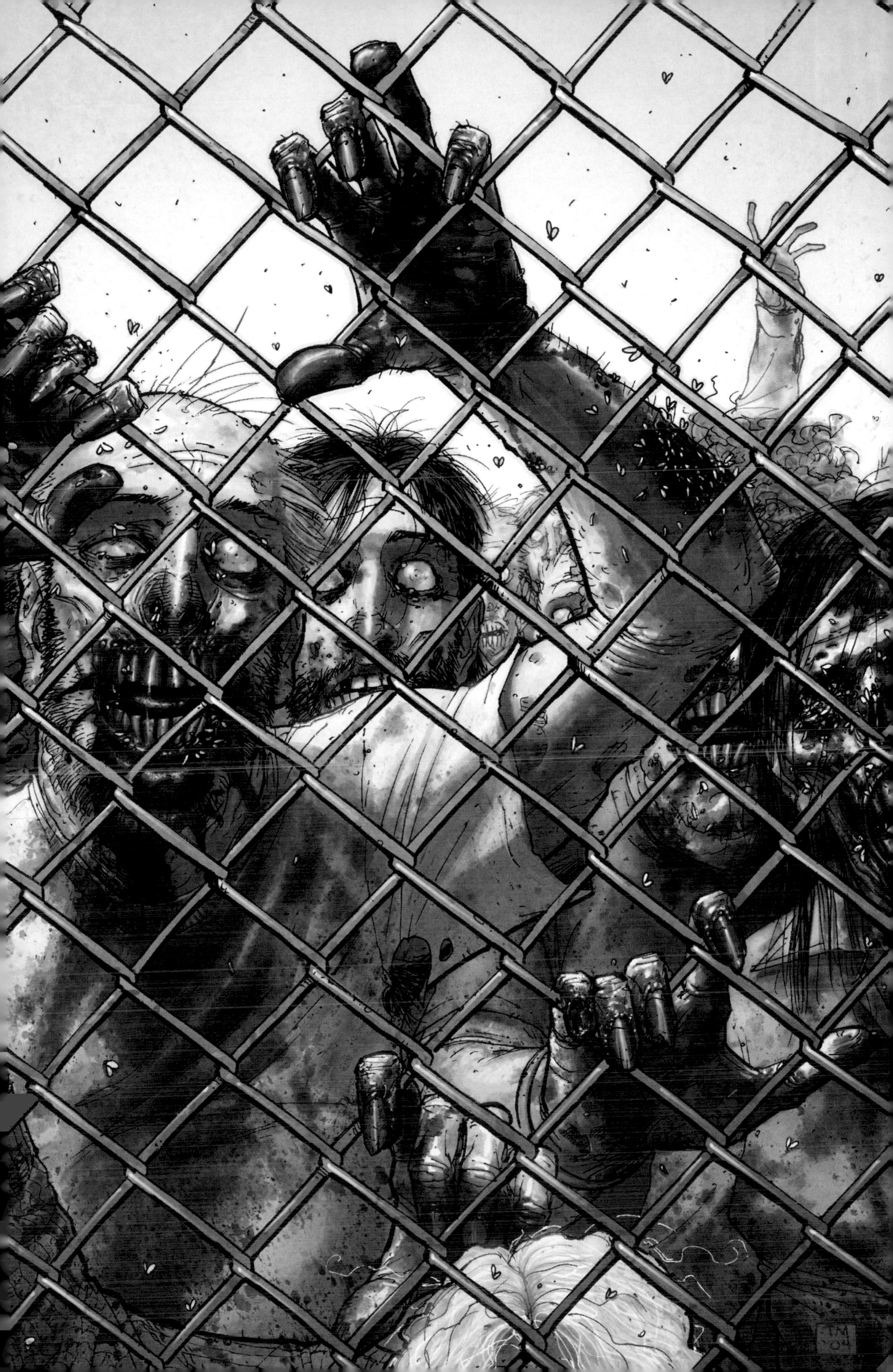

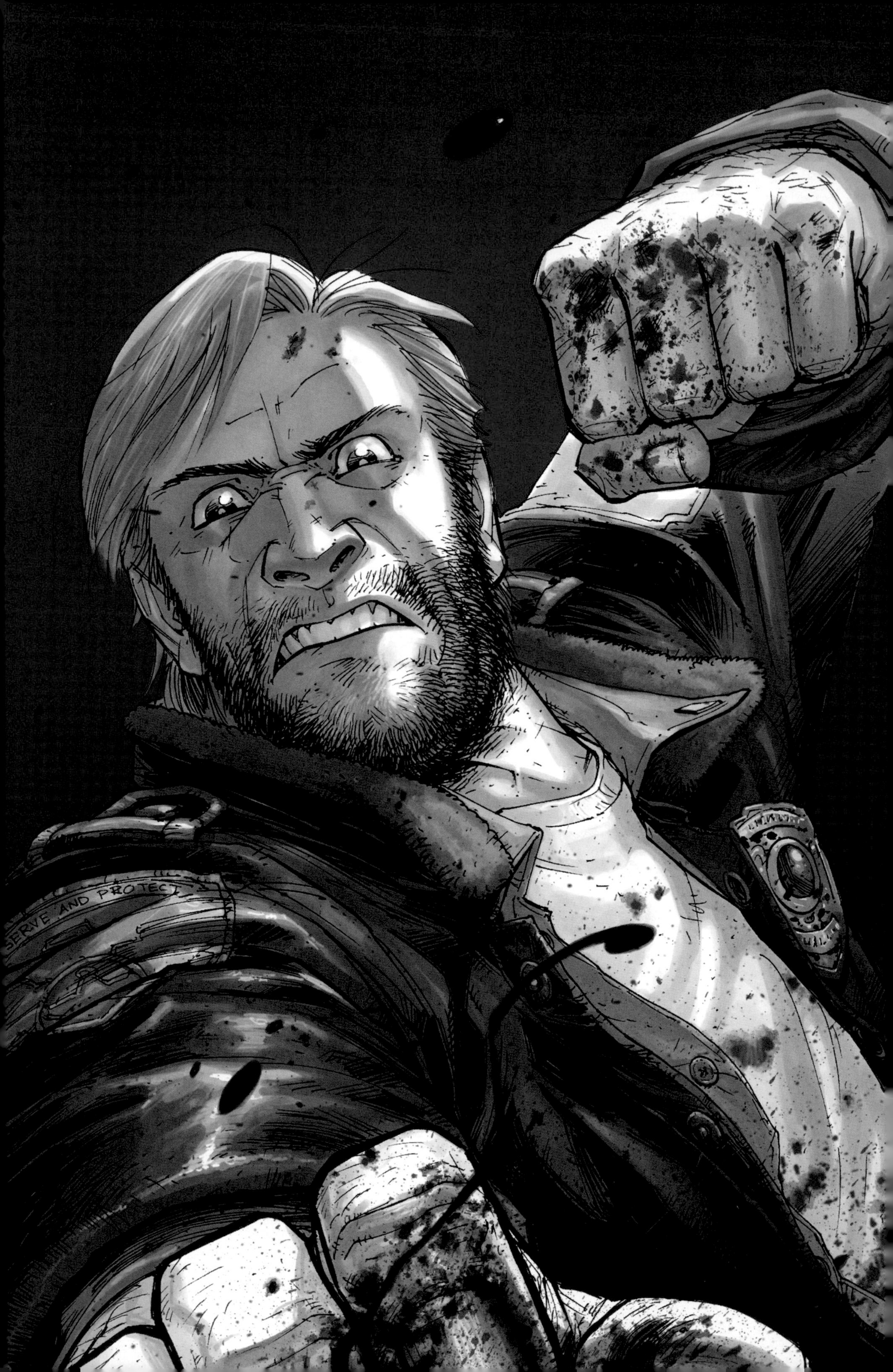
SERVE AND PROTECT

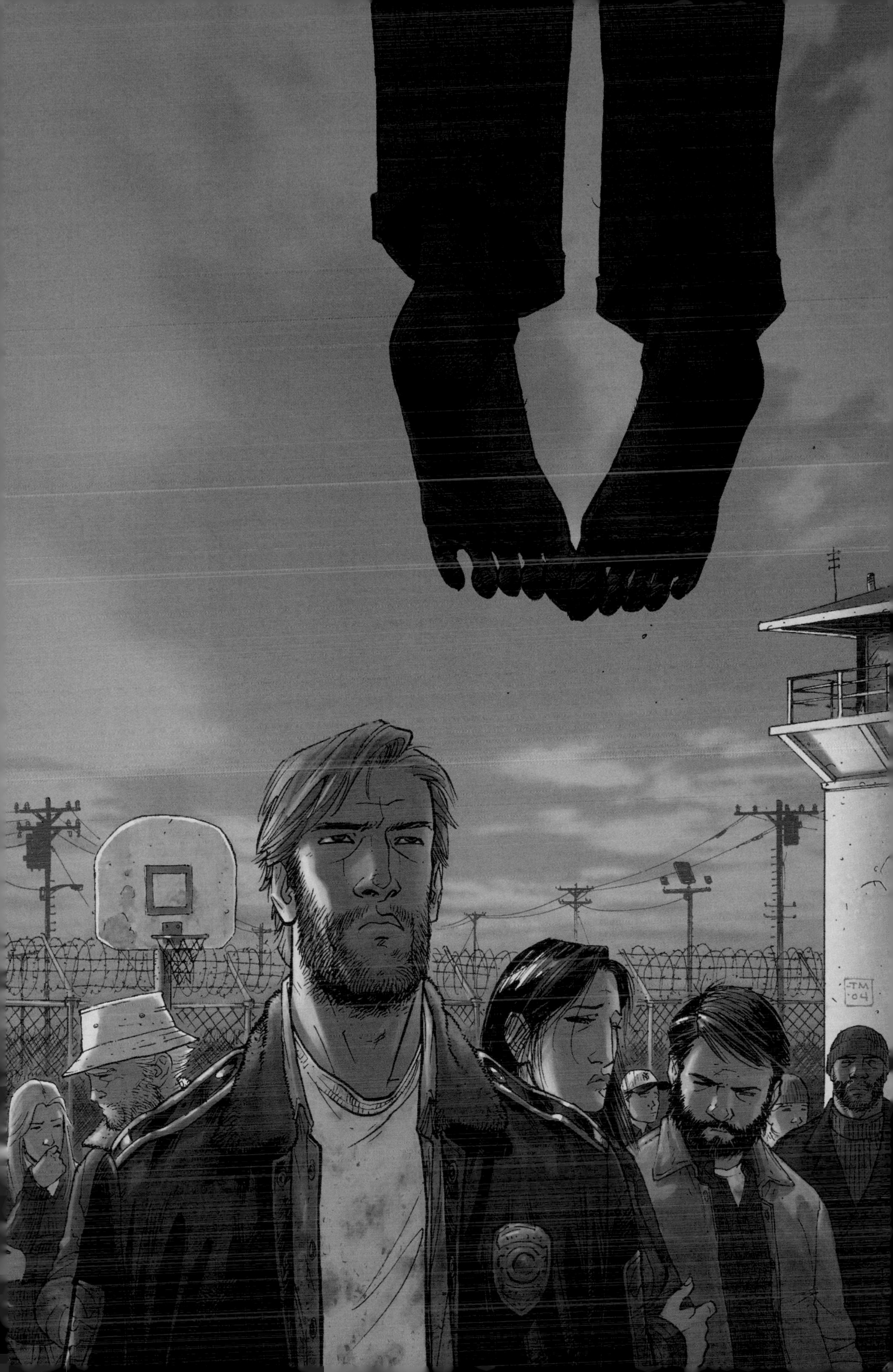
TM
'04

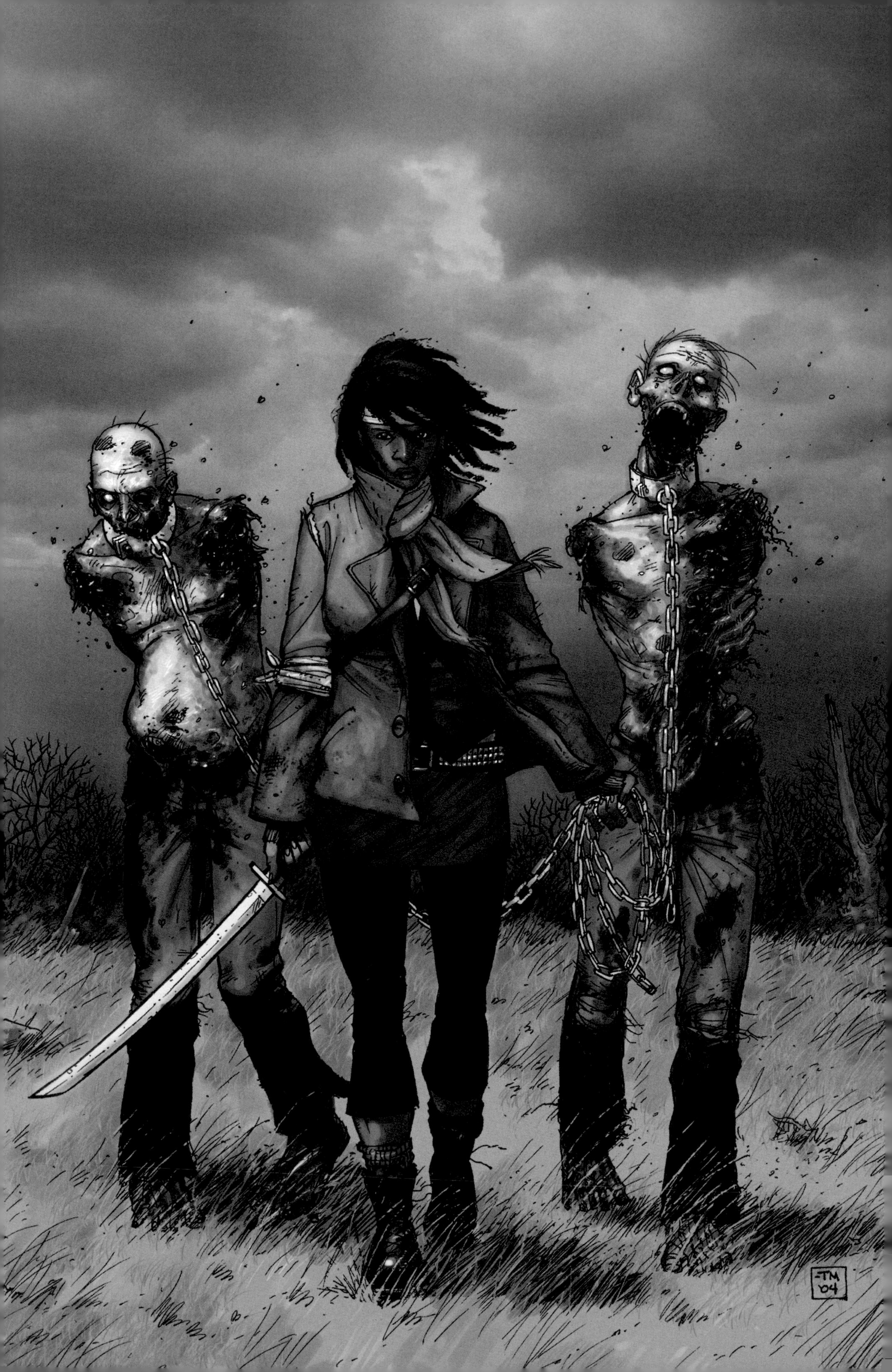
TM
'04

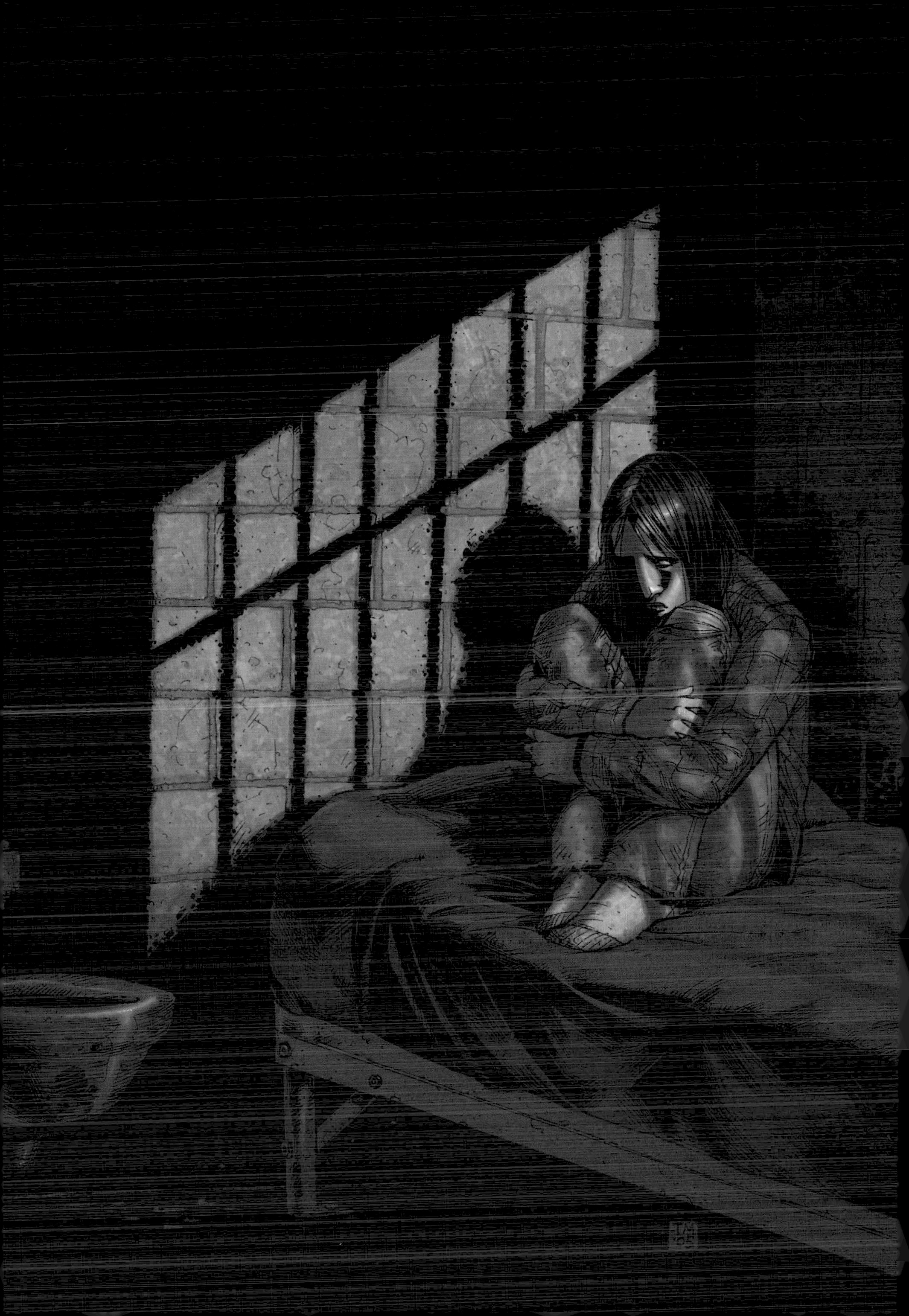

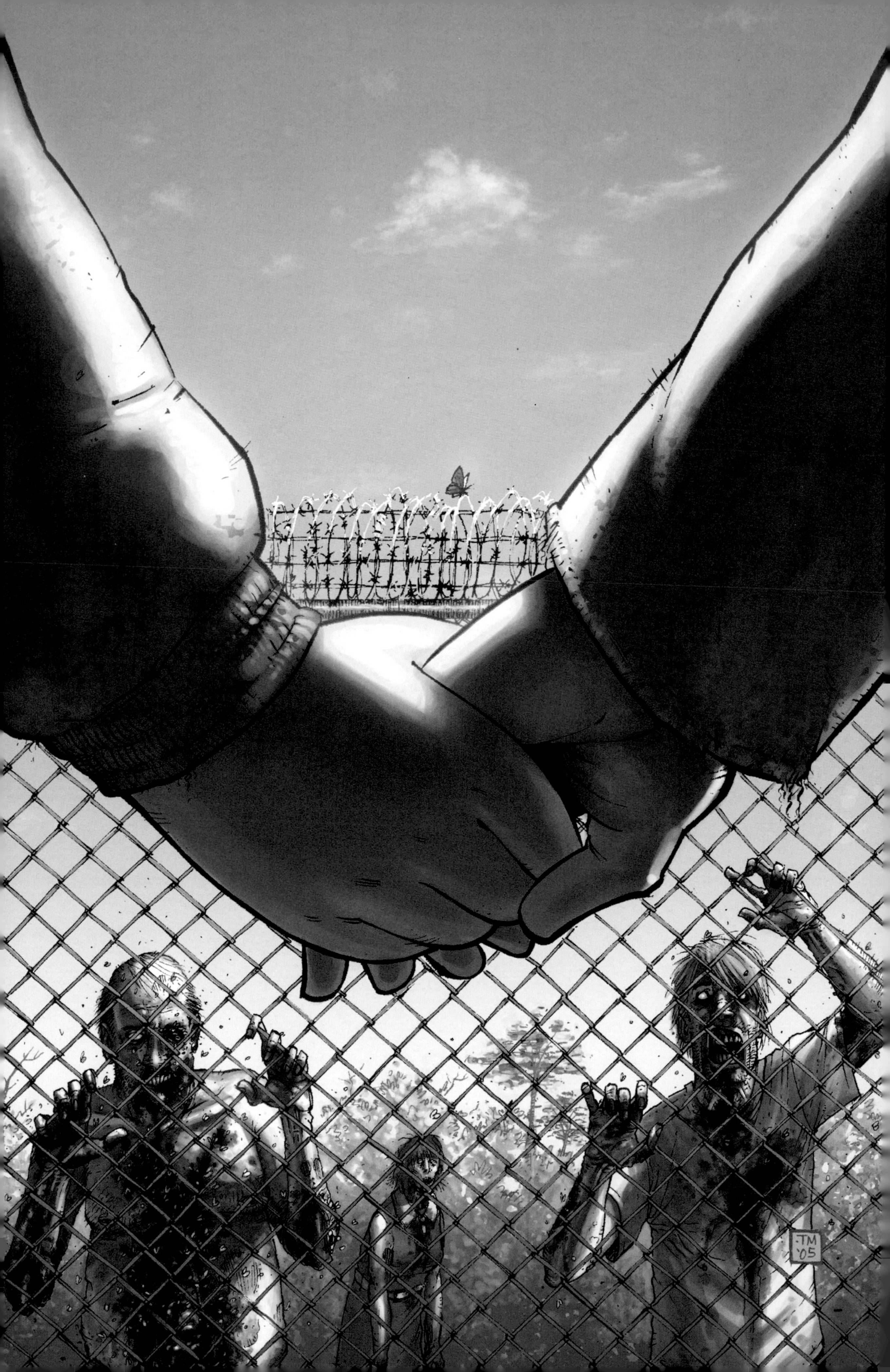
TM
'05

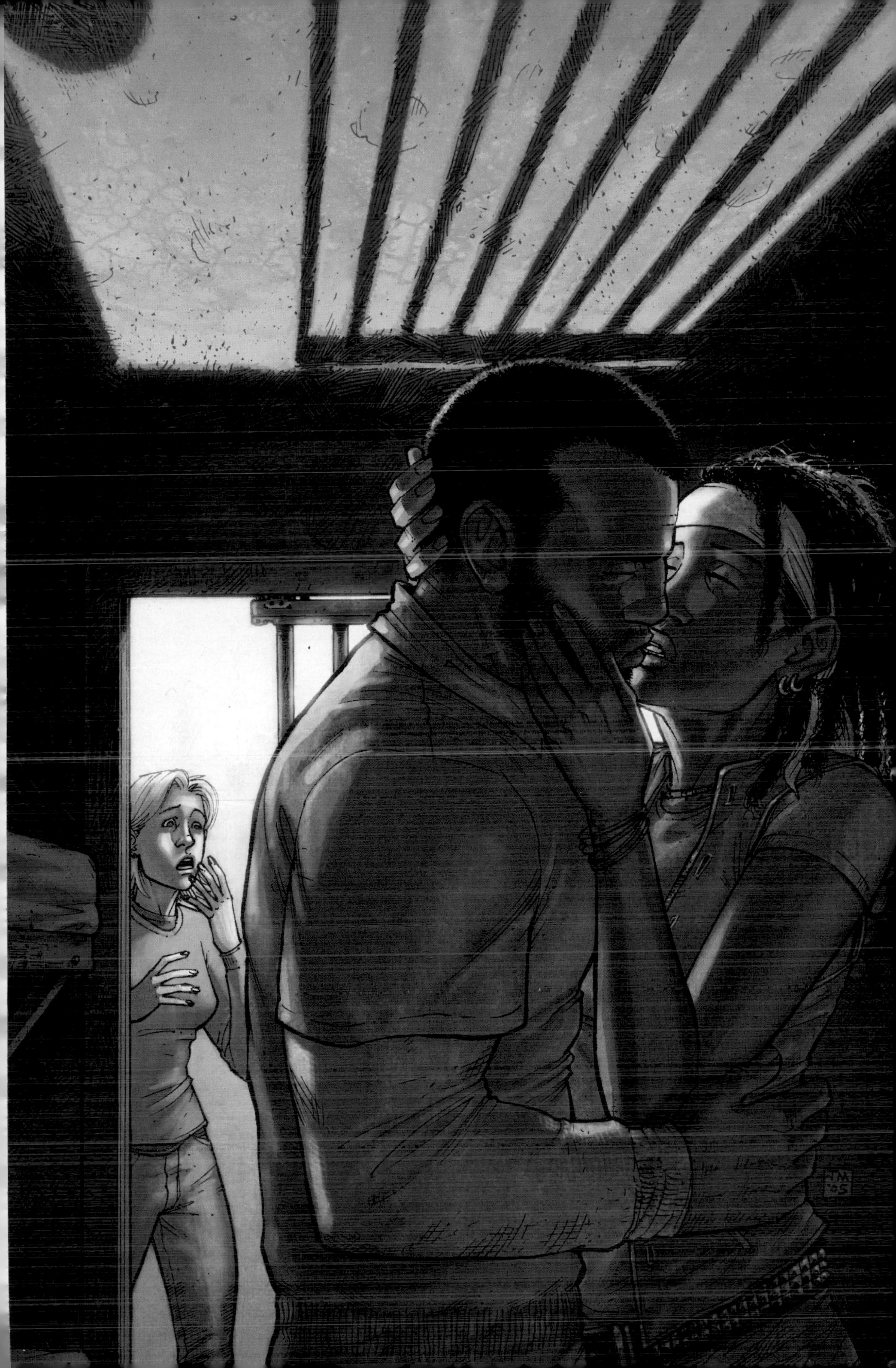

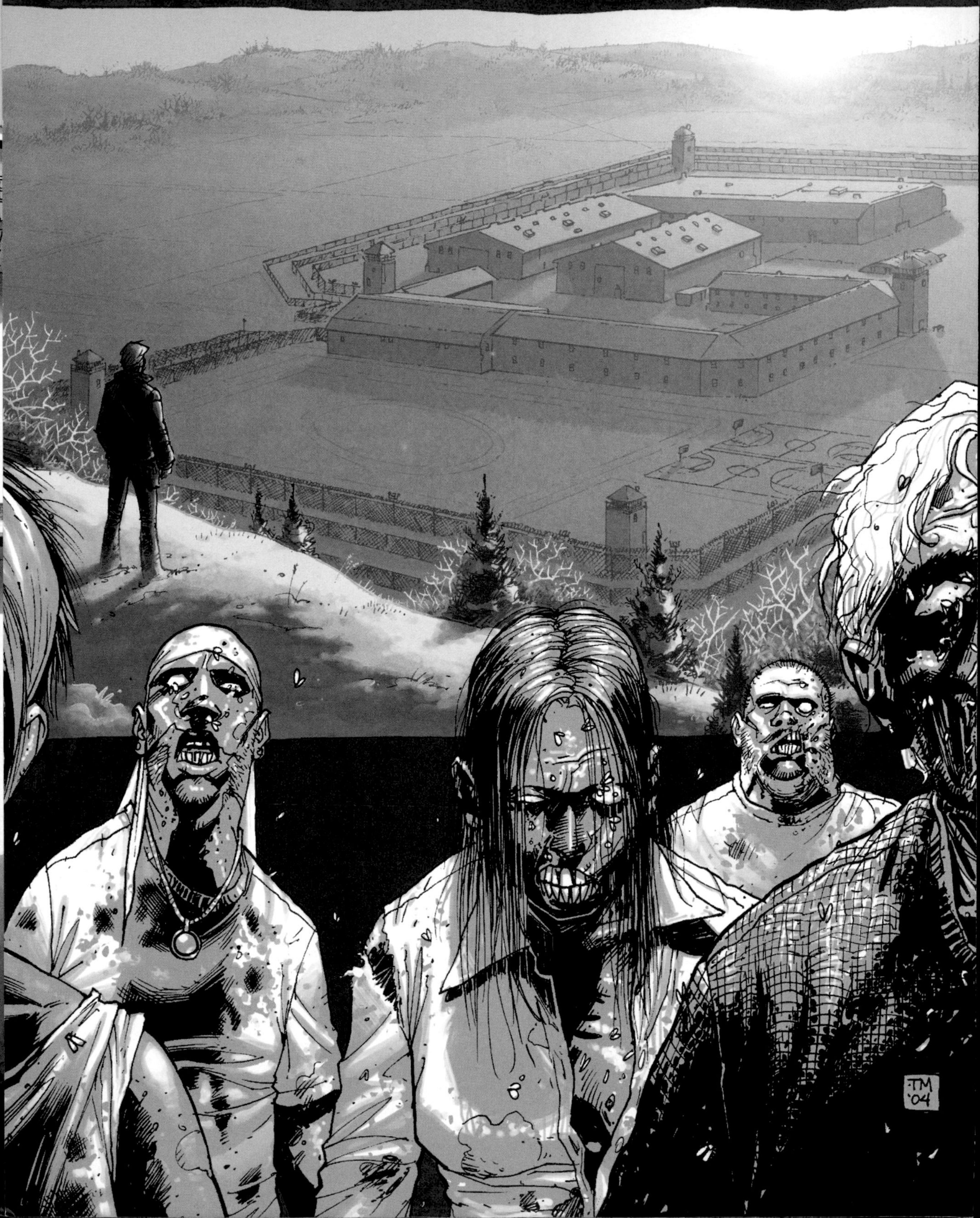
TM
'04

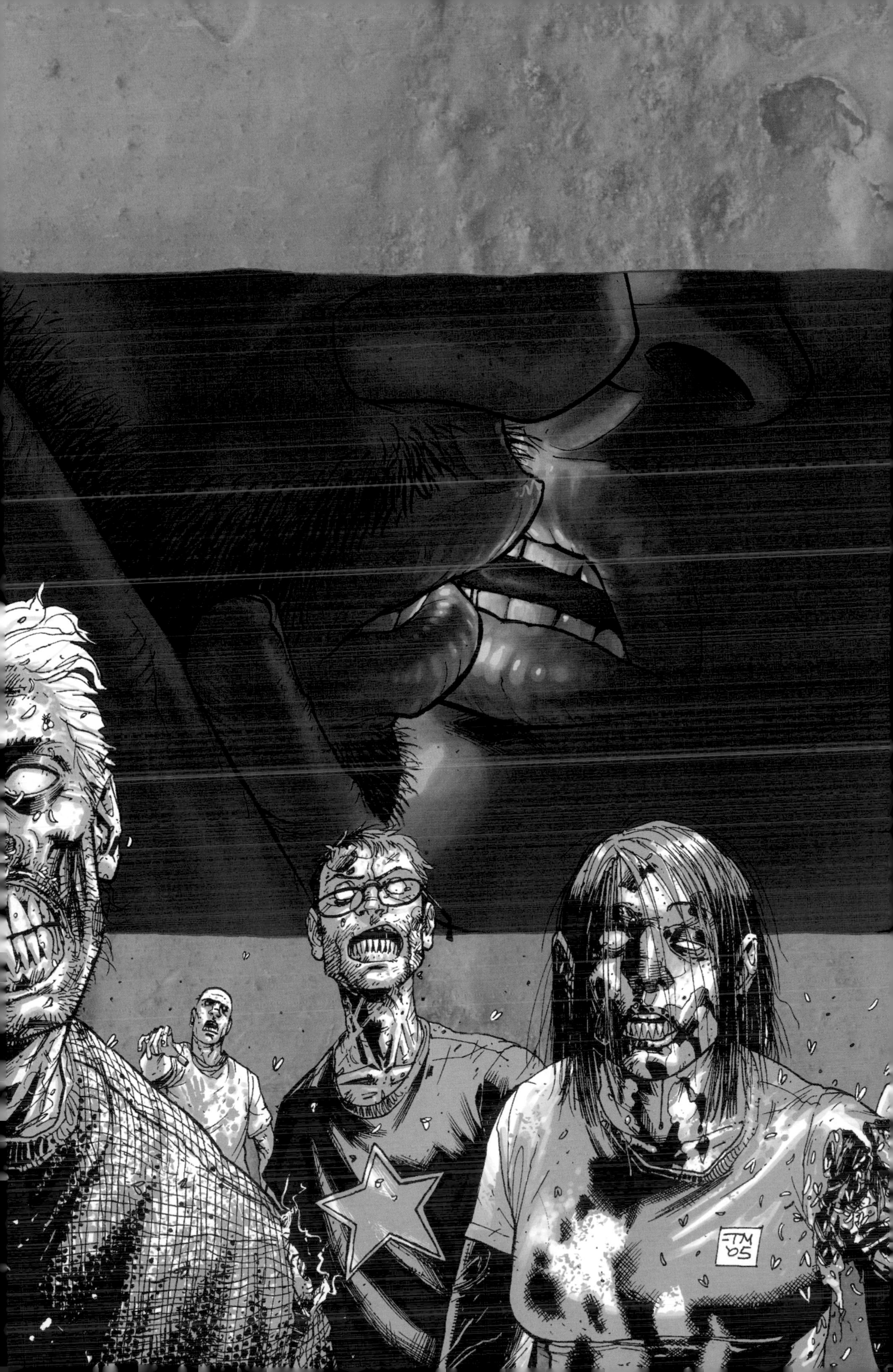
TM
'05

MORE GREAT BOOKS FROM ROBERT KIRKMAN & SKYBOUND!

THE ASTOUNDING WOLF-MAN

VOL. 1 TP
ISBN: 978-1-58240-862-0
$14.99
VOL. 2 TP
ISBN: 978-1-60706-007-9
$14.99
VOL. 3 TP
ISBN: 978-1-60706-111-3
$16.99
VOL. 4 TP
ISBN: 978-1-60706-249-3
$16.99

BATTLE POPE

VOL. 1: GENESIS TP
ISBN: 978-1-58240-572-8
$14.99
VOL. 2: MAYHEM TP
ISBN: 978-1-58240-529-2
$12.99
VOL. 3: PILLOW TALK TP
ISBN: 978-1-58240-677-0
$12.99
VOL. 4: WRATH OF GOD TP
ISBN: 978-1-58240-751-7
$9.99

BRIT

VOL. 1: OLD SOLDIER TP
ISBN: 978-1-58240-678-7
$14.99
VOL. 2: AWOL
ISBN: 978-1-58240-864-4
$14.99
VOL. 3: FUBAR
ISBN: 978-1-60706-061-1
$16.99

CAPES

VOL. 1: PUNCHING THE CLOCK TP
ISBN: 978-1-58240-756-2
$17.99

GUARDING THE GLOBE

VOL. 1: UNDER SIEGE TP
ISBN: 978-1-60706-356-8
$16.99

HAUNT

VOL. 1 TP
ISBN: 978-1-60706-154-0
$9.99
VOL. 2 TP
ISBN: 978-1-60706-229-5
$16.99
VOL. 3 TP
ISBN: 978-1-60706-552-4
$14.99
THE IMMORTAL EDITION, VOL. 1 HC
ISBN: 978-1-60706-241-7
$34.99

THE INFINITE

VOL. 1 TP
ISBN: 978-1-60706-475-6
$9.99

INVINCIBLE

VOL. 1: FAMILY MATTERS TP
ISBN: 978-1-58240-711-1
$12.99
VOL. 2: EIGHT IS ENOUGH TP
ISBN: 978-1-58240-347-2
$12.99
VOL. 3: PERFECT STRANGERS TP
ISBN: 978-1-58240-793-7
$12.99
VOL. 4: HEAD OF THE CLASS TP
ISBN: 978-1-58240-440-2
$14.95
VOL. 5: THE FACTS OF LIFE TP
ISBN: 978-1-58240-554-4
$14.99
VOL. 6: A DIFFERENT WORLD TP
ISBN: 978-1-58240-579-7
$14.99
VOL. 7: THREE'S COMPANY TP
ISBN: 978-1-58240-656-5
$14.99
VOL. 8: MY FAVORITE MARTIAN TP
ISBN: 978-1-58240-683-1
$14.99
VOL. 9: OUT OF THIS WORLD TP
ISBN: 978-1-58240-827-9
$14.99
VOL. 10: WHO'S THE BOSS TP
ISBN: 978-1-60706-013-0
$16.99
VOL. 11: HAPPY DAYS TP
ISBN: 978-1-60706-062-8
$16.99
VOL. 12: STILL STANDING TP
ISBN: 978-1-60706-166-3
$16.99
VOL. 13: GROWING PAINS TP
ISBN: 978-1-60706-251-6
$16.99
VOL. 14: THE VILTRUMITE WAR TP
ISBN: 978-1-60706-367-4
$19.99
VOL. 15: GET SMART TP
ISBN: 978-1-60706-498-5
$16.99
VOL. 16: FAMILY TIES TP
ISBN: 978-1-60706-579-1
$16.99
ULTIMATE COLLECTION, VOL. 1 HC
ISBN 978-1-58240-500-1
$34.95
ULTIMATE COLLECTION, VOL. 2 HC
ISBN: 978-1-58240-594-0
$34.99
ULTIMATE COLLECTION, VOL. 3 HC
ISBN: 978-1-58240-763-0
$34.99
ULTIMATE COLLECTION, VOL. 4 HC
ISBN: 978-1-58240-989-4
$34.99
ULTIMATE COLLECTION, VOL. 5 HC
ISBN: 978-1-60706-116-8
$34.99
ULTIMATE COLLECTION, VOL. 6 HC
ISBN: 978-1-60706-360-5
$34.99
ULTIMATE COLLECTION, VOL. 7 HC
ISBN: 978-1-60706-509-8
$39.99
COMPENDIUM VOL. 1
ISBN: 978-1-60706-411-4
$64.99
THE COMPLETE INVINCIBLE LIBRARY, VOL. 2 HC
ISBN: 978-1-60706-112-0
$125.00
THE COMPLETE INVINCIBLE LIBRARY, VOL. 3 HC
ISBN: 978-1-60706-421-3
$125.00
THE OFFICIAL HANDBOOK OF THE INVINCIBLE UNIVERSE TP
ISBN: 978-1-58240-831-6
$12.99
INVINCIBLE PRESENTS, VOL. 1: ATOM EVE & REX SPLODE TP
ISBN: 978-1-60706-255-4
$14.99

SUPER DINOSAUR

VOL. 1
ISBN: 978-1-60706-420-6
$9.99
VOL. 2
ISBN: 978-1-60706-568-5
$12.99
DELUXE COLORING BOOK
ISBN: 978-1-60706-481-7
$4.99

SUPERPATRIOT

AMERICA'S FIGHTING FORCE
ISBN: 978-1-58240-355-1
$14.99

TALES OF THE REALM

HARDCOVER
ISBN: 978-1-58240-426-0
$34.95
TRADE PAPERBACK
ISBN: 978-1-58240-394-6
$14.95

TECH JACKET

VOL. 1: THE BOY FROM EARTH TP
ISBN: 978-1-58240-771-5
$14.99

THIEF OF THIEVES

VOL. 1: "I QUIT."
ISBN: 978-1-60706-592-0
$14.99

THE WALKING DEAD

VOL. 1: DAYS GONE BYE TP
ISBN: 978-1-58240-672-5
$9.99
VOL. 2: MILES BEHIND US TP
ISBN: 978-1-58240-775-3
$14.99
VOL. 3: SAFETY BEHIND BARS TP
ISBN: 978-1-58240-805-7
$14.99
VOL. 4: THE HEART'S DESIRE TP
ISBN: 978-1-58240-530-8
$14.99
VOL. 5: THE BEST DEFENSE TP
ISBN: 978-1-58240-612-1
$14.99
VOL. 6: THIS SORROWFUL LIFE TP
ISBN: 978-1-58240-684-8
$14.99
VOL. 7: THE CALM BEFORE TP
ISBN: 978-1-58240-828-6
$14.99
VOL. 8: MADE TO SUFFER TP
ISBN: 978-1-58240-883-5
$14.99
VOL. 9: HERE WE REMAIN TP
ISBN: 978-1-60706-022-2
$14.99
VOL. 10: WHAT WE BECOME TP
ISBN: 978-1-60706-075-8
$14.99
VOL. 11: FEAR THE HUNTERS TP
ISBN: 978-1-60706-181-6
$14.99
VOL. 12: LIFE AMONG THEM TP
ISBN: 978-1-60706-254-7
$14.99
VOL. 13: TOO FAR GONE TP
ISBN: 978-1-60706-329-2
$14.99
VOL. 14: NO WAY OUT TP
ISBN: 978-1-60706-392-6
$14.99
VOL. 15: WE FIND OURSELVES TP
ISBN: 978-1-60706-392-6
$14.99
BOOK ONE HC
ISBN: 978-1-58240-619-0
$34.99
BOOK TWO HC
ISBN: 978-1-58240-698-5
$34.99
BOOK THREE HC
ISBN: 978-1-58240-825-5
$34.99
BOOK FOUR HC
ISBN: 978-1-60706-000-0
$34.99
BOOK FIVE HC
ISBN: 978-1-60706-171-7
$34.99
BOOK SIX HC
ISBN: 978-1-60706-327-8
$34.99
BOOK SEVEN HC
ISBN: 978-1-60706-439-8
$34.99
BOOK EIGHT HC
ISBN: 978-1-60706-593-7
$34.99
COMPENDIUM TP, VOL. 1
ISBN: 978-1-60706-076-5
$59.99
COMPENDIUM TP, VOL. 2
ISBN: 978-1-60706-596-8
$59.99
DELUXE HARDCOVER, VOL. 1
ISBN: 978-1-58240-619-0
$100.00
DELUXE HARDCOVER, VOL. 2
ISBN: 978-1-60706-029-7
$100.00
DELUXE HARDCOVER, VOL. 3
ISBN: 978-1-60706-330-8
$100.00
DELUXE HARDCOVER, VOL. 4
ISBN: 978-1-60706-616-3
$100.00
THE WALKING DEAD: THE COVERS, VOL. 1 HC
ISBN: 978-1-60706-002-4
$24.99
THE WALKING DEAD SURVIVORS' GUIDE
ISBN: 978-1-60706-458-9
$12.99

WITCH DOCTOR

VOL. 1: UNDER THE KNIFE TP
ISBN: 978-1-60706-441-1
$12.99

TO FIND YOUR NEAREST COMIC BOOK STORE, CALL:
1-888-COMIC-BOOK

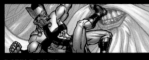

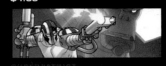